B. Mo...

S0-ADJ-853

THE FALL RIVER LINE

MARCUS AND AMY KINCAID
Investors in the line, their lives and fortunes were entwined with the Fall River ships

AUGUSTA KINCAID
Their beautiful russet-haired daughter, her courage and determination would shape lives and fortunes

ARIA KINCAID
Tempestuous and passionate, she was her sister's bitter rival for the love of

LUKE WAKEFIELD
He rose from cabin boy to a man of power, but a dark fear haunted him . . .

———————

"Courage and love abound"—*San Diego Union*

"All the elements of great reading are there—politics, romance, famous people, family scandal, war . . ."—Toledo (Ohio) *Blade*

The Fall River Line

Daoma Winston

St. Martin's Press
New York

THE FALL RIVER LINE
Copyright © 1983 by Daoma Winston.

First published in Great Britain by Century Publishing Co. Ltd. 1984

St. Martin's mass market edition/June 1986

ISBN: 0-312-90184-4
Can. ISBN: 0-312-90402-9

10 9 8 7 6 5 4 3 2 1

For Jay Garon, and his hometown,
the historic city of Fall River

Acknowledgments

With thanks to Reference Librarian Eileen Stafiej and her staff at the Fall River Public Library, Fall River, Massachusetts; Florence C. Bingham, Curator, the Fall River Historical Society; and John F. Gosson, Curator, the Marine Museum at Fall River.

And, for providing me with additional materials, to Evelyn Winston Freedenberg, Silver Spring, Maryland; Regina and Raymond Guay, Kensington, Maryland; Sam Gourse, Providence, Rhode Island; Joan Slouis, Washington, D.C.; and Avis B. Markstrom, Bristol, Rhode Island.

Note: Plot requirements led me to make some small changes in the ships' sailing schedules.

Prologue

Amy and Marcus Kincaid were different kinds of people. He was a big man, burly, with a reddish-gold beard and sideburns and a loud, booming voice. He never sat down, but flung himself onto a settle and sprawled, so that floors and furniture creaked under him, and his step made the brass chandeliers rattle. He wore a black coat, wide-shouldered but fitted at the waist and flared at mid-thigh. His gray scarf knotted once at the throat was of silk. The trousers, a darker gray, were narrow, straining at his broad thighs. It had been an expensive outfit, but worn now and close to outgrown as well. His grandparents had been in the tallow business, and better than comfortable, but his father frittered away a small fortune. Marcus, along with his younger brother Parish, had inherited nothing. So now, at twenty-six, Marcus was just beginning.

Amy, the same age as her husband, was alone in the world, an orphan since childhood, raised by a wealthy and generous aunt named Jane Oliver. Amy was small, spare, with tiny hands and narrow, high-arched feet. Her heart-shaped face was rarely lit by smiles, and her eyes were wide, measuring, a cool blue. She wore her dark hair pulled straight off the forehead in a tight spinsterish chignon. Her gown was spinsterish too, dark gray, with only a stiff white bow at the throat to brighten it, and bound at the waist with a loose-braided belt that drooped at her narrow hips. They had married because she needed a husband and a life, and Jane Oliver had liked him. And he, hardworking and ambitious, needed a start, and her money would help him.

It was of money that they were both thinking when Amy said, 'I doubt that you should do it, Marcus. It's one thing for Richard and Jefferson Borden, but another for us. They have the ironworks, and the railway completed to Fall River. A shipping line will only increase the value of those two. But we have no part of either. So if you buy into the line with what

1

you've brought back . . .' Here she stopped, sighed. Finally with another sigh, she went on, '. . . if the investment were lost, we'd have nothing.'

Her husband leaned back in his chair and wondered how to explain it to her. He wasn't a man to whom such discussion came easily. He wasn't a patient man either. But now he was trying to be both.

Outside, the chill wind of a Massachusetts late September ruffled the dark waters of Mount Hope Bay, and a cool salty mist spread from the Taunton River to veil the town of Fall River. With the early falling dusk, its busy port had grown silent except for the snap of halyards on the sailing vessels and the creak of barge ropes.

Inside the gray clapboard house it was warm, snug, the comfort a luxury to Marcus. He felt remembered cold in his legs and moved to thrust them closer to the fire.

'Would you like something?' Amy asked immediately.

'No, thank you,' he said. Then, 'Amy, I don't want to go away again. It would mean another three years. An endless time to be so far from home. And only this investment will keep me here.'

'You must do what you think best.' She had expressed her opinion. The decision was up to him.

But he knew that the words she spoke were not the words she meant. He saw it in her face – her sweet, plain face.

'Amy, listen. The Bordens are always successful. They started with making barrel hoops – and look at the ironworks now. If they think this line will turn a profit, then it will.'

'Yes,' she agreed. But her tone was dry.

'And I see it for myself.' He went on, enthusiasm kindling, in spite of himself, in spite of her. 'I can imagine great ships sailing out of Fall River. Travelers and goods from Boston, from all of New England, embarking here, loaded from off the train cars, and going on to New York City. On *our* ships, Amy. Think of it.'

'If they embark. If they are loaded. And if the ships sail.'

'Amy! For God's sake . . .'

'You needn't swear.'

'No, no. I'm sorry.' He stopped. It was so hard to tell her what was in his mind. They'd been married three years, but it had been nearly three years since they had last sat down to talk together. They were still virtually strangers. And that the talk had to be about money made it even more difficult. The agreement when they exchanged their vows had been that it would be theirs. *Theirs.* But now he knew she thought differently.

The wind suddenly seemed loud as the silence grew longer between them. It lashed the trees around the house, rattled the window panes, and hissed monotonously in the chimney. Still, to him it seemed gentle compared to the long howling gales he had experienced on the whaling voyage from which he had returned only a few days before.

He drew a deep breath, remembering the stink of the ship's manufactory, where whales were reduced to precious oil and bone, and where, in a moment's carelessness, he had lost the smallest finger of his left hand. Here there was the sweet scent of pinewood burning in the fireplace, of beeswax polish and starched linens. The scent of Amy.

But how to explain it to her, he asked himself again. It was only his good fortune that the Bordens, knowing him, having known his grandparents, were willing to accept him as a partner in the venture they were organizing as a family affair. And it couldn't fail. Wouldn't fail. By the end of this year of 1846, the Mexicans would be defeated and the whole of the American continent would belong to the United States. There would be a great surge of goods out of New England, south to New York, and from there to the rest of the country. Fall River was growing, too. It had seven textile mills, and soon there would be more. The business section and homes destroyed in the 1843 fire were already being rebuilt. The future was bright, and he, they, could be part of it. Only how to make Amy understand?

When he finally spoke, it was to take a different tack entirely. He said, 'We have the house. Even were I wrong, we'd have a roof over our heads.'

A grim smile touched her mouth, and he knew he'd made a mistake. Another mistake.

She said, 'Yes, Marcus. Thanks to Aunt Jane Oliver.'

'Thanks to her indeed.'

Amy said nothing. He went silent too.

Aunt Jane Oliver. The mad old lady to whom he owed so

much: the voyage, and its profit. The treasure he'd brought back. The house. Even Amy.

It had been Aunt Jane's idea to bring them together. The old woman, still sharp, her black eyes alive in her shrinking face. Perhaps already then she knew she was ill and unlikely to recover. She worried about Amy, the same age as himself, and was concerned to see her settled. But Amy was a quiet girl. There were no suitors climbing the path to her house. It didn't matter to Marcus. Amy was sweet and intelligent. She had every skill that he imagined a woman would need to be a good wife, and eventually a good mother.

And he was an honest man, which was one of the things Aunt Jane had said to him. 'You're honest, Marcus Kincaid. You've done well by your brother, too. You're an honor to your family. It's true your father was a fool, and wasted his inheritance so that you have none. But an honest man can make his way. At least that's my opinion. Although I know many a man who wasn't who made his way as well.'

Marcus had said nothing. He didn't like the reference to his father even though what the old woman said was true. But Marcus had grown up tasting bitterness only in very brief moments of self-doubt. He might be his father's son, but he was different. He promised himself that he'd renew the family fortune, restore the family name.

Aunt Jane made the offer in plain words. 'Marcus Kincaid, my Amy needs a husband. If you will promise to be good to her, to care for her . . . if you will be the husband I begin to fear she will never find for herself, then I will settle on her, for your use, whatever you need to share in a charter, so that when you go whaling it'll be as a partner seaman, not as ordinary crew.'

And so it had been.

Now Amy said, 'It's the risk I worry about.' But she slanted a cool, disapproving glance toward the mantel where he had arranged a display of his treasures, and wondered whether the pale gray-green lion he called celadon porcelain, the four-inch cloisonné vase, the laughing dog in ivory were really symbols of what she feared. That Marcus was like his father – a man whose head and sense could be turned by useless fripperies. The bolt of China silk in palest blue that she had carefully put away in linen wrapping would one day be useful perhaps. But what use could these small gleaming ornaments be?

He saw her glance and understood. 'They cost only a pittance.' It was true. The whaling ship, storm-wracked in the Behring Sea, with carpenter and cooper unable to effect the necessary repairs, had limped southward and by good luck made it into Canton Harbor. There he'd thought to buy some China silk for Amy and was directed to the enclosed foreign enclaves where agencies for trade were permitted. He'd found the silk and seen the porcelain, all of it brought into Canton from the interior where no aliens were allowed to go. These, on the mantel, were only a small sampling of what he had purchased. Three sea chests were filled to the braces; but when he saw Amy's reaction, he'd left the rest still packed.

'A pittance can become a fortune,' she answered now.

'Oriental treasures are an investment, Amy.'

'Perhaps. But meanwhile they earn no interest.'

By Jesus, he thought, the woman uses a harpoon when a hatpin would do.

He rose, stood before the fire, and spread his hands.

When Amy had first noticed that the left one lacked the smallest finger, and saw how often he jammed that hand into his coat pocket, she asked him how he came to lose the finger. He shrugged the question away, saying it was nothing.

Now she wondered about it again, but this time she didn't ask. She said, 'I'll make us some tea, Marcus,' and at his nod, hurried into the kitchen. There, busy with kettle and cups, she considered what was most important to her. It seemed out of character that he should have spent much for small exotic dainties of no real value. She also knew of the three packed sea chests. Still, she had no sense of the worth of such things. Perhaps he *had* spent only a pittance, and perhaps he was right, and one day they would prove the investment he believed. Until then there was the thirty thousand dollars. No more, no less. What was most important?

Aunt Jane Oliver had asked her what she thought of Marcus Kincaid, Amy remembered, and remembered the shrug she'd given in reply. Aunt Jane had said, 'Say something, girl. Do you hate him? Do you fancy him? Do you think he's a good man?' After a bit, Amy had replied, 'I don't know.' 'Go on like that,' the old woman snapped, "and you never will.' Amy

5

hadn't answered. Aunt Jane said, 'What do you think you have to know about the man? And what do you think you can ever know about a man? Any man? After how many years?'

Amy chuckled dryly. 'I don't think either you or I have grounds for opinion, Aunt Jane.'

'Oh, don't be so bold, miss. You don't know all that much of me. And I'll say frankly, the same of me for you.'

'Aunt Jane,' Amy said, 'you're being difficult. You've known me since you took me in when I was newborn. You've known my friends, and all I've ever done.'

'I haven't known your thoughts, girl. I doubt anyone ever would. And that's why I'm asking, What do you think of Marcus Kincaid?'

Amy had finally answered, 'I like him. What I know of him, that is.'

'You don't find that he turns your stomach?'

'No.'

'Doesn't make you fearful?'

'No.'

'You don't feel any small something in your chest when you get a glimpse of his russet hair?' Amy didn't answer.

'Well?' the old lady insisted.

'I don't know what you mean by "small something".'

Jane Oliver said, 'Don't lie to me. Every girl, some time, will have that feeling. Unless she's been locked up behind brick walls. And even then I suspect she'd be caught by a voice or a whistle.'

'Aunt Jane,' Amy said, 'you are a very wise woman.'

'The conversation is closed,' the old lady said.

Now, with the kettle steaming, Amy filled the pot, and thought, Well, yes, she had felt that small something in her chest at the sight of Marcus's russet hair. And felt it when she heard him stride across the room. And the three years he'd been away were longer, it seemed to her, than the twenty-four years before she met him. She picked up the loaded tray.

From the other room there came a great clatter and a slam. A trembling shook her, but she steadied herself, waiting until she was quite sure, her hands clasped firmly so that she wouldn't drop tea and cups and cakes, then went slowly toward the front parlor. She expected it to be empty. She thought Marcus had gone banging out, angry, perhaps never to return. Never to sit down and talk with her again. But when she reached the room, she saw his broad back at the window. He was struggling with the shutter. He set the hasp, pulled the window down, and drew the draperies.

'The air's freshening for a storm.'

She set the tray down, poured his tea, and offered him a slice of cake. He accepted and ate it in two gulps, crumbs dusting his waistcoat.

'You're a fine baker,' he said.

'Thank you.' She took tea for herself, and with the cup raised to her lips as if for protection, said, 'Marcus, you know you are free to do exactly as you please in this matter of money. You've no need of my permission.'

He sat staring at her. Then said, shortly, 'I know that.'

'Well, then?'

'It's our lives together. I want you to understand, to agree. I won't do it if you fear I may be wrong.'

The answer took her aback. It was so far from what she had expected. She wondered if it were true. But only for an instant. It was true – she saw it in his face. It wasn't a way of getting around her. Trying to get her to say, 'Yes, yes, go ahead, do whatever you want.' He was saying what he honestly felt.

She put her cup down, no longer needing to hide behind it. 'Aunt Jane trusted you. And proved it, too. Not just with the money she gave you but also with the house. She placed it in both our names.'

'The greatest trust. I felt so when I read her letter about it.'

'I felt so when she told me.'

'But *her* trust is not what I ask of you, Amy. Not Jane Oliver's trust. Your own.'

'I know,' Amy told him. Her cool glance went once again to the mantel. The ruby eyes of the carved ivory dog seemed to wink at her. It crossed her mind that she'd have been more impressed if Marcus had brought back sets of porcelain dishes. Well, perhaps he had. There were, after all, three sea chests still to be unpacked. She said casually, 'Now that you've discussed it with me, and I've had time to consider, I want you to invest with the Bordens. *Want* you to. That is my answer.'

He let out a great roar of laughter and bounced out of the

7

chair and came in quick noisy strides toward her. She had just taken up her cup again, and he hesitated, then snatched it away and set it down with a thump. He kissed spilled tea from her wrist, and swept her into his arms, crushing her against him so that her flat, thin, and bony body seemed nearly in danger of breaking.

Later, in the big bed in the upstairs front room, he made love to her for the second time since his return. The first night they had been together after the long voyage, he had fallen upon her, a hungry man deprived too long, a man whose means of satisfaction had never been satisfying. Although he didn't hurt her, it had been no joy to lie in his arms then.

But now, now he wooed her tenderly, and kissed her, and told her something of his dreams and they became her own.

When the night was done, she was more regretful than glad to leave him sleeping in his bed, and to go down into the kitchen - smiling as she had never quite smiled before - to heat washing water, and boil the coffee, and mix the batter for johnny cakes, and smiling still, to hum behind her teeth a small song.

PART I
1847 to 1877

Chapter 1

The town of Fall River was first established in 1659 on land traded from the Pocasset Indian tribe for a variety of clothing and household goods. It was known as the Freeman's Purchase and then as Freetown. Some twenty years later a second group of sites was forcibly taken by the Plymouth government and sold to a combine of settlers. The two areas together were named first Fallriver, then Troy, and finally, in 1834, Fall River, from the Indian word *quequechan*, which meant 'falling water,' and came from the Quequechan River that flowed from the Watuppa ponds through the town and into the harbor on Mount Hope Bay.

From 1803, when it was incorporated, and for sixty years thereafter, the town, under its several names, was divided by state boundaries, so that part of it was in Rhode Island and part in Massachussetts. In 1862, the boundary was moved two miles south and the whole of the town became part of the Commonwealth of Massachusetts.

In 1846 it had a population of 12,000. At water's edge, there were docks and wharves and warehouses, and a railroad track that connected Fall River to Boston. From the harbor the town rose upward on a series of narrow granite ledges cut into a steep hill that hung above the bay and the Taunton River that emptied into it.

It was a bustling and growing place, with seven textile mills, an ironworks, shops, saloons, markets, and banks.

And it was there that the Bay State Steamboat Company was

organized with capital stock of $300,000. Its fleet consisted of two coal-burning sidewheelers, the chartered *Massachusetts* and the *Bay State*, newly completed by shipbuilder Samuel Sneedon of New York at a cost of $175,000. The *Bay State* was the largest inland steamer then sailing in American waters, with a length of 315 feet, a beam of 40 feet, and a 14-foot hold.

She made her maiden voyage from Fall River Harbor on May 19, 1847.

At dawn of that day Marcus Kincaid lay sleeping beside his wife. He dreamed of a ship, a gleaming white sidewheeler, her flags afloat on a steady breeze. When Amy touched his cheek and whispered, 'Wake up. It's time,' he opened his eyes and saw the first flush of morning at the windows, and said sleepily, 'No, no, Amy. She sails this evening. After the boat train arrives from Boston.'

'It's time for the baby,' Amy said, gasping in sudden pain, then as it eased, laughing.

In a single convulsive movement that shook the four-poster bed, he was out from under the coverlet and reaching for his clothing. 'Parish!' he bellowed. 'Hey, Parish. Wake up and dress and run for the midwife! Parish! Hey!'

'There's no need to rouse the neighbourhood,' Amy protested.

'Parish!' Marcus shouted until he heard his younger brother's querulous question in the hallway. 'Run for the midwife, I say. It's time.'

Then, entangled in his shirt, stamping into his boots, he turned back to Amy. She was pale now. Beads of sweat shone on her upper lip. A pang tightened his belly. 'Are you all right? Is it bad?'

It was a question he was to ask with increasing frequency as the slowest day he had ever known wore on.

At noon he sat on the window seat looking past elms misted in spring green to the Fall River docks below. There the new *Bay State* was moored, surrounded by two-masted schooners and donkey tenders and coal barges. He had staked his and his family's future and fortune on her success; but now, as he tugged his reddish beard and squinted into the sunlight, only a part of his mind and a small part of his heart was centered on her. Once more he asked anxiously, 'Is it very bad?'

Amy, white-lipped, her small hands clenched, was unable to answer. She managed to shake her head at him over the great mound of her belly.

'It's no worse than it should be for the moment,' the midwife said.

Marcus ignored her while he considered if there was anything else to be done. Parish had pumped up the huge buckets of water and now sat in the kitchen, waiting for word. Marcus himself had opened the chest Amy had prepared over the months. Sheets and blankets, wrappings and buntings were stacked close to hand.

He felt totally useless. He supposed it was natural enough, for that's how it was, that a man should be completely necessary at the beginning of this thing and absolutely unneeded at the end of it. Still, there ought to be something.

'What can I do?' he asked finally.

Now, with the pain momentarily subsided, Amy could say, 'Go down to the ship. There's nothing to keep you busy here.'

'I want to be with you, Amy.'

'Please. I must concentrate. It's the only way. And I can't do it, not while you watch me so anxiously. Go to the wharves, and I'll send Betty Gowan for you when it's time.'

Amy had allowed herself the one luxury when she knew she was with child. She hired Betty to come in at breakfast and leave after dinner. The girl was only sixteen, but strong and willing, and lived not far away with her parents.

'You're sure you're all right?'

''Marcus!' But she was laughing.

He bent to kiss her cheek. She was no longer plain to him. Pregnancy had rounded her once flat body, put color in her cheeks, warmed her pale blue eyes. Their nine months together had brought joy to them both.

'You'll send for me on the instant?'

She managed a nod, though her teeth settled hard into her lower lip.

'We'll send for you, Mr. Kincaid,' the midwife said importantly.

Parish sat at the kitchen table over a cup of coffee. Betty leaned into a cabinet, the back of her neck red under her braided black hair. Marcus looked from the one to the other, smelling

11

guilt in the steamy room. No doubt that Parish had been up to something, but Marcus wasn't sure what. He could never be certain with Parish. Now his brother sat tipped dangerously back in the wooden chair, a thin hand beating a quick tattoo on his knee. He was slim, tight-strung. His hair was a very dark brown, his mustache narrow. At twenty-five he was a worry to Marcus because he had settled to nothing at a time when a man of that age was no longer to be considered a boy. Only a few days before, Parish had left his apprenticeship at the bank. He did not like bookkeeping, he'd said. It was a strain on his eyes, his back. It was a strain on his soul.

In part Marcus blamed himself. He had cosseted Parish too much at the beginning, and Amy, too kind-hearted to be firm, had finished the job while he lived with her in the years Marcus had been away. Not that Marcus would chide Amy for it. Parish could tease tears out of a serpent and sweets from a stone.

'Will it be long?' Parish asked, shoving aside his coffee cup. 'What does the midwife say?'

'That all's as it should be. I don't know how long it will take. I'm going down to the wharves.' Marcus looked at Betty. 'You'll come for me as soon as there's word?'

She turned, curtsied. 'As fast as I can.'

Marcus asked if Parish wanted to go too.

He yawned, rose. 'Why not? Anything's better than sitting here.' His tone was casual, concealing a long-held dislike of Amy. He didn't care if she were delivered of a boy or a girl or a puppy. It was all one to him if she screamed in pain or cried out in bliss. Until Amy, Marcus had had time for no one and nothing but his younger brother. After Amy, Parish considered, he was left to fend for himself while Marcus took to the whaling ship and came back rich enough to invest in a shipping line and would give his brother not a cent, but only the roof over his head.

Still, he thought, following Marcus, he had a dollar coin in his pocket, begged off Betty, and that was something.

Together, they went into the brightness of the sun, Marcus, as always, striding ahead. They walked quickly along five steep blocks past where the fire-blackened buildings of Franklin Street were still being restored, along a second slope, and into the quick bustle of the docks, where the *Bay State* strained at her hawsers.

They were hardly at her gangplank when Marcus heard his shouted name, and turned, and there came small Betty, dashing after them, the ribbons on her cap flying, her face wreathed in a smile.

Even as he told himself that all was well, else why would Betty smile, he saw the flying ribbons and blessed Amy, who'd said a sixteen-year-old girl needed ribbons on her cap to make her gay.

'It's a girl,' Betty said, laughing. 'She came almost the moment you left the house.'

Marcus yelled, 'Hooray! Hooray!', and set out for home at a run. Breathless, flushed, beard and russet hair disheveled, he burst into the upstairs bedroom.

'Amy, my love!'

She seemed to be drowsing, but when he crossed the threshold, she opened her eyes. 'I hope you're not sorry I've given you a daughter.'

Against her shoulder she held a small bundle of white bunting. She gently turned back a fold to reveal a tiny head covered with silken red fuzz.

He laughed, though he felt close to tears at the miracle of it. 'How can I be sorry? But for the hair, which is surely mine, she's a small replica of you.'

'Hold her.'

He bent, reached without hesitation, and when Amy put the baby into his arms, he felt as if all his life he had been waiting for that moment. With a smile at Amy, he went to the window. He turned the infant so that her wide-open eyes, Amy's eyes, seemed to look down at the Fall River docks. 'Look,' Marcus said. 'Look, and always remember. There's the *Bay State*. She sails today, for the first time, on your first day of life. Which is good luck for her and for you, too. For she'll be the making of our future and our fortune.'

'I think,' Amy said from her bed, 'that we shall name her Augusta.'

They had spoken of it before. If a boy, the child would be called Marcus. If a girl, Marcus had leaned toward Amy. Amy had favoured Augusta, which was Jane Oliver's baptismal name.

Marcus turned. 'If you say so, then Augusta it shall be. And when it seems too grand for her, we can call her Gussie.'

He sat on the edge of the four-poster, handed the baby into Amy's arms. 'And you? Are you all right?'

'You can see.' She smiled at him. 'I never looked it, but it appears that I'm well made for childbearing.'

He held her hand until he thought she was asleep, the infant once again settled against her shoulder. When he rose, she said softly, 'Marcus, you must sail with the ship as you planned before.'

'You're sure you want me to?'

'You said it yourself. She's our future and fortune. Yours and mine and little Gussie's. You must look after her for us.'

He kissed her. 'Then I'll see you on my return.' He touched the infant's cheek briefly, took up his already packed carpetbag, and went downstairs.

'She's a pretty girl,' he told Parish. 'And Amy's fine. They're both resting from their ordeal now.'

'Oh, I thought I'd see them,' Parish said, feigning disappointment. Then, 'I see you're going on the *Bay State* after all.'

Marcus nodded.

Parish's mouth slanted under his narrow mustache. 'I'm glad you're a sensible man.'

'I must be.'

Parish ignored that. 'Since you're going, I'll go too.'

A few minutes later, after he had collected a change of shirt and collar, they walked together back to the docks. He said, 'I hope you're not sorry in this enterprise, Marcus.'

Marcus didn't answer. It was useless to try to counter Parish's doubts. Parish would believe what he wanted to believe. Besides, Marcus was committed. It was too late now to wonder.

'The arrangement, ship and rail, it's awkward,' Parish went on. 'One day passenger and cargo ships will go direct from Boston to New York. What then?'

This Marcus couldn't ignore. He said, 'It's a slow and dangerous voyage around Cape Cod, and in the open seas. Our inland route, through Narragansett Bay and into Long Island Sound, is safe and sure.'

It was late afternoon by then, but the docks were still alight with the western sun. They were crowded with carts and wagons and carriages of all description. Teams of horses whinnied and stamped and shied as dogs played chase and snarl around them, and sea gulls swooped and screamed overhead. The dockmaster, a tall blond man with drooping mustaches, compared bills of lading against the manifest as cargo was stacked for loading. Crates of cotton and threads from the mills for the factories of New York. Hoops and staves and hasps from the ironworks.

Marcus watched for a moment, then went on board. He was more than the Bordens' silent partner. He was to be their eyes and ears as well. He would travel the *Bay State* as a passenger, then report back to them. Already he knew the vessel from stem to stern. He'd been over it many times since it was brought up from the shipyard.

'You'll have things to do,' Parish said. 'I'll take a look on my own.'

Marcus went on alone, and was glad of it. He walked slowly, as if without plan, along decks and gangways. He found nothing to criticize. There was only polished brass, gleaming wood. The swinging oil lamps in each of the forty-eight cabins were properly trimmed. The sheets and towels were fresh. The wash basins of English porcelain shone. The water pitchers were full. It was good to see the care lavished on the passengers' accommodations, for which they would pay an additional dollar over the two-dollar deck fare. It was the same in the public rooms and cargo holds.

The monthly payroll for the entire ship would be a few pennies below $2,000. The captain, called the commander, would receive $31.25; the first pilot would draw $18.75. Added to the running expenses of coal and food, it was plain that a goodly income would be required to earn a profit.

Yet Marcus was smiling when he returned to the deck. He was sure all would be well. It was deepening twilight now. As he pulled his pocketwatch from his waistcoat, he heard from the distance the slow chuff and rattle of the Boston train. Bells ringing, a white curtain of steam billowing from beneath it and twin clouds of black wood smoke pouring from its square stacks, it hove slowly into view.

In an instant a small army of dockworkers flung itself on the open flatcars, quickly hauling down crated baggage and additional cargo. From Boston fishing fleets there came great wooden barrels of fish and live lobsters in salt water bound for the markets of New York. From Taunton there were stoves and silverware, and boots and shoes and slippers from Lynn and Natick.

Amid the confusion of the laboring stevedores, daintily appareled ladies stepped down from the train and made their way across the busy docks. Gentlemen in bowlers and tall hats stepped carefully around piles of horse droppings. A young boy swept hastily at these, always a few paces away from actually clearing a trail.

As Marcus watched, two men carrying a barrel between them passed before a team of horses, which whinnied and reared in their traces. The men lunged back, the barrel falling between them. It burst open and from it spilled a gray wriggling mass of eels. In an instant they slithered in all directions, spreading quick pandemonium. Women screamed shrilly. Men shouted. The dogs barked wildly and dashed away.

The young dockworker flung his broom down, positioned an empty crate, and threw himself at the heaving mass. With great sweeps of his bare hands he gathered the ugly things up and dumped them into the crate and then gathered more, while all about him men stood watching. Soon the dock was clear. What eels the boy hadn't managed to recapture had escaped for good. The men who had dropped the barrel took up the crate and brought it to the ship. The boy went back to his straw broom.

Marcus sent a deckhand for the sweeper. When the boy came, he looked frightened. His hands were white-knuckled fists at his sides; his throat worked inside his collarless shirt. Shadows of apprehension lay in his light gray eyes.

Marcus looked down from his great height, rubbed thoughtfully at his reddish beard, then let himself slump against the railing. It shortened his formidable height. He was glad to see the boy move a step closer.

'What's your name?' Marcus asked.

'Luke Wakefield, sir.'

'And how old are you?'

The boy stared, didn't answer. He didn't know what he could have done wrong, but whatever it was, if it cost him his work, then he didn't know what he or his mother would do. He was

16

twelve years old, small and slight because he was under-
nourished, but he carried a man's responsibility on his narrow
shoulders.

'What's the matter?' Marcus asked. 'I only ask your age.'

Luke told him in a breathless stammer.

'You show uncommon common sense for any age. I saw how
the other men stood and watched while you went after those
eels.'

Luke said nothing, but he wiped his hands on his thighs,
remembering the slime against his palms and how his gorge
had risen at the feel of it.

'You work at the docks on a steady basis?'

'I try to go to school too.'

'That's a good thing. But you work because you need to, of
course. Do you have a family?'

'My mother,' Luke said briefly.

'All right.' He was thinking of his infant Gussie when he
went on. 'I believe you can do better than dock sweeper. Let
somebody else attend to the dung. Come by to see me in four
days time.' He gave directions to the house on High Street.
'Will you be there?'

Luke said he would, then turned away quickly so that
Marcus wouldn't see the relief that filled his eyes. He hadn't
been in the wrong. This big, deep-voiced man thought there
was better work for Luke to do. Perhaps there was hope after all.

As he took up his broom, the dockmaster demanded, 'What
did he want?' and when Luke explained, puckered his mouth to
whistle. 'Not bad. You know who he is?'

'No,' Luke answered. 'Nor do I care. As long as he gets me
more pay.'

'It's Marcus Kincaid. Friend of the Bordens, and they're the
line's owners. He can get you more pay, if anyone can. But
mind now, when you go to see him, wear a clean shirt. And if
you don't have one, then come to me for it.'

Luke grinned his thanks and bent over his broom. He didn't
know how it would be. He knew only how it had been until
now. They had come to America below decks in filthy steerage.
A family then – his father, his mother carrying his infant
brother, born only twenty-four hours before they embarked at
Liverpool. Disease had swept the crowded compartments

17

where they huddled. Stench and filth spread from bulkhead to bulkhead. Of the four of them, only two, Luke, then eight years old, and his mother Nelle, survived. And when the dead infant was taken from her arms, she crumpled away into a pale, stricken silence that seemed like death itself. By the time the ship docked in Boston, she seemed to come to herself again. She spoke enough to answer the questions rightly, but all the while she held a small bundle of rags in her arms. And it was Luke who had to lead her ashore, to find a room for them. It was he who brought her to Fall River two years later. Day after day, night after night, she sat still cradling a small bundle against her. She spoke when she wanted to, answered questions when she understood them. But her reason was gone, and there seemed no way ever for her to return to what she had been before.

It was thirty minutes after seven. There was still a light in the western sky, but smoldering oil lamps lighted the wharves. The clamor had risen. It seemed to Marcus that most of Fall River had turned out to watch the *Bay State* depart.

He wished that Amy were with him to see the passengers embarking, and dockworkers pushing loaded barrows, but by this time, he thought, she would be holding small Gussie to her breast, suckling the baby whose birth day it was. He was missing that sight to see this one, and regretted it too. He told himself he'd see Gussie at her mother's nipple another time.

The train was emptied now, the candlelight at its windows gone dark. The flatcars were bare of baggage and cargo. Wagons and carts and teams had all gone. Beneath his feet the ship began to throb with life.

'All ashore that's going ashore!' The cry was repeated through public lounges and gangways. Those not sailing departed slowly, while the passengers lined the rails, waving their last goodbyes.

Marcus stood on deck while the whistles blew, the hawsers were flung free, and the *Bay State* backed slowly from her berth out into the waters of Mount Hope Bay.

As the wind ruffled his russet beard, he raised his eyes to the darkening heavens and prayed soundlessly that his judgement had been good. That the line would prosper and endure.

When he turned away, heading for the saloon deck with the thought of finding Parish, he noticed a deckhand working with great coils of rope. The man was tall, big-shouldered, plainly strong, with a shock of uncombed black hair, high cheekbones, and glittering black eyes that were fixed on Marcus himself. Marcus didn't know him and was about to move on when the third mate, Hal Davis, stepped from the shadows and shouted, 'Hey, you, Willie, get on with it. How long need it take you to roll a coil?'

The man called Willie stared, his big hands motionless on the rope.

'Get on with it, damn you!' Davis bellowed. 'Or can't you figure out what I'm talking about?'

Willie dropped the rope, head lowered, shoulders bunching. A hot wave of menace flowed from him. He was set, ready. Hal Davis hated foreigners, and he'd wanted his brother for the job Willie had gotten. Since the day Willie was hired, the third mate had made his feelings plain. Now Willie had had enough. Of Davis. Of the job.

But Marcus moved so swiftly that he was between the two men before they knew where he had come from. Genially he engaged the third mate in conversation. It was a great day for the Bay State Steamboat Company, wasn't it? And the weather was fine. It would be a good voyage, wouldn't it? When would they see the first light? And when would they round Point Judith?

By the time the third mate had answered all these questions, Willie had thought better of starting a fight, taken up his ropes, and with a last look at Marcus had gone below. There, busy with other chores, Willie Gorgas thought of the big reddish-haired man, dressed in fashionable clothing and fine linen. He was all that Willie wanted to be, dreamed he might one day be. For now, at seventeen, he worked the ropes, swabbed the decks, croaked out a foreign-sounding 'Yes, sir,' and 'No, sir,' was barely understood and hardly understanding of what was said to him.

The first real memory Willie had was of a stormy afternoon, far away in the Carpathian Mountains. He was riding in a cart with ten other boys. He knew that he was seven years old. He knew his name. He knew nothing else about himself, nor where he was going, nor even where he had come from. Sometimes he dreamed of a burnt-out stone cottage in a burnt-out field. But that was only a dream. His name and age were real. Thunder roared through steep ravines; lightning flashed along the bare ridges. The worn old nags bucked. Suddenly, the cart's axle broke, and it overturned. Boys were flung in all directions. Willie picked himself up, his knees scraped raw and bleeding. Both hands were gouged. While the other boys scrambled together, Willie fled. Beneath darkening skies, he raced away alone. He ran without knowing why and without looking back.

Some time after the storm had passed, he fell, exhausted, into a farmer's haystack. At sunrise he awakened.

He found an egg and ate it raw. He drank water from a well. When the farm dog barked at him, he ran again.

Slowly he made his way through strange countryside until he reached a river. He hid on a barge, and when he was discovered the man laughed, fed him, and put him off at the next town. What had worked once could be made to work again. He tried the same trick, but was beaten, threatened with drowning. When he tried a third time, he was found and whipped and killed the man who did it with the man's own knife and fled before it was discovered. That night he went to a barge captain, offered to work for his food, and was taken on. It took Willie years, but he made his way across Europe. By then he had heard of America. He was determined to see it. At fifteen he signed on the ship that he jumped twelve months later in Boston Harbor, and soon after that he found his way to Fall River where he had heard there were jobs. He didn't care what he did, nor how he did it, except to survive. But now, polishing brass doorknobs and thinking of Marcus Kincaid, Willie began to care. He knew there was only one thing he wanted to be: a man like that. A rich man. A man sure of his power.

In the dining saloon of the forward cabin the tables were lit by tall, tallow dip candles. At the stroke of eight, Captain Joseph Comstock came in with his guests. He was broad-shouldered and bearded, wearing a long dark coat and a top hat, the emblem of his rank. He removed his hat, set it aside, and took a chair. Marcus and Parish joined him while the other passengers were seated.

Later that same summer, President James Polk, returning from a brief sojourn away from the pressures of the Mexican War, would dine with Captain Comstock, and when they reached Newport, the president, received by thousands of citizens at Long Wharf with cannonading and rockets, would stand on the afterdeck and deliver an impromptu speech.

But the captain was as attentive to his guests this evening as he would be to the president, and as the luxurious fifty-cent table d'hôte dinner was served, the room filled with whispered conversation and laughter. Course after course was consumed. Fish, soup, beef, and fowl. Fruits and sweets and puddings and nuts. Rum, whiskey, and coffee by the bucket.

Parish stirred restlessly. He was bored with the talk. He cared in no way that plans were already being drawn up to install lighting gas in the Capitol at Washington City, and that, as the speaker went on, it was only the beginning. In a few short years such lighting would be found in every home in the nation; it would be the end of the whaling industry, for who would need sperm oil then? Parish cared only that he had but a single dollar coin in his pocket and wanted more. As soon as he could, he excused himself.

Marcus would have gone with him, but he was interested in the conversation. That he had left the whaling business behind before it died, even if it had a few more years, pleased him. But now his attention was claimed by a small girl sitting across the table from him. She was about five, with a square, sullen face, a pug nose, and dark brown eyes that contrasted oddly with her rough-cut blond hair. Her tiny plump hands moved quickly between the food placed before her and her mouth, so that she consumed what appeared to be a prodigious amount for her size. Next to her sat a man whom Marcus took to be her father, although engaged as he was in a discourse related to finance with the man on his right, he paid no attention to the little girl.

With his own newborn Gussie in his mind, Marcus was fascinated by this child. He smiled at her. She stared back at him expressionlessly as she stuffed a huge end of buttered roll into her mouth. She coughed on it. Her father reached behind him, pulled out a folded journal, and slapped her smartly on top of the head, saying, 'As sure as my name is Hiram Graystone, General Zachary Taylor will have the Mexican War over in a matter of months, and our American flag will fly in Mexico City.'

'Even if,' another man said dryly, 'the legislature of Massachusetts has passed a resolution calling the war wanton and unjust and unconstitutional. As it most assuredly is.' His voice was soft, magical. His face was pale as if he suffered from ill health. He was on his way to New York to embark on a European tour.

Captain Comstock addressed him. 'Mr. Emerson, if you agree with that assessment, then why do you believe this war is being fought?'

'For profit, sir. For material good,' Ralph Waldo Emerson answered, and then added softly, '"Things are in the saddle and ride mankind."'

Hiram Graystone's beard split on a cackle. '"Profit? Material good?"' he repeated mockingly. 'And what else is there?'

The little girl squirmed. Once more her father slapped her smartly atop her head. 'Be still and listen, Mabel. If you're to understand how to deal with the property you'll one day inherit, you must learn.' He pointed his beard at Emerson. 'Say what you like about profit, I call the war simple justice. Americans live on the land in Texas and California. It's American land.'

'Land?' Emerson murmured, smiling. 'You see? Material good. No more.'

'There *is* no more,' Hiram Graysone retorted. He swung around to confront Mabel, his mouth thin and unloving. 'Now what lesson have you taken from these remarks?' he demanded harshly.

Her small pug nose wrinkled. 'Land is good,' she said finally.

He nodded, then said to the table at large, 'She's not the son I had hoped for, but only the best I could do.'

Small Mabel's face went a harsh flaming red, then a bloodless white.

It was too much for Marcus. His instinct was to pull the journal from Hiram Graystone's hand and belabor him about the head with it. Instead, he flung down his napkin and leaned toward Mabel. 'I have a little girl too. She was born only this morning. Her name is Gussie.'

Captain Comstock smiled. 'We must have a toast to your young daughter, Mr. Kincaid. And at the same time to Miss

Mabel Graystone, who is with us tonight.'

It was a graceful thing to do, Marcus thought. But Comstock was just such a man. However, Hiram Graystone ignored the comment, ignored too the anguish on his daughter's face. He was a man whose soul was as dried out and pursed as his wrinkled face. Son of a Vermont farmer, he loved land not for its product but for its interest and rentals. He had married for them, connived for them, and was embittered when his wife ran away with another man only because she left behind for him to raise a daughter rather than a son.

Now, instead of raising a glass to Mabel, he looked at her coldly. 'Go down to the stateroom to bed.'

It was in Marcus's mind that the child was too young, too small. How would she find her way? But she nodded, rose, and waddled rather than walked into the shadows at the far end of the room.

Hiram Graystone said to the table, 'Ah yes, there are great opportunities in this expansion. Texas, California.'

'If they be free states, that is,' one of the men at the table observed. 'Otherwise they'll be trouble.'

Hiram shrugged. 'We'll have a compromise.'

Captain Comstock rose, excused himself, and soon afterward Marcus too left the dining saloon to walk slowly along the deck where the young, the less well-to-do, were making themselves comfortable on benches and chairs provided for those who had paid only the deck fare.

A silver moon laid a bright path across the bay. Soon now the twinkling oil lights of Newport would flicker in the darkness, and in a little while the ship would dock briefly at Long Wharf to take on more passengers bound for New York, and more cargo too.

A couple passed him by. The man was young, square-jawed, smiling. The girl was beautiful and demure. The glow about them brought a warmth to him. Perhaps they were honeymooners; surely they seemed so, holding hands tightly, and were going down now to share their first night in marriage. He hoped so. He would like to think that the beautiful *Bay State*, on her maiden voyage, would become part of the memory of their first time together. There was a goodness in love, and the girl looked eager.

Smiling to himself at his thoughts, Marcus started for his

stateroom; but then, because they had only the one key between them, he decided to find Parish first. It took him just a few moments.

Parish was in the saloon bar, seated at a table in a lamplit corner with three other men, drummers by the looks of them. His face was flushed. His eyes glittered. But his slim hands were steady holding the cards.

Marcus stood beside him. 'It's late, Parish. And we must talk.'

Parish flicked a quick sideways glance toward Marcus. He had tripled the money he had teased from Betty Gowan. Given another half an hour he'd triple the sum again. Given a full hour . . .

But Marcus laid a thick hand on his shoulder. 'Parish.'

'Yes, yes. You're right. It *is* late.' Parish smiled genially at his fellow card players. 'I'm, sorry, gentlemen. Perhaps another time?'

It was just as well, he decided, as he followed Marcus out. There'd been the beginnings of suspicion in the eyes of one sharp-faced fellow. It didn't do to wait too long before withdrawing. It didn't do to be too greedy either. Perhaps Marcus had done him a favor without intending to. But he said nothing of that.

Marcus was frowning at him. 'I don't want you to play on this ship.'

'A friendly game's no harm,' Parish protested.

'Friendly game!' Marcus sighed. 'What did you win?' But he didn't wait for a reply. 'I don't know what's to become of you.'

'Don't worry.'

'But I do, you know.'

'I'll make my way.'

'I hope so.'

Parish didn't answer. He stopped to look out. Marcus paused with him. The lights of Newport drew closer.

Soon the *Bay State* docked. Late as it was, a noisy crowd stood on Long Wharf. Passengers embarked, some having been rowed from adjacent islands, and the dockworkers hauled more cargo aboard. Then, with three quick whistles, the ship once again got up steam and was on her way.

It was time to retire. Silently the two men went to their stateroom. Marcus let them in, lit the oil lamp.

Parish flung himself down, seemingly asleep in the same instant.

But Marcus was wakeful, his mind ranging far as he took off his boots and stretched out on the fine purple linen.

It was 178 miles from Fall River to New York. The *Bay State* should make that distance in eleven hours. They had just left the Newport docks. In a little while they would round Point Judith, and there would be the sea. But it was a quiet, windless night. The ship would be steady. And soon after passing the Point Judith light they would enter Long Island Sound. At six in the morning, with the sun nearly risen, they would dock at the pier in New York.

There was a whisper of footsteps in the corridor outside. Parish sighed deeply. Then all was still again except for the steady rhythmic turn of the wooden paddle wheels.

Marcus smiled into the dark. The line was under way. And there was his new Gussie, his Amy. The future lay bright before him.

Chapter 2

On January 24, 1848, gold was discovered on the American River in California. Since word traveled slowly in those days, the find was not yet well known when, only nine days later, at Guadalupe Hidalgo near Mexico City, a treaty ending the Mexican American War was signed between the United States and the Mexican government. It provided that the Americans would pay $15 million and assume claims against the Mexicans of $3,250,000 in exchange for territory from the 42nd parallel south to the Gila and Rio Grande rivers. Over the years this land would become the states of California, Texas, and New Mexico, as well as most of Arizona, the Oklahoma panhandle, the larger part of Colorado, southwestern Kansas, and Wyoming.

It was only in August of 1849 that news of the American River gold strike was widely published on the East Coast, and it was then that Parish Kincaid read of it in the *Boston Advertiser*, when he was visiting that city. He immediately rushed to South Station to take the first train to Fall River.

He was afire with the thought of gold – and he wasn't the only one. The train was full of men carrying all they owned in packets and carpetbags. They were traveling to Fall River to board the *Empire State*, a new 1,598-ton sidewheeler, built for the Bay State Steamboat Company a year earlier. She would leave soon after the train's arrival, bearing these gold hunters to New York, from where they would go by ship around Cape Horn, or by rail to St. Louis and stage or wagon across the continent.

Parish was determined to be with them, but he had no means for the trip. When the train chugged up to the Fall River wharves he was first off, and went immediately in search of Marcus.

He found his older brother engaged in conversation with the dockmaster, and drew Marcus aside. 'I would like to ask a favor.'

'And what's that?' Marcus studied the thin tense face, and, knowing the look, prepared himself.

'I need a stake. One hundred dollars. I know I could do it on that.'

'Do what?'

Parish waved a hand at the men ambling across the wharves. 'They're going to prospect for gold in California.'

'And that's what you want to do?'

'It's where the future is,' Parish answered.

'That may be,' Marcus said, openly doubtful. 'But I judge you'd do better to stay here and settle down to a trade.'

'I want to go,' Parish insisted. 'If you help me now, I'll repay you tenfold.'

'No. And I've business to attend to.' Marcus turned abruptly away. It was his own fault that Parish had remained an irresponsible child. Now Marcus had to put an end to it. He said, 'You're a grown man. It's time you learned you must work for what you want.'

Red-faced, shaking, Parish strode away. There was so little time left. He heard the sound of it passing in his mind.

Hurrying, he went to the house on High Street. Within moments he had stuffed shirts and toilet articles into a carpetbag. He had no plan. He only knew that gold was his future. He had to go.

There was Amy's voice. The cry of the new baby girl, Aria. Two-and-a-half-year-old Gussie's prattle. Betty Gowan's giggle. All known and familiar to him – the sounds of home. The thought gave him only brief pause. There was nothing for him here, and this wasn't his home. He remained on sufferance and suffered for it. But what should he do? Even as he asked himself, he knew.

They were here, on the second floor. No one was below. In the kitchen was a bowl where Amy kept coins for the ice man, the firewood man. And in the front parlor ...

He went down, careful of his boots on the stairs. He was only a moment emptying the bowl. The chore in the front parlor took longer. Moving soundlessly on the English carpet, he put his bag on the settle, opened it; then he went to the mantel. The celadon lion and the ivory dog that Marcus had brought back from the city of Canton still stood on the mantel. Parish ignored them. He considered them Kincaid's folly when he considered them at all. But there was a small silver snuffbox and two silver candlesticks sitting beside them. These he could easily sell in New York. He felt no guilt at taking what wasn't his. He believed that Marcus owed him. His brother had returned from the whaling voyage with a small fortune, which he ought to have shared with Parish. A portion had been Parish's due.

Candlesticks and snuffbox went into his carpetbag. He was smoothing the shirts over them when Amy appeared in the doorway.

She wore a white blouse layered with ruffles at the throat. Her full skirt belled at her hips. She had lost the spinsterish look she had had when she married Marcus, but Parish didn't notice the changes in her. He disliked her as much as ever.

'Oh, Parish, it's you.' Her smile was warm, loving. He didn't notice that either. 'I thought I heard someone here. But I believed you were still in Boston.'

He kept his thin face expressionless. 'No.'

'Is something wrong?'

'No,' he repeated.

'Did you have any luck?' She was holding Aria, who waved small pink hands around her dark head, and from behind her came Gussie to throw her arms around his legs.

'Unca,' she shouted. 'Unca, you home.'

Her eyes, at birth as blue as Amy's, had become a strong glowing green. Dimples played in her flushed cheeks. Already she could speak many words, could understand most of what was said to her. Parish disliked precocious children. He patted her once, then put her aside. To Amy he said, 'I had no luck in Boston because there's nothing I want to do there.' He went on, 'I'm going.'

'Going?' she echoed. 'But Parish, where? Why? What are you talking about?'

Her concern was evident. She had, he knew, always liked him. It was too bad he couldn't return the compliment. But it wouldn't do to offend her now.

He said, 'Just down to New York on the *Empire State*. I'll be back very soon.' But out of the corner of his eye, he noted that Gussie had climbed onto the settle and was busily digging in his carpetbag.

Before he could get to her to stop her, out came a shirt. From its folds the silver snuffbox fell to the floor. The sound of it was like thunder exploding in the room, but his voice, yelling, 'Gussie, stop that!' was even louder.

Amy gasped. Aria screamed suddenly. Small Gussie's wide green eyes grew even larger with fright.

With the tick-tock of the clock in his head, Parish bent to swoop up the box. 'I need it, Amy. For going to California.'

'No,' she said, as he stuffed it into the bag. 'No, Parish. That's not the way. You must discuss it with Marcus. Be sure he'll think of something. He'll find a place for you. Perhaps with the line, if you like. You mustn't go so far away from us.' Her voice was gentle, not accusing. 'You belong here. With your family.'

'No, Amy.'

'I don't care for the silver,' she said softly, 'but I can't let you leave. Not like this.'

He caught up the bag, went to the door.

'Wait,' she cried, and was after him quick as a thought. After him, and clinging to his arm, while Aria wailed louder and

Gussie, scrambling down from the settle, flung her small self at his knees.

He kicked the child away and pushed so hard at Amy that she staggered back and fell into the wall. Her face was as white as her blouse, its ruffled neckline torn and darkened with sweat from Parish's hand. He cursed and fled, taking the carpetbag with him.

As he raced out, planning a circuitous path to the docks lest he meet Marcus on the way, he heard the three combined cries and Betty's shrill interpolations.

'What is it?' she was asking. 'What's happened?'

Amy's blue eyes were full of tears. A reddish bruise spread on her arm. But holding the screaming infant Aria, she knelt, clasped Gussie. 'It's all right,' she said. 'It's nothing. Uncle Parish didn't mean it.'

Betty cried again, 'What's the matter?'

'Nothing,' Amy answered evenly. 'It's nothing, as I've said.' Hugging both children to her, she sank into a chair. Poor foolish Parish, she thought. To be reduced to such behavior. How desperate he must be.

Meanwhile Betty's eyes had fallen upon the mantel. She saw empty space where silver ought to have been. With a gasp, she hurried into the kitchen. Yes, it was as she had suddenly feared. The household money was gone from the bowl. Parish, who had once begged to borrow a dollar from her small savings, had fallen to stealing now.

She was telling Amy about it when Marcus came in.

He caught her last words: '. . . and the bowl's empty.' He saw the anguish on Amy's face, the torn and stained ruffles at her throat. He heard Aria's whimperings, looked at Gussie's streaked cheeks.

But when he asked gruffly what the trouble was, Amy didn't answer. Betty blurted out with a gush of tears what had happened. She'd heard more than Amy realized. How Amy had begged Parish not to go, how he'd taken the silver and shoved her so hard she'd almost fallen, holding the baby in her arms. And how Betty herself had given him a dollar because he teased her for it, and known even then that she oughtn't to do it. Wringing her hands, she told it all, and then, when Marcus dismissed her, she ran sobbing into the kitchen.

29

Face pale under his russet hair, Marcus said, 'I apologize to you, Amy. I'll go and get the silver back.'

'No. Let it be. I don't care about it.'

'I do.'

'Let him go, Marcus. It means so much to him, it means nothing to me.'

'The snuffbox and candlesticks belonged to Aunt Jane Oliver.'

'They are only *things*. Forget them and pity Parish instead.'

He touched her cheek gently, smoothed Aria's dark curls, and kissed Gussie's tears away. Then, even as Amy asked him not to, he left the house.

It was close to twilight now. The air was thick and sweet with the scent of roses. He didn't notice. It was as if he breathed sulphur as his bootheels pounded on the cobblestones.

First he looked through the gatherings on the wharves. He saw the dockmaster checking his manifests, but didn't speak. He went into the warehouses, just to be certain. Then he boarded the *Empire State*.

He found Parish below decks in the common sleeping room. The place was crowded, blue with cigar and pipe smoke, the air already heavy with fumes from the oil lamps. Amid the deep rumbling voices, a fiddle sang sweetly. A throbbing accordion played along. Packets, tin cases, trunks, and crates were secured in the corners.

Marcus took it all in as he spied Parish, made his way toward him. Gold fever, he thought. A disease as much a contagion as cholera. The understanding softened him. But only a little.

'Why did you do it?' he said to Parish.

'There was no other way. You refused me, didn't you? What else could I do? And I've only borrowed the silver. I'll return the value to you tenfold, I promise.'

Parish's words in his uncaring voice, his look so casual too, stiffened Marcus as nothing else could have. Understanding no longer mattered to him. Pure hard rage gripped him. 'Keep the silver and be damned to you. You're no longer a brother of mine!' he roared. With the image of Amy's white and tear-stained face, her torn ruffles before him, he grabbed Parish by the shirt, jerked him to his feet.

The other men in the place went silent, backing off, eyes watchful.

'So don't come puling back when you're starving. I saw the bruise on my Amy's arm. I heard my children screaming in fear. Just don't come back.'

Parish raised his hands to thrust Marcus away and Marcus was on him then, bowling him over. He whipped Parish down with hard crashing blows to the face, until coming to his senses, he felt blood on his fists and saw Parish lying still beneath him. Rising, Marcus paused, looked down at Parish for a long moment, then left the ship to hurry back to the house on High Street.

In a little while Parish laboriously dragged himself to his feet. He cleaned his face as well as he could, flung away his bloodied handkerchief, and huddled alone in the midst of the mill workers who had quit their jobs, the artisans from Boston, the roustabouts and drummers and hostlers, all dreaming, as he did, of California gold. All on the way to find it.

The ship throbbed. The paddle wheels began their slow turn. The whistle blew. The *Empire State* was on her way.

The next that Marcus and Amy heard of Parish was three years later. It was the occasion of Gussie's fifth birthday, and the fifth birthday of the first sailing of the *Bay State*: May 19, 1852.

The two were celebrated together. And with good cause, Marcus considered. Gussie was healthy and bright and beautiful to behold. And the steamship company was a success after a good start. In 1850, the same year the *State of Maine* was added to the line, and just three years after its beginnings, the company had paid dividends of 6 percent a month for ten consecutive months. Its earnings had built the *Empire State*, and would soon lead to the acquisition of another ship.

Amy had arranged a late afternoon luncheon and invited Luke Wakefield to join in the festivities.

He was seventeen now, tall, lean. His dark hair was neatly trimmed to his collar, his face still smooth shaven, though he thought to grow a mustache as soon as he could.

Although they had been hard, filled with back-breaking and hand-blistering labor, the past five years had been the best he had known. And he had Marcus Kincaid, and Amy too, to thank for them. He remembered clearly the day he had first come to High Street. It had been mid-afternoon. The lilacs in the front yard were at full bloom, dripping purple and white blossoms over the footpath. He opened the gate in a fence covered with pink climbing roses. His hand shook when he touched the brass door knocker. He wore a clean shirt provided by the dockmaster, and steam-pressed trousers. He was still shaking when he left. But he was smiling too. For Marcus had given him a letter to the general manager of the Bay State Steamboat Company, and directions to take it to the office on Anawan Street.

Some had resented him when he'd first come aboard. Hal Davis, the third mate, sneered, and cursed him later, when Marcus stopped to talk to him.

But Luke's new life had begun with the Kincaids, and he had them to thank for it.

As he made his way to Gussie's birthday party, stopping to buy her a puppet doll and a tiny stuffed bear for Aria, he considered what he must do. That morning he had heard on the docks from a seaman returned from Sutter's Creek that he'd met Parish.

So it was through Luke that Marcus heard for the first time in three years about his younger brother. But, mindful of what he knew of the quarrel, Luke gave only the barest information.

Marcus listened, grunted, said nothing.

Later, Amy drew Luke aside to ask for more details. He had to tell her that Parish was gambling for a living in the wild towns spawned by the gold rush. She nodded, turned away, and never spoke of it to Marcus.

It was Gussie's day. She wore a white frock, with tiny lace ruffles at the throat and yoke. Her russet hair was a bright halo around her head, and her green eyes sparkled with excitement. Later – and she was already looking ahead to it – they would all board the ship and make the voyage to New York. Meanwhile three-year-old Aria lurched busily between the adults, greedily demanding attention in any way she could until she came finally to Luke, pulled at his trousers.

He took her up, smiling. How much his life had changed in these past five years. From a place of absolute hopelessness he had moved into a situation of unimaginable opportunity. He was getting his schooling, which he saw he needed as much as he needed his pay to support his mother and himself. The more schooling he had, the more he could earn as time passed. He was thankful that learning came easily to him. And he loved his job... the three quick whistles that signaled the ships' departures, the feel of the decks under his feet, even the small cramped quarters where he now worked with the purser. Amy, though not old enough to be so, was more mother to him than his own, who was more like his child. So at last Luke had a family again. He was as grateful for that as he was for all else Marcus had made possible for him.

Heart full, he held Aria on his lap, hugging her.

Gussie came and said, 'We'll go with you today on the *Bay State*.'

'Yes,' he said. 'And we have a fine day for the voyage.'

'It's my ship. I love it.'

'So do we all, Gussie.'

'I love Luke, too,' she went on. Her green eyes fixed on his face.

When Luke grinned, bent to kiss her cheek, Aria turned red and screamed, 'My Luke,' so he kissed her too. She snuggled cooing against his shoulder.

Amy and Marcus smiled at each other, but Gussie stood frozen and still until Marcus took her by the hand and led her to the window, and then raised her up in his arms, saying, 'You see the ship? And the wharves crowded with people, and the carts and wagons pulled up at the warehouses?'

Gussie craned her neck, studied the scene below. 'I see, Papa.'

'That's just how it was the day you were born, my Gussie. The same day that the *Bay State* went on her maiden voyage a few hours after. And I raised you up in my arms and took you to the window, tiny as you were. I told you to remember it. For that ship, the one you call yours, is our future and fortune. And so is her line. And that she first sailed on your birthday is good luck for her, and for you too.'

Aria whimpered, and Amy took the child and cradled her, but even then she made soft unhappy sounds in her throat. Amy sighed. Young as she was, Aria had already begun to resent any moment that was Gussie's.

'And Mama?' Gussie was asking. 'Where was Mama then?'

'Why, she was in the big bed in our room, watching us, you and me at the window, and smiling, and happily telling me what she had thought to choose for your name.'

33

'And Aria?' Gussie asked, with a sidelong look at her complaining sister.

'Aria had not yet been born. That was to come later,' Marcus went on, holding Gussie while he told her of that first voyage of the *Bay State*. How he had dined at supper with the ship's commander, Captain Comstock. How Mr. Ralph Waldo Emerson, the writer and lecturer, had been there too. He described the whole of the trip, never once mentioning his brother Parish, and went on to speak of the voyage back when the *Bay State*, encountering the Stonington Line's *Oregon*, as the two ships left New York, set out to race her and won hands down, arriving in Newport in 9 hours and 15 minutes. 'And it was on just such a day as this that it all began,' he ended.

Gussie considered for a while, still looking down into the harbor. Sea gulls wheeled there and curls of sparkling sunlight seemed to skip across the currents. 'I remember it,' she said at last, as her father put her on her feet. She looked up at him. 'I remember that day well.'

He laughed. 'No, my Gussie. I don't think so.'

'I do,' she insisted. 'I'm sure.'

'No person remembers the day he was born,' Amy said. 'It takes more than a few hours to develop the faculty of memory.'

'But I *do* remember it,' Gussie cried. 'I'm sure I saw it that day.' Small, obdurate, she looked at the others, certain in herself.

And thus it was that she always thereafter recalled her fifth birthday, but it seemed to her that she recalled the day she was born, too. For she pictured it so strongly in her mind the way Marcus had described it to her. The new *Bay State*, her colors flying. The train steaming onto the wharves under clouds of black smoke. The ladies and gentlemen picking a path through crates and carriages to climb the gangplank in laughing groups. The whistle blowing. The steam billowing. And then the slow rhythmic dip and slide of the wooden paddle wheels.

At luncheon, Marcus raised a glass of lemonade. 'This is to our Gussie, five years old today. And to the Fall River Line, no matter what she's called, also five years old today.'

So the two, Gussie and the steamship company along with its ships, became linked to her in her heart and mind, and even then she felt that they were a part of one another, blood relatives whose ties could never be severed, and that every journey began and ended with the Fall River Line, and every dream too.

Ten-year-old Mabel Graystone had a dream too. Looking from the train window, she saw it plainly: She was grown up. Her hair was shining blond and braided in a high coronet. She was tall, very slender, and dressed in black, the most fashionable widow's weeds anyone had ever seen. But she was no widow. For beside her stood a tall handsome man. He was dark-haired and aristocratic of visage. And she leaned against him, while her father's coffin was lowered into the ground...

The image faded as the train's bells rang and its cars rattled onto the Fall River wharves. With the dream's fading, small fat Mabel was swept under a current of fright. Her hand crept out to clutch her father's coat.

'What do you want?' he asked.

She looked up at him, unable to speak.

'Well?'

'It's nothing,' she managed.

'Get your things together. We're about to stop.'

She gathered a small reticule, a parasol with a broken handle. She put on a plain, out-of-style bonnet that went well with her out-of-style cape.

'I hope you'll remember your manners,' her father said grimly. 'There'll be people for you to meet aboard the ship.'

'Yes,' she said softly.

'Yes? What does that mean? Will you remember your manners, or won't you?'

She stared as him, seeing the color rise in his bearded face. It was useless. She would never be able to please him. Even as she thought that, fear swept her again and tears filled her eyes.

'The girl's an idiot,' her father grumbled as the train jerked to a stop. He continued in the same vein, murmuring to himself but loud enough that she could hear, as he got to his feet and climbed down, not waiting for her.

Breathless, she followed him across the wharves and up the gangplank. He had already been given his large brass stateroom key on the train, so after checking in at the purser's office, they went directly there.

'Put away your things,' he said.

She did that, took off her bonnet.

'We'll go up to the saloon.'

Again he went ahead. Mabel trailed after until he said over his shoulder, 'Come along. I don't want to have to wait for you.'

The passengers had begun to gather in the forward cabin.

One party in particular caught her eye. There were two little girls, one with reddish hair, the other with black curls. Their father was tall, bearded, and his hair was reddish too. A good-looking younger man was with them, and a pretty woman, who was probably the children's mother. They were all laughing. Mabel's heart shriveled with envy.

Her father caught her glance. 'The Kincaids,' he said. 'At least you have a good eye for who's important. You've met Mr. Kincaid before. Do you remember?'

Mabel shook her head.

Hiram Graystone grunted. 'No, no, I suppose you wouldn't. But we'll remedy that by making his acquaintance again.'

He spent some little time talking with Marcus while Mabel stood tongue-tied beside him, and then, sourly, he dragged her from one group to another, introducing her and thrusting her forward into an unsteady curtsey, while she barely managed to whisper a choked 'How do you do?'

That ordeal and then the ordeal of dinner over, he allowed her to retreat to the stateroom. There, snug in her bed at last, she remembered her dream again and burst into tears.

Chapter 3

Over the next few years several ships were added to the line, and paid for by its earnings, which were rumored to be over 50 percent per annum.

To celebrate the construction of the new *Metropolis*, Colonel Richard Borden gave a party. The *Metropolis* was a huge steamboat, 342 feet long, with two smoke stacks and four boilers, and an engine cylinder of 105 inches in diameter, the largest ever cast up to then. Before its installation, Colonel Borden's twenty-two guests were seated to lunch within its iron walls. Afterward, when the tables had been cleared away, a horse and carriage cantered through, followed by 103 marching men.

Amy's dress of China silk, its blue deepening the blue of her eyes, was from the bolt that Marcus had brought back from Canton Harbor for her. Aria and Gussie were clad in white. The two small girls were introduced to the other guests, and listened as the adults conversed.

Gussie, seven by then, couldn't restrain herself. 'What's the cylinder?' she demanded to know of her father.

He explained that it housed the engine.

'Then where's the engine now?' she asked, looking at the iron walls.

'Still in New York, my Gussie.'

'And when will I see it?'

'Before 1854 is out, the *Metropolis* will be launched.'

'And we'll ride her to New York?'

'We will,' he said, smiling down at her.

As the line prospered, so did the Kincaids. Marcus bought a horse and carriage and had a stable built to keep them. But, mindful of his father's extravagances, he delayed implementing the addition to the house Amy had designed, and he took advantage of those opportunities of further gain that presented themselves to him. He became agent for a number of textile mills, making use of his frequent trips to New York by buying cotton there for transshipment to Fall River.

It wasn't with deliberate intention, yet every act of Marcus's encouraged Gussie's earliest feelings about the line. He took his ladies, as he liked to call them, with him when he traveled. He made sure that they met the men who sailed on the ships. Thus, when she was still learning new words, Gussie understood that the captain of the *Bay State* was called the commander to differentiate him from the two pilots, who were also captains in rank. She learned the number of men on the crew lists, their jobs and years of service. And, because Marcus was like a gambler who has placed his whole stake on one roulette wheel number and could only stand by frozen to watch it spin, he lived and breathed the line; and so did Gussie. The ships were subject for dinner-table conversation. Their cargo was recounted. The passenger figures tallied. In good weeks, Marcus was ebullient; in bad weeks, he was downcast but determined. Amy remained serene either way. She was happy with her lot and with what Marcus gave her, and listened only to agree and encourage. Aria paid no attention. But Gussie listened to learn, as wide-eyed and charmed as a child absorbing a fairy tale.

Then, as if fate itself connived to enmesh her in the line, two of the major events of her early years came to her through Fall River Line ships.

The first was when she was nine years old. It was July 26, 1856. They were aboard the *Empire State* when she left Fall River at fifteen minutes past seven with 225 passengers on board.

The ship had already had a checkered history. Early in 1849, in the year after she was commissioned, she had suffered a serious fire while docked at the Fall River port and had been repaired at a cost of $120,000. Then, in April of 1853, one of her flues had burst and a blaze resulted. Her captain and a few passengers were able to put it out with hoses, while another ship came alongside and removed most travelers and their baggage. Only a few months later, again back in commission, she was off Plum Island in Long Island Sound when she was rammed by a schooner running with the wind and lightless at night. The schooner went on, but the captain, fearing injury to the steamship, was forced to anchor until she was towed safely to New York.

It was because of that history that Amy considered the ship to be less than lucky. But Marcus had laughed at her when she mentioned it privately to him, and she said nothing about it when the *Empire State* left Fall River.

It was a hot and calm evening. The family had dinner with a group of other passengers. The talk was largely about Senator Charles Sumner of Massachusetts, who was still in serious condition, having been beaten on the Senate floor by a southern congressman. The senator's survival was uncertain. Speaking of it, Marcus said, 'But nothing will change his mind about the need for the abolition of slavery.'

Later the family walked together on the foredeck for a little while, then retired to their stateroom. Aria, then seven years old, fell asleep instantly. But Gussie was restless. She felt the deep throbbing of the engines as if it were a heartbeat. She felt the life of the ship around her. She wanted to see what was happening in the lounges. She wanted to watch the docking at Newport. Marcus forbade the former, agreed to the latter. They stood together while more passengers embarked, and more freight was loaded. When the ship was under way again, the two returned to the stateroom.

Amy said, 'You must go to sleep now, Gussie. You'll be very tired tomorrow as it is.'

There was no use in further protest, Gussie knew. She lay down beside Aria, and listened to the sounds of the ship. When she was younger, Gussie had spent hours imagining herself commander of the ship, certain that one day she would captain the *Bay State*. She would stand in the wheelhouse, looking through the windows across the bridge, and confer with the pilots. By now, though with regret, she had given up that fantasy. There were no girl commanders, nor pilots, nor deckhands. There were no girls on the crew. But it didn't matter. She was still of the ships. She smiled to herself. And one day she would marry a man who belonged to the ships.

Marcus had blown out the oil lamp and sat talking quietly with Amy. At about nine twenty-five, some two and a half miles eastward of Point Judith, a sudden roar drowned out the sound of the paddle wheels and a hot blast of steam poured along the main deck and up the companionway from the starboard boiler.

He guessed instantly what had happened. 'We've got to get all of you outside,' he said. He grabbed life preservers, rushed Amy and the children, still in their bedclothes, aft and out into the open air. Others had had the same thought. The place was crowded. Pale faces gleamed in the dark, seeming to float above the shifting deck. Shrill voices blended into what seemed to Gussie to be a single continuous shriek that pained her ears and made her heart thump faster in her chest. It was hard to stand in the mass of shifting bodies, to see in the night's blackness. What was happening? Would the *Empire State* go down? Gussie fought back her fright. No. It couldn't happen. It wouldn't.

'You'll be all right here,' Marcus said, and hurried away to see what he could do to help.

A dense body of steam filled almost every part of the ship. The lights in the gangways had gone out. Half-clothed passengers stumbled fore and aft, shouting questions, tripping over sofas and chairs and other people, and screaming as they fell.

By the time Marcus reached the engine room, the third engineer, Ezra Williams, had managed to wade through scalding water to turn the valve that stopped the engine. He was badly burned, his shirt wet and shredded, clinging to his blistered arms and face and chest. As Marcus reached him, Ezra collapsed. Marcus helped carry him to the saloon, where he was laid on a hastily collected mattress and treated with oil and flour. There were other casualties, and they too were brought in and cared for.

On the aft deck, confusion increased as more people scrambled into the open air. But Amy stood quietly, braced against the shoving bodies that thrust against her. Aria clung to her and Gussie was close beside her, staring wide-eyed at the crowd and wondering what was happening. Small tingles of fright stung her, but she tried to ignore them. Nothing bad could happen to her on the ship. But still, she had to see, to know. She craned her neck, twisted this way and that, peering into the dark. It was impossible. The shadows were thick. The people were solid barriers. She let the movements of the others gradually ease her away from Amy's side until she was at the fringes of the excited group. With screamed questions and exclamations ringing in her eyes, she went to find out what was going on below.

She slid a small hand along the rail, feeling her way down the dark gangway. Fear touched her again. Again she tried to ignore it. Nothing bad could happen to her on the ship, she told herself. The steam was hot, very wet. It beaded her cheeks, clung in thick mist to her hair. Its smell was sour and burned in her nose and throat. Now, frightened once more, she wanted to go back to her mother, back into the open air where she could breathe. But she wouldn't allow it. Though her hands shook, she went on. Near the bottom her slipper caught and she stumbled. For an instant she managed to cling to the rail. Then she fell five steps into nothingness, her arms wildly reaching for support that wasn't there. One knee scraped a sharp projection.

The fall seemed endless. Suddenly, before she crashed into the deck, she was snatched up.

Willie Gorgas squinted coal-black eyes at her. 'You wait, little girl.'

'Thank you,' she said, her voice shaking.

'You hurt?'

'No.' She brushed her scraped knee. 'No, I'm all right.'

Her heart still thudding, she turned away to continue on. She had come this far. She would see what was happening.

But Willie Gorgas said, 'Up to the saloon. Not below,' and swung her around, giving her no time for argument. 'Is bad there. Is dangerous.'

She went back the way she had come, coughing on the bitter air, and he watched her until she disappeared into the dark at the top of the gangway. That was what he wanted, he told himself. A child of his own. Someone to belong to him. It was bad to be alone. Sighing, he headed for the gentlemen's cabin where there were more injured to be seen to.

Shortly thereafter the ship set out to return to Fall River, traveling on one boiler.

At one o'clock on Sunday morning, she steamed slowly to the docks. They were empty. Only a few lights flickered at wooden poles. Some small vessels creaked against the pilings. But by the time the *Empire State* was secured, word had spread. Lamps were lit. A crowd had begun to gather. The roadways filled with carriages and wagons.

Marcus immediately went for the Bordens. The two brothers and their wives, roused from sleep, dressed quickly and hurried to the stricken ship. After delivering the children into Betty Gowan's care, Marcus also returned to the ship. There, with Amy, the Bordens, and the six doctors who had already arrived, he set about helping the injured.

At noon, he stood beside Ezra Williams, passing unguents and bandages to the doctor who worked over the burned man. Ezra murmured incessantly out of a delirium. His wide-open but unseeing eyes stared from deep within the raw swollen tissue of his scalded face. His bared chest, scored raw and red by boiling water, gleamed now with salves as it rose and fell slowly on shallow breaths. Then, suddenly, as Marcus leaned closer, Ezra's disjointed murmurings faded. His burned lips sagged open. His chest fell, and did not rise again.

The doctor stepped back, sighed. 'He's gone.'

Others followed after in the hours of that long day. The death toll reached eleven passengers and five crew members.

A coroner's jury convened in Fall River and decided the explosion was an accident for which no blame could be affixed. Over the years the records of the event would be lost, and those terrible hours and the toll they took would be forgotten.

But Gussie Kincaid would remember that night as long as she lived. The acrid smell of scalding steam, the confusion of screams and cries and prayers.

The second event of her childhood that left a lasting imprint on her came three years later, when she was twelve.

It was the autumn of 1859. By then, Gussie was quite tall, slender. Her long reddish hair fell nearly to her waist in thick smooth waves. Her face had become heart-shaped, its dimples deeper than ever. Already she had begun to lose little girl ways and to assume the demeanor of a young woman.

She and her father were alone in New York, Aria having fallen ill on the day of departure so that Amy had stayed home with her. Gussie had been glad to leave, escaping the worst of Aria's temper tantrums.

Marcus had taken care of his business in New York with dispatch, while Gussie was entertained by the family of one of his associates. She was taken to see Bryant's Minstrels at the Mechanics' Hall, and fell asleep that night humming 'Dixie Land,' which later became known simply as 'Dixie.' She saw F. H. Conway's *Pike's Peak* at the Old Bowery Theatre. She read news reports of the National Women's Rights Convention recently held in the city, and saved for her mother copies of its resolutions. The main one requested that the states eliminate from their constitutions the word 'male,' and suggested passage of laws enabling all citizens to vote. It asked where in the Declaration of Independence was it said that women and Negroes should be deprived of their inalienable rights.

There had been much to do, to see. She was full of high spirits when they embarked on the *Metropolis* and set out for home. It was late October, the same day that John Brown went on trial in Charles Town, Virginia. He was accused of rebellion and murder in the attack he had led on the Harper's Ferry ammunition depot while trying to get arms to be used in the fight to free southern slaves.

The night was stormy as dinner was served in the dining saloon. The conversation was equally stormy. Just as the country was divided on the issues of slavery, so were the passengers at the table. Listening, Marcus recalled that Senator Charles Sumner, returning to Washington City not long before, after recovering from his wound, had said at that same table that already many southern students were leaving their northern schools to return home. On the journey to New York, Marcus had suspected that several of the young men he had seen were just such students.

Now someone said, 'Brown should be hanged immediately.'

'Yes,' someone else agreed. 'He should be made an example.'

Young Gussie opened her mouth to remonstrate with the two, but then remained silent.

There were others to defend Brown and his party. Ralph Waldo Emerson, returning to Boston from a lecture at a New York lyceum, declared that he believed the man to be a new saint, and the men who followed him the same.

Marcus noticed that the captain was silent, and recalled that silence later. Marcus too said nothing. He was pro-abolition, believing that no man who held slaves could ever be free himself.

There were many he knew in Fall River who were more concerned with the issue as it affected trade than with its moral implications. Still, the Massachusetts Underground Railroad had been active in moving escaped slaves through Fall River for a good number of years, and had become even more so after the passage in 1850 of the Fugitive Slave Act, which gave federal commissioners the right to hear cases related to runaway slaves, and established penalties for those who helped them.

In response to that act, New York, Massachusetts, and other New England states enacted what were called personal liberty laws. The state provided counsel for anyone arrested by federal marshals as a fugitive, required that he be tried, forbade state officials to issue writs or aid claimants, and forbade state jails to hold them. There were heavy fines and prison terms for any who broke those laws.

Still, slaveowners and bounty hunters moved with impunity

through most areas. Billboards and newspapers offered descriptions of runaways, and rewards for their return.

The arguments went on, back and forth across the table, impassioned speakers not distracted by the many fine courses put before them.

Gussie listened intently. She had read Harriet Beecher Stowe's *Uncle Tom's Cabin* just a few months before. Amy had told her that on the day the novel first appeared in book form in 1852 it had sold three thousand copies, and since then uncounted thousands more. The book had deeply affected Gussie.

Hiram Graystone was not to be influenced by emotional or moral arguments, however. He was firm in his conviction. Those states that wished to have slavery should have it; those that did not, must not. And private property of any kind was inviolable. As far as he was concerned that was the end of it. He looked at his seventeen-year-old daughter. Mabel gave him a dutiful nod, chewed on her steak. When his gray-streaked beard parted in a faint and rare smile, her eyes were suddenly awash with tears for which she knew no reason. She was used to her portion and accepted it. Tall, ungainly, stout, she avoided the looking glass because of its power to hurt her, and frequented the dining-table for the relief it offered.

After the meal was over, Marcus suggested that he and Gussie have a walk on deck. Wrapped warmly in a shawl, she went with him.

'What will happen?' she asked.

He sighed deeply. 'I think there will be war. And soon.' It was the last thing he wanted, but he knew the slavery issue would have to be settled.

He was about to go on, to explain it to Gussie, when the ship's second mate, Carl Hansen, hailed him. 'Do you have a minute for a few words, Mr. Kincaid?' At Marcus's nod, the man looked at Gussie, then dropped his voice to say, 'Privately, sir.'

Marcus raised his brows, but requested that Gussie step inside. When she had gone, he asked, 'Now what is it, Mr. Hansen?'

'There's a man on board who is recognized to be a bounty hunter.' Hansen's face conveyed dislike, and worry too.

'And how does that concern you?'

The mate rubbed his dark mustache. 'He creates a problem that wasn't foreseen in New York. With the captain's permission, I have two people for the railway hidden down below. We must get them ashore in Fall River, undetected, and put into the right hands.'

Marcus knew, of course, of the federal penalties designed to prevent interference with the return of runaway slaves, but he didn't think of them as he said, 'There must be a means to divert the man when we've reached the docks.'

'It'll be difficult, sir. It would be better if it didn't come to that.'

'Of course. It would be best if the two seemed to be traveling with their owners. He'd have to believe he's mistaken in his identification.'

'Yes. And perhaps the diversion you spoke of, to keep him from getting too close.'

'I could be the owner,' Marcus suggested.

'I fear you're too well known, Mr. Kincaid. He might easily have learned on the ship who you are.'

'Perhaps,' Marcus agreed. 'Who then?'

'I don't know, sir. It's why I've come to you.'

'A young lady,' Marcus said thoughtfully. He jammed his left hand into his pocket, warming against his body the place from which the smallest finger was missing. It was some fifteen years since the accident on the whaling ship, yet when the winds grew cold he still felt it. 'A young lady,' he said again. 'Coming to New England to visit her Yankee relatives, and being escorted by trusted family slaves.'

Hansen nodded, his eyes agleam in the dark.

Marcus thought first of Mabel Graystone. She was just the right age. And she was plain enough, poor girl, so that a man would give her only a cursory glance. But then it seemed not a good idea. Hiram Graystone's opinions were very strong. She might share them. The lives of two people were at stake if Marcus made a poor choice. There was one person he *could* trust. He told Hansen. The man protested – 'She's very young, sir.'

'Young but quick-witted. I believe she can do it, with a bit of help. And no harm can befall her. We'll be right there to see to that.'

'If she agrees without persuasion.'

Marcus was certain she would. With that settled, the two men discussed the needed diversion.

'Send Willie Gorgas to me,' Marcus said finally. 'He'll know what to do when we explain what's required.'

At five-thirty the next morning the *Metropolis* whistled at the Borden Flats light and entered Fall River harbor. Soon she was secure, the gangplank in place.

Big Willie Gorgas was first down, but once on the dock, he lingered, eyeing the passengers as they began to come off. Very soon he saw the man who had been identified to him the night before in the gentlemen's sleeping room.

It was George Raleigh, age twenty-five, out of South Carolina, bounty hunter. That was all Willie Gorgas knew about him, but it was enough for him to approach the coming encounter with enthusiasm. He hated slavery. It was easy for him to imagine himself in chains: at twenty-seven, lines had already begun to score his face under his thick black beard, and his big hard body had begun to wear. He would have been hard put to explain it in his guttural English, but he knew what he felt. He was married now, and only the month before his wife had borne him a son. But the child was sickly, and his wife Annie was a sharp-tongued shrew. He was still a deckhand, with hopes for little more, because he had brawn but not much language. He thought he knew what a slave must feel. Besides, beyond the issue, he would have done any favor Marcus Kincaid asked. It was as simple as that.

Willie watched as George Raleigh came slowly down the gangplank. He was a tall, loose-jointed man, wearing a wide-brimmed black hat on dark blond shoulder-length hair. He had a drooping blond mustache, high cheekbones, and squinting blue eyes.

He already knew that if he showed arms he could have been arrested in New York, and probably he would be in Massachusetts. He had had some experience in tracking runaway slaves before, and earned good money at it; he intended to do the same here, in Fall River.

But George Raleigh was wary. In 'Philadelphia several months before, he'd stopped a runaway and the man yelled for help. A mob had formed out of nowhere. Before federal marshals could be called, George had been kicked, pummeled, and beaten. In the melee the slave had disappeared.

George wouldn't let that happen again. With the capture of these two he was after, a man in his middle years and a slightly younger woman, he'd earn some four hundred dollars. He'd been following them for two weeks, but hadn't dared to approach them at the pier in New York; there were too many people about. When they'd disappeared into the ship and he hadn't been able to find them aboard, he was certain they were there still and would have to come off some time. He'd been watching at Newport but hadn't seen them. Now they were at the end of the line.

He lounged against a railing and set himself to wait. He knew he could easily pick out the two black faces among all the white ones.

Willie Gorgas waited too.

On the *Metropolis* Gussie gave a final touch to her russet curls, adjusted the flowers on her small hat, pulled the veil into place over her face, and stepped into the companionway.

Marcus smiled at her. 'Ready?' And at her nod, 'You're not afraid? If you are, you must say so. There's time to change your mind.'

'I won't change my mind. I want to do it. I'm not a bit afraid.'

When he'd asked her the night before, her reply had been instantaneous. 'Yes, yes, of course, Papa. I can do it quite easily. I'll put up my hair. Borrow a bit of veiling ...'

She felt honored that her father trusted her with so delicate a task. It made her a part of history. All night she had waited for this moment.

Now, even though her heart beat quickly, she touched a bulkhead for luck. This was her ship. Nothing bad could happen to her here. Smiling, she followed Marcus to the foredeck, where two people were waiting in the early morning fog.

'My daughter Gussie,' Marcus said softly to them. And to Gussie, 'Mr. and Mrs. Burton. But you must call them Jeb and Auntie Marge, you know.'

Gussie smiled at the two. 'You'll forgive me, I hope.'

The man nodded. The woman stared impassively.

Gussie stepped between them. 'I'll do the talking if anyone

stops us. Even if you're asked a direct question.'

'Remember, Gussie, Willie Gorgas will be there too,' Marcus said. 'And I'll come as quickly as possible with the carriage. For surely it'll be better not to attempt to board the train for Boston this morning.'

Gussie raised her chin, stood straight and tall as she went slowly down the gangplank, the Burtons on either side.

Overhead the sea gulls wheeled and swooped and shrilled against the low-hanging mist that enwrapped the wharves where the train waited and the stevedores had already begun their unloading.

'It was a nice trip, Auntie Marge,' Gussie was saying as the three reached the dock. 'Still, I'll be relieved to reach our destination. Concord, was it not, Jeb? It'll be strange to see our Yankee relations after all this time, won't it? I wonder where they stand.' Her voice and speech had softened. There was the soft hint of a drawl in her words, as she and her companions reached George Raleigh.

For a moment, he stared in confusion. The faces of the two were right. He was fairly sure of that. But the clothes were different from in New York. And what were they doing with the white girl? They'd been traveling alone, of that he'd been certain.

He lunged forward to block the way as they set foot on the wharves. 'Burton,' he said sharply, 'you're both of you to come with me to a federal marshal. I know who you are, and to whom you belong.'

'Sir,' Gussie said sweetly, 'are you speaking to me?'

'To these people. Runaways,' he drawled. And added, 'Ma'am,' in mockery.

She smiled as sweetly as she had spoken, but her eyes flashed green fire. 'Runaways? Indeed? How can you say so? These are my people who are taking me to relations in Concord. Yankee relations to be sure. But kin nonetheless. And who are you to interfere with us?'

'I'm George Raleigh,' he retorted, 'And these people belong to Jonathon Corram in South Carolina. I've papers to prove it and prove who they are, too.'

'Prove what you like,' Gussie said, still smiling, 'it makes no never mind to me. I know who I am. And I know my Jeb and Auntie Marge.'

'And can you prove *that*?' George demanded. He was uneasy at the prolonged conversation. People were standing to watch, to listen. He thought of his gun, but didn't dare draw it.

'Let us pass,' Gussie said quietly. 'We three have nothing to do with you, and need prove nothing to you either.' She heard the soft, frightened hiss of Marge Burton's breath, felt waves of silent fear from Jeb Burton. But beyond George Raleigh's shoulder she saw Willie Gorgas moving in, coming closer. His dark eyes glinted beneath his lowering brows. There was a slanted grin on his mouth.

He had been slow to move because for an instant he was uncertain. Marcus Kincaid had said the two would be with his daughter. But the girl looked years older: hair piled high, face veiled. Tall and straight and smiling. But then he knew her. She was dissembling so well that she'd fooled him almost who had known her since she was a tiny child.

Oh, he was going to enjoy this, he thought. He lumbered close, and with an elbow thrust forward like a club slammed into George at mid-back. The blow knocked him off-balance and Willie had him by the shoulder, spinning him around. In his guttural foreign accent, Willie growled, 'Hey, watcha doing?' As he spoke, he pushed at George and pulled and dragged him this way and that.

The bounty hunter's frustration boiled over. 'What the hell!' He managed to gain his balance, fists doubled and lashing out.

There were shouts. The train's bells rang; its whistle hooted. Nearby horses snorted and reared and stamped the ground.

Gussie and her charges moved quickly away from the brawl that followed. They climbed into the carriage and Marcus immediately drove away.

That afternoon George Raleigh returned to the wharves. He talked to the dockmaster. Shortly after, he went to the Kincaid house. At his knock, Marcus opened the door.

'I'm here about the Burtons,' George said. 'If you don't produce them, I'll go for a federal marshal.'

'I don't know what you're talking about.' Marcus grinned in his beard. 'If I ever saw you before I don't remember it.'

'We traveled together on the *Metropolis*, Mr. Kincaid. You and me and those runaway slaves.'

'And some other eight hundred people.'

'Which included your daughter. She'll tell you what

happened. If you don't already know.'

'My little daughter Gussie? Or my smaller daughter Aria?'

'I want the Burtons,' George said.

'Go get your marshal,' Marcus said. 'I know nothing of any Burtons. And no Burtons are here. If your marshal has the proper warrants, then he can look for himself.'

The couple was already hidden in a tiny cupboard in a house off South Main Street. Well after dark, it had been arranged, they'd be driven by carriage to the next stop in Boston.

George knew it was no use. He left Marcus and walked back to the center of town, wondering what to do. He was nearly out of money. He could kiss goodbye to the four hundred dollars he'd thought to earn.

When he saw a 'Help Wanted' sign on a hostlery, he decided to go in and investigate.

Chapter 4

'I wish it could be different, Marcus.' Gaylord Wenton pressed out his cigar and leaned back in his chair. He took a deep breath before going on. 'But this blockade of southern ports announced yesterday by President Lincoln will make future cotton deliveries impossible.'

'I realize it,' Marcus said. 'And soon, I think, the president will demand an end to all commercial relations between the northern and southern states. The declaration of insurrection requires it.'

It was nearly two months since February 4, 1861 when Jefferson Davis had been chosen provisional president of the confederacy, and seven days since southern soldiers had fired on Fort Sumter in Charleston.

Wenton chewed the ends of his mustache. He was a man of Marcus's age, a Georgian, but well traveled.

'What will you do?' Marcus asked.

'We'll sell to England. If a way is found out of New Orleans.'

'I meant *you*, Gaylord.'

The southerner didn't answer. Marcus understood. Neither of them knew what was to come, what part he would play in it.

For nearly ten years they had done business together, Wenton delivering cotton to New York, Kincaid buying it for Fall River's mills. They had found each other trustworthy, and had had a profitable association. There had been but one subject which, by common consent, they avoided during their frequent meetings. It was the issue of slavery versus abolition, which had divided the country from its beginnings and was now bringing it to war.

They were finishing their meal when Luke joined them.

Gaylord, who had a son the same age, was fond of Luke. He pressed strawberry pie on him, and coffee, and spoke enthusiastically about a play he had seen the night before. Soon Luke departed on some errands.

Marcus and Gaylord walked outside into the bright sunlight of the April afternoon. On the crowded sidewalk, they stood together for a moment. Then Gaylord put out his hand. 'God keep you, Marcus.'

'And you, Gaylord.'

It was with a heavy heart that Marcus waved down a hansom and directed it to the pier, where the *Bay State* was preparing to depart.

He and Wenton had made many farewells over the years. But this one, today, represented an ending. There would be more endings soon.

Marcus considered what he should do. There were not many choices. His income would drop without the cotton commissions. Dividends from the shipping line could be expected to drop too if the textile mills had no yardage to ship to New York factories. He wished now that he'd built that addition to the house for Amy. If he'd done so when she first spoke of it, they'd have it. Now it would have to be delayed even longer.

It seemed to Marcus that the times had brought a sober mood to the passengers. The embarkation was quieter than usual. When the ship sailed at 5:00 p.m., however, she carried a full complement and the holds were loaded too.

After dinner Luke came up from the purser's office and asked him to walk on the foredeck for a little while.

It was a dark night. The sky hung black and starless overhead as the ship steamed up the Sound. The flashing white light of Stratford Shoal blinked at them while Luke said quietly, 'I must tell you about a decision I've taken.'

Marcus knew. He had fought heartsickness in the past few days, for the thought had been at the back of his mind: If there was war, Luke would go. There was confirmation in Luke's face.

For a moment, now, Marcus was overwhelmed. There was a shaking in his big body. Sweat suddenly drenched him.

Luke went on, 'I volunteered yesterday. I didn't discuss it with you before because I knew what I had to do.'

Marcus affected a calm he didn't feel. He was still shaken by his fear for Luke. But he said quietly, 'I'd have wanted to talk against and for at the same time. And, no matter what I said, you'd not have listened.'

Luke grinned. 'You're right. I'll be going with the Massachusetts Seventh Regiment. Mr. Buffington has organized it, and joined himself. But I heard that he's been advised to resign. It's said he'll be needed in the House of Representatives in Washington City.'

'And when do you go?'

'At the end of the week.'

'So soon,' Marcus said. 'It moves quickly now. After a long beginning.' Marcus paused. Then, 'And what of your mother, Luke? Have you provided for her?'

The two men were close enough for Marcus to ask. He was an outward person. He spoke and acted his thoughts. Luke, grown now, was slower, quieter. He walked lightly and spoke softly. But he had within him the same force, a wiry strength that sustained him. Now heat rose in his face. He felt it and was glad of the dark. It was difficult to speak of Nelle. She was as she had been since he was eight years old. He had recently turned twenty-six. He supported her, visited occasionally to see how she fared. But he never referred to her unless asked, and had never suggested that the Kincaids meet her. He was ashamed of it, but couldn't help it. Her madness lay like a long shadow over him. He feared it could claim him unless he kept separate from it and her. At last he said, 'I've made arrangements. She'll be cared for.'

'You're sure?'

'I am.' And then, face hot again, and unwillingly, 'But if you'd not mind, I'd give the people your name. In case there was an emergency. So that I could be reached if it were necessary.'

'Yes,' Marcus said, hiding his pity. He understood what it cost Luke to speak of his mother. 'And give me her address, too. I'll look in on her to be sure all's well.'

Luke choked back a refusal. He didn't want the two halves of his life to meet at any point. But Marcus might need to see Nelle one day. How could Luke know how long he would be away, or what would happen? How could he know even that he would come back? 'Yes,' he said. 'You must have it.'

Slowly Marcus walked through dawn quiet streets. There would be changes. His income would drop, but that was only a small part of it. There was more. He had been feeling the conflict ever since his meeting with Gaylord Wenton. The talk with Luke had only intensified it. His pride demanded action of him. How could he stay at home when other men went? It was his country too. But what words would he use to explain everything to Amy?

The sun had just risen when he reached the house. All was silent. When he raised a hand to the door, she opened it, stood smiling at him. It was as if she had already guessed the momentous thing that was about to come upon them.

He washed, brushed his beard, and went into the kitchen. Coffee was boiling on the stove, johnny cakes sizzled in a pan, and there was ham frying.

She served the two of them and sat down. 'How was the journey? And did you see Mr. Wenton as planned?'

'Yes.' Marcus drank half the cup of coffee down, waited while she took the pot and refilled it. Then, 'You know about the blockade?'

'Yes. The paper was full of it.'

'We'll not be able to do business any more, Amy.'

'I understand. But what of Mr. Wenton?'

'I asked. He didn't say.' Then, 'Luke spoke to me as we were coming home.' Marcus took a deep, steadying breath. 'He has volunteered, Amy.' Marcus put down his fork, rubbed his beard, waited.

Small cat claws of pain scratched her throat. She looked into

53

Marcus's face, then turned away quickly, fighting back tears. At last she said, 'I'm sorry. I wish he had waited.'

'He couldn't avoid it.'

'He could have delayed.'

'If every man did, then we'd have no army, would we?'

When she said nothing, Marcus added, 'It's his duty.'

Once again the small cat claws scratched her, but this time deep in the heart. Not Marcus. No, no. She couldn't bear that. She waited until she could safely speak, and at last, with a long, direct look, she said: 'Marcus, I don't want you to go.'

He was so relieved that he hadn't been forced to say it himself that he burst out laughing.

'No,' she said, her voice hot with a rare anger. 'No, I'm serious. I don't want you to go, and I see it's what you're thinking of.'

He sobered then. 'If it's Luke's duty, then it's mine too. I'm only forty-one and hearty. I haven't been sick a day in my life. I can shoot a gun as well as the next man.'

'I'm forty-one too,' she said quietly.

'And what's that got to do with it?' he demanded. 'I'm speaking of volunteering myself, not you.'

'I'm expecting, Marcus.'

With a yell, he leaped to his feet, knocking back his chair. He grabbed her, swung her into his arms. 'Is it true, Amy?'

'Of course it is. But if you don't put me down, it may not be.'

'Oh,' he gasped. 'Oh, my dear. I'm sorry.' Paling, he set her gently on her feet. 'I'm sorry,' he repeated. 'I didn't think.'

'I know,' she said, smiling. 'I felt much the same myself when I realized it.'

He held her then, but gently, looking down into her face. 'Is it all right?'

'Yes,' she said. 'I think so. Even though I'm not as young as I was. Still, I'm hearty too. But just the same, I shouldn't like to be alone these next six months or so. Nor alone either when my confinement comes.'

He thought of the day Gussie had been born, with the *Bay State* standing in the harbor and his brother Parish waiting in the kitchen. 'Nor shall you be alone,' he said firmly. 'I'll be with you.'

'I know it's contrary to your own wishes. I'm sorry for it.'

'You mustn't be.' He made sure that nothing of what he felt showed in his face. If she needed him, then he must sacrifice anything. Even his pride.

She asked, 'Are you happy that we'll have another child?'

'Of course,' he told her. His arms tightened, but with care, and he held her against him and looked down at her. Her eyes were still the cool clear blue they had been, but her cheeks were rounder now, and for the first time he saw a few threads of white in her pulled-back dark hair. 'How could I not be happy? But you must be careful and not strain yourself.'

'I'll be fine,' she told him, and then asked when Luke would be leaving. After Marcus had explained, she went on, 'We must have him for family supper. Be sure to arrange it so we can be together.'

She stopped speaking. Marcus heard the unuttered words in his mind. *One last time.*

No one was quite sure when Gussie became Augusta. Perhaps it was when she had put up her hair and worn a veil to deceive George Raleigh, even though, at Amy's insistence, she had allowed her hair to fall to her waist again the same day. Perhaps it happened more gradually over the next two years as she began to understand her feelings for Luke.

In any event, it was as Augusta that she referred to herself, thought of herself. And it was Augusta that she was now called. Except by Luke, who still called her Gussie, and tweaked her curls, and didn't seem to realize that she was now fourteen and grown up within, even though she might not yet show it as much as she one day would.

Now she stood at the window, watching the road below. The late afternoon sun shone in her red-gold hair. Her eyes were bright with held-back tears. Her form was slender and shapely in blue poplin, and at her mouth there were two dimples, one above the other. When she smiled, they flashed together. But now she wasn't able to smile. Her lips were drawn tight. Luke was going away to the war – going away, perhaps never to return. It seemed the end of the world to her. The end, at least, of her world.

When he appeared on the road, a small gasp escaped her. He wore blue cloth, black high boots. The uniform made him a stranger, but a stranger with familiar features. A tall slim body, supple, yet with broad shoulders. A crop of curly black hair. A soft, well-trimmed mustache set over a mouth usually sober, but surpassingly sweet when he smiled.

She held her breath to choke back another gasp. For his sake, she mustn't give way. Saying goodbye would be difficult for him too.

And then, from below, she heard Aria's shrill, 'Oh, Luke, Luke, you can't go away and leave. What do I care for the stupid war, or stupid old Lincoln! You can't go away!'

Twelve-year-old Aria had no dignity, Augusta thought without rancor. She was still a child and acted like one.

And it was as a child that Luke held her and soothed her and laughed over her dark head at Amy and Marcus.

When Augusta reached the foot of the stairs, she took in the scene at a single glance. She said, 'How are you, Luke?'

'Well enough, Gussie.' He grinned, putting Aria aside, while she fought him and clung to him at the same time.

Amy, watching, was troubled. It wasn't the first experience she'd had with Aria's tempestuous nature. She had seen it too often to overlook. That the girl was so uncontrolled of her feelings worried her. It reminded her, in some way she didn't understand, of Parish, who had been gone thirteen years and of whom they'd heard nothing for more than nine. Perhaps it was a certain headstrong quality. In any event, Amy intervened. 'Aria, if you continue so, you'll make Luke's evening with us a chore instead of a pleasure. Go and wash your face, comb your hair, and compose yourself.'

Pouting, shoulders sagging, feet dragging, Aria disappeared up the stairs.

They sat in the parlor. The brass chandelier was lit. A small fire burned on the hearth to dry the late April damp.

Betty Gowan, married now to a cousin also named Gowan, served salted walnuts and biscuits with cheese, and Marcus was liberal with the sherry decanter.

Luke sipped the drink slowly. What he had done was real to him now. He looked from Marcus to Amy. This was his real family. And he was going to leave them.

'Do you think it'll be long?' Amy asked.

'Some say it'll last a matter of days,' Marcus said. 'Some say it could be years.'

Amy, Marcus, the girls. The girls. Luke thought of them that way. The girls, who were like the younger sisters he'd never had. Living or dead, he would treasure them all, always.

From beneath lowered lids Augusta studied him, memorizing the set of his eyes above his cheeks and the shape of his mouth. For a time memory would be all she would have of him. The future was already become emptier for her. Her fingers suddenly burned. She hungered to take his face between her hands, and stroke it and know it by feel as well as by sight.

Instead, she folded them tightly together and asked, 'Do you know where you go first?'

'Down to Washington City. A whole company of us together.'

'On the *Bay State*,' Marcus put in, smiling. 'Your ship.'

'And from there?' she asked.

Luke had risen to set his glass on the mantel. 'I don't know yet,' he said, leaning over to tousle her hair, as if she were a four-year-old, she thought resentfully. And he added, to make it worse, 'You mustn't worry your pretty head about that,' while she fought the need to seize his hand and kiss it.

'I hope it's not through Baltimore.' Marcus's face was fierce. 'The Sixth Massachusetts Regiment was attacked there by a mob of southern sympathizers. I hear four soldiers were killed, and many more in the mob. And several bridges were burned to keep other Union troops from proceeding.'

'But we'll go through. If not by train, then on foot,' Luke said.

Augusta shivered at the quiet determination in his voice. Nothing would stop him, she thought. 'Will you write to us?' she asked. 'We'll so much want to hear from you.'

Once more he tousled her curls, as if humoring a child, she thought. He said, 'Of course I'll write. When I can.'

Soon Betty came to say that supper was ready. They were at the table when Aria reappeared. She was composed when she came into the room. But as she sat down and looked at Luke, her face reddened. Tears suddenly sprang from her eyes. 'I can't help it,' she sobbed. 'I know I'll never see you again.'

'Aria, stop that this instant,' Marcus said.

She turned her wet face to him. 'Don't you care?'

It was the same when it was time to say goodbye. Luke hugged her, and again she burst into tears, while Augusta said softly to him, 'Come home as soon as you can. Come home safely.'

But when Luke had gone, Aria happily settled to a game of chess with Marcus. Augusta retired early, and spent the night crying soundlessly into her pillow.

The *Bay State* was crowded. Four months after the first bombardment of Fort Sumter, New England militias were still forming up and traveling south.

The forward lounge was noisy, the air thick with blue smoke through which the chandeliers shone dimly.

Amy sat beside Marcus, looking at the gathering of soldiers. In every young face she saw something that reminded her of Luke. One had his long jaw, another his pale gray eyes; a third had his sudden smile and his thick dark hair. She sighed. They had twice heard from him since he'd been gone. She, writing for Marcus and herself, had answered immediately, and Augusta had written separately. But there had been no replies as yet. They didn't know where he was now, nor how he fared.

Again she sighed, shifted her body. It was ungainly, weighty with seven months growth.

'Are you all right?' Marcus asked.

'Yes.' She smiled at him reassuringly. She had insisted that she make the trip with him. It had been a hot summer, a trying one for both of them. He had been troubled to stand back while so many others of his age joined the Massachusetts regiments. She had been concerned for him and tried to conceal the discomforts of her pregnancy. She had thought the journey would lighten both their spirits.

But now she was sorry she'd come away from home. There was a discomfort low in her back, and small tides of nausea rose up in her throat.

A howl of laughter burst from a group of soldiers sitting close by.

'Freely poured spirits make for high spirits,' Marcus said to her.

She agreed. Her forced laugh made him look at her.

He rose quickly. 'Come on, Amy. I believe the fresh air and quiet of the deck would be better for you.'

She got up, took his arm. Outside, a silver August moon rode the eastern horizon. The ship steamed through quiet waters.

It was beautiful, but she was glad when he suggested they retire. She drifted into uneasy sleep, listening to the whisper of the paddle wheels. Hours later she awakened, aware of knifelike pain and a hot dampness at her thighs.

In the same instant Marcus was on his feet. 'Amy! What is it?'

'I fear it's the baby,' she gasped.

'No,' he said. 'No. It can't be.'

'Marcus, I'm sorry. I must...' she gasped and choked for air. 'I must have help, Marcus.'

He tucked the coverlet around her, kissed her. He dressed quickly. 'I'll ask the purser. There'll surely be a regimental doctor aboard. I'll only be a moment.'

They were in what was called the Race, that dangerous area at the mouth of the Sound between New London and Montauk Point, where many a sidewheeler had come to grief. But all was quiet as the *Bay State* steamed on.

Through the purser, Marcus found a physician, commandeered a cabin boy to run for heated water, and hurried back to Amy.

She was pale, sweating. After a quick examination the physician said softly, 'There's nothing I can do. Except give her a bit of laudanum.'

Hours later an infant boy was born. He was tiny, wrinkled, and blue of face. Though the physician slapped his bottom hard, and breathed into his small gaping mouth, he never took a living breath.

The *Bay State* had docked in New York before Amy knew of it. After Luke told her, choking back his own grief, she remained in her stateroom. She stayed there all that day and on the journey back to Fall River. She spoke of the infant only once. That was to ask, 'Was it a boy or a girl, Marcus?' and when he told her, she said, 'I'm sorry.'

He was free, then, to do as so many of the other men were doing. He could satisfy his pride and convictions, and go. Amy no longer had need of him. That was what he told himself weeks later. But when he saw the shadow that lingered in her eyes, he knew better. She needed him. And he needed her as well. He couldn't leave her now.

Chapter 5

By 1863, despite the difficulties posed by the war in the south, a company called the Old Colony Line had extended its railroad all the way from Boston to Newport, and offered to buy out the Borden brothers' Fall River Line. The Bordens were amenable but insisted that the Bay State Steamboat Company should be included in the sale.

Marcus had a choice. He could sell his shares, or hold on to them and go with the new owners. It was hard to decide. He worried it over in his mind for a time before he discussed it with Amy.

They were traveling to New York with the two girls. Though Marcus no longer dealt in cotton, he continued his frequent trips.

The line was only moderately affected by the war economy. There were fewer passengers traveling for pleasure, but soldiers filled the gentlemen's cabin and sat drinking in the lounges. The hold of the *Empire State* was packed with Army blankets, with boots and tunics and barrels of powder from the factories of New England. From New York these war goods would be delivered to depots for distribution wherever the Army marched. But Marcus was uneasily aware that when the war ended, his commissions, at least partly based on these goods, would end too. He had the future to think of.

He said to Amy, 'I'm not sure what I should do.'

She looked past the vase of flowers that sat on the table between them. He thought she was prettier than the roses. He was about to tell her so when she said, 'You must do what you think best. We'll manage somehow.'

'I don't know what's best, and that's the truth of it. If I did, I wouldn't be muddling around in my thoughts.'

Aria pushed back her chair. 'I'm finished eating. May I be excused?'

At the same time, Augusta asked, 'Papa, what do you mean? I don't understand.'

He nodded at Aria, who slipped away. Then, to Augusta, 'I have a choice. Either I keep my shares or allow them to be bought out.'

'Bought out? But how can they do that?'

'They can.'

'But *we* are the line.' Green eyes wide, she stared at Marcus. 'Of course you must go with the new company. How can you consider otherwise?'

'It's a matter of business only,' he told her.

She looked around the dining saloon. 'This ship, all the ships, they are ours. The line is ours. It isn't just business.'

He forced himself to smile. In his heart he agreed with her, but his heart mustn't be allowed to decide for him. He would consider a while longer before he made his decision. To Augusta he said, 'We'll see.'

She bit her lip, didn't answer. She pushed the food around on her plate, with no appetite, until, finally, unable to bear it any longer, she too asked to be excused to walk on deck.

Amy nodded. She understood as well as Marcus did what Augusta was feeling.

At the door the girl looked back. How beautiful a room it was! It was her home. One of several, along with the *Bay State*, the *Metropolis*.

The foredeck was nearly empty, but a woman stood alone at the rail. She was wrapped in a dark shawl and her dark skirts belled out around her. Behind her a man and a second woman waited.

With a start of surprise Augusta realized who the solitary lady was: Mrs Lincoln. Augusta had heard that the president's wife often took this ship when visiting her older son who was a student at Harvard.

With a smile, a murmured 'Good evening,' Augusta moved away. She found a quiet place, leaned her arms on the railing, and wondered what her father would decide.

'Lump,' Hiram Graystone said. 'A lump.'

Mabel moved slowly beside him, saying nothing.

'Ugly, unkempt. Who'd want you?'

'Yes, Father,' she said softly.

'Yes, yes, yes,' he cried. 'Is that all you can say? All the men at the table. Did you speak to one? Did you look at one?'

'No, Father.'

'I want you to get married.'

'I know '

'I want a grandson.'

'I know.' Her voice was expressionless, but there were tears in her eyes.

He said savagely, 'Well, what are you going to do about it?'

'I don't know,' she answered.

'Twenty-one years old. A spinster. What have I worked for all my life?'

'I don't know,' she said again.

'I shall go to bed,' he said disgustedly. 'I suggest that you should do the same.'

'All right,' she agreed.

But a few minutes after entering her stateroom, she hurried down to the dining saloon, having first made certain that her father had retired for the night.

Hungry for a bit of late supper, she sat alone, a plate of cold fish and creamed eggs with coleslaw before her, and listened to the conversation.

'The proclamation he has issued says it very plainly. All men between twenty and forty-six years of age must go. There are two alternatives: one, a substitute may be purchased; two, an exemption may be purchased for the sum of three hundred dollars.'

Mabel listened, but it meant nothing to her. She ate quickly, stuffing the food down until she could take no more. Yet she still felt hungry when she finally put down her fork.

Amy and Marcus walked slowly around the deck. They were speaking of the proclamation too, but indirectly.

'I'm forty-three,' Marcus said thoughtfully.

'You'll very soon be forty-four,' she countered.

'Does that matter?'

'Do you want to go so much, Marcus?'

She saw the tightening of his face. Yes, yes. He wanted to go. Were all men mad? Duty. Honor. A just cause. She knew the words. Yet she shuddered to think of what could happen. It had been so long now since they had last had word from Luke. Could she bear such a long silence if it were Marcus who was gone from her?

It was dark, but Marcus didn't have to see the shadow in her eyes to know it was there. Though she never spoke of the infant lost, he knew she had forgotten no more than he had. He said finally, 'No, Amy. I don't suppose I want to go all that much. But some days there's a part of me . . .'

'I want you to be happy.' She took his hand, clung to it tightly.

His fingers clasped hers. 'Do you still have your design for the addition? Perhaps we should think of it again.'

In the morning, docked in New York, they were told of the riots sweeping the city. Attacks on draft offices had begun in the same hour that the first call-up lists had been posted; now they had spread. Roaming bands were assaulting Negroes. Deaths had already been reported.

When they went to the upper deck they saw tall towers of black smoke rising over the city, and heard whistles blowing and bells ringing. The streets near the docks were crowded with police wagons careening wildly around stalled hansoms and struggling, shouting people.

Marcus insisted that Amy and the girls remain on board while he attended to his business. He returned soon. It was impossible to transact commerce that day.

Later that week, he made his decision. In the same month he became a shareholder in the new Boston, Newport and New York Steamboat Company, which was owned by the Old Colony Railroad Line.

The transfer of ownership brought two changes. Marcus no longer served as eyes and ears for anyone, and it was suddenly announced and put into immediate effect that Fall River would no longer be the terminus for the Fall River ships. They would dock at Newport. It was there that cargo was loaded, and there that passengers debarked and entrained for Boston.

Marcus had argued against the change, and argued again to alter it once it became reality. He accomplished nothing. He ended by telling Amy, 'They'll soon get tired of complaints from the passengers who have to dïne as the ships round Point Judith and find the high seas not much to their liking.'

It was Thanksgiving. Marcus and the family sat at the table.

Snow blew against the windows, and fell in thick soft flakes on the already white lawn.

He bowed his head to give thanks.

Augusta closed her eyes and prayed for Luke's safety.

Luke lay on his pallet, shivering inside the worn blanket. His head ached. His beard itched. He was hungry and had been for so long that he couldn't remember when his belly hadn't hurt with it. The man next to him moved, and that hurt too. They were crammed so close together that even taking a deep breath was dangerous. There were seven of them in a stone cellar large enough for three and too shallow to stand without bending over.

Not that Luke could stand yet. Nor even knew if he'd ever be back on his feet again. In the beginning – or at least what was the beginning for him – there had been twelve men in the same cellar. Five had been carried away.

Out of the dark a voice said, 'I calculate it to be November. That's right. November. It puts me in mind of the day of Thanksgiving.'

Somebody laughed.

Luke felt cold wind on his face – draught – and blessed God for it. Without the air that seeped in from some unseen crevice, they'd all have been dead by now. Not only the five.

'We had goose,' the voice went on dreamily. 'Fat sweet tender goose. From Canada. My Pa used to take up his musket and go over and get it. Let everybody in the state of Maine have turkey. We had our goose. And cranberries, of course. Potatoes whipped up, and brown gravy...'

Somebody yelled, 'Shut up, damn you!'

Luke opened his eyes. It was dark. He couldn't see. It didn't matter. There was nothing to look at anyhow. He shut his eyes again, rolled to his side.

The day of Thanksgiving. November. He wondered if that were right. He'd lost so much memory there was no way for him to be certain. From Taunton they'd gone by boat and train to

Washington City, and made camp at Kalorama Heights until August, then to Camp Brightwood. In March they embarked at Alexandria. Later he fought at Williamsburg, still later at Antietam. There had been a Christmas, marked for a few hours, but he wasn't sure when that was.

He remembered clearly, though, a hot summer night. He'd been riding with the other men. They were scouting well ahead of the company. Almost, for a little while, he had forgotten what they were there for. The honeysuckle was so sweet. The dark hummed with locusts. Ahead of them great swarms of white moths rose up like rippling veils.

Suddenly, the shadows exploded. There were flashes of fire. Thunder rumbled around and over them. All three went down. Horse hooves drummed close by and passed and came back again. It was all he heard for a long time. Drumming horse hooves. Some time later he was aware of voices. And he was aware of pain until it swallowed him into darkness once more.

The next he knew he was here in the stone cellar. He recognized none of the others with him. Little by little he learned that he was a prisoner of war, and lucky to be alive. He had had a bad head wound and his face had been cut. He became accustomed to the once a day visit at dawn by the soldier in gray, who brought water and a half a bucket of gruel and set it down in a corner, his hand holding his musket steady. Eventually Luke became accustomed to the sound of the door closing, the iron bars falling into place.

Eyes closed, shivering in his torn blanket, he let himself drift. Amy. Marcus. The girls. He pictured them one by one. Then he imagined the Kincaid house on High Street. In his mind he walked inside and stood beneath the brass chandeliers. There was a fire burning in the parlor. He stood at the hearth, warming himself, and looking at the pieces on the mantel. A girandole of crystal set with five candles that Amy had had from her Aunt Jane Oliver. The lion of pale gray-green porcelain that Marcus had called celadon, the four-inch cloisonné vase, the laughing dog in ivory. The exotics that Marcus had brought back from his stop in Canton Harbor so long ago. And next to them the clock under a dome of glass, its small parts magically working together.

There was a sound. Iron bars. Luke raised his head slowly. A pale dawn appeared when the door swung open. Cold wind burned his face.

'Food, water.' The soldier in gray set the two buckets in the corner, but this time he didn't immediately retreat to slam the door behind him. This time he waited. When no one moved, he asked, 'What's the matter? Nobody hungry here, nobody thirsty?'

Somebody chuckled. 'Is this a new game?'

Luke pushed himself up to an elbow. The voice was different, the stance too. The musket pointed to the dirt floor. This was a new man.

'Fall to,' the soldier said. 'For what it's worth. And I wish there were more.'

Luke crawled to the corner. He took a spoonful of gruel, swallowed two sips of water. He could feel the guard watching him.

When he turned to go back to his pallet, the man asked, 'That's all you want?'

'The others.'

'It'll last for them. Or I'll get more.' Then, 'What's wrong with your head?'

'Don't know. But I'm better than I was.'

'Which doesn't say much, does it?'

'Wakefield,' a voice called out of the dark, 'ask the damn reb where we are since you're so conversational.'

The guard spoke to Luke. 'You're on a farm just south of Richmond. Libby was too filled up.' With that he stepped backward through the door and slammed it so hard that bits of clay fell from the roof of the cellar. Iron bars thudded into place.

'Richmond? Did he say Richmond?' One of the prisoners asked.

Luke didn't answer. What did it matter where they were? He let himself sink back into sleep.

Later there were whispers, movement. The sounds brought him awake. Someone was saying, 'He's dead, I tell you.'

Close by Luke saw two men huddled over a ragged pallet.

The men yelled, the six of them left. They yelled as loudly as they could. Much later the door opened and lantern light spilled through.

'What now?' the guard demanded.

'We have a man that needs burying.'

The guard came in, his place at the door taken by another man. He too held a musket at the ready.

The first soldier stood over the corpse, swung the lantern briefly, and nodded. Then he looked at Luke. 'You're Wakefield?' he asked. 'From Massachusetts, are you?'

Luke said he was, unsurprised. He was still wearing his insignia on the remains of his uniform.

The guard said nothing more. He pulled the corpse out. The door was slammed shut. The iron bars fell into place.

Luke forgot the exchange of words by the time the cellar was sealed shut again.

But the guard didn't forget it. His name was Christopher Wenton. That night he wrote to his father Gaylord, and mentioned the Yankee prisoner named Wakefield who came from Massachusetts.

There were only the two of them left. Willie Gorgas and Johnny Franger. Just the two of them out of the whole patrol.

Willie said, 'I guess we were lucky.'

'Maybe,' Johnny agreed. 'But we'd been luckier still if we'd been able to get away.'

Willie paced the small square of dirt before the lean-to of shredding blankets. 'The rest of them, they're dead. They won't be getting away. And we've got a chance.' The words were mispronounced and spoken with an unfamiliar rhythm. But it didn't matter. Johnny Franger had no trouble understanding.

He squatted on his heels, drew a design in the dirt. 'You're right, Willie. We're lucky. We're going to be all right.'

'I want to be out,' Willie growled. 'That's what I want.'

'And that makes two of us again.'

'You have any idea where we are?'

'Hell, to begin with.' Johnny raised pale eyes to the dead line, which was marked by a row of fires kept burning night and day and patrolled by always careful guards. One step too close to the dead line and the guards fired. He went on, 'Also called Andersonville, I think.'

'How long can we hold out, do you suppose?'

'As long as they make us, Willie.'

'No,' Willie growled, his black eyes glinting. 'No. I want to go home.'

Not that home was so much, although he didn't say so to

Johnny Franger. Only anything was better than this. The rations were water and cornmeal, and little of either. Sometimes a bit of maggoty pork was included. The air stank from a large swamp in the middle of the area that was used as a sink. The mosquitoes and flies and ants were ever present and voracious. Bloodhounds used to track runaways kept up a constant terrible howl. So anything was better.

Willie was hungry, in pain. His broken arm needed fixing if it was to mend right; his foot needed attention, too. They'd been captured four weeks before. They'd been shipped by train for two nights, had walked the rest of the way and into the stockaded acres. He was ready to go home, even if home wasn't what he had hoped it would be. He hadn't wanted to leave his son even as he'd thought about volunteering. But Annie was a nag. He'd married her because he was lonely, locked in himself. Because she had a warm body, and in that time, a nice laugh. But she had changed so quickly it was like a demon possessed her. And when the war came, she'd said, not once, but many times, 'So you're for abolition and the niggers, are you? Then how come you don't go with the others? How come you're still doing your job and earning your pay right here? And you say you're American. Just like all foreigners. Want what you can get but won't pay for it.'

She said it once too often, if she didn't mean it. But she did. She hated Willie and he knew it. He got drunk one afternoon and stumbled out of the rum shop and signed up before he got sober. When he did, it was too late to change his mind. He was relieved. It would be good to be away from Annie. And he'd get home to his son. He'd made up his mind.

He met Johnny in New York, and learning they were both from Fall River seemed a miracle then. The miracle was that they'd been together ever since.

'So do I want to go home.' Johnny's voice dropped. 'And maybe there's a way.'

The thing about Johnny Franger was that he always had an idea. Willie admitted to himself that he didn't often have ideas. He knew what he wanted but he didn't always know how to get it. Johnny did.

'What way?' Willie asked.

Johnny gestured to the small group that stood near the lean-to. Willie slid closer, squatted down and bent his head.

Johnny scarcely moved his lips around the words when he said, 'Would you try?'

'Yes,' Willie breathed.

'Then I'll think about it.'

Later that day a detail came in with a horse and wagon. It moved across the fields, gathering dead bodies that were thrown into the wagon and carted away. In mid-afternoon, Willie and Johnny stood near the dead line. They watched as the corpse-laden wagons rolled out. Beyond the stockade, deep ditches had been dug. The bodies were pitched into them. Boards were laid over them and covered with a layer of dirt.

Together, silent, Willie and Johnny retreated to their lean-to.

In the morning, two soldiers came in. 'You get up!' one yelled. 'On your feet.'

Some of the prisoners rose. Others, wounded or too weak, lay still. Although he could have, Willie didn't move either.

'You!' A musket pointed at him. 'Work detail.'

Willie lay motionless.

The guard came to stand over him. 'What's the matter, Yankee? Somebody shoot your ears off?' He was very young, with fiery red hair and a thin mustache.

'It's the foot,' Willie said, thrusting his blood-encrusted boot forward.

'Couldn't understand you,' the guard drawled. 'You one of those mercenaries the Yankees hired to do their fighting for them?'

Willie scrambled up. Roaring curses from his childhood, he threw himself at the guard. He heard the explosion, smelled gunpowder. But he felt nothing. The second shot stopped him. It was as if he had flung himself at a stone wall. He wavered on his feet for an instant before he fell.

He rose up out of blackness on a current of pain. His chest was afire. He screamed and heard the sound echo back at him.

At dawn, when he opened his eyes, Johnny Franger was bending over him. 'You'll be all right,' Johnny told him. 'They got somebody in to take the ball out of your chest, and the wound's been cauterized. If you made it through that, you can make it through anything.'

'I'll make it,' Willie said softly.

'Just don't try that again. It was lucky you weren't killed on the spot.'

'I'll try it again,' Willie said. 'Yes, I will. And I'll kill the man that shot me.'

Johnny hunched closer, his head on his arms. 'Home,' he said dreamily. 'God, how that woman can cook. Stew, and johnny cakes. And a sweet woman, too. Not too smart in the attic. You follow me, don't you? But sweet. Never talks back. Just, "Sure, Johnny," and, "Whatever you think, Johnny." I'm a lucky man in what I've got waiting at home. And the boardinghouse, neat as a pin, bringing in good money every week. And...' Softly, he went on, enumerating his claims to good fortune as if they were talismans against the prison camp, the war.

Willie only half-listened. He was busy thinking about the guard's red hair and thin mustache, how he walked and moved and raised his musket to fire.

Chapter 6

In 1865, the Boston, Newport and New York Steamboat Company shifted the terminus of its line from Newport back to Fall River. The *Bay State* and the *Empire State* and their sister ships and freighters once again snugged to the wharves at the foot of Central Street, and blew their whistles at the Borden Flats light.

In that same year, but earlier, Marcus received word from Gaylord Wenton that Luke had been captured. Marcus never knew that Wenton had sent two messages before but both had gone astray.

He had been handed the missive as he stood on the docks near a freighter that had only been tied up moments before. The bearer had thrust it into his hand and darted away into the crowd before Marcus could do more than ask, 'What's this?'

He scanned the few words quickly and let out a shout of joy.

'Luke's alive!' It had been hard to think so in the face of a silence that had lasted nearly two years. Only Augusta had clung stubbornly to her faith that Luke would return. Marcus understood, but it worried him. She was just weeks short of eighteen now and beautiful beyond description, yet she showed no interest in the many men who came to court her.

Homeward bound in the carriage, reins in his maimed left hand, the message in his right, he read the words again. Luke was imprisoned, Wenton wrote. He was not well. It might be possible to arrange his release for a payment of five thousand dollars damages for his services against the Confederacy.

'It's ransom,' Amy whispered when she heard of it after he burst into the house shouting the news.

'Perhaps. And I don't care. I shall have a draft in that amount by tomorrow morning.'

'How will you deliver it? Surely you don't think to go south in these times.'

'Mr. Hansen, you know him, now first mate on the *Metropolis*, used to have contacts with the Underground Railroad for escaped slaves. It's possible he'll have some ideas how to help me reach Wenton.'

Aria, hearing the news, seemed unaffected. 'Oh, how nice,' she said, and wandered off. But Augusta said softly, 'Is it true, is it true?' while light suddenly brightened her green eyes and color burned in her cheeks. And she had to read the message, to hold it in her hands that suddenly shook.

Marcus said gently, 'You mustn't take this too much for granted, Augusta. We can't be certain we'll be able to carry through.'

Hansen looked doubtful when he heard the story. 'It sounds like a ruse, Mr. Kincaid. You'll likely lose your money and not see Luke Wakefield again.'

Marcus knew that himself. But he jammed his left hand in his coat pocket, and said firmly, 'I must try.'

For many reasons Carl Hansen would try anything for Marcus. But the biggest reason had become Augusta. For years he had looked upon her with a fond paternal eye; now his feelings were no longer fatherly. So he said, 'If you're determined to take the risk, then I believe there's a way. I have a friend in New York who occasionally makes trips south and across the lines. If he's able to deliver the money to Gaylord Wenton, he will.'

Marcus passed over the draft along with Gaylord's last known address in Richmond.

Four weeks later Luke was standing on the Fall River wharves. He still wore his blue uniform, but now it was patched where it had been torn, and streaked and stained. His boots were cracked, the laces held together with knots. His head wound had healed, but the dark unruly hair under his forager cap was touched with silver, and over his right temple it was marked by a crooked white streak an inch wide. Just below his right eye there was a dark red dent. It could pass for a birthmark but was actually the filling in of new tissue where a ricochet had struck him.

He was clean shaven and thin, nearly rigid with apprehension. For, as he looked at the early morning bustle, he felt like a stranger. Wondering at himself, he turned to glance back at the *Bay State* on which he had just arrived. He'd recognized most of the crew, had visited with the captain in the wheelhouse. Now the captain waved at him. A deckhand shouted, 'See you soon.'

It was all familiar, and yet he felt as if he were in a dream. He was light-headed with a deep quiet happiness. He was home. Yet he also was heavy with unease. Were the Kincaids changed? Would they see much change in him? So much had happened since they were last together.

He had thought that he would die in the dank cellar in which he'd lain so long. Instead, late one night he was suddenly shaken out of a nightmare and hauled to his feet, with a whispered 'Come on!'

He was pushed into the dark. Air perfumed and sweet touched him. Overhead silver stars winked. The rumble of a cart pulling up sounded like thunder. 'Go on. Get up. And be quick!'

He had only a glimpse of a bearded face as he obeyed. There was no time to say 'Thanks,' to ask what had happened, to learn where he was going. The cart jerked away into the night and he with it.

Later, from Marcus he learned of the message from Gaylord Wenton and what Marcus had done; but neither he nor Marcus ever learned that the five thousand dollars delivered as ransom stuck to no man's fingers, but went directly from Wenton to pay the Englishman who delivered to him a wagonload of muskets and barrels of powder.

The day that Luke arrived in Fall River was the same day that General Robert E. Lee surrendered to General Ulysses S. Grant at Appomattox. The sun was shining on the southern town, but in Fall River an April mist hung on the wind, and dark storm clouds edged with white blanketed Mount Hope Bay.

For a little longer Luke remained, surveying the early morning scene. He took in one slow breath after another. Freedom. This was what it felt like. Hope. The future. Finally, with a tired sigh, he picked up his sack and set out for Liberty Street, where his mother lived. But already he was thinking ahead to when he would see the Kincaids. Marcus. Amy. The girls. Memories of them had sustained him amid the noise of the battlefields and in the deadly silence of the stone cellar in which he'd been imprisoned. His real family.

He had been away close to four years now, but the change in his mother's boarding house bewildered him. The building was smaller and seemed much older. Window frames and porches were in disrepair. What had once been a pleasant garden was now a dump, where hordes of children raced between overflowing trash cans and piles of garbage. On the front steps a gaggle of women made loud comments on the passers-by. They remarked upon Luke as he approached them – the white streak in his hair; the scar on his face which turned livid when he heard them; his tall form; the tattered uniform. He apologized and moved past them on the steps. Four years, and all was changed. He would have to find new quarters. He couldn't live here.

His mother had remained the same. Her hair was white. She was small as a child. She greeted him with a blank stare, a twisting of the lips.

He looked at her, feeling the familiar mixture of pity and guilt, and asked, 'How are you?' She said nothing until he went on, 'Mother, it's me. Your son. Luke.'

Then she nodded, clutched the same dirty bundle of rags to her breast. 'I see you. I know you.'

'Have you been well cared for?'

'Yes.'

There seemed nothing else to say. He remained for a little longer, more to satisfy himself than her, for she, after those few words, ignored him. Soon, though, he left her. Her madness was a burden. It was always a relief to put it behind him.

Even as he felt the relief, however, he asked himself if the taint that had led her to become a child clutching a bunch of rags was in him too. Quickly he shrugged the question away.

It was raining when he came down to the street. The women and children had disappeared. A cart rumbled past. Somewhere a dog barked. He was even more tired than he had been before. Slowly he walked up to South Main Street. He followed along it, looking at the new buildings set among the old. He crossed a bridge over a slimy stream and zigzagged into North Main. When he reached Bedford, he turned right.

The Exchange Hotel was only a few blocks up the hill. He was relieved that it was still there, and still much as he remembered it. Wet through, hair soaked under his cap, shivering with sudden chill, he went inside.

The rates were higher than he had expected. He told himself he couldn't stay there long; but his room was clean, comfortable. It seemed the essence of luxury to him. He sat down to rest for a little while but it was impossible. Impatience drove him. Soon, cleaned up, hair combed, still wearing the only clothes he had, he was out on the street again. The rain had stopped. The air was fresh, with a touch of spring warmth. The lilacs were thick with dark purple buds that would soon burst into myriad lavender stars.

It wasn't far to the Kincaids. By the time he reached the gate, the sun had come out. He paused there. Through the worn soles of his boots, he felt the uneven herringbone brick path. He didn't remember the path, and as he followed its turn toward the porch he realized that there was a long low addition, invisible from the street, attached to the house. And on its roof was a widow's walk that hadn't been there before.

He stopped to admire the changes. Bright sun rimmed the white railings, glinted off the windows bracketed in black shutters, and lay in pale ribbons on the white clapboard walls.

As he stood there, a woman came around the corner of the house. She carried a wide-brimmed hat on which ribbons fluttered amid a nest of yellow daisies. Her red-gold curls were tied high at the back of her head. Her face was small, heart-shaped, with deep-set green eyes. Her curved full lips were accentuated by two dimples. Her pale green gown was plain and untrimmed except for a full ruffle at the ankles; its very simplicity made more apparent the slimness of her waist and the slender curve of her hips.

Luke didn't know her, yet he did. He took a half step, paused, and said uncertainly: 'Gussie? Is that you, Gussie?' And asked himself if it were possible. She'd been a child of fourteen when he left. And now . . .

'Luke.' Her lips moved soundlessly on his name. Color swept into her cheeks. She flung her hat aside, gathered her skirts in both hands, and ran to him. But just as she reached the circle of his wide-opened arms, she stopped. Her color deepened even more. 'Luke,' she said. 'Oh, how good it is to see you.'

He couldn't speak, could only stand and smile at her. He had felt old, tired, scarred. She had come running toward him, her face alight. And he was renewed, made young, joyful as he had never been before.

'Oh, how good it is to see you,' she went on softly. 'We had no word that you were coming. And only a little while ago, down street, I heard rumors of the surrender and thought of you. And now you're here.'

She had always loved him, but there was a difference in that love now. She felt it in her body. A yearning had spread through her at the first sight of him. A hunger she had never known before. She wanted to touch him, to smooth away the reddened scars on his face, to run her fingers through his unruly hair and kiss the white streak over his temple. The difference between what she had once felt and what she felt now made her cautious. She was too old for childish demonstrativeness.

Even as Augusta and Luke smiled at each other, he bound by the same constraint that held her, Aria came bursting out. The younger girl leaped the porch steps and threw herself at Luke. She wrapped her arms around him, and kissed him on the cheek, the ear, the mouth. She cried a welcome greeting, and shouted for her parents, hugging him tighter still. Augusta stood by watching, and Luke, coping with Aria's excesses, continued to look at Augusta with his heart melting within him.

75

Then Marcus was there. The big man gripped his hand, pounded his shoulder. Amy held him close, and blinked back tears.

Inside, seated in the parlor, there were questions, answers. Luke told the little he could remember of the past four years. Where he had been, the patrol in which he had fallen with the head wound that had left the white streak in his hair, his time in the stone cellar.

Marcus spoke of hearing from Gaylord Wenton when Luke described the night he had been taken from there. So finally Luke understood what had happened.

Marcus said, 'Gaylord had a son. He must have known of you through Gaylord, and recognized your name, I think.'

'Thank you, Marcus. You've saved my life for the second time.'

Amy rose to her feet. 'Enough talk of the war. Augusta tells me there's been rumor of a surrender. We must talk of the future.'

Once again Luke's eyes went to Augusta.

Marcus and Amy both saw that, and exchanged glances. Later, when Luke had gone and the girls were upstairs, Amy and Marcus sat together in the parlor. It was shadowed, lit only by a single lamp. The windows were open, and a soft breeze stirred the curtains.

Amy watched as Marcus stretched out his legs, and lit a cigar. Her lady friends might sniff, but she saw no reason for him to linger on the back steps to smoke when he could sit at ease in his own home to do it. She had no dislike for tobacco as long as it was smoked rather than chewed. 'It's been a good day,' he said finally. 'A day to remember.'

'Yes,' she said. She wondered how to say what was in her mind. She'd been troubled for some time. It was because of Aria. The girl's nature had never calmed. She remained, at sixteen, as excitable, her spirits as out of control, as when she was a child. But she was no longer a child. Amy foresaw problems. Several times, she knew, when they were traveling, Aria had left Augusta sleeping in their stateroom and gone to spend hours with passengers, always male, on the ships. There were crew members of the *Metropolis* who had, as tactfully as they could, told her of the girl's adventuring. When Amy spoke of it, the girl called the reports lies and vowed Amy unfair to disbelieve her. Some comment Amy might doubt, but Carl Hansen's word was good. She knew him well. Further, he had been paying obvious court to Augusta and had felt obliged to drop a few careful words to Amy.

'You're frowning,' Marcus said. 'What is it? What's wrong?'

'I should like to see the girls settled.'

He chuckled. 'Ah, I know now. It's that demonstration of Aria's, isn't it? You didn't like the way she greeted Luke. But it's only her way. She's still a child for all her sixteen years. She doesn't know how her actions look or what they could mean to others.'

'Perhaps not. But I wonder, Marcus. I suspect that she has . . . has strong needs.'

Marcus laughed. 'If so, then she comes by them honestly, doesn't she?'

Amy blushed, smiled. But she debated within herself. Ought she to tell Marcus what she had heard about Aria, what she knew for herself as a fact? She decided no. It would upset him mightily. It could anger him. She saw no way in which the knowledge would help. Finally she said, 'I believe some girls should marry early.'

Marcus answered through a billow of blue smoke. 'You're wise in such things. If you think that, then I agree. But I must tell you, I shouldn't like to see Aria married first. Augusta's only eighteen, but if her younger sister is wed and she is not, she'll feel a spinster in her heart.'

'Yes,' Amy said. 'You're right, of course.' She remembered how she had felt, twenty-three and unmarried, before Marcus came into her life. She smoothed the rep of her skirt over her knees. Then, 'You saw how Luke looked at Augusta?'

'I did indeed.'

'He has always been dear to both of us. And to Augusta, too. I'm sure of it.'

'She loves him,' Marcus said flatly.

Amy smiled again. There was no need to say more. Their marriage had been arranged by Aunt Jane Oliver and it had been, still was, good for both of them. Neither Marcus nor Amy saw any reason why it should not be the same for Augusta and Luke. And with Augusta married, they would soon find a suitable husband for Aria too.

*

Augusta sat before the looking glass, whalebone comb in hand. Dreamily she looked into the dreamy green eyes that were reflected there. This was the day she had thought of for so long. This was what she had waited for. Luke was home at last!

She went over every moment of her first glimpse of him. The tall, dark-haired man, forager cap tipped low, who paused at the gate and looked up at the house. For an instant, he was a stranger. Perhaps a friend though, coming from Luke, with word of him, she had thought. And then, her heart clenching inside her, she had known. It was Luke himself, in the flesh!

She knew now more certainly than ever before why she had not encouraged Carl Hansen and the others who had showed interest in her. She had been waiting for Luke to come home. Had it not been for the war, she would probably have had a year's tour abroad, which was what many of the girls had before they settled down either to marriage or spinsterhood. Now the waiting was over. Luke was back. She wondered what to do, what she could do. She wondered if Luke felt for her anything like what she felt for him.

That same night Luke lay in his bed not far away at the Exchange Hotel, thinking of Augusta. She was so young. He was twelve years older. He remembered that she had been born on the day that he first met Marcus Kincaid. He asked himself if the age difference would matter. He wondered if he had enough to offer her. And he wondered, suddenly sick at heart, how she would feel were she to meet his mother.

The *Metropolis* steamed slowly past the Borden Flats light. Marcus and Luke stood at the rail in a pink dawn.

It was five days since Luke's return. The time had gone quickly. He had moved his mother to a new boardinghouse. He had gone to the company's offices to see the general manager, and learned that the *Bay State* would soon be retired. He was assigned to the *Metropolis* as assistant purser, which meant an increase in pay. He was returning now from his first trip.

During the making of these arrangements to resume his old life, he had thought only of altering it. He wanted to talk to Marcus, but didn't know how to begin. He was troubled by his age. Perhaps he was too old for Augusta. And even with the promotion he had so little. She deserved everything. Would love be enough? Would Marcus and Amy think so? And what of Augusta? How did she feel about him?

'Are you settled yet?' Marcus asked. 'Having been away for so long, it can't have been easy for you to come home.'

Luke said, 'It's as if I was never gone. The past four years already seem like a distant dream.'

'But they've marked you.'

'Yes. I think so.' Automatically Luke's hand went to the scar on his face. He looked at Marcus.

'Yet you're not truly changed. You're still the boy I've known all these years. The boy I've thought of as a son.'

'Not such a boy any more, I fear.'

'No. And I'm glad of it, Luke.' Marcus rubbed his reddish beard. 'Do you know, I think Augusta is deeply fond of you.'

Luke said slowly, 'I'm in love with her, Marcus.'

Marcus grinned. He clapped Luke on the shoulder. 'Then I can leave the rest to you and Augusta. Speak to her, man. Speak to her at once. If you feel that way, there's no reason to wait.'

'I will,' Luke cried joyfully.

At twilight that evening he asked if Augusta would walk him down to the wharves. Before she could answer, Aria said, 'We'll both go with you to see you off.'

He said gently, 'Aria, you weren't invited. I'd like to speak to Gussie privately.'

Aria's eyes widened; her lower lip jutted. The slim young body went rigid with indignation. 'All right,' she said loudly. 'If you don't want me, then go alone.'

Amy said, 'Aria, I shall need you at home.'

The girl flounced out, banged the door behind her.

'Gussie?' Luke asked.

She had been silent during the scene, wishing that Aria were not so forward, wishing too that it had not been necessary to hurt her feelings. At the same time there was sudden hope in her. If Luke wanted to be alone... Aloud, Augusta said, 'Yes, I'll come with you. It's a beautiful evening.'

Smiling, Amy watched the younger people go out. She believed she knew what was about to happen.

They stood in a sheltered corner. The big whitewheeler was aglow with lights. The docks swarmed with stevedores carrying crates. The tall arm of a derrick moved up and down, swinging great loads into the hold.

Although they weren't touching, she was so aware of him, of his tall lean body, that she felt as if his whole being enwrapped her. It had always been thus. His presence created a small special world for her. She waited, tremulous, hoping for him to speak.

But he was silent, thinking that if Marcus were in error, and Gussie didn't love him, then his question would spoil everything between them. They could not even be friends any more. Dare he risk it? At least, as it was, he could see her, be with her. He could feast his eyes on her, and dream. But he wanted more of her. Her love, and a future together. He tried to think of the right words, assembling a small speech in his mind.

Finally Augusta asked, 'Do you think you'll like being with the *Metropolis*?'

'Very much. Though I'll miss the *Bay State* when she's retired.'

It was the first Augusta had heard of it. Her eyes widened. 'Retired, Luke? They can't do that! She's my ship. She sailed on her maiden voyage the day I was born.'

'I know. But that's how it is.'

'That's how it is,' she repeated softly. 'Things change.' She remembered when she had dreamed of being a boy and standing with the pilots in the wheelhouse. She remembered when she first realized that she would never captain the *Bay State*, but that her destiny would still lie with that ship, and all the others of the line.

'Not everything changes,' Luke was saying.

She raised her eyes to his. There had been something in his voice that made her forget the ships, that set her atremble. Now, now was the moment when her life would be decided. For to be without him meant nothingness. And to be with him meant being alive. Her yearning for him was become a sweet singing in her blood. She wanted to belong to him, to belong to him and have him and know him, and feel his arms about her and his breath on her lips.

'I won't change,' he went on, having finally found the right words. The simplest of all words. For he knew there was no risk in love, none beyond the risk of life itself. 'I'll always love you.

Would you marry me, Gussie?' And he waited, holding his breath and hungering to take her into his arms.

To be his, and to belong to him. That was what she had always wanted. There was a glow on her face. Her two dimples flashed joyfully. She put her hands into his and whispered, 'I will, Luke. I will.'

That same night a play called *Our American Cousin* was being performed at Ford's Theatre in Washington City. As President Lincoln and his wife sat in a box near the stage, the door slowly opened at the back. A man stepped through. He raised a pistol and fired.

They had been making plans. A neighbor came banging at the door to tell them the news.

'He's shot and near to dying!'

'Just now,' Amy cried. 'Just now, when peace is come.'

'It's the worst thing that could have happened,' Marcus said.

Augusta was silent, only wishing that Luke were with her. Only wanting his arms around her while she remembered the night, years before, when she had seen Mrs. Lincoln, enwrapped in a black shawl, walk slowly along the deck of the *Empire State*.

The next morning, the president died. A trembling Andrew Johnson was given the oath of office.

All over the country, in coastal cities and mountain villages and prairie towns, Americans watched as their flags were lowered to half-mast, and prayed that the United States, again one, could survive this latest blow.

Chapter 7

Willie Gorgas looked older than thirty-five in the bright sun of late May. There were white flecks in his dark beard, and deep lines gouged his cheeks. His thick shoulders were stooped. Though he walked quickly there was a noticeable hitch in his gait. He wore a black coat, its left sleeve neatly pinned under the stump of his arm. His gray trousers were tucked in freshly shined boots.

Stepping onto the main deck of the *Empire State*, he said, 'So. We're on the way, Johnny.'

Johnny Franger laughed. He was a small man, light on tiny feet. His hands were narrow, and quick with a deck of cards. His face was thin, bright-eyed under a cap of ginger hair. 'It seems to me we've been on the way for a long time.'

'And walked for most of it, too,' Willie answered.

Heading for the purser's office to get his key, Willie looked for familiar faces. There was no one he knew. But the purser himself looked up when Willie said his name. 'Gorgas? Willie, is that you?' and with his eyes on Willie's stump, 'Of course it is. How are you?'

'Good,' Willie said, recalling the man's face but not his name.

'And you're on the way home?'

'Yes.'

'Then welcome to you.' And with a grin, 'And here's your key. You get the best room in the house.'

If it wasn't the best, it was close to it, Willie knew. It was like a stateroom that Marcus Kincaid would travel in. Briefly Willie wondered where Marcus was, how he fared.

Johnny whistled as he followed Willie in. 'Now this makes it worth it all, doesn't it?'

Willie nodded, but didn't answer.

Soon after the ship steamed away from the New York docks,

the two men went to the lounge. They settled in deep chairs, with a pitcher of ale and two mugs on a small mahogany table before them.

'Have you thought about it?' Johnny asked. 'About what you're going to do?'

'I have.'

'And?'

'I'll go see the company's general agent. But what work does the line have for a one-armed man?'

'Wait until you hear what the man says.' When Willie didn't answer, Johnny went on, 'And besides, we'll have the hundred and fifty apiece bounty.' That was what they had been promised when they signed on. A bounty of one hundred and fifty dollars for serving the full hitch as volunteers in the regiment.

Willie took a deep swallow of ale. He was on the way home. But was it real? Was it happening?

Johnny spoke, but Willie didn't hear him. In his mind he was listening to distant sounds. The rumble of caisson wheels on rutted roads. The thunder of faraway cannon. His own deep-throated screams. He hadn't wanted help. He would have ignored the wounded arm until whatever was going to happen happened. But they'd dragged him to the hospital tent, with him not strong enough to fight the three guards off, and one of them the man who'd shot him, and Johnny Franger running along beside yelling, 'No, no! I'll take care of him,' because everybody knew about the hospital tent. They got him there, tied him down. He heard the two doctors arguing. One said, 'No, there's time to save it.' The other said, 'It's got to go.' He was still screaming 'No!' as they poured whiskey into him. The stump healed slowly, but heal it did. His strength came back to him. He was ready when the chance finally came.

In mid-February they were called out to repair a bridge. It was cold, the sky thick with snow clouds. Yet they sweated, working under the muskets of the two guards. One he'd never seen before, the other he recognized from another time. He had the stump of his left arm to thank the man for. Willie kept his head down, but his eyes were fixed on that guard. The storm broke suddenly. Lightning flashed across the sky while snow lashed down in great icy whips, swirling, suffocating.

'Into the wagon,' the guard yelled, his musket ready. The other one stood aside, watching. One prisoner climbed on, then another. Johnny went up. And as he did, Willie lowered his head and charged. The musket spat fire, but Willie didn't see it. He heard in his head his own screams as he bore the guard to the ground. His right hand clenched around the man's throat. Clenched. Tightened. Meanwhile Johnny had jumped from the wagon onto the second guard. They'd fallen together. Only Johnny had gotten up. He pulled at Willie's shoulder. 'Come on. Let's go.'

And while the snow spun around them, they ran into the tall pines, and Willie remembered another time he had run, fleeing to save himself.

They traveled by night to avoid both armies, and went on foot because that was the only way. They didn't want to be stopped, questioned. Maybe to be sent south again. They lived off the land.

Now Willie stared into his ale and wondered still if it were real.

He would be home in the morning. Annie would greet him with her usual sneer, he supposed. But there would be his son, Willie. The boy she called William. It was what he had come back for. Otherwise there'd be nothing for him in Fall River - him, and his half left arm. There'd be nothing. Except young Willie. With the thought of the boy, his strength flowed back. There was everything for him in Fall River.

'I pinch myself,' Johnny Franger said. 'Do you feel that way? I've got to pinch myself to be sure it's me. And that it's happening.'

'Yes,' Willie said.

'By all rights, I ought to be dead. And that's the truth. I should have starved to death, or else got shot for tripping near the dead line. I ought to have had tick fever or diarrhea or typhoid fever or dropsy or scurvy. Instead, I'm going home. And Ellie'll be waiting. Smiling, sweet. I guess I'm the luckiest man in the world.'

'It's good to be lucky.'

Johnny was turned away. He swung back to say, 'I know how right you are.' He grinned. 'When I look over there, at that woman, I count my blessings. There's that, and that's what I could of ended up with. And then there's my own little Ellie.

You'll see what I mean when you meet her.'

'Yes,' Willie said. His glinting black eyes briefly studied the group of people sitting nearby. Although he had seen two of the three many times before, it was a long time ago, and they had changed. Mabel Graystone and her father Hiram were sitting with a man named Arthur Fields.

Willie studied them a moment more, then turned back to his ale. Rich people, people of power. They had everything. But some day he'd have power and money too. He didn't know how yet, but some day he'd have everything. For his boy Willie.

If Mabel Graystone could have read Willie Gorgas's mind, she would have laughed. He thought she had everything. And she was thinking to herself that she had nothing. She'd been alive for twenty-three years, sad and terrible years, and there was nothing to show for any one of them. Not even a single joyful memory. Her dull glance swept the lounge. The girls were beautiful to look on, their waists tiny, their hair shining. Mouths, eyes, alive and glowing. She was the only plain one in the whole saloon. The others were flowers among flowers. And she was the weed.

Her father said, 'Mabel, I'm speaking to you.'

'I'm sorry, Father. I didn't hear.'

'Mr. Fields is asking have you traveled before on the Fall River Line, or is this your first voyage?'

'First voyage?' she repeated blankly.

'No, no, girl. That's no answer,' Hiram sneered at her. 'Is your mind wandering again?'

She looked directly at Arthur Fields for the first time since her father had made the introduction and pushed him into a seat. She said, 'We go to New York very often, and always on one of the Fall River Line ships.'

'I, too,' Arthur said, smiling. 'It's surprising we've never met before.' He was a man of thirty-two, thin of face, with a soft pale mustache and soft pale gray eyes. He had long narrow hands, and between them he clasped a book, his fingers unconsciously caressing its cover. He saw her glance and said, 'Whitman. Have you read him?'

Again she gave Arthur a blank look. 'Whitman?' She wished there had been some way to avoid this encounter. It could end only one way. Badly.

'Walt Whitman, Miss Graystone. The poet.'

'The poet,' she repeated. From between her lips, without apparent reason, there issued a loud raucous laugh. Her face turned red. She was afraid that she would suddenly burst into tears.

Her father pulled at his nearly white beard. 'No, Mr. Fields. Mabel doesn't read foolish stuff. She has no time for poetry. She reads financial journals and leases and mortgages. It's all she can do to keep up with our financial affairs, although I've been grooming her since her infancy to deal with the property she'll one day inherit.'

Arthur Fields uncrossed, then recrossed his knees. He regarded his boots thoughtfully. He was himself a man of some property, having inherited it from his parents and grand-parents. But he had never, among his acquaintances, heard such open discussion of one's private affairs or what one owned. There was something almost indecent about it. And the girl. What was her name? Martha? Mary? No, Mabel. Poor thing. But what could one expect with such a father. Arthur Fields wondered how soon he could politely make his excuses. When Hiram had bumped into him, apologized over-profusely, and insisted that Arthur join him for coffee, Arthur had accepted because it was easier than to refuse. Now he wished he'd sent the man on his way.

Aloud, Arthur said, 'I see, I see. So time's the limiting factor. Still, I find a good book very relaxing.'

'A good book? That piffle Whitman writes can't be called good.'

'There are some who think so.' Arthur allowed himself to look at Mabel. Her round face was a dull red. Her thick blond hair was piled into a messy knot on the top of her head from which loose ends shredded to hang limply around her cheeks. Her shoulders were rounded within an unbecoming cape of ruffles. He reached for his coffee and sipped at it. It was a pity she didn't know how to make the best of that bosom since it was full enough to invite the eye.

'And you,' Hiram asked, 'aside from the reading of poetry, how do you pass your time?'

'I travel. I study.'

'Can you make money at that?'

Arthur Fields coughed, put down his cup. There it was

again. The man was impossible. Money, business. It was all he could think about. Arthur had had enough. 'One manages,' he said coolly. He rose, bowed. 'I'm sorry. I must retire now. I'm happy to have met you, Miss Graystone.' And to Hiram, 'And you too, sir.'

He turned quickly away from their acknowledgements and walked across the lounge. There, in a corner, he spied Boston friends and sat down to talk with them.

Hiram, watching, said, 'You are disgusting, Mabel.'

'Yes, Father,' she answered, watching too.

'Stop saying, "Yes, Father."'

'I'm sorry, Father.'

'I bring you a young man, and what do you do? You laugh like a woman crazed for no reason. You don't say a word. You offer him no encouragement.'

'He doesn't want to be encouraged.'

'Look at him. He had to retire, he said. He's not retiring, is he? Except from you.'

'I did nothing to offend him, Father.'

'You did nothing. Yes. Nothing to interest him either. And I want a grandson, damn you! Who'll pass on my name for me, damn you? Who'll own what I've labored for all my life when I die and you die? Who'll carry on the Graystone name then?'

She sat very still. What could she say? How could she answer? She dreamed of lying in a man's arms. Her body hungered for love. Inside this shell of fat, this lump, there was a young and fetching woman. But what was the use? No one knew she was there, hiding.

She glanced across the lounge at Arthur Fields. He was leaning forward, smiling at the woman sitting next to him. He held out the volume of Whitman's poems and the woman took it, her hand plainly lingering on Arthur's.

Mabel turned away.

'We might as well go to bed,' her father said.

'I'd like something to eat,' she answered.

'Now? You've just finished your meal.'

She raised dull brown eyes to his face. 'I'm hungry.'

He shrugged his disgust. 'Do as you like.'

Later, she lay alone, listening to the sound of the paddle wheels. The food she had eaten lay like a stone in her chest. It lay like a weight of sorrow in her heart. She pictured Arthur Fields. Pale eyes, pale mustache, smooth long hands. One day they might meet again. She hoped so. She wanted very much to repay him for his snub.

Willie walked slowly up the hill. Johnny had turned off at his street, and in a little while, he would be home, hugging his sweet wife.

And soon Willie would be home, too. Alone. That was how it had always been. Alone was how it still was. Annie wouldn't want it any other way. But at least there would be Willie, or William, as she called him. It wasn't going to be easy. Willie would have to find a way to make peace with her. He would have to find a way to put up with her. Already he could almost hear her shrill, 'And so you've come home with one arm, have you? Then what do you suppose you're going to do?' But there would be a way. There had to be a way.

He tried to imagine himself feeling the way Johnny Franger felt. Looking ahead. Happy. Hands tingling for the feel of breasts. It was no good. Coming home to Annie put a sour taste at the back of his throat, and that was all.

He saw the house ahead, paused for a moment, and then limped on. He went slowly around to the side, let himself in. The place had an unfamiliar look. There was the smell of corned beef and cabbage on the stairs. When he knocked at the door, it opened on a face he didn't know.

'Mrs. Gorgas?' he said questioningly.

The woman stared at him. 'I don't know her.'

'But where's she gone?'

The woman shrugged.

He went down a flight, tried again. There he was told to try down the street, at a gray house.

That time when he knocked, he was recognized. It was Mrs. Heit, small, dark. She said, 'Mr. Gorgas, you'd best come in.' And when he followed her into the kitchen, she went on, 'And sit down. I have something to tell you.'

'My boy? My boy?' he asked gruffly.

'He's well. He's out in the back. I'll call him in. But in a minute. First...'

'Something's happened,' Willie said.

'Your wife died, Mr. Gorgas. She had the lung sickness.

Nobody knew a way to get word to you.'

The sour taste at the back of his throat was suddenly gone. Annie was dead. He need never again hear her shrill voice. But his relief vanished in the instant. 'My boy?' he rasped.

'We took him in. There was no place else for him. And one more with three of mine didn't matter. He's six now and a good lad.'

Willie rose. 'I want him.' And then, softly, stumbling on the words, 'Thank you for what you did.'

'Sometimes people help each other,' she answered. She went to the window and called. Soon there was the thump of running feet on the stairs. The door flew open. Six-year-old Willie flung himself in and came to a quick rocking stop. He had a shock of dark hair. His eyes were black, bright. He was tall for his age, and thin, but his hands were large and so were his feet. He was big Willie all over again.

Willie opened his one arm – but William looked uncertainly at Mrs. Heit.

'It's your father, come back from the war,' she said.

'Papa?' the boy said questioningly.

'You're a fine big boy,' Willie said. He let his arm drop. He could be patient if he had to. 'I won't go away any more, Willie.'

The boy looked at Mrs. Heit. 'He's your father,' she said helplessly.

The boy turned to Willie, studied him for a long moment. Finally he said, 'My name is William. William. Not Willie.' And then, 'What happens to me now?'

It was a good idea. At least that's how it seemed at the beginning. They would be among friends. The room was big and clean. The food was good. Johnny's wife, Ellie, could look after William when Willie was out hunting for work.

Ellie was just as Johnny had described her. Pretty, sweet, loving. Her face was round and dimpled. Light brown hair enwrapped her head in thick braids. She was plump and curved and soft, with no hard angles to her, and her voice was soft, too. She was so much what Johnny had described that the unexpected happened.

Willie Gorgas began to want her. Even more unexpected was that she fell in love with him.

There were six roomers. Willie and William got the breast of chicken when she served chicken, the largest cut of fresh peach pie when she served pie. Their clothes were kept in order, and at no charge. Their boots were shined.

Another unexpected thing that happened was that Johnny Franger changed. He wasn't the same man he'd been in Andersonville. He didn't grin and tell jokes and laugh over his deck of cards. Unlike Willie, who looked but couldn't find a job that suited a one-armed man, Johnny didn't look for work at all.

He was content to spend his days in the kitchen, drinking ale. Sometimes when Ellie pleaded with him, he would do a small repair. Sometimes when he wouldn't, Willie would do it for him. Thus, after Johnny ignored the broken back step for weeks, and Willie himself fell over it, Willie set out to repair it. He learned very quickly that he could use the stump of his arm for more things than he'd thought. He fixed the step, and when he saw the flooring was rotted out, he laid a new floor and railing. Then he did the other small jobs that needed to be done. The experience emboldened him to apply for any job he heard of. He'd learned he could somehow manage to do a man's work.

One day he was walking by a hostler's. He heard a man swearing. '... come in drunk! It's for the last time. Get out of here! I don't need your kind of help.'

Willie waited until a small man staggered out and away, then went inside. If one man got fired, maybe there was room for another.

The stable was dark, but Willie walked through a bar of sunlight so that George Raleigh got a good look at the lined, gaunt face, the black beard, the tall hulking form with only a stump for a left arm. He knew the man but not the name. Six years and some back, when George had been trailing the runaways, this man had dumped him on the wharves and held him up so that the two had gotten away. George rubbed the back of his hand across his long blond mustaches. Well, what did it matter? It had worked out for him, hadn't it? Worked out better for him than it had for this poor fool.

'I'm looking for work,' Willie said. 'You have any here?'

George looked at Willie's stump. 'You've been south.'

Willie nodded. He moved the stump at his shoulder. 'I can do more than it looks like.'

'You have a name?'

Willie told him.

'Then you're hired.' George thrust a pitchfork at Willie. 'Get these stables cleaned out. Then load up and run the team down to New Bedford. We're got a shipment of fish to pick up and bring to the *Metropolis* before ship's sailing tonight.'

It had taken no time for George to recognize Willie. It took Willie a few weeks to remember George. Willie had gone further, seen more strange faces. A lot more had happened to him. But one dawn, when he walked into the stables, George moved his head in a certain way, and the past shifted and spun and came forward into the present. George Raleigh was the bounty hunter.

But by then the incident on the wharves no longer mattered. Willie never told George that he had met him before.

Willie worked, and saved what he could of what he earned, and wanted Ellie, and did the chores around the house. Meanwhile Johnny Franger drank his ale and played his cards at the kitchen table. At first the drink made him surly. But soon surliness became simmering rage. Ellie could do nothing right. The house wasn't clean enough for his taste, although he made more mess than anyone else. His shirts were too wrinkled to wear, the food was slops for pigs.

Ellie grew more and more silent, and Willie wanted her more and more. He wanted the house, too. After a while, because he did the work and made the decisions, he began to feel it was his. He so much felt it was his that when Lottie Dimot moved in, and began to bring in men friends for an hour or a night, he decided he had to put a stop to it. Johnny was willing to close his eyes. Lottie was a quiet girl and paid her high rent on time. But Willie was bothered. He didn't object to Lottie's trade, only to having it in the house where his boy lived. When he told Ellie that Lottie would have to go, she agreed, but Johnny complained loudly. Neither Ellie nor Willie listened, and within the day Lottie Dimot was gone.

But Willie didn't forget her. She was a whore and made a living at it. Willie thought about it all the time. And watched Johnny. And wanted Johnny's wife.

Chapter 8

Marcus wanted to give Augusta and Luke something of substance to build on as Aunt Jane Oliver had done for Amy and him. He could afford it. His investment in the three chests he'd brought back from the whaling ship remained untouched. The yearly dividends from the shipping line still held, and soon, with the war's end, cotton would be harvested again and his commissions would begin coming in.

He considered buying them a small house but then decided instead they must live in the addition at home and have a sum equal to the purchase price of a house to invest as they pleased.

One morning, over breakfast, he told Amy about it.

'And they'd be here with us,' she said softly.

'I admit I like the idea.'

She touched a bluish bruise that had recently come out on her wrist, looked up at him. 'Ah, yes. So do I. But you must leave the choice to them.'

'Suppose they prefer the house?' he demanded.

'So be it.'

'I'll discuss it with them this evening.' Then, 'And did you know today's the day the *Bay State* is leaving?'

'You've told me twice, Marcus. You're as sentimental about that ship as Augusta is.'

'With cause to be. Look where she's brought us.'

'With or without her, you'd have done well. If it hadn't been the shipping line, it would have been something else.'

'Still, she's our beginning,' he said, and chuckled. 'How could I be otherwise about her?'

'And she's a fine ship.'

'Yes, but she's like a woman just over the bloom. All the little tricks and tucks don't hide what's happening to her. We could paint and polish until doomsday and it would be the same.'

'Why, Marcus, I hadn't thought you'd even noticed.'

He gave her a horrified look and jumped up. The floor shook

as he stamped around the table and grabbed and hugged her, crying, 'Amy! Not you! Not you!'

'I tease you,' she said, laughing, with her cheeks suddenly as pink as the silken bow at her throat.

At eleven that same morning Augusta walked down Ferry Street to the wharves, and stood looking at the *Bay State* moored in her berth next to the much larger *Metropolis*. The small ship's gangplank was lowered. Augusta slowly went up to the main deck. At first Aria had said she wanted to come, then she had changed her mind. Amy had chores at home that wouldn't wait. But Augusta was glad to be alone. So much of her was invested in the ship. The *Bay State* had been hers, and her, from her actual beginning. The rhythm of Augusta's life had been set by her comings and goings. She awakened to the three-whistle signal of arrival. Her evenings began with the three-whistle departure signal. Her father's absence and presence, and now Luke's, were all related to the ship.

She touched her lips, then touched the railing. Goodbye, she said silently. Goodbye, and fare well wherever you go from here.

She waited on the wharves for a short time. Soon there came the throb of engines. A cloud of smoke slowly rose up into the blue sky. There were shouts of command. The gangplank was raised, the hawsers freed.

She watched as the *Bay State* slowly steamed away across Fall River harbor. Then, with a last wave of her hand at the empty ship, she turned her back and looked at the *Metropolis*. The *Bay State* was retired, but this ship remained, and was part of her; and there would be others, newer, larger, and even more beautiful.

She was smiling when Luke came in the carriage to meet her.

They drove out to the Watuppa ponds through crowded roadways, past the mills where cotton was made into cloth amid the clank and rattle of gears and pulleys and wheels, past markets, shops, and stables. The way was always uphill and the houses grew fewer and soon the fields were colored with wild flowers.

'Hungry?' Luke asked, as he pulled up and got down to tether the horse.

'A little. I don't know what Betty's fixed for us. She insisted that I mustn't peek. It's supposed to be a surprise.'

He helped Augusta down, took a blanket, and spread it on the ground near the trunk of a fallen tree. He hefted the basket. 'It seems enough for a party instead of only two.'

'Perhaps that's the surprise.' Augusta brought out sandwiches of ham salad, whole ripe tomatoes, a small stoneware container of chicken, thinly sliced cucumbers on buttered white bread. At the bottom of the basket, there was a package wrapped in a white linen napkin. When she opened it, she found cookies in the shape of a sidewheeler. 'The *Bay State*,' she said. 'How good of Betty!'

'She knows how you feel.'

Augusta raised her eyes to his. 'It's the end for the *Bay State*. But not for the line. There must always be changes. And always new beginnings.'

He drew her close, kissed her gently. 'I'm glad you see that.'

It seemed that was a good time, the best time. She served him a sandwich, a tomato, bread with chicken, and poured tea from the jug. Then she said, 'I've been thinking of something, Luke, but haven't quite known whether to speak of it or not.'

'And what's that?'

'Your mother,' she said simply.

His face went sober. The scar on his jaw reddened. He put aside his plate. 'My mother?'

'I'd like for her to come to our wedding, Luke.'

A wave of sickness swept him. He felt sweat on his brow. Icy sweat. He brushed it away with the back of a shaking hand. Nelle – he didn't want to think of her, the weakness that had destroyed her. The weakness that was in him too. He said roughly, 'You don't know her.'

'I don't. That's true. But I've seen her. It was when you were away. My father went to look in on her. He wanted to move her elsewhere when he realized how things were. I went with him then. But your mother refused to go. She was, I think, fearful of us.'

'It's better where she is now. I've seen to that.'

'Of course.' Augusta waited. When Luke didn't speak, she went on, 'I'd like, in some small way, to make her a part of our lives. To have her at our wedding would be a beginning.'

'No,' he said. 'No. I cannot.'

'Why?' Augusta asked softly.

'Gussie, you've seen her so you must know.'

'But I don't know. And she's your mother.'

'She's mad,' he said. 'She's been like that since I was a boy of eight or so.'

'It wasn't by her own choice.'

Nor had it been his choice to remember so little of the past four years. Still it had happened. It was the weakness in him. What he had always feared made plain. 'I can't help how she is,' he said. 'And I'll do what I can to help her. But I can't do what you ask.'

'It would trouble no one.'

'It would trouble me. I'll take care of her as long as she lives. I owe her that. But don't expect me to ... to ...' He stopped. He was out of breath suddenly. Pulses beat in his temple and throat and the sickness built up in his chest.

'To be with her, to see her,' Gussie finished for him. 'That's what you mean, isn't it?'

He nodded, but didn't speak.

'It is,' she said. 'But why, Luke?'

'And I don't want you to either. Leave her to herself as I've always done. It's better that way. Just leave her, and let me be the judge of what's best in this. I know. I know.'

'Why are you afraid?' she asked.

'Afraid,' he repeated dully. 'Yes. That's it, isn't it? Fear. But remember, I'm of her, her son, her flesh. When I see her, I see what I could become.'

'Oh, no, Luke! You're nothing like her. Nothing.'

'How do you know that?' he asked. 'How could anybody know?'

'My heart tells me.'

'Gussie, Gussie, you're so young, only eighteen. You don't know life yet. You don't know people and what they can do or be.' Faint recollections drifted through his mind. Rebel soldiers stealing boots from Yankee corpses. Renegade Yankees taking blankets from dying Yankees. Lifeless bodies flung on carts. He went on heavily, 'Let me decide this, for I know what's best.'

'Very well,' she said. 'I mean no harm to you, or to your mother.'

95

'Of course not.' He took up his plate, although he had no appetite, and began to talk of other things.

Augusta listened and replied, but all the while she thought about Nelle Wakefield.

They were married on a Sunday in late June in the garden of the house on High Street. It was a still, cloudless day. The sun was bright, the sky blue.

Augusta wore a white gown of China silk, its waist snug through the bodice and dropped to below her hips where it belled out in a series of layered flounces. The sleeves were long and narrow, edged at the wrists with tiny white flowers made of satin, a motif repeated at the high neck.

There was such a glow of happiness about Gussie that when she came out on her father's arm, a small silence descended, and Luke felt tears suddenly burn in his eyes.

Was it real? he asked himself. Could it be happening to him? Then Augusta smiled at him. The already brilliant sun became brighter. When they had exchanged their vows and he had put the ring on her finger and she had put the ring on his, he bent to kiss her. But before he touched his lips to hers, he whispered, 'I love you, Gussie.'

And she said, 'And I love you, Luke.'

Later that same day, in the honeymoon stateroom on the *Metropolis*, they lay in each other's arms, bodies and breaths melded together, and then there was no need for words.

Aria had listened through the planning, watched through the preparations, and laughed gaily through the wedding. While she seemed happy for Augusta and Luke outwardly, inside she burned.

That they were to live here, in the house, made it all the worse. She wasn't there on the evening Marcus made his proposal. Augusta, listening, had smiled, kissed him, and said, 'Papa, thank you,' and looked at Luke, then gone on, 'Of course we'll live at home with you. And to invest whatever you give us is sure to be wise.'

Luke saw then, with faint unease, that the decision had already been made. She hadn't asked him what he thought, how he felt. She had announced what she wanted and assumed that he would agree. It was the same in connection with his mother. For some reason Gussie felt a need to know Nelle Wakefield. So Gussie proposed to do so, and never mind Luke's own feelings. In the case of the house, Luke wasn't sure. Perhaps it would be better for them to start off alone. Yet her eyes were shining, Marcus was looking expectantly at Luke, and it was suddenly impossible to express his doubts. He owed so much to Marcus already. Now he would owe him one thing more. He said, 'If it's what you want, Gussie, then we'll do it. And thank you, Marcus, for making the offer.'

Aria knew only that Betty and her mother were now in the small sitting room off the hall, polishing the furniture with lemon oil and awaiting the huge bouquets of roses that Aria had been sent out to gather and held in her arms.

She went in, a smile on her lips, but a fury in her soul. Her fingertips bled where the roses had pricked them. She felt as if they'd pricked her heart instead.

Luke had always been hers, Aria's. 'My Luke,' she could remember saying when she was little more than a baby. 'My Luke.' Now he belonged to Augusta.

They were expected to return after their week's honeymoon in New York on the following morning. That night they would lie abed together – in Aria's own house.

Already Aria imagined how it would be. She, alone, would lie abed too. It would be the same as it had been on their wedding night. She had lain staring at the ceiling of her room and felt Luke's hands on her, on *her* instead of Augusta. *She* writhed to his touch and lifted herself to him. She felt the prickle of her nipples as they rose to his kisses. She would be his. While Augusta lay in his arms, Aria would pretend that it was she herself he held. And in the morning Augusta and Luke would exchange small secret smiles, and Aria would watch, and ache, and hate them both. It had always been that way. Aria had always been left out. There were Marcus and Amy, Luke and Augusta, but only Aria herself who had no one. Although always, always, she had dreamed of Luke and wanted him.

That dream was ended now. She burned and knew of only one way to quench the fire that consumed her . . .

'Are there enough roses, do you think?' Amy asked.

97

'I think so.' Aria could barely breathe. The room was full of the sweet scent and it choked her.

'Perhaps we should have a few more,' Amy said, pointing to a tall, slim vase of crystal.

'All right,' Aria agreed. She went out into the garden again, but this time she didn't stop at the rose bushes. She walked on through the garden into the road, and down to the wharves. There, aware of the covert glances sent her way, she wandered about until nearly dark. She was looking, but not sure of what she was looking for.

When she finally reached home, Amy said, 'Where did you go? We were worried for you'

'To the wharves,' Aria answered. She didn't care if her mother had worried. No one cared for her, why should she care for anyone else?

'But you didn't say. I thought you'd gone to pick more flowers in the garden.'

Aria shrugged.

Amy said softly, 'I know it's difficult for you, but your turn will come. You're only sixteen, Aria.'

'I don't know what you're talking about,' Aria retorted.

'I think you do.' Amy smiled. 'We've all had such feelings. We must all learn to deal with them.'

Fierce hot color burned suddenly in Aria's cheeks. Her hatred was *her* secret. Her feelings were her own. She wanted no one's pity, not even her mother's. She wanted only what was due to her – Luke, whom she had always loved, taken from her by Augusta. But aloud, Aria said, 'I've no feelings to deal with, Mama. It's just that I dislike being a child and treated as a child.'

'It will pass. It will pass quickly, believe me.'

'Oh, Mama,' Aria groaned.

Amy laughed, but she decided that she had been right when she had spoken to Marcus about her concern for Aria. The girl should be married, and soon. But for now, Amy knew she must do something to ease Aria's feelings and to distract her attention.

Later that night she spoke of it to Marcus. 'She's jealous. Not so much of Luke, but that Augusta is grown. Free.'

'Then take her down to New York. There are plays to see.

Museums. All sorts of things. Do a bit of shopping and sightseeing. Just the two of you together.'

It seemed to Amy a very good suggestion. She told Aria about it, and they began to plan the trip together.

But when Augusta and Luke returned home, something happened to make Amy wonder if a trip to New York would actually be enough to distract Aria.

The family was gathered, waiting, when the young couple arrived. What Amy saw in Augusta's eyes told her that all was well between them. After they had greeted each other, first Augusta and then Luke kissed her. And then Luke bent his head to kiss Aria's cheek. Amy saw how the child deliberately turned so that her lips were beneath Luke's. She saw the slender arms go up and around Luke's neck. And saw him color deeply and pull back.

She didn't know that he had felt the touch of Aria's tongue within his mouth, had felt her passion and sensed a deep answering response in him. But what Amy knew was enough to make her worry.

Three days later, she and Aria boarded the *Metropolis*. Luke was back at work. He greeted them at the purser's window, saying: 'Aria, you look very nice.'

'Why, thank you,' she answered, laughing. 'And why not? I've borrowed Augusta's hat. Didn't you notice?'

He looked again and saw that it was true. The hat was small and white, covered with pink flowers. It was one that Gussie had worn on her honeymoon. 'That's right,' he said, handing over a key for the stateroom assigned to them. 'And it's very nice on you, too.'

He tried not to think of how she had kissed him, and how he had felt. She was a child, he told himself, and he was her brother now.

She said, 'I'll come and visit with you later.'

'We'll be busy here until well after the dinner hour. Suppose, when I have some free time, I find you.' He was careful to speak to Amy as well as Aria.

Amy answered. 'We'll expect to see you later then.'

The two went down to their stateroom. They unpacked some nightclothes, freshened up, and returned to the deck in time for the 'All ashore that's going ashore!' call.

Soon the ship steamed into Mount Hope Bay. She was crowded with passengers, women in their travel finery, groups of men laughing together.

It was to the men that Aria looked most often. She studied each one as she passed them. There were only a few that interested her. Those that did, she marked in her mind.

Later, when they had eaten and gone into the lounge, she sat beside her mother, prim and proper on the outside, but wanton within.

While Amy conversed with a group of Fall River people, Aria yawned and squirmed, and finally whispered that she would go out to the afterdeck for some air.

Amy told her not to be too long. Smiling, Aria agreed. She took her light shawl with her and went quickly through the companionway. She had timed it exactly right.

A tall blond man emerged from the shadows, walking slowly toward her. He was one she had chosen as interesting. He was about twenty-five, with a sleek coiffeur of wavy golden hair. She pretended to lurch and stagger.

He accepted the cue, caught her arm to steady her, and said, smiling, 'Let me help you, miss.'

'Why, thank you.' She smiled up at him. 'I believe I've turned my ankle.'

They spoke together for an hour.

His name was Harry Purlin. He had pale blue eyes and thin straight lips. He sold leather goods in the small New England towns to the north of Fall River. Before they parted, they made an appointment to meet a little later.

Aria returned to the lounge and sat with Amy, and then, after a brief visit with Luke, retired. As soon as Amy had fallen asleep, Aria slipped out to meet Harry Purlin again on deck. They spent most of that night in a passionate embrace on deck, mouths and bodies locked together, only drawing apart when a crew member passed, and closer than before once he was gone. Though Harry urged her, she refused to go to his stateroom, promising that some other time she would. He assured her he'd be on the *Metropolis* when she and her mother were to return to Fall River.

She didn't really believe him. But on the return journey he was on board again, and managed to avoid a meeting with

Amy, who had no idea even that he existed. Once again, while Amy slept, Aria and Harry spent hours together. She still refused to see his stateroom, but he knew the darkest corners of the deck, and leaned her against a bulkhead and held his body pressed to hers, while his hands caressed her, and she ground herself against him, all the while pretending it was Luke's arms that held her, his mouth that pressed hers.

She spoke gaily of the trip to Marcus and Augusta, showed the new slippers she had bought, and the tortoise-shell combs for her hair, and told them of the sights she had seen. Amy, listening, smiled at Marcus, believing all was well, and absently stroking a large blue bruise on the inside of her elbow.

But then, in mid-August, Harry Purlin came down from Boston on the boat train and boarded the *Empire State*. Aria met him there. And when the ship sailed at seven-forty, she went with him.

She left no note, and took only a few things with her in a carpetbag. Some ribbons, two gowns, her light shawl.

Harry had said they'd be married in New York. She neither agreed nor demurred. She knew he was lying, thinking it necessary to persuade her. To her, however, he was merely a ticket away from Fall River. She spent two weeks with him. They quarreled whenever they went out because she flirted with anyone who looked at her and he feared trouble from it. When it was time for him to return to his leather goods route, she accepted the money he gave her and kissed him goodbye. An hour later, she moved out of the hotel room. There were other men. She never once thought of going home. At the end of the week she found work in a small milliner's shop off Thirty-fourth Street.

Chapter 9

Amy's face was pale. She gripped her hands together so fiercely that their fingertips were white. She said in a shaky voice, 'It frightens me that I could have been so blind. After all, I knew the child was troubled.'

'Don't blame yourself, Amy. We share the blame for this. If there's blame, that is, beyond Aria's own.'

'Thank you, Marcus.' Amy forced a weak smile. 'But I fear that doesn't help us find her. And as for the blame in her, we can't weigh it until we know what happened.'

It was nearly ten days since Aria had gone. There had been no word from her. But Luke had been told that she'd been seen leaving the *Empire State* in New York in the company of a tall blond man. The steward who mentioned it to Luke didn't know the passenger's name, but said he had seen the man a number of times before. Luke gave that small bit of information to Marcus, who immediately went to Boston to the Pinkerton Agency.

On his return home, he seemed confident that Aria would soon be found. But a week later there was still no news of her, and Pinkerton's man knew only that she hadn't been arrested, hadn't been registered in any hospital, nor in any of the hotels at which she had earlier stayed with her parents or, in fact, any at which they had stayed without her. He also told Marcus that Aria wasn't in the morgue.

It was a difficult time for all of them. Amy blamed herself. But Marcus, while worried, grew more and more angry at Aria. The house shook when he walked through it, and the chandeliers rattled, and his temper exploded as it rarely had before. Augusta and Luke, settling into married life together, were also affected. She was instinctively aware, and uneasily so, that Aria's disappearance had something to do with the vows Augusta and Luke had exchanged only recently. Augusta remembered how Aria used to say, 'My Luke. My Luke.' How Aria had wept when Luke had gone away to the war. She had thought that Aria's love was a child's love. But now she remembered what she had felt for Luke at Aria's age.

Luke for his part remembered how Aria had kissed him the day of the wedding – her tongue in his mouth, her passion. He remembered how he had felt. And how he had thrust her away. But he didn't speak of his thoughts to Augusta, nor did she speak of her thoughts to him. Instead, she said merely, 'What do you think could have happened?' and he answered, 'I don't know. We can only hope that we'll find out soon.'

Then, at the end of the first week in September, when the *Metropolis* docked in New York, Luke was handed a message. The moment he saw his name, written in a round girlish hand, he knew it was from Aria. He stopped the boy who had brought it to him, gave him a coin, and asked, 'Where did you receive this?'

The boy pointed over his shoulder with a dirty thumb.

'But where?'

The boy shrugged, pulled from Luke's restraining hand, and ran off, shirt tails flapping.

I'll be at the corner of Broadway and Grand, right near the entrance to Lord & Taylor at 2 pm. Will you? There was no signature. But he needed none.

He pulled a watch from his pocket. He had half an hour if he was to be on time. He hurried out to the street and hailed a hansom. It was a slow trip. Carts and wagons and carriages rode wheel to wheel, their drivers shouting imprecations to each other. Pigeons waddled and strutted over piles of dung. Horses neighed and snapped. Hawkers offered their wares in every imaginable tongue.

To Luke the place was a strange land, and he was an uncertain traveler. When they stopped finally, it was exactly two o'clock. He paid the driver and got down. His pale eyes searching, he squinted in the bright sunlight. There was the ornate entrance into Lord & Taylor's. Couples strolled by, hand in hand. A number of single women walked around him with purposeful strides, their heeled boots tapping the sidewalk. Groups broke to circle him and closed again once they were past. A huddle of men loitered at the corner. A one-legged man leaned on his crutch, a soldier's hat held out in mute plea.

Luke took it all in, his heart sinking. He'd had to force himself to come. For Marcus, for Amy. But Aria was nowhere to be seen. She wasn't here. Then why had she summoned him? What had happened?

Across the roadway there was a building set back from the street. A low stone wall separated its minute grounds from the walkway. A woman wrapped in a blue shawl ate her lunch there. Close by her, another was reading a newspaper. The upper half of her was covered by the newssheet; the lower half, a dark blue skirt embroidered with white butterflies, suggested nothing to him. But then, slowly, the sheet was lowered and Aria raised her dark head, smiling.

He hesitated for a moment. Then, thinking of Marcus and Amy again, he waved and dashed into the road. There was a clatter of wheels. A stream of obscenities pursued him as he gained the safety of the sidewalk.

'Aria!'

Her wide-open arms caught him, held him. She hugged him tightly, laughing.

He held her too, not thinking then that the embrace was too close. He thought only of the joy his news would bring when he returned home. He said, 'Aria, in the name of God, what's happened to you? What have you done? Why?'

'I've left home,' she said. 'As if you didn't know.'

'Of course I know. But why did you do it? And how? And do you realize what you've done?'

Her dark eyes danced with mischief. She smiled. 'The why and how make a long story. Surely you have time for me today? Time to hear it.'

'Yes, yes. But you must come back with me.'

'Why must I?'

'Your parents, Augusta. You can't imagine what it's been for them.'

'I can't, and I don't care to. All I know is that they've survived. They *have* survived, haven't they?'

'That's no way to talk,' he said. He stepped back from her. 'Let me look at you. Are you well? How have you managed?'

'I've managed nicely.' She smiled again, turned slowly on her heels. Her skirt flared out and the white butterflies seemed to flutter with the movement. 'Look at me, Luke. Don't I seem well to you? Can't you tell how nicely I've got on on my own?'

He nodded slowly, agreeing. 'You seem to have done better than those at home. Your mother and father are heartsick with worry for you.'

'And Augusta?'

'Gussie too.'

'I can imagine,' Aria said tartly.

He ignored her tone. 'Why have you done this?'

'We'll speak of that later,' she promised, sliding a hand under his arm.

'Aria, you know I don't have all day. Either sit here with me on the wall and speak of it now, or come with me to the ship. We can talk there.'

'I want to show you where I live. And besides, as for going to the ship, I don't trust you.'

'Trust me?'

'Perhaps you'll lock me in a stateroom and carry me back to Fall River by force.' She laughed as she said it, and her eyes sparkled; it was plain to him that she was enjoying herself.

But he said soberly, 'I'd like to drag you back, whether you want to go or not. And I'd like to give you the spanking of your life, which is what you deserve. But I won't do either because neither would accomplish anything. You'd run away again if I used such methods. And you'd forget the spanking before I would.'

'How right you are.' She spun away from him, walked in quick noisy steps toward the intersection.

Luke had to follow. He couldn't allow her to disappear into the crowds. For Amy and Marcus's sake he had to learn where she lived, why she had left home, when they would see her again. He hurried after her, calling, 'Wait, Aria. I'll come with you.'

When he had caught up with her, she told him, 'Of course you'll come. And you won't be sorry either.'

For a few blocks they walked side by side in silence. Then she said, 'Do you hate me, Luke?'

'Hate you? Of course not. Why should I? I've known you all your life, and loved you all of it too. Why, Aria, I think you've done yourself and your parents a serious wrong, but surely that doesn't make me hate you?'

She stopped suddenly, pointing. 'We go in here.'

It was a hotel plainly. There were boxwoods outside, and a wide brass-bound door. Within were tall palms in big redwood buckets, and thick carpets.

'This is where you live?' he asked. He found it hard to believe. It was an opulent place.

'Yes. For the time being.'

'How do you afford it? You surely didn't have much saved to take with you.'

Her answer was a soft laugh. He stopped, put a hand under her chin, and tipped her face up. 'And what does that mean?'

'That?'

'The laugh.'

'Think what you like.' She stepped into an elevator. He didn't know what to think. There had been something about her laugh that made him uneasy. It had told him something, but he wasn't sure what. He followed her, looking through the brass rails as the white-gloved attendant closed the door and turned the wheel. The elevator rose slowly over the lobby. He looked down on the heads of ladies wearing large feathered hats and gentlemen whose bald spots shone in the dim light. When the car stopped on the third floor, he walked behind Aria down a long carpeted corridor.

At the end of it, she unlocked a door, flung it wide. 'Come in.'

The room was bright and clean and neatly decorated, but it had no lived-in look. He saw nothing of hers except on the dresser: a hairbrush and some bottles of perfume, and a filmy robe hanging on the armoire door.

'Sit down,' she said.

But he remained standing. 'Tell me. Why have you done this? Why leave your family, your home? What shall I say to your parents?'

'You know why I went away,' she said. She drew off her hat and dropped it on a table. Slowly she pulled her gloves from her hands. Now, fingers linked before her, she stood watching him.

'I know?'

'Oh, Luke, Luke, I always thought that you loved me best. Loved me more than anyone else.'

'What are you saying? Of course I love you, but as a man loves a child. You're only a little more than sixteen. What do you expect of me?' Even as he spoke, he felt within him a deep stirring. A pulsing of senses.

'And is sixteen so much younger than eighteen?' she asked.

'It is.'

'Two years,' she scoffed. 'Two small, unimportant years.'

'When the time comes, you'll understand.' The pulsing was stronger. A spreading hunger. And mixed with it was guilt. She was Gussie's sister. He looked at the door.

'The time is now,' Aria said. 'And I don't understand.' Her voice broke, but after a moment, she went on softly, 'I loved you when you were a scrawny boy. Before they put the scar on your face. Before they put that crooked white streak in your hair. I loved you then, as I love you now.' She stopped speaking, turned away.

But he had seen the quick-welling tears in her eyes. He went to her and swung her around to face him. The mark on his face was red. His eyes glowed silver. 'I'm sorry if I've hurt you. But it will mend, believe me.'

Her dark head dropped. Her slender body swayed against him. 'I'm a woman,' she whispered. 'And that's how I love you, and always have.'

But he was thinking of the blond man with whom she had left Fall River. Perhaps she was no longer the child she had been. Luke didn't know. He couldn't tell. It seemed she was alone now. The room suggested nothing else. But he didn't want to ask her.

It was as if she had picked the thought out of his mind. She let her head fall to Luke's chest, whispered, 'I'm so alone. There's no one in this world for me.'

'Nonsense. You have your family. You have me. One day you'll fall in love and marry and have children.' His quiet words belied the pounding of his heart. He wanted her, wanted her. And he was ashamed. Once again he looked at the door, but he didn't move.

She went on, 'I thought to fill my emptiness with someone else. Another man. No one you know. So I came away with him. But it was awful. Worse than before. I've left him, Luke. He couldn't take your place.' She didn't tell Luke that when she and Harry Purlin parted, she'd worked one day in the milliner's shop and then left it. Since then she'd been with a number of men, and been paid for her pleasure so well that she could afford to stay in the hotel to which she had brought him.

'Then come home where you belong,' he said. 'You needn't be alone. Just come home.'

Now her wavering body pressed close to him. She burrowed her face in his shoulder. 'I can't, I can't. And I won't!'

'Then what shall you do?'

'I don't know,' she moaned. She raised her tear-wet face. 'Oh, Luke ... if only it had been different.'

He smoothed her hair back from her cheek, and she pressed it to his hand, and took his hand and kissed it, and burst into a fresh storm of weeping.

He lifted her, carried her to the bed, and put her down. 'You must be calm now,' he said, sitting beside her. 'We must decide what to do. I want you to be happy and safe, Aria. I want to make everything right for you.'

She didn't answer but took his hand, and again she kissed it, and even as she did so, she drew him closer and closer still. The light in the room was fading. The shadows had moved in from the corners.

She whispered feverishly, 'Always, always, from the beginning, you were *my* Luke. *Mine*. I loved you best and most. And then you turned away from me.'

'No,' he said. 'No, Aria.'

'Yes,' she said softly. 'And I know why. It was my father and mother. You acceded to their wishes. But I don't care. I love you still.'

He rocked her, comforted her, as if she were still a small child who had fallen and cut her knee, and he was trying to assuage the hurt of pain as well as of fear. But she wasn't a child, as the hunger in his body knew, and without even realizing it, he crossed the narrow step between comforting and lovemaking. She, eager, guiding, in response to his sweeping urgency, only kept saying his name – 'Oh, Luke, Luke, my Luke.'

He heard only love, hunger for love, in her voice and nothing of the triumph she felt. It was for this that she had sent him the message so he would come to her. For this sweet excitement that she had waited and planned. His lean body over hers. Yes. His weight on her. The mindless, anguished thrusting of his hips. Oh, yes. But more. The revenge. The hurt for Augusta.

Luke heard only the love in Aria's voice, and heard it still when they lay back, entwined with each other, and she said softly, 'Now you are mine.'

The words brought him back to himself. He was bathed in sudden cold sweat, sickened. The clean neat room seemed ugly, streaked with filth. The warm air held a disgusting stench. He pulled away abruptly. His flesh seemed to burn where it had touched hers. He heard himself mutter, 'What have I done?' and wondered at the words. Why did he ask? Of whom was he asking it? Surely he knew what he had done. But that was now. Only moments before what had he known? Only that he was a man drowned in a mindless hunger. A man who had forgotten the most important part of himself – his love for Gussie. A man who broke when tested too far. Why else had he forgotten so much of the war? Why else had he forgotten Gussie for those long dangerous moments just now. A man like his mother . . . like poor mad Nelle Wakefield. He couldn't look at Aria. He buried his face in his hands.

And she was saying, 'You've made me happy. You've given my life back to me.' Her eyes were bright, clear, joyful. When he looked at her, she smiled.

He shook his head slowly back and forth. He couldn't understand what had happened. He had loved them both, Aria and Gussie, like sisters. The sisters he'd never had. There had been no other thought in his mind until the April day he had walked up High Street and paused at the gate and seen Gussie come around the corner of the house. Then what had he done now? And why? He loved Gussie, he owed his life to Marcus and Amy. How could he have betrayed them? Betrayed himself? Except through a strain of madness that made him weak when he should have been strong.

'Forgive me,' he said quietly, rising to his feet. 'I have no excuse, Aria. All I ask is that you forgive me.'

'I cherish our love.' She rose, walked before him, nude and lovely, to take up her peignoir. She wrapped herself in it. 'I always shall.'

Silent, his face turned away, he dressed.

She had lit the lamp, and in its pale glow he saw her smile. He saw the triumph he hadn't recognized earlier. She had planned it – the child Aria. It was the reason for her message, the reason she had asked that he meet her. But why? There was no time now to question, to ponder. He must get to the ship.

She said, 'You'll be back in two days?'

The scar on his jaw stood out red and his eyes were silver ice in the white of his face. 'This must never happen again. And it won't, Aria.'

She didn't answer but her lips tilted in a small smile.

'I must tell your parents where you are.' It was the end of everything for him. He knew it. He would lose Gussie, lose the friendship of Marcus and Amy. For when they met with Aria, she would surely, out of spite, reveal what he had done to her. But he had to tell them, no matter what the consequences. He had to.

'It doesn't matter,' Aria was saying. 'I'm free of them. And I mean to stay that way.' She turned, went to the window.

He spoke to her slender back, repeating: 'I must tell them. They have the right to know where you are. That you're safe at least.'

'I told you. It does't matter. All I care about is that you come back to me.'

'I won't, Aria. Forget me. Forget what's happened.' Even as he said it, he wondered at her lack of concern. Why didn't she care that her parents would learn where she was? How was it that she didn't fear facing them?

Again she gave him that small tilted smile. There was no beauty in her face now. Her eyes seemed empty, the curved lips cut in cold stone. Luke wondered how he could have wanted her, or thought he did in a weakness of flesh born of the mind's madness. Even in such a state she ought to have repelled him then as she sickened him at this moment. He took up his hat and hurried out.

The purser glared at him while he apologized for being delayed. He tried to immerse himself in the affairs of the office, the passengers. He took and responded to compliments and complaints; he made adjustments, smiling pleasantly. But he was like a man in a nightmare, moving through familiar chores. He actually retained little of what was said to him, and forever after, he remembered nothing of that sailing except that the purser once asked him, 'Luke, are you ill?' and he'd managed to say, 'No, sir. I'm fine.'

By dawn, when they docked at Fall River, he had himself under some sort of control.

He finished his work on the ship, and went to the house. Gussie was in her usual place on the widow's walk. She waved at him. Quick pain flashed through him. Soon she would know how he had betrayed her. But he buried the thought and went inside. By then she had come downstairs. They had breakfast together. When they had finished, he pushed back his chair, drew a deep breath. 'Gussie, I must tell you. I've seen Aria.'

'You have? Where is she? How is she? When will she come home?' Gussie's heart-shaped face was alight with relief; her green eyes glowed. 'Oh, Mama and Papa will be so happy, Luke. How did you find her?'

'So many questions,' he said heavily. 'And I have only a few answers.'

'But she's all right?' Gussie asked quickly.

'Yes. She seems to be.' He was remembering how Aria had writhed against him. Remembering her avid mouth. He said, 'She's alone. There was a man but she's left him. She doesn't mean to come back. Nothing I could say seemed to change her mind.'

'Do you know what happened? Why she's done this?'

He shook his head. The less he said of that now the better. Gussie would know the truth soon enough.

'You must tell Mama and Papa at once.'

'Yes. In a little while.'

She waited, but he said nothing more, and she didn't press him. He was obviously troubled; his lean face was furrowed with lines she had never noticed before. The scar was darker than usual. What had Aria done? What had she said to him? Gussie put a hand on his shoulder. He seemed to shrink at her touch. She said gently, 'My parents will be grateful.'

He bowed his head and didn't answer.

'We must go to her immediately,' Amy said.

'I don't believe it will help,' Luke told her. 'You must be prepared for that. But I think you should try.'

Marcus strode back and forth, bootheels banging on the floor. 'I don't understand it. I don't understand it. But, yes, of course, we'll go. And if I have to, I'll drag her back by the hair of her head.'

'Marcus, please!'

His face flamed dangerously red. 'I will. I will,' he bellowed.

He said the same thing the next morning as the three of them approached the hotel in which Luke had left Aria. 'I'll drag her back,' Marcus said. 'No daughter of mine will behave so.'

'You must let me speak first,' Amy said softly. 'Don't threaten her. Don't argue with her. Only listen.'

Luke drew a deep painful breath, knowing what was to come. She would tell them how she had always wanted him and had run away because of that and how he had come to her and they had lain together. His life would end with those words. Those he had loved most in this world, Marcus, Amy, most of all Gussie, would hate him. They would see him unclean, a leper, who defiled them all. As he saw himself. But there was no answer when he knocked at the door. The three of them looked as each other and then went down to the desk to enquire.

Luke stood there, his heart sinking with pain for Marcus and Amy, with relief for himself, as he heard the clerk say that Aria had left.

'Left for where?' Marcus demanded loudly. 'When? How did she go?'

The clerk shrugged. 'I'm not her keeper. I just see from the ledger that she's gone.'

Amy bit her lip, turned away.

Luke and Marcus both asked further questions. They consulted with the white-gloved attendant who ran the birdcage elevator. They described Aria to the doorman. But it was a waste of time. Aria was gone. That was all anybody could tell them. There was nothing to do but give up and return to the ship.

When they sailed that evening, Amy stood at the railing, her cool blue eyes fixed on the city's jagged skyline. She clasped Luke's fingers tightly and whispered, 'We'll hear from her soon, I know. She'll write to us or come back.' —

But as the *Metropolis* steamed slowly from the pier, Amy shivered and blinked back tears.

It was Christmas Eve of 1865. Outside, snow fell in hard, wind-driven flakes. Inside, a fire burned on the hearth in the sitting room, where Augusta leaned over the small table, wrapping the last of the gifts. It was long and narrow and held a muffler she had knitted for Luke. She pressed a silver star on the blue paper, and smiled. This was only one of several she had prepared. But her real gift was something else that wouldn't be delivered until early May. She would tell him about it that very evening, however.

He came in soon after, his face red with cold. He took off his greatcoat and gloves and went to stand at the fire.

'You look chilled,' she said.

'I am. Your father and I walked a long way, speaking of the future of the shipping line now that the war's over.'

'It will go on,' she said. 'The reconstruction will begin.' Her certainty was in her voice. The great ships would always sail from Fall River to Long Island Sound and New York.

Luke smiled at her faith and loved her for it. He himself was not so sure. But he didn't speak of his doubts. He glanced at the table, 'I see you've been busy.'

'Yes. In a little while we'll take them into the parlor and put them under the tree. But I have something to tell you first.'

His eyes narrowed. She looked so grave. He wondered what had happened. With that came the swift thought of Aria. Had there been word after these months? He had felt saved by her disappearance. It had given him back his life. Almost he had begun to think that his painful memories were no more than an evil nightmare. Aria had run away. He had received a message, gone to her, had tried to persuade her to return. And there was nothing more. It was what he wished with all his heart. Almost. But not quite. So that no matter how deeply he tried to bury the evil dream that was reality, his guilt weighed heavily on him.

Augusta said, 'What's the matter? You look almost frightened.'

'No, no.' He was impatient now. 'What is it, Gussie?'

'I suspected it at the end of September,' she said. 'I waited to be sure. And then waited for the right moment. And this seems to be it.'

He stared at her, not comprehending.

'We're going to have a baby.'

'Gussie!' Her name was an anguished whisper. He was

113

overwhelmed by conflicting feelings. Guilt stung him. Joy warmed him. He didn't deserve such a gift. But oh how he wanted it.

She waited, smiling, but grave still.

At last he collected himself and swept her into his arms, holding her slender warmth against him tightly. 'What·a Christmas Eve gift you've given me!'

'And I hope you're pleased?'

'Of course I am.'

She hid her face in his shoulder. He *was* pleased, she told herself. That briefest of hesitations, that paling and look of breathless shock, had been surprise. Yet she knew him so well. She knew him as well as she knew her own heart. Then what was wrong? What had he first thought of when she told him about the baby?

Chapter 10

Through the long hours of a pain-wracked night Gussie whispered between clenching teeth the names of the various lights between Fall River and New York: *Borden Flats, Bristol Ferry, Mussels Bed Shoals . . .*

And as the sun rose on a May morning in 1866, Kincaid Wakefield was born. He had red-gold hair like his mother and his father's silver-gray eyes. When Augusta put him into Luke's arms for the first time, Luke said hoarsely, 'Thank you, Gussie,' and blinked to hide his sudden tears.

On an evening in late June, when Kin Wakefield was a month old, Luke kissed Gussie and the infant goodbye and crossed the wharf to the gangplank. There he turned to wave once before he boarded the *Metropolis*.

It was an easy trip. The weather was fine. The passengers were gay. He planned to go shopping. He wanted a gift for Gussie, and something for Kin too. But the next morning, when the ship docked in New York and he stood on the wharf, a small drunken man jostled him and demanded his name and asked for a dollar. Luke ignored him. The man waved an envelope under his nose, crying, 'A dollar or you don't get this.'

Luke thrust the money at him and took the envelope. It was a message from Aria. It gave an address, asked that he come to her.

He stared at the round girlish handwriting for a long moment, then crushed the scrap of paper in trembling fingers. *Be damned to her! I won't go – I don't want to see her again!* His thoughts seared him. Anger. Guilt. No! And then, while he sank in both, there came a memory. Marcus, so tall before him, leaning a hip against a railing to shorten himself and lessen the distance between them.

It was no good. Luke could curse through the day, the night, and the rest of his life. He had to go to Aria. He owed it to Marcus and Amy.

He found, upon inquiring, that the place was not far away. He walked the distance in long quick strides, not noticing the pushcarts loaded with produce, some of which had come down on Fall River Line ships from the fields of New England, not noticing the wagons and carts that crowded the narrow streets. He thought only of Aria. He would see her, hear her out, try to persuade her to return home. That was all.

The address led him to an old wooden house that looked about to fall down. Its front stoop was littered with soggy newspapers and the rotted peels of fruit. A small brown mongrel dashed at him, barking, as he knocked at the door. He booted it aside, but not hard. A short, very stout woman opened the door and peered at him suspiciously. The mongrel kept its distance but continued to bark. Over the noise, Luke asked for Aria.

'Down there.' The woman jerked her head toward the dark corridor behind her. 'She owes me money.'

'I'll pay it,' he said.

But the woman didn't step aside. 'She's bad off.' A fat grimy hand came out, thumb sliding suggestively from the smallest finger to forefinger. 'And I had the doctor yesterday.'

'I'll pay, I told you. Let me see her.'

When the woman moved aside, he went down the corridor in quick hard steps. A door sagged open on broken hinges. He pushed it in.

Aria lay on a cot, her face as gray as the walls of the room, as gray as the thin sheet that covered her. Her dark eyes glittered with fever. She held an infant to her breast.

'So you've come,' she whispered, as Luke stood there, speechless and staring.

'What's happened to you?' he asked finally. But he knew. He'd last seen her at the end of September. Now it was late June. The child was his. Born of a few moments' madness. The memory of it singed him in sinew and nerve. Disgust brought sour bile to his throat. He swallowed hard to keep from retching.

'It's just as I planned. Or nearly so,' she told him.

'I see.' He kept his voice soft. Hating her, hating himself, he went on, 'And why have you sent for me now?'

'That was a part of the plan, too.' A faint smile touched her lips. 'You must take the boy home with you, Luke. I've named him Caleb. You may do as you please about that. Only you must take him home.'

'And you?' Luke asked, remembering somewhere at the back of his mind the sweet glowing child she had been.

'I had thought to have the boy delivered to you and Gussie, as a keepsake of me. I had thought I'd go far away, having had my revenge, and never see either of you again. But that's not to be.'

It was hot in the room, unbearably so, yet he saw that she shivered. She was plainly ill as the landlady had said. Her languor was more than the exhaustion of having given birth. 'What's wrong?' he asked.

'I'm dying, my Luke.'

'Dying?' he repeated. He couldn't tell. She had always been prone to wild fancies. And he heard in his mind a voice cry, 'Die then and be done with you!' But she was Marcus and Amy's daughter, and Gussie's sister. For those three he fought down hatred and disgust. He said, 'I'll find a doctor or midwife.'

'Promise me you'll take our son to Gussie to raise.'

'Aria!'

'Promise me.'

'I'll get help.'

He was at the door again when she said in a fierce hot whisper, 'Promise me.'

'Yes. Of course I promise.' The words wrenched from him,

low, breathless, echoed back at him as he hurried out.

The woman who had let him in told him the midwife was just across the street. He raced to find her. She went with him, grumbling that the girl was young and strong. There could be nothing wrong with her.

But when Luke led her to Aria's cot, the midwife drew in a deep breath and leaned over where Aria seemed to be sleeping. She raised the infant from the girl's limp arms. 'Childbed fever,' she said softly. 'And I can't help her now. She's gone. God bless her.'

He put bills into the midwife's hand without counting them and sent her away. Holding the infant, he sat for hours beside Aria. Numbed now, he considered everything. It had been her plan to avenge herself of an imagined wrong, of a love unrequited. To destroy Gussie. To destroy himself. The infant mewed like a kitten; he stroked its dark fuzzy head gently. So small, so innocent. Created from Aria's hate and his blind lust. He could abandon the child, give it away. Aria was gone. She wouldn't know. She couldn't tell. There was no one left to reveal the truth. He could forget forever what had happened.

The stout landlady came and grumbled that she was owed money. The rent, the doctor. He thrust bills at her and pushed her out, shutting the broken-hinged door so hard against her that it slipped from the frame and banged against the wall. He paid for that too. He carried the baby in his arms when he went down to the street to make the necessary arrangements; and when, finally, he boarded the *Metropolis*, he still held the infant in his arms. In the hold, Aria lay in a plain wooden coffin.

He gave the child to the womens' cabin attendant to care for on the journey. She did her work that night, holding him to her breast and feeding him every several hours on milk mixed with water and sugar, boiled and then cooled, from a twist of soaked cotton. He went at it as if it were a warm and comforting teat. As soon as Luke heard the ship's whistle blow at the Borden Flats light, he retrieved the infant.

When the ship landed, he left his work to an assistant and hurried to the house on High Street. Once there, though, he hesitated at the gate. This would be an irrevocable act. Once done it could never be altered or changed or withdrawn. Was there another way to deal with the helpless mite he held so awkwardly against him? He saw none. With a deep breath, he went in.

Gussie was inside the door waiting for him. The light shone in her red-gold hair and in her eyes. Even as she greeted him with her warm, welcoming smile, the glow in her green eyes faded to bewilderment as she looked at the baby in Luke's arms.

He said gruffly, because he was forcing the words from an unwilling throat, 'This is Caleb. He is Aria's son.' It was the most he could bring himself to say. He wanted to go down on his knees and tell her the rest of it and beg for her forgiveness. But how could he? How could he explain it to her when he couldn't even explain it to himself? In a mad moment he had betrayed her, betrayed too all that he was. The child he held was the result. Whatever he said would only hurt her. And there was no way to soften the blow.

'Aria's son?' Augusta said at last. The words were softly spoken but they fell like small cold stones into a breathless silence.

'Your sister has died. I received a message when I reached New York that I must go to her. She spoke a moment to me, asked that I bring the child home. I promised I would before I went for help, and when I returned to her she was already dead.' He paused, waited, hearing the echo of what he had said in a voice so cold and hard and unfeeling that it had burned like acid in his throat.

Augusta said nothing. She looked into the infant's tiny face, feeling as if the earth had been cut away from under her, and what had once been solid ground was now become a quicksand in which she was sinking. Aria's son. A month younger, perhaps only weeks younger than Kin, who lay sleeping in his cradle. And Luke had brought the baby there because Aria had had his promise. Why had Aria turned first to Luke for help, then, to fulfill her demand? Augusta remembered how he had faltered when she told him she expected their first child. It was Christmas Eve. The firelight had flickered on his face. His silver eyes had flickered too. And then he had swept her into his arms.

She knew – her heart told her. He held Aria's son, as he had said. But it was *his* son, too. She imagined herself saying,

'Luke, the boy is yours, too. Why do you lie?' How would it help to force the truth from him? What would it accomplish? She had no answers. She knew only that it would change them both forever. How this thing had happened between him and Aria, Augusta didn't know. Why, she didn't know. But she loved him. There was shame in his face, and guilt, and defiance too. Yet she still loved him. Then what was important? Aria? The infant Caleb? Luke.

He held the infant and hated it. Why had it survived its birth? Why hadn't it drowned in its mother's blood? Overwhelmed by his guilt, he put the child into Gussie's arms, saying, 'I promised her, Gussie. As she lay dying, I promised.' And because of what was in his own heart and mind, he went on, 'If anything happens to him, I'll kill you.'

The color rose in her cheeks. The threat in that cold, even voice meant nothing to her. It was only a measure of his anguish. But she said, 'The child is without sin. No harm will ever befall him from me.' She paused, breathless.

'Thank you,' he said softly.

At last, white-lipped, trembling, she said, 'You've known me all my life ... can you believe I would do injury to a baby?'

'Forgive me,' he said slowly. 'I'm sorry for saying that.' He knew he had spoken out of his own guilt, but he couldn't bring himself to say so. And he sensed there was no need. Gussie understood too well.

'We'll raise him with Kin,' she said now. 'The two boys together.'

The infant mewed and turned his tiny face to her breast. She told herself that she loathed him. To the day of her death, or his, she would hate him for being Aria's child. But she held him lightly, and even in that terrible moment, she vowed to herself that he would be cared for with Kin, and the same as Kin, as long as she lived.

'I must go and tell your parents,' Luke said at last.

'Yes,' she answered. And as he turned to the door, 'Wait. I'll go with you. We'll do it together.'

Aria was buried two days later. Amy clung to Marcus, seeming smaller than she had ever been. He too was pale for once, and shrunken in size.

They expressed no doubts when Luke told them that Aria had eloped with a man she had met on the *Empire State*, the same tall blond salesman about whom they had originally heard, that she had been abandoned when she became with child, and had died alone of childbed fever. Whatever they thought they kept to themselves. Although they took baby Caleb to their hearts, they never spoke of Aria again. But Amy remembered her and mourned her and wondered how she had failed her.

Chapter 11

The speculations and profiteerings of Wall Street were always the subject of conversation in New York but were less well known in Fall River. Thus it was that the Boston, Newport and New York Steamboat Company was taken over by the Narragansett Steamship Company in 1867, and fell into the pudgy, acquisitive hands of James Fisk, one-time Vermont peddler, while word of the possibility was still only rumored in Fall River.

Augusta first heard of it one blustery afternoon in March when Marcus said heavily, 'It's done, you know. They'll merge with the Bristol Line and make the home port Fall River.'

Luke shook his dark head. 'It's hard to know what'll happen. We both know the man's not to be trusted. During the war he was down in Washington making blood money profits by overcharging the War Department, and since then he's been in New York, building a fortune for himself with his tricky deals. Still, from our point of view a merger with the Bristol Line may not be such a bad thing. It's been offering us strong competition for both passengers and cargos. And there are the two new ships Dan Drew has ordered.'

'I know, I know,' Marcus said. 'As you say, the merger may be a benefit. But Fisk ownership could be something else again.' He sighed deeply. 'But what's to be done?'

'You can sell your shares, I suppose.'

'I doubt I'll have a choice. Fisk'll probably force me to it in the same way he got the Bristol Line originally.'

Luke was silent for a moment. Then, 'If he does, I'll go to work elsewhere.'

That was too much for Augusta. 'You mean you would give up?' she demanded indignantly. 'You mean you won't even fight for what's yours?'

'There may be no choice.'

'Then make the choice. We've been in the line from the beginning. It doesn't matter who controls the shares. What are they but paper? We've always been a part of it. How can you talk of throwing away twenty years?'

'Twenty years,' Marcus said softly. 'In May.' He dropped his napkin, rose to his feet. 'I'll go up to see your mother, Augusta.'

Augusta and Luke exchanged a glance. Since Amy had fallen ill, Marcus had changed. The strength seemed to have gone out of him. It was noticeable in his voice, his walk. He no longer bellowed. He no longer stamped his boots on the stairs.

Now he paused at the threshold of the room they had shared for so long. Amy lay still on the piled-high pillows. Her face was white, her lips too. Her thinness exposed her cheekbones and the tiny sharp angle of her chin. There was a large blue bruise on her temple. Such bruises had become a commonplace. He didn't know when they had first begun to appear, but he knew they were related to the blood sickness the doctors could neither identify nor cure. That was how it had begun. First an occasional bruise on her arm. Later others had appeared and faded. And then the weakness had set in, and the wasting away. And always lately, the pain.

How could it happen? he asked himself. When had it really started? She had been more than usually quiet in those first weeks after Aria's death, so that, even though Amy hadn't spoken the girl's name, he knew she mourned. But that was natural and right. He did the same, even knowing that Aria's sins had been paid for by her death didn't assuage the pain. And there was the boy, Caleb. Amy loved him and cosseted him as she did Kin. But slowly Marcus had begun to see that all was not right with her. She sat so many hours in her chair. She rarely came to greet him in the garden. She never climbed to the widow's walk to wave to him. The blue marks became more frequent, and as they did, her smile began to die...

Suddenly now, as he watched, she opened her eyes and looked at him. It seemed, for a moment, as if she didn't know him. Her gaze was blank, empty. It smote him like a blow. He gasped with pain. He was seeing death and knew it, and couldn't bear it.

Then she smiled faintly. 'Why are you standing there like that?'

'I thought you were sleeping.' He came to her side, stood close by, wanting to throw himself down next to her, to hold her tightly to him. But he didn't touch her. Even the gentlest caress was pain for her these days.

'I wasn't sleeping. And if I had been I'd have wished you to waken me. To sleep is to waste time.'

'But you must rest.'

'I shall.'

That was as close as they came to speaking the truth they both knew.

'Is there something I can do for you?' he asked. 'Will you have tea, toast? A small sherry perhaps?'

'Sherry. That would be nice.'

He hurried down to get it because if she accepted a few sips of the spirits it meant she was in pain. The doctor had given her laudanum, but after a few times, she had refused it. 'I lose my senses in sleep,' she had told Marcus. 'I mustn't do that. I must savor what I have. I want to hear the boys laugh, and Augusta's voice when she speaks to Luke. And I want to talk to you.'

It was his idea to try the spirits – sometimes it helped and sometimes it didn't.

When he returned, her eyes were once again closed. He stood beside her, waiting, and saw her smile, and asked in a hoarse whisper, 'What, Amy?'

'I was thinking,' she answered, her eyes still shut. 'The chinoiserie. So much of it left in the sea chests. All this time. Perhaps we should have unpacked the lot.'

'Perhaps, Amy.'

'My beautiful blue gown...'

'Here. Let me give you the sherry.'

She opened her eyes as she accepted the small glass. Over its rim, she smiled at him. Her face was thin again, thin and plain as when he'd first known her, and her body too. But to him she was beautiful. He turned away, swallowing hard. She mustn't see.

'Later,' she said, 'when you come up again, would you bring me the small lion from the mantel? I should like to have it with me.'

'I'll go now.'

'Later,' she said again, and laughed, for he had plunged from the room with his words. She heard his footsteps thud on the stairs. He sounded like her Marcus. The way he had always been until only a few months before. When she was no longer able to fight off what sickened her and at last was forced to take to her bed.

He came hurrying back to put the small lion into her hand, and as she murmured her thanks, her eyes closed. 'I can rest now,' she whispered.

'Do. I'll be right here.' He sat close by, still careful not to touch her. He leaned his head against the chair back. Slow tears coursed down his cheeks and melted into his beard.

The door slammed. There was noise in the hallway. Augusta looked up expectantly.

The boys: Kin, Caleb. Where the two toddlers went there was always commotion. They prattled incessantly. They shared a curiosity that had no bounds. They must touch and tap and try and taste whatever they saw, even to reaching out to grab for the moon, to stroke the sky. And yet they were so different already. Not only in appearance – Caleb's dark hair and light eyes; Kin's russet hair and blue eyes. But in their manner, too. Caleb was always first, two steps ahead although he was the younger by a month. He cried loudest when he was hurt, screamed loudest when he was angry. It had been Aria's way also. But Augusta didn't dwell on that. Without speaking of it, both she and Luke, she knew, had watched for signs of Aria in the boy. Yet such signs no longer mattered to her. She found it hard to remember now what she had felt for Caleb when she first beheld him. He was, from the beginning, his own person, and he adored her, depended on her, made himself a part of her as she could never have imagined he could be under the circumstances as she thought she understood them. In this single year he had become as much her son as Kin was.

'Mama,' Caleb stumbled over the threshold. His cheeks were red from the cold, his eyes shone silver. 'Mama! Eat!'

'Eat, Mama!' Kin echoed, making a crooked path across the room.

She kissed them both, watched as they bumped together and fell and clambered up to go to Luke. He swung Kin to one knee and reached for Caleb to do the same.

There was, in that movement, only the briefest hesitation, but Caleb screamed in instant anger.

The boy knew, Augusta thought. Somehow he sensed the smallest holding back.

Luke caught him up, held him, soothed him, while Kin contentedly played with his father's cravat and dug his head into his father's shoulder. Smiling, speaking slowly in his deep voice, Luke was saying, 'Well, now, what's this? Here you are. Right here on my knee. Then what's this shrilling about?'

But he understood. Try as he might to be even-handed, when he looked on Caleb, Luke saw Aria again. He saw the living embodiment of an act for which he couldn't forgive himself. An act with which he could never come to terms. For it had made him like his mother. Like poor Nelle Wakefield, who even then continued to sit in her chair, empty-eyed, and clutching a bundle of rags. It was made even worse by the knowledge that in the nearly two and a half years of their marriage, he and Gussie had grown more in love, although it had seemed impossible, than they were at the beginning. More in love. Yes, yes. He felt it. But there was between them an invisible wall. Love and passion bound them close. Yet the barrier was there. The barrier was his betrayal; Caleb was its product. And, though she had never charged Luke with it, he was certain she knew. For, just as Marcus had never spoken of Parish Kincaid once he had gone, so Gussie never spoke of Aria.

Now, having quieted Caleb and hugged both boys, Luke set them down and sent them off to beg milk and gingerbread from Betty Gowan. Even if they couldn't ask for it in words, she would know what they wanted. Betty had a son of her own, now three years old, cared for by her mother. Her husband had died at Bull Run. She was a buxom woman of thirty-six now, but seemed to have no interest in remarriage. Her life was filled by her family at home and what she considered her other family in the Kincaid-Wakefield house on High Street.

When the boys had gone to Betty, Augusta said thoughtfully, 'My father will be down again in a little while. I think you should speak to him further about our shares.'

'You will do it, won't you, Gussie?' Luke responded. 'No matter what the subject, you'll have your say. This affair of the line is your father's concern. And mine too, I suppose. Why not leave us to it?' There was no annoyance in his voice. He was stating an observation made many times before.

'My father's. And yours,' she retorted. 'Men's business. That's what you mean.'

'Yes.' Suddenly he smiled. She was beautiful when the indignant color rose in her cheeks. 'I suppose that is what I mean.' He knew that she couldn't help it. She had been raised to feel, to think, that the line was hers. But it had never been. It had once belonged to the Bordens. Then to those others in Boston. Now to Jim Fisk. But Luke had heard Marcus on the subject so many times, he understood.

She was saying, 'It's my business too.'

He said thoughtfully, 'I wonder how Fisk was able to get the Bristol Line in the first place. Daniel Drew has the reputation of being no mean adversary. But Fisk pulled it off. And now I wonder what he'll do.'

'There's only one way to find out, and that's to ask him.'

'Ask him?' Luke laughed. 'My God, the man's a Wall Street mogul. How could anybody just ask him what he intends?'

'How indeed? By walking up to him, and saying, "Sir, what do you intend to do with the Fall River Line?"'

Luke grinned. 'You mean, "Sir, what do you intend toward my daughter?"'

She waved the teasing aside. 'I'm serious, Luke.'

'You make it sound so easy.'

'It is,' she said.

He got to his feet. 'Leave it to your father.'

'He can't think of it now. You know that.'

'He will when he has to.'

Augusta considered the problem for a few days. Her father was so plainly occupied with Amy's illness that nothing else mattered to him. Luke, who owned no shares in the line, would never attempt to usurp her father's position. There was no one to speak for the Kincaids but herself. Having decided that, Augusta announced that she would take the *Metropolis* to New York on Friday. Betty would manage the boys without her. Marcus would watch over Amy. Luke tried to dissuade her, but on Friday, when the *Metropolis* left, she was on board.

It was a cold and windy evening. Mount Hope Bay was crested with long white rollers. An occasional small floe of ice was bumped away by the prow of the ship. The sky was dark, without moon or stars.

But in the lounge it was warm and light.

For Mabel Graystone, it was too light. She preferred a certain dimness. It was easier on her eyes, and kinder, she thought, to her face. She bulked large in the deep chair, her black gown flowing around her. A big paper-filled carpetbag leaned against her knee. She had inventories and mortgages to study, plans to evolve, but she didn't bother with them now. Somberly her mind ranged back over the past few months. Her father had died suddenly in the first week of January. By his will she had inherited property in New York, Chicago, and as far away as Fort Worth in Texas. It should have been enough for her, but she had the feeling that there ought to be more.

She was going to New York to see a man who had handled some of her father's affairs. She would learn how well based her suspicions were by the time she had finished with him. It was a chore to which she looked forward.

But at the moment she had something else to think about. She took up the round gold watch which hung on a chain on her large bosom. It had been her father's, worn in his waistcoat pocket. Now, like everything else, it was hers. The time was eight-fifteen. She was careful not to look toward the large central staircase. Arthur Fields was late by ten minutes. He had said he'd join her at a few minutes after eight. Well and good. She supposed it was like him to be tardy, although until now she wouldn't have guessed so.

He'd appeared at her father's funeral, saying, 'I'm sorry for your trouble, Miss Graystone.' His gentleness had surprised her. That he came at all astounded her. She imagined that he had had his reasons, whatever they were, and never expected to see him again. But later in that week he came to call, and earlier this month, he had proposed marriage to her. She had asked for a while to consider it, and that same day she had gone to Pinkerton's. The logo of the detective agency, a single ugly staring eye, had very nearly put her off. But she couldn't believe that he loved her, so there had to be another reason. She suspected he was a fortune hunter. She had to know. So she forced herself to go in, to engage in the interview, ask her questions, provide the necessary information. Within a few days, she had the answer. He was a respectable person, with a comfortable inheritance of his own. Soon after, she accepted his proposal.

How she wished that her father were alive! He had seen her humiliation when he dragged Arthur to meet her. If only Papa could see her triumph now. At the thought a grim smile appeared on her lips.

'My dear, forgive me.'

She looked up, the smile fading.

Arthur stood over her. 'I was delayed below. A Boston friend wanted to introduce me to Charles Dickens.' Arthur paused, brows raised.

She said nothing. Charles Dickens. What was he to her?

'The British journalist,' Arthur said. 'He's here, staying in Boston, and commuting to New York and Baltimore and Washington to give lectures.'

'Yes?' she said.

'A brilliant man.'

'I dislike being kept waiting, Arthur.'

'I'm sorry, my dear.'

'Well, sit down then. Don't loom over me like that. I shall get a crick in my neck from staring up at you.'

He sat beside her, looked over the lounge. 'A goodly crowd for this time of the year.'

She ignored that. She said, 'I've been thinking. When we marry, I should like to keep my name.'

'Keep your name, Mabel? My dear, that's very irregular, isn't it? I mean, we *will* be married.'

'It's different. But what do I care? I shall be Mabel Graystone-Fields. With a hyphen. It has a nice ring to it.'

'But why? I don't see the need.'

'My father's name must live,' she said harshly. 'I hope you understand that, and won't try to persuade me otherwise. After all, your name will be there too. Graystone-Fields. That's what I said.' Her cheeks were suddenly pink, her large eyes glistening with tears.

'If you like, and it's so important to you, then why not?' He took her plump hand and smiled at her. 'We neither of us fear to be different.'

'I've drawn up an agreement.' She reached down into the carpetbag, without hesitation drawing out a stiff sheet of paper covered with black writing in ink. 'It details everything, I think.'

'An agreement? I don't understand. What kind of an agreement do we need between us, aside from our marriage vows?'

'The name. That's one thing. I shan't want you changing your mind when it's too late.' She paused to look at him. 'And then, of course, there's the property.'

'What property?'

'You know very well what I mean. All that I've inherited from my father.'

'I see. That. What of it? I have enough of an income to support us. And I intend to do just that. I don't want what your father has left to you.'

'Just so. That's what it says in this agreement. That you'll allow me to use Graystone-Fields as my name, that you'll support me and whatever progeny we have, and that you renounce now and forever any claim for any reason on that which belongs to me before our marriage.'

'It's all so irregular,' Arthur said quietly. 'When there's a marriage usually the fortunes are joined, and descend to the children in the fullness of time. I see no cause for this kind of paper.' He withdrew his hand gently from hers, laced his long slender fingers together. 'I regret that you do.'

'You don't see it, and you regret. I do see it, and I don't regret. What was my father's is now mine. Mine, nobody else's. It goes to my children. And to nobody else.' Her voice grew louder, more harsh with each word. By the time she was forced to stop to take a breath, it was almost a screech.

He said hastily, 'I don't mean to be argumentative. If that's what you want, then it's perfectly acceptable to me. I was only commenting...'

'You accept?' she asked.

'Of course I do. I have no need of your money. Nor do I want it. Whatever you like I will do.'

She thrust the paper at him. 'Then sign it, Arthur. Sign it.' But she paused. 'No, no, wait – let us go to the purser's office. We ought to have witnesses. Yes, that's right.' She rose ponderously, her black gown flowing around her. 'Come.'

He shoved the paper into a breast pocket, caught up her carpetbag, and followed her.

At the purser's office, Luke listened, nodded. Arthur signed his name. Luke signed his, but his mind was on Augusta. She would be in the upper lounge, waiting for him. He was in a hurry to finish in the office and go up to her for a little while.

'There,' Mabel said, 'that's done.' And a great bray of laughter burst out of her. 'And a good thing for you, too. For if you'd reneged, I'd have sued you for breach of promise.'

Arthur, pitying her with all his heart, remembered Hiram Graystone and cursed him. The man had been cruel beyond measure to Mabel. 'Come along, my dear,' Arthur said gently. 'Let's go up and have supper.'

The next morning Augusta had a breakfast of coffee only and returned to her stateroom. She was determined to make a good impression, the best possible one. In a few hours she would see James Fisk. She reviewed what she knew of him. He was a Vermonter originally, but he had lived in Washington during the war, and then in New York, pursuing his financial interests. She wondered why in this period of the south's reconstruction he had left the opportunities offered by his associations in the capital, and instead plunged into the world of Wall Street. Now he associated with Jay Gould, and was known to have somehow outsmarted Daniel Drew, a man noted for shrewdness as well as religiosity. Fisk had offices at Twenty-third Street and Eighth Avenue in Pike's Opera House, often called Erie Palace after the Erie Railroad, one of the enterprises over which he had gained control.

Augusta dressed carefully for the encounter. Her traveling suit was of a dark blue, with a fringed shirt, sealskin cape, and a long full skirt that flared at her slender hips. A white lace fichu showed at her throat, and small white feathers decorated the narrow rolled-brim hat she wore tipped forward over her red-gold curls.

She was one of the first passengers to disembark, although she paused for a few words with Luke and kissed him goodbye, ignoring his 'Gussie, your father wouldn't like this meddling, if he knew.' During the slow hansom ride, she linked and unlinked her gloved fingers, and nervously practiced an opening line.

But when she alighted at Pike's Opera House, and presented herself at the door to which she had been directed, her nervousness had left her. She had nothing to fear. She had come on a legitimate errand.

The man who welcomed her was florid of face, with a carefully trimmed and well-waxed pointed mustache. His hair was dark, parted at the center. He was stout in such a way that though he wore the most expensive of clothes and a large diamond stickpin, he looked disheveled, as if he had just stepped from his bed. His smile, the flash of his look from her hat to her shoes told her that he had an eye for a pretty woman.

She set out to make use of that information. Dimpling, she bowed slightly. 'Mr. Fisk, I thank you for seeing me even though we are unacquainted.'

'A pleasure, my dear girl.' He waved a ringed hand at an upholstered chair. 'Seat yourself, please do.'

She sank down, leaned forward. 'You must wonder at this. I'm a stranger to you. And this is, of course, an intrusion.'

He beamed on her. 'I am delighted, I assure you.'

'I've come because you're the only one for me to turn to.'

'To turn to?' he echoed. 'You must explain that. It has - what shall I call it? - something of a desperate ring.'

She supposed he imagined she had come to beg for money. She said quickly, 'It's about the Fall River ships. About your new Narragansett Steamship Company.'

'The merger of the Bristol and the Fall River Lines.' He nodded, eyes alert now. 'And how does that concern you?'

'My father, Marcus Kincaid, owns shares in the Fall River Line.'

'Ah yes, you are a Kincaid, are you? But when you introduced yourself . . .'

'I'm Mrs. Luke Wakefield. And my husband works for the line, he is assistant purser on the *Metropolis*. Perhaps you have seen him? A handsome man, dark-haired, but with a white strike near his temple, the result of a war wound. Except for when he volunteered with the Massachusetts Seventh, he has always worked on the ships. He was a dock sweeper as a boy, then cleaned cabins. And my father...'

'Yes, I see,' Jim Fisk cut in. 'Your father has shares.'

'He has always had them, from the beginning. He invested with the Bordens, who started the line. I was born on the day the *Bay State* sailed her maiden voyage. It was their first ship.' She hurried on, forgetting that she was speaking of her father, of Luke. 'I'm worried what will happen. It means so much to me. It's been my whole life.'

He was charmed. Not so much by her beauty, although there was that too, but by her emotion. He understood it. For he, too, loved the ships. He said, smiling, 'My dear, what do you think will happen? The line will go on.' He leaned forward so that his full stomach rounded over the top of his trousers and pushed out his long coat. 'But it will go on as it has never been before. I shall make her the queen of the inland waterways, and each ship will become a great floating palace. I have plans, my dear girl.' His eyes gleamed. A smile of delight suffused his fat pink face. 'Commodore Cornelius Vanderbilt shall see what Admiral James Fisk can do when he sets his mind to it.'

She cried admiringly, 'Why, you're not what I thought you'd be.' And it was true.

'And what was that, I wonder?'

'I – I – ' She stammered in quick search of polite words. She had expected him to be a libertine, thoroughly disreputable. After all, she had heard of Mrs. James Fisk, who lived in Boston, and whom he so rarely visited. And heard, too, of his mistress, Josie Mansfield. Augusta had also imagined him to be old. Yet he was probably very close to Luke in age. Aside from that, she saw a lightness in the man. He did not seem bad to her. And how could he be? When he spoke of his ships, it was with love. The kind of love Augusta understood. She said finally, 'You care for your ships, I see that. I expected you'd be interested only to see the profit.'

He laughed, plucked the pointed ends of his mustache. 'Is

that so wicked? Is hoping for a profit for a man's investment a sign of his mortal sin?'

'Of course not! I hope for the same.'

'And you shall have it, my dear Mrs. Wakefield. Mrs. Luke Wakefield. You see, I remember your husband's name.' He got to his feet, extended a pudgy hand. 'Now, let me take you to tea at the Waldorf. They serve delightful pastries of cream and strawberries. And we'll talk of something besides profit and business and the new Narragansett Steamship Line.'

But, knowing from the gleam in his eye what he wanted to talk about, she prettily begged off, saying she had errands to do before the ship's sailing that evening, and promising, when he urged her, to return to see him another time.

The talk that night in the dining saloon was mainly of Andrew Johnson.

Listening, Augusta forgot her joy in having accomplished what she set out to do by meeting with Jim Fisk.

The men speaking were strangers to her but she had heard their opinions many times before.

One said, 'He's a southerner in his heart. Andrew Johnson doesn't want to know the sense of the Senate.'

Another lit a black cigar. 'We'll impeach if he continues.'

Augusta could bear no more. She leaned forward, said softly, 'The president is trying to heal the nation's wounds, to carry out Abraham Lincoln's policies. You two care only for revenge.'

Both men smiled condescendingly, and then, turning away from her, one said to the other, 'Will the Senate convict in an impeachment proceeding?'

'That remains to be seen,' came the answer on a blue plume of smoke.

In May of 1868 the Senate voted on the accusation of high misdemeanor as charged in Article XI of the impeachment documents. President Andrew Johnson was vindicated by a vote of 35 to 19, with the one vote necessary to prevent the two-thirds majority requirement.

Thus Andrew Johnson was able to complete the four-year term to which Lincoln had been elected, but had not been able to serve.

In November of the same year, Ulysses S. Grant was elected to the presidency.

Eight months later, in June 1869. Augusta and Luke, with the two boys and Betty to look after them, were on board the *Providence*. Like the *Bristol*, she had originally been built for Daniel Drew's Bristol Line. He had paid $675,000 for each ship before their launchings in New York in 1866. James Fisk got them for $125,000 apiece and commissioned them for service in late 1867. Both ships were already equipped to carry 1,250 passengers, 250 in 200 staterooms. Each one had three decks, with tiers of cabins, large spacious saloons with mahogany finish, and elegant galleries from which could be seen the soft glow of gas chandeliers and the gleam of bronze fixtures below.

When Jim Fisk acquired the two vessels, he had them refurbished. He ordered 200 canaries for each, every bird named for a man Fisk himself knew. They were scattered throughout the hallways and lounges of the ships. The officers had been put into impressive uniforms. The commanders and pilots no longer dressed in tall black hats and black coats; now they wore blue, trimmed with gold braid. On both ships there were full staff bands.

The passengers seemed to like the changes. There were plans afoot for the design and construction of two new ships. Fisk had had an admiral's uniform made for himself and a dress styled much the same for his sweetheart Josie Mansfield.

Augusta and Luke left Betty with the two boys in the main deck saloon, and walked on the second deck together. It was a beautiful night. The sky was black velvet, sprinkled with diamonds. The air was sweet. Music and laughter hung on the faint breeze.

Six months earlier Luke had been promoted from assistant purser to assistant to the general manager, a change he welcomed because it meant that he could be home more often with Gussie and the children. Marcus had long before realized, when he received his dividends as usual, that the new owner wasn't going to force him to sell out. But it hadn't mattered to him, Augusta had seen. Amy's illness was all he cared about. He never even considered enough to wonder how it was that no move had been made against him by Jim Fisk. Luke, of course, connected Augusta's visit with that, for she had described her meeting with Jim Fisk in careful detail. Luke didn't tell her so, but it rankled a little that he felt she was responsible for his promotion, even though he knew he had earned it.

As assistant to the general manager, his job was much like the one that Marcus had performed long ago for the Bordens. Luke enjoyed it. He had no one chore, but dozens of them. He sailed on no one ship, but on all of them. It was his responsibility to foresee a problem before it developed.

He was on the *Providence* now because of a meeting that Jim Fisk had set up. Leaning on the rail beside Augusta, Luke told her, 'I must make sure all goes well with the dinner.'

'It sounds important.'

He grinned. 'Mr. Fisk will be entertaining the President. They'll embark together in New York.'

'The President? Oh, Luke, how exciting!'

'He's on his way to the Boston Peace Jubilee. And Mrs. Fisk will be accompanying him for a change. He's given special orders about the menu. The wines, the brandies, even the cigars.'

'I'd like to be a fly on the wall. To know what they talk about.'

'I'll be there, somewhere close by. Perhaps I can play the fly for you.'

She leaned close to him, feeling the rhythmic turns of the paddle wheels like a pulse in her body. For the moment, she cared nothing about Jim Fisk, nor even President Grant. She cared only about Luke. She touched her fingertips to his mouth. 'Shall we pretend that we're honeymooners again?'

'We could be,' he said. His voice was warm, the words truly meant. Yet the scar on his face gradually reddened.

Augusta leaned against him. He stepped away, saying, 'Let's go to the grand saloon and have some champagne.'

'A lovely suggestion,' she agreed lightly, knowing that something had troubled him and willing it away.

They drank from fine crystal, and in a little while, his face relaxed. 'You're very beautiful,' he said.

She smiled, didn't answer. It was pleasant to be told that she was beautiful, to know that he saw her thus. But the condition of beauty meant nothing to her. It was not her accomplishment.

It was given. Still, if it was part of why Luke loved her, then she was grateful for it.

His attention left her for only a few moments when he noticed that several men ensconced in easy chairs set close to the railings of the galleries above sat with their legs crossed, one knee over the other, so that from below anyone could see chalked on their boot soles the numbers of their cabins. He said nothing to Augusta, but she saw the direction of his glance.

She said, 'That means precisely what I think it means, of course.'

He raised his brows.

'They're inviting whichever ladies are interested, aren't they?'

'Gussie! How do you know such things?'

'I'm not a child, Luke.'

'Still...' He stopped himself, smiled. Then, 'We can't change the nature of man.' Hearing the words, he thought of himself with Aria and winced.

But Augusta said, 'I don't propose that we should.'

'And perhaps the gentlemen are shy.'

'Perhaps. But what does it matter? We have no control over their morals.'

'Mr. Fisk believes people should do what they want to, and as long as it makes him money, he doesn't care what they want.'

She laughed softly. 'You don't understand me, do you? You expect me to insist that the stewards go and tell those gentlemen to clean off their boot soles. You expect me to demand that they, and the ladies for whom they search, go elsewhere for their pleasure. But we can't do that. Mr. Fisk said these ships would be floating palaces. Pleasure palaces. And all passengers have their own idea of what their pleasures must be.'

'As long as it's kept within reasonable bounds and harms no one –'

'Oh, there's harm, I fear. But not such that we can prevent.'

Once again Luke thought of Aria and wondered when he would ever be free of his shame.

The next day at five-thirty there were crowds moving slowly up the gangplank. The *Providence* glistened white in the late afternoon sun. Looming high over the other ships, flag-

135

bedecked and scrubbed and polished from keel to pilothouse, she did indeed look like a floating palace, Augusta thought as she stood watching.

Suddenly there was a bustle. Admiral Jim Fisk, resplendent in his gold-trimmed uniform, strode to the foot of the gangplank. A small group of men, some seven or eight, came along the dock and paused there. It was President Grant and his party. The President wore a plain dark suit. He was burly and short in the leg. His beard was full and dark, streaked with gray, and concealed his expression.

Later, when the evening was over, Luke told Augusta about the dinner in the private dining saloon. He had been in and out, had heard only some of the conversation. The mirrored room was lit with gas chandeliers, the table perfectly appointed, and the menu the most extravagant that Jim Fisk could devise. Jay Gould, his partner, was there, and Andrew Boutwell, the Secretary of the Treasury, among others.

It was, Luke said, peculiar how President Grant had so little to say. He ate heartily, drank wines and brandies, and smoked the cigars Fisk presented to him. He seemed to listen while Fisk first, and then Gould, expounded on the gold market and how the President with an ill-considered act could destroy it and destroy the productivity of the nation too. The government must at all costs hold onto the gold it had accumulated, Gould explained. Never once did the President commit himself to an opinion. When the evening was done, he smiled pleasantly at Fisk and Gould, thanked the white-gloved Negro stewards who served him, and finally said good night and withdrew.

Three months later, having learned of the approaches by Fisk and Gould to his brother-in-law Abel Corbin, and having put a stop to them, the President ordered that the Treasury sell gold. The result was known thereafter as Black Friday, for it was on Friday, September 24, 1869, that the market collapsed. Fisk and Gould, and many other investors, were wiped out. Most were permanently destroyed, but Fisk and Gould were soon back in business.

That particular debacle had no effect on the ownership of the Narragansett Line, but by then Jim Fisk had begun to tire of it. He put aside his admiral's uniform, traveled less frequently on his ships, and began a new series of maneuvers to add to his fortune.

Early in November of that year a storm blew in from Mount Hope Bay and covered Fall River in snow. Even so, the *Metropolis* arrived on time. When Marcus heard the three-whistle signal, he got up and went to the window. He had been wakeful. It had been another long night. Here and there on the wharves lights flickered in the dark of dawn. Lanterns swung near the waiting train.

He washed in the cold water in the basin, ran a quick brush over his head and beard, without looking at himself in the glass. Quietly he went down the hall to Amy's room.

It was dark, silent. Suddenly too silent. He stood at the threshold, holding his breath. Outside, a branch scraped the side of the house; a horse-drawn wagon rumbled slowly by. His heart gave a sudden jump against his ribs. His breath clogged in his throat. He lunged for the lamp on the mantel. Hands shaking, he managed to light it. When he turned to look at Amy in its pale glow, he knew.

He threw himself on the bed beside her, clasped her cold hand in his, no longer fearful of causing her pain.

Chapter 12

Soon after Christmas, Augusta realized that she was with child again. She told Luke first, and was warmed by his pleased reaction. Then, hoping to cheer her father, she immediately told Marcus. But since Amy's death, he cared for nothing. He received Augusta's news with a forced smile.

Still he *did* try to carry on as usual. He spent much time with Caleb and Kin, answering their three-year-old questions, dividing hugs and whirls in the air between them. But even as the red faded from his beard, so his joyful zest had faded to resignation.

One night in midwinter he prowled restlessly from room to room of the house on High Street. Wherever he looked there were reminders of Amy. Not that he wanted to forget her, but the reminders brought him pain. He decided he had to get away.

The next evening, wearing a greatcoat and high rolled-brim hat, with Luke at his side, he boarded the *Bristol*.

He knew the ship well, having traveled on her many times before. But it struck him how different he was from the old days when the instant he stood on the *Bay State*'s deck, he had begun his proprietary observations. He had no such proprietary interest in the *Bristol*.

Luke excused himself to go to speak with the captain in the wheelhouse. Once Marcus would have gone with him. But no more. Now he settled himself in the saloon on the second deck. Soon the ship was under way. Once Marcus would have been on the main deck to observe the sailing. But, again, no more. He tipped his head back, squinting in the gaslight, and listened as the band began to tune up for its concert.

When he saw Willie Gorgas, he raised a hand in recognition. Willie Gorgas didn't seem to notice him.

Tall, his thick shoulders bunched, Willie was walking with Johnny Franger, who was aggrievedly saying, 'What I want's a drink.'

Willie didn't answer. Johnny drunk meant trouble. Leading the man outside into the icy air, he said, 'You had enough already. You don't need more.'

'You set yourself above me,' Johnny retorted. 'You and your one arm, and your funny talk that's hardly English.'

Though Willie and his son still lived in Johnny's house, they were no longer friends. Johnny was eaten up with jealousy. Willie worked too hard, earned too much. And he wanted Johnny's wife.

Willie wouldn't deny it. He'd been with George Raleigh for a year and parted with him on good terms because he'd stumbled on a job at a ship's chandler on Anawan Street. From there he could listen to the whistles and hoots and warning bells that echoed over the harbor. And there he learned about men who needed clean quarters and a home-cooked meal. So the house was always full, earning more money than ever, for which Johnny never said thank you, though Ellie did, and often. That angered Johnny, too.

Now he said, 'I meant to do you a good turn when I brought you home with me. But I never meant to do myself a bad one.'

'You didn't,' Willie said. The heat was rising in him. He wished he hadn't let Johnny join him on the trip to New York.

'Oh, didn't I?' Johnny jeered.

'You want me to take my boy and move out?'

'No. What for? It's too late now.' Johnny gave a gap-toothed smile. 'Ellie wouldn't let you, would she?'

'She's a good woman,' Willie growled. 'Don't talk against her.'

'A good woman woman loves her own husband, not another man!' Johnny yelled. 'You think I don't know what's been going on?'

'Nothing has,' Willie said through his teeth, head coming down, black eyes aglitter. 'Nothing. Don't talk bad against her, I say.'

'Sure you'd say no. What else? But I know it's true. She's opened her legs to you, you and your one arm and your funny talk. She's taken you in.'

'It's a lie,' Willie said softly. 'She's a good woman.' His one hand jerked Johnny to face him. 'A lie. I wish it was true. But it's not.' His one hand curled at Johnny's throat and tightened in a grip of iron. The smaller man writhed and kicked. 'A lie, goddam you! A lie!' The smaller man's eyes bulged out; his mouth was wide and his tongue dripped foam. Willie held him in that tightening grip and shook him. Soon his drumming feet stilled. His head fell to the side.

Willie sighed deeply. He shook Johnny's body once more, then lifted it and dumped it over the railing, and went inside.

Marcus looked past the window at the Borden Flats light flashing white against the dark of the sky. There was the murmur of voices around him, the song of the canaries, and the strains of the band's music, but all seemed muted and far away.

It was nearly a year since Amy's death. There had been a very quiet Christmas, lightened only briefly by Augusta's announcement that she would be having a baby at summer's end. With the advent of 1870 he had reasoned that he must become active again. He could not allow himself to continue to pace the floor. He was forty-nine now, but that didn't mean he was in his dotage. Still, he didn't feel right and hadn't for some time. Something had gone out of him. He lit a cigar, blew a thick plume of smoke. He tasted the tobacco in his throat, felt it burn in his chest. Foul, foul. He put the cigar out.

There were people around him. Ladies in veiled hats and velvet gowns. Men in dark suits, with high stiff collars on their shirts and silken ties. He listened without interest to their conversations, picking out stray words: Worth's for gowns, of course... The best hotel is the Waldorf... Reconstruction... Universal voting rights for males... The Knights of the Ku Klux Klan. Once he would have cared. Now the talk meant nothing to him.

Rising, he nodded at an acquaintance but didn't stop to speak. The cold air of the forward deck burned on his hot cheeks and made his eyes water.

He hurried out of the wind into the companionway and found himself breathing hard and staggering from a sudden weakness of the legs. As he passed it slowly, a canary in a golden cage suddenly went silent. He glanced at it, but he was thinking of Amy. He could have, should have, given her more. Given her everything. But he'd thought there was time still. And always he remembered his feckless father and felt the need to prove himself different. At least Augusta would have the house, the shares in the line, and remaining in the sea chests the beauties he had invested in in Canton so long ago. He cared for none of them with Amy gone. He said her name in his mind. Amy. Amy. But what good did it do? She was gone. He would have to learn to be without her. As he had learned to be without Parish, a once beloved brother, who betrayed that love. As he had learned to be without Aria, a forever beloved daughter, who had betrayed that love. But Amy was a part of himself. How could he be without that? And why had it happened? How? He couldn't make sense of it. The time they could have had together. He had called the line their future and fortune. The fortune had come, the future too. And she was no longer here to share it with him.

He stumbled to his stateroom, sank down in a chair in the dark.

The *Bristol* stopped at Newport to take on a few passengers and more cargo.

Marcus listened, but didn't go out. He knew how it would be. Long Wharf would be alight with flares. There would be a hurried bustle. Those embarking would be wrapped in furs. More and more, Newport was host to the affluent of New York. In summer the ships were filled with them, the holds stacked with their chests and even their carriages.

He pressed his hands to his head. Within his skull he felt a pounding, and as the ship resumed her journey, he felt the rhythm of the paddle wheels in his own body. A deep, hard throbbing. He pulled feebly at his cravat. It seemed to be shrinking, choking the wind from him. But he couldn't get it off, and let it go. Slowly, very slowly, the dark of the room seemed to turn red. Through it he saw the Point Judith light flash white and felt in his body the ship's heave on the Atlantic's waves.

There was a sudden quick jolt in his head. A hard blow, but within. He flung his head back, bracing for the next one to come. The dark red of the room brightened. It became a blinding glow. Then slowly, slowly, it dimmed. With the next heave of the ship, he fell sideways, gasping for air . . .

When, in the early morning, the ship docked in New York, the cabin boy, unable to rouse Marcus, went in and found him. He lay sprawled on the floor near the chair from which he had fallen. His usually ruddy face was white; the wide-open eyes stared at the ceiling; his mouth hung awry in his limp beard.

Luke was summoned. He found it hard to believe. He helped raise Marcus's body to the bed, felt his father-in-law's cold face and hands, and covered him with a blanket. But still Luke felt that Marcus must suddenly rise up and bellow, 'Damn it, it's only a joke. I'm too young to have died! Damn it, man! What do you think this is?'

While the ship's whistle blew, the gangplank went down, and the passengers left, Luke remained with Marcus. He remembered their first meeting when Luke was twelve years old. How the man had towered over the boy. Now that boy was a man of thirty-five. And most of what he loved in his life, and what he was, too, he owed to Marcus Kincaid.

Luke tried to think of a gentle way to tell Augusta, but the moment he arrived alone at the house the following morning, she knew. She paled, whispered, 'Something's happened to Papa.'

'Yes,' Luke said, and he told her how Marcus had been found.

'He missed Mama so much. And I shall miss him,' Augusta said finally. Then, looking at Luke, 'Now there's only the two of us.'

Over the next few months, as the season changed from winter to spring, Augusta began to notice how large the house was, and how empty. There were the two boys, always coming and going, bickering and making up. There was Betty Gowan, and Augusta herself. And Luke. But somehow there was also an emptiness that was never filled.

She kept busy. Her pregnancy in no way caused a curtailment of her activities. Kin, Caleb, Luke, their home, all claimed her attention. The line did, too. Daily she climbed to the widow's walk to watch the ships arrive and depart. She remained conversant, through questioning Luke often, with every aspect of them. But her interests ranged further afield as well. There was her concern for women's suffrage. Abolition, and then the war, had temporarily detracted attention from that issue, and in 1870 only in the territory of Wyoming did women have the right to vote. She established a study group that met weekly at the house to exchange information and ideas on the subject.

Luke was aware of her activities, of course. What had been private reservations slowly became very real misgivings. It seemed to him that always Gussie must put her nose into what he believed to be man's business. And as for women's suffrage - he had only to think of his mother, poor sad Nelle with her bundle of rags, to realize how weak women were. How they would break when faced with life's difficulties. Only briefly, then, did he recall that just five years before he too had shown signs of a similar weakness. That he too had been mindless and out of rational control. Quickly he put that recognition aside. He told himself he wouldn't have minded if Gussie devoted herself to the usual charities and good works. It was just that she didn't know where to draw the proper line.

Then, one bright day in April, when he had been on the docks and returned home to clean up and change clothing before the evening meal, he heard a whisper in the front hall.

Gussie was saying: 'Come in, come in. You needn't be afraid. This is Luke's house. And he's here.'

Frowning, he went to see. Augusta smiled at him. He thought how beautiful she was. But then his eyes fixed on the woman with her. Small, thin, white-haired; wrinkled of face and dull of eye. It was his mother, Nelle Wakefield. He swallowed a wave of sickness. He had supported her for years, continued to support her even now. But he couldn't remember when he'd seen her last. This time he was unable to put aside his feelings. Seeing her brought them back in painful intensity. Luke was of her flesh and blood. Her madness was in him. And he had proved it. From afar he heard the shrill of Caleb's laughter and shuddered within himself.

Augusta gently propelled the older woman toward him.

At last he said coldly, 'How are you, Mother?'

She nodded, didn't speak.

'You're well?'

She nodded again, clutched the bundle of rags more closely with one arm and clung to Augusta with the other.

'I've brought your mother here to stay with us.'

Luke could say nothing. There was no way to get words past the lump in his throat. He kept moving his head up and down up and down, feeling the false smile frozen on his mouth. Why had Gussie done this? Why hadn't she spoken to him of it first?

Kin and Caleb came trotting in from the back of the house. They were four years old now. Kin was slim, his hair russet instead of red gold, with a serious, narrow face. Caleb was square, rosy of cheek, with a ruff of dark hair that no amount of brushing down would smooth. They both stared hard at Nelle Wakefield, but she didn't seem to see them.

'These are your two grandsons,' Augusta said, introducing each by name.

For once they didn't hurl a dozen noisy and nosy questions at Augusta, at Luke. They stared at the older woman, intimidated by her lack of response to them.

'I'll show you to your room now,' Augusta went on gently.

Later, when she returned alone, she said, 'You could at least pretend to try to make your mother welcome.'

He paced the room, hands gripped tightly behind him. 'Gussie, you've gone too far this time. You ought to have told me what you were thinking of before you brought her here.'

'I wasn't thinking of it. If I had been, I would have spoken to you. I just went to see her and I realized ... realized ...' her words trailed off. It was for him that she had done it. So that he would accept his mother as she was and thus find peace within himself. After a moment, Augusta sighed. 'It wasn't good for her in the boardinghouse. I've thought so for some while. And today, when I saw how it was with her, I couldn't bear to come away without her.'

'And so, without a by your leave, or a by my leave either, you brought her with you.'

Augusta stood a bit straighter. Her face was exactly the same as before her pregnancy, but her body was fuller. She said, 'We have so much.'

'Yes.'

'We can share with her and miss nothing.'

'I suppose.' But there was still a lump in his throat. His mother was mad, and he knew it. He had never felt anything for her but pity and obligation, and even that, over the years, had been drained out of him. Now there was nothing left. He didn't want to see her, live with her. He didn't want to be reminded of what his childhood had been. He didn't want to be reminded of the weakness they shared and the guilt that weakness had brought him.

Gussie said softly, 'With Mama gone, and Papa too, it has seemed empty here to me.'

'You'll soon have another baby to take your time. And you'll surely find my mother more trouble than you expect.'

'I'll do the best I can for her.'

'I realize you will,' he said. 'But you don't know what's involved.'

'I shall learn,' Augusta told him firmly.

As the months passed, and he came to be accustomed to his mother's presence, Luke was surprised at how little it bothered him. He simply accommodated to it.

She asked for nothing, and seemed to take up so small a space that her presence could hardly be considered a burden. Sometimes he heard Augusta talking to her, and it was as if she were speaking to a contemporary, a complete human being, not a maimed soul who heard little and understood less.

One day as he listened, Augusta said, 'Mother Wakefield, it's a beautiful morning. Will you walk down to the wharves with me when Luke goes? I'll show you the ships and you can see for yourself the place where he works.'

Luke held his breath, waiting. The words came softly from her. 'I'm afraid.'

'To walk with me?'

'The ships,' Nelle Wakefield answered.

And with good reason, Luke thought – the deaths of her husband, her infant son. There was no madness in fearing the ships when you saw it as she must see it. Gussie had said the madness came from outward circumstance, and it was so. But something in her had allowed it. He knew. He knew.

He went in, told Augusta, 'Perhaps it would be better not.'

'We'll see,' she said, and smiled at the older woman. 'Let's go up now, Mother Wakefield, and see what the boys are doing.'

Clutching her bundle of rags, Nelle followed Augusta from the room.

She didn't go to the wharves that day, but later in the month she was there, waving, when Luke sailed on the *Bristol*. Thereafter she went often to watch the ships leave the Fall River wharves.

One day the bundle of rags was gone. In its place she held a small doll. He asked Augusta about it. She said, 'The doll is better.'

'Nothing at all would be better still. Rags or doll, what's the difference?'

'The rags don't look like an infant. The doll does.'

'I don't see your meaning,' Luke said.

'It's a narrowing of the distance between the real and unreal.'

Luke saw that Augusta was right, and blessed her for her understanding.

In August they were down street together, Luke noticed that Augusta was pale, and hurried to drive her home in the carriage when she said she was tired. She was silent on the way, but there were small beads of perspiration on her upper lip and deep shadows ringed her eyes.

She refused to go to bed as he suggested until early afternoon, when the first pains came. Only then, with all prepared, did she give in.

Their daughter, named Amy after Augusta's mother, was born after a long and difficult delivery. It was winter before Augusta was herself again.

By May the difficult time seemed past, and on the 19th, her birthday, she and the boys and infant Amy, along with Nelle Wakefield and Betty Gowan, sailed with Luke on the *Providence*. The two older women shared a stateroom with the children, and the baby was brought to Augusta only at feeding time. Luke had carefully planned the whole affair, and was relieved that his mother seemed not to realize that she was once more on board a ship, the place where the catastrophe which had destroyed her life had begun.

When he saw that all was well with the others, he arranged that he and Gussie have dinner together in the dining saloon. He chose the food, the wine, and ordered special roses for the occasion. Gussie was lovely in a blue gown with matching blue-braided trim, her figure once again slender and supple.

'To your birthday,' he said, lifting a glass. 'And to you.'

'To the line,' she answered. 'Twenty-four years old today. May it live forever.'

Augusta and Luke had been home for two days when Caleb came down with what, at first, seemed a cold. His nose ran, his eyes watered, and his voice was husky when he told Augusta, 'I'm tired, Mama. I hurt all over,' and laid his head in her lap. She touched his burning cheek, while Kin pulled at her skirt, whispering, 'Mama, what's wrong, Mama?'

She carried Caleb to the nursery, and wrapped him. An hour later she sent Betty Gowan for the doctor, because, although he had whimpered a few times, she hadn't been able to rouse him to speak or to take even a single sip of hot sugared tea.

It was the beginning of a two-month-long siege. The disease that had struck Caleb was called some sort of paralytic disorder by the doctor. He had seen only a few cases of it before, and always in the summer months. He knew of no specific to cure the boy, but only suggested that which would break his fever, keep him comfortable.

Through long nights, Augusta sat beside the small bed,

whispering to him. Once or twice in the dark hours he would open his eyes and then slowly close them again. Sometimes he shifted his right leg, but the left one was always still. She rubbed it with hot towels and flexed it at the knee. but it never responded to her touch.

When Luke was at home, he sat beside her. His silver eyes were somber, moving from Caleb's thin pale face to her. He would remember the morning he had brought Caleb, an infant, home and put him into Gussie's arms, saying, 'If anything happens to him, I'll kill you.' It was his own guilt that had spoken then, as it was his own guilt that so burdened him now. It was Gussie who had freely, fully, accepted Caleb, not Luke, and within himself he knew it.

Sometimes at night Kin would call out, 'Mama, I need you to hear my prayers. I need you, Mama.'

'Go,' Luke would say. 'I'll be here with Caleb.'

She would wash in steaming water – her hands, her face – then swiftly change into another gown. Hurrying into the hall, she would find small Nelle Wakefield, the doll clutched in her arms, waiting in silent hope. Augusta would stop, hug her briefly. And then, while Kin knelt at his bedside, she would sit with him, listen as he said, 'Now I lay me down to sleep . . .' and when he was finished, 'And please make my brother Caleb well again.'

Eyes full of tears, she would tuck Kin in, stop to stroke tiny Amy's cheek, and then, hurrying again, she would return to Caleb.

Time dragged by. She refused to leave Caleb except when, morning and evening, she went up to the widow's walk to watch the incoming and outgoing steamers. Day by day the boy seemed to shrink until he made hardly a dent in his bed, his small body barely discernible under the light coverlet. But Augusta spoke constantly to him, her voice a soft persuasive whisper, 'Caleb, say good afternoon to me. Caleb, here's Papa. Tell him hello.'

One day, sitting with her, listening, Luke closed his eyes against sudden tears. Aria's son. And his. And Gussie's, too. For it was she who comforted the boy in his trouble, and she who cared for him. And whatever Luke had said to her once had no meaning to it and never had had any. When it was time for him to go, he rose. He put a hand on her shoulder. 'Gussie, I love you. I always have.'

It was more than five years now since she had known what had happened between him and Aria. Yet his words seemed to come from then, and not from now. She loved him. What else mattered? She went with him to the door, and there she took his hand, and looked up into his face. 'And I love you, Luke. And always have. And always will.'

A week later, Augusta was sponging Caleb's face, wondering how long he would lie thus – silent, wan, helpless. If only she knew what more to do for him. Then, beneath her fingers, she felt his cheek move. His lips trembled. 'Caleb?' she said softly. 'Caleb?' His lashes fluttered. Slowly, slowly, while she held her breath, he opened his eyes and gazed at her, whispering, 'Mama? Caleb's so hungry.' And he shifted his legs and reached up with his thin arms and clung to her.

That was the beginning. Within days his cheeks turned pink and his eyes grew bright again. But when Augusta took him from his bed and set him on his feet, he fell and couldn't get up. It was weeks more before he learned to walk again.

One night when Caleb's illness was well behind him, Augusta sat in the parlor with Luke. All during the boy's illness she had thought of it, and now finally, she felt it was time to speak.

She said, 'Some day, and very soon, I think, we must begin to tell Caleb about his mother.'

Luke stiffened in his chair, turned his head to look at her. 'Gussie, why? You're his mother.'

'I feel that I am. But it isn't so.'

'He thinks it is and that's what matters.' What could she tell him? That Aria was his mother? And his father – what of that? Who would Gussie say was the boy's father?

'Caleb and Kin are too close together in age to be brothers,' Gussie said. 'One day they'll know it.'

Luke rose. He went to the mantel and picked up the small marble lion. He turned it carefully in his fingers, and looked at it without seeing it. At last he said hoarsely, 'Of course there are some who know that the boy is Aria's son, but there's no one to

148

speak of it. So leave it, Gussie. When he asks is time to tell him, not before.'

'It may be difficult for him then,' she said softly.

'Leave it,' he repeated, his voice hard.

She nodded slowly, knowing that for now she would heed him.

Chapter 13

On January 6, 1872, at the Grand Hotel in New York City, Jim Fisk was shot by his rival, Ned Stokes, and died a day later.

When Augusta first heard of it, she shivered. Fisk had been only thirty-seven years old. The same age as Luke. It was hard to believe that the man who had commissioned himself an admiral, who had made fortunes and lost them and made them again, was really dead.

She went up to the widow's walk and looked down at Mount Hope Bay. The wind was cold, the town mantled in snow. The boat train sent clouds of black smoke over the busy wharves.

Changes. The *Bay State*, the line's first ship, was six years gone, and within this season the *Empire State* would be retired too. On them she had lived much of her young life, and much of it had depended on them.

But with the changes there were continuities. Below, the *Metropolis* was taking on her passengers. Lanterns lit the docks. Lights flickered and danced among the black shadows.

Augusta wondered what would happen now, and wished that Luke were home . . .

Months later the *Bristol*'s and *Providence*'s sweet singing canaries were auctioned off, and so was Jim Fisk's gold model of his favorite ship – the one on which he had entertained President Grant only three years before. The Narragansett Line was sold to the Old Colony Railroad Company, and became the Old Colony Steamboat Line.

This time Augusta didn't have to make a special plea to be

allowed to retain the original stock of the Bay State Company that had by now been transferred several times. Luke discussed it with the general manager, and he, very shortly, talked it over with the new owners. The shares were converted with a reasonable profit accruing to the Wakefields, and Luke remained in the job he had had since 1867.

But even though Fall River was growing, with fifty-five cotton mills and fifteen new textile corporations, there was a noticeable drop in the line's business. Competition from other shipping companies and from the railroads was steadily increasing.

In 1873, Jay Cooke and Company, a prestigious banking firm, declared bankruptcy, the first sign of what was to become a country-wide economic depression that led to 10,000 business failures.

To Mabel Graystone-Fields, that three-year collapse was a boon. While others suffered, Mabel prospered. She bought land at tax sales for a pittance of what it was worth. She foreclosed on the second mortgages she held the day they fell due. She had gone into moneylending, extending small loans and accepting only land as collateral. When payment was due, she received full principle plus interest, or she took a deed to the land instead. In the nine years since Hiram Graystone's death and her marriage to Arthur Fields, Mabel's real estate holdings had increased by more than a third, her liquid assets by nearly double.

She had, briefly, in 1868, taken a few months away from her business to be delivered of a son. She named him Bennet Graystone-Fields, and when Arthur protested that he hadn't realized what she intended, she whipped out their pre-nuptial agreement and thrust it under his nose.

'You see. It says right here that I could use the name Graystone-Fields, does it not? Does it not?' she shrilled.

He read the words over. 'Yes. It says you may use that name. It says nothing about your child, our child, using that name.'

'If it's my name, then it's his name,' she cried triumphantly.

Arthur, tired of the scenes she made when thwarted, argued no more.

Bennet Graystone-Fields at the age of eight was a small chubby boy with very round pink cheeks and a small double chin. His eyes were brown, always anxious. His ears, over-large, stuck out beneath a crown of golden blond hair.

Now, in the autumn of 1876, he sat in the train and peered out at the countryside. The maples were red and yellow. The creepers were scarlet on gate and wall. Cloudless above a veiling of black smoke from the engine, the sky was streaked with the black silhouettes of birds flying south. He watched, wishing he were a bird. It would be nice to fly. He slid a glance at the back of his mother's head. Her large black hat, with its lace tail, was tipped forward. If she let him. But would she? Even if he could fly, he doubted it. She never let him do anything he wanted. But how could she stop him from flying? If he knew how. His eyes went back to study the birds but they were gone. Now there was only the veiling of black smoke and the empty sky above it. He craned his neck, wriggled.

'What is it' Arthur Fields asked, lifting his eyes from the book he held. It was Mark Twain's *Roughing It*, published in 1872. Arthur had read it three times already. This time, more than ever, he wished that he could escape to the exciting southwestern frontier about which Twain had written. It was difficult now to remember why he had married Mabel. He recalled the large jutting bosom that had looked soft and warm and delightful. He recalled her large brown eyes, wounded eyes. Her father had been a hard man; Arthur had thought that love would gentle her. He had been wrong. Only cruelty of the kind she had known all her life would deter her. It wasn't in him. And there was the boy...

'Birds,' Bennet was saying insistently.

'Ah, yes. What about them?'

'I saw some flying by.'

'Yes. It's the time of year when they migrate.'

Mabel turned in her seat. 'I don't understand how they can take *my* money to pay *your* debts.'

He shook his head at her, knowing what was to come. He gave a meaningful sideways glance toward Bennet.

Mabel ignored his wordless response. 'How can they?'

'I'm not sure I understand it myself. What's in the claim is apparently their argument. As man and wife, I am responsible for your debts.' He sighed. 'And you are responsible for mine.'

'But the money is *mine*. My own, Arthur.'

'Shall we discuss it later?' It had already been discussed a dozen times. It was the reason they were going to New York. These past few years had been as unkind to Arthur as they had been good to Mabel. His fortune seemed to have dissolved though, he didn't quite understand how. He had debts outstanding and evidently the debtors had determined to collect what was owed from Mabel. She was astounded when the papers were served. She raved for two days. Then she said, 'We're going to see about this,' and before he knew it, he and Bennet were at South Station and boarding the boat train.

She said now, 'I think you've done this to me, Arthur. I think you told them they could try it on me. But I shall fix you, and them.'

'I did nothing, and you know it. We must allow the attorneys to work it out for us.'

But Mabel had years since conceived an intense distrust of attorneys. After her father's death, she had hired one to sue the lawyer who had handled her father's affairs. She was convinced that some of her property had stuck to his fingers during the settlement of the estate; her attorney had investigated and assured her otherwise, but she never believed him. She decided that he'd been bought off, and was working hand in glove with the lawyer who had been trusted by her father. Now she read the law books herself, hired an attorney only when she needed him to represent her in court, and never used the same one twice.

'You say you did nothing,' Mabel went on, her voice rising. Her eyes began to flash fire.

Heads turned to look at her. Small Bennet went pale. He leaned his head against the window and pretended to sleep.

'We'll talk of it later,' Arthur said quickly. He too closed his eyes.

Mabel stared balefully at him, but just then the train whistle blew and the clatter of the wheels slowed. White steam hissed through the black smoke cloud that hung over them. She gathered up her carpetbag and reticule, preparing to descend.

Soon the train jerked to a stop. The passengers made their way down, across the wharves to the gangplank of the *Bristol*, and swarmed aboard.

Mabel clasped Bennet's hand and dragged him along beside her. He had to trot to keep up with her, his short fat legs pumping in a desperate race to keep from falling. Arthur followed along more slowly. In the past few years his mind's fatigue had spread to his body.

Mabel didn't look back. She understood Arthur – let him walk behind her. It didn't matter. Bennet clung feverishly to her hand, and where Bennet was, Arthur was sure to be. She didn't care. Except that she wasn't going to permit anybody to collect her money to pay off *his* debts. She would not.

At the purser's office, she said, offering the brass-colored key she had been given on the train, 'I don't want this stateroom. It's a mistake.'

The purser raised his brows, but suggested another.

'No,' she told him, 'That's the same mistake. I want to be lower.'

Arthur said quietly, 'Purser, please make the change.' He accepted a new key, pocketed the refund, and turned away without further comment.

'So it was you,' she said furiously, moments later in the stateroom. 'You reserved that expensive cabin! What for? Why did we need it?'

'What does it matter?' Arthur asked. 'It's my money. I thought to please you, but since I didn't we are here now.'

'Your money.' She took a deep breath. After an instant's ominous silence, she said, 'I wonder how much longer your money will last.'

'I wonder too,' Arthur answered.

She grimaced, part smile, part snarl. 'And then?'

'I don't know.'

'Don't worry, I'll take care of you,' she told him, and then she burst into a great bray of laughter.

Bennet, silent witness to this exchange, burped loudly. The ship was still at the dock, but he felt queasy. His stomach seemed to contract and expand. Waves of heat and cold spilled through him; his hair prickled on the back of his neck. 'I'm hungry,' he said in a small voice. 'Mama, I'm awfully hungry,' after which in a great geyser all that he had eaten for breakfast and lunch and afternoon tea gushed from his mouth.

Mabel delayed dinner until after the Newport stop. By then Bennet had been cleaned up and was no longer complaining that he wanted to eat. He yawned, his sad brown eyes heavy, the lids drooping, while, finally, he picked at his evening meal.

Mabel looked with satisfaction at the company at the group table she had insisted on joining. They could eat, as a family of three, at any time. But the group table was a golden opportunity. Here sat Thomas Edison, a man who had his own inventing firm, and Hamilton Fish, Secretary of State for President Grant, and small ancient Cornelius Vanderbilt, a man reputed to have a fortune of almost $100 million.

These men were the reason she had waited so long for her dinner, herself nearly weak from hunger. She had wanted Bennet to see them. They were to be an object lesson to him, even if Edison ignored her to concentrate on his cold salmon, and Hamilton Fish kept his eyes on his mock turtle soup, and old Vanderbilt seemed hardly to know where he was. But Bennet looked more asleep than awake. She pinched him. 'Give your attention to these gentlemen. Listen to what they say. Learn, learn! One day you'll have a fortune to build on. You must know how to deal with what you get and how to proceed.'

The boy straightened, cast a sad eye at the others, then slouched again.

When the men began to speak, it was not of financial matters. There was talk of the Centennial Exposition in Fairmont Park, Philadelphia; of the Battle of Little Big Horn, in which George A. Custer, disregarding his commanding officer's orders, had attacked Sitting Bull and his Indian warriors and died in the battle that followed with 265 of his men. Hamilton Fish spoke sadly of the candidacy of Republican Rutherford B. Hayes, which made Mabel wonder if he had hoped to be president himself one day.

Meanwhile she listened, pinched Bennet when his head drooped, and finally, in a pause, said loudly, sighing, 'I don't know what a poor woman's to do.'

'Mabel,' Arthur whispered. 'Mabel, please.'

She looked at him and grimaced, then swung to face the others. 'Can you guess our errand? We go to New York to defend ourselves against an unbelievable depradation. Sirs, you don't realize the plight of women. You do not. And, I warrant, you do not care either.'

Arthur placed his napkin on the table, pushed back his chair, and put out his hand to Bennet. The boy rose from his seat, but Mabel thrust him down. 'Stay here.' She neither looked at nor spoke to Arthur as he left the dining saloon, but went on: 'My very livelihood is threatened by my foolish husband's debts. My livelihood, I tell you. And who's to help me?'

There was an exchange of glances at this rhetorical question, a scuff of chairs on the thick carpet, and with small bows, brief apologies, the others disappeared to the sound of Mabel's harsh inexplicable laughter.

William Gorgas was watching. The big woman dressed in black was like a ship. The small boy who stumbled after her was like a dingy caught in her wake. William was seventeen years old. Not too old to sympathize with the child, to understand what he must feel. Not yet too old to be beyond such emotions himself.

William was tall, lean. He had a thick shock of well-combed black hair and shining black eyes. His mouth was soft, but sharply defined, his hands big, thick-knuckled, but unscarred. He wore the best of suits and excellent handmade boots. But for most of his life, and particularly in the past two years, he had felt that he was being dragged by his father through meetings he didn't want to attend.

This trip was the same. Old Willie, which was how William thought of his father, had insisted that William go with him, saying, 'It's time. I want you to have the best so you can know the best.'

His father's guttural accent made William shudder. He said, 'Papa, I'd rather wait a while.'

'What for? We'll stay at the Fifth Avenue Hotel, see the sights. And you'll meet some people.'

William agreed, knowing it was no use. No matter what he said, he'd end up going. He'd be embarrassed by old Willie and embarrassed for him.

It was that way now. Old Willie had spoken little at the dinner table, but it seemed too much to William. He couldn't look at his father. He had to get away. Saying he was tired, he excused himself and retreated to his stateroom.

Left alone, Willie finished his meal in silence, drank his coffee, had a brandy, and went out to stand on deck. He wished young Willie hadn't left him. There was much to talk about. He wanted to tell his son how once he had scrubbed the decks of the *Bay State*, and polished her brass. He wanted to explain about the chance America offers, if only a man would take it. But the boy had asked to go to bed. Never mind. There'd be time for talking.

A breeze came up. In the main saloon the band was playing. The canaries were gone, but the *Bristol* was the same. It was six years and some since that cold winter night when Willie had stood on the same spot and squeezed the life out of Johnny Franger. Now he thought briefly of what had happened after ...

When the ship had docked at Newport, Willie got off. He spent the day there, and picked up a returning boat, which was the *Providence*, back to Fall River. He acted surprised that Johnny wasn't there, and told Ellie that her husband had gotten drunk in Newport and gone off on his own. It was several days before she became worried. He'd disappeared that way a number of times before.

The following week, Willie read that a man's body had been found washed ashore on Aquidneck Island. He mentioned it to Ellie, and accompanied her when she went to see if it was Johnny. By his clothes, she thought so, and so did Willie. Since nobody asked what had happened to him, there were no official questions about his death. Ellie and Willie brought him home for burial. Eight months later they were married.

Soon after that Willie bought an old house in Tiverton. He was planning to fix it up as a boardinghouse. But before the work was done, he happened into Lottie Dimot on the street, and had a good idea. He hired her to run the house. She brought in girls, collected the money, and after taking her cut, turned the rest over to Willie. It was a profitable arrangement for both of them.

Within a year Willie duplicated it in New Bedford with one of Lottie's girls. Two years of savings gave him the money to buy a house with a large lot two blocks off North Main Street in Fall River. There he established the Fall River Gorgas Inn. Ellie knew nothing of the two whorehouses. She helped him design the inn, but was content to go on running the original boardinghouse for a few increasingly selected guests. There was William to think of, after all. Willie had his plans. William also knew nothing about the whorehouses.

Now the boy had almost finished two years at college. Harvard had been a fine place to send him. He had made friends there, Willie was sure, even though he himself had never met them. Young Willie had learned how to talk and act. He was what his father had hoped he would be: a gentleman, like Marcus Kincaid.

In New York the two of them would go to the best tailor they could find. The boy would start learning the inn business. Soon he'd know it inside and out. Too much schooling would soften him. That was why Willie had determined it was time ...

When he went to the stateroom, he found the boy staring out of the porthole.

'I thought you wanted to go to bed, Willie.'

'Papa, please call me William.'

His father shrugged. 'William then.'

'I was thinking,' the boy said tentatively.

Willie didn't ask about what. He knew. The boy wanted to stay in Cambridge another two years. But the inns were ready and waiting.

Willie rubbed his beard. 'Listen, it's all for you. Everything I built up. For you.'

William sighed. 'Sure. I know,' and slowly took off his cravat.

Chapter 14

It was a hot August day. The white lace curtains hung limp at the window. Luke heard from outside the sound of the boys' quarreling. They were ten now, an age for curiosity and argumentation, he supposed. And Amy, at six, was learning to be the same from them, although he wished she wouldn't. As he went to the window, he heard Betty Gowan's cautioning, 'Hush, you're making too much noise,' and in the silence that followed, the chirp of birds and the hum of bees. In the distance a tug hooted and barge bells rang.

Augusta, though, heard nothing. She lay sunk in a strange sleep. *Gussie*, he whispered to her in his mind. *Gussie, wake up. Wake up. It's enough now. I can't bear it.* She did not respond. It would be the same if he had spoken in his loudest voice.

Only a week before she had been at the Seamen's Mission, helping to ladle out bowls of stew. He could imagine how she'd looked then, her slender figure leaning across the huge vats, arm outstretched. A curl loosened from her chignon, falling across her cheek. Her eyes following each man, her smile dimpled and warm before he turned away.

She'd been tired when she came home that afternoon, but she'd walked with him to the docks, and looked on with the same pleasure as usual as the *Providence* holds were loaded.

She waited until he boarded, then blew him a kiss before she climbed into the two-seater he had bought for her to drive the short distance home.

He arrived back in Fall River two days later. The house was silent when he went in. Gussie hadn't been on the widow's walk waiting for him; she wasn't in the parlor, nor in the kitchen. The children came running to him. Amy threw herself at his legs and clutched them, weeping. Between them, Kin and Caleb told him: 'Mama's sick in bed.'

He hurried in to see her but met Betty Gowan at the door. Her worried face frightened him. She said, 'Oh, I'm so glad you're at home finally. Augusta has a fever. I've had the doctor twice, but he doesn't know what to do.' There were tears on her cheeks, and she wrung her hands in her apron. Even the blue ribbons on her cap were limp.

Luke went in. Augusta lay still. She seemed small as a child. Her face was pale but for an ugly red blush on her cheekbones. Her lips moved although she didn't speak.

Her fingers trembled slightly when he touched them.

His heart sank. He remembered how Amy had trembled at the slightest touch in her last illness. When he could speak, he whispered, 'Gussie, it's Luke. I'm here now. What can I do for you?'

But she didn't answer, nor open her eyes. He was suddenly

more frightened than he'd ever been in his life.

There was a whisper of sound at the door. He turned to look. His mother stood there, small as a child, pale. In her arms she clutched the doll that Gussie had given her.

He shook his head at her, turned back to Gussie.

Suddenly his mother stood beside him. Her eyes came up to his in a quick glance. Carefully she laid the doll on the foot of the bed. Then she leaned over Gussie, and pressed a kiss on her burning cheek.

In a hoarse voice, Nelle Wakefield whispered: 'My daughter, my daughter. We need you. We all need you so. I do, and the children. And most of all, there's Luke.'

Gussie was still. The room was still. Tears stung Luke's eyes as his mother soundlessly left the room. The doll lay on the bed where she had left it. She would never touch it again.

Later he spoke to the doctor, who called the illness a brain fever, and said, 'I have given her what I can think of, and have investigated in Boston. I'll continue to do that, of course. But it's up to her constitution, Luke. She must fight it through to survive.'

Alone, listening as the doctor's surrey clattered away down High Street, he asked himself if this was the punishment. For a few short moments, his love for Gussie had failed. Was this the price to be paid? Was he to lose her forever? And if so, why must she pay the even greater price? Shaking, his long body atremble as it had never been before, not even in the worst of the time in the stone cellar, he hunched on the settle.

A hand as light as a leaf, a dry and withered leaf, touched his shoulder. Luke raised his face.

Nelle Wakefield said softly, 'There's a veil, almost impossible to see through. A deadening of light. A darkening shadow. But the ears hear, Luke. We must find the right words.'

He looked into the small wrinkled face, into a gaze once blank, but now alive with compassion and pain.

'We cannot lose her,' his mother said.

'No,' he croaked. 'No.' And with the refusal, the tears he had fought back since he first saw Gussie as she was now suddenly could be contained no more. He wept, and his mother held him as she had once held a bundle of rags and, later, a doll. She held him, and rocked him, and promised, 'We won't lose her, Luke.'

A November snow was on the ground, veiling the trees the day he came home after a hard trip with gale winds off Point Judith and icebergs in the Sound. Betty came rushing to greet him. 'Augusta's improved! She woke up yesterday afternoon and asked for you.'

The children gathered around him. Little Amy, thumb in her mouth, clutching Nelle Wakefield's gown with her other hand; Kin, Caleb. They were a family. No one of them different from the other. No one of them separate. More than ever Luke was determined that Caleb should never hear the truth. He would ensure the secret, he promised himself as he hugged them, and saw his mother's smile for the first time that he remembered, and then hurried away to burst into the bedroom.

Gussie lay high against the pillows, her thick red-gold hair in two shining braids. She put out her arms to him.

He cried, 'Gussie, Gussie...' and after that could say no more.

She clung to him, whispering, 'It seemed so long, so long a time, and I was dreaming all the while. There were shadows. You, your mother. And voices far far away. Sometimes they were fainter, and all light seemed to be fading. And then – then I heard the calling to me –'

A few days later they realized that something was wrong with her legs.

The small, perfectly formed fir stood in the corner. It was strung with popped corn and cranberry ropes, and slivers of silvery paper icicles. Spread on the floor beneath it was a country scene: snow made of cotton, a tiny wooden barn, a farmhouse, miniature horses harnessed to a surrey.

Somewhere at the back of the house Amy was complaining to Betty in a high-pitched voice. Listening, Augusta frowned. Of late, Amy too often sounded that way. The child needed to be taken in hand. Betty had too much to do, even with Mother Wakefield trying to help. The two boys and small Amy. And an invalid...

The thought was pain. Augusta shut her eyes tightly. No, no. It couldn't be. Her whole body was alive with small pulses and flutterings. Her whole body. She was alive. She was well again.

But her legs hung below her hips like two dead sticks. Clothed now in stockings and slippers, they appeared perfectly normal. But they no longer functioned as they once had. They would no longer hold her weight, flex, move. They would no longer walk, nor run. She felt young in every part of her. That she would turn thirty in four months didn't matter. It was only her legs that aged and imprisoned her.

She smoothed the gown over her lap, her thighs. There was no feeling. She pressed the joint of her knee. Nothing. It was still the same – the same horrible nothingness. She didn't believe it possible, yet it was so. She was well, she told herself. The long nightmare was over. It had passed. This too would pass. But when? How long would she be captive in her chair, the shawl around her shoulders, the books piled beside her? How long must she listen to the children run past the door and not stop? How long must she kiss Luke goodbye, then never go to the widow's walk to see him leave?

She would have to remain in the chair until Luke came to take her to the supper table. He was at the docks now, but soon he would return. They would have the meal, he would settle her in bed, and there she would stay, with Mother Wakefield and Betty looking after her, until he returned on Wednesday. Oh, how she longed to go with him. How much she wanted to feel beneath her feet the polished decks, to listen to the sound of the paddle wheels and the wind whispering at the wheelhouse, and the music in the saloon. Oh, how she wanted to see the Point Judith light again.

Suddenly, she straightened up. Her eyes glowed.

When Luke came in, she said, smiling, 'I've had a wonderful thought. Do you suppose it would be possible for me to go with you this evening?'

'Go with me? I'm not sure that's a good idea. The weather's not pleasant. There'll be little to amuse you this time of the year.'

'I don't want to be amused. I just want to go.' It was the idea of the ships. The ships. Hers. So many things had happened to her on the ships. The *Empire State* where, after the explosion, she had seen death for the first time, and learned what courage was. The *Metropolis*, when she had seen at first hand what slavery meant.

Always, morning and night, she heard the three-whistle signal and her spirits lifted. Perhaps the ship would bring a miracle to her. There had been others, after all. She herself had survived, and when she had first opened her eyes, she had seen the doll on the chest and known that even as she was well again, so Mother Wakefield was too.

Seeing the look on Gussie's face, Luke decided quickly. It was against his own inclination, for he was fearful. But yes, of course she must go. And why not when it might do her good? 'If you don't think you'll find it too difficult –'

'It'll help me.'

It would make her happy, Luke thought. That was reason enough to take the risk. He carried her into the bedroom and set her on the edge of the four-poster bed. She was as light as a child. As light as when she *was* a child and he had carried her about. And she looked so young.

'Could you ask your mother to come in?' she said. 'I'd like to take some things.'

He found his mother in the kitchen, told her of the plan. She nodded, smiled, and went in her slow silent walk to help Gussie.

But Betty grumbled, 'She'll catch her death of cold. And what for? To sit alone in her stateroom, staring at the walls, and thinking.'

'Augusta wants it, so don't discourage her,' Luke said.

To Augusta, Betty said with a smile, 'So you're going too, are you?'

'I should have thought of it sooner,' Augusta answered, while Nelle Wakefield nodded.

It was a rush, but Augusta was ready when it was time for Luke to leave the house. She kissed Kin and Caleb and Amy and told the three of them to be good, to listen to Betty and not make trouble for her. She squeezed Betty's hand, looked into her anxious eyes, and said, 'Don't worry while I'm gone.'

Luke lifted her easily, one arm at her small waist, the other under her useless legs. When they left, Augusta looked back. From the widow's walk, her cloak billowing around her, Nelle Wakefield raised a thin hand in farewell. It was a short ride in the surrey to the docks. There, with the boat train unloading, he carried her up the gangplank and to the stateroom he had

162

arranged for earlier. After she had taken off her outer coat, wrapped a thin woolen shawl around her shoulders, and smoothed her hair, he took her into the *Providence*'s second deck saloon.

Though the canaries were gone now, there was other music as the band members tuned their instruments.

'You'll be all right here?' Luke asked.

'Of course, Luke.' How could she not be? She was home.

It worried him that he had to leave her, but there was the usual inspection to do. There were staff he must speak to. And the ship would be leaving soon. He said, 'I'll see you in a little while,' and went off.

She leaned back in the deep chair. Soon the passengers began to descend the wide staircase in groups of twos and threes. Ladies wrapped in furs and heavy shawls, gentlemen carrying their hats under their arms. The saloon rippled with excitement as the call, 'All ashore that's going ashore!' sounded.

Augusta savored the thrum of the engines and remembered having lunched in the iron cylinder of the *Metropolis* before that ship was launched. She was gone forever from her berth in Fall River, having been retired in 1874. Augusta wondered what the ship was doing now, steaming where, serving whom. She felt the slow gentle movement beneath her. Beyond the big window close to which she sat the Borden Flat light flashed and faded, flashed and faded, and the dark waters of the bay reflected back puddles of gold from the saloon's chandeliers. Now she was warm, confident. It was the beginning. She dropped both hands to her lap, smoothed the skirt over her thighs. Somehow she must teach herself to walk again.

From two women behind her, there came muted conversation. 'I always used to stay at the Fifth Avenue, but I'd like a change. It's just that I don't quite know where...'

'Perhaps if you ask the purser...' her companion remarked, and went on, 'I do wish I knew what the music will be this evening.'

'Perhaps if you asked the purser...' her friend retorted.

Augusta smiled to herself. If every passenger on the ship brought to the purser such queries, there would be nothing but chaos. Still, how, except by word of mouth, was one to find a hotel? And, without a program, how could one know what the band would play?

She was turning those questions over in her mind when Carl Hansen came to say a few words to her. He was resplendent in the blue uniform that Jim Fisk had originally designed, the gold braid indicating years of service. When he left her with greetings·for the Christmas just past and good wishes for the new year shortly to come, there were others. Crewmen of every rank came for a few moments. They were all her family. She gloried in seeing them again.

Later, after she had had dinner with Luke, he carried her back to their stateroom. She was ready to rest by then, and he still had affairs to attend to.

She sat straight against the piled-high pillows, leaned forward, grasped her right leg by the knee, and lifted it slowly. Then, gasping with effort, she placed her heel on the soft sheet and slid her leg flat again. Four times, five times. There was sweat on her face when she switched to the left leg. Four times again, five times. At last it became impossible; she could perform the movement no more. She lay back, listening to the wind, to the slap of the rising waves on the portholes. The ship was rounding Point Judith now.

She was smiling when Luke came in.

'You're all right, Gussie?'

'I'm fine. I'm glad I came with you.'

'Then we'll do it again.'

'Yes,' she said. 'Oh, yes.'

Four months later the April sun was flooding brightly into her room. Augusta pushed herself up from her chair, leaned on it to rest, then flexed her left leg. It would hold her weight now. It would move as she directed it. But there remained a long way to go.

Luke carried her into the parlor when he was home. He took her down to the wharves, and to church on Sundays. He took her to performances at the new Academy of Music, opened in January the year before, at the corner of South Main and Pocasset Streets. It became a commonplace to see Mr. Luke Wakefield lift his wife into his arms and carry her into South

Park. She was determined not to accept that as a permanent condition.

Now, though tiring, she clung to the chair and flexed her leg again and again.

When Luke came in, he protested. 'I've told you. You mustn't try to stand when you're alone. You'll have a fall.' He was afraid something would happen. She was alive only by what seemed a miracle to him. He feared any risk.

'I'll not fall,' she said. 'I'm improving. Nothing will stop me.'

'Of course you're improving. And of course nothing will stop you. We both know that.' He swept her into his arms. 'But tell me, what do you want? Where do you want to go?'

She touched the white streak over his temple lightly, then said, 'Put me down.'

'I'll carry you, Gussie. Just say where.'

'I want you to put me down.' This time her voice was sharp. He set her in the chair, stood back. 'What's the matter?'

'I don't want you to carry me.'

'But I like holding you.'

Her eyes flashed. The color rose in her cheeks. 'I think you don't realize what you like. Having me dependent on you. Your child. To be pampered and cared for and carried about. But I don't want you to condescend to me so. I'm an adult. I have a will. And strength. I will *walk* again.'

'You will,' he said, seeing that his fear had made him more hindrance than help, and knowing that he must find courage to match her own.

A few days later he brought her a crutch, and stood watching as she pushed herself to her feet and leaned on it and smiled at him. She'll walk, he thought. If anyone could do it, it would be Gussie.

At night, when she was alone and the house was still, Augusta tried. She let herself slip from the edge of the bed to the floor, and lay on her stomach pushing with the toes of her left leg, trying to push with the toes of her right leg. Slowly, slowly, there were small sensations. First pain. Very bad at first, then easing away into an odd throbbing ache. Later there was feeling. It came and went. She learned to crawl inches at a time.

She chose goals to work toward. The marble-topped wash-stand. Then the big chair near the window. Then the wardrobe. Finally the chest where Nelle Wakefield's abandoned doll remained as silent witness to Augusta's efforts, to the miracle that made them possible. Gradually, one by one, she moved to touch them. Yes, yes. She had done it so far, but by crawling. Eventually she taught her right leg to hold her up. She leaned on the crutch and walked with it and that was much better than before. But there was still a way to go.

Day times the study group came to talk. Its members spoke of Victoria Claflin Woodhull, the first woman ever to testify before the Congress in Washington, asking that women's suffrage be supported. The group's ladies were all agreed on that, but not on Mrs. Woodhull. She was not a woman of good reputation. Augusta said she didn't care what the woman's reputation was. If women were to achieve the vote, then they would have to say, 'Damn reputations. Do you agree or don't you?' The others decided they could go along with that. And when they took their leave, and Augusta was alone, she practiced once more.

At the end of June, she awakened early one morning. She heard the whistle of the *Providence*. Luke would be traveling back on her. Augusta sat up slowly. The sky was a faint pink, the sun just beginning to rise. She got up, reaching for her crutch. She would have to hurry if she were to be on time.

Half an hour later, she pulled the surrey to a stop on the wharves. She was wearing a large white hat, dangling big bows of pink veiling. Her gown was white, too, trimmed with pink beads and pink embroidery at the cuffs and skirt. She looked at the crutch, and sighed, and eased it under her arm.

When she was ready, balanced, she moved slowly toward the *Providence*'s gangplank. The deckhand at the foot of it saluted her. 'Mrs. Wakefield?'

'Has my husband come down yet, do you know?'

'Not yet, ma'am.'

'Then I'll wait here.'

'Shall I go and get him for you?'

'Oh, no, thank you. I'll just wait.'

Moments later, Luke came across the main deck and saw her. He waved, walked more quickly.

As he started down the gangplank, she moved toward him. But then she stopped. She balanced herself, leaned the crutch carefully on a rail. And then, straightening, with her eyes fixed on him, she walked slowly, slowly, but steadily and surely into his arms.

PART II
1877 to 1907

Chapter 15

Augusta watched from beneath half-lowered lids as the closed drapes billowed on the warm breeze of a late September afternoon. First the room was flooded with golden sunlight. Then pale shadows arose.

Sunlight, shadow. Sunlight, shadow. It had a rhythm. Like the rhythm of the Borden Flats light. The rhythm of Luke's fingers, now slowly stroking her back. There were no words to describe the feelings evoked by his touch. A delicious sweetness. A languor. A melting within her flesh.

She smiled, moved closer to him. His arm warm under her shift. His breath warm at her temple. How good it was. The loving. And this aftermath. The lying together in oneness.

But already, everything that had been completely forgotten while he kissed her and stroked her and they joined with so much pleasure that nothing could intervene, already that everything was beginning to make itself known.

First there was the tick of the clock. It seemed to grow louder, measuring off the time she had with Luke. And then, beyond the locked door, there were voices. Seven-year-old Amy's shrill whine, boisterous Caleb, and quieter, murmuring Kin, whose very softness concealed an unimaginable stubbornness.

Amy was saying, 'But I want to tell them something. It's important. It can't wait.'

'You must be patient until they come out. This is the private time. We have our private times. And they have theirs.' It was Caleb, sounding very grown up for eleven. In a few years, his voice would begin to change, and he would show signs of facial hair. And oh so suddenly, he would no longer be her little boy, Augusta thought. *Her little boy.* Had she once believed for an instant that she hated him? Had she once watched him, seeking in him some part of Aria? It seemed impossible now. He was hers. Like Kin, like Amy. Her child.

Kin's whispered comment was only background to the noisy struggle, the rattle at the doorknob. But Augusta knew he was there. Sweet Kin, so like her father Marcus in appearance, with cheeks that flushed easily and russet hair. But it was a skin-deep resemblance only. Kin was turned inward, thoughtful, and careful of his affections, like Luke.

Luke's stroking hand didn't falter. He said with wry amusement, 'Children!'

'It's Amy. She wants a talking to. And she shall have it in a little while.'

'She wants a spanking.' Luke pulled Augusta closer. 'But perhaps a talking to will help. Never mind for now. My mother will be along to attend to her.'

Augusta kissed his bare shoulder. 'Yes. We're lucky in her. And in so many other ways as well.'

It was hard now to remember the desperate months when it seemed she would never walk again. The unending hours of kneading her legs and stretching them, and dragging herself on aching arms to learn to move. It was hard to recall being carried from room to room, from house to carriage, gown trailing and heart always sinking. There were no scars of that illness left on her. She was as new, and thankful for it.

'I wonder what time it is,' Luke said.

'Don't think of it,' she said softly.

'Oh? Why not?'

'Because I'm not ready yet to part with you.'

He leaned over her. The dimples beside her mouth deepened as he watched. Her eyes glowed green at him through their fringes of dark lashes. Now she was stroking him, light feathery touches of silken fingertips. The drapes billowed and fell. The golden sun came and retreated. 'I won't think of the time,' he said, and pressed his mouth on hers.

'Wait,' she told him. She rose from the canopied bed and slipped off her shift. 'Wait, so I can feel all of you.'

The sounds from the hallway faded as she went back into his arms.

Later, when she was dressed again, she stood before the mirror, putting up her hair. Luke stood behind her, his hands busy at his cravat. Watching the reflection of his face, she asked, 'Is it the same for others, do you suppose?'

'The same?' he echoed. He was thinking ahead now to the *Providence*. He would be sailing on her that evening. She would be carrying a full complement of passengers, some from Boston and Fall River, but many from Newport. Much of that town's development could be laid to the establishment of the Fall River Line. From 1854 to 1874 alone, there had been land sales worth $13 million. Mansions called cottages had been built on Bellevue Avenue facing Cliff Walk. The people who lived in them were beginning to move many of their belongings back to their New York homes for the winter season, thus there would be heavy cargo in the holds as well as valuable goods in the sleeping quarters. Recently there had been some problem with shipments disappearing, and several thefts reported on the *Providence*. Luke was considering how best to prevent further incidents of that kind. No crewman, and no one from the general manager's office, could spend all his time moving around the ship and keeping watch. Perhaps he would have to bring in a new man.

'You aren't listening to me,' Augusta said. 'You have a certain faraway look. I was wondering if it were the same for others. In the bed.'

Luke's hands went still on his cravat. Momentarily he forgot the *Providence*, and smiled at her. 'I don't know. Perhaps it is. Yet somehow I doubt it. Else why would there be so much discontent?'

'It may be the nature of man,' she suggested. 'Man, as in human beings, as well as man in male.'

But it was a subject he did not want to pursue. Males were not always loyal to their wives. He was one who hadn't been. How was he to judge? How dare he try? Even now he could not explain what had happened to him with Aria. And his years on the ships, observing people, had led him to realize that regardless of what the pretense might be, the reality was otherwise. His single misstep, for all its consequences, was minor compared to the behavior of some. And not just the male animal either. There were woman equally hungry for different partners. Hadn't he seen enough shadowy figures glide through dim companionways to tap on cabin doors to know?

Augusta was asking, 'Do you think it's discontent with what one has that makes for adultery?'

'Who knows?' He bent his head to kiss her. 'I must be off to the wharves now.'

'You'll be back for early supper?'

He nodded, and went out.

The moment the door had closed behind him, there was uproar in the hall. The children. All three clamored for his attention.

Usually she'd have gone to his rescue, but this time she ignored the noise. She stood at the looking glass reconstructing the conversation, and recalling the inflection of his words. It had been foolish of her, in her happy complacency, to talk so. Some subjects were best let alone. That was one of them. Suppose he thought she was deliberately reminding him...

She had made no plans before, but now she considered it. Nelle Wakefield would be at home to oversee the children. The new helper, Marge Gowan, had proved herself competent, and an apt pupil to her cousin Betty's instruction.

One day not long after the one in June when Augusta had begun to walk again, Betty had said, 'I must talk to you, Augusta,' and they had both sat down at the kitchen table over cups of coffee.

There had been a flush on Betty's cheeks, and Augusta had thought that she looked, then, remarkably young for a mature woman of forty-six with a fifteen-year-old son. After a throat-clearing and a few nervous sips of coffee, Betty said, 'If you weren't well I wouldn't be doing it. But as it is...'

'Doing it?' Augusta asked.

'Leaving you,' Betty said, and hurried on to explain that some while back, at church, she'd met a widower, a man with a grown son. At first she'd ignored the man, but lately they'd gone out, and now he had proposed marriage. Augusta had once met him. His name was George Raleigh. Long before, he'd been a bounty hunter.

'I remember him,' Augusta said. 'We were on the *Metropolis*.

He was after two poor souls –' Anger welled in her voice.

'He's different,' Betty assured her. 'He stayed on in Fall River. And now he's as good a Massachusetts man as any.' She went on to say that he owned his own stables, renting out wagons and carriages and horses.

A few days later she had brought Marge to meet Augusta. The girl was seventeen. She had worked as a carder at the Pocasset Mills for the past year, but lately she had begun to cough, an ailment common to textile workers. She was slim, as dark haired as Betty, and good with the children.

Between them, she and Nelle Wakefield would manage nicely. Augusta decided that she would sail with Luke on the *Providence* that evening.

The large saloon was almost empty. The chandeliers had been dimmed. The band had played its last music and put away its instruments until the morrow. The *Providence* steamed slowly through the Sound, most of her passengers bedded down for the night.

Augusta waited for Luke, enjoying the near solitude of the large chamber. It was always a pleasant time for her. The lull in the ship's excitement while the life, above and below decks, went on.

When, finally, Luke came, he looked tired. The lines around his eyes seemed deeper. She rose at once. 'Shall we go down to the stateroom?'

'Let's have some air first.'

She saw that he was troubled, but she decided not to ask him what was wrong. When he was ready, he would tell her. But she was glad now that she had come. Perhaps there was some way she could help him.

Outside it was cool, quiet. She pulled her cloak around her, leaned against the rail. The sound of the paddle wheels was as familiar to her as the beat of her own heart.

At last Luke sighed. 'It's an unpleasant thing sometimes to discover the truth.'

'Yes,' she said. 'What do you mean though?'

'I've been asking questions for weeks. Watching. Assessing the men on the ship.'

'It's the thefts,' she said. She had known about the problem for Luke had mentioned it.

'The losses aren't inconsiderable. The line has made every penny good. It mustn't keep happening. So I had to act.' He turned to face her, his silver eyes narrowed. 'But it was ugly. And sad. And I wonder, now, if perhaps I've made a mistake.'

'You've found out who was responsible?'

'Yes.' He went on to describe how it had been. And who it had been . . .

He had asked his questions. From the answers he received, he had eliminated the Fall River and New York dockmasters, and finally all but two deckhands who helped with the loading. He questioned the one, and was certain of the man's innocence. He questioned the other, and was certain he knew something. A longer, more heated session led to more information. Hal Davis, a man of sixty-five, third mate on the *Providence*, who had sailed on the *Bay State*'s first voyage, was responsible for the last check in of cargo. Once he had moved certain crates in, he turned them over to a chosen deckhand who, with an impostor stevedore, simply removed the crate from the ship along with legitimately delivered goods. Davis had a brother who picked it up and sold the contents in Bristol and Boston and New Bedford.

The third mate, never promoted in thirty years because he had been a hard man to work with, with a reputation for contentiousness and foul language, had broken down when Luke approached him.

He had clutched his bald head, tears streaming down his face. 'What will I do?' he cried. 'Where will I go? You were always old man Kincaid's favorite, and married his daughter. So you've had everything. But I have nothing. And no one to turn to.'

Luke had finally told him, 'I'll have to see your papers taken away, Mr. Davis. You can't be an officer of the line any longer.'

'Then give me something else,' the man had pleaded. 'Let me prove you can trust me. I'll tell my brother to go to hell. And be straight with you forever.'

Luke gave him a chance as a deckhand. Davis went from pay of thirty-five dollars a month to twelve. But now Luke was wondering how wise he'd been.

Augusta slowly shook her head. 'No, no. You oughtn't to have done it. For all you've helped him, you'll not be able to depend on him.'

'There's something other than this situation,' Luke said. 'The more I've thought of it, the more I've come to see that we need a special person aboard whose work it is to keep an eye on just such problems.'

'A Pinkerton man,' she suggested.

'I think so. I'll discuss it with the home office as soon as I return to Fall River.'

She slipped a hand under Luke's arm. 'As for Hal Davis... I'm glad you can be kind. But I hope you'll never have reason to be sorry you were.'

Below decks, in the forecastle, called the glory hole by the hands, Davis sat by himself, and swore. He cursed himself for being a weak old man. He cursed his younger brother. He cursed the ship, the Sound, and the world into which he had been born. But loudest and longest of all, he cursed Luke Wakefield...

The next evening, at 5:00 p.m., the hawsers were released. The *Providence* moved slowly from Pier 28 on the North River. From the third deck, Augusta watched as the ship steamed majestically around the southern point of New York City. Bordering the shore, in the direction of the East River, there were bands of green, with footpaths lined with trees just beginning to turn to autumn yellow and red. The big white ship passed beneath the bridge being built between New York and Brooklyn. It was called the Wire-Bridge, and had been under construction for the past five years. It was estimated, Augusta had heard, that it would take another five years to finish, and that the cost would be $10 million. Then there came Hell's Gate, once a rocky jagged whirlpool. Now, widened and deepened, its hazards for navigators were reduced so that nothing of its former terrors remained. Further along the East River there were small islands, gleaming green in the setting sun. Soon they would reach Execution Rock, and then Eaton's Neck.

Smiling, Augusta went inside to wait for Luke in the saloon. She greeted several passengers she knew, then settled in a comfortable chair to listen to the music and watch the couples promenading on the galleries above.

Almost immediately she became aware of someone staring at her. It wasn't the sort of complimentary glance to which she had long been accustomed. It was an open and concentrated look, which brought an itch to the back of her neck. She tried to ignore the sensation. She took off her veil-trimmed hat and set it aside. She smoothed the blue swirl of her gown and drew off her elbow-length gloves. At last, unable to contain her curiosity, she turned to look.

Across the saloon, beyond the groups of strolling people, a man stood at a tall carved wooden pillar. He had grayish-brown hair, a bristly mustache. His face was long, narrow, with high cheekbones and thick dark pouches beneath his eyes. He wore a dark suit of the finest quality and what was plainly the best of linens. His boots gleamed, as well polished as his gold-headed Malacca cane. One of his hands lay lightly on the shoulder of the boy who stood with him, and the boy too, some fourteen years of age, was dressed in good apparel. Augusta was sure she had never seen either of them before. But both man and boy continued to stare at her.

She felt a small chill ripple down her back. How odd that strangers should affect her so. And strangers they must be. She swung away, determined to ignore them.

But, only moments later, the two stood before her. The man bowed. 'Mrs. Wakefield?'

She raised startled eyes to his. 'Yes. I am Augusta Wakefield.'

'Augusta! How it suits you. And how grown up, too. When I last saw you you were called Gussie.'

'You knew me when I was a child?'

'Indeed I did.' Parish Kincaid allowed a faintly reminiscent smile to curl his mouth. He had recognized Luke the moment he saw him on the aft deck. Augusta he hadn't known. But, having admired her for some small time, he'd asked a steward who she was. So he'd known how this beautiful woman had come by her reddish-gold hair. He said aloud, 'I'm Parish, your father's younger brother. And this,' he indicated the boy beside him, 'this is my son, Peter.' The mouth beneath the bristly mustache continued to smile. The dark eyes were veiled. Parish wondered what she knew, what she remembered, what Marcus or Amy had told her. He had known the risk, but considered it negligible. So much time had passed since he left Fall River. He went on, 'I see that you don't remember me.'

'Parish,' she said slowly. 'Uncle Parish. Of course.' The name, the title, came back in a swift rush, and with it, another sudden chill. But she rose, smiling warmly. 'It's been so long, hasn't it? And we've had no news of you.'

'You'd forgotten all about me.' He hoped so. It would be much simpler if nothing remained in her mind of those last few moments before he left the house on High Street, pursued by her cries and the infant's screaming.

Augusta ignored his remark, embarrassed to admit it, but wondering how it could have happened. Her parents had never spoken of him. He had been there, she almost remembered that, and then suddenly he was gone, and never mentioned again. It was odd. And until now she had never wondered at it, nor ever thought of him.

He said, 'I've been in California. Now Peter and I are returning to Fall River to live. He shall see where his roots are. And I'll see home for the first time since 1849.'

'You'll find it different, I fear.'

'Of course. I expect to.' He gestured to her chair. 'Please. Do make yourself comfortable,' and when she seated herself, he sat down beside her, his glance sweeping the saloon. 'The town will be as different to me as the *Providence* is from the *Bay State* and the *Empire State*, both of which I knew well.'

'I too,' she said. 'And both are gone now. The *Bay State* went for scrap and the *Empire State* is an excursion boat.'

'But the line itself endures.' Parish smiled. 'Your father was right. It was indeed a good investment, although I confess I didn't think so then.'

'You've had no news of our family for many years?' she asked.

'None. California's a long way from Massachusetts. I wrote sometimes, but there was never any reply.' None of that was true. He had never written. But he knew Marcus and Amy were dead. Before embarking on his return, he had made sure to learn what had happened in Fall River.

Augusta was saying, 'Then I must tell you, Uncle Parish. Both my parents are dead.' She still found it hard to say the words, even harder to believe them. There were times when she found herself listening for Marcus's heavy footsteps, awaiting the joy of Amy's laugh.

Parish allowed a moment of silence. She mustn't realize with what indifference he had first heard that news and now heard it once again. But finally he said, 'I'm sorry. I'm too late then. I had hoped it would be otherwise and we could all be together once more.'

The boy, Peter, until then silent and unmoving, shifted his weight and said suddenly, 'We're cousins, aren't we?' and smiled at Augusta.

'We are indeed. And you have more cousins. My sons, Caleb and Kin. I wish they were on this voyage with me. You'd find them company, although they're a few years younger than you.' She looked at Parish. 'The boys are very close together. Just 10 months apart actually, with Kin the older. We have a daughter, too. Amy. After my mother.' It was casual as she said it; there was nothing for Parish to remark upon.

But it was important for Augusta to explain. And that was what Luke had insisted. She herself feared the deception. It was true there were very few people who remembered that Luke had brought Caleb to Fall River when the boy was an infant. And those, like Betty Gowan, were sworn to secrecy. Still, Augusta had always felt uneasy about it, although she had given in to Luke.

'And you had a baby sister, didn't you?' Parish asked. 'I seem to remember . . .'

'Yes. It's Aria you mean.' Augusta drew a deep breath. 'She too is dead.'

'Ah,' Parish sighed. 'A pity.' He leaned toward her, 'But you, here you are. Lovely, and grown up. Married, and with children. It's hard to believe. Your husband's Luke Wakefield, isn't he?'

'Yes. How did you know?'

'I remember him from when he was a boy, perhaps the same age as Peter.' It was from Luke that Parish had thought there might be trouble. He didn't want Augusta's feelings for him to be corrupted by Luke's memories. But it was a chance, only one of many, that Parish had determined to take. He went on, 'It'll be good to see him again,' and at the same time had a moment's flash of memory. The ship's sleeping quarters, shadowed – the men standing back, music and laughter fading – and Marcus grabbing him by the shirt front, eyes flashing rage...

When Luke joined them a little later, Augusta immediately saw that he did not share Parish's open pleasure at the meeting.

'It's been a long time,' Parish told him.

Luke nodded. He was remembering how Parish's name had never been spoken once he was gone. How Marcus's face had flamed when he, Luke, had brought word of him picked up on the wharves, and how sad Amy had looked when she questioned Luke later about Parish's whereabouts and well-being. He knew Marcus had thrashed Parish, but didn't know why. He didn't have to know what had happened. If Marcus had turned against his younger brother, then there had been good reason.

Parish, smiling, pressed ahead determinedly. 'We're returning to Fall River for good, Peter and I. I want my son to know his origins. And that's where the Kincaids began. In Fall River.' He looked at Augusta. 'I want him to know his relations too. There are so few of us left, Gussie.'

Luke eyed Parish's diamond stickpin and the ring on his finger. The man had done well for himself. But Luke wasn't impressed, and knew he never would be. Marcus had wanted nothing to do with his younger brother. There must have been cause.

Later, when they were alone, he said as much to Augusta.

She protested, 'You're not fair, Luke. Parish was hardly more than a boy when he left.'

'He was a man in his early twenties. And he didn't measure up to your father.'

'But who could have?'

'He didn't try.'

'You were only a child yourself. How could you know? Probably, if there'd been time...'

'No. I doubt they'd have ever made it up.'

'It's in the past and no longer important,' she said.

'But has he changed? That's what I wonder.'

'Changed? From what?'

Luke shrugged. 'What does it matter? We needn't see much of him.'

*

Parish had other ideas. He was a Kincaid, and so was Augusta. And because of the Kincaid connection the Wakefields were at the center of life in Fall River. Parish proposed to use them for his own purposes. But he soon learned that neither Luke nor Augusta was interested in society, and they rarely went out of an evening. By his standards, their lives were genteel and conservative. Luke was immersed in his work with the line, and Augusta, as he saw it, was concerned only with her family. Parish was surprised that they continued to live in the house once inhabited by Marcus and Amy, and that though it had been enlarged, it was nothing like the palatial home he had envisioned. Still, it didn't matter to Parish. They knew everyone; they had respect and reputation. He had no feeling for Augusta beyond a faint dislike. She reminded him of Marcus in her coloring, of Amy in her form. He considered that taking her down a peg or two would afford him amusement. But first he needed her help.

He was tired of being an outcast. At fifty-five, he was at last ready and well able to settle down to a quiet and pleasant life, and that was what he intended to do. No one was going to stop him. At the same time, he wanted to establish a bond with Peter. They had, until now, never lived together. The boy had been farmed out, first living with a family, then later sent away to school. For too long there had been no room in Parish's life for a son. He was making room now that he had begun to feel the burden of time forever lost.

He had started as a gambler and parlayed a small and uncertain fortune into a fortune in gold. He owned a mine, parts of two others. His income was secured in investments in New York and San Francisco. Peter's mother had died in the same year as the boy's birth. She had been a dance hall singer. He'd married her out of loneliness, and found her unbearable thereafter. She left him and the child for a piano player of dubious talent, and was shot to death in a bandit attack on a carriage on a Mexican road. Parish neither knew nor cared about what had happened to her lover.

Soon after his arrival in Fall River, with Augusta's help, he bought three acres on Highland Avenue. By the end of the next year, he had built a great stone house and furnished it richly with carpets from Axminster and glass from Brussels.

He enlisted Augusta's assistance in locating what he called servants and what she called help. It amused him to learn that even in 1878 there were no servants in Fall River. There was live-in help, as Marge Gowan was, and live-out help, as Betty Gowan had been. In Newport, of course, there were the usual distinctions: butlers, cooks, upstairs and downstairs maids, grooms and gardeners. After much discussion, he turned to Newport for his staff.

He enrolled Peter in a private day school, and on the strength of Marcus Kincaid's name, managed to get himself invited to join the Quequechan Club on North Main Street.

That winter, when he gave a small musicale, he made sure to consult Augusta about the date, the flowers, the catering, and the ensemble he engaged. Later Augusta insisted to Luke that they attend.

'We should,' she said when he objected. 'For Parish's sake, as well as for Peter's. It'll seem odd if we're not there.'

'Let them look after themselves.'

'They're my relations.'

'Yes. But you don't know them, and never have. There's no obligation.'

'I'm afraid I've already accepted,' she said, smiling.

'All right. Have it your own way. If you have to.'

He had been so grudging in the consent she hadn't asked for that Augusta decided in future to discuss with him before rather than after any further invitation Parish offered.

Chapter 16

A few days later Augusta sat reading the line's sailing schedule in the newspaper. Arrive... Depart. Fall River, Newport, New York. As she looked at the hours listed, she remembered a conversation overheard some years before on the *Providence*. *What will the band play tonight?* one woman said. And another: *Can you tell me of a good hotel in New York?*

Someone else asked: *When will we pass the Sakonnet Point light?* And finally, the suggestion: *Let's ask the purser.* But the purser, as Augusta knew from Luke, had too much to do to answer these same questions a hundred times a night. How then to tell the passengers what they wanted to know?

She looked again at the sailing schedule. The line prepared it for the newspaper to print so as to keep the public informed. She saw immediately how it could do the same for its passengers.

It must publish a small newspaper, or pamphlet, with advertisements to defray the printing expenses. It could include the band's programs, which for the past year had been printed and given out on the ships. There could be select menus of the ships' dining saloons, suggested chefs' recipes, information about the lighthouses, the tides, and the harbors on the routes.

She waited excitedly for Luke to return home.

He was barely inside the front door when she described what she had in mind.

He said, smiling, 'You're doing it again, you know.'

She didn't ask him to explain. She understood. 'But I'm as much a part of the line as you are. Why shouldn't I make suggestions? If I were a man...' She paused as he laughed. 'Well, if I were, I'd be...'

'You'd be captain, pilot, and first mate. Doing three jobs instead of one.'

'You know what I mean,' she said ruefully. 'And the idea just came.'

'I *do* know,' he said. And hugged her. 'Don't mind my teasing.'

But it hadn't been teasing. They both knew it.

Later, in the big four-poster bed, he said into the dark, 'Are you happy?'

'Happy?'

'Sometimes I think I'm so much the older. Perhaps you miss something. Perhaps our lives together aren't the same for me as for you.'

She moved closer to him. Burying her face in his shoulder, she whispered, 'There's nothing more than what we have. Nothing more that I could miss.'

*

Luke didn't forget Augusta's idea. He presented it to the line's board of directors, and on May 19, 1879, her thirty-second birthday and the thirty-second birthday of the Fall River Line, he put into her hand the Fall River Line *Journal*, Volume I, No. 1, the first house organ ever to be published in the United States. It was a ten-page booklet, six by nine inches in size. On the front page there were advertisements for John and James Dobson's carpet emporium on Washington Street and French's Hotel near the courthouse in Boston, and two shops there which sold pianos. Inside were more advertisements, and also ships' sailing schedules, and a group of jokes, riddles, and small items of Fall River interest. The journal was to come out monthly, and though it would change in size and content, it would be published and distributed on Fall River Line ships for fifty-six years.

Later that evening, Augusta stood at the rail of the *Bristol*. A cool breeze lifted the curls at the nape of her neck, and billowed in her light cloak. She tried to remember the first celebration that she'd had aboard ship. She thought she was five, but wasn't certain. She might have been younger or older. She had in mind an image: Her father lifted a glass to her and said in his booming voice, 'To our future and fortune, Gussie. To you, and to the line!' And at the same time as he spoke, she heard the three-whistle signal and the paddle wheels began their familiar music.

Luke spoke at her elbow. 'Dreaming?'

The image of her father's face disappeared. The sound of his voice and the music of the paddle wheels stilled. She laughed. 'I was thinking of long ago.'

'Parish is aboard. I've just seen him on the main deck.'

'Oh? Is he? And Peter too?'

'Yes, Peter too.'

Luke made no attempt to conceal the dislike in his voice. She pretended not to notice, but was glad that there came a diversion in the form of Caleb.

'Mama! Mama, guess what!' The boy tugged excitedly at her arm. 'Guess who's aboard?' His eyes shone. He pressed against her, with Kin close beside him, while Amy thrust past the boys to hurl herself into Augusta's arms.

'Yes, I know. Uncle Parish is aboard. And Cousin Peter.'

'That's not who I mean. Someone else. Someone important, Mama.'

'Now let me see.' She glanced around with an exaggerated stare. 'Who could it be?'

'Do you give up?' Caleb demanded.

'I think I must. With all the passengers traveling this evening, how can I guess which one you mean!'

'Oh, but he's special, Mama. It's the president. President Hayes.'

She glanced at Luke. 'Is it so?'

'Yes. He's returning from a lawyers' meeting in Boston.'

Caleb jumped from one foot to the other. 'You see? I was right. Someone important.'

She smiled down at Caleb. 'You won't trouble him, will you? I'm sure he'd like to make the voyage in peace.'

Caleb shook his head solemnly. 'I won't, of course not. He's our guest, Mama.'

Our guest. The words touched her. Thirteen-year-old Caleb was mostly still a boy, but there were moments when he was nearly manlike in his understanding. More, he shared her feeling for the line.

'Tell us the story,' Amy shrilled. 'Tell us about Grandpa Marcus and the Fall River ships. And when you were a little girl.' Amy's hair was midnight dark, braided into two thick plaits secured by pink bows. She wore a pink and white jumper on her wiry nine-year-old body. Her dark eyes shone like new-washed coals in her small face.

Luke held Augusta and she held the three children within the loose circle of her arms. She spoke softly, her eyes fixed on the distant silver stars. 'Grandpa came back from a whaling trip a long time ago. He looked for a way to make his living. For there was another Amy, your grandma, to be taken care of. And he heard of the Bay State Steamboat Company that was then being set up...'

Slowly, her eyes aglow with moonlight, her voice low and compelling, she told them about the start of the line: how its first ship sailed the day she was born, and how her father had held her up to the window of the room that was now Caleb's and Kin's so that she could see and remember it.

Caleb listened, holding his breath. It was a story he had heard

184

many times before, but it always seemed new to him. He loved the sound of it, the very words. *Your future. Your fortune.* He knew the ships. They were to him, every one, individuals, as alive and real as human beings. He knew their crews and was as at home with them as he was at home in the house on High Street. He knew every light between Fall River and New York, and often chanted them to himself before falling asleep: Borden Flats, Bristol Ferry, Mussels Bed Shoals, Hog Island. He could go on until the last one before New York's East River, Blackwell's Island. His father, he knew, had gone to work for the line at the age of twelve. Already Caleb was a year older. But, as Augusta said, times were different now. First Caleb had to finish school. Then Luke would find him a place on the line. Caleb could hardly wait. He already imagined himself wearing the blue uniform, beginning to earn the gold stripes that stood for years of service.

Kin was different. He cared nothing for the ships. He sulked through every voyage, hiding away in the boys' stateroom with a book for as long as he was allowed to. He made fun of Caleb's ambition. Now, wriggling, yawning, Kin said,' Mama, you've told us the same thing before.'

'Many times before.' Augusta laughed. 'And no doubt will again.'

'Go on,' Caleb urged her. 'Tell us more. Finish it.'

Amy pressed her cheek against Augusta's arm. 'Just tell about Grandma Amy. Tell me about her. And how I'm like her.'

But Luke decreed it was time for the children to go to bed. As they went down the companionway toward the stateroom, three men walked ahead of them. They wore dark suits and highly polished boots, and spoke softly in deep rumbling voices.

Luke said quietly, 'The man in the middle is Rutherford Hayes.'

As Augusta nodded, Amy pulled free of her mother's hand and bounded down the companionway, her pink frock streaming behind her, piping: 'Mr. President! Mr. President, I want to say hello'

'Amy!' Augusta cried, and started after her. 'Come back. Be quiet –'

But it was too late.

The three men turned. The tallest of them stood smiling for a moment. He was heavyset, with a sandy-red beard shaped to his full face, and dark deep-set eyes, and a great prow of a nose. He bent down from his height to Amy and said, 'How do you do? Tell me what your name is.'

She was speechless with surprise for an instant. Then, 'I'm Amy. And that's my family.'

By then Augusta had caught up with the child. She put a hand on Amy's shoulder, curtsied. 'Sir, I'm sorry we've disturbed you.'

He smiled, bowed. 'Don't be. I'm pleased to be recognized,' and added with a glance at the two men with him, 'at least by my friends.'

They exchanged good nights, and the president and his men disappeared into a stateroom.

Luke said quietly, 'That mustn't happen again, Amy. You're much too forward and inconsiderate.'

Unrepentant, she answered, 'I only wanted to say hello.'

Luke sent the children off, and led Augusta into the saloon for a glass of champagne. There, in the gaslight, she once again examined the Fall River *Journal* before rolling it into her reticule so that she could show it to Nelle Wakefield when they returned home.

But the journal remained untouched for weeks thereafter. For, when she and Luke came back to Fall River, they found the older woman abed. She had had a spring cold that lingered. Over the past two days it had worsened. She was small under the heavy quilt that Marge Gowan had put over her. Her body shook with chill.

'Augusta,' she whispered through blue lips. 'Daughter, thank you.'

'Hush,' Augusta said. 'Save your strength, Mother Wakefield.' She had already sent Luke for the doctor. Now she prayed that he would hurry.

He wasn't long in coming, but there seemed little that he could do. It was a congestion in the lungs. Nelle Wakefield was old and frail. Time would tell.

It was terrible to be so helpless. Augusta set about nursing her. For five days and nights, she sat with Nelle Wakefield, sponging her burning brow, tucking the heavy quilts around her when she shivered, seeming even to breathe for her when her own breath choked and rasped in her throat.

Sometimes Nelle Walefield gasped words, broken sentences. 'A good life . . . wasted, wasted.' And, 'But love . . . blessings on you . . .' Augusta remembered the bundle of rags Nelle had once clutched to her breast, remembered the doll. How far away the woman had been until the day Augusta herself had needed her. What a moment it had been when Augusta opened her eyes and saw the doll on the top of the chest, and Nelle leaning toward her, her eyes clear and worried.

At dawn of the sixth day, while Luke was away, he heard later from Marge Gowan, Augusta cried out, awakening all in the house, and sent Marge for a kettle of boiling water. She quickly built a cover over Nelle's face and let the steam fill it. But the blueness in the old woman's cheeks and lips only increased, and with Marge holding one small leaflike hand and Augusta the other, Nelle Wakefield slipped quietly away into death.

When he heard the news on his return, a great emptiness spread through Luke. It was as if he had lost his mother twice over. Once when he was eight years old and they were on the ship and her husband and infant died and something within her died too. And now, once again, she was gone from him, but this time there was no chance of her recovery. He wished that the lost years could be retrieved, yet was grateful for the time that they had had.

It was a small funeral. Only Luke and Augusta, along with the three children, and Marge Gowan with Betty Gowan Raleigh, were there. But Parish came with Peter, and laid a large wreath on the fresh grave, and later in the week, when Luke was away, the two came to pay a condolence call.

Peter was fifteen now, tall for his age, with something of the same quiet and watchful look that Parish had.

It was only during that visit that Augusta realized how Caleb worshipped Peter, hanging on his every word, imitating his walk, attempting his quiet way without much success, but attempting it anyhow. Kin, she saw, was distant with his cousin, and hung back with little to say, which for him was much as usual. Amy, so often boisterous, sat still, regarding Peter with the eyes of an adoring puppy.

When Luke returned several days later, she told him about the visit.

'Whatever Parish does has a reason,' was all Luke said.

She added nothing more, remembering how she had prickled with gooseflesh when she first saw Parish on the ship.

Weeks later she recalled it again. Parish had come by to pick up Peter, who had gone with the boys on a day trip by boat to Oakland Beach to hear the Rhode Island military band play. He visited with Augusta for a little while. He set the gold-headed Malacca cane near him, stripped off his gloves.

Marge Gowan brought tea and cakes on a tray.

Parish watched her quick graceful movements through narrowed eyes, thinking of her cousin Betty when she was young. But when the girl left the room, he said to Augusta, 'It's peculiar that you don't send Kin and Caleb to the day school. I should think you would. Consider your position in town.'

'We see no reason to do that.'

'But as people of wealth, as leaders of the community . . .

She smiled at him. 'Wealth, Parish?'

He shrugged, a wry expression on his seamed, narrow face. 'You take after your father, indeed. Marcus was always tight-fisted.'

There was dislike in his voice. She heard it and stiffened with surprise.

'I never found him to be so. He was always most generous. When he could be.'

'But he didn't feel often that he could be,' Parish said lightly. He smiled at her. 'Still, my judgment may have been soured. You know how boys are. Often they want the moon, and when they can't have it, and don't understand –' his eyes flicked sideways at the mantel. He remembered the gleam of silver on it. Candlesticks. A silver snuffbox. Now there remained the caladon lion and ivory dog . . . Marcus's oriental follies. But Augusta, he knew, remembered nothing of the day on which he had left this house. It was just as well. Even the faintest criticism of her parents was dangerous. Soon he said a few words about Nelle Wakefield and departed.

After he had gone, Augusta sat thinking. It was natural for Parish to assume they were wealthy. He saw only the surface, nothing beneath. He knew of the shares in the line, and the house, and he made his assumptions.

What he didn't realize was that competition for passengers and shipping had grown more and more fierce in the past few years. New steamship companies had been formed, and in an effort to gain custom, some had cut their fares to as low as one dollar. She and Luke had agreed that the Fall River Line must not charge below a dollar and fifty cents, fearing that undesirable passengers would be attracted were that allowed. It was what had happened on other lines, they knew. Pickpockets, stateroom thieves, and unrespectable women had begun openly to prey upon travelers. There had been some such incidents even on their own ships in spite of the Pinkerton detectives hired to serve on board after the Hal Davis problem. Luke had argued his opinion, and Augusta's, before the company board of directors. When they finally agreed, the new rate was set.

But, even so, by summer's end the Fall River Line had carried a record 400,000 passengers, and still could pay no dividends because of these low rates.

Parish might have wondered scornfully aloud why they didn't move to Highland Avenue and send the boys to private day school, but he didn't understand that Luke and Augusta had no income at present other than Luke's salary with the line. It allowed for no luxuries.

When they discussed the situation, she looked at the mantel where the celadon lion and ivory dog sat. 'Papa's investment,' she said finally.

'Gussie! You can't mean you want to sell those things!'

'Of course,' she said calmly. 'That's why he left them to us. For when we needed them. And we need them now.'

That evening, after he had gone, she went to the attic and opened a sea chest. She lifted out a teapot. The china was cool to the touch. Papa's fingers have handled this, Augusta thought.

Smiling to herself, she climbed to the widow's walk. The *Providence* moved slowly away from the wharves, her flags fluttering in the salty breeze. The whistle blew three sharp blasts. Overhead the gulls swooped and screamed. She watched until dark fell, and the ship's running lights faded away in the shadows.

At week's end, Luke, still with reservations, accepted the wrapped package of six small pieces. He sold them in New

York for three thousand dollars. It was a sum equal to what they could have expected to receive in dividends if all had been well with the line. What he sold had come from the chest; the celadon lion and ivory dog remained on the mantel next to the girandole used long ago by Jane Oliver.

Marcus's folly, as Parish had once thought it, had at last begun to pay off.

Chapter 17

In January of 1880, Charles Stewart Parnell mounted the stage at the Academy of Music to appeal for donations in support of the Irish cause. Disputatious crowds spilled out onto the footways of Pocasset Street and around the corner onto crowded South Main.

The event was still being argued over at midsummer on the *Bristol*. It was the subject of that conversation on the deck from which a bored Peter and Caleb withdrew to make their way by a circuitous route to the forecastle.

The 'glory hole' had wooden bunks built into the bulkheads, tall lockers, and several scarred tables. A single gas light cast midnight shadows on the bare deck.

The boys weren't supposed to be there, and knew it, and that made it all the more exciting to them.

Peter had made the arrangement with Hal Davis but hadn't known the way, so he'd brought Caleb along to act as guide.

There wasn't a place on the *Bristol* that Caleb didn't know. He'd explored the ship many times while Kin sat reading in the stateroom they shared. For Caleb, it was a chance to prove to his cousin that the *Bristol* was as good as Caleb's own plot, just as the mansion on Highland Avenue was as good as Peter's.

It didn't matter to Peter if they were supposed to be in the glory hole or not. He was a Kincaid, Caleb was a Wakefield. Peter considered that the two names made it all right. And he'd been bored. He cared nothing for Irish nationalism. He'd kept thinking about the talk he'd had with the deckhand, Hal Davis, when he'd mentioned he wished he could join in a game. Davis had squinted, laughed, and rubbed his beard. He understood that sixteen-year-old Peter wasn't welcome in the card room. He'd been half teasing when he invited Peter to join him and a few others below decks. But there Peter came, stepping cautiously down the ladder.

Hal Davis welcomed him with a grin. 'I thought you mightn't make it.'

'Why not? I said I would,' Peter returned. He pushed Caleb forward, introduced him.

'Oh, I know him,' Hal said, while the two other off-watch men nodded. 'He's welcome to play if he wants.'

But Caleb didn't care for gambling. He stood watching while Peter joined the three men at the table. They had only an hour, so the game moved swiftly. Peter, like his father, knew dice well, and liked to win.

There was little conversation until Hal Davis said, slanting a look at Caleb, 'Why, I've known him since the first time he came aboard the *Metropolis*.'

'The *Metropolis*? Me?' He knew the ship, having sailed on her many times before she was retired when he was seven years old. But he didn't remember that Hal Davis had ever sailed on her.

When he said so, Hal Davis laughed hoarsely. 'It was before you'd have known me or anybody else. When your father carried you on, an infant in arms. Coming up from New York, you were.'

'Me?' Caleb said again. Gaslight reflected in the man's small eyes and glinted on his bald head. There was a twist of malice to his lips. Caleb, recognizing it, was as much bewildered by that as by the words that made no sense to him.

'That's how it was,' Hal Davis went on. 'It was you all right. A few weeks old, as I made it then. And fed by the matron every few hours. Boiled milk, she gave you. From a bit of cotton to replace the teat you wanted and couldn't have.'

Caleb felt his cheeks begin to burn. He didn't know why, but he was suddenly frightened. All he wanted was a reason to climb the ladder, to get away from the glint in the old man's eyes.

But he had no excuse. He watched as Peter threw a last roll, and crowed over his triumph. The men laughed and pushed his winnings toward him.

Peter got to his feet. 'Another night perhaps?'

The men agreed. Hal Davis said, 'Come down whenever you want,' and looked hard at Caleb. 'But you don't have to tell your father everything you do, do you?'

Caleb said nothing to that. He and Peter climbed out of the forecastle. When they were back on deck, Peter asked thoughtfully, 'What was the old man talking about?'

'I don't know.'

'Weren't you born in Fall River?'

Hot color rushed into Caleb's cheeks. His gray eyes darkened. 'I was. Of course I was.'

'Then I wonder what you were doing in New York. And why you came back without your mother.'

Caleb shrugged. 'Who knows?'

'Perhaps he's made a mistake,' Peter suggested. 'He's old enough to be fuzzy in the head.'

Caleb nodded, but didn't answer. He didn't want to talk about it any more. He wished Peter would go away.

Later, in his stateroom, he asked Kin, 'We were both born in Fall River, weren't we?'

Kin didn't look up from his book. 'Sure.'

'We used to go on the *Metropolis* a lot, didn't we?'

'I don't remember,' Kin said. 'Maybe we did and maybe we didn't.'

Amy reared up. Her black braids hung on her small shoulders. Her eyes were bright. 'I remember the *Metropolis*.'

The boys ignored her. She sighed, burrowed beneath the blanket, and soon fell asleep.

In a stateroom on a deck below, Parish listened while Peter recounted his adventure in the glory hole. It was the kind of thing Parish would have done himself at the same age, and it didn't trouble him that Peter had made some small winnings from the deckhands who were willing to take that risk.

Then Peter said, 'That man, Hal Davis, is peculiar. He was making a big thing about knowing Caleb when he was an infant and came up from New York.'

'Came up from New York?' Parish's narrow face grew

thoughtful. 'What was he talking about?'

'I don't know. But that's what he said. And something about boiled milk.'

'I've a notion the man's a sot,' Parish said casually. And then, 'What did Caleb say?'

'Nothing. He just turned red and stared.'

It was two weeks later, a hot cloudy afternoon with a sultry wind coming off Mount Hope Bay. Parish's meeting with Betty Gowan Raleigh was entirely accidental. He had ordered a piano from New York, and it was to be shipped up to Fall River for him. He needed a team, a heavy wagon, and several strong men to bring it to his house on Highland Avenue. He went to Raleigh Hostelry to make the arrangements, and Betty was there, waiting for George to finish his business.

Parish knew her as soon as he saw her. She was close to fifty now, with silver strands in her modishly dressed dark hair, and a plumpish figure. But she had remained remarkably pretty. He smiled at her and told her so.

She colored, introduced him to George.

'We, Betty and I, go back a long way,' Parish said easily, sizing George up with a quick glance.

George Raleigh had filled out, but he still moved with grace. He was forty-six. His once long and once blond mustache was trimmed and white, and his hair was shorter too, though full over the ears. He had had to work at convincing Betty, when he met her at church, that he wasn't the same man who had been a bounty hunter in his youth. But it was true. He'd not gone home after he came to Fall River. He served in no army. He never spoke of his past, nor thought of it even. That life and place seemed far away. He had worked hard and married and minded his own business. And after his wife died, he raised his son alone. He and Betty were happy together and he was good to her and her Davey.

George looked Parish up and down slowly. The man seemed dry, too spare to have juice. With a wink at Betty, a grin at Parish, George said, 'My wife and I go back a long way too.' He was referring to their first meeting, when he had come to the house on High Street to find the two runaways already en route to Boston and freedom.

Parish didn't understand. But Betty did. She smiled, moved away, while the men discussed their business together. Listening, she thought how prosperous Parish seemed: his fine clothes... the gold-headed Malacca cane. And now a piano to come up from New York. It had been different once. He'd begged a dollar from her. And there'd been the stolen silver, the money gone from the sugar bowl, the babies weeping... Amy's white face and torn shirtwaist. It gave Betty a peculiar quiver to see him again. She had been fond of him. She remembered it too well, although he seemed a different man to her now.

When the arrangements were made to have the piano picked up at the wharves and delivered to Highland Avenue, Parish thanked George, turned away to speak to Betty. 'May I give you a ride home? My carriage is outside.'

'Why, no,' she said. 'But thank you. I'll wait for George, and we'll go home together after doing some chores down street.'

'Ah, we have so much to talk about,' Parish said smiling.

'Maybe another time,' she told him. She didn't mean it, and promptly forgot about him.

But at the end of the week he appeared at her house, hat in hand. 'May I come in for a visit with you?'

She welcomed him because long before they had known each other, and she didn't know how to turn him away. But Parish's quick searching eyes made her uncomfortable, and she suddenly found herself remembering the touch of his lips on the nape of her neck.

After he'd put aside his hat and cane, he drew a dollar bill from his pocket. 'I haven't forgotten that I owe you this, along with my thanks.'

'Owe me?' she echoed.

'You loaned me a dollar on the day I left Fall River. A dollar in hard coin, as it was then. And it brought me good luck too.'

'I remember,' she said. 'And I'm glad for the good luck.'

'And you also remember the silver,' he told her.

She didn't answer.

'Of course you do.' His voice dropped, became confidential and regretful. 'And so do I. I look back on my behavior then and I cringe with shame. I was so desperate, Betty. I didn't know what I was doing. If my brother Marcus and Amy were alive, I'd go down on my knees to them.'

'What's past is past,' Betty said. 'Why think of it now?'

'Because I've lost so much time. There's such a terrible hole in my life. I wonder about so many things. For instance, I remember Augusta as the child Gussie. A beautiful little girl. But there was a baby in Amy's arms. Aria, I think her name was. Augusta tells me she died. But I don't know how, or when.'

'She left home when she was sixteen,' Betty said. 'She was less lucky than you were after your leaving. She died that same year in New York.'

'A pity. She was so young...'

'Yes,' Betty said briefly, then, 'But why do you care?'

'Family. It comes to mean something as you age, I suppose. In any event, that's why. Marcus was my only brother. His children are all that's left. Except for my own Peter.'

So Aria had died at sixteen in New York. And Luke had come home from there with an infant. But when was that? Parish asked himself.

At the end of his visit, when he had finished the tea she gave him and talked on of his plans for a little while, he paused as he was leaving to ask, 'The Wakefield boys, my grand nephews, how old are they?'

'Fourteen,' Betty said, 'or thereabouts. There's only some ten months between them. Kin's the older.'

Parish smiled, said goodbye, and was on his way.

He had no proof except Betty's nervousness, her suddenly wary eyes and voice. It was enough for him. There was something odd about Caleb Wakefield's origins. And Luke had brought an infant home from New York only weeks after young Kin was born. No proof, but an inward certainty. Caleb was Aria Wakefield's bastard.

What he didn't know was that Peter had overheard the whole of the conversation with Betty, and had drawn the same conclusion Parish himself had drawn. The boy had arrived to meet his father at the carriage, as previously arranged. He'd come up to the house, and hearing the talk through the open window, had paused to listen.

When he realized his father was making his farewells, Peter retreated to the footpath, so he was there when Parish joined him.

Still, Caleb would probably never have learned the truth

except that one Saturday, at twilight at the end of summer, he and Kin had been throwing a ball back and forth in the yard. The ball went spinning past Caleb and through the open door of the stable, to disappear in the shadows within. Caleb went after it, and found Peter bending over Amy, holding her in his arms, and kissing her hard on the mouth.

Caleb said through gritted teeth, 'Let her go.'

Peter pushed Amy away, and stepped back. 'I've been trying.' He grinned. 'Your small Amy can be a leech.'

Caleb glanced at Amy. 'Go inside.'

'I think you misunderstand,' Peter said quickly.

'Go inside,' Caleb repeated to Amy.

'Mind your own business,' she flared. 'Cousin Peter loves me. And I love him. And when I grow up, we're going to be married.'

'You're only ten years old. It'll be a long time before you get to marry anybody.'

'That's what you think,' Amy retorted. 'You're not Papa. You can't tell me what to do.'

'I can tell Papa,' Caleb answered, 'and let him decide if he wants Peter to kiss you hidden away like this.'

Peter's temper boiled over. He didn't like being unjustly accused, and he didn't like Caleb's ordering him about. He demanded coolly, 'What's all this to you? Why do you care so? She's not your real sister. How could she be? You weren't even born here. You came up from New York just after Kin was born.'

Caleb heard Hal Davis's words in his mind: *When your father carried you on, an infant in arms. Coming up from New York, you were. A few weeks old as I made it then. And fed by the matron every few hours ...*

'Or is it that you want her for yourself?' Peter asked. 'Is that it?'

'You're disgusting!' Caleb yelled. 'How can you talk like that about Amy?' Even as he launched himself at Peter, the older boy's words sank in. 'Of course she's my sister,' he yelled. But was she? If he'd been brought from New York – was he Caleb Wakefield, or someone else? Damn Peter, damn him! For what he'd said as well as what he'd done to Amy.

She ran to the house, weeping. She was frightened now. Peter had been teasing her. Suddenly she'd stepped close to him, and wrapped her arms around him, and gone on tiptoe so she could press her mouth to his. She had held on tightly while he struggled, laughing, and tried to put her aside. Suppose he told? What if Papa heard? And Mama? How could she explain what she felt?

Kin rushed in to try to stop the fight. Peter was the older, the larger, but Caleb had the strength of rage and terror. He wanted to destroy Peter's words, and Peter with them. He knocked Peter to the ground and flung himself on top, pummeling with doubled fists at Peter's face. No, no. It wasn't true. It wasn't. It couldn't be. Amy *was* his sister. He was Caleb Wakefield. He had to be! A great gout of blood poured from Peter's mouth. He lashed out with booted feet.

Kin shouted. He bent to grab at the two struggling figures, and was himself kicked and slammed off his feet.

The boys were finally separated by Luke, who seized both, pulled them apart, and lifted them up to stand before him. 'What's this?' he demanded.

Caleb and Peter slid sideways looks at each other. Caleb couldn't speak. His chest heaved. There was a bleeding scratch on his face; his eyes were too bright, silvery yet shadowed. *Born in New York. Not Amy's brother. Nor Kin's. Not Luke's son. Not Augusta's.* The words rose and fell in his mind. Pounding drumbeats of pain.

It was Peter who finally spoke. He felt foolish for having blurted out what he knew. He was close to a grown man. He ought to have laughed at Caleb's unjust accusation. He ought to have made Amy explain that it was she who had so suddenly slipped her arms around his neck and pressed his mouth with hers. Instead, he'd let himself be stampeded. He didn't know what Luke would say if he told the truth, but he knew his own father, Parish, would be coldly amused at him, and in the end, angry if he were banned from the Wakefield house.

'It's nothing,' Peter said softly. 'I'm sorry. I oughtn't to have fought Caleb.'

'Nothing,' Luke repeated, watching Caleb's expressionless face.

The boy concealed his relief. Nobody need know what Peter had said. Nobody need ever talk of it. Then it hadn't happened.

It wasn't real. He nodded too.

'If it's nothing,' Luke went on, 'you must be friends again.'

'Of course,' Peter said. It was his fault, and he would somehow make it up to Caleb, even though he'd been so unjustly accused.

'Yes,' Caleb said, thinking that it didn't matter that it was Peter who had told him, only that someone had.

His anguish didn't show on Caleb's face. There was no way for Luke to guess that the boy was shaken to his very soul. Why had Peter said he wasn't Amy's brother? If he wasn't, then what was he? How could he have been born in New York, brought to Fall River as an infant? And why, why, did the possibility that he wasn't Luke's and Augusta's son seem true to him when it was most certainly a lie?

Always, before, he had been like Marcus, his grandfather. Open in his feelings, quick in his temper. Fast to anger, fast to forgive. Now he became a brooder, quiet, withdrawn. Now he took solitary walks on the bank of the Taunton River, wandered the roads of Bogle Hill and Corky Row, and then spent sleepless hours listening to the wind sigh in the eaves.

The change in him came in such small steps and so gradually over the days that no one connected it with the fight he had had with Peter. That, it was considered, was over with and done. It was forgotten.

But by autumn, when the creepers were turning scarlet on the fences and the maples golden, Luke realized that the boy was unwontedly silent at the supper table, and that he no longer went down with him to see the ships off at sailing time. He blamed it on Caleb's age. The boy was nearing fifteen. It was a time of many changes, of dreams and fears. A burdensome time.

Augusta saw it and was troubled. She knew that Caleb was growing up. But still – still – there was an uneasiness in her she couldn't explain. Even in growing up from a child into man a person remained true to his nature. Where had his sudden high color gone? Where his heavy walk and quick temper? Why did she feel, always, as if he were a top that was wound too tightly?

When she spoke of it to Luke, he said, 'Yes, yes, I see it. But it's the time.'

'And Kin? I see no such changes in him, although he's the older.'

'Each one acts in his own way.'

'We must do something.'

'Gussie, Gussie, it's always the same with you.' Luke smiled to take the sting out of the words. '"We must do something," you say. As if something can be done. In this case, it cannot. So let it be. He'll grow through it and come out the other side.'

'He's suffering.'

Luke smiled at her again. 'So have we all.'

But that didn't matter to Augusta. Caleb mustn't suffer, not if she could help it. If others had, then that was wrong and a pity. Someone ought to have helped them, too. It was not in *her* nature, Augusta told herself, to sit by and do nothing.

So one evening, when Luke was gone to New York, and Kin and Amy were occupied at a game of chess, and Caleb stood staring out of the window, she asked that he come to the parlor to help her wind skeins of wool into balls.

It was the first week of November. James A. Garfield had just been elected president, and Sarah Bernhardt was about to begin her American tour by appearing at Booth's Theatre in New York City.

Augusta planned to talk first of these events as a way of setting him at ease.

When he came, soon after, to join her, he stood in the doorway watching her. The lamplight made her hair gold. Her face seemed young. She realized he was there, and looked up. She smiled, her dimples showing. 'Thank you, Caleb.'

He looked about him. 'The wool?'

She gestured to the table. 'It can wait a minute. Sit down.' She patted the settle beside her.

But he sat on the carpet at her feet, and looked up at her, waiting.

She saw that his eyes – eyes so like Luke's that their silver gaze brought a breathlessness to her – didn't quite meet her own. She forgot the just past election and the coming Bernhardt performance. She said softly, 'Tell me what's wrong?'

He was silent, choked. Her directness had caught him by surprise. He had thought to help her wind wool. He had planned no words; he didn't know the right ones. If what Peter said was true, then his father and mother had deceived him all his life. He wasn't a Wakefield, a Kincaid. He wasn't anybody.

He didn't belong here, nor anywhere else. He was a fraud as he fell asleep, whispering to himself the names of the lights between Fall River and New York. A fraud when he trod the decks of the *Bristol* and the *Providence*. A fraud when he stood in the wheelhouse with the pilot and watched the approach to the Fall River wharves while the ship's whistle blew. A fraud when he rode home past the mills as their big windows began to glow with light.

He had always known there was something different about him. His father wasn't the same to him as he was to Kin. It had been a fact since his first aware moment. And it was what made it so easy to believe Peter.

Now Caleb slowly shook his head. He just didn't know the words.

'You're very nearly a man,' Augusta said. 'There's nothing in you, or in your thoughts, we can't speak about. I don't wish to intrude on your privacy, believe me. But you're troubled. I see it. So I too am troubled. You must trust me to help.'

'Help?' he cried. 'How can you help me?' And then he burst out, 'But just tell me, why do people tell lies?'

'Lies?' Her face was thoughtful, her voice calm. But inside, her heart had begun to beat more quickly. Lies. What was in his mind? She went on, 'Of what sort do you speak? There must be different reasons for different lies.'

He looked down at his knobby hands. 'I don't know.'

'There are lies out of fear. To hide a wickedness. There are lies out of love. To protect someone dear. There are lies out of greed.' When he said nothing, she said, 'You ask about a specific lie, don't you?'

He felt the shaking begin anew inside. Ever since he'd first heard the words from Peter, the same shaking had come and gone. It rattled his bones and made his heart jump. When it stopped he felt for a little while as if he were dead.

'Don't you?' she said softly, leaning toward him.

'Yes.' He drew a deep breath. He wanted to go on, to tell her. But it was too hard. He couldn't say the words. He couldn't get his tongue to move them out from behind his teeth. He didn't have the strength to form them.

'Was it, perhaps, a lie that was actually never spoken? Perhaps a lie that was lived?'

'Yes,' he said again, and the color rushed suddenly, shockingly, into his face.

For an instant he was her old Caleb again, like her father, showing his feelings. She expected the boy to leap up now, and bellow and stamp about the room, shaking the floor, while he shouted his accusations at her.

Instead, Caleb remained seated, and as the color faded, he seemed to shrink, retreating into obdurate silence again.

So she knew. Her question had come from the deepest part of her. From an old fear that this would happen. That one day she and Luke would be called to account. She and Luke. For they had done it together. They had lived the lie and brought Caleb to live it with them. They had called the boy 'son,' but never said, 'You are *our* son.' She had taught him to call her 'Mama' but never said, 'I am your mother.' She slid down from the settle to sit close beside him, her gown bunching up around her. She put a slender hand on his shoulder. 'You can say to me anything you must, Caleb. You can ask of me anything you must.'

'There was someone on the ship – I heard him say . . . that he had known me when I was first born – when Papa brought me from New York.' Eyes fixed on her face, watching, distrustful. '. . . It would mean that you're not my mother.'

Her fingers tightened into his shoulder. She said calmly, 'But I am your mother, Caleb. It's true. It's true, I tell you. It's also true that I did not bear you from my body. But in every other way there can be, I've been a mother to you. I've loved you, taken care of you. You're a part of me. And you've always been my son. You, my son. In every way that matters.'

So his last blind hope was gone. Without knowing it, he had wished for a denial. He winced and nodded at the same time. 'You didn't bear me. But you've given me my life. I understand that. But then who did bear me? Who are my parents?'

'We are your parents. Your father and I,' she answered.

'No,' he said hoarsely, his silver eyes agleam with held-back tears, 'no, I mean my real parents. I need to know the flesh and blood I come from.'

'We are,' she insisted.

'It isn't so,' he told her. 'It's what you want me to feel. And it's what I do feel, and shall always be grateful for it. But now I must know the rest of it, the truth.'

'I did not carry you in my body,' she said. 'That's all I can tell you.' She remembered the day Luke had brought the infant home and put him into her arms and his small head had snuggled to her breast as if he belonged there.

'And my father?' Caleb was asking. 'Do you know who he is?'

She was silent for a long while. Knowing so much, the boy should know the rest of it. But she couldn't bring herself to speak. She couldn't force herself to tell him of Aria. She would never make true what she had only surmised and made herself forget. At last she said, 'I cannot talk of it.'

No matter what he said, that was what she answered. Finally he understood that she would not give in.

Before he went to bed, he kissed her.

The next morning, when the *Providence* docked, Caleb was waiting at the foot of the gangplank. He was very pale, with dark rings under his eyes, and his mouth tight. There was, in that moment, nothing of the boy about him.

Luke, still on the main deck, saw him and hurried down to the wharf to ask quickly, 'What's wrong? Is everything all right at home?'

Caleb nodded. Later, when Luke's chores were finished, they rode in the direction of home together. The mill whistles had just signaled the start of the working day. The roadways were nearly empty. He pulled up near a bridge.

'Caleb?' Luke asked.

The boy turned. Silver eyes met silver eyes. He said, his voice harsh and shaking, 'Mama is not my real mother. I know that. I asked her. And she has told me. And now I ask you. Who were my parents? Why did they abandon me to you? Why did they not want me?'

Luke, taken by surprise, felt turned to stone. The scar on his face colored. His hands became big fists on his knees. The past was risen up and on him. He didn't know what to say. At last he asked, 'Where did you hear of this?'

'What does it matter? Isn't it enough that I know? That I must learn the truth and I ask you for it?'

'We are your family. We love you,' Luke answered. 'Isn't *that* enough?'

Slowly Caleb shook his dark head. 'I must know.'

'Caleb . . . leave it be. There are some things in life that can't be explained.'

How to explain to this child, to this boy not yet fifteen, what it was that turned a man mindless? How explain that he could love one woman and still implant his seed in another woman's body.

'I can't leave it be,' Caleb was saying. 'Who is my father, my mother? Where are they now?'

Your mother's in her grave, Luke thought. And your father sits beside you.

He drew a deep breath. 'I'll say only this. I am your father. *I* am. Can't you see it? When you look at me, you see yourself. When I look at you, I see myself. Accept that and be content. Nothing is changed. You are my son.'

'You're my true father?'

'I swear it.'

Caleb nodded, turned away. He snapped the reins. The horses snorted, went on. He said nothing more on the drive. He was testing the idea of it. Balancing it against what he felt. Was he Luke Wakefield's son? He didn't know. When they arrived at the house, he went inside and, avoiding the others, went immediately to bed.

Luke told Augusta about the boy's questions. She asked, 'Did he believe you?'

'I don't know,' Luke answered. 'I couldn't tell.'

'I'm frightened for him,' Augusta said softly.

'So am I, God help me. And him.'

She waited for a moment, thinking before she spoke, then suggested in a near whisper, 'Perhaps this is the time, the best there'll ever be, to tell him all of it.' She didn't want to hurt Luke. Only for Caleb's sake could she force herself to look into Luke's face and say those words.

The scar at his temple darkened. His face grew hard. Within, he wanted to weep. For what he had done to Augusta, to Caleb. Aloud, he said, 'I can't. I've told him I'm his father. That's all he needs to know.'

Chapter 18

In early 1881 the New York, New Haven and Hartford Railroad and the steamboat companies that serviced the Boston to New York runs ended their three-year rate war by fixing the one-way fare for passage at four dollars per person. The Fall River Line was party to that agreement.

By late June, when the *Providence* steamed slowly away from the wharves, passenger travel was higher than ever. The ship carried a full complement, and her holds were loaded. The waters of Mount Hope Bay were dyed crimson by the sunset. Overhead the gulls wheeled and shrilled, diving into the pink lace of the ship's frothy wake.

Inside, the gaslit chambers were already aglow with light, and from the saloon there came the first sounds of music.

Willie Gorgas looked at the well-dressed passengers who moved around him, listened to their cultivated speech, and began to feel that maybe he had made a mistake. This was enemy ground now. He shouldn't have brought his fight here. Ellie had told him not to do it, but he'd ignored her. He had to see young Willie. And it was his right. He was young Willie's father. The boy couldn't pretend it wasn't so. Once Willie had wanted the boy to be on the other side – to have the wealth and power that would put him there. It no longer mattered. It had lost him the boy. He began to feel a deep burning hatred for the pretty women in their big feather-trimmed hats and tiny belted waists, with silken hands bejeweled with rings, who politely averted their eyes from his one-armed body as they passed him by. He wanted to smash the men accompanying them, tall and straight and whole, in their narrow trousers and fitted coats.

Ellie had said, 'Wait, Willie. It'll be all right. Just give William time.'

But Willie had already given him time. He hadn't been able to wait any longer. It had been five long years. He'd made sure the boy had everything he needed to continue his schooling. Even though he'd wanted him to begin with the inns and learn them the right way. The inns: the Fall River Gorgas Inn, the New Bedford Gorgas Inn, the Boston Gorgas Inn. All for young Willie – an empire built slowly by a runaway from the Carpathian Mountains... but all for young Willie.

Now Willie leaned his one elbow on the ship's railing. He was still a big man, burly in the shoulders and heavily muscled in the back, but at fifty-one, he was becoming stooped. There were times when the stump of his left arm ached so badly he could hardly stand it. His beard was black and white, his dark eyes sunken. The lines in his face were become caverns. He dressed well. His Ellie had seen to that and it had become a habit with him. Still he had a shaggy unkempt look. His trousers bagged at the knee; his cravat was never properly tied. How could it be, he asked himself when he noticed. It was a two-hand job, and he had only one. But actually it was because he didn't care.

All he wanted was for things to work out the way he had planned them, and he wondered why they didn't...

They'd gone to New York together, just the two of them, to buy clothes for young Willie. A good boy, handsome, strong, and sensible. At least that's what Willie had thought. He'd been all right in every way. He hadn't argued when Willie told him two years at Harvard was enough. That it was time to stop and make a start in the business.

But when they got home, sitting in the kitchen, with Ellie serving them a big breakfast, the boy had said, 'Papa, I'm sorry. I'm going back to school. I want to finish college.'

'I need you to help me.'

'I'm going to finish school,' the boy said stubbornly. 'Then I'll be ready, I promise. As soon as I graduate. I know what I'm doing. I know what I want. You'll see that I'm right.'

'You've got enough schooling,' Willie growled.

William's mouth tightened. He shook his dark hair. There was a glint in his dark eyes. More than ever he looked like his father. But there was a smoothness to him. His hands were uncalloused: they'd never pitched manure from a stable; never shoved crates across the wharves; never polished brass, nor secured hawsers. Young Willie fit it. He looked like he

205

belonged. Old Willie didn't, and never had, and never would. He knew the difference. He was glad to see it and repelled by it at the same time.

Ellie had put platters of eggs and ham and toast before the two, and each time she came between them, she made small talk in her sweet voice, trying to divert them.

They both ignored her, stared at each other in angry silence.

At last William pushed back his chair and got to his feet. 'I'm sorry, Ellie. I don't want any more.' He looked at his father. 'I'm going, Papa.'

Willie got up heavily. His shoulders were bunched, his eyes flamed. 'No. No, you're not. You sit down and eat, and we'll talk.'

'Talk more? Why, what for? What's there to say?'

'So you understand.'

The boy answered, 'There's nothing to understand.' He turned toward the door.

Willie grabbed him, swung him back, shoved him against the wall. 'You listen.'

'You can't change my mind.'

'Listen!' Willie yelled, and slapped the boy hard across the face.

Ellie cried out.

Willie's breath rasped loudly in the silence that followed.

At last the boy said, 'That won't stop me either,' ducked around Willie, and ran from the room.

Willie was sorry. But it was too late. Within the hour William had gone. Days later there was a letter from Cambridge. William wrote that he didn't mean to go against his father, or hurt him and Ellie, but he had to finish college. Willie sent him money. It was acknowledged with thanks. Willie sent more money, and continued to. He had plenty. It was all for young Willie anyway. William wrote again, with thanks. But that was all there was between them. At first Ellie had said, 'Go visit him, Willie,' but, though he wanted to, he didn't. 'It's up to the boy,' he told her. Later Ellie began to counsel patience. 'Wait. See what happens. It'll be all right.'

Willie worked. He visited the inns. He dropped in on the whorehouses. Lottie Dimot got rich and fat and moved to a good hotel in New York. Willie found another woman to run her place. He made his payments and collections and did his banking. Life went on.

Finally, this week, Willie had seen the name of William Gorgas listed in the Fall River *Daily Herald*. The boy had graduated in the class of 1881. Though Ellie had once again cautioned him to wait, he immediately took the train to Boston and went on by hack to Cambridge. He hadn't been able to locate William. But he had overheard a group of graduates talking about the party they were having on the *Providence*. Old Willie decided that was how he'd see young Willie, and talk to him, and maybe be able to make things right again ...

But now he was beginning to wonder. What would William say? How would he act?

The answer to his questions came sooner than Willie expected. The ship had hardly cleared the Borden Flat light when young Willie, walking on the canvas-covered deck with three friends, came abreast of him.

For a moment, father and son stared at each other. Then William set his shoulders, seeming as if he would move on.

Willie said harshly, 'I've got to talk to you,' eyeing the three men with his son. They were beardless and without mustaches, as was the way now at Harvard, and wearing the best of fashion. Young Willie plainly belonged with them. Yes, he had joined the enemy.

He did not speak until, his face expressionless, he waved his friends away. Then, turning to his father, he asked, 'Is this meeting an accident? Or did you assume that I'd be aboard and chase me down?'

'I wanted to see you. I'm sorry for what happened. You know it. I don't have to say more. You're my son.'

'I'll talk to you later, Papa,' the boy answered. 'There's something I have to do first.' Hands doubled into fists, he walked away.

He was thinking, *I've got to tell her. Now, right away. She has to know*. But how? How? The question rankled. He was a grown man. A graduate of Harvard. But he still didn't know how to explain away his earlier lies. At the beginning he'd said he was an orphan. It had sounded plausible. A bank was trustee for his estate. It made so much sense he could almost believe it himself. Fall River seemed far away. Time seemed endless. But now he had to tell her.

'Gorgas,' her father had said. 'What kind of a name is that?' Others had wondered, William supposed. But they'd been too polite to ask. Not Mary English's father, though. He liked to say he was a relation, distant, of course, of the Cabots and Lowells and Lodges and Peabodys. More likely his family had sold their families yard goods. At least that was what William now comforted himself with. But he'd said then that it was Austrian, he thought, and a long way back, though he wasn't sure how long. His shrug suggested counts of the court, and secret love affairs with royalty. So much for Willie Gorgas with his hunched shoulders, and one arm, and heavy accent. And so much for Ellie, too, the plump cook and maid and keeper of the boardinghouse. William's shrug had been good enough to put John English off, and Mary too, William supposed, until they were safely married. Which was what he had wanted ...

Old Willie watched as William walked away. He was content. As far as he was concerned, he had made the beginning. But two hours later, when he went into the dining saloon, he froze in mid-step.

William sat at a small table, smiling over a centrepiece of fresh tea roses, at a woman. A child sat on the woman's lap. She had curly hair and dark eyes that he knew as well as his own, which had looked back at him from the looking glass for so many years. They *were* his own. William had a wife, a daughter.

Willie had never known about either. There sat a girl child, his granddaughter, a stranger to him, who was her flesh and blood.

Willie's gorge rose. The music faded. The glow of the room was shadowed. The laughter sounded as screams in his ears. He turned, stumbling, and bumped into a couple crowding up behind him. With a muttered apology he dragged himself away.

He knew William had seen him come in, and now watched him leave. But he had to be alone for a time. He stood in the shadows on deck until he had managed to empty his heart of rage. There was a reason. He'd understand once William explained. Finally Willie went to the purser's office and determined the number of William's stateroom, ignoring the man's attempt to make conversation.

William himself opened the door. He'd thought to prepare Mary, to tell her his father was on board, to describe him a little, so she wouldn't be too surprised. But he'd delayed. Now it was too late.

His father pushed him back, a hand at his shoulder, and looked beyond him to Mary, to the baby.

There was nothing to do but say lightly, 'Papa, I want you to meet my wife Mary.'

Willie stared at her, said nothing.

'And this is our daughter, Di-Di. Short for Diane, which is a name in Mary's family.'

The infant gave Willie a round unblinking stare.

In a voice that shook, Mary said, 'How do you do, Mr. Gorgas?' and turned to William to ask frigidly, 'Your father?' She was trembling. An icy knot formed in the pit of her stomach.

Willie ignored her. He demanded of William, 'What's this? How could you do it and not tell me?'

'Or me?' Mary echoed, although she wasn't referring to the same thing.

William shrugged, only answering her. 'You can see, Mary.' He indicated the shambling one-armed man, black and white beard unruly, gruff-voiced and foreign, who was still staring at them.

Mary held the baby tightly. She was a slender woman of twenty-four, wasp-waisted and large-bosomed. Her thick blond hair was rolled in intricate coils around her head. Her cheekbones were high, her nose patrician. Her eyes were a deep cold blue.

William said to his father, 'I was going to come to see you. I was going to explain. But later on.'

'I'm here. Explain now.'

'We married two years ago,' Mary said. 'Di-Di is a year old. Just in case you're wondering.'

'I do not wonder. The child is my granddaughter. Any fool can see that.' Willie pulled at his beard. 'It's a joy to know of her. I ask only, Why did you do this? Why? You said you wanted to finish school, and went back, and married.'

'I *did* finish,' William said quickly. He didn't explain that he had delayed his graduation for several years, to keep the money coming, to avoid facing his father.

'Yes. But... but to marry without telling me... to have a child...' Willie's eyes glanced sideways at the infant. 'Time wasted – Why?'

'I was going to tell you, Papa.'

'But you didn't. Not when you got married. Not when your wife had the child.' Willie's head went down. 'But I see. I understand.'

Mary Gorgas said nothing. She looked over Willie and through him and around him. It was as if he had suddenly disappeared.

'You'll come into the business the way we always said?' Willie asked suddenly. 'This foolishness of yours is over now?'

'Yes,' William answered. 'Of course I will.'

Mary Gorgas still didn't speak.

Willie knew what she was thinking as she looked down her straight nose at him as if she smelled some stinking thing that had suddenly appeared before her. He was a foreigner. Her handsome Harvard boy William was the son of a lousy foreigner named Willie Gorgas who, after all these years, could hardly speak good English. He couldn't strike at her, not with the big fist that no longer had the strength it had once had. He couldn't slap her as he had once slapped his son.

But he had words, broken words to be sure, still words he knew she could understand. His temper, always uncertain, exploded. His shoulders bunched. He rasped angrily, 'Don't sneer at me. My money bought the clothes you wear, and paid your rent. My inns, the Gorgas inns that I made by myself, and my whorehouses too, they are what you live off, even if you didn't know it until this minute. It's true. It's true, I say. So how are you better than me?'

William's breath hissed. Red flooded Mary's face; her arms tightened around the baby, and the child whimpered.

Willie looked once more at the infant, then backed from the stateroom, growling, 'Think about that, you two.'

As the ship moved into sudden fog not far from Newport, the foghorn sounded, low and mournful. Bells rang. The rhythmic splash of the paddle wheels slowed.

William listened for a moment, then looked back at Mary. 'I'm sorry,' he said one more time. 'I was wrong. I admit it. But I loved you. I love you now. I'm not sorry for that much.'

'You lied to me.' Mary paced the room slowly. Her gown swung from her bustle, whispering a counterpoint to her every movement. 'You lied, William. And if my father ever –'

'Do we have to tell him?'

'We *won't* tell him.' She glared at William. 'So, in the end, you'll make a liar of me, too.'

'Mary... Mary... think! Would you have married me? Be honest. Would you have?'

'No,' she said coldly. 'No. No. No.' Her voice broke. 'I wouldn't have. Not if I'd known. Although I love you.'

'Then you understand.'

She swung back to face him. Her mouth was pale, and her cheeks. Her cold blue eyes were like chips of ice cut from an Arctic lake. 'My understanding doesn't matter. My father must never know. And I don't want to. Do you hear me, William? I don't want to either. If I see that man again, if you allow him to come anywhere near me...'

'Then what do you want me to do?'

'The responsibility is yours. You make the decision you must. I have made mine. I will never see that man again. Nor will Di-Di.'

'Mary...'

'You must arrange it. I don't care how.'

He looked down at his hands. 'We're speaking of my father'

'Yes,' she said coldly.

Suddenly he raised his face. 'He's a wealthy man.'

'I don't care to hear about it. Whorehouses.'

'Do I give it up and have nothing?'

'It's your decision.'

'If I do, then what will we have?'

'*You'll* have nothing indeed.' She gave him a tight-lipped smile. 'I love you. But if we can't have a marriage, then I'll return home to my father.'

'Mary!'

'You must decide.'

'Do you want me to give it up?'

'It's your responsibility,' she said. 'I've told you. You're the

211

liar. Now mend your handiwork.'

He spent the night sleepless, thinking about it, twisting it this way and that. He saw no answer. He had to have the money. Mary would never change her mind. He knew her well enough to know that once she set her heart on something, it was useless to argue. It was the means she had used to force her father to allow her to marry him. She would use those means again, this time against William himself.

He found his father at breakfast. The ship was docked. There were passengers leaving. But Willie sat over his coffee, staring into the smoke from his cigar.

'May I join you?' William asked.

The older man nodded.

That morning William looked older than his age. His face was gray, his hands unsteady. He said, 'I have to talk to you.'

'Sure.'

'It was a shock to Mary. What you said.'

'Sure. And *I* shocked her, too. But seeing her, the baby, that was a shock to me.'

'I'm sorry, Papa.'

'You keep saying that. You're sorry. To her. To me. What does it get you?'

'Not much.'

'Then maybe you better not say it.'

William leaned forward. 'I have to know. What are you going to do?'

'Do?'

'About me.'

'What makes you think I'm going to do anything about you?'

'I know you're angry. I know I've hurt you.'

'So what?' Willie rasped. The boy was all Willie had wanted to be, dreamed of being. He said quickly, 'I'm going to give you the inns, lock, stock and barrel. It's not what I expected. I figured we'd work on them together, you and me. We'd build more and more of them. But you have a different plan. Okay. Do what you want. They'll be yours.'

'And you?' William breathed.

Old Willie grinned. 'I've still got the whorehouses, and I'll keep them.'

A wave of nausea swept William. Whorehouses. Mary's lips,

212

white and twisted, throwing the word at him in a harsh whisper. 'Whorehouses, William. If my father knew...' And then, 'I don't care what happens. I'll never see that man again. Do you understand me? Never, never, never!' And William's quick whisper, 'All right, Mary. Whatever you want, I'll do. I promise. Whatever you want.'

'I could divorce you for your lies, William. But I'd have to say what lies they were. And I couldn't bear the shame of it. I couldn't, not for myself, nor for Di-Di. She must have everything, and that means background too.'

He'd said, 'I swear nobody'll ever know, Mary.' Her mouth thinned. 'You're right. No one will know.' No one. Except William. And Mary. And old Willie.

William looked his father in the face. 'Thank you, Papa.' There was nothing more to say now. He got to his feet slowly, and slowly walked away. At the door, he stopped, turned to look back. Old Willie leaned his one elbow on the table, his head bowed over the big fist under his chin. Fighting another wave of nausea, William stumbled out to the deck, and up the stairs, his bootheels ringing on the iron treads. He must tell Mary quickly that their future was secure. Di-Di would have everything.

Behind him, he heard a high-pitched yelp of pain. He cast a fleeting glance in that direction, then hurried on.

'Clumsy little idiot! What's wrong with you? What were you looking at?' Mabel Graystone-Fields demanded as she dragged at Bennet's arm.

He hung against her, a dead weight, his face paling.

'Come on,' she said again. 'What's wrong with you?' She was a formidable sight in rusty black, with a cloak around her, a darned place on her gray shirtwaist.

Tears stood out on Bennet's cheeks. He had been mesmerized by the long slim legs moving ahead of him, how they had scissored up the steps. He didn't know what had happened. He gulped and choked but didn't move because he couldn't.

Arthur, behind the two and a few steps down, always trailing, an appendage often overlooked, saw what was wrong. Bennet's foot had slipped through the open riser. The harder Mabel tugged at him, the more off-balance he became, the tighter the

213

trapped foot was wedged. Arthur said, 'Wait, Mabel,' and would have gone on to explain, but she cried, 'Wait! That's what you always say!' and with a grim laugh, 'For what?'

'Let the boy be. Don't pull at him. His foot is caught.'

'Caught? How?'

Bennet gasped. 'In there. You see?' and pointed.

She jerked away from Arthur. 'Do something!' And to Bennet, 'Stop crying. It can't be all that bad. It's nothing. Nothing. Clumsy idiot! Thirteen years old and look at you!'

Arthur knelt. As gently as he could, he turned Bennet's foot. The boy screamed and retched. Mabel's voice grew shriller as she continued her tirade. Against Arthur, against Bennet. Finally, she cried, 'I shall sue! The first thing I do when we return to Boston is to file a suit!'

Bennet wept harder. His plump shoulders shook, and his fat body trembled. Even when Arthur had finally managed to slip his foot from the boot, and then to work the boot free, he cried and gasped and shuddered.

'Now stop,' his mother said. 'You see? There's nothing wrong. Only a bit of a red bruise. It'll be gone by tomorrow.'

'But it hurts.' Bennet leaned all his considerable weight on his right foot. 'Mama, it hurts something terrible.'

'There's nothing wrong,' she said firmly. But even as she spoke, the foot swelled observably.

'I think there may be a doctor on board,' Arthur said. 'Perhaps it ought to be looked at.'

'Looked at!' Mabel seized Bennet's arm. 'For what? It'll cost three dollars. Maybe even more.'

'I'll pay for it,' Arthur said wearily.

'You'll pay,' she sneered. She dragged Bennet, who hopped and staggered and wept, up the stairs. 'You'll pay?' she shouted over her thick shoulder at Arthur. 'With what? You don't have a penny left and you know it. You eat by my grace. And travel by my grace. And my money!' All this at the top of her lungs, a great robust shout heard by dozens of passers-by.

Arthur endured it, his thin face set. She was a woman of pure vitriol, and everything she touched she burned. He felt nothing for her now, and wondered if he ever had. But there was Bennet.

In the stateroom, the boy sank down, keening. Mabel washed his face with a cloth soaked in cold water. She busied herself at

214

her luggage and drew out three bottles of liniment. She rubbed all three foul-smelling stuffs on Bennet's swollen foot, saying meanwhile, 'There's nothing wrong. A bit of a bruise. Oh, what a baby you are. Thirteen, and listen to you!'

Arthur watched, listened, but said nothing.

He said nothing the next day when, after they landed in New York, Mabel dragged Bennet from bank to bank, from Wall Street to Longacre Square, the boy white-faced but no longer weeping, no longer complaining, limping along beside her while Arthur trailed after.

'You see,' Mabel said that evening as they returned to the *Providence* for the journey home. 'You see, it's better now, isn't it?'

Bennet nodded.

'I told you. The best thing is to walk on it. I was right, wasn't I?'

He nodded again. But the pain brought vomit to the back of his throat, and when Mabel announced that she was hungry and they would eat the moment the ship sailed, he groaned aloud. Arthur groaned with him, but silently.

On July 2, 1881, President James A. Garfield was waiting for a train in the Washington, D.C., Station when he was shot by an assassin named Charles J. Guiteau, who was captured on the spot.

Mabel Graystone-Fields heard the news while on her way to the Old Colony Steamship Line's office in Boston. She shrugged, hurried on. Once there, after forcing the excited passenger agent and the office manager into a corner, she presented her complaint of responsibility in the injury of Bennet's foot against the steamship company, the captain, pilot, officers, and crew of the *Providence*.

On September 19, President Garfield died of his injuries. A day later, Chester A. Arthur took the oath of office and assumed the presidency.

At the end of that week Mabel Graystone-Fields returned to the Old Colony office to inform the passenger agent that she had just filed a suit for civil damages of $15,000 against the company.

The trial of Charles Guiteau began on November 14. He was

convicted on January 24, 1882, and executed on June 30 of that year. By then Mabel had received a draft of $5,000 in settlement of her uncontested claim in the matter of the injury to Bennet's foot on the *Providence* and had already invested it in a good piece of land on Aquidneck Island.

But on her very next voyage on the *Providence*, her triumph became her defeat. After a meal of New England boiled dinner, with a side order of baked beans, topped off with bread and fruit pudding, Mabel retired to her stateroom alone, wishing now that she had brought Bennet with her instead of leaving him in Boston with Arthur. Sighing, she disrobed and put on a capacious sleeping gown. She washed in tepid water, then pulled the chamberpot from beneath the bed. As she settled to use it, the *Providence* moved into the open sea at Point Judith. The ship rose and dropped suddenly. So did Mabel. The chamberpot shattered beneath her. With a scream she leaped up, clutching her torn and bleeding buttocks. Weeping, cursing, she spent the rest of the night trying in vain to remove from her burning flesh two long shards that had pierced her.

At five o'clock in the morning, when the cabin attendant came to bring her the hot washing water she had ordered the night before, he found her pale and composed. She was dressed, standing against the wall. He saw the remains of the chamberpot and its contents staining the carpet, and two bloody towels. He saw how pale she was and how rigidly she stood. He asked, 'Madam, are you all right?'

Through clenched teeth, she answered, 'Yes, yes, go away.'

'I'm sure I can locate a doctor, madam.'

'No,' she gasped. 'I have no need.'

Plainly she had the need, but the attendant knew her too well to argue. He told the chief steward, who consulted with the purser, who examined the passenger lists. There were two passengers on board who were listed as doctors, but one was honorary and the other had a degree in religion; neither were physicians. The purser went up to the wheelhouse and spoke to the captain, who decided to see for himself.

Within moments he knocked at Mabel's stateroom door.

'Go away,' she yelled.

'I must see you,' he said firmly, and knocked once more as he went in. He took in the scene quickly. The broken chamberpot, the bloody towels. He said, 'Mrs. Graystone-Fields, you must have help.'

Her pale face became red. 'No.'

'I have a trained first-aid person aboard.'

'I will not have it.' She clung to the wall for support.

'You must.' He was thinking of the suit she had brought before, and what she would do now. 'I order you to allow yourself to be treated.'

'No one will touch me,' she cried.

'Very well. Then I shall write a statement describing what has happened here, and in the presence of the cabin attendant and the purser, I shall read it to you and then sign it. It will make clear that you, by your own carelessness, broke a Fall River Line chamberpot and cut your behind with it, and then, on being offered assistance and treatment, did willfully refuse it.'

With a shrill, 'How dare you?' and a groan of pain, she gave in, and lay face down on the bed.

The deckhand, waiting in the corridor, entered with hot water and bandages. The captain, smiling now within his beard, withdrew.

The ship docked an hour later. Immediately thereafter a quiet Mabel limped down the gangplank and walked with slow careful steps to where the Boston boat train waited.

Chapter 19

The first iorn-hulled ship to sail Long Island Sound was launched in June of 1883 by the Fall River Line. Her name was the *Pilgrim*. She had been designed by the eminent naval architect George Peirce at a cost of $853,000. Thomas Edison installed one thousand incandescent bulbs for the new electrical lighting, even to entwining strings of them around the two masts. There were sleeping accommodations for 1200 passengers and a grand saloon that easily held 1000 people. The decks were canvas-covered and all the corridors were thickly carpeted.

At the end of October the *Pilgrim* was waiting on the Fall River docks for the boat train from Boston, her flags flying, smoke stacks capped by smoke that spun away on the wind off Mount Hope Bay.

Augusta paused on the carriage step to look up at the ship. 'She's a beauty,' she said to her husband as he offered his hand to help her to the ground. A quick pulse beat in Augusta's throat. She felt a tingling of excitement go through her. She had already traveled on the *Pilgrim*, had explored the saloons and lounges, and stood in the wheelhouse with the captain and pilot, surveying Narragansett Bay as they sped toward Point Judith. Still the experience remained fresh to her, as wondrous as it had been in the beginning, on her first sailing thirty-one years before.

'It's going to be crowded,' Luke told her.

'That means you'll be busy,' Augusta said, laughing. 'But at least I'll have the best of company.' Amy, Kin, and Caleb were going with them on this trip.

The children scrambled down from the carriage, Kin as always laughing, Caleb not as eager as he once had been, and Amy surging forward, ready for adventure.

In a group they climbed the gangplank and went into the entrance hall. It was a large room, with a thick lush carpet; beautiful carved high-backed chairs of the finest mahogany were set around the paneled walls.

It was there that Parish greeted them. Peter was with him.

'I didn't know you'd be going to New York,' Augusta said.

'A last minute decision. We're to visit the Metropolitan. Peter's come down from school to see the production of Gounod's *Faust* with me.'

'You must be looking forward to that.'

Parish nodded at Augusta. His mustache was nearly white now, his face narrower than ever. He leaned heavily on his cane. 'We're both looking forward to it,' he answered.

But Peter said nothing. It was to please his father that he was going. At twenty years old, he was not much interested in opera, nor in his father's companionship, although they continued to share an avid interest in gambling. Except when they were playing cards, his father's presence was a damper. and even more so when the Wakefields were there. Still, Peter had hoped for this trip. He had found in recent years that Caleb was often an enthusiastic partner in his adventures.

Caleb never referred to the fight they had had, what Peter had told him then, never referred to Amy either. Now Peter allowed himself a quick look at her. Her thirteen-year-old body did not tempt him, although she had small perky breasts that showed through her pink shirtwaist, and her feet and ankles were beautifully trim. One day she would be a lovely woman. But now he was interested in something a little more mature. He wondered if Caleb were too, and with that in mind, said, 'Meet me for a walk on deck later?' before he and his father went off to their stateroom.

Caleb agreed with a nod.

Luke, as always busy, went first to speak to the captain, then down to the kitchens that served the dining saloon. Provisioning the *Pilgrim* was a complicated affair. For this trip they had taken on such staples as 500 quarts of milk, a barrel of flour, 60 pounds of coffee, 200 pounds of sugar, 270 dozen eggs, 2,200 pounds of meat, 300 pounds of fish, 40 pairs of fowl, 50 quarts of berries, and 300 loaves of bread. They had also loaded 3,000 oysters, 1,500 clams, and five dozen assorted game. After talking to the first cook and the butcher, Luke went in search of Jim Reilly, a new man on the ship.

Kin had left his mother to read in his stateroom. It was, for him, the best way to pass what he considered a boring journey. Amy had gone to the wheelhouse, and from there planned a systematic exploration of the various decks.

Augusta went down to the grand saloon. Already its new electric chandeliers cast a soft glow, lighting her russet hair and bringing out the green of her eyes. She sat alone, out of the way of the always shifting groups, and observed the scene, a smile deepening her dimples, her slender hands clasped in her lap. She wore a pale gray traveling suit that had high puffed sleeves. A large white bow nestled under her chin. Her hat, tipped forward over her brow, was pale gray too, and decorated with a single white feather.

She was like a lighthouse beacon to Jim Reilly. The instant he stepped into the lounge, his eyes moving in quick assessment of the people there, she caught his glance. He couldn't look away.

He didn't know her name, from whence she came, or where she was going. But in a single instant, he found himself breathless. He was a tall man, broad-shouldered but not heavy. His hair was dark brown, neatly combed, with longish sideburns and a small mustache. His collar was stiff, his cravat a dark blue. He had a quick smile that lit his blue eyes and softened the square line of his jaw. His was an Irish face, although he was American born, his parents having emigrated from County Cork as bride and groom.

After staring at Augusta for longer than he realized, he forced himself to turn away. He had a job to do. This was his first sailing on the *Pilgrim*. He had already familiarized himself with the ship. Now, by the time they left the Fall River wharves, he would have once again covered each deck. He'd have located whatever known problem makers there were. He'd have sized up the guests, in particular watching for any possible adventurer or adventuress too, who might be hoping to victimize the wealthy and prominent aboard. Even as he walked the length of the grand saloon, his gaze resting lightly here and there, he kept thinking of the beautiful woman he had seen, and wondering who she was . . .

The ship had made her stop at Newport. As she rounded Point Judith, the wind struck. In the dining room, there was the tinkle of glass and the scurry of stewards. The chandeliers in the grand saloon swayed, sending long dark shadows racing across the room. The music of the orchestra grew louder, covering the moans of the wind in the masts and guy lines.

In the staterooms, the pitchers rattled in the mahogany racks on the bulkheads. The chamberpots skidded along the floor, and the cupboard doors creaked and swung free.

The *Pilgrim* plowed steadily on; soon she passed the Block Island light and reached the Sound.

Augusta rose, preparing to retire. That was when Luke finally joined her, bringing Jim Reilly with him. He introduced the younger man, then went on, 'Jim's been with Pinkerton for several years. But he's new with the line.'

Jim Reilly smiled, took the hand she offered him. 'I'm glad to meet you, Mrs. Wakefield.'

'And I you. Welcome to the Fall River Line.' She didn't know that already he was in love with her. She saw a nice young man, a man some ten or twelve years younger than herself. She wondered if he were perhaps too nice for his job.

· He said, 'She's a beautiful ship. I'm happy to be working on her.'

'We're proud of the *Pilgrim*,' Augusta responded.

Luke explained Augusta's longstanding interest in the line. While Jim appeared to listen, he hardly took the words in. What did they matter? He was twenty-five years old, and for the first time in his life, he was in love. He had thought before that he had been, but always the feeling died. This time it was different. Already he knew that. And the woman was married. By the way she put a light hand on her husband's sleeve, Jim judged she was happily married as well. That seemed not to matter either. He was in love. Nothing of what he felt showed on his face. But when he had his few hours sleep that night, it was to dream of Augusta and to whisper soundlessly her name against his pillow.

At dawn that morning, the lighted *Pilgrim*, her masts sparkling with their glowing incandescent bulbs, sailed beneath the newly completed Wire-Bridge, which would later become known as the Brooklyn Bridge.

An hour later, Augusta was at breakfast in the dining room in the afterhold. There, too, the many chandeliers were aglow over the tables and serving counters. She and Amy were discussing their plans for the day. Amy wanted to go shopping on Fourteenth Street. Augusta suggested a visit to the Metropolitan Museum of Art in Central Park. Kin was with them, but plainly, his thoughts were not. Augusta was about to ask after Caleb when he finally appeared. There were dark circles under his bloodshot eyes; his face was pale. She looked at him, wondering if he were well. When he refused food, but asked only for coffee, and quickly, she asked, 'What is it, Caleb?'

He shook his head, didn't answer. She saw that his hand trembled when he picked up his water glass and emptied it at a gulp.

Later she understood. For when Luke joined them, he said, 'Caleb, I'd like to speak to you privately after your meal.'

Caleb flushed, nodded. He'd been stupid, and he knew it.

Naturally Luke would find out. How could he fail to? But Caleb hadn't been able to stop himself once he got started. Peter had said there'd be a girl for them. He'd been excited, waiting. Then Peter hadn't brought anybody. So they'd started drinking in Peter's stateroom. One glass of dark rum after another. And what then? Caleb wasn't certain. He had a faint recollection of being sick, and going out on deck. Being sick again. The wind in his face, his hands clinging to the rail. Somebody had helped him get to his stateroom, had even taken the brass key and unlocked the door for him.

He had stumbled inside, muttering to himself.

Kin had rolled over, groaned, 'Shut up, Caleb. You've woken me up,' and flung a book at him.

Caleb had sunk down on the berth. The door had closed softly. Who had done that? It was all faint in his mind. Who had found him at the railing? Where had Peter gone? What had Caleb done after he left Peter's stateroom?

A few minutes later, alone with Luke, he rubbed his hands together, then dug at his burning eyes. He felt like a child, not a man of seventeen.

Luke said, 'Are you better?' At Caleb's nod, Luke went on coolly, 'You certainly still look the worse for wear.' There was an unusual sternness in Luke's face and manner. He was troubled, wondering what exactly he ought to say.

Caleb shrugged. 'I didn't sleep well.'

'You ought to have slept very well indeed. You were very nearly unconscious, as I gather.'

'I was not,' Caleb retorted. And then, heatedly, 'And I hate your spying on me. I hate it.'

'Spying?' Now Luke's voice dropped to almost a whisper. 'What an odd word to use. I have friends on this ship, and you're known. You're my son.'

'But am I?' Caleb asked.

Inside, Luke winced, but he said softly, 'You are. I've told you.' And before Caleb could reply, he went on, 'My friends worry about you. And so do I.'

'There's nothing to worry about. I'm all right. You can see that, can't you?'

'I see nothing of the sort. And there's a good deal to worry about. You drank yourself close to insensibility. You're too

222

young for that, believe me. Start now and you won't survive to grow old. Where were you, Caleb?'

Caleb said nothing.

'You wouldn't have been served in the bar or lounges. Not to be brought to that condition. So you were drinking privately. And that's worse than anything.'

'Who's the friend that tattled on me?' Caleb demanded, thinking of Parish.

But he was wrong, and realized it when Luke said, 'It wasn't tattling. It's part of his job. You met him yesterday, which is how he knew you. Jim Reilly.'

'The ship's detective,' Caleb said contemptuously. 'Oh, I see, I see. He was trying to get on your good side.'

'He was doing us both a favor. It's the drinking privately that frightens me, Caleb. If you're with others, enjoying yourself, perhaps it's possible to overdo. You aren't so experienced that you'd realize what was happening. But to drink just for the sake of it –'

'I'm sorry,' Caleb said. 'It won't happen again.'

'You were with Peter, weren't you?'

'What does it matter?'

'I think you were.'

'All right, and what if I was?'

'He's three years older than you. He at least ought to know better. It's not the first time he's led you into unacceptable behavior.'

'I'm responsible for what I do,' Caleb retorted.

'If you want to call your behavior responsible.' Luke frowned at him. 'I wouldn't like to forbid you Peter's company. He *is* your cousin. Still, I can't allow him to corrupt you by his bad influence.'

'It's not Peter,' Caleb said stubbornly.

It was true. What Caleb did was from his own feelings, not his cousin's urgings. Ever since he'd learned that Augusta wasn't his mother, he'd felt a stranger in his family. When Luke said, 'I'm your father,' Caleb asked if it were so because he had to. He didn't quite believe it. He wanted it to be so, but wondered if it were. He wondered about his mother. That unknown woman who had carried him. He felt an alien, and knew he would always feel that way. He belonged nowhere.

The foundations of his life had been swept away. The ships that had once been his joy meant nothing to him now. Because he wasn't a part of them. Their history wasn't his. Augusta's, Kin's and Amy's . . . their history was theirs. But not his. More and more he was angry. It burned in him, only overflowing sometimes but always there, a constant pain from which he knew no relief. When he looked at Augusta, saw her smile, her direct gaze, he felt a sickness sweep him. It was all lies. His whole life was a series of lies, lived by him, told to him.

Luke said quietly, 'I hope you'll do better, Caleb. I'm proud of you. I love you. I want for you to have a fine and healthy life as a good man.'

With a pretense of shame, Caleb said, 'I'm sorry. I know it was wrong of me.'

Luke accepted the apology with a nod. 'If you're troubled, tell me of it. Let me help you. I will if I can.'

But what help could Luke give him? Caleb wondered. Could he give back to Caleb that lost innocence that came with learning the truth? Augusta wasn't his mother. Then who was? In the name of God, he thought, who was?

'I hope you'll remember our talk,' his father said. 'For if you show such behavior again, and have been with Peter, then I'll be forced to forbid you his company.'

A few months later, Luke proved he was as good as his word.

It was just before Thanksgiving. When Caleb was sure that Luke would be on the *Providence* that trip, he agreed to meet Peter on the *Pilgrim*.

Peter had brought with him two girls, tarts from Boston, who, he assured Caleb, would do whatever he wanted.

They were in the cabin together. Caleb wanted, and didn't want. He was a virgin still and fearful. But the wanting was stronger than the fear. His body ached with it, his pulses drummed. He didn't know where to start, or how, or what to say. Finally one of the girls disappeared with Peter.

The other, who said her name was Clara, said to him, 'Well, what about it?' and ran a long fingernail down his cheek.

'Wait,' he said thickly.

'God! What a baby,' Clara said, and flounced out.

Caleb sat and fumed, drank and fumed. Where had she gone? What was she doing? She was supposed to be for him. Peter had arranged it. Now Caleb wanted her under him, so he could feel her body and know what it was like. He was exploding for want of her, drunk and afire, when suddenly she came back, and said, smiling, 'Mad at me, sweetheart?'

He reached for her, and she began pulling at his cravat, and crooning, and pushing him down so she could lean over him, her mouth pressed down on his.

Now he was suddenly sickened. Her pinched face looked old to him. There was the smell about her of a man's soap, the smell of sweat, too. Her giggle was ugly and shrill. He said heavily, 'Go away.'

'You're scared,' she jeered, her long nails raking his face. 'What's wrong with you?'

He caught her wrist, held it so she couldn't scratch him. 'Quit it. Leave me alone.'

'Listen! Who do you think you are!' she shrilled. 'You're going to pay me, you know. Whether you do it or not!'

He reared up, thrusting her back. He couldn't stand the sight of her, the touch of her flesh. All he wanted was to be left alone.

'Damn you!' she cried, clawing at his face again.

He knocked her aside, and she yelped, tried to scramble to her feet. But he was on her, a red madness sweeping him, so that afterward he was never sure what had happened: why he had grabbed her and held her and hit her as hard as he could.

She screamed, doubled over. He let her go, and she tumbled to the floor.

As he stood staring at her, shivering, there was a knock at the door. He thought it must be Peter. He looked down at the girl again. At Clara. Blood on her mouth, her gown ripped. So still he thought she must be dead. Terror nearly felled him. Augusta, Luke. What would they say?

Another knock. He turned the key, opened the door.

Jim Reilly stood there, looking worried. He said, 'There's been a report...' and brushed Caleb aside, closing the door softly.

In a single step he knelt at Clara's side and touched his fingers to her throat. 'She's alive, thank God!'

Sobered now, Caleb thought, *She's alive! I didn't kill her!* He choked out, 'I hit her. I just – lost my head.' Then, unable to contain himself any longer, he leaned over the sink and was violently sick.

Jim revived Clara and led her outside, where he gave her

twenty-five dollars of his own money to help her forget her torn gown and swollen mouth.

Later, he had a few words with Peter Kincaid, and when the *Pilgrim* returned to Fall River, neither Peter nor the two girls were aboard.

But Caleb was, subdued, trembling when he remembered the red madness that had seized him, and fearful of more trouble to come.

Then, just after the new year, Augusta and Luke heard that Parish had been felled by food poisoning in New York. A few days later, he died. He was buried in Fall River at the start of the following week.

Caleb, along with the rest of the family, saw Peter at the Oak Grove cemetery, and afterward at the house on Highland Avenue. He seemed shocked but had himself well in hand. Soon after, he stopped to see the Wakefields, to tell them he was closing the house and returning to college to finish the term while he decided what he wanted to do next.

The trouble that Caleb had been expecting came in mid-February. He was returning home from school late one afternoon when a girl called to him from just across the road from the house. It had been snowing, but now it had stopped. The air was crisp, cold. The boulevard lamps flickered in the twilight.

'You, Caleb Wakefield,' the girl cried. 'Wait a minute,'

He stared at her, clutching his books.

'You remember me, don't you? Clara. From the ship.'

'Clara,' he said softly, and knew what was coming. He had been cold before. Now he was frozen to the bone.

'Me. And in the flesh.' She asked how he was, what he was doing, and when was he coming to Boston, where she saw Peter now and then, she informed him. When Caleb just stared at her and didn't respond, she seized his arm. 'I need some money, my friend Caleb. I know you can help me.'

'But I can't. I have no money,' he said hopelessly.

'You can get it. You have to.'

'Ask Peter.'

In fact, she had tried it on him, and he'd laughed, and told her to go to hell. She said to Caleb, 'You're the one who hurt me. So you have to help me. And I mean it. You hurt me a lot and I

226

need the money.' She was breathing hard now, clutching his arm.

'It's no use,' he told her. 'I can't.' He broke free of her, ran to the house. Inside, he heard his mother call to him, but he hurried to his room and hid there.

Clara went down to the wharves. Shivering, she asked in the line's office and was told where to find Luke. Within minutes, she had cornered him near the warehouses. She told him about the voyage on the *Pilgrim*, about Peter and her friend, and what had happened with Caleb. She demanded money. She didn't mention Jim Reilly.

Disgusted by what he had heard, Luke gave her fifty dollars and saw her on to the train for Boston.

It began to snow again as he walked along North Main Street. By the time he reached home, his hair was frosted white and he had a pain in his throat. He took off his greatcoat and hung it on the halltree, then went to warm his hands at the fire in the parlor. Augusta came to kiss him. She offered him coffee, and when he refused, returned to the kitchen to help Marge prepare supper. Luke sent Amy for Caleb. While waiting for him, he looked at the celadon lion on the mantel and took down the ivory dog to examine it, thinking of Marcus and wondering how he would have handled this situation. Sighing, Luke returned the small statues to their places. He wasn't Marcus. He must do what had to be done in his own way.

White-faced, Caleb listened as his father said, 'I had a peculiar encounter today,' and went on to describe it. And then added, 'She learned where you lived from Peter, of course. And you were brought together with her by Peter in the first place. This time I truly blame him more than I blame you. He's a person of the poorest judgement, and now that Parish is dead, there'll be no restraints on him, although there were few before. You're not much better than he is, Caleb, but I admit that I look for a little less from you because of your lack of experience. So – although I don't expect that the occasion to do so will arise frequently – I must forbid you to have anything to do with Peter Kincaid.'

This time Caleb didn't argue. It had nothing to do with Peter; he was sick at heart and ashamed. He didn't know how to explain what had happened to him. He knew only that always

always always at the back of his mind there were insistent questions. Who am I? Where did I come from? Who was my mother? Is Luke really my father? Why am I lost? There were questions. And there were no answers.

Two nights later, he leaned over sleeping Kin, and whispered, 'Goodbye,' and went to peek at Amy for a last look. Then, clutching his portmanteau, he went silently down the stairs past Augusta's closed door, stepped outside, and disappeared into the shadows of the silent, snow-covered street.

Chapter 20

This time it was Augusta who realized what had happened. It was noon, but dark outside. Thick snow clouds lay over the harbor and town. The smoke stacks of the mills belched black against the sky's gray, and the roadways gleamed with a thin skin of ice where they had been cleared.

Augusta came down to say, 'Luke, Caleb's not in his room. His bed hasn't been slept in. And no one has seen him since last night.' She sounded frightened and her eyes were shadowed with worry.

Luke understood immediately, but hoped he was wrong. Within hours, however, he knew that Caleb, like his mother Aria, had run away. And, as with Aria, it was impossible to find him.

They searched in New York and in Boston. They spoke to Peter. Jim Reilly spent days at it, and had the help of friends at Pinkerton's too, all to no avail.

Luke thought that he was living through a familiar nightmare, and knew now as he had never known before what Marcus and Amy must have suffered through the long sleepless nights and terrible imaginings, which, in Aria's time, had come to pass. Still, there was no way but to go on.

Augusta said, 'We're his family. He loves us, he knows we love him. We'll hear from him, Luke. He'll come back.'

'It's my fault,' Luke answered. By then he had told her about

Caleb's involvement with the girl from Boston, and what had happened thereafter. But when he spoke of guilt, he meant something else. They both understood that. Caleb had wrestled with resentment and bewilderment ever since he learned that Augusta wasn't his mother. All the boy had done since then stemmed from that shock to him. It had been Luke's insistence that led to their concealment of the truth. More, it had been by Luke's act of sin that Caleb had been born at all. 'It's my fault,' Luke repeated, burying his face in his hands.

Augusta stroked his hair. It was still dark, except for the narrow white streak that lay over his temple, but amid the dark there was now silver. She noticed it for the first time, just as, for the first time, she saw the lines in his face when he finally looked up at her and asked, 'But how can I change it?'

'You can't. And you mustn't blame yourself. No matter the excuse, Caleb was wrong with the girl. And wrong too to run away. When he's less ashamed, he will understand. We'll hear from him.'

At the end of the month Augusta read that a battered body had been found off the Massachusetts coast. She was frantic until she learned that it had been identified as one among the 103 people lost when the steamer *City of Columbus* was wrecked off the Gay Head light in January.

In October, the Naval War College was founded at Newport, and Augusta and Luke went to the formal opening ceremony. Both of them searched the crowd there for a glimpse of Caleb's face, and afterwards looked along the streets for him, too.

That spring, again in Newport, this time to see the famed Lillian Russell perform, Luke saw how Augusta's eyes scanned the theater audience and knew what face she was looking for.

In May they were on the *Pilgrim* together. Augusta had made the trip with him because one of the deckhands had said he'd seen Caleb on the New York pier the day before. At dawn, with the first rays of the sun aglow on the horizon, they were up and dressed and had already breakfasted, so anxious were they to land. A sudden hard jolt threw them, along with others, to the deck. There were screams and cries, bells began to ring. Neither Augusta nor Luke was hurt, and within moments, they knew that no passengers had been injured. The *Pilgrim* had gone aground on unmarked and submerged rocks near Blackwell's

Island. Miraculously, in spite of a 125-foot gash in the bottom, the ship didn't take on water and was able to proceed to her New York berth.

The delay strained Augusta's every nerve and resource. Forever after she wondered if, had she reached the city on schedule, she would have found Caleb. For, when they finally docked, although she spent hours questioning the longshoremen and porters, asking if they had seen a seventeen-year-old boy alone, and describing Caleb to them, she had no word of him.

There came a day on the *Bristol*, as Luke stood at the top of a flight of stairs, when he saw from the corner of his eye a movement. And then he saw Caleb.

Caleb! At last! Luke was in midstep. He yelled, threw himself backward. He mustn't let the boy get away. He must reach him. But suddenly there was nothing beneath Luke's feet. He reached into empty air with both hands and sprawled to his hip and elbow. Then, off-balance, he fell in a great tumbling heap down the iron steps.

A crowd gathered quickly. Passengers, crew. Then Jim Reilly came and sent them away.

Luke knew nothing for several hours.

Jim had him moved to a stateroom, and sent to the purser to learn if there was a doctor aboard. In a little while a small, pudgy, bearded man appeared. He poked and prodded at Luke. He gently turned his head this way and that. 'Let him rest. We must see what the damage is before we know what to do.'

When Luke opened his eyes, Jim was sitting with him.

'I saw Caleb,' Luke said. 'Out of the corner of my eye. You must go and look for him.' Then Luke blinked, his pale face suddenly paler, his silver eyes narrowing in pain. 'It's bad,' he gasped. 'Tell Gussie –' The rest was mumbled, not comprehensible.

The ship sailed on. At dawn she passed the Borden Flats light and her whistle blew the usual three times.

Augusta, wrapped in a light shawl, stood on the widow's walk and watched her move into port. The *Bristol*. She thought of Jim Fisk and how he had loved that ship, and wondered about the canaries that had once lived aboard.

Then, faintly smiling, she went downstairs to prepare for

Luke's return. Marge Gowan was still abed and not expected to arise so early. Amy was sleeping too. Kin was in Boston at school, preparing to enter Harvard the following year.

It would be just Augusta and Luke. She set the table for two, put the coffee on to boil. There was plenty of time, for Luke would have things to do in the general manager's office before he came home.

The sound at the door was much sooner than she expected. When she didn't hear Luke's call, she went to see.

Jim held one end of the litter, Carl Hansen the other. Their silhouettes were tall and ominous against the pale light of the spring morning sky.

She saw the pallor of Luke's face. 'What is it?' she gasped.

Jim motioned her aside, led the way in and past her across the hallway, saying soothingly: 'He'll be all right,' and to Hansen: 'Easy here. We'll have to swing around.'

They maneuvered through the narrow doorway. In a little while, they had settled Luke in bed.

Later she learned from Jim what had happened. How Luke had thought he'd seen Caleb and turned to go after him, and had fallen down the stairs. The doctor on the ship said that he'd bruised his hip and arm and had received a bad head blow. He would recover with time.

She listened, nodded. Finally, she whispered, 'And Caleb?'

Jim slowly shook his head.

'You *did* look?'

Jim saw how her slender hands shook as she entwined them, and her lips, asking the question, shook too. He would do anything to make her smile again, but it was beyond his power. He said, 'I *did* look, believe me. Caleb was not on board.'

She sighed, bent over Luke. 'How is it now?'

'Better,' he answered.

And that was what he said for weeks thereafter. No matter that pain lashed him in excruciating waves, that his nights and days were sleepless. He said, always, that he was better. But he could walk only with Augusta's aid, and could sit up only for a few hours at a time. The doctor said tendons in his hip and back had been damaged and must heal. He made the effort to move and paled with pain, sweat standing out on his upper lip and forehead.

Augusta encouraged him, wincing inside to see him suffer, but smiling at him still.

He improved, but it was a gradual thing. Even as his determination remained constant, his spirits flagged more and more.

He lay abed, watching Augusta go about her chores. How beautiful she was, her heart-shaped face more lovely to look on now than when she was a girl. Her red-gold hair was the same color. Her form, in the maturity of her thirty-seven years, more inviting than ever. And he was a lump, a stick. Old, old. The twelve years between them seemed an eon now. He bit his lip, turned his face to the wall. What good was he to her? For all he loved her and wanted only to give her joy, he had brought her heartache. What good was half an old man to Gussie?

Peter came one afternoon for a visit. It was the first time he had been to the house since Caleb left home, and the first time they had seen him since just after his father's death. He looked well, and carried the gold-headed Malacca cane that Parish had once held between his elegant hands.

He had brought chocolates for Augusta, and for fourteen-year-old Amy Louisa May Alcott's *Little Women*. For Luke he brought cigars.

He sat down, crossed his slim legs, and, ignoring the cool welcome both Augusta and Luke gave him, asked: 'How does it go, Luke?'

'I'm better,' Luke said, as always. He kept his temper with difficulty. It would have been a pleasure to order Peter from the house. But what good would that do?

'Is there any news of Caleb?'

'None.' Luke spat the reply out, his voice hard.

'You made too much of that, you know.'

Augusta told him, with icy anger, 'Your part in that was reprehensible.'

'I didn't realize what a child Caleb was,' Peter said regretfully. He went on, 'And how is Kin?'

'Fine,' Luke said briefly.

'If you'd sent him to the day school, he wouldn't have needed the year in Boston preparing for Harvard.'

'Perhaps. But it'll do him good.' Luke asked no questions of Peter.

But the boy went on, 'I shall graduate the end of the month.' When Luke made no comment, he added, 'And then I'll return briefly before going abroad.'

Augusta left the room to answer a knock at the door. When she returned, Jim Reilly was with her.

Jim hesitated when he saw Peter, but Luke waved him to a chair and Augusta went to ask Marge for tea.

Peter regarded Jim thoughtfully, concealing his dislike. The ship detective was, Peter considered, more at home in the house than he had reason to be. He was also, Peter considered, more friendly to Augusta than he had reason to be.

Jim stayed only long enough to discuss some of the line's affairs with Luke, to deliver an envelope of papers, and to have a cup of tea.

When he had gone, Peter said, 'I hope you'll soon be on your feet again.' And added, 'How old is Jim Reilly?'

'How old?' Luke repeated. 'A few years your senior, I should think. Twenty-five or twenty-six.'

'A mature enough age, I suppose.'

Luke said, 'It would seem so to you. He certainly does a good job on the line, which is what he's hired to do. And he's a good friend to us.'

'Oh, I see that,' Peter said, with a faint question in his voice. 'A very good friend.'

He had no reason for it. Except that Jim Reilly, in doing his job, had interfered with Peter's pleasure, and embarrassed him as well, which annoyed him. The man was young and handsome, and Augusta was beautiful. And Peter was bored, which was why he had come here. He knew that Luke and Augusta must blame him, and dislike him. He was curious to know how they would behave toward him. Now he had found out. He considered their well-bred coolness hypocritical. They ought to have sworn at him, remonstrated with him, perhaps even thrown him out of the house. Since they didn't, he was pleased to make what trouble he could.

Amy was waiting on the path outside. Her thick hair, as dark as Luke's, was restrained in a pink ribbon, but burst out beneath it in a mass of shining curls. Her deep-set dark eyes gleamed flirtatiously. 'Oh, Peter,' she said, putting a hand on his, 'I so rarely see you now.'

'I've been away at school, as you know.'

'And besides, my family doesn't like you any more.'

'And you? Do you blame me too?' he asked, already knowing the answer.

'Caleb's grown. He ought to be able to look after himself.' She tossed her head. 'But never mind him, or Mama and Papa either. What of you? Now that you're finished at Harvard, what shall you do?'

'I'm going abroad. I want to see England and France.'

'Alone?' she asked, her eyes widening.

'Oh yes,' he said lightly. 'Quite alone.' It was how he always was, always had been. Growing up, he'd scarcely seen his father. Until they came together to Fall River, he'd hardly known him, and even then they'd lived as polite strangers. He saw suddenly that his discomfort with the Wakefields was a flower of that seed. He was jealous of the mysterious and invisible bond that had always bound them so closely and kept him outside.

'I wish you weren't going away,' Amy said softly. 'You may not have noticed, but I'm grown now.'

Smiling, he leaned toward her, whispered, 'I've noticed.'

She raised up on her toes, her lips only inches from his. He remembered another time when she had lifted her mouth to his and slipped her arms about his neck, and then Caleb had come. This time no one came. Peter kissed her, gently at first, and then, as passion stirred, more deeply, while she clung to him. When finally he took her arms from around him, she was trembling.

'We shouldn't,' he said. 'I'm too old for you.'

'Too old,' she scoffed. 'Why, in another year I'll be sixteen.'

'Your parents,' he murmured, with a glance at the house.

'They can't stop me from loving you. So don't go away. Wait a little. And then I'll go with you.'

'I'll come back,' he said. 'And if you still feel the same...' It was a game to him. It pleased his vanity. And besides, it was one more blow against the Wakefields.

'Do you promise?' she was asking. 'Do you, Peter?'

' I promise,' he said solemnly. 'I'll come back for you.'

She kissed him one more time, and then stood watching while he mounted the two-seater, snapped his reins at the horse, and drove away.

The faint question so deliberately allowed in Peter's voice lingered in Luke's mind when he was alone. It would have meant nothing to him before. But now, debilitated, sunk in his spirits, it echoed inside him. Jim was young, fine-looking. What did Gussie see when she looked at him? What did she see when she looked at Luke?

Jim came often to spend an hour or two of an afternoon before the *Pilgrim* sailed. He brought news of the crew, of the ships, the wharf gossip of which there was plenty. He sat at ease, smiling. He loved Augusta Wakefield, but he was determined that she should never guess it.

And she, welcoming him, was always the same. Friendly, warm. He was a family friend, young, thoughtful. He had done all he could to help them with Caleb.

One night she said to Luke, 'Jim ought to be married, you know. He would make some girl a wonderful husband.'

'You think so?' Luke asked.

'Yes, I do.'

'How can you tell?' he demanded. 'By what you know of him, I mean.'

'I can tell,' she said, smiling.

'So you think. But there are masks to put on and take off. Things are not always what they seem.' His tone was heated. A flush had come to his cheeks.

'What are you talking about?' she asked.

'You may think him good-looking, nice – all that a woman would want...' Luke stopped. He knew himself that jealousy was overwhelming him. She must know it too.

But she only looked thoughtfully at the chest of drawers where she had put a huge bouquet of hydrangeas. It was as if he hadn't spoken. She said, choosing her words carefully, 'If only Amy were a bit older. It's too soon to think of it. But in a few years, if Jim were still available...'

'He's much too old for her.'

'Much too old?' Augusta repeated. 'Oh, do you think so? The age difference is the same as between you and me.'

He was silent, his eyes averted.

She said lightly, 'I don't think much of that argument. No, no. In a few years time...'

Luke gave a great shout of laughter, 'Gussie, Gussie, how

you do think ahead! And that will do fine. Think all you like. But don't meddle.'

She came and sat on the edge of the bed. 'You've laughed! The first time I've heard that sound in a good while.'

'We're the same,' he said, smiling still. 'You making your plans, while I say, "No, no, wait, don't try to arrange."'

'The same,' she whispered. She leaned closer, drew him to her. Her hand moved slowly over his hip. Her lips pressed to his. He allowed the sweetness of the embrace for only a moment, then shrugged her away.

'Luke, why?' she asked softly.

'I can't. Not now. If we must wait until I'm well, then I cannot bear to begin.'

She took his face between her hands and said with her lips lightly against his, 'As I am to you, so you are to me. And I need you, want you, in the same way.'

'Gussie,' he whispered.

She slipped away for a moment to set the latch on the door. Then she was back, and she took him into her arms. And later, when he was relieved, his passion spent, she lay with him for a long time, and held his face to her bared breasts, and smiled and stroked his cheek.

Luke returned to the ships at summer's end. He was well by then, the spring back in his step, the smile on his lips. There was still no word from Caleb, and though Luke knew when Augusta thought of the boy, which was often, he too had begun to feel that one day they would hear, as she had always said.

She traveled with Luke occasionally, busied herself with her study group, which still raised Luke's brows, and spent time at the Seamen's Mission as well.

One day, when she had just returned home from there, she received a summons from Kin's school. Luke was gone to New York. She set out for Boston on the next train.

When she arrived, she went immediately to the school, to Kin. But instead of finding him in his room, she learned that he was in the infirmary. She was directed to stop at the office of the headmaster.

The man was her own age, but gray of hair, with a lined face and serious eyes. He explained that Kin had developed a chest illness; the school doctor feared consumption, but refused to state it as a certainty. Kin would have to be taken home at once.

Augusta's heart sank. Consumption. A malady of the lungs. Cure was uncertain. It was a disease that was rampant. Yet until now she had known no one who had suffered it. She said, rising, 'Let me see him.'

'It will be best for you to be cheerful,' the headmaster told her. 'You mustn't alarm the boy.'

'I'll be cheerful,' she said.

But it was hard when she saw Kin to keep the smile on her lips.

'Mama,' he said weakly. 'I'm sorry for this.'

'Sorry to be ill? Well, I expect you are. But we'll soon have you well again and back at school.'

'I don't think so.' He was short of breath, too pink of cheek. His eyes sparkled, but with fever instead of health.

'We shall see.' She was tart now. 'I don't know a reason to be so dim.'

'I feel it.'

'Indeed?'

She made the arrangements, and brought him home to Fall River in a hired hansom.

By the time Luke returned with the *Providence*'s arrival from New York, Kin was settled in his room and a new routine had been established for the house.

Augusta or Marge brought him his meals. When he could, he walked about the second floor. The rest of the time he was propped on pillows. He dreamed, he read a little. He brooded weakly on the illness that had struck him down.

Summer's green faded and was replaced by autumn's red and gold. Winter mists began to gather over Mount Hope Bay.

Augusta and Marge planned meals designed to tempt his appetite. Soft milk puddings and roasted fowl and potatoes mashed with home-whipped butter.

Luke brought him newpapers and books from New York, and sat with him, discussing the presidential campaign and the merits of Grover Cleveland, the Democratic Party nominee as opposed to the Republicans' James G. Blaine.

In the beginning, Amy had spent a few hours of each day with Kin; but as his illness lingered, she grew impatient with him, and one day, when her mother reproached her for avoiding Kin, she said, 'But no one thinks of anyone but him any more. It's always Kin, Kin, Kin.'

'He's ill,' Augusta said gently.

'It's not my fault he is,' Amy cried, ' and I'm tired of it. If he's to be well again, he must try. But he doesn't. He's enjoying himself!'

'Amy!'

'But it's true, Mama.' Amy tossed her head and her eyes flashed. 'He lies there, like a king on the hill. You're at his command. And when he's home, Papa is too. And he wants me to be the same. "Amy, let's play chess." "Oh, Amy, get me that book on the mantel." "Amy, open the window – no, shut the window –"'

Even as the girl mocked her brother's demands, the small china bell that Augusta had left by his bedside began to tinkle.

Amy smiled triumphantly. 'You see?'

It was true, Augusta knew. Only moments before he had rung for a cup of tea. Earlier he'd asked for something else. Now again he was calling to her. She was troubled. He mustn't become a permanent invalid.

When Jim Reilly came for an hour, she suggested that one day perhaps Kin would go out for a ride. Jim agreed it was a good idea. But after days of suggesting and finally insisting, she couldn't get Kin to go out. 'I'm too tired,' he said. 'It's no good, Mama.'

In November, Grover Cleveland was elected, the first Democratic president in twenty-five years.

By Christmas Kin's flush had faded. The fever left his eyes and he coughed rarely.

In May of the following year he had his nineteenth birthday. He came down to the parlor for a few hours, but then, coughing into his hand, he retreated to his bed, while Amy gave her mother an 'I told you so' look, and Augusta pretended not to notice.

By the late summer of 1885 the doctor pronounced him cured. Luke and Augusta decided that he should return to the preparatory school, then go to Harvard. He agreed that he would, but without much enthusiasm.

One Wednesday he sailed on the *Pilgrim* with Luke. That he

went was a major victory for his father and mother. He had been lethargic for so long. He had little energy and no interest. But it was on that trip that he met Tom Gavin, and Tom's sister, Barbara.

The two were returning home to New York from Newport where they had been visiting friends. Barbara was twenty-one, small, very curved at the bosom and hip. Her blond curls were dressed high on her head under the small blue bowl of her hat. Her eyes were a matching blue, and warm. Her smile was bright and quick.

She had been nursing a disappointment when she and Tom boarded the ship. She had thought to be engaged in Newport. Instead, she had watched the man she wanted hover over her best friend. Until the moment she saw Kin Wakefield, she had thought her heart was broken for good. Now she decided it wasn't. She examined him from head to toe. He was tall, slender. His hair was dark and curly, his face clean shaven. He had an interesting air about him. She leaned close to her brother. 'Go meet that man over there.'

'How?'

'Dammit, Tom, you can think of something. Just try.'

Tom, at nineteen, and already apprenticed to a lawyer in New York, was full of ideas. He started across the grand saloon, determined to bring back the tall angular man at whom his sister pointed her dimpled chin. It was, Tom knew, the only way he'd get any peace. Barbara always managed, somehow, to have her whims satisfied.

He circled around Kin, stopped, started to speak, stared for a moment. Then, with a grin: 'I'm sorry. I thought you were someone else. A friend from Newport. Now I see I'm mistaken.'

Kin smiled, gave his name.

Tom thrust out his hand. 'In any event, I'm delighted to know you.'

They spoke for a few moments more. Then Tom said, 'Oh, I'd better get back to my sister. Come and meet her.'

For want of anything better to do, Kin agreed. Soon he was exchanging greetings with Barbara, meanwhile thinking she was the prettiest girl he had ever seen. Her skin looked so soft he longed to touch it, her mouth so sweet he yearned to taste it. And Barbara was deciding that she was determined to have him.

239

He was much better-looking than the man she'd wanted in Newport and lost to her best friend.

Chapter 21

Bennet looked enviously at the three people leaving the grand saloon together. They were within a year or two of his own age, but how different. The men were slim, their bodies hard and masculine in elegant clothes. The girl looked like a walking doll, her head with its blue bowl-shaped hat tipped mischievously. They were good to look at, and moved with grace and sureness. While he... he... He made himself sick.

'What's wrong with you?' Mabel Graystone-Fields asked. 'You're making the most appalling face.'

'Nothing,' Bennet answered. His mouth set in a sullen pout. There was sweat on his plump cheeks.

'Something is.' His mother leaned closer. Her voice was shrill when she went on, 'You better tell me, Bennet. I'm asking you: what's the matter?'

No privacy, he thought, not even in his mind – and certainly not in his life. She had to peek, to pry. She had to know. If she could climb inside his head, she would do it. If she could read his guts, she would do that too.

'Bennet!' Her voice was raised in warning.

He'd learned that the only defense was to give just a little. He said, 'I was thinking of Papa.'

'Seventeen years old and he's thinking of his papa!' Her voice rose until it was an ugly gasping shriek. 'His papa. As if he ever did anything for you. Tell me, what did he ever do? What, what? I demand to know. What did he do?'

Bennet shrugged hopelessly and slid a little deeper into his chair. It was no use. There was no way to stop her. He pretended he was dead. He was deaf and dumb and blind. He lay in his coffin, hands folded on his chest. It was no good. She stood over him, screaming. He gave up the imagined scene, the candlelight and flowers, and looked at her.

Her eyes blazed in her round and sallow face. Her black hat had slipped to the back of her head, resting uneasily on her straggly knot of hair. 'What do you think I am?' she cried. 'A rich woman, hah! A woman who can ignore her business because she has so much? I do what I have to do.'

Bennet didn't answer. He'd been hoping that she would change her mind. But she hadn't. They had just a little while before they departed Newport's Long Wharf. Until then, there was hope. She could still have left the boat there, returned to Fall River, and gone on to Boston. There would have been a way, if she had wanted to. But she hadn't wanted to.

The conductor had come with the telegram. 'Mrs. Graystone-Fields, I'm sorry. It's urgent, I hear. This has just come for you.'

She snatched it without thanks, unfolded it, and read. There was the murmur of voices around them. The train wheels rattled and clacked on the uneven tracks. Bennet held his breath. At last she said, 'It's your father. He's ill.'

'We can rent a carriage in Fall River,' Bennet said quickly, 'or take the train back. Either way, we'd better go home.'

'Go home? Are you crazy? A woman about to be widowed can't rely on others. She must take care of herself. And besides, he's in the hospital. He doesn't need us. There's surely nothing seriously wrong with him. And it'll cost. I wonder how he thinks to pay for it. He doesn't have a cent, Bennet.'

'We should go back,' Bennet said softly.

'You're a sweet, kind-hearted boy,' she said, and then came her great shouting bray of a laugh. 'A sweet, kind-hearted boy.'

Bennet felt neither sweet nor kind. He worried for his father. He wanted more than anything to return home to be with him. Bennet was frightened to think what might be happening. But his mother had already decided against it. So he sat, heavy and ill at ease, aching inside, and wondered what was wrong with his character. Why didn't he get up and leave her? What would they find when they finally returned to Boston?

'I'm hungry,' Mabel announced. 'Let's eat.'

Limping, he followed her to the dining room in the afterhold. His foot, injured years before, had never healed properly. By the time she had taken him to a doctor, it had been too late to do anything for it. So now he wore a specially constructed boot and did the best he could. Generally he managed, but if he hurried, he was prone to lose his balance and fall. And a fall was difficult. He was very stout; once he was down, it took a strong man to get him to his feet. He often felt a dull throbbing ache in the bad foot, but he never mentioned that, always concealed it from her. If she knew, she would dig out her foul-smelling unguents and smear them on, so that for days he would be forced to stumble about in a cloud of stink.

Mabel watched him settle in his chair. Seventeen, she thought. That was when the animal urges began to control the male. Probably that was what was wrong. Perhaps she had been slow to realize it. It didn't occur to her that he might be worried about his father. Arthur was so long a nonentity to her that she supposed he must be that to others too. Her worry was for Bennet. He was her son, her heir. Her father's heir. Often, in the night, she spoke to her father as if he were still alive and could hear her. 'Papa,' she'd say, 'aren't you proud of me? Do you see what I've accomplished? Nobody has put anything over on me. Not on Mabel Graystone. See? You worried for nothing. I'm as good as any son. And there's *my* son Bennet to prove it. Bennet will carry on. When I die there'll be Bennet to do your name and mine proud.'

But at the moment, Bennet worried her. She decided to provide for those dangerous male urgings of his, lest they lead him to escape her control. Once he got that nonsense out of his system, he would be all right. Poor fellow, there was so little he could do for himself. So she would have to do that too, yes, even find a woman for him.

Now that her mind was made up, she moved quickly. She always ate fast, but this evening she positively raced through the elaborate meal, although she refused no courses. She rushed Bennet into a choking fit that turned his face purple. Then, waiting while he caught his breath, she said, 'Come on, Bennet. What's wrong with you?' and finally got to her feet and surged out, leaving him behind.

She walked slowly along the deck, ignoring the full moon, the soft breeze that ruffled the waters of the Narragansett Bay, and the gleam of the Block Island light. She didn't see what she was looking for, so she went down to the grand saloon and walked slowly through it, particularly eyeing the girls who sat together, laughing. And the girls who sat alone. Finally she found what she sought. The girl was a redhead, slender, very pretty, with a small piquant face and a tiny high-bosomed body. Just to be sure, Mabel watched.

In a little while, she was certain. There was no doubt of it. The girl was a whore. Satisfied, Mabel approached her.

It took only a few minutes to complete the arrangements. Since Mabel knew no other way, she was direct. She sat down next to the girl, said, 'I have a seventeen-year-old son. He's a good boy, so you needn't be afraid of him. He needs a girl to give him some little life. Can you do that?'

Jeanette Hall giggled. 'This is a first for me. I usually deal with papas.'

'Mind your mouth,' Mabel said sharply. 'I don't want him to know about me. Pretend you were attracted to him.'

'Pretend is my middle name,' Jeanette said, which was true. If Mabel had asked her, she would have said her name was Clara, the name she used on the ship. But Mabel didn't ask her.

'Will you do it?' Mabel asked.

'For twenty-five dollars.'

'Twenty-five! That's ridiculous!' Mabel returned.

After some haggling, the price was agreed on. Mabel would give Jeanette fifteen dollars.

'You'll have to show him to me,' Jeanette said.

'You'll see us together. Then I'll leave him. You take over from there.'

'It's funny. You're funny.'

'Just do what you get paid for doing,' Mabel said grimly.

She joined Bennet in the dining saloon, hurried him through the last of his third dessert, and walked close to him, overshadowing even his bulk; until they were on the deck. Then, spying Jeanette, Mabel said, 'I shall go below to read. Take the air as long as you like.'

She sat in the grand saloon. With a sheaf of papers held close to her face, she appeared to be concentrated on her reading. In fact, she saw neither words nor figures. She was thinking about Bennet and the small red-headed girl, and grinding her teeth. After a while, she relaxed. She puckered her lips and whispered silently, 'Papa, I had to do it. It was the only way to control him. You'd have done the same if you were me.'

Jim Reilly, surveying the saloon, noticed her moving lips, and paused, as he walked by, to observe her. He had seen her in conversation with Jeanette Hall, who had called herself Clara to him. And only a few moments before, he had walked by the girl on the deck. They hadn't spoken. She had deliberately turned her head away, and Jim had already told her that if she made trouble, she'd never be allowed on a Fall River Line ship again. She said sweetly that she'd made no trouble and never would again. He let it go at that. It was impossible as long as the passengers wanted them to keep these girls away.

Meanwhile Bennet stood on deck, leaning against the rail. He wondered what was wrong with Mabel. Why had she suddenly decided to leave him alone when she never did? Soon Jeanette edged closer. She smiled at him, and he, though startled, smiled back. It was all the encouragement, and more, than she needed. In a small little girl voice, she asked if he knew the time. He took from his waistcoat pocket the gold watch his father had given him years before. She leaned toward him, saying, 'Oh, thank you so much,' and giggled. 'Not that I really care. It was just an excuse to talk to you.' He stared at her, feeling heat in the bottom of his belly and fire on the back of his neck. When he didn't answer, she pushed against him. 'Don't you like me even a little? Don't you want to be my friend?'

He was frightened, but he allowed her to lead him, tiny hot fingers wrapped around his wrist.

As the two of them passed Jim Reilly, he gave them a quick searching glance. He immediately identified Bennet, the sulky and stout boy always kept in tow by Mabel Graystone-Fields. Now Clara, who was years older than he, had him in tow. Having seen Mabel in conversation with the girl, Jim understood. He laughed silently as he continued his rounds.

Below, turning on the light, Jeanette said, 'This is better, isn't it? We can really talk here.'

But they spoke only a little. Frightened Bennet was maneuvered in the direction he wanted to go without knowing how to get there himself. He sank down on the bed, the heat still burning but worried about what to do next. Jeanette leaned over him, crooning, 'My, you're a sweetheart. My, I'm glad I came on board. Wouldn't it have been awful if I'd missed meeting you?'

Later, he agreed it would have been.

Before they parted, he gave her fifteen dollars. She giggled as she thanked him, and he asked why. 'Your mama's going to pay me in the morning.'

He laughed too. He thought it was funny. But he knew then how scared Mabel was of losing him. She'd even buy him a woman to keep him. He said, 'Just be sure you collect what she owes you. It's not always that easy.'

Jeanette did indeed manage to get her fee from Mabel the next morning. But that was before Bennet had risen. He didn't see her that day at all, although he looked for her.

He dutifully followed Mabel through her business appointments, heard several times that a statue known as 'Liberty' had been delivered that week, a gift of the French people, and would eventually be set up on Bedloe's Island. He heard also, in Wall Streeet, that there was soon to be a three-mile stretch of electric street railway in Baltimore. However, he hardly listened to what was told to him. He was too busy thinking about Jeanette, and her small hands caressing him, and her breasts hot on his chest.

But she wasn't on the ship when he and Mabel returned to Fall River. He searched for her on the Boston boat train, determined to find her again.

When they arrived home, they found that Arthur was still in the hospital. 'I suppose that's just as well,' Mabel said grimly. 'They won't let him out until I pay them.'

'Let's go see him,' Bennet suggested.

'Tomorrow's soon enough,' she said.

But the next day she claimed business demanded her attention. 'I can't take off. I'm desperate. A woman must always take care of herself,' she cried. It had always been that way, Bennet realized. She had no time for Arthur and never had.

She was, Bennet was beginning to see at last, more than a little eccentric. He had hardly thought about it before. He had accepted what she gave him, the way they lived, without question. It was all he had ever known.

But now he began to wonder. She had lived as if they were poor, their accommodations since Arthur's money ran out grotesquely meager. Her clothes were always second hand, his the cheapest that could be bought. Yet he knew she had a fortune in liquid assets, and more in land and buildings and mortgages. She had it. And one day it would be his. She needed him to inherit it. *She needed him.*

When that understanding hit him, it changed his life forever.

He saw his father that afternoon. Arthur's thin face was as gray as his thin hair. He smiled faintly, held Bennet's hand, and whispered 'Good night' when Bennet left.

By morning Arthur Fields was dead.

Mabel, on hearing the news, simply nodded. She saw him through his burial and out of her life, and immediately set out on the boat train for Fall River, determined to make the *Pilgrim's* sailing that evening.

Bennet started looking for Jeanette as soon as he limped up the gangplank. Pudgy face intent, squinting, he wandered the public rooms and decks. Each time Mabel caught up with him, she demanded, 'What is it? What are you doing? What's wrong?'

But she'd already guessed. Jeanette Hall – that's who he was after. Mabel began to think she might have made a mistake. She'd wanted Bennet to be a man, but she hadn't counted on how like a man he would be.

She decided to find Jeanette Hall first. She'd tell the girl enough was enough, and make sure she understood. If there was trouble, then Mabel assured herself, she'd know how to handle that too.

But when she found Jeanette, the girl was hanging on Bennet's arm. Mabel glared at the two of them, and sailed on, her black gown billowing behind her.

Later she sat in the grand saloon, pretending to listen to the ship's concert, and glaring over the pages of that month's Fall River *Journal*. When Bennet finally joined her, she said, 'That woman's not respectable. You must have nothing to do with her.'

'I don't care about that,' Bennet laughed. 'And neither did you when you paid her to sleep with me.'

Mabel's raucous laugh bubbled up, but she fought it back. Choking, she snarled, 'What a lie! How can you talk that way to me?'

'I'm sorry, Mama.' His round face flushed. His brown eyes filled with tears. But his mouth set stubbornly. He wasn't going to give in and she'd better find out quickly. He got to his feet.

'Where are you going?'

'Out,' he answered.

'Where?'

'You don't want me to tell you,' he said. His plump body made a half bow. He left her alone.

Jeanette was waiting. She wore nothing but a thin silk robe. Her nude body glowed pink and small within its folds. Her hips were slim, boylike. Her breasts were barely more than soft pink nipples. He put his lips to them.

'What did she say?' Jeanette asked.

'Never mind,' Bennet answered, raising his head. He seized her at the waist, his thick fingers meeting around it. 'Never mind. I'm here, aren't I?'

In the morning, while Bennet slept soundly, there came a knock at the door of Jeanette's stateroom. She slid from the bed and opened it.

Mabel's thick hand fell on her shoulder, dragged her into the corridor. 'You leave him alone,' Mabel said.

Jeanette giggled. 'I like him, Mrs. Graystone-Fields. He's a very nice boy. And he likes me, too.'

'Just leave him alone. I'll give you a hundred dollars.' The words were breathless. Mabel could hardly believe herself what she had just said. One hundred dollars. It was a fortune. But Bennet was worth it. Bennet's life was worth it.

'All right,' Jeanette sighed. 'If you insist.' She accepted the money, tucked it away.

Satisfied, Mabel returned to her stateroom. By the time she reached there, Jeanette had already awakened Bennet, told him what had happened, and showed him the one hundred dollars. Bennet assured her he would give her double that amount to see him in Boston and to meet him the next time he made the trip to New York.

A deck below, Willie Gorgas looked at his reflection in the glass, sighed, and gave his thinning hair a last swipe before putting away his comb. Now he studied the room. Everything was in order. He was packed. In a little while the ship's gangplank would go down. He would be in New York.

Every time he made the trip he thought of Ellie and how she

247

had always said to be patient. But Ellie had died two years ago. He lived on in the house as he had always lived. The house that had once belonged to Johnny Franger. The house where he'd first met Lottie Dimot and got from her the idea that had made him a rich man.

He had given William the inns. The papers had been prepared by a Boston lawyer, and handed over. William was there to accept them. He said, 'Thank you, Papa,' and quickly looked away.

That was all. And that meeting was the last Willie had had with him. He knew William and Mary had moved to New York, and taken baby Diane with them. A year after the transfer of the property, five years ago, Willie had gone to Boston. At South Station he hired a hack that deposited him on a narrow street near Harvard Yard.

He found the house and asked for William. Nobody knew him there. Suspicious eyes raked Willie up and down. He made a few more inquiries. Nobody admitted to hearing of a William Gorgas. So Willie began to understand. He was an outsider, a foreigner. When, later, he heard about the move to New York, it made sense to him.

At home, Willie thought about it more. It wasn't William's fault. The boy belonged to a different world, an American world. He was glad he'd given the boy the inns. Willie waited, as Ellie had told him to do, but he never heard from William.

He held out as long as he could. Then he went to New York. He'd gotten the address of the big brownstone from the manager of the Fall River Gorgas Inn. A butler opened the door, giving him a funny look. Willie lowered his head, daring the man to turn him away when he asked for William.

When he was ushered in, his boots whispered along plush carpets. There was the scent of roses in his nostrils. A uniformed maid came to stand beside the butler. 'Who do you want to see?' she asked.

'I told him,' Willie said, with an impatient look at the butler. 'Mr. Gorgas. Or else Mrs. Gorgas,' he added as an afterthought.

The maid uneasily examined his face, his clothes. At last she backed from the room.

When the door slammed open, it was Mary who confronted him. Red-faced, her hands made into small fists, she demanded coldly, 'What do you want? What are you doing here?'

'I came to see my granddaughter,' Willie said. 'Diane, my granddaughter,' he repeated.

'Get out!' Mary Gorgas screamed. 'Get out! He promised. He swore to me. He said I'd never have to see you again.'

'William?'

'William!' she screamed.

'I don't believe you,' William said softly. 'You're making it up.'

'Get out, I say!'

Willie backed slowly from the room. The butler pulled open the door. Willie staggered down the steps of the brownstone. But he didn't go far. He waited at the corner. He stood there in the rain through a long morning. By noon, when he was more determined than ever, the front door opened and Mary Gorgas came out. With her was Diane, sitting up in a large high-wheeled English pram with a stack of satin pillows behind her. She was nearly three years old as he calculated it. She had golden curls and wide black eyes and a small, delicate frame. He stood still, eyes watering, his one arm aching, and watched a nursemaid in a long blue cape push her away with Mary Gorgas strolling along beside them.

Since then he had seen Diane a few other times. And today he would see her again . . .

The ship's whistle blew. There was a slight jolt. Willie took up his small bag and went to the main deck. The crowds were gathering there. Soon the gangplank went down. Willie was one of the first off.

He took a hack to Central Park and walked the rest of the way. The traffic was heavy. Horse cars and wagons clogged the streets. There were pushcarts and vendors shouting their wares and prices, and everywhere he looked there were new buildings. He compared it to Fall River and shrugged. A different world.

The door of the brownstone opened just as he reached the corner. A woman in a white uniform came out. She held Diane's small hand. The two walked to the corner, with Willie following after them. They crossed the street, turned into a tree-lined lane. He went with them, taking the short cut to Central Park. Once there Diane would walk sedately beside her nursemaid, and run a little too. And after two hours they would return home again.

Willie sat on a bench, and watched, his one hand fisted on his knee. The arm he didn't have ached; the stump ached. Inside him there was an ache too.

When Diane ran down the path toward him, he looked up and smiled at her. 'Hello, little girl.'

She stopped suddenly and stared at him, her lips like a tiny pink flower and fright widening her eyes.

'Hello,' he said again.

'Diane,' the nursemaid called. 'Diane, come here at once.'

'Hello,' he said for the third time. Then, 'Don't be afraid of me.'

But she turned and ran away, crying, 'Nanny, Nanny, is that the Bogeyman?'

Heartsick, his eyes stinging with tears, he watched her flee.

Chapter 22

That fall Amy put up her hair, braiding it into a thick black coronet, secured by two of her grandmother Amy's whalebone combs. She was readying herself for Peter's return even though she had not had a single letter from him since his departure. Then came word indirectly that he had become engaged to an English girl.

She covered her hurt, yet it festered in her. He had promised to come back but hadn't meant it. He had played at love with her, and shamed her. And nobody cared. Nobody knew her heart had been broken. Her mother and father were concerned only with Kin.

Now, listening to the voices from the parlor, her lips compressed tightly. Kin. Kin. Kin. That was all she ever heard. Ever since he'd been ill, it seemed to Amy, the whole of each waking hour and every conversation was devoted to her older brother. For all she could see, it would continue that way for the rest of her life. Now that he was well again, it was still the same. Kin. Kin. Kin. As if nobody else had feelings, and hopes, and fears, and dreams. As if nobody else suffered. Tears stung Amy's eyes. She dashed them away. What was the use of weeping? She'd lost Peter. She was alone.

She heard Kin's voice. It was louder, much louder than usual.

'It's what I want to do,' he said, a familiar stubbornness in his words.

He would win, as he always did when he set his mind on it. She put her hands over her ears and ran upstairs.

In the parlour, Kin went on, 'I've thought about it. And I've decided.'

'I see,' Augusta said softly.

Luke was silent for a moment. Then he sighed, saying, 'Harvard is the oldest and most prestigious school in the country. Most consider it a privilege to study there.'

'I'm not most people. I'll learn more as an apprentice to a lawyer.'

'Then, perhaps in Boston...' Augusta stopped at Kin's vehement headshake.

'Boston's out,' he said explosively.

'Oh?' She began to realize that there was more to it than he was saying.

Luke said, 'But you must think ahead. If you study in Boston, or even apprentice yourself there, you'll be in the right position for later on. The line will give you great opportunities –'

'But I don't want to work for the line. It's time our family went in another direction.'

'Why?' Luke demanded.

It was what Augusta was asking herself. Why must Kin feel that way?

Kin said, his face flaming now, 'There's a world beyond Fall River. I want to see it and know it.' He added, 'And I'm going to.'

'If not Fall River, and not Boston, then where?' Augusta asked.

'New York, Mama. That's where I want to be.'

'If you're set on it,' Luke said, 'then all right. But I still don't understand.'

'And how will you find a place?' Augusta asked.

Finally Kin allowed himself to grin. 'I already have one. It's where Tom Gavin works. Davis and Davis on Forty-third Street.'

'And you've probably found a place to live as well.' Augusta's voice was dry.

'Yes. I'll board with a family Tom's recommended to me.'

Augusta smiled at him. 'Then it's settled.' She suspected it had been settled long before this discussion was begun.

He nodded, relieved.

'And do you start soon?'

'The first of October.'

'It *is* soon,' she said ruefully.

Only weeks away, yet it seemed eons to Kin. Eons until he would see Barbara. The mere thought of her name in his mind set his blood burning. He felt a stirring in his groin and got up quickly. 'If you'll excuse me...'

In his room, driven by restlessness and hunger, he paced back and forth. Barbara. Barbara. Her mouth warm and sweet under his lips. Her arms sliding slowly around his neck. Her small round belly pressed against him...

Two weeks later he sailed on the *Bristol* for New York.

He returned for three days at Christmas.

Augusta studied him anxiously. He looked well, did not cough, and he seemed happy. She told Luke it appeared so far that the move had been a wise one.

Kin, walking the snowy familiar streets of Fall River, wondered that the buildings seemed so small, the roads so empty, the life so drab. He could hardly wait to get back to New York. To Barbara. He saw her some time every evening, and when he was away from her, at work at the big desk in the lawyer's office, or in bed late at night, he dreamed of her. She had allowed him only quick kisses, embraces. In his dreams there was more.

He wanted to marry her. But his earnings barely supported him, and Barbara, the daughter of a wealthy manufacturer of corsets, was accustomed to the best. Tom insisted that it didn't matter, that Barbara loved Kin. But Kin couldn't see a way.

One night, when they were having dinner together, she looked across the candlelit table at him and said softly, 'I should like to see your home and meet your family.' Small flames seemed to dance in her blue eyes. 'Do you think they'll like me?'

'Of course they will,' he assured her.

'Then I wonder why you haven't spoken of it yourself?'

He answered, 'I never thought of it.'

'Never thought of it? Why, what an odd thing to say.'

He smiled at her. 'Not so odd. All I've ever thought about since we met is you, Barbara.'

She leaned back, smiled. 'I'll go with you to Fall River as soon as you can arrange it.'

Within two weeks, they set out on the *Providence*. Barbara had a stateroom to herself, while Kin had a place in the men's dormitory.

They ate dinner together, after watching the sunset. Later, warmly wrapped against the chill air, they stood on deck, listening to the foghorns echo through white shadows of mist. She whispered, 'It's almost like being married, isn't it? Being alone like this.'

'If only we could be,' he said fervently.

'My father would give you a job with his firm.'

'No,' Kin said. 'I'd rather finish the apprenticeship. In the long run it'll be better.'

'You'd rather do that than marry me?' she asked, a small pout on her lips.

'It's for you too.'

'I know. But I love you so, Kin.'

'You'll wait for me, won't you?'

'I want you so much, so much. I don't know if I can,' she said sadly.

Later, when he walked her to her door and unlocked it for her, she said, 'Come in for a minute.'

He hesitated, then followed her.

She closed the door softly, leaned her narrow shoulders against it. 'This is like being married too.'

He kept his eyes fixed on her face. 'I love you, Barbara.'

'Oh,' she said. 'Oh, it's so hard.'

'Don't, Barbara. Darling, don't.' He drew her into his arms, seeing tears fill her eyes. 'It's going to be all right. As soon as I can make it on my own ...'

'Yes,' she sighed. 'Whenever that is.' She raised her face so that their cheeks touched, and then, as she slowly turned her head, their mouths brushed lightly. With a groan he pulled her against him, her breasts crushed to his chest. Molded together, they swayed, kissing until they were breathless. Slowly, hardly aware of it, he sank down to the bed, drawing her with him.

What happened then was no surprise to Barbara although it was to him. It was what she had planned. If Kin was going to pose obstacles to their immediate marriage, she would remove them. She used the one sure weapon at her command.

The visit with Kin's parents went smoothly. She considered Fall River quaint and told Kin so. She was glad when they returned to New York.

Over the next month she was loving and complaisant one night; another she was moody, withdrawn. A third she was a gay tease, ducking her head from his caresses. He was in a fever of constant longing. Morning, noon, and night he ached for her body, and had it often but never enough.

When she was sure it was the right time, she appeared at the office, pale with rice powder, very quiet, and said that they had to talk.

Still, when they walked together, she was silent, biting her lips and wringing her hands. Finally, with much persuasion, he managed to get her to tell him what was wrong.

'Oh, Kin, I'm so frightened,' she said. 'I don't know what to do, where to turn.'

'What's the matter?' he asked quickly. She was ill, he thought. There was some terrible trouble...

'I'm pregnant.'

His relief nearly overwhelmed him. He stopped on the sidewalk, laughed, and put his arms around her, ignoring the whistles and stares of passers-by. 'That's nothing. We'll get married.'

'Oh, Kin, how I love you,' she cried.

They were married in March 1886 at Grace Church in New York.

Barbara's father and her brother Tom were there, and so were Luke and Augusta, with Amy the single bridesmaid. Only later did they learn that Kin had given up his apprenticeship and gone to work for Mr. Gavin's corset concern.

Barbara and Kin had been married for two months when she said, one evening, 'Kin, I have something to tell you.'

He stroked her arm. Her skin was soft as satin, and scented. He could hardly listen to her for the sudden drumming in his ears. His blood was rising. He wanted her.

'Kin?'

'Yes.' But he was drawing her closer. 'Barbara . . .'

'Not now. Not now, I say. Something's happened. You must listen to me.' They were married. Nothing could change that. She'd shown everybody that she could get a handsome husband. She was a wife now, and could do whatever she wanted. It was no longer necessary to pretend.

'I'm listening,' Kin said.

'I'm so sorry. But I . . . I've lost the baby. Today . . . just after you left . . .' her blue eyes were wide. 'I felt so strange. And then . . . then . . . there was the blood.'

'Oh,' he said. 'Oh, I'm sorry.' But he felt nothing. He didn't care. He had what he wanted. Not that night, for he said no, it was too soon. Not the next, for she said it was still too soon. But then, after that, it was as it had been before. They were lovers as well as husband and wife. Except when she withheld herself either to tease or lead him. And he, obsessed by his need for her, followed wherever she wanted.

The first time Amy saw Sean Callahan was on the *Pilgrim*, when she and her parents were returning from Kin's wedding to Barbara.

Sean was three years older, nineteen, but matured by a hard life so there was nothing of the boy about him. He was of medium height, but had thick shoulders, well-developed forearms, and a broad chest over the slimmest of hips. His hair was bronzed by the sun, with a touch of red, his eyes hazel and fanned with squint lines. He had a slow, swaying walk, and a soft laugh, and when she heard it, she laughed too, although she didn't know why. One thing she knew, he was nothing like Peter. And that was what she wanted.

The second time Amy saw him was on the Fall River wharves. It was then she decided she was in love with him. Her eyes followed him as he spoke to the dockmaster, as he moved with the stevedores. He was a deckhand, one of ten, and earning fifteen dollars a week. He had been in the country for five years, and lived in Boston with an aunt and uncle.

At first Sean hung back. 'You'll lose me my job with your carrying on,' he told her, when she lingered by him too long on the ship. 'I've things that must be done, and you're interfering.'

'I'm not,' she said. And, 'I don't care.'

'And then who'll feed me?' he asked, but he was laughing.

'You'd find a way.'

'I would that,' he answered, 'for I don't like being hungry.'
But he winked before he turned away.

The next time they met it was because she was waiting for
him at the docks. She watched her father and Jim Reilly come
down from the ship together, and, hidden by a wagon, saw
them disappear into the general manager's office. When Sean
appeared, she nodded her head at him and quickly walked off.

He followed her for a block, catching up with her on Anawan
Street. 'And what do you think you're doing?' he asked.

She smiled, took his arm.

By the end of the month he was waiting for her at the foot of
High Street whenever he could, and she was slipping out to
meet him.

He said, 'You're making a mistake, my girl. Your folks won't
let me have you or you me.'

'Of course they will,' she said. 'They'll have to.'

'You'll see that I have the right of it.'

When, one Sunday afternoon before the sailing of the
Pilgrim, she brought him home to meet Augusta and Luke, she
realized that it would be more difficult than she had thought.

Her parents were both polite to him, but it was a cold and
forced courtesy that made it obvious he didn't suit them. There
was too little to talk about. He was quiet, only answering the
questions they put to him, plainly ill at ease, and embarrassed
by his thick brogue.

For a little while Amy watched, listened, then she took
matters into her own hands. She rose, smiled at Luke, at
Augusta. 'I want to tell you. Sean and I are going to be married.'

There was a shocked silence.

Color rose in Sean's face. His big calloused hands knotted
and the muscles bulged in his forearms. They had talked of it
between them, but he hadn't expected her to make the
announcement now, so baldly, with him there. But he said
sullenly, 'I love the girl.'

Augusta and Luke spoke at the same time, stopped, looked at
each other. Then Luke said, 'No, Amy. You're too young.'

It was the first reason that came to mind. There were others.

The memory of his youth: hordes of children, raised in grinding poverty... the stench of it... the shame of it. Amy hadn't been born to that. She must never know it.

'I'm old enough to know what I want,' she said. 'And old enough to love.'

She would show Peter, her parents. Somebody wanted her. Somebody cared for her.

'You're not to see this man again,' Luke said. His voice was soft, but his lips were white. He looked at Sean. 'You understand.'

Sean's hazel eyes flashed with hatred. He wasn't good enough for the likes of the Wakefields. It was his brogue, his manners, his clothes. And it was his church, too. 'I understand,' he said.

'You won't stop me, Papa,' Amy cried.

Luke didn't look at her. He went to the door. 'I'll see you out, Mr. Callahan.'

He considered that the end of it. But Augusta knew there was more to come.

She tried to talk to Amy. The girl wouldn't listen. 'I love him,' she said hotly. 'You and Papa can't keep us apart.'

'We want the best for you. Wait a little, six months or so, and see what happens,' Augusta pleaded.

But Amy had her own ideas. In April, less than a month after she first met him, she and Sean were married by a priest in Boston, and afterwards, they went to a hotel. She was eager. He was forceful. They exhausted themselves in passion, and could hardly bear to separate when Amy went home to tell her parents.

But Sean wouldn't go with her. 'They've thrown me out once, and they'll do it again. You know the why of it. I'm not good enough for their English blue blood. I've got me pride too, remember.'

'Then I'll go by myself,' Amy said.

Defiantly, her face flushed, she stood before her parents and showed them her wedding ring.

'Oh, no,' Augusta cried, 'No! You can't have been so foolish!'

But Luke heard Amy out without saying a word. The color faded from his face except for where the scar burned red.

Then, finally, in a voice harsh with anger, he said, 'So you sneaked away and married him!'

'I didn't sneak,' she cried. 'I went with him!'

'Sneaked,' he said again. 'Knowing how I feel. How your mother feels.'

'I don't care,' Amy repeated. 'I know how I feel. I love him!'

'And we love you,' Augusta broke in. 'Doesn't that mean anything? Are we, your father and I, nothing to you?'

'You've thrown away the good future we'd hoped you'd have,' Luke said. 'Thrown away all that I've worked for. And for nothing! Nothing, I tell you.' He drew a deep breath. After a moment he went on more quietly, 'All right, Amy. What more is there to say? You've made your choice, haven't you? Now live with it.' Without another word, he left the house. He went down to the wharves, and later, when the *Providence* sailed, he made an unscheduled visit on her to New York.

Meanwhile Augusta argued with her hotly. 'It was very wrong of you. You ought to have waited. You should have gotten to know Sean Callahan better.'

'But you'd still have been against him,' Amy cried.

'Your father's concerned only for your good. And so am I.'

'I know what's good for me,' Amy returned.

'You think so now. But I'm not so sure of that.'

'I don't care. I'm married. Nothing you and Papa say can make me sorry. And if he doesn't want to see me again, he needn't. I have Sean now.'

'You have Sean,' Augusta repeated. 'You think he's all you need. But there's more to life than that. We're a family. You can't break that bond so easily.'

'Tell Papa,' Amy answered.

'He knows, ' Augusta said heatedly. 'It's you that doesn't.'

But Amy shrugged, and packed her clothes, and left before the hour was out.

In May the *Empire State* burned and sank at Bristol, Rhode Island, while serving as an excursion boat. When Augusta heard the news, she thought that one more part of her life was gone.

Chapter 23

It was just before Christmas. The big tree filled a corner of the parlor.

Luke looked at it, then turned away. 'You've seen her, haven't you?' he said to Augusta.

'I had to. I couldn't bear the worry. It's been nearly nine months.'

'And?'

Augusta said nothing.

'Tell me.'

'She's well. But she's expecting.'

'As she will be for the rest of her life,' Luke said bitterly.

'But she loves him.'

'I don't want to hear of it.'

Augusta went to the mantel. She touched the celadon lion, then took down the ivory dog, feeling its smoothness a comfort. She said, 'I can't turn my back on my child, Luke.' Caleb was gone from her. Kin had his own life. There was only Amy.

'She's turned her back on you.'

'No. She hasn't. She's young. She didn't know the way to deal with her feelings.'

'I forbade her to see Sean Callahan. And she married him. I told her, and now I tell you, she's made her choice.'

Augusta said softly, 'This isn't like you.'

'I can't bear it.' He buried his head in his hands. 'To know what it will do to her. Everything will be hard. And she asked for it. A man like him. A mick. And hardly off the boat at that.'

'Oh, Luke, that isn't you. And what does it matter?'

'I never felt an Englishman since the day I put foot on these shores. But he makes me feel like one. I could see the old hatred in his eyes. He came here, with his Irish heart and Irish memories, and took my daughter from me.'

Augusta stared at him. 'But Luke, you've never felt so about

Jim Reilly. And he's Irish too. What is this now?'

'Sean is another sort from Jim. And you can see it as well as I can.'

'I don't see it. I see only two young people who are starting out together. What Sean Callahan is doesn't matter.'

'It does, though.' Luke didn't look up at her. Hunger. Fear. Separation. That's what a man like Sean Callahan meant to him. He himself had escaped it. Now Amy had willfully gone back to it. He went on painfully, 'I know how it'll be for Amy and her children. As it was for me so long ago. The same. Until I met your father, and he changed my life. She returns to that, a choice she's made, for herself and the children she'll have. And I'll not be a part of allowing it. I cannot.'

'It's done,' she said softly.

'Gussie, I've never said to you, "I forbid this or that." I say it now, for the first time. I forbid you to see Amy. Let it be. Let her go her own way. Whatever happens will happen. When she wants to return to us, she can. But without Sean Callahan.'

'She'll never do that.'

'How do you know? How can you tell?'

The thought of Aria was between them again. They had been too close for too long not to realize when their minds were joined. Amy was so like Aria they could predict what their daughter would do by what Augusta's sister had done. Their eyes met, fell away. They didn't speak of it.

Augusta brooded on it for days, then, finally, she decided – she would see Amy. If not here, in her own home, then in the place where Amy lived.

She knew from Jim Reilly where that was, and went there one midday. It was sleeting when she arrived in Boston and took a hack to the address. It was a short, dismal street, a lane of dirt, with icy sewerage-strewn gutters, and houses a generation away from their last coats of paint.

Amy's room was heated by a stove that emitted a foul smoke. The floor was splintered. The furniture was sparse, its wood scored and cracked.

Amy let her mother in and stood waiting.

'I've brought you a few things,' Augusta said.

'Thank you.' It was hard not to throw herself into her mother's arms. She ached for an embrace. But pride held her back. Her dark eyes went around the room. The place was awful, probably worse even than her mother had expected. But Amy didn't care. She had done what she wanted. Still . . . still . . .

'How are you feeling?' Augusta asked.

Amy patted her large belly. 'We're fine, I think. It should be soon.'

'And Sean?'

'What do you care?'

'I care because he's your husband.'

'I'll tell him you said that. I think he'll be pleased.'

'Amy, what good does this do?'

'Why did you come, Mama? To gloat?'

'Do you think so?'

'I don't know,' Amy cried.

Augusta smiled. She put her arms out, drew Amy close. 'You're still my girl. Always, Amy.'

'Yes,' Amy whispered. 'Oh yes, Mama. I miss you. And Papa too. And my home.' She looked wildly around the room. 'Sometimes I think I'm dreaming. I'm having a nightmare and soon I'll wake up and everything will be the same.' She came to a sudden stop, drawing a deep gasping breath. Her eyes filled with tears. 'No, no, I don't mean it. I love Sean.'

'Then it'll be all right.' Augusta put an envelope on the table. 'There's a little gift for you. And I've brought you some things for when the baby comes.'

'Oh, Mama, thank you.'

'You'll let me know?'

'Of course,' Amy said, 'if you really want to hear.'

'My only daughter? My first grandchild? What do you think?'

Just before year's end Jim Reilly told her that Sean and Amy had moved to a house in Fall River. Two days later he told her that Amy had had a son and named him Kevin. The same afternoon Augusta drove herself to Corky Row.

It was another dismal street, another dilapidated house. But at least it was closer to home, Augusta thought.

Sean opened the door to her and stood barring the way. 'What do you want here, Mrs. Wakefield?'

'I've come to congratulate you on your new son,' she said. 'And to see how Amy is.'

He had been celebrating his recent fatherhood, and still showed the signs of it. His hazel eyes were bloodshot and there was a flush on his cheeks. His voice was rough, and his brogue thicker. He waved her in.

Augusta loosened her cloak and looked around. The room was neater than the one in Boston, but very small and crowded with what was plainly second-hand furniture. A crib stood in the corner. Amy sat at the table, the infant in her arms.

'Hello, Mama.' Her face was thin, the thick black braids straggly, but her smile was warm.

'Are you well?'

'Oh yes. It wasn't nearly as bad as I expected it to be.'

'Bad?' Sean laughed. 'Why, she was like a cow dropping her calf. It was nothing. Five hours. And bang!'

'I'm glad,' Augusta said. She looked down at the boy. It was hard to tell yet whom it was that he resembled. His fine hair was reddish. His eyes were screwed shut. But she fancied she saw a squareness in the tiny jaw. Perhaps Kevin looked like his father. 'A beautiful boy,' she said softly.

'Not yet,' Amy answered. 'But he will be.'

Sean stood near the window, looking down into the snowy street. He wanted to send Augusta away. He didn't like her coming. He hadn't wanted to make the move from Boston to Fall River, but he'd had to. A cousin of his had come from Ireland and his aunt and uncle needed the room. Besides, living in Fall River, he had more time with Amy. He didn't have to travel so far to the harbor.

Just the same, seeing Augusta bothered him. It shamed him and scared him. Sean knew how Amy had always lived, and it wasn't like this. But who could he blame for that? He'd warned her, hadn't he? He'd told her what it would be. She'd chosen him, and now she was stuck with him. But how could he know she'd always want him? How could he be sure? And here was her mother trying to bribe her again. Like the last time she'd come with her money and gifts.

He'd told Amy then he was having none of it. He'd warned her, she'd better not take anything the standoffish, too-good-for-the-micks Wakefields offered her. He knew gifts with strings when he saw them. He'd warned her.

He stood quietly, but raging inside, until Augusta had gone.

Then he said loudly, 'Well, damn you! If you want to go home to High Street, then go!'

'But I don't want to.' She rocked the baby in her arms. 'Why would I?'

'That's what she came for, isn't it?' he demanded furiously.

'I think she came to see Kevin.'

'And why should she care? He's my son. Mine! Let her let him be. He'll never be good enough for her.'

Augusta had brought with her the quilt off Amy's bed. It was a patchwork, done in many colors. They had spoken of it. Augusta, pointing to a pale blue square, had said, 'Your grandma wore that dress when you were a little girl. Grandpa Marcus had brought the silk back with him from a whaling trip when he was a young man.'

Now Sean pushed it to the floor. 'And this . . . what do you need this for?'

'You won't give her a chance,' Amy said softly.

'She's trouble-making.'

'No. You're wrong.'

'Wrong? Don't tell me that. I know what I say. She'll take you, and the boy with you, if ever she can.'

'No, she won't. She wants only to see us sometimes.'

'Don't "No, Sean" me!' he yelled, slamming his fist on the table, and then slamming his way out the door.

He was gone all that night, but not on the *Pilgrim*, where he should have been working. He came home late the next afternoon, drunk and staggering, to collapse on the quilt she had spread on their bed.

The next week Augusta went to see Amy again. There was a dark bruise on the girl's arm, another on her cheek. 'I fell down the stairs,' she said, when Augusta asked. 'It was a silly thing to do.'

'I hope you weren't carrying the baby.'

Amy flushed. 'No, no, I wasn't.'

'How fortunate,' Augusta said dryly.

Amy's eyes didn't quite meet her gaze. She was restless, her hands folding and unfolding over each other. She picked Kevin up, put him down. He slept through the handling as if he were used to it. Augusta understood from where the bruises had come, but she said nothing.

'Did Papa ask about the baby?' Amy wanted to know.

He hadn't asked, in fact. But Augusta had told him. He'd listened, but hadn't spoken.

'She'll be a good mother,' Augusta had said.

After a long silence, he'd answered, 'I don't care.'

Those words she didn't repeat to Amy. But Amy understood him well enough. When Augusta rose to leave, she asked, 'Why are men different, Mama?'

'Are they?'

'Sean...' A blush colored Amy's cheeks. 'He's always angry when you...'

'When I come to see you?'

Amy nodded. 'And Papa... I suppose he is too?'

'Then would it be better for you if I didn't visit? Is that what you're trying to tell me?'

'Perhaps. For a little while...'

'I see.' Augusta had been afraid that would happen. But much as she hated the thought of it, she saw no way. Amy must come first, not Augusta's own feelings. She bent over the baby, kissed him tenderly. When she straightened, she said to Amy, 'If you should need me...'

'Need you?' Amy bit her lip. 'Why would I? I have a husband now, and a baby son.'

'But you'll remember, won't you?'

'I'll remember,' Amy said.

On December 30, 1888, the *Bristol* steamed into Newport Harbor and settled at her berth at Long Wharf. The hawsers were knotted, the gangplank lowered, and soon after the passengers departed. Only a little while later the ship's alarm bells began to ring.

'Fire!' came the shout. 'Fire in the kitchens!'

A billow of black smoke almost instantly rose over the ship. The quiet docks came alive with cries, horses neighing, and the rattle of wagon wheels.

From below decks, the crew raced to help the kitchen hands. Sean was among them, manning a station on the bucket brigade. His shirt stuck to his body, soaked with sweat from the intense heat. He choked on the blistering air as he passed the heavy buckets on. Reaching, turning, thrusting, with the deck

264

growing hot beneath his feet and his ears deafened, his throat burning, he worked mindlessly with the others. Then, with a roar, the kitchen grease pots exploded into a sheet of flame. One finger of it enshrouded him, setting his shirt afire and singeing his flesh. With a scream, he fell to the deck.

When Augusta heard the news, she hurried to Amy. The girl was white-faced, shaking. She held small Kevin in her arms, and beneath the year-old infant, her belly bulged. Her skirt and shirtwaist were worn. She wore a shawl with holes about her shoulders. 'I don't know what to do,' she said.

'Jim tells me that Sean will recover.'

'But how?' Amy shuddered. 'What will he be?'

That evening Luke said, 'You've seen Amy, haven't you?'

'I went to her when I heard about Sean. She's very frightened.'

'He'll do. Though it will be several months before he can work. And he'll be paid while he's off, according to the line's usual policy.'

'But what of after?'

'He won't be a deckhand. It's expected there'll be some permanent trouble with his arms.'

'And what will Amy do? She's expecting another child.'

Luke flushed. 'It's proving just as I feared it would. Before God, I don't know what the girl's to do.'

'We must help her.' Her voice shaking, she repeated the words. 'We must help her, Luke.'

His jaw hardened. Amy had made her choice. She had gone Sean Callahan's way instead of her family's way. For him, she had turned her back on her own, and traded his love for theirs. She had cared nothing for their fear, their pain. Then they must not care now for hers. He said gently, 'No, Gussie, I'm sorry, I won't have it. There'll be no help from me as long as she remains with him.'

'You can't mean to let her and her babies starve,' Augusta cried.

Silently he turned away.

The next day, when he was gone, she unpacked three small pieces of chinoiserie. She sent them to Boston with Jim Reilly, who sold them for close to a thousand dollars.

Sean was just home from the hospital when she went to see

Amy, taking the money with her. He glared from his bed in the corner. 'What do you want?'

'To know how you are.'

'I'm fine. I'm in top spirits. I'm better than I've ever been in this world,' he said, waving both bandaged hands at her. 'What did you think, that I'd be out dancing a jig?'

She knew by his thickened and slurred speech and his shiny hazel eyes that he'd been drinking again. She wondered how often that happened.

She stayed only a little while. The moment the door closed behind her, Sean snarled, 'And look at you, Amy, the picture of your mother. Your nose stuck in the air and your brows frowning at me!'

'You didn't have to talk as you did,' Amy said softly. 'She only wants to help.'

'I don't want her damnable help!'

'I do. I shan't let Kevin go hungry.'

'He won't go hungry, damn you!'

'Then what'll we do until you go back to work?'

He didn't answer that. Instead he yelled, 'You think you're too good for me. That's what it is. You should have stayed on High Street where you belonged.'

She had heard it before, too many times, and was to hear it again.

At home, over dinner, Augusta asked, 'Will Sean have a job waiting for him when he's ready?'

'Yes.' Luke put down his knife and fork, and looked at her grimly. 'But I don't know how long he'll last in it.'

'Why? What do you mean?'

'The man's known to drink on board. He's had several chances already. Because he's Amy's husband. Jim Reilly's spoken of it to me twice, not knowing what else to do.'

'I see.' She closed her eyes tightly. If Sean lost his job, it would be the harder for Amy.

Three weeks after he finally returned to work, Luke told her that Sean had been fired.

'For drinking on board?'

'Fighting with a passenger while drunk.'

'I must go and see Amy,' was all Augusta said.

'What good will it do?' The man's hopeless.'

'No one's hopeless. We must find a way to give him another chance.'

' Not with the line,' Luke said firmly. 'I'm sorry. That's one thing I'll not do for you.'

'Then I won't ask you to,' she said. 'But there'll be some other way.'

She asked among her friends. No one needed help. Finally she spoke to Betty. George Raleigh agreed to see Sean, and hired him, and within the same week had fired him for brawling with another driver.

At the end of the month, when Augusta went to see Amy, the top-floor rooms were empty. 'They've gone to New York. It was three days ago. And I can't say that I'm sorry. Although I pity the girl and her baby,' the landlady told her.

Augusta had a letter soon after. It said very little. Just that Amy and Kevin were well. She expected the new baby soon. Sean was working as a teamster.

In midsummer Augusta, no longer able to bear not seeing Amy, embarked with Luke on the *Pilgrim*.

She sat in the grand saloon after dinner, reading the *Century Magazine* with interest. The article was about the *Pilgrim*, and described her enclosed paddle wheel boxes and Italian Renaissance decor. Luke, sitting with her, wondered if the opening of the new Thames River drawbridge would affect the line's business, for it meant the beginning of through railroad service between Boston and New York.

They were both distracted from their musings by the entry into the grand saloon of President Grover Cleveland. He was with a party of five, three men and two women. He was a good-looking man, and a bachelor, yet Augusta considered that it wasn't politic of him to be seen returning from his Buzzard's Bay home in the company of these ladies, particularly when his paternity of an illegitimate child had been mentioned in the national press.

Later, in their stateroom, she mentioned that to Luke, but he said it seemed the president didn't care, so why should she? She decided she'd bring the issue up at the next meeting of her study group to learn what her friends thought.

The next morning she watched as the ship passed the Statue

of Liberty, its coronet and torch dyed pink by the rising sun.

After breakfast, she and Luke parted. When the ship docked, she went first to see Kin at the Gavin Manufacturing Company. After a brief time with him, she went by hansom to visit with Barbara for a little while.

Then, with a clear mind, she started off anxiously, to where Amy lived.

But, when she arrived, the Callahan family was gone again. No one knew where, or cared, it seemed.

Fighting back tears, Augusta returned to the *Pilgrim*. All that night she lay wakeful, tormented by memories of a small, bright-eyed little girl with unruly curls, aching to hold her close once more, and asking herself what had happened, where had they gone?

It would be several years before Amy was heard from again.

Chapter 24

With the completion of the Thames River drawbridge in 1889 and the beginning of through rail service between Boston and New York, Luke's concern was proven justified. All the Sound lines suffered a large cut in business, including the Fall River Line. The effect was worsened in September of that year when the Joy Line, operating out of Providence, reduced its one-way fare between New York and Providence to a single dollar.

Still, the ships steamed out of Fall River harbor, flags flying from their masts, lights aglow. And Augusta watched them leave, with the gulls sailing over them, and watched them return, with the gulls swooping to meet them.

Then, in July of 1890, Barbara and Kin had a conversation in their home in New York.

'I'd like to name him Luke after my father,' Kin said.

'But I'd thought to name him for my brother. For Tom, who brought us together.' Barbara's blue gaze was dreamy. 'Thomas Wakefield. It has a nice ring to it, don't you think?'

'Very nice,' Kin agreed. 'But for our next one.' He grinned. 'If you agree, that is. But for our first born I prefer Luke.'

'I don't know,' Barbara said. 'Why for your father?'

'Because.'

'Oh, all right,' she said ungraciously. 'Whatever you want. I don't really care.'

Kin bent and kissed her. 'You're wonderful, and I love you.' Then, 'I'll write and tell them now, and ask them to come for the christening.'

She sighed. 'I suppose you have to.' Then she brightened. 'We'll have a big party afterward.'

'Party?' He looked doubtful. 'What for?' But when she took his hand and cupped it around her breast, and smiled up at him, he said, 'Sure, if you want to,' and was content.

It was that conversation that led to Augusta's trip with Luke in the middle of the month.

They embarked on the *Puritan*, another ship designed by George Peirce and added to the fleet a year before. She was a four-deck steamer, with feathering paddle wheels and an all-steel hull. She had 321 staterooms, an uninterrupted promenade deck, and at 420 feet was the largest of the line's fleet. Serpentine newel posts decorated the gallery stairs, which led to an area carpeted in red and gold. A large portrait of Governor John Endecott hung in the center, and outward there radiated long corridors of white and gold.

It was only six weeks after Augusta's forty-third birthday, and the line's forty-third anniversary.

She looked around the beautiful white and gold dining saloon and smiled.

Luke raised his glass to her. 'To you, Gussie. And to the line.'

'Our future and fortune,' she said softly, thinking of the certainty in her father's voice when he had said that to her.

She was fashionably dressed in dark blue silk, with ruching at the throat and wrist. Her waist was narrow and flat, her bosom and hips curved. There were the faintest of lines in her face, but her eyes still glowed a bright and alive young green, and her dimples were as deep as ever.

A man sitting at a table not far away suddenly turned his head and smiled and nodded at her.

She realized with a start that it was the former president,

Grover Cleveland. She returned the greeting and looked away quickly. He was a private citizen now, and traveling with friends. He must be allowed to enjoy himself in peace.

'I'm happy we're going,' Luke said to her. He was as lean as ever, his face brown, his eyes pale silver – the same silver that was spreading from the white streak into the rest of his hair from its place over his temple. 'I want very much to see Kin. I wish they'd move to Fall River.'

'It's too quaint,' Augusta said, and smiled. 'You know how Barbara feels.'

'Quaint indeed. And I suppose we are too.'

'Perhaps we are.' But Augusta was thinking of Amy. Where was she now? How did she fare? And of Caleb. What of him? She felt as if there was a hole in her heart that would never be filled until she saw the children again. Now, trying to imagine their faces, she found that she couldn't. What she saw in her mind's eye was blurred and fading. But her pain was sharp.

Across the dining saloon, Bennet Graystone-Fields said to the steward, 'I'll have the lobster, yes. And then a steak. A good thick one. And mind you, well done. If it's bleeding when you bring it, I shall send it back. With the lobster, vinaigrette beans. And with the steak, roast potatoes and peas and brown bread. And first I'll have a plate of cold salmon. And a dish of white grapes.'

Mabel listened, nodding her approval. It sounded a proper meal to her, money well spent, she considered, although she rarely considered money well spent. This, however, was different. It was for food, for sustenance. She had eaten that way all of her life, and found it agreed with her. Her body was tall, strong, and very full. Wedges of flesh draped over the edges of her chair. Her cheeks hung in folds. She had two chins. She no longer imagined that there was inside her a young and pretty girl whom no one knew. She had forgotten that fancy. Now she asked, 'And what about dessert?'

'Pie of any kind you can imagine,' the steward said politely. 'And lemon cakes, pudding, and . . .'

'Lemon cakes,' she said. 'And after that I shall see.'

Bennet smiled at her. 'We have time to order dessert, Mama.'

'I'll order now and be sure I have it when I want it. It's the forethought that counts. If you remember that in your business dealings . . .'

'I have no dealings yet,' he told her.

She slapped her hand on the *Wall Street Journal*, a financial publication that had attained a good reputation in the year that it had been appearing. 'Read this. Study it. It must be your Bible. And then you'll be ready. You shall help me when I need it.'

'You'll never need it,' he said softly.

She smiled, taking the words for a compliment instead of an expression of his despair. 'We'll see what we see. Meanwhile you must learn.'

He cut in, 'Listen, Mama, I shall need an increase in my allowance. A large one.'

'An increase? A large one? Have you gone crazy? What for?' Her face had turned red, her voice risen.

He didn't answer her. He just looked at her, his brown eyes soft, a faint smile on his lips.

'What for?' she repeated, her voice now rising in a shriek. 'I demand to know. You need nothing. I provide. What do you lack? Tell me that, ha? And what do you think I am? I work hard. How can you ask me to throw my money away?'

'I just want an increase in my allowance,' he said mildly. He remembered clearly when at that look on his mother's face, that note in her voice, he'd begin to shake and shiver and sweat. All the time he was growing up, she had terrified him. She had terrified his father, too. His father had never gotten over it and died to escape her. But Bennet, at twenty-two, was no longer afraid of her. He had come to see that she needed him. Indeed, she needed him as much as he needed her. Bennet, in spite of everything, was good-natured. He preferred not to fight unless he had to. So he ignored the small things and concentrated on the large. He considered an increase in his allowance to be one of the latter.

Glaring at him, she said, 'Your father ought to have left you something. Any man would have. But no, not he.'

'He had nothing.' Bennet's smile widened. 'You can afford it, Mama.'

'By God, I do think you've gone crazy! What will you spend my money on? Tell me that, ha?' She didn't wait for an answer. She let her shoulders sag, her face crumple under its mass of hair. Her voice broke on a sob as she said, 'Oh, it's so hard. To be a woman all alone in the world. To know what to do. To protect yourself, your only child. The world is so wicked.' She shot a narrow glance at him. 'Why, Bennet?'

'I shall be taking an apartment. A suite of rooms. Lodgings. For myself.'

'Lodgings for yourself!' Now, suddenly, her face purpled. Her eyes bulged. Her massive nest of graying hair jerked back and forth as she shook her head. 'Pray tell me why,' she demanded through gritted teeth.

The steward brought the cold salmon and grapes and a basket of hot rolls. He slid wine and butter closer to Bennet. Bennet waited until the man had withdrawn. Then, with careful and finicky motions, he buttered a thick slice of bread and popped a grape into his mouth. Then he said, 'I want to.'

'It's that girl.' Mabel said it flatly. She knew her Bennet. And this was Mabel's own fault. Jeanette had proved to be tougher than she looked. Mabel had been unable to scare her away, even to buy her away. She had tried both. Jeanette had giggled, told Bennet, and now this was the result.

Bennet said pleasantly, 'I'd like to have a place of my own.'

'What for?' Mabel asked.

'So I can sometimes be by myself.'

'What for? Why do you have to be by yourself?'

He bit into the bread and took up a forkful of salmon.

'Oh, Bennet – do you know how you've hurt me? All I've lived for since the day you were born is you. You, my son. How can you do this to me?' She peered at him to see what effect her words were having. She saw none. She dropped her head.

The steward brought Bennet's steak, put it before him. The roast potatoes were in a silver tureen, and garnished with peas. 'Very nice,' Bennet said, beginning to eat.

Mabel ignored her own food. She shrieked, 'Bennet!'

Grover Cleveland turned his head and looked away again. Richard Morris Hunt, traveling with a party of Vanderbilts, glanced sideways. There were sibilant whispers from half the dining saloon.

Mabel clutched her massive bosom with both trembling hands. 'Oh, how it hurts.'

'What hurts?' he asked, his mouth full.

'What you tell me.'

He continued to chew, then swallowed. 'I'm sorry, Mama.

But I would like an increase in my allowance.'

She pretended not to have heard him. With an effort, she smiled benignly and began to eat, trying to catch up with him.

But he finished first and didn't wait for her. He folded his linen napkin neatly, excused himself, and rose. He limped slowly away from the table, allowing her to have a full view of how difficult it was for him to walk on his bad foot. Then, when he was sure she had seen him and was looking now, he allowed his legs to collapse from under him. He fell in an untidy heap, gasping so hard that his round hips and thick thighs quivered.

With a cry, Mabel rushed to his side and dropped down beside him.

Luke and a steward hurried to help her rise and reassure her, while two other stewards lifted Bennet to his feet.

He thanked them with dignity, said, 'Goodnight, Mama,' and went outside for a walk in the air.

Later, in his stateroom, Jeanette snuggled to him, and asked, 'Well? How did it go.'

'I'll get my allowance.'

'And we'll have an apartment together?'

'Not together. That wouldn't be right. But just down the hall from each other.'

'And we'll get married, the way you said?'

He smiled at her so hard that his cheeks quivered. 'Of course. I told you. One of these days we'll get married.'

'Oh, we'll have fun,' she giggled.

'We surely will,' he agreed.

Two days later, Willie Gorgas stood alone at the rail of the *Pilgrim*. He wished he hadn't gone. He guessed he was getting old, else why would he have done it? To go down there. To walk up to the place, knock, and wait, and then, standing there, have the door closed in his face.

Mary had finally come to let him in and said coldly, 'What do you want?'

She knew. Of course she knew. But he told her anyhow. 'I want to see my granddaughter,' he'd answered.

Her lips had curled. 'Speak up, man. I don't understand you.'

'Have some respect,' he'd shouted. 'I'm your husband's father.'

'My husband has no father.'

It took him a minute to know what she meant. Then he didn't believe it. A son couldn't deny a father that way. It couldn't be. 'It's a lie,' Willie yelled. 'William would never...'

Her curled lips made an ugly smile. She said nothing.

Willie knew it was true. William had allowed his father to die. Willie Gorgas was no more. The old man whose black eyes glittered with anger was only a husk. He was dead in his son's heart, dead in his son's memory. Then how could he be alive? He shouted, 'Let William tell me.'

'All right,' she said softly. 'You'll hear it from his own lips.' She left the room.

William was standing behind the closed door of the library. The room was paneled in dark mahogany with a red plush carpet and red satin drapes at the window. But his face was white. His tall body seemed to sway. Mary said, 'Go and tell him, William. I'm tired of this. What will the neighbours think? The servants? Suppose we have company when he comes. Go and tell him to stay away from here and away from us.'

'Mary...'

Her lips tightened. 'It's your fault,' she said harshly. 'If you'd told me the truth we'd never have come to this.'

'But I didn't know.'

'Whorehouses!' she returned. 'Can you imagine what'll happen if people find out?'

'Mary...'

'The Belmonts, the Oelriches, the Vanderbilts – can you imagine?'

'I can't...'

'I don't care for myself,' she said softly. 'It's for Diane. She's so lovely, so good. I want her to have the best. The best, William. And so do you.'

He nodded, straightened his shoulders. Slowly, he edged the door open and looked into the foyer.

Willie stood waiting.

As William watched, the outer door swung back. Diane came in. She wore a white pinafore and white slippers. A tiny white bonnet perched on her curls. She looked like a small angel as she smiled uncertainly at Willie.

Then her nanny took her by the hand and drew her away, saying, 'We must go now. It's time for lessons.'

'Wait,' Diane said. 'I want to ask . . .'

But her nanny pulled her out. 'I'll call your mother, Diane. I will, if you don't come.'

At the door, the girl paused to look back, her eleven-year-old face bewildered.

When she was gone, William entered the foyer and looked at old Willie. He seemed smaller than William had remembered him to be. His shoulders were bowed. The pinned sleeve of his jacket had loosened around the stump of his arm. His beard was very nearly all white. He said, faltering, 'Willie? William?'

William opened his mouth to speak but no sound came out. His hands hung limp at his sides. He was empty inside.

Willie whispered, 'But I'm not dead, boy, at least not yet,' and went stamping out of the place.

'It was the only way,' Mary said later. And as she handed William a Scotch and soda, 'You had to do it. You had no choice.'

William didn't answer. He had done nothing. But why say so. As always, his father, old Willie Gorgas, had had the last word.

'Whorehouses,' she said softly. 'It's the last we'll hear of them, William.'

And slowly, feeling as if his head should fall from his neck and go spinning across the thick pile carpet, he nodded and nodded and couldn't stop . . .

Willie, leaning against the rail, knowing nothing of the conversation, nodded and nodded in much the same movement, and stared across the dark waters of the Sound, and backward, across the dark years of his life.

Caleb Wakefield walked slowly along the promenade deck. A warm mist rose up off Mount Hope Bay. The stars were fading. There had to be some way to approach his parents. But although he'd considered it ever since the ship's sailing the night before, he hadn't decided how.

He wasn't sure what they would say, do. He wanted the

meeting to be right. A lot depended on the rightness, although he tried to tell himself that it didn't matter. If it was good, then it was. If not, he'd get along.

Getting along had been something he'd learned to do since he left home. But he was tired. He wanted more. He thought he saw how to get the more.

He smoothed back his hair, using both hands in a gesture that had become habitual to him. At twenty-four, he was a very good-looking man. Lean but broad-shouldered, his dark curls glossy, his pale gray eyes shining from his face. He looked so much like Luke that, after the first glance he'd given his father, the question of paternity had been answered.

He was, as Luke averred, Luke's son. Knowing that gave Caleb a certain strength. As Luke's son, he had rights. He was glad now that he had decided to return home, which was the way he still thought of it.

Within months after his arrival in New York he'd realized that by running away he'd given up what should rightfully have been his. Which was at least a part of whatever the Wakefields had. By then he'd understood what he hadn't known before – money was everything. Without it, a man was a bellboy, wearing a uniform that didn't quite fit, at the mercy of those who could pitch pennies as tips, and give orders, and demand service and courtesy without saying thanks. Money was power. Very quickly, once he knew that, he maneuvered himself from bellboy to chief bell captain, from a business hotel to a luxury hotel.

The opportunities improved. He soon had a bank account. He found women for men. He placed bets. he arranged card games. But what he had become nagged at him. He wanted money, but something else too. It took time for him to see that there was profit in going back to his beginnings. But he didn't want to go as a supplicant. Even so, he still had no plan when he embarked on the *Pilgrim*.

But now, suddenly, he saw a way: let them think the meeting was accidental. Once again he smoothed his hair. Then slowly, nodding a 'Good morning' at a steward, he went along the companionway and sauntered into the dining saloon.

When, from the corner of his eyes, he saw Augusta and Luke seated at a table, he continued by, his head turned slightly away.

Augusta's eyes widened. She remembered how once Luke had thought he'd seen Caleb, and only imagined it, and she thought now that perhaps it was the same. Perhaps Kin's new baby, young Luke, the christening, the party afterward, even being in New York, had all combined to bring him forward in her mind. So now, out of her wish, she imagined she saw him. But then she heard Luke's gasp.

He pushed back his chair and half rose. 'Gussie! It's Caleb!'

And she realized it was so. Caleb. A grown man – hesitating. A light in his eyes and a frown between his dark brows. Hesitating as if trapped between warring feelings. A desire to stop, a need to flee.

But she wouldn't allow that. She too rose. Arms reaching, she cried, 'Caleb! Caleb!'

And, floating it seemed to her, treading on air, she covered the small distance between them, and threw her arms around him. 'Oh, Caleb! How wonderful!'

Luke was right with her, his hand outstretched.

Caleb said quietly, 'Is it possible that you both look the same?'

'We're not. And neither are you.' Augusta held him tightly. 'Sit down with us. We'll have coffee and talk.'

And when a steward had brought a third chair, brought fresh coffee and hot rolls, they began to speak, all three of them together, and stopped and grinned. Then Augusta said, 'You were coming home, weren't you?'

Caleb looked startled. 'Coming home? Why do you think that?'

'You mean you weren't?'

'I was going to Boston. I have some business there.' It was a lie, of course. He had no business, though he hoped one day he would. He went on, 'I'd have taken the direct train, but –' he sighed – 'sentiment led me . . .'

'To us,' Augusta cried, her eyes alight with joy.

Luke told him, 'We always wanted you back, so when we saw you . . .'

'I never thought of it,' Caleb said, but gently, regretfully.

The sadness in his face and voice made it easy for Luke to say, 'Would you think of it, Caleb? Surely by now you realize that we both love you. There was never an intent to injure you.'

277

'I knew that all along,' Caleb said. 'I simply felt I had no right to be with you.' It had taken him too long, he decided. He ought to have returned before to what was rightfully his.

'Now you must see that you do belong. And it was never a matter of right,' Luke said.

Augusta clasped her hands tightly to keep from touching him. 'You're part of us, Caleb.'

'I must consider,' he said softly.

'Do you have to go back to New York? Have you obligations there?' Luke asked.

Caleb shook his head. 'Only my employment. I haven't married. I'm alone.'

Augusta beamed at him. 'Then it's settled.'

'Slowly, slowly,' Luke said, smiling. 'Allow Caleb to decide.'

The ship's whistle blew three long blasts. They were passing the Borden Flats light. By the time the *Pilgrim* was tied up at the Fall River wharves, Caleb had agreed to go on to Boston to complete his fictitious business, then to return home for at least a few days and think about what he should do.

Within two weeks he had moved his few belongings from New York, was working in the line's general manager's office, and considering his next move.

Chapter 25

It was a steamy Thursday afternoon in August of 1892. South Main Street was busy with shoppers. The trolleys clanged their bells at loaded wagons blocking the way. The horses neighed and stamped amid their droppings.

Augusta eased the basket on her arm, and smoothed her gloves. She decided it was time to go home. It was too hot, and too crowded down street.

She waited at the corner for a break in the traffic. Behind her she heard, 'Isn't it terrible? Can you imagine?' And then, 'I wonder if it's true? Both of them, they say. And with a hatchet, too.'

A police wagon clanged by. Suddenly the intersection was full of people all moving in one direction. Augusta allowed herself to be carried with them, wondering what had happened. As she moved, surrounded by a crowd, along Second Street, she heard the Borden name mentioned. By the time she reached St. Mary's Church, she had heard the details. Lizzie Borden was being arrested for the killing of her father and stepmother. When she saw the silent, staring mob outside the house, Augusta choked and turned back. Every step she took on the blocks toward High Street, she faced groups pushing the other way. Young women and old, men and boys, babes in arms even. It seemed as if every mill in the town had emptied, every store closed, every bank vacated. In the thousands they came, avid, whispering, and hurrying to the house of death.

That evening in a trembling voice she told Luke what she had seen. And added: 'I don't believe it.'

'We must wait and see,' he told her. 'We know nothing of what happened.'

The pros and cons of the case were argued in the shops and drinking places and mills. They were talked over in Augusta's study group, where several of the women had gone to church with Liz Borden, and others speculated over what her relationship was to Colonel Richard Borden and his brother Jefferson, and how the scandal would affect their families, since all the Bordens were cousins of some kind.

Augusta finally announced that the subject was closed. The group had to consider matters of more lasting moment. In November there would be an election. Grover Cleveland would be running for the presidency again; Adlai Stevenson would be candidate for the vice-presidency. The ladies grumbled but accepted her decision. The fate of the nation was surely more important than the death of two sad souls in Fall River. But when the meeting was over, they returned to the subject again.

It did not end until June of the following year when the trial was held in New Bedford's Superior Court, and Lizzie Borden was acquitted. Soon thereafter she moved with her sister Emma to a house called Maplecroft on French Street, and resumed the quiet life she had lived until the mysterious death of her parents.

Later in the same year, on a cold winter day, Willie Gorgas

walked along Central Street a few blocks from the Fall River Gorgas Inn. He leaned heavily on his cane as he paused at a curb. He was tired, dizzy. The blue twilight was thick with mist. He thought of William, and then, with longing, of Diane. Sighing, shoulders hunched, he stepped into the street and into the path of a horse-drawn wagon. There was a shout. A horse neighed wildly as it knocked him off his feet. Wagon wheels rolled over him. His last thought was of a small blond girl, crying: 'Is that the Bogeyman?'

In 1893 also, even before the newly elected president took office, Cleveland was warned that a financial panic was brewing. At the end of October, the Philadelphia and Reading Railroad filed for bankruptcy. The prices of grain, cotton, and steel fell. The stock market was constantly unsteady. By May of 1894 panic had set in. More railroads collapsed. A run on the banks caused some 500 of them to close.

But at the same time the New York, New Haven and Hartford Railroad Company took over control of the Old Colony Railroad and Steamboat companies, including the Fall River Line. As substitute for outright purchase, the New Haven effected a 99-year lease with set fees, and included as a part of the agreement the promise to return to the Old Colony, at expiration of the lease, all ships, wharves, and warehouses in the same condition as at the time of signing. Since the New Haven had taken over the Providence and Stonington Steamship Company a year before, this was the second step in what was to become a monopoly of transportation facilities in southern New England.

At the time it seemed reasonable to Luke and Augusta, and in no way affected their lives. Their shares in the Old Colony were converted. Luke's job remained secure, and so did Caleb's.

But the younger man was concerned. 'It's the same as a new owner,' he said, frowning. 'A ninety-nine-year lease! What does that mean? Who among us will see the wharves returned?'

Still, the Fall River ships sailed.

By then, Caleb was working on the *Plymouth*, a new boat, in service only two years, that had been designed especially for winter travel, with less passenger space and greater cargo area.

He was twenty-seven. Those years that he had spent away seemed part of another life to him. He knew now that he had returned to where he belonged. What had first brought him back, scheming and hating, no longer mattered. He stayed for love. For the love of the ships, for love of Augusta and Luke. And for love of Rosalie Burns, whom he expected to marry at the end of December, a month hence.

One evening, aboard the *Plymouth*, he gave his hair a final brush and set his cap on his head at a jaunty tilt. It was time for him to make his rounds.

He climbed down the steps, started along the companionway, thinking of Rosalie. It was on just such a night that he had met her some five months before. There was a high wind. Whitecaps ruffled the bay and spun a fog cocoon around the ship, dulling her lights to a pale glow. Rosalie had been standing at the rail, the wind blowing her fur cape, sparkling droplets shining in her hair. She was a pretty sight to behold, and he paused to admire her. He might have gone on, except that she turned to him and cried, 'Oh, isn't it wonderful!' and laughed, and at the same instant, the ship dipped hard. She fell into the rail and then away from it, and he caught her in his arms to keep her from tumbling to the deck.

She was a Fall River girl, he soon learned. He knew of her family, although he had never met any of them then. He saw her as often as he could thereafter, and only a few weeks ago, she had accepted his proposal...

In a little while, when he was free, he would meet her. They'd have a coffee together, and she'd tell him about the shopping she'd done in New York and the progress in arrangements for their wedding. Once he'd have sworn that he could never feel as at peace with himself as he did now. Once he'd thought all hope of happiness had eluded him. But now, with the ship's deck under his feet and Rosalie in his mind, he felt that he had everything he wanted.

A familiar voice cut into his reverie. He stopped, turned to look.

Peter Kincaid smiled at him. 'Surprised?'

'Of course! I didn't know you were in this country.'

Peter said, 'Nor did I know you had returned to Fall River. When was that?'

'About three years ago.'

'And returned to the line, too, I see.'

'Yes,' Caleb said. 'But what of you? What are you doing here?'

'It seemed a good time.' There was something still boyish about Peter, even though he was now thirty and wore a small Van Dyke beard. He sighed. 'I didn't expect to have to do it, but I did.'

'Return, you mean?'

'This last year's business failures have been bad for me. I didn't have much choice. There's something left, of course. And the house too. But my rambling days are temporarily over.'

'That sounds bad.'

'Oh, believe me, I'll survive.'

'Have you married?'

'Me?' Peter looked horrified. 'Certainly not. I'm unmarried, unsettled, and unconcerned.'

Caleb grinned at him. 'Every man to his own. I've recently become engaged.'

'The more fool you, when there's so many fish in the sea.'

'I can tell you, there comes a time when a man decides he wants only one fish.'

'Some men,' Peter said. He walked with Caleb, asking for news of the Wakefields. He shook his head at news of Kin's little son Luke and pulled his beard at word of Amy's marriage and subsequent disappearance. When Caleb went into the saloon, Peter followed him.

Caleb found Rosalie where he expected, and introduced her to Peter. The three of them had coffee and cakes together, and then Caleb had to return to his duties. He looked back from the doorway, saw the two leaning toward each other in earnest conversation.

It was an image he was to carry with him forever. Peter's head bent forward and Rosalie's bright one. Her curls almost touching Peter's cheek . . .

'Are we ready?' Augusta asked. They had only a short distance to go to the Central Congregational Church at Bedford and Rock Streets, but she didn't want to have to hurry.

Luke grinned at her, his leathery face alight, squint lines deepening at his eyes. 'We are.'

'And so am I,' Caleb said, coming down the steps to join them. He had a tall hat under his arm. He wore a long black morning coat and striped trousers. His luggage was already in the carriage. There was nothing more to do than take his greatcoat and leave.

Augusta was smiling at him. Luke felt in his waistcoat pocket once more for the ring, then he pulled the door open.

There was a clamor in the roadway. A cart rolled up. A young man leaped down. Caleb recognized him as a boy who worked for Rosalie's parents. Suddenly frightened, Caleb hurried to meet him, calling ahead, 'What's wrong?'

The boy stuck an envelope into Caleb's hand, mumbled a few words Caleb didn't understand, and rushed away.

Augusta's face had paled. She clung tightly to Luke's arm.

Caleb looked at them, then down at the envelope. He opened it slowly, unwillingly – *Peter and I will be married by the time you read this. Forgive me. Rosalie.*

He crumpled the note in his big hand. To Augusta and Luke, he said, 'There'll be no wedding.'

'Caleb!' Augusta's pained whisper.

'What's happened?' Luke's quick question.

Caleb couldn't speak. He thrust the note into his father's hand and went into the house. Alone, he sank into a chair and buried his face in his hands, shaking with anguish, burning with anger. Rosalie... all he wanted. Peter, the spoiler. He clenched his fist and beat his knee until both were numb.

Two hours later, in uniform, and ready to go back to work, he boarded the *Puritan.*

'All ashore that's going ashore!' The cry went up along the decks and companionways. Flags danced in the moist June breeze. Goodbyes were shouted, and white-gloved porters retreated, no longer carrying baggage. With a ringing of bells the gangplank went up and was secured. There were three blasts of the ship's whistle, and the *Priscilla* moved slowly away from Pier 28 and past New York's skyline.

It was the ship's third scheduled trip after being commissioned earlier that month. At 440 feet in length, she was the largest vessel of the Fall River Line, carrying 1,500 passengers in 359 staterooms and 1,022 berths. She took on 200 tons of coal every trip, had ten boilers and 30 furnaces. George Peirce had designed the *Priscilla* and it had cost $1.5 million to complete.

The grand saloon was 142 feet in length, 30 feet in width, and 24 feet high, with panels decorated in seven different colors. The dining room on the main deck had windows on both sides with panels of leaded glass in a floral design; the same motif was repeated in the leaded glass table lights. The green and red carpet was patterned in the Oriental style.

It took a crew of 196 to service the *Priscilla*, including among the others two first pilots, two quartermasters, fourteen deckhands, and 68 waiters.

But neither the beauty, the size, nor the newness of the vessel made any impression on Mabel Graystone-Fields as she watched the busy harbor slide away from the wide wake left behind.

It was Bennet who concerned her. She didn't know how to get at him any more. Once she had been all-powerful in his life. Now she took second place. It wasn't right, it wasn't fair. True, she had his promise never to marry without her permission. But still...

She said softly, 'Bennet, you won't forget?'

'No, Mama. Of course not.' He had said it before. Not once, not twice. More times than he could remember. 'I won't forget. I promise.'

'What's a woman to do,' she sighed, clutching her portmanteau to her.

Bennet slid a look at her. She seemed well. Her face was full, her brown eyes clear and bright. She didn't look as if she had been at death's door three times in the past five years. In fact, Bennet was pretty certain she hadn't been. But how could he be absolutely sure?

The day he moved to his new lodgings, with Jeanette already ensconced next door, Mabel had ranted and raved, calling hell's fire and damnation on his head in the one moment, weeping brokenly the next, and in the third, wringing her hands and shouting to the ceiling: 'What should I do, Papa? I've been caretaker of your money all these years. Who should I leave it to when I die?'

Bennet had gathered the last of his things, his hat and cane and gloves, listening quietly; finally he pressed a firm kiss on her cheek and departed. He had lunched with her the next day and the day thereafter. He ignored her questions about with whom he ate his dinners and spent his nights. At the end of the week he received word that she had had a heart attack. Of course he went to her. She was gray of face and gasping for breath when he arrived. The doctor had gone, she said weakly. He predicted she might recover. She grasped Bennet's hands, pleaded with him to come back to her. He soothed her and smiled at her and agreed to have lunch with her the following day. Over the next month he developed the habit of allowing her to lengthen the mealtime. He balked though when she tried to prolong the day into night. Jeanette was waiting for him. One midnight there came a pounding at his door. Jeanette moaned, 'Oh dear, what's that?'

When Bennet went to see, he was handed a message. His mother was dying. He dressed quickly and hurried to her. That time her lips were blue, her face sallow. She gasped, 'Thank God, you're in time. I'm dying, Bennet.'

He thought she might be, and sat close beside her, whispering, 'What can I do for you?'

'My dear son, how good to have you with me. And now, if only I could have the comfort of peace of mind. If only I could be sure ... sure ...'

'Sure of what, Mama?'

'Some day, you must – you must marry.' She stopped, choking for air.

'Don't think of it,' he said.

'But I do, I do. Only promise me, my son. Promise that it will be only with my permission.' Her head fell sideways on the pillows. Her mouth gaped.

He felt tears rise in his eyes. Poor Mama. She was frightened, in pain. Softly, he said, 'I promise, Mama.' She recovered soon after. It was then that his suspicions first began. Was she as ill as she seemed to be?

When Jeanette broached the subject of marriage, he said, 'I've been thinking of it.' The next time she raised the question, he told her, 'Yes. It's a good idea. When the time is right.' He never mentioned his promise to Mabel, considering it no affair of Jeanette's.

Now he said to his mother, 'I'll go down to my stateroom for a little while.'

'Dinner will be served soon,' she said, color rising in her cheeks.

'I'll join you.'

285

'Good. They say the cooking's excellent.' Her voice was pleasant now that she had had her way and could begin to concentrate on the food.

With a nod, Bennet left her. He found Jeanette awaiting him in the stateroom.

'It's nice here,' she said. 'But not where I want to spend my life.'

He ignored the luxury of bed and carpet, the elegant shade on the light, the drapes at the porthole. 'You'll be out later. I'm going to dine with Mama now.'

'But I'm hungry,' Jeanette wailed. 'I want to eat, and then walk in the grand saloon.'

He said softly, 'First I'll take care of Mama.'

Jeanette sank down in a chair. She smoothed her red curls from her face and shrugged. 'Do what you like.'

She knew that he would, no matter what she said, and no matter how she pouted. She enjoyed the arrangement. She had more than a thousand dollars hidden away in a bank and was certain there was more to come. He was pleasant and undemanding, and he'd promised to marry her some time. What more could a girl want?

Before he left her, he said, 'When I return, I'll take you down to dinner.'

'You will?' She jumped up to plant a kiss on his ckeek. 'You're wonderful!'

He met his mother on the main deck, and together they went into the dining saloon. She sailed ahead as usual, finding seats at a large table where four men were already seated.

She announced her name, and Bennet's, as soon as they were seated. The four men introduced themselves: a Morgan, a Vanderbilt, a Harvey, and a Belmont.

Having offered that courtesy, the four returned to the conversation interrupted by it. They were grim. The depression of 1893 was continuing into 1894. Gold reserves were still shrinking. It was expected that 640 banks would fail before the end of the year, and 22,500 miles of railroads would end in receivership.

Mabel listened in some bewilderment. She had not been affected by what had happened in 1893, except that she had been able to pick up a few pieces of pretty property at good prices through foreclosure auctions. She didn't expect it to be any different this year, nor the next either. Still, she sent Bennet a significant look. A Morgan, a Vanderbilt, a Harvey, and a Belmont – he was having dinner with the most important financiers in New York.

When the men had excused themselves, she told Bennet so.

'Yes, Mama,' he said, without interest.

'It is among such men as those that you will make your mark.'

'Yes,' he repeated, his mouth full of mashed potatoes.

When, finally, they had finished the meal, he took her for a walk along the deck, then, while she fumed at him, he bade her good night and walked away.

A short time later he was in the dining saloon with Jeanette. She looked around, and said once again, 'You're wonderful!'

The light from the round opalescent ceiling lamps was soft. The table lamps with their floral shades glowed faintly. The mahogany tables and chairs, the fine linen cloth and silver and china all shone with the patina of unremitting care.

The menu was a thick affair of foods and wines suitable to every taste.

Bennet ordered for the two of them. A Boston stew first. Then two relishes: euchered figs, sweet gherkins. Then Finnan Haddie, broiled in cream. To follow, he chose an extra porterhouse steak for four, with mushrooms. He decided, since he had already eaten one meal, that that would be enough.

Their stew had just been served to them when he saw the steward suddenly freeze. A hush fell across the large room.

He looked up, his spoon halfway to his lips, as Jeanette gasped, 'Oh, look!'

Framed now in the large double doors with their shining and carved mahogany arches there stood a woman. She was tall, wearing a large pink plumed hat and a long sequin-decorated gown, which fit tightly over her 42-inch bust, clung to her narrow 27-inch waist, and hugged her 40-inch hips to bell out in a pink froth around her ankles. Her arms were covered with above-the-elbow pink gloves of the softest kid. For a long still moment, she stood in the doorway. Then, looking neither to left nor right, she walked across the hushed room, with the head steward dancing ahead of her, and seated herself regally at a table for four. Only now did she permit herself to smile and look at her escort, and to begin, slowly, to remove first her left glove, then her right. She was the actress Lillian Russell, whose name had been Helen Louise Leonard before she left Iowa for a career far from her birthplace.

The man with her was James G. Brady, known by many as Diamond Jim. A super salesman, who had a three-carat diamond in the ferrule of his cane, he was of a size to suit the lady. He weighed 250 pounds, and had a bulldog jaw and several chins. Small shrewd dark eyes gleamed in his round red face.

They had met in 1893 at the Columbia Exposition in Chicago, when both were guests of the Palmer House and Lillian was playing the Columbia Theater on the Midway. He was so impressed with her performance that he gave her a gift of diamonds. In the year since, they had become fast friends, but without the intimacy of lovers. Lillian was married, but she lived with her husband only occasionally. Lillian and Jim Brady had much in common. They loved gambling. They enjoyed confiding in each other because they were both lonely. And they were experts at eating. They were on the way to Newport, where Lillian was to perform and Jim would visit friends.

When Jim Brady took up the menu, Bennet brought his spoon to his mouth and swallowed his Boston stew, while Jeanette breathed, 'I never thought I'd see that. Never, never.'

And at the next table Mary Gorgas said quietly to her daughter Diane, 'Di-Di, sit up straight.' And to William, 'Did you see that presence?'

William smiled, said nothing.

'Diane!' she said, barely moving her lips. 'Do you hear?'

'Yes, Mama.' The girl straightened her slender form and raised her chin. But her face was blank. There was no light in her eyes. She was treated like a little princess by her parents, had been surrounded by servants and English nannies for as long as she could remember. Now at fifteen she felt like nothing more than a prize horse, for which her parents were already seeking a suitable stud.

'You're beautiful,' Mary Gorgas said. 'You must make use of it.'

'Yes, Mama.'

'As she has. But in a more respectable way, of course. I would die rather than see you a performer.' Mary drew a deep breath, and went on, 'I believe we'll no longer call you Di-Di. It's a childish nickname and has no dignity. You're grown now. We shall call you Diane.'

'Yes, Mama.' Diane sighed.

'You'll like Newport. It's the right place for you.' Mary was about to go on, but suddenly she stopped. Her blue eyes darted to where Lillian Russell sat with Diamond Jim Brady. A smile touched Mary's lips. She waved for a steward.

Within moments he had brought the actress and her escort a bottle of champagne. As he presented it, he nodded in the Gorgas direction.

Lillian raised her golden head and smiled and bowed in her chair. Jim Brady beamed, although he habitually drank nothing but lemon soda and orange juice.

Mary lifted her hand in a genteel wave. Moments later she leaned toward Diane. 'Go and ask her to write her name on your menu.'

'Mama! I can't!'

'Don't be ridiculous. She'll be pleased. Performers are always pleased to have attention paid to them.'

'It's too embarrassing.' Diane was close to tears. She looked at her father. There was no help there. She didn't expect it. William always agreed with his wife.

This time, in fact, he wasn't listening to Mary, nor aware of Diane's glance. He was wondering if it would be possible, after they had been in Newport for a few days, for him to go on, alone and without Mary's knowing about it, to Fall River. He wanted to see old Willie's grave. Ever since he had received word that his father was dead, he had thought about it.

'Papa, do I have to?' Diane pleaded.

He looked at her but didn't answer.

Mary hissed, 'Now you listen to me, miss. I don't want to hear another word. Take this menu over there. Smile your best and curtsey as you've been taught, and do what I tell you to do.'

Diane took the menu unwillingly.

'You know it's no good to argue with me. I know what's best.' Mary's voice softened. 'Oh, my darling, I have such plans for you. I've given my life to those plans. Now do this for me.'

Diane rose gracefully. The folds of her blue gown swayed as she walked to the nearby table, curtsied, and offering the menu, said in a whisper, 'Miss Russell, may I have the very great honor...'

The actress beamed at her, signed her name with a flourish, and said, as Diane retreated, 'What a delightful child.'

Later, when leaving the dining saloon, she paused to say a few words to Mary, who looked at her adoringly, introduced herself and William, and ended by contriving that they hear the evening concert together.

When the *Priscilla* docked at Long Wharf in Newport, they left the ship together, having exchanged addresses and promised to meet for tea that afternoon.

Chapter 26

In September of 1895, Amy Wakefield Callahan boarded the *Puritan* with her three children. No one recognized her. Although she was only twenty-five, she looked ten years older. There was gray in her dark hair and grim lines streaked her brow. Her white shirtwaist was patched at one elbow and frayed at both cuffs. Her full black skirt was gone rusty with washing. Although she'd never before been on the *Puritan*, she saw many familiar faces among the crew but didn't identify herself, nor stop to smile or speak. Briefly she wondered about the *Providence*, not knowing that the ship had been retired a year before.

She hurried the children from the entry hall into their stateroom, ignoring their questions until she had locked the door.

Then, sinking down on the bed, she said: 'We're going home. Kevin, we're finally going home.' He was eight years old now, old enough to understand. 'Home, Ray.' The boy was six. He knew the word, but he didn't know what it meant to Amy. He chuckled, excited about the ship. 'We're on the way, Gussie,' Amy whispered. Gussie nodded. She was small, wan. She wasn't sure what 'on the way' meant. At five she knew only that she was all right as long as she was with her mother and could reach to touch her mother's gown or hand.

'And it's about time too,' Amy said, her voice breaking. She swallowed hard. She wasn't going to cry any more. She reminded herself of that. She had made her decision.

How long was it since she'd seen Sean? Two years, three? She was no longer certain. They'd quarreled one night. He'd said in a fierce hot whisper, 'Damn you, you lie like a stick beneath me! There's no love in you for me. There's nothing. You're a dry old woman!'

She *was* a dry old woman. She'd had five babies in seven years, and only the three remained. She was frightened there could be more, so the body that had once welcomed him no longer did. And she heard herself crying, 'Sean, no! Be careful!' and weeping when he wasn't.

'You're no damn use to me,' he'd told her.

It was a quarrel like all the others before it. She could remember nothing different about it. It ended with Sean yelling that she thought she was too good for him and that was the trouble.

She'd screamed, 'I'm tired of hearing that. I married you, didn't I? Doesn't that prove that I love you?'

He'd dragged her up from the bed and slapped her across the room. While she stood there, glaring at him, he'd dressed and stormed out. And that wasn't unusual either. But he had never come back. She'd expected him the next day, and the week that followed. By month's end she realized he had gone for good. There was no food in the house, the rent was due. She left the children with a neighbor and went into the streets in search of work. She found a job ironing in a laundry. Somehow she managed. The children grew.

Time passed. Then she realized that the flesh was falling away from her bones. On the coldest days she was warm, and there was a flush high on her cheeks and her eyes burned feverishly. The cough came on her later, and with it the memory of Kin. His illness that had required those long months abed ... feedings with milk puddings and thick soups and beaten cream. She had no money to spare for a doctor. She had no time to rest: there were three babies to feed. She didn't care for herself any more. It was only her babies who mattered. It came to her often that she would gladly trade her life for theirs – if she could only give them something. But how? How could she manage it? Then one night, seeing no future ahead, she knew what she had to do...

The stateroom was dim. Small Gussie sat close beside her on the edge of the bed. Kevin huddled at her feet. Ray stood on tiptoe, peering out of the porthole.

The ship's whistles blew. Bells rang. 'We're on the way,' Amy said again, feeling as if she were already home. This was a new ship to her, but she belonged to the Fall River Line, was part of her family. She remembered the day she had called out to the president, and he had stooped down and smiled at her. She put her arms around Gussie, and said softly, 'A long time ago, way before you were born, and way before I was too, when your grandma first came into the world, a ship called the *Bay State* waited in Fall River harbor. She was smaller, and not so elegant as this, but she was the first one of the line. And your great grandpa, his name was Marcus, you remember, held the infant Gussie up, and showed her that ship, and told her about the brand-new Fall River Line, and that it was her future and fortune.'

Amy's voice trailed away. There was too much to tell. She had no strength or breath for it. She would trade her life for theirs. There was no other way.

She took from her purse a small vial of laudanum, and from her pocket the note she had written before leaving New York.

'You must be good,' she said to the three children. 'I want you to lie down now with me, and go to sleep.'

'Is there nothing for supper?' Kevin asked.

She shook her head.

'Can't we go look at what's outside?' Ray demanded.

'You'll see in the morning,' she told him.

When she turned out the light, small Gussie cried, 'Mama, it's dark in here.'

'Then close your eyes,' Amy whispered.

She quickly swallowed the contents of the vial and lay down, gathering the children close to her. Holding them tightly, she lay back, staring wide-eyed into the shadows

The whistles blew at the Borden Flats light. The sun was just rising. The bay was a deep pink now, and the sky above was aglow with scuttling clouds.

It had been an uneventful trip, but Caleb was glad it was over. His joy in the line, in his life, were gone. He was glad when the voyages ended, but given one day ashore, and he was relieved to depart again. It had been that way ever since Rosalie left with Peter.

'Caleb!'

The tone of voice startled him. He turned quickly from the railing.

'The purser asks that you come with me.' It was the second mate. Dark-haired, dark-eyed – and worried-looking now, although usually carefree.

'What is it?' Caleb said.

'A steward reported children crying in one of the staterooms.'

'Well?'

'He knocked, but received no answer. He says it's been going on for a long time.'

Caleb followed the man to the main deck and into a companionway. He was thinking that some woman had left the children alone to spend a stolen night with her lover, and slept so well in spite of it that she didn't know the time.

As they neared the place, they heard the sound clearly. A small whimpering, a desolate weeping. Was it one child or two?

The men exchanged glances. The mate shrugged. It took only a moment to get the door open.

Although the room was shadowed, they saw the scene clearly.

A woman lay on the bed, her eyes open and fixed on the ceiling. Two small boys sat near her, crying. A tiny girl, curls tousled, burrowed against the woman and moaned.

Caleb went close, and then closer. His gorge rose as he looked into her face. When he'd last seen her, she was fourteen, with shining black eyes and runaway black curls. Now her eyes were dull, and her hair streaked with gray. But he knew her. 'Amy!' Caleb whispered. 'My God, it's Amy!'

His hand shook as he pulled a sheet over her, and took the three children into his arms and held them as tight as he could.

There was no time for the expression of grief in those first few days. But grief was there, a heaviness in the heart, a shadow to cloud the eye's vision.

Luke and Caleb attended to the funeral arrangements: brief services at the Congregational Church on Bedford Street, the interment at Oak Grove Cemetery near to where Marcus and Amy were buried. Crewmen of the Fall River Line's ships were pall bearers. Afterward Marge served a lunch of cold meats and salad and brown beans and dark bread.

Then there were the children, whose everyday needs required immediate concern. Rooms had to be aired, made comfortable for them. Their inadequate clothing had to be supplemented. And that was only the beginning.

Augusta, with Luke standing beside her, held them close, and told them that their mother was gone. Kevin only nodded. He had understood. Ray stared blankly, asked, 'But where? And when's she coming back?' Small Gussie's lips moved, but no sound came out. Her hands fluttered wildly before her face. Kevin said softly, 'She doesn't talk any more. She used to. Some. But now she's stopped. And never says a word.'

Augusta fought back the need to weep. No time . . . no time now for that. She would try with Gussie, learn first if the child could hear. Try to help, if there was a way to help. If she had spoken before, she could speak again.

The next afternoon Betty Raleigh came. One of her step grandsons brought her in his new electric brougham. His name was Gowan. He and his twin brother, Arthur, both worked in their father's teamster business. It had thrived under their grandfather, George Raleigh's hands, expanded when their father Rafe took it over. George had had a stroke a good number of years before. Betty had cared for him until his death. His son Rafe, and the boys, remained close to Betty.

She was sixty-four now, and leaned on a cane. Her face was round, her hair white. She said gently, 'I'm sorry for this, Augusta.'

Gowan Raleigh listened while the two women spoke together. He tried to picture his grandmother a servant in this house. He knew it was so because she had told him tales of her life here, but it was hard to imagine. Finally he excused himself, saying he had errands. He would return in an hour, if that was all right.

'He's a fine-looking boy,' Augusta said when he had gone.

'They both are,' Betty agreed. 'I've been lucky in my life.'

'You were willing to take the chance.'

Betty smiled at her. 'Maybe I didn't know that when I was doing it.' She went on to ask about Caleb, and, with the connection clear in her mind – and in Augusta's too – mentioned that there had been news of Peter Kincaid and his wife. Rafe Raleigh had just bought Peter's Highland Avenue house. The Boston lawyers who had handled the sale had told him that Peter and Rosalie were living now in San Francisco.

Marge Gowan brought in tea, and stopped to visit with Betty. Marge had long since lost the cough she had had when she first came to take the older woman's place, but her face remained thin and sallow. She pulled her hair into a tight knot on the top of her head and wore small glasses on her nose, and seemed to have resigned herself to spinsterhood. After she left the room, Betty said, 'She gives up too soon. After all, I was two years the older and more when I married George.'

When Gowan returned, Augusta went with her to the door. Betty smiled at her grandson, shook her head. 'I don't know about that thing he drives. Brougham he says they call it. As if it were one of those nice comfortable carriages. Can you imagine it, a carriage that has no horses. And how it scares them when it goes down the road!' She put her small wrinkled hand on Augusta's. 'Send for me, if you need help.'

But Augusta never did. For again there was no time.

At the end of the week Sean appeared at the door. His face was flushed. His body was stiff in his shabby clothes. The smell of whiskey hung about him. 'I want my children,' he said.

Marge stared him up and down, and took off her glasses and put them on. 'Talk to Mrs. Wakefield.'

When Augusta came into the room, he said, 'I heard of Amy's killing herself. I'm here for my children.'

Without a word Augusta took from inside the Bible on the mantel the note which Caleb had given to her.

He read the words addressed to her and Luke: *I'm sick and cannot go on. I can give them nothing. For my sake, will you love my babies and forgive me?*

'I don't care. I want my children.' He dropped the note on the table, then wiped his hand on his coat.

'You had abandoned them, and her,' Augusta said coldly. 'She was bringing them home to us.'

Sean shrugged. 'It's nothing to me what she was doing. She was mad at the end. And she's gone now.'

'She wanted us to raise them, Sean. To do what we could for them.'

'She knew nothing of what she wanted.'

'Sean, no!'

'They're mine – and I'll have them!'

'If you loved them, you wouldn't take them away.'

'I'll do what I can for them. That'll have to be enough.'

'But you never did before,' Augusta said dryly.

Sean's face flamed. His fists doubled. 'Damn you, woman, I did what I could. It was never enough, so I got out. But now I'm back.'

He'd had to leave Amy. He'd known it that last time they were together. Her love turned from him, her eyes hating him. He'd had to leave her, lest some time, in his anguish, he killed her. But he wouldn't tell this woman of that. Let her think whatever she wanted of him. He'd tell her nothing, but he'd have the children.

Quietly, reasonably, angering him even more, Augusta said, 'You must think of it. We can give them a better start in life than you ever can. And there's Gussie. Did you know that she doesn't speak?'

'It takes some longer than others.'

'Perhaps. But it may be something else. She spoke before ... before Amy died, Kevin tells me. But who knows what's happened to her since? Here, with Luke and Caleb and me ...' Augusta thought of Nelle Wakefield. She had come back. Perhaps Gussie could.

'You can't buy them,' Sean said harshly, 'and that's what you're trying, no matter how you put it. If it wasn't for you, Amy would be with me still. She was always divided between us and broke under the burden of it. That's done, though. So I'll take them away with me now.'

Augusta's cool voice had an edge. 'Who'll care for them while you work?'

'My aunt and uncle.'

'And how can they manage?'

He laughed. 'Three more won't matter in that brood. And I'll give them all I earn. They'll manage as well as you. Maybe better in some ways.'

'No,' she said quietly. 'It won't do, Sean. I can't let you have them.' But she understood the lengths to which he would go.

He said harshly, 'You won't stop me.' He went into the hall and yelled out: 'Kevin, Ray, Gussie. You kids, come down here!'

There was a scurry of feet in the upper hallway. The children came. First Ray, because he was always the fast one, Augusta had already learned. Then Kevin, more slowly, with a look of suspicion. Small Gussie stayed at the top landing. She peered down, shaking her head from side to side.

Sean held the boys by their shoulders. 'You're coming with me.' And then, 'Go up and get your sister, Kevin.'

'Daddy?' the boy asked questioningly.

'Who else would it be? Go on now.'

Kevin led foot-dragging Gussie down.

Augusta asked, 'Must you do this, Sean? Couldn't you wait a few days? And then...'

'Then what?'

'Why, we could talk more about it. Perhaps come to some agreement.'

The muscles corded in his thick arms. His flushed face grew even harder, and his brogue was heavier as he went on: 'I'm their father. There's to be no agreement between us. I want them. And no matter what you say, I'm taking them with me now.'

Augusta saw how pale Kevin's face was, and how wide his eyes. Ray seemed to be holding his breath. Gussie trembled and shook her head.

By her argument, she was making it worse for them. And it was impossible to refuse him, with the children there to hear what invective would come. She managed a smile. 'Very well. You must do what you think best.' But her voice shook on the words, and she hurried on: 'We must pack the children's things. Will you sit down and wait or do you want to come and help us?'

She knew he'd never allow the children out of his sight, fearing some deception she might use against him. It didn't surprise her when he said, 'I'll go with you,' and followed up the stairs.

The forced smile remained on her lips while she packed the new clothes she had gotten the children, while she hugged them, and kissed them, and promised to see them soon, even then knowing that Sean would not allow it.

When he picked Gussie up, the little girl screamed, held out her arms to Augusta.

Augusta winced inside but said softly, 'Never mind, my darling, I'll come to visit as quick as I can.'

But it was to be three and a half years before she saw the children again.

Chapter 27

In the 1870s Cuban patriots led an unsuccessful revolt against Spanish rule. They made another attempt in 1895 but failed again, although the Spanish weren't strong enough to destroy them. William Randolph Hearst and Joseph Pulitzer, publishers of competing newspapers, interested themselves in the rebels' cause and began to print sensationalized stories of Spanish oppression, agitating for American intervention. Theodore Roosevelt supported them.

The following year Congress issued a resolution that accorded the Cuban rebels belligerent status and offered Spain assistance in any negotiations. Within weeks, Spain refused the offer. The rebellion dragged on. Support for the rebels increased, and although William McKinley, inaugurated in March of 1897, was wary of interfering, he at last sent the U.S.S. *Maine* to Havana to protect American lives and property. On February 15, 1898, the ship blew up, with the loss of 260 lives. The pressure for war immediately increased.

Secret orders were sent by Assistant Secretary of the Navy

Theodore Roosevelt to Commodore George Dewey at his Hong Kong base to prepare his ships to attack the Spanish Pacific Fleet in the Philippines should there be war.

Meanwhile the State Department assured Spain that the United States did not intend to annex Cuba, and suggested an armistice between Spain and Cuba. Spain acceded, but President McKinley asked Congress for authority to use whatever means necessary to gain Cuban freedom. Congress adopted such a resolution, and the president signed it. On April 25, war was declared.

By then, Augusta had seen Sean Callahan's name listed as one of those who died in the explosion of the *Maine*. For a single long moment she sat very still, thinking of him, of Amy. Then, with a glance at the watch pinned to her shirtwaist, she leaped up. She hurried into her bedroom to put on her hat. She snatched her cloak from the halltree on the way to the door.

As she opened it, Marge appeared at the head of the stairs. 'What is it? Where are you going?'

'I must find Luke at once,' she answered. 'It's in yesterday's newspaper that Sean Callahan died in Havana. And that news is days late. We must go to Boston immediately.'

She said the same thing when she found Luke at the offices near the wharves. She had known he would be there. The *Plymouth* had been docked for two hours. It was his custom to stop and make his report and learn what had occurred in his absence before he came home to breakfast with her.

She stepped into the warmth of the room, her breath coming in small white plumes and her ungloved hands red with the late February cold.

Luke saw her and came quickly to meet her. 'What's wrong?'

'Sean's dead. We must go to Boston for Amy's children.'

'Wait,' he said. 'Not so fast.' He put her into a chair. 'Now tell me.'

So she told him what she had read, and he listened gravely, and at last he nodded. 'Yes, we'll go. But it may not be easy.'

'I know,' she said. 'But we must try. If Sean's relations are not amenable, then we'll go to the law.'

Already she had prepared her arguments. She was determined to be fair but firm. She and Luke were the children's grandparents; they could best take care of them. She knew she was in the right, but she didn't know what to expect. She only knew Sean's hatred.

It was cold and damp in Boston. A freezing rain glazed the roadways.

Luke hailed a hack. When they were on the way, he said, taking her icy hands, 'Now, Gussie, you will be calm.'

'I will. But I'll do what's necessary to have Amy's children.'

'You realize that perhaps they'll not know you?'

'They will,' she said.

He held her hand tightly all the way, and as he helped her down from the hack, he brushed a kiss on her cheek.

Her dimples flashed for a moment. Then she turned to the house. It was of three stories, old, showing signs of decay. The slippery steps were of cracked brick. The door had been so long unpainted it was impossible to guess what color it had once been.

The woman who answered their knock was small, gray-haired, and worn. Augusta thought instantly of Nelle Wakefield, and wondered if Luke did too.

His voice was gentle, asking, 'Mrs. Callahan?'

The woman nodded, looking first at him, then at Augusta. 'You're Amy's parents, aren't you?'

'We are.' Augusta drew a deep breath, said softly, 'I'm sorry for your loss. We learned of Sean's death only today.'

Mrs. Callahan moved aside, asked them in.

The kitchen to which she led them was clean, the floor scrubbed bare in places, the window sparkling, although blotted with sleet outside. She waved them to chairs, and stood before them, hands clasped in her apron. 'I know why you're here,' she said in a thick brogue.

'The children,' Luke told her.

'Are they well?' Augusta asked.

'They're well,' Mrs. Callahan said.

'If we could see them . . .' It was Augusta, straining in her chair.

'If you hadn't come to me, and soon, then I'd have come to you,' Mrs. Callahan said.

Augusta and Luke stared at her.

She went on, 'I have a sick husband. I'm not young any more, as you can see. I can still do my cleaning work . . . but for how

300

long? And then how'll I manage? What I want – what Sean would want, for he was a good boy, no matter what you think of him – but all that counts for nothing now. It's the children. Kevin, Ray, Gussie.' On the last name, her voice shook. 'Gussie,' she repeated. 'I'd have brought them to you, believe me. When I had the price of the tickets,' she added. 'For I can't care for them. Not without Sean's pay.'

'You shan't be sorry,' Augusta said softly. 'You'll see them. We'll make sure of that.'

'Thank you for saying it. And meaning it too. But it's a long way from here,' she looked around the kitchen, 'to your house in Fall River.'

'Only fifty miles, Mrs. Callahan. We can manage it, I'm sure.'

'I don't mean the miles.' The older woman smiled bitterly. 'It's the lives, I mean. Sean chose the one for them. I choose the other now.'

Augusta rose. 'You must love the children,' she said. ' And we shall too.'

It was a year later, the last year of the 19th century.

The Treaty of Paris, ending the Spanish-American War, had been signed. The independence of Cuba was established. The Philippine Islands, as well as Guam and Puerto Rico, were formally ceded to the United States for a payment of $20 million.

By then Augusta knew that her life, and Luke's, was changed forever. It was like having a new family. Kevin was eleven years old now, a tall, very thin boy with red hair and high color and blue eyes. Ray was ten, smaller, with sandy curls and surprisingly dark eyes. Gussie was eight, with Amy's dark glossy curls. She still couldn't speak.

Augusta had taken her to doctors in Fall River and Boston and, finally, in New York. Nothing was found physically wrong with her. The doctor in New York told them about an illness with some similar symptoms discovered by a Viennese physician named Freud, and predicted it not impossible that her speech would return as mysteriously as it had left her.

But Augusta wasn't content to wait and see what would happen.

She asked Kevin about it, when it had begun. He said, 'She's always been like that. Isn't that right, Ray?'

That was like Kevin. Augusta had already learned by then that Kevin always looked to Ray for confirmation although he was the older. He was unsure of himself and needed his brother's support.

Ray had shrugged. 'As far as I can remember.'

Small Gussie looked from one to another of them. Smiling, she shook her head vigorously.

Augusta had wanted to take her into her arms, to hold and rock her. She refused herself that luxury. 'But do you hear me, Gussie?' she said.

The child nodded, fluttered her hands.

'Can you try to talk to me?'

Gussie's smile dimmed.

But Augusta hadn't given up. Meanwhile there were outings and shopping adventures. There were a number of visits to see Sean's aunt and uncle. Then, one day, they were told that Mr. Callahan had died and Mrs. Callahan had moved to New Jersey to be with her daughter. There was no reason to go back. But there were other things. When a telephone was installed, the children had to learn to use it, just as they had learned to use the electric lights that had been brought in a year before. There were bicycle rides and picnics, and trips to New York on the ships with Luke.

Soon Kevin and Ray could recite the names of all the lighthouses between Fall River and New York, and if they were to miss one, Gussie would shake her head and rush to write it down for them. Soon all three knew the crews by name. And knew the ships too, both above and below decks.

Most evenings they went with Augusta to the widow's walk atop the house and looked past the elms and pines, now grown tall, to the harbor below, watching with held breath as that night's steamer headed across Mount Hope Bay, her two smoke stacks sending trailing scarves of black against the blue of the sky. Most mornings they were awake when that day's steamer whistled at the Borden Flats light and slowly made her way to the wharves where the boat train was already awaiting her arrival.

Often Augusta would gather the three of them around her and tell them, as she had told Caleb and Kin and Amy, the stories about her own childhood. The ships were her future and

302

fortune, and they were the same for Kevin and Ray and small Gussie, too.

Luke, too, told them about the line. How once there had been only three ships, and now there were so many more, and how once the cold of winter brought ice to the wash basins in the staterooms, but now they were all steam warmed, and instead of candles there were electric lights as at their home, even though most others in Fall River were still lit by gas.

Sometimes he would take them through the new Fall River Line terminus, still under construction but nearly finished, and show them the thick walls and broad arches through which the boat trains from Boston could pass to stop within only a few yards of the ships.

Luke traveled less that winter. He was sixty-four, still tall and lean and straight as he had been as a boy. The white streak in his hair seemed to have spread so there was little of the dark left. But his eyes were the same clear gray that sometimes looked silver, and his slow smile was as warm as ever, even when he felt unaccountably tired, and his shoulder ached, and he was breathless at odd moments.

Kin and Barbara had come up from New York with young Luke, who was nine, for the Christmas holidays. The boy had met Amy's children for the first time, and they immediately became fast friends. Luke had already been promised a trip back for Easter, although Barbara was not enthusiastic.

Now Augusta looked around the parlor. The tree was wilting. It would have to come down tomorrow. And the decorations would have to be packed for use next year.

She heard Luke's step in the hall and turned, smiling, to ask, when he came to the door, 'Are you ready?'

They were to go to friends for a late supper and to celebrate the advent of the New Year and a new century. Already they would be late, for he had dawdled over dressing.

He asked, 'Do you really want to go?'

'Is something wrong?' she asked.

He rubbed his shoulder. It ached again, and he was tired. But it was nothing new and he didn't want to spoil her evening. 'No, nothing's wrong. I just thought it might be nice if we were alone together, to see 1900 in.'

She wore a gown of blue, her narrow waist cinched in a wide

cummerbund of matching silk. The high collar was ruffled and reached almost to the tips of her ears, framing her face. Her eyes glowed with light, and her dimples flashed. At fifty-two she was more beautiful than she had been as a young girl. There was a strength in her face, and a certainty too.

She said, 'If you'd rather stay home . . .'

'No, no, You've promised we'd come. It was just an idea . . .' He took up her long fur-trimmed cloak.

She allowed him to help her. He fastened the neck closing, then bent to press a kiss on her forehead. 'We've had a good life.'

'Yes,' she said, smiling.

'You've made it so.'

'Well, thank you for that. But I think we both have.'

The celebration bells were still ringing when they returned home. She identified them by their different sounds – St. Anne's, St. Mary's, Notre Dame, the Congregational's deep tolling. The mill whistles were still blowing too. And in the harbor, tugs hooted. But inside the house it was quiet.

The children were in bed. Marge had retired. Caleb was in New York. A small fire burned in the hearth so that the parlor remained warm.

Augusta took off her cloak and put it away.

Luke watched her. 'I see you now as you were when you were twelve years old.'

'A long time ago.'

'It doesn't seem so to me.' He sat down in a chair near the fire, stretched out his legs. The evening had dragged on for him. He was glad, finally, to be at home.

'Would you like a cup of tea?' she asked. 'It was a cold ride back.'

'No, thank you,' he said.

'Shall we go to bed now?'

'You go ahead. I'll come along in a minute,' he told her. He needed a little while to summon the strength to walk the few steps down the hall.

She started across the room, but at the door she turned back. The room was dim. A shadow lay across his face. 'Luke?' she said softly.

He saw a blaze of light and the wet boards of the wharf, and the mass of eels shining, and he grabbed for them, heaving them up, and felt their slimy bodies between his fingers and flung them into the crate and seized more. And their heads butted hard at his chest and throat. Then the haze became a brilliance with Gussie at the center of it, her russet hair aglow. And as she came toward him, running now, he saw her fling her big white hat away and throw her arms wide, and heard her call 'Luke, Luke' as she came into his arms . . .

'Oh, Luke,' she whispered. 'My Luke.' She bent over him, knowing even then, knowing in the midst of her disbelief, that he was gone from her.

She passed the five days to the funeral enshrouded in that same disbelief. But there were moments when she was alone, after seeing the subdued children to bed, and discussing the funeral arrangements with Caleb and Kin, when the reality assailed her. The silence of the room in which she had spent her life with Luke would hum with his name. A great sob would burst from her aching throat, and behind her muffling hands she would weep and moan and ask herself how she could go on alone. And later, when the well of tears had dried and she stared into the dark, clasping a cold pillow against her, she would ask herself why she hadn't known. Why hadn't she sensed the silent weakness that had brought him down? They had been so close, sharing breath, love. Then why hadn't she felt what was happening to him? Finally, then, drifting mercifully into an uneasy sleep, she would waken enwrapped again in disbelief, and rise, feeling as though he were away on one of the ships and she would see him at breakfast soon after the arrival at the wharf. And then, sometime, her gaze would fall upon his empty chair and the sight of it would stop her breath in her throat.

The day of the funeral was cold and bright, with the sun glittering on snow-covered bushes and lawns.

Heavily veiled, in black, Augusta stood by the grave. Gussie pressed close on one side, Caleb on the other. She was unaware of them in that moment, as she was unaware of the other mourners, Luke's friends, numbering in the hundreds, who had come from Tiverton, and New Bedford, and Boston, to see him buried. As the minister spoke, she made her own farewells, and refused to be drawn away when the first shovel of dirt fell on the coffin lid, but stood there, watching. He was gone. Now he was gone from her.

She was quiet on the drive home from Oak Grove with Caleb and the three children. She climbed down from the carriage and walked steadily up the path to the house, and there, before the steps, she suddenly faltered and raised her head to look at the windows. No, no. I can't go in. It's empty for me with Luke gone, and only what I remember of him left behind. She saw his silver eyes, felt the touch of his hand. She heard his deep voice saying, 'Gussie, Gussie . . .'

Then small Gussie, who could not speak, and never had, put out her hand and took Augusta's arm, drawing her closer, and stammered, hoarse and rasping, 'Grandma, don't be afraid. I'll take care of you.'

For a moment, Augusta was rigid. If only Luke could hear. If only he could know. Ah, how happy he would be. To know that Gussie could speak. Luke . . . Luke . . . And then, melting, she knew that she must be glad for both of them. For herself. For Luke.

Crying, but laughing too, she bent down and hugged the child, saying. 'Thank you, Gussie. Thank you.'

Later that evening, when the children had gone to bed and the house was quiet, she went in search of Caleb. She found him in the living room, sitting before the fire.

He looked up at her. 'You should rest now. You've had a tiring day.'

'Soon,' she answered, and sat beside him on the settle, taking his hands. 'There's something I must say to you.'

'To me?'

She had begun to rehearse the words as soon as she determined to do this one last thing for Luke. But it was for Caleb, too. 'We buried your father today. If there remains any question in your mind, then ask me. I'm free now to answer you.'

'I know he told me the truth. He was my father,' Caleb said, wishing that he had said those words to Luke. 'I hope he realized before . . . before . . . that I had accepted that.'

'I know he did.'

Caleb looked at her drawn face. 'I have no questions.'

'Are you sure? I want you to have peace within yourself.'

'No, Mama. I have no questions.' But even as he spoke, the familiar shaking began inside him. Who had borne him? Why had she abandoned him? Was she tall and fair? Or small and dark? And how had his father known her? How had Caleb himself come to be?

Augusta knew. She said quietly, 'For your father's sake, because it was too painful for him, I've said nothing all these years. Your mother was named Aria. She was my younger sister. She died soon after your birth in New York. She loved you, and wished that you be brought home to me. Your father promised her on her deathbed that he would. And he did.'

'Aria,' Caleb said, testing the name on his lips. 'Aria.' Augusta's younger sister – very nearly a child at the time of his birth.

Augusta went on, 'There's no more I can tell you. How this came about, I don't know. Your father couldn't speak of it to me.'

'You forgave him.'

'I loved him,' she said.

'Thank you,' Caleb whispered.

Chapter 28

Barbara Wakefield sighed as she mounted the *Puritan*'s gangplank. She much preferred to travel on the *Priscilla*, but this was one time when she didn't mention that. If she had, Kin might have suggested that they stay over in Fall River another day.

She was anxious to go. The town grated on her nerves, and funerals were unpleasant. She had rather liked her father-in-law, but he was dead and buried. There was no way to bring him back. She paused to wait in the entry hall for young Luke and Kin. They always dawdled, young Luke hanging back for one last look at the ship from the vantage point of the wharves. Barbara hoped he wasn't going to grow up to be another

Wakefield obsessed with the ships and the line and all that went with them. She had helped Kin escape that snare. But now young Luke was beginning to show a certain enthusiasm she'd just as soon not see.

When they reached her, she said, 'I'd like to go down to the stateroom first thing.'

Kin agreed, while Luke danced impatiently beside him, asking, 'Will you take me up to the wheelhouse, Papa?'

'Later,' Kin said.

But later Barabara decided she wanted an early dinner, so they went to the dining saloon.

They were finishing coffee when Barbara said, 'I don't know how your mother will manage, Kin. Three children to care for. Alone, and at her age.'

'It'll be difficult, I suppose.'

Young Luke listened to his parents. He wished he had been able to stay longer with his grandmother. He liked the way she had time to smile at him. 'Grandma Augusta will manage,' he announced. 'She always does.'

Barbara asked, 'And how do you know that?'

'I can tell,' the boy said. And added: 'She has two dimples right next to each other.'

Kin chuckled. 'That's proof of efficiency, of course.'

'Don't encourage him to sound like a dolt,' Barbara snapped.

'What's a dolt?' Luke asked.

Barbara looked at Kin. 'You explain it. I'll go to bed.'

'So early?' Kin looked worried.

'I'm developing a headache.'

'Oh, poor darling. Can I get you something for it?'

'A good night's sleep is all I need,' she told him, gathering her gloves and reticule, and rising.

Moments after she had gone, Caleb joined them. 'Barbara?' he asked.

Kin explained, while Luke squirmed in his seat, asking, 'Will we go to the wheelhouse?'

'I must see to your mother,' Kin said.

Caleb offered to take the boy, and went off with him when Kin agreed.

Kin went down to the stateroom. He tiptoed inside to stand over Barbara, and sighed when he saw that she was sleeping.

He'd hoped to lie down with her while the boy was adventuring with Caleb.

She watched through slitted eyes while he turned disappointedly away. When he reached the door, she said softly, 'Kin, is that you?'

'It is,' he said. 'I'm sorry if I awakened you.'

'But you didn't, my dear. And I feel so much better after my little rest. I was waiting.' She threw back the quilt. 'I was waiting just for you.'

Mary and William Gorgas boarded the ship at Newport. When they had left her fur cape and his greatcoat in their stateroom, they went immediately to the dining saloon for a late supper.

Mary's blond hair was silvered but coiffed as perfectly as ever. Her figure was plumper than it had been but beautifully gowned. She wore an emerald necklace with emerald drop earrings to match, and a green dress, and over her shoulders a small ermine cloak that she had carried on board.

William's hair was still dark and there were only a few lines in his face. But he no longer looked like a young man. He walked slowly, and slouched, and he had the habit of repeatedly nodding his head.

Mary's ruse with the champage, and with Diane, years before, had worked. Lillian Russell and Diamond Jim Brady had proven friendly. They had arranged all the necessary introductions and had exchanged many entertainments with the Gorgases, even to making sure that they attended the glorious dinner Jim Brady had given to celebrate winning $180,000 by betting that William McKinley would win the 1898 election. Lillian had been particularly fond of Diane, and although the girl was shy and hung back, had seen that she had important opportunities. With Mary guiding her, Diane had availed herself of them.

They had bought a pleasant house on Bellevue Avenue not far away from the Breakers, Mrs. Vanderbilt's cottage, at that time still being built. Their own place overlooked Cliff Walk, so they changed its name to Cliff Mansion.

Now, as they sat together over coffee, neither Mary nor William spoke to each other; both were thinking of Diane.

At a nearby table, a man said, 'Before the year's out Brigham

Roberts will be unseated from Congress and back in Utah.'

'The ladies' influence,' his companion said. 'Polygamy's not in good odor with them.'

'Even without the vote they have their means.'

'And bless them,' a third man said.

'Bless them,' William repeated, nodding and nodding.

'And, of course, it's outmoded,' the conversation went on. 'Polygamy, in the twentieth century!'

There was laughter at that. Then one of the men said thoughtfully, 'We'll soon see nothing of horses and carriages, but only automobiles. And, very soon, flying machines running aloft. Electrical lighting in every house and public place. And more and more of those subway trolleys, like the ones in Boston and New York.' He smiled. 'It's a wonderful time to be alive.'

'Amen,' was the answer.

William nodded and nodded, and said, 'Amen.'

Mary shook herself, as if coming out of a dream. She looked around the dining saloon, seeing a few faces she recognized, but not many. Most of the Gorgas's Newport friends had long before returned to New York for the season. They would attend the Metropolitan Opera; their daughters would have their debuts.

Mary wondered if she had been wrong to rush Diane. She too could have come out in New York, if Mary had willed it so. Diane could have done anything.

Mary drew a deep breath. Diane had done exactly what Mary had always wanted for her. Then why was Mary asking herself ridiculous questions? Diane was happy and would no doubt write soon to say that she and Charles Farr were having a child.

Charles. Lord Farr.

Diane. Lady Farr.

A smile spread across Mary's face. It was what she had always wanted. It was what she had raised Diane to be: Lady Farr.

William leaned close. 'What are you smiling at, Mary?'

She shrugged.

'I wonder if there'll be a letter from Diane waiting for us.'

'Perhaps.'

But William didn't think so, although he didn't announce his doubt aloud. Diane hadn't written in six months. Why should she write now?

Poor girl. How William worried about her! She was still so young. Only twenty-one, and married for three years . . . To blot out the thought of what had happened, he leaned toward Mary again. 'Do you want anything else?'

'No,' she said.

'Then let's go to the grand saloon.'

She nodded, rose. As they left the dining saloon, she directed warm smiles at the people she knew. But she didn't stop to speak. She knew better. If she did, William might embarrass her by going on.

He was in one of his moods, she saw. She understood. He too was thinking of Diane. But he didn't realize that the marriage was for the girl's own good. They had been grooming her for just such an opportunity all her life. Of course she'd had to accept it once it had come to her.

'Diane always liked this ship,' William said, as Mary and he took seats in the grand saloon.

'Yes,' Mary agreed, an acid note in her voice, and her gaze drifting to where the orchestra still played.

At least there was no Jesse Light and his violin now. No Jesse Light with his golden curls and gentle blue eyes. How Diane, so good, so beautiful, could have supposed herself in love with such a man, Mary couldn't imagine. But that was what Diane had imagined. By then, she had already accepted Charles Farr's proposal. Of course she'd demurred at first. But Mary had made her see how ridiculous she was being. Diane was not, as she claimed, too young to be engaged to be married. Sixteen was quite a usual age. And in spite of what she said, two months was quite long enough to know him. He had come well recommended. He was of a very good English family and had a manor in the county of Suffolk. He was nice looking, tall, dapper, slender. He *did* seem to drink more than Mary would have liked, but he was not a drunk, as Diane had said.

So there had been no excuse, from Mary's point of view, for what Diane had done. She was wearing Lord Farr's ring when she ran away with Jesse Light. Mary and William had stopped her, of course. They couldn't allow her to ruin her life forever. They'd brought her home within days. But it hadn't been in time. Before they'd found her she'd been despoiled.

Mary sent Charles home to wait for a year, while, as they told him, Diane recovered from her nervous collapse. He'd said he'd wait. He did. For William made it worth his while to do so.

Diane had an infant daughter. She wept and screamed when Mary took it from her. It had been hard on Mary too. But she'd had to do it. For Diane. The girl couldn't marry a lord with a bastard child in her arms. When notified that Diane was well, Charles returned. They were married in New York in 1897, and sailed immediately for England.

In the three years since, they had seen her only once. She and Charles met them in London. They had no time alone with Diane. Charles was constantly attentive, and always charming. Diane had little to say.

William wanted to go for another visit with Diane. But Mary wondered if that was a good idea. She decided to wait and see.

'I hope there's a letter,' William said again.

Mary didn't reply. If he was going to be in one of his moods, she wouldn't encourage him.

He saw her jaw harden. He remembered that she had once been a pretty girl, but something had happened to her face since then. Now she had a bulldog look. In a little while, if he wasn't careful what he said, she'd remind him about the whorehouses. As if they mattered to him any more. As if anything did, aside from Diane.

Poor child. Why had he allowed it to happen? Mary marrying her off to that English drunk. Mary pretended not to know, but what was the use? Everybody knew how, on that trip to New York to shop for Diane's trousseau, he'd slipped all over this very ship, yes, it was the *Puritan*, and drunk himself into such oblivion that he'd gone to sleep in the womens' dormitory, and would have remained there, if the horrified matron hadn't run him out.

And Diane loving that violinist in the band, though William didn't know how they'd met, or when or where, and didn't know either how Mary had found them. But he'd seen Diane when Mary brought her back. How pale the girl had been – white as snow and ethereal as mist. For days and nights Mary talked, never stopping. And for months Diane never stepped out of the house. And then, one day, she was slender again. Mary had said, 'You must write to Charles Farr, William.' So he did. It wasn't much of a letter, but Charles came anyway, and the two were married.

Diane went away to England.

She went away.

He looked at Mary, thinking for the first time how much he hated her. After a moment he said, 'My father used to work for the Fall River Line. Did I ever tell you that?'

Mary turned red. Her mouth grew tight.

He went on blithely, 'Yes. He was a deckhand on the *Bay State*. Before he went to the war and lost his arm. Before he started the first three Gorgas Inns.'

'It's ancient history,' she said quietly.

'And before the whorehouses too,' he said, and got to his feet and walked quickly away, leaving her alone.

Chapter 29

In mid-June of 1900 President William McKinley was nominated for a second term by the Republican Party, with Theodore Roosevelt as his running mate. Both men were elected in November.

In March of 1901, President McKinley was inaugurated.

On September 14, Theodore Roosevelt became the 25th president, when McKinley died eight days after an assassin's attack.

When Kevin came running with the news, Augusta thought of another presidential killing and remembered how she had recalled his widow. Now, again, she mourned, not only the dead man, but his wife too. More than ever Augusta understood that part of the woman had died with him. In the year and a half since Luke's death, Augusta had learned that something of her was gone for good. She would go on, but she wouldn't be the same.

There were nights when she would reach for him and find emptiness. There were days, when in the midst of an all-consuming occupation, she would suddenly be overwhelmed with loneliness, and times when her ears would be filled with familiar sounds, yet she would raise her head, straining to hear his voice.

Still, she had Amy's children to care for and love. Caleb at home except when he was on board the *Priscilla*. Jim Reilly came often to visit. Her interest in the line continued, and her involvement with her study group increased as it began to consider the position of women in the new twentieth century.

As time passed she learned to accept the wound of Luke's loss as another part of her.

By 1902, Fall River was often called Spindle City after its most important industry: it had ninety mills, with eighty-three thousand looms and three million spindles. From them, thirty-two thousand workers produced fifteen hundred miles of cloth each day.

In addition to the mills, it had two electric companies, two telegraph companies, and a suburban railroad and trolley system. There was also a poor farm, a public library, a police patrol-wagon division, as well as two theaters competing with the Academy of Music. These served a population of eighty thousand.

The Fall River Line, however, was not as prosperous. Increasing competition for passengers and shipping had led to a continuing drop in revenue, and therefore in dividends.

Augusta, with more responsibility than ever, and without Luke's earnings, less income than ever, became increasingly alarmed. For the first time she went into the attic and made a complete inventory of the chinoiserie Marcus Kincaid had brought back from his whaling trip.

Porcelains of palest green, carvings in jade. Delicate tablewear edged with gold. Vases and light holders of cloisonné. Studying the treasure, she felt as if her parents, Amy and Marcus, were standing beside her.

She was a child again, and Marcus was telling her about the time he had lost his littlest finger, and describing the foreign enclaves of Canton.

She was startled from the past into the present when Kevin asked if he could come in.

She called out that he could, but he must be careful, and smiled at him when he pulled open the door and then froze.

'Grandma!' Kevin's voice went from bass to tenor in the

single word. He was sixteen, with a faint bronze fuzz on his upper lip. 'Where did you get these things?'

She told him about Marcus's voyage to the Behring Sea, and he listened, wide-eyed, sighing when she paused. 'Oh, Grandma, I wish I'd lived then.'

'It was a hard life.'

'But exciting. And look what he brought back with him.'

Later he told Ray and Gussie about the treasure in the attic.

'Is it valuable, do you think?' Ray wanted to know.

Gussie looked thoughtful. She was her mother all over again, but a smaller version at the same age. At twelve, her body was straight and graceful. Her black eyes sparkled; her hair was black and curly. She listened while Kevin and Ray speculated about the treasure, and finally said, 'We're costing Grandma too much money.'

Both boys stared at her. 'What do you mean?'

'That's why she was studying what she has up there. She's thinking about selling it.'

'You don't know what you're talking about. Grandma's rich.' That was Kevin.

Ray, who was small still, but thick in the chest like his father Sean, and with Luke's dark hair, turned red and blurted, 'Gussie, you're crazy!' Before Gussie had begun to speak, he'd never have said that. Now, though, she needed no special treatment.

'I'm not crazy,' she retorted, unperturbed. 'Wait and see.'

Later, when she was in bed and Augusta came in to kiss her good night, Gussie said, 'Why were you looking at the China things today?'

'I wanted to see what was there.' Augusta took up the doll on the chest. It had belonged to Nelle Wakefield once, and now it was Gussie's. Her dress was a bit worn. Augusta decided to make a new one.

Gussie said, 'You're going to sell some, aren't you? Because we cost you too much money.'

Augusta sat on the bed. She smiled, cupping Gussie's cheeks in her hands. 'What makes you say that?'

'I know.'

'It isn't that you cost so much. But I'll probably sell a few pieces.'

315

'When you do, I shall go with you,' Gussie announced.

Thus it was that the two of them boarded the *Priscilla* on a foggy July evening.

The horns of tugs and barges boomed eerily across the harbor. The boat train came hissing with unusual suddenness from out of a white shifting shadow. The ship's lights were muted by the thick mists what swirled around.

Jim Reilly came to greet the two. 'Augusta, Gussie.' He divided his smile between them. He had loved Augusta for all the time he had known her, and that was sixteen years. Small Gussie was an extension of Augusta, and beginning to be like her, so it was easy to love her too.

'Will it be a crowded run?' Augusta was asking.

'No. There'll be something like five hundred after the Newport stop.'

Augusta said nothing about it to Jim, but she took that to be a sign that she had made the right decision. It was the end of the first week in July. Allowing that the weather was poor, that was still a scanty passenger load for a ship designed to carry 1500. In her stateroom there were two small packages of well-wrapped porcelain figurines, and in the hold there was a carefully packed crate, carried on earlier by one of the stevedores. Augusta determined that she would drive a hard bargain for them.

Jim knew nothing of her concern. He went off to complete his pre-sailing rounds, with a promise to meet her later in the grand saloon.

At seven-forty, the *Priscilla* moved slowly away from Oliver's Wharf, enwrapped in white mists.

Curtained by the outside fog, the big windows of the dining saloon reflected the warmth and gaiety within. Augusta sat waiting for Gussie to decide what she wanted for dinner.

The child went over the menu for the second time. Her eyes were on the steak. But it was too expensive, she had decided. Porterhouse, with baked or mashed potatoes, was a dollar and a quarter for two people. But she was only one, and doubted she could do such a portion the justice it deserved at that cost.

Augusta asked what was wrong, and Gussie sighed, saying she didn't know. Perhaps she had no appetite.

Augusta ordered small steaks for each of them, with salad and potatoes, and watched Gussie hungrily eat the food, wondering why the child had hesitated over the menu. It wasn't like Gussie not to know her own mind.

Later, in the stateroom, when she had kissed Gussie good night, and tucked the coverlet around her, she understood.

Gussie said, 'Grandma, after you sell the China things, will you have enough money?'

So that was on Gussie's mind when she couldn't order her dinner! Augusta sat on the edge of the bed. 'There's nothing for you to fear. We shall manage very well.'

'I know,' Gussie said. 'But I want to help.'

'You do help.' Augusta kissed her again, and went up to the grand saloon, touched nearly to tears at Gussie's concern.

Alone, Gussie closed her eyes tightly against the light. It bothered her, but it was worse to try to fall asleep in the dark. She had never talked about it with her grandma but her grandma seemed to understand that the dark meant being frightened and unable to talk, and always waking up in strange rooms. The dark meant remembering the night on the ship when she had lain in the berth beside her mother. Her mother was very still, and warm. So warm that Gussie snuggled closer, comforted by the softness of her breast, and drowsing. There were no loud voices. There was no fear. Only the thump thump thump of her mother's heart against Gussie's cheek, and the distant thump thump thump of the paddle wheels. Then, quite suddenly, the sound against her cheek was gone, and slowly slowly the warmth and softness went too. Gussie burrowed closer, but knew it was no use. She was alone, alone . . .

Now although her breath came fast and she clutched the pillow, she said aloud, testing the sound of her voice against the silence, 'But Grandma came for us. She made it all right again.'

At about the same time, in Fall River, Kevin leaned over a chessboard, frowning.

Ray said, ' Make your move.'

But Kevin swung away from the board. 'Gussie's probably right. We're costing Grandma too much. And that's why she's selling those pieces from the attic.'

Ray blinked, looked around the room. He sounded younger than fifteen. 'Do you think it'll be the way it was before? Will – will we be poor?'

317

'There's three of us, Ray, three, for Grandma to take care of.'

'What can we do?'

'Grandpa was working for the line when he was twelve. Maybe if I talked to Uncle Caleb –'

Ray looked shocked. 'But you have to go to school.' And added slowly, 'So do I.'

'Plenty of people don't after sixteen,' Kevin said.

The boys stared at each other, silently listing the jobs they could do. There were the mills. There were several markets. The banks often used messengers.

At last Kevin said, 'But all I really want to do is work for the line the way Grandpa did.'

'Me too,' Ray agreed.

Meanwhile, on the *Priscilla*, Augusta visited with friends in the grand saloon.

The vessel stopped in Newport, took on passengers and freight, and made its departure still in dense fog, with extra lookouts on the bow since even the nearby flashing white beacon of Goat Island Lightship was blotted out.

It was dark in the pilot house. The captain, the pilots, and the quartermaster stared past the running lights into the white mist. When they heard the Castle Hill bell, the course was changed for Point Judith. Moments later, from somewhere ahead in the cottony thickness, there came the sound of a steamer's whistle. It sounded as if it was beyond Brenton's Reef Lightship.

Immediately the captain ordered the *Priscilla*'s whistle to be blown every half minute. But there was no further warning from the other steamer.

Now the only thing heard in the pilothouse was the soft whisper of water at the bow, the beating of paddles from amidships, and the ship's signal blasts.

Suddenly one of the bow watchmen shouted an alarm. A black hull loomed close. The *Priscilla* shuddered from stem to stern at a mighty blow into her port side. Within seconds the other ship was disengaged and floated away to be lost again in the fog.

Augusta had just told her friends goodnight and risen to her feet when the collision occurred.

Jim Reilly, near the bottom of the staircase, had been coming to speak with her.

When the *Priscilla* shook and shuddered and settled hard at her head, Augusta was thrown off her feet.

Jim saw her go down. He leaped the last few steps and pushed and shoved his way through a barrier of stunned people.

As he lifted her in his arms, the chandeliers dimmed and then went out, leaving the grand saloon in darkness.

Around him there were screams, cries of pain, shouted questions. But he was suspended in time, aware only of Augusta. He had never before held her close. He knew that he, his love, was different now. There was no going back to what it had been before. But he said only, 'Don't be frightened, Augusta.'

She gasped, 'What happened?'

'There's been a collision.'

She drew away. 'I'm all right. You'll be needed.'

He steadied her on her feet, not wanting to let her go. 'Are you sure you're not hurt?'

'I'm not. But I must go to Gussie.'

'I will. Stay here until we know what's happened.'

He left her, hurried down to the stateroom. Gussie was peering from the open doorway, her eyes big in her face. A surge of passengers filled the corridor. He fought his way through it, then took her up to the grand saloon.

On the way, he learned from a crewman that one deckhand, sleeping off-watch in the forecastle, had been killed, that water was gathering in the below decks forward compartments but the bulkheads were holding, and that water had just reached the dynamo in the engine room and the steering engine was no longer operable.

He left Gussie clinging to Augusta and hurried away to do what he could.

The stewards were going from cabin to cabin, rousing those passengers not already awakened, telling them to put on life preservers and come up on deck. The lifeboats were swung out in readiness for evacuation should the captain order it. The ship's whistle continually blew a distress signal.

Some cargo was jettisoned. Three hundred and seventy-six barrels of fish just loaded at Newport were thrown overboard along with kegs of Fall River beer and bolts of cloth from its mills. A few smaller crates were left undisturbed. Among them was the one belonging to Augusta.

319

By midnight, forty minutes after the crash, there was still no help from Newport. Then, out of the fog, came a passenger liner. She had a gaping hole in her side, and her forward compartment was flooded. She was the *Powhatan* of the Merchants and Miners Line from Baltimore to Providence, with 131 passengers aboard. Speaking by megaphone, the captains of the two ships exchanged information. The *Powhatan* had been sounding her whistle regularly. Until a few minutes before the crash, the *Priscilla*'s whistle had been clearly heard. How the two ships had come so close was not understood. The *Powhatan*, unable to tow the *Priscilla* because of her own damage, stood by. She had offered to take on the *Priscilla*'s passengers, but her captain decided that could be too hazardous, and that since he expected rescue from Newport at any moment, he could afford to wait.

But it was four o'clock in the morning before the Fall River Line's eastbound freighter, *City of Fall River*, came carefully through the fog and heard the *Priscilla*'s distress signal. The freighter could not tow the large ship's bulk, but hove to, adding its own whistle to the *Priscilla*'s. At dawn, with the fog beginning at last to lift, the *Puritan* approached.

Several hours passed before hawsers were successfully attached and the *Priscilla* was towed into Newport.

Augusta and Gussie came down the gangplank together. When Augusta looked back and saw the damage done to the *Priscilla*, she shivered as if the wound were in her own flesh.

It was an emotional docking, with many passengers weeping and praying. But now it was time to find a place to rest until the next New York-bound steamer came in. Augusta looked at the watch pinned to her bosom. They had something like twelve hours to wait.

Jim Reilly caught up with her. His face was drawn with fatigue. His hair was tousled, his clothing wrinkled and dusty. 'Augusta! Are you all right now?'

She smiled at him. 'We're fine.'

She explained that she was going to the telegraph office to let Kin and Barbara know that she was delayed and would be arriving the following morning.

He said he would find a place where she and Gussie could stay, and rushed off. By the time she had sent her message, he had returned.

He had found a room in a boardinghouse a block away from Long Wharf. He led the way to it. Before leaving her, he held Augusta's hand. 'I'll be at the ship. If there's anything you need, send for me.'

For the first time then she remembered the crate she had had shipped with the cargo. She mentioned it to Jim; he promised to locate it, if it was still on board, and to make sure it sailed on the ship with her when she resumed her journey.

'Thank you,' she said, turning away quickly. She was unwilling to deal with what she saw in his face. She was unwilling to think of it now.

When she and Gussie were in their room, the child asked, 'What's wrong with Uncle Jim?'

'I think he's upset about the accident.'

'He doesn't look the same, nor act the same.'

'He'll be himself, you may be sure, when we next see him.'

But Augusta wondered. She remembered how he had held her. The darkness closing in. Close by, the cries, the weeping. And she remembered how she had felt. It had been three years since a man had held her. Her response had startled her. Until then she hadn't realized how much her body had needed to be held so . . .

Four days after the accident, the *Priscilla*, with a twenty-five-foot square patch over the hole in her prow, steamed to the New York dry dock.

By then, Augusta and Gussie had spent two days with Kin and Barbara, and had sold the chinoiserie that they had carried with them, as well as that packed in the crate, which Jim had located and shipped to them. When Kin heard about his mother's intentions, he said, 'But they've always been in the family.'

'There's more in the chests. And the money will be a help these days.'

'The line *seems* prosperous,' Barbara said, a question in her voice.

Augusta didn't answer her. She wished now that she hadn't spoken of selling some of her father's pieces.

After she had gone out of the room, Barbara told Kin, 'It's the three Callahans. She'd be well off without them.'

'They're my sister's children,' Kin said quietly.

'I know,' Barbara snapped. 'Who said they weren't? But that

doesn't make them less expensive.' After a moment she went on, 'With time, those pieces will become even more valuable. To sell them now actually represents a loss.'

Kin said nothing. Whatever his mother did was all right with him.

'And,' Barbara added, 'that's a loss to you as well. Because if she hung on to them, they'd someday be yours.'

'And Caleb's,' Kin said softly.

Barbara shot him a narrow-eyed look. She rose and began pacing the floor, her arms wrapped around her. 'I think you should talk to her.'

There'd be no loving that night, Kin knew, if he didn't. More and more he saw how Barbara handled him. Always by offering, or refusing, her favors in bed. He knew, but he gave in anyway. 'I'll talk to her before she leaves,' he said.

When he spoke of the value of the China treasure, as he called it, and its importance as an investment, Augusta listened but said nothing. She and Gussie had been shopping, and had gone to the Metropolitan Museum. They'd walked miles through Manhattan. Passing Longacre Square at Forty-second Street and Broadway, they had seen an enormous new building under construction. A newsboy told them it was to house Adolph Ochs's *New York Times*. Soon the place would be called Times Square.

It had been a day that brought back thoughts of Amy, of Luke. Augusta was tired, her spirits flagging too.

'If you spend it, it will be gone,' Kin went on.

'But that's what I must do,' she told him.

'Perhaps you should sell the line's shares, invest in something better.'

'I shan't do that,' Augusta said firmly.

When Kin repeated the conversation to her, Barbara decided to talk to Augusta herself. But the right time never came.

The next evening they stood on the dock together. The *Puritan* loomed over them.

'You look well,' Barbara said, 'in spite of everything. It's a relief to us. Kin was worried for you. And I too, of course.'

'Then you could come to see Grandma more often, instead of always asking when she would come here.' Gussie, once she had learned to speak, had also discovered the pleasure of saying what she thought.

Barbara pretended she hadn't heard. It was a habit of hers, Augusta had noted before. She overlooked whatever she didn't want to know.

Bells rang. Wheels rumbled. Men shouted. Bales of cotton tilted on wagons speeding by. A warm damp wind riffled the ship's flags.

Augusta drew a deep breath. It was good the trip was ending and she was leaving for home. She loved Kin, and managed to get along with Barbara, and seeing young Luke was always a joy; but they had their own lives and she had hers.

Plainly, though, Barbara wasn't sure that was quite as it should be. She looked Augusta up and down, having first given Gussie a cool frown.

'Yes. You *do* look well. That's a charming dress.' There was a faint question in her voice.

'Thank you,' Augusta said, smiling.

Her gown was a deep blue, with high puffed sleeves and a big white bow at the throat. Her hat was white with blue veiling. She carried a white parasol.

Gussie, having heard the faint question , responded to it. In a voice that dripped honey, she said, 'Grandma's gown is better than widow's weeds, Aunt Barbara. Though she was gorgeous in black. You ought to have seen how the men looked at her . . .'

'Gussie!' But Augusta was laughing.

Barbara however didn't laugh. 'That's an extremely unsuitable remark.'

'Oh, you can't fool me. You think Grandma has to be in black, as if that's what reminds her that Grandpa's gone.'

'You're impertinent, Gussie Callahan!' Barbara said shrilly. 'Fourteen-year-old girls should be seen and not heard.'

Gussie grimaced, raised her eyes to the heavens as if asking for patience.

Augusta said hastily, 'You'll send young Luke for a visit this summer, as we decided?'

'For as long as you like, and can endure him,' Barbara promised.

'It's no burden,' Augusta assured her. 'And I know he'll be happy with us.'

'Surely happier than he can be in a New York summer.'

Augusta saw with relief that the passengers were beginning to board. She touched her lips to both of Barbara's cheeks, thanked her, and hurried up the gangplank, with Gussie dancing beside her.

One moment the girl was a grown-up young lady, a few seconds later a hoyden. That was Gussie. A wave of love swept Augusta. How fortunate she was to have Amy's children. Gussie, all directness and warmth. Kevin, who loved the ships. And Ray, who was slowly outgrowing his diffidence.

She looked for Caleb, but didn't see him. He would probably be at the pilothouse.

She stopped at the purser's officer for her stateroom key.

'I wonder where Jim is?' Gussie said.

Heat touched Augusta's cheeks. She had been watching for Jim too, and wondering how she would feel when she saw him. They had been good friends for so long. But in an instant after the *Priscilla*'s accident that had changed. She said, 'Perhaps he's not on the *Puritan*.'

'He ought to be, with the *Priscilla* in dry dock.'

As Augusta opened the stateroom door, Gussie asked, 'Why did Aunt Barbara keep saying that – about how well you look, as if she was surprised? As if you shouldn't.'

'I think you misunderstood.'

'I did not. That's what she meant.'

Augusta didn't answer. There was nothing to say. Gussie was right, of course. Not only Barbara, but others, too, seemed to think they could tell her heart by how she dressed her hair and what gown she chose.

It was of no importance to her. She knew the dull numbed despair of the first year after Luke was gone. How, in the night's stillness, she reached for him. And how, even now, three years later, she continued to, and continued to awaken trembling, as if she had dreamed his death and then discoverd the dream was true.

'Tell me,' Gussie said, 'are you very unhappy?'

'No, but there are moments...' She was thinking of Jim again.

'Aunt Barbara doesn't understand. She's a cold fish. You can't expect too much of her.'

'One can't expect too much of anyone,' Augusta said.

'Shall I try to find Jim?'

'If he's on board, and has time, he'll find us.'

'I'm sure he will,' Gussie said, and looked pleased.

Later the two stood at the railing. Augusta thought of Luke, and how many times he had stood beside her in those last moments before the ship's departure. Now Gussie tugged her arm. 'There's Caleb. He doesn't see us.'

No, Augusta thought. He didn't see her, nor Gussie. His face was blank, his mouth narrow. She had seen that look many times before, and pitied him. It meant to her a fear of love. He had been hurt too many ways. Where once he had been outgoing and explosive in his feelings, now he lived behind a barrier of his own making. She had seen the change in him when he fell in love with Rosalie, but when Rosalie had run away with Peter the older wound began again to fester with the new.

He was thirty-six now, and in his prime. Augusta wanted to see him in love, married. But he was grown wary. Three times that Augusta knew of, he had been on the verge of engagement. Each time, at the last moment, he had drawn back. Was it that he was fearful? Or was he punishing any girl who loved him for Rosalie's fickle behavior?

As Augusta watched, the look on his face changed. He'd seen her and young Gussie. He came to them. 'Are you all right? No ill effects from the accident?'

'No ill effects,' Augusta told him.

'And your visit with Barbara and Kin?'

'Aunt Barbara was disapproving,' Gussie said. 'Of Grandma.'

'Jealous, no doubt,' Caleb said, laughing.

'That's what I think.'

Augusta said hastily, 'And Luke will be coming up to spend some time with us in Fall River.'

'Another recruit,' Caleb said. 'I'd better tell you right now that both Kevin and Ray are working on the ship. They're handling baggage, and getting blisters for their pains.'

Gussie smiled triumphantly. The boys had finally seen that she was right. Grandma *did* need help. They were doing what they could.

So that was what had come from their questions about the chinoiserie, Augusta thought. How good they were! How proud she felt!

Caleb went on to say that they'd asked him for jobs. He'd

been able to find them and had been certain of her consent.

Augusta smiled. 'But just for the summer.'

'Of course. I've told them that.'

'Aunt Barbara is getting fat,' Gussie said.

'Plumpish,' Augusta amended. She suspected that Barbara was pregnant, but didn't say so.

'I suppose I can't get a job on the ship too,' Gussie said.

'You cannot,' Caleb told her.

'It's terrible to be a girl. I can't do anything. It's not fair.'

'You can take care of your grandma.'

'Grandma doesn't need taking care of. She's perfectly able to take care of herself, and anybody else who comes along.'

'I do think you're right,' Caleb said. But his attention had wandered.

A tall slender girl walked by. She was beautiful but oddly dressed. Her gown seemed too warm for a July evening. The shawl around her shoulders was thick. Her blond hair gleamed in the sun, and her features were small, perfect. Although she looked abstracted, she carried herself like a queen. Caleb told himself that she would be the next one. He didn't know her name, but he would find out.

She was dressed too warmly for July because where she had been in England it had been cold. Her air of abstraction covered a bone-deep fatigue. She had arrived just that day, and now she was on the way to Newport. She was frightened to think of what she had done and worried about what would happen next. Her mother, her father. It had been three long terrible years since she'd seen them, five terrible years since she had left home. In all that time, by the second, the hour, and the day, she had known nothing but humiliation. She knew she would remember the pain of it for the rest of her life.

She found herself looking quickly around now. She couldn't help it. Had Charles Farr followed her? She knew he didn't care what she did. Still, ever since she had left the manor house in Long Melford, she had felt as if he might be coming after her. Not because he wanted her, but for her money, and for spite too.

There was a tall officer looking at her across the crowded deck. She turned away quickly, went to the purser's office, and got her key.

She would settle into her stateroom, stay there, and collect

326

herself as well as she could. She had to be ready when she arrived at Newport. She had to be able to deal with her mother and father . . .

Only moments after she left the purser's office, Caleb was there, asking about her. 'I think I recognize her, but I can't quite think of her name,' he said.

'Farr. Mrs. Diane Farr,' the purser told him. 'For Newport.' The purser grinned. 'I haven't seen her for a long while. But she used to be Diane Gorgas. Made the trip from New York to Newport often. I remember her folks very well.'

Caleb said her name softly to himself. Diane Gorgas Farr. Oh yes, he knew her, although he, like the purser, hadn't seen her for years. He smiled faintly. The time between didn't matter. It had only improved her.

In her stateroom, Diane took off her large hat, set aside her shawl. She sank to the edge of the bed and looked around, but she hardly noticed the luxurious decor. What she saw was the beginning of freedom. Yet she knew she was only part of the way there.

She must be strong. From the moment she landed at Newport, she would have to fight. Her mother most of all. Her father too, although he was somewhat less stubborn. But she was determined. Her small fists knotted until the knuckles turned white. Her lips thinned. She would never go back to Charles. The nightmare of the past five years was finished.

In the looking glass Augusta saw Gussie's reflection. The child was sleeping soundly, clutching the pillow to her cheek. A faint smile touched Augusta's lips. What joy had come into her life with Amy's children! Gussie, so stalwart and loving and perceptive; Kevin and Ray, both steady, and wise for their years. It was a wonder that they could have been so unmarked by the shadow of Sean's defection and Amy's death.

Yet for all that the children had brought her, they could never touch her with the feeling that Jim had given her. The sense of wholeness. The sense of suddenly being a woman again. That moment when he had caught her up in his arms as the ship shuddered had changed everything between them. She had known, and recognized his knowing too, that nothing would be the same for them again. They could no longer be the friends they had been for so many years. There was more to come.

Slowly she took down her hair. It gleamed red gold in the dim light, the soft waves falling to her waist. She ran the brush through it. The sound it made was like the caress of fingertips on silk. When she put the brush down, she leaned close to the glass. There were a few lines at her eyes; her smile had left tracks around her mouth. But even as she sighed, her dimples flashed.

Jim. How would it be when she saw him? What would he say?

Later, in bed, listening to the steady rhythm of the paddle wheels and the distant ringing of watch bells, she felt a quickening in her, and savored the lift of expectation, and smiled into the dark.

Chapter 30

He was on the wharves, waiting, when the *Puritan* docked.

She saw him as she came down the gangplank. The sun was just then rising. Sky and harbor and earth were pink. The children called out to him, but Augusta only raised her hand, suddenly taken with shyness. Suppose she had imagined that moment between them. Suppose she had misread the concern of friendship. She was, after all, twelve years the older. There had been the same age difference between her and Luke. But that had been nothing. Men grew older at a pace unlike women.

When Jim came to her, and smiled and took both her hands in his, she forgot her shyness and her questions. There was no more doubt in her. She had neither misread nor misunderstood.

'I'm glad you're back,' he said. 'I've been waiting a very long time.'

The change from friendship to courtship was almost imperceptible. She had seen Jim often before. But then it had been informal. He had visited, stayed for a meal. Now, though, they went out. They dined sometimes at the Gorgas Inn. They went to the Academy of Music one night to see *Way down East* by Lottie Blair Parker. Another time they saw *The Climbers* there. Sometimes she traveled to New York to visit Kin and Barbara and young Luke, and she and Jim had a day of exploring. The children had always liked him, and now they happily accepted him.

Still, there were times when having a readymade family interfered. Jim wanted Augusta to go to New York with him and to stay over to see Lillian Russell perform with Weber and Fields, but Gussie was to give a recitation at school that evening. Another day they had planned a picnic, but Ray needed help with his studies. Jim seemed not to mind, and Augusta herself thought the incidents inconsequential.

But then, just before Thanksgiving, Jim said: 'I have a special outing planned for tomorrow. I'll come for you at three. Is that all right?'

'Yes. But what's the outing?'

'You'll see.' He grinned at her. 'I want it to be a surprise.'

The next day it was snowing lightly. Kevin and Ray went ice-skating at Beattie's Quarry. At two-thirty Ray came staggering in. His clothing was wet; he had lost his stocking cap and his mittens. At fifteen, his face looked pale and aged.

'Grandma, oh, God, Grandma, it's Kevin. I'm afraid that he's in the quarry.'

'What are you talking about?' Even as she spoke, she caught up a cloak and thrust her feet into boots, and ran toward the door.

Following her, Ray sobbed, 'The police are there, and some passers-by stopped. But they haven't found him. I had to come and tell you myself. Because it's my fault.'

In the carriage, she heard the rest. How Kevin and Ray had argued, and Kevin had gotten angry and walked away. The snow got thicker and thicker, and at first Ray thought he was hiding, but then he got scared and started to yell for Kevin. And Kevin didn't come and didn't answer.

She slapped the reins harder and yelled at the horses, then shouted over the wind at Ray, 'It'll be all right,' while tears streaked down her cheeks.

From the distance ahead, she could hear the call, 'Kevin Callahan! Kevin! Kevin!' and saw the faint glow of swinging lanterns.

She pulled up at the quarry and flung herself down, with Ray tumbling after her.

One of the men rushed up to say, 'Mrs. Wakefield, don't worry, he didn't go through. We've gone over the ice two times. There's no break in the quarry. He's somewhere about. You'd best go home and wait.'

But she couldn't go home. She waited near the carriage while the men searched the woods as the early dark fell, and Ray stood close to her, rigid with fright.

Then, suddenly, a shout went up. A tall shadow stumbled into the roadway. Even through the curtains of snow, she knew it was Kevin.

He came toward her, croaking: 'I got lost! I don't know how it happened, but I went in circles in the woods.'

Ray hurled himself at his brother and hugged him.

'I'm sorry,' Kevin said. 'It was my fault.'

'No, it was mine,' Ray cried.

On the way home, Augusta asked what the quarrel had been about, but neither boy would tell her.

It was only when she pulled up in front of the house that she remembered that Jim was to have come for her at three o'clock.

He was waiting on the steps. Snow sparkled in his hair and on his shoulders. Seeing him, Ray burst out: 'It was Jim, Grandma. Kevin said you're going to marry him! And I was saying you wouldn't. You wouldn't leave us for anything.'

'I won't leave you,' she said gently, as Jim hurried to meet her.

He listened while she explained what had happened. Then he turned to Kevin. 'Are you all right now?'

'I'm fine, except for feeling like an idiot. Imagine me getting lost.'

He and Ray went inside.

Augusta said, 'I'm sorry, Jim.'

'No message,' he said quietly. ' And Marge not here –'

'She was visiting Betty Raleigh when Ray came for me.'

'And no note on the door even.'

'I was so frightened,' she said.

He followed her in, and waited until she first made sure that Marge was heating soup for the boys, then went in to dry her hair and change her gown. When she returned to the parlor, he said, 'We need to talk.'

'I'm sorry for what happened. Shall we try again tomorrow?'

Gussie was reading before the fire. Kevin and Ray came in from the kitchen to settle down at the chessboard.

Jim looked at them for a moment, then suggested a ride. She agreed, knowing that he sought a private conversation.

Soon she was bundled in a warm carriage robe and riding along Eight Rod Way, the horse hooves clopping in the soft snow, the lights bobbing ahead of her.

It seemed as if the two of them were alone in the world. There was no sound beyond those they made, and no movement, and no light.

Then he said softly, 'We're so rarely alone. The children are always between us.'

'But this ... today ... it was an emergency, Jim.'

'You forgot me,' he said. 'Now tell the truth. Didn't you simply not remember that I was to come?'

'Jim, please! In the moment, with Ray weeping, and so frightened ...'

'But you see –' He paused to swallow. The words weren't easy. Facing the truth wasn't easy. He had loved her for so long, and needed her for so long. He couldn't be satisfied now with less than everything. 'You see,' he said again, 'it'll always be that way. Kevin, and Ray, and Gussie ... they'll always come first with you. All your life, they'll come before me.'

'There's no first or second,' she told him. 'There's only love. Enough to share.'

'Not for me, I fear.' He let the reins slacken. The horses slowed. 'The surprise I had for you was twofold.' When she started to speak, he shushed her. 'Wait. I was going to take you to Nicolet's and ask you to choose a wedding ring.'

'Jim!'

'I want you to marry me. But before you answer me, I must tell you something.' He drew a deep breath. 'Pinkerton's has asked me to leave the Fall River Line and go on to something else. They're opening a new office in Omaha. They want me to organize it and run it for them. I'd like you to come with me.'

Her heart gave a sudden jump. Omaha? Where was it, what state even? For an instant she couldn't remember. Except that she knew it was far away. Another world.

'To Omaha?' she repeated faintly.

He wanted to drop the reins and take her into his arms. He

wanted to hold her and tell her not to be fearful. Wherever they were, as long as they were together, they would be happy. Instead, he said, 'I know it's a long way.'

She breathed, ' And the children?' There was an aching in her now. Kevin, Ray, small Gussie.

'You see? They're your first consideration. Always. Forever.' Then, 'You needn't give them the whole of your life. Caleb can look after them,. Or Kin and Barbara. Besides, the boys are nearly grown, and soon Gussie will be.'

'Leave them!' she said. 'Leave Fall River?' Now the aching encompassed her and became her being.

'Will you think about it?'

'I will, Jim.'

But she already knew the answer.

It was the week after Thanksgiving. The day was cold and gray. A damp wind sent soggy leaves flying along High Street. Only a little while before, Augusta had heard the *Priscilla*'s signal at the Borden Flats light. Soon the ship would dock. The boat train would load and chug away. In less than an hour, Jim would be at the door.

She lit the light under the coffeepot and set the table, then whipped eggs and sliced bread. Those preparations done, she wrapped herself in a cloak and went quietly past the rooms where the children were still asleep to stand at the widow's walk. Past the bare elms and tall scraggly pines, she could look down on the harbor. There came the *Priscilla*'s running lights, aglow in the fine mist. There, faintly, came the sound of her bells.

The *Bay State* and the *Empire State*. The *Metropolis*. The *Providence*, retired in 1900, and scrapped just this year. The *Bristol*. The *Puritan* and *Pilgrim* and *Plymouth*. And now the *Priscilla*. Each one an individual, a reality. A part of her life, her family. As much a part of her as the children were.

When she heard Jim walking on the path, she went down to meet him, took his coat, and led him into the kitchen.

He gave her a searching look, but spoke only of inconsequentials while they had breakfast. Caleb would be along soon. It had been a slow trip. There had been fog again, and some ice in Narragansett Bay. The *Priscilla* was now so fit it

332

was hard to believe she had ever been damaged. Augusta winced when he spoke of that. It reminded her of the night she had realized how much she missed being a woman.

Finally, when he had finished his coffee, he put down his cup. 'Will you go with me?'

Now was the moment. Now she must say it, and face what would come of it. To be alone again, and without the warmth of love. To remember what was lost through the still hours of the night. A pulse flutterd within her. A trembling. Finally she said, 'I cannot.'

He said nothing for a long time. He sat with his head bowed and his mouth grim. At last he told her, 'Then I shall go alone.'

She let her breath out, and folded her hands in her lap so that she wouldn't reach to touch him. How much she yearned to. To feel his strength. To have it hers. But no, she mustn't, couldn't. She whispered, 'Yes. Yes. I thought you would. And it's best. Truly, it's best, Jim.'

'I'll always love you,' he said, when he was leaving.

She closed the door behind him, then ran up to the widow's walk and watched until he was gone, and the sound of his footsteps had faded, and the road was empty and still.

Chapter 31

Three times Mabel Graystone-Fields had collapsed on her bed and sent for Bennet. Each time he had hurried to her side, had held her fat hand and repeated his promise not to marry without her consent.

But he had never asked for it, being satisfied with things as they were. Except for the fact that Jeanette occasionally reminded him that he had said they would marry, and pouted when he put her off, she suited him very well. They laughed a good deal together, and made love, though not as frequently as they once had. He had put on a substantial amount of weight, going from plump to fat, and limped heavily. She had filled out, which made her more womanly looking but a bit less to his taste. Still, the good balanced the bad in his mind, and he was a gentle man, as well as shy, and wouldn't have known how to change the situation even if he had wanted to.

In May of 1905, a Western Union boy appeared at Bennet's door and thrust a yellow envelope into his hand. Bennet examined its outside, then fished in his pocket for a dime. He flipped it to the boy before returning to the easy chair near the window and propping his bad foot up on an ottoman.

'Aren't you going to open it?' Jeanette asked. Her hair was still very red. Now she wore it high in stacks of curls. Her face was small, triangular, with deep-set eyes that peered from beneath kohl-darkened lashes.

'I imagine it's from my mother,' Bennet said.

'Just the same, you never know. It could be important, couldn't it?'

'Perhaps.' He slid a fat thumb under the flap and carelessly pulled out the message. Having scanned it, he tossed it aside.

'What's it say?' Jeanette asked. She was always curious, but even more so about anything to do with Mabel, who was a self-declared enemy, although they'd had nothing to do with each other for a long time. Bennet had proven that Jeanette had nothing to fear from the older woman, but Jeanette knew they remained rivals and was always on the alert. Her savings had grown substantially. She enjoyed her life as it was and had no intention of returning to what it had been like before she had the good fortune to be approached by Mabel.

'I'll have some champagne,' Bennet told her, leaning forward just slightly to see better into the roadway below. It was a favourite occupation of his.

She popped the cork and filled a large glass for him, then set the bottle back in the silver ice bucket. It had come with the breakfast served by the hotel. Bennet never allowed a drop to go back.

When she handed him the glass, she asked, 'Aren't you going to tell me?'

'It's Mama, of course. Who else would send me a telegram?'

'And what does she say?' Jeanette was alarmed now. Mabel never spent money wastefully. The message had to be important.

'That she's dying. Again. And I've to come to her at once.'

'Oh, Bennet...'

He shook his head. 'Don't pretend. You don't care.'

'But aren't you going?' Jeanette asked. She was worried that Mabel might recover and disinherit Bennet out of spite.

'Later,' Bennet said.

'It might be real this time,' she told him.

'It might be.' He emptied his glass, smiled at her pleasantly. 'And what if she changes her will?'

'If it's true, she won't,' Bennet said.

He refused to talk about it any more, and spent the day watching the roadway through the window. He enjoyed seeing the traffic go by. There was an occasional electric brougham, riding high and soundlessly. Sometimes he saw a Duryea, and once in a while a Packard, one of which only two years before had made the trip from San Francisco to New York in 52 days. Along with these, there were the usual surreys and hansoms and loaded wagons. Their maneuverings made for an exciting view.

Later in the afternoon she asked him again, 'Aren't you going?'

'After dinner,' he told her.

But when they had dined, he was heavy with food, and wine-logged, and his foot hurt. He decided to go in the morning.

As he was finishing his usual gargantuan breakfast, he received another telegram. This time, after he had opened it, his hand trembled, his face paled. Finally he said, 'Mama's died.'

'I'm sorry,' Jeanette told him.

A momentary exultation swept him. He had outlasted her! He was free – the long struggle was over! 'You aren't sorry,' he told Jeanette, 'and neither am I.'

Still, when he went to the rooming house and the landlady led him to Mabel's bed, saying, 'Poor soul, she called for you all day and night,' Bennet's eyes filled with tears and he had to mop them away so he could see her face.

She was at peace. She hadn't needed him for that. Bennet sat beside her. He had thought to tell her all his grievances, but now he felt no need. The battle was won. He could forgive her and pity her. He sat with her for a little while, and then, limping, he left her.

The first thing he did was to settle his father's unpaid

335

medical and burial bills. Next he made Mabel's funeral arrangements and went to see her lawyers. Then, having done his duty by her as he saw it, he left her to the undertakers and her affairs to the attorneys, and took Jeanette on a shopping trip to New York.

They sailed from Fall River on the *Providence*, a new ship given the older one's name. This *Providence* was built in Quincy, the first of the Fall River ships to be built in Massachusetts, and once again designed by George Peirce, although he died before she went down the ways. The ship was smaller than the *Priscilla* but had nearly as many staterooms and almost as much freight capacity. The interior was decorated in the French Renaissance style, and had a telephone in every cabin.

By the time she made the stop at Newport, the new *Providence* was nearly full.

Bennet sat in the grand saloon with Jeanette, watching the passing parade. She saw how his eyes followed the young ladies. There was one in particular, a very slender girl, who looked to be nearly a child by her form. His gaze returned to her again and again.

Jeanette clasped his plump hand. 'You told me that we'd be married.' And, widening her eyes, careful to keep her voice at almost a whisper, 'Then why don't we?'

'We will,' he said. 'I've been thinking about it. There's one thing, though.'

He proved that he had indeed been thinking about it by pulling from his pocket a pre-nuptial agreement. It didn't occur to him that he was doing just what his mother had done before him. He had drawn it up the evening he learned of his mother's death, and had had his lawyers study it for any weakness. It specified that Jeanette would relinquish all rights to his fortune, and that the properties and estates he owned would remain intact and on his death be distributed as his will disposed, in consideration of which she would receive now an immediate payment of $10,000. In effect, the contract was identical to the agreement that his father had signed many years before, except that he had received no money.

Chewing her lip, Jeanette read it several times. Then she asked, 'What does it mean?'

'You don't get anything after I die except what I leave you in my will,' he answered. He didn't tell her that he had not yet written one.

'Nothing?'

'Only what I leave you in my will.'

She looked at him blankly. 'If that's what you want...'

He showed her a draft for $10,000. 'And this. Now.' As she looked at it, he added, 'I have to protect the Graystone fortune.'

'There's none but you.'

'That could change,' he told her.

Together they went down to the purser's office. The purser watched while she signed her name: Jeanette Clara Hall. Then he signed his own. Bennet handed her the draft, saying, 'And this is the consideration.' The purser nodded.

Bennet smiled at Jeanette. 'We'll get married as soon as we get back to Boston.'

In New York, she bought three gowns at Worth's, and then, because he was in a good mood, he bought three more for her. He also bought, for himself, a Duryea, the first of his automobiles.

On the return trip, Jeanette saw how his eyes strayed. She deliberately befriended a slim, dark-haired girl named Coty James. Coty had blue eyes and white skin and hips the width of a board. She spent the dinner hour with them, and retired to their stateroom with Bennet for an hour or two after, while Jeanette took a stroll on deck.

Bennet and Jeanette were married at the end of the month, and for their honeymoon sailed to New York again. This time they took the *Priscilla*.

They had an elaborate meal in the dining saloon, walked in the grand saloon, and strolled for a little while on deck. By the time the ship reached Newport, Bennet was sound asleep and Jeanette was wondering how much money she could save in the next few years.

As the *Priscilla* steamed away from Long Wharf, leaving the lights of Newport behind, Mary Gorgas said to the purser, 'Lady Farr. My daughter.'

'Mrs. Farr,' Diane said wearily. And then, smiling at the man, 'You do understand?'

337

'Mrs. Farr,' he repeated, charmed and willing to accommodate her in all things.

'You're still married to Charles,' Mary Gorgas said under her breath.

'But not for long.'

Mary's chest puffed out and her jaw thrust forward. Her eyes glinted dangerously, 'Diane, I've told you! You will not have a divorce!'

Behind her a waiting passenger coughed politely. Before her the purser moved interested eyes from her to Diane.

Diane accepted the key he offered her and turned to her mother. 'It may take a while,' she said, 'but you're not going to stop me.' Then, smiling at the purser and the waiting passenger, she walked away.

As she let herself in to her stateroom, she wondered why it had taken her so long to learn how to deal with her mother. Her earliest memories were dominated by the sound of her mother's voice. 'Stand up straight. You're a lady, you must act like one.' And: 'I know what's best for you. You must listen to me.' And: 'You'll do what I say.' There had seemed no way to escape that voice. Or had she even thought of it? She suspected she hadn't. Not until she was sixteen and Charles Farr came into her life. How she despised him! Even now the thought of him could make her flesh crawl. It had been the same then. His whiskey breath and soft hands. Except for her hatred of Charles, she'd never have had that brief affair with Jesse Light...

She took off her plumed hat and slipped the garnet beads from her neck. With her chin on her hand, she looked into the glass and into the reflection of her eyes. She tried to remember Jesse's face, but couldn't. There was a blank in her mind where he ought to be. It had all been wiped away, or perhaps just buried, by what came after. Those six months of virtual imprisonment... always knowing she'd not be allowed to keep the infant she was to bear.

Diane jerked away from the looking glass. She rose, clenching her hands, to pace the room. From far away she heard the distant sound of music. In her mind, she heard her infant's cry as her mother took the baby from the room. The girl would be eight years old now. What would she look like? Would she be blond like Diane, like Jesse Light? Or would she be dark, like William? Where did she live? And how? Who loved her? Who read to her at night? Once she was gone, Diane had cared for nothing. She hardly remembered her wedding day. She had moved through it pushed by her mother, pulled by her, until, finally, she and Charles had boarded the boat train. They spoke briefly of the weather and then lapsed into silence. When they arrived at the ship in Fall River, Charles told her, 'We'll have some champagne and go straight to our stateroom.'

She had accepted three glasses of wine in hopes it would dull her. She needn't have troubled. Charles mounted her with no pretense of interest. After a little while he rolled away, saying, 'There, that's done. Now you can't claim the marriage hasn't been consummated.' He barely touched her again. When they finally reached Long Melford, she understood. On the grounds of Melford House was a caretaker's cottage. Charles visited it every day, and spent most of his nights there. It was where his mistress lived. When Diane learned about it, she wasn't surprised. It explained Charles to her as well as anything could.

He never spoke to her, hardly looked at her. Evening after evening they dined together in silence while the butler served them. Night after night she retired to her room, cheeks burning with shame.

Gradually she gained the confidence to go beyond the grounds of Melford House. She visited the church and Melford Hall. She went into town and wandered along Hall Street, its only thoroughfare. She lingered outside the Bull, an inn that dated from the seventeenth century, and daydreamed before the stone and wattle cottages from an even earlier time. She went out into the fields where a cattle fodder called rape lay golden in the summer sun. Five years passed and she was hardly aware of them.

Then one day as she was walking in the garden maze, she came face to face with Charles and his mistress.

He demanded coldly, 'What are you doing here?'

Diane's face burned with humiliation. Fighting tears, she hurried inside. There, pacing, wringing her hands, she said to herself, *This will not be my life any more.*

She left Melford House with one small bag, and took the train from Sudbury to London. The next day she boarded a ship, and 10 days later arrived in New York. The same day she embarked for Newport.

It was two o'clock in the morning when the hack deposited

her at Cliff Mansion. An affair of some sort was just coming to an end. Ladies in full evening attire were descending the marble steps, diamonds sparkling at their throats and ears. Their escorts carried elegant canes and wore silken top hats. Diane thought briefly of Charles as she entered the house.

Her mother stared at her, cried, 'What are you doing here?'

Her father shouted with delight and joyfully opened his arms to her, then stood back, nodding and nodding.

'I've come home,' Diane had said.

'And where's his lordship? Where's your husband?' Mary demanded.

'I've left him.'

It had been impossible to convince Mary that evening that Diane could no longer be bullied or driven.

Now, two years later, Mary sometimes believed Diane and sometimes she didn't. It no longer mattered to Diane. She was determined to be free from Charles, and she knew it was only a question of money. He had made that clear in correspondence with her parents. It might take another year or two before it was resolved, but she could wait. She was twenty-five and free for the first time in her life. There was the child – somehow she must be found. And there was Caleb.

Now came a knock at the door. Diane stood still, waiting until it came a second time. Then, slowly, she opened it.

Caleb said smiling, 'Come up on deck for a little while.'

'I suppose I could,' she answered doubtfully. She didn't want to sound too eager. He was, she had decided, the kind of man who must not have his way too easily.

'Please. It's been a long time since I saw you.'

It had been two months and four days; she had counted them off. But she said lightly, 'Oh, not as long as all that.' And then, 'But yes. Just give me ten minutes and I'll meet you.'

Twenty minutes later, she joined him. He took both her hands in his, and turned her so that the moonlight fell on her face.

'You're so beautiful, Diane.'

She thanked him absently, more aware of the deep tone of his voice than of his words.

He went on, 'Have you thought about it?'

She nodded, feeling his fingers tighten around hers.

'And?'

'Caleb, I don't know. It might be a very long time. Charles is being difficult about the divorce.'

'I've told you I'm willing to wait.'

'Then we'll see,' she said softly.

He tipped her face up, his thumb under her chin, and looked into her eyes and said, 'I want you. I shall never stop wanting you.'

In the dining saloon the Fall River people were still discussing the mill workers' strike that had been settled the previous January after a six-month work stoppage involving 25,000 operatives at 71 mills, controlled by 33 corporations. On July 20 of the previous year the Manufacturers' Association had announced an industry-wide wage cut of twelve and a half cents. That night the Textile Council, which represented five craft unions and was associated with the New England Federation of Textile Workers, an American Federation of Labor affiliate, called for a strike on July 25. The manufacturers refused to back down. Instead, they closed the mills. The furnaces went cold, the sky over the smoke stacks turned clear and blue, the machinery fell silent. The capital of the affected mills totalled $25 million. There were 2.3 million spindles involved. The combined losses were later calculated to be some $5 million.

The Fall River Line suffered large decreases of freight revenue as a result. For the six months of the stoppage no wagons transporting bales of cotton were unloaded into its holds. No finished cloth was shipped to New York.

The strike was lost when the mill workers could no longer hold out. They accepted the twelve and a half cent wage reduction effected the previous July, and agreed to have their future wages set by the state governor, who would base them on mill profit margins.

Opinions ran strong as to who was responsible for the losses suffered by the mills and the workers, and the city of Fall River itself.

Finally one of the disputants, a director of the Pocasset Mills, leaned toward Bennet to ask, 'And what is your opinion, Mr. Graystone-Fields?'

Bennet had just begun his second helping of cream pie. He put down his fork and looked blankly at the man. Then: 'I have no opinion. I give no time to such matters.'

The man sat back, whispering to his neighbor behind his hand. Jeanette, sitting beside Bennet, noticed. But Bennet himself did not. He had turned his head to look at an adjacent table. Jeanette noticed that, too.

Two girls sat there. They were identical twins, perhaps fifteen years old. They had jet black curls and very fair skin, and small slender bodies. They carried on between them an animated conversation, with many flashing smiles and much laughter.

Soon after, in the grand saloon, Jeanette struck up a conversation with them. Their names were Gay and Joy Brown, and they were traveling with their aunt and guardian, who was resting in their stateroom. After a little while, Jeanette said, 'You must come and meet my husband,' and when they did, he smiled fondly at Jeanette before smiling fondly at the twins.

They spent an hour together before going off to bed. By then Bennet knew that they had been orphaned early, that money was in short supply in the Brown household, that they went to public school, never had enough clothes, and that they were both, in his opinion, utterly charming.

He met Mrs. Brown in the dining saloon early in the morning, and took her and the twins to share an elaborate breakfast with him.

They rode the boat train together to Boston, and parted with friendly hugs and promises to meet again. It was Jeanette who wrote down the Browns' address, and who, several weeks later, when she saw Bennet's boredom, sent the three an invitation to lunch.

It was over lunch that Bennet suggested he pay for the twins' piano lessons, and then that they began calling him Uncle Bennet. That was the last time that Mrs. Brown joined the girls in their visits with the Graystone-Fields family.

In November just before Thanksgiving, he took them to New York. They spent the time there shopping. He sat and watched while they paraded their choices before him. He was particular about color, fit, design, and concerned himself with every

detail, from their slippers to the bows they wore in their hair
On the ship coming back they paraded the clothing again.

Bennet sat on his chair like a sultan of Turkey, his paunch
extended between his thick knees, sipping a glass of
champagne. Joy pirouetted in a gown of white organdy with
pale lavender dots, great bell sleeves trimmed with lavender
braid, and a white hat encircled with lavender flowers perched
on her saucy curls. Then Gay tripped in. She wore blue lace and
spun a matching blue parasol, with a large blue flower in her
hair.

As he watched, murmuring his approval, his round face grew
flushed, his eyes bright. And afterward, he took Joy to bed in the
privacy of his stateroom while Gay and Jeanette made
conversation together. Gay pouted when it appeared he favored
her twin. But Bennet proved he was impartial, for soon he
called Gay in.

At Christmas, he gave both girls marmot coats and muffs and
a blue fox cloak to Mrs. Brown.

Jeanette didn't mind. Now that she saw what he wanted, she
was determined to provide it. She had signed the pre-nuptial
agreement and married him because she already knew what a
good thing she had. Bennet was generous with the household
money and with gifts. She knew that he would continue to be,
and from what she had saved before, she knew her future was
assured.

Chapter 32

Over the next two years Jeanette thought often of that future.
She was lonely. There was no longer much time for champagne
sessions with Bennet, hardly any for the giggly conversations
they had once had, and none at all for lovemaking.

She kept him surrounded by young girls, knowing that he
needed them. He didn't take each of them to bed, but he wanted
to treat them and teach them. He spoke of their clothes and

schools and friends, and of leaving them money in his will. He did have his favorites, and these Jeanette observed closely. Eventually, she paired them off with available young men. When Bennet had competition, he dropped them.

Jeanette was careful to give him no competition. She had her own interests to look after. She teased from him diamond necklaces and great ropes of pearls and golden bracelets, saying, 'You want me to look as fine as any of the ladies on board, don't you?'

He did indeed, and he outfitted her in jewels that shone brilliantly among those worn by the Belmont and Vanderbilt women who traveled on the ship with them, gossiping about the murder of Stanford White that year on the roof of Madison Square Garden, and bemoaning the fire that had burned the *Plymouth* to the water's edge in Newport harbor the past March.

Bennet spent his time practicing his hobby of taking up with young girls, and perfecting the means of pursuing it, on which he would spend the rest of his life.

Without effort on his part, and in the hands of his attorneys, the fortune Mabel had left him more than doubled. By 1907 he was worth some $4 million.

By then, too, President Theodore Roosevelt had been in office for two years of his first full term, and had received the Nobel Peace prize for helping to end the Russo-Japanese War. The International Workers of the World, known as the Wobblies, had been organized for two years. And San Francisco was being rebuilt after devastating damage by an earthquake and fire the year before.

By then, too, when Bennet took a Fall River ship to New York, he rented four staterooms for himself and Jeanette, and the young ladies he called his wards.

Thus when he embarked on the *Priscilla* in mid-May of 1907, he was surrounded by a small harem of young, beautiful, and well-dressed girls.

He had turned thirty-seven that year. His hair had begun to gray. He wore a small mustache and goatee that were graying too. His face was full and florid, and on his lips there was always a small shy smile.

After a stop at the purser's office for the stateroom keys, which he himself distributed to the girls, he went to the dining saloon on the main deck and ordered a sumptuous meal to be served in an hour. Then he took Jeanette and his girls out on the forward deck to watch the bustle of departure.

Caleb and Diane stood together at the head of the gangplank. He still wore his blue uniform, with the gold stripes on the sleeves, each one indicating five years of service with the line. Since their marriage in January, she had been trying to persuade him to leave his job. Thus far he had refused, but he knew that he'd soon give in.

They watched as, below them on the wharves, Kevin hopped down from a carriage and offered his arm to Augusta. She stepped lightly to the ground. Gussie followed her.

'She's lovely,' Diane said. 'And you take after your father, of course.'

Caleb grinned at her. 'Of course.' There were no shadows in Diane's eyes now, and no sign of how she had wept the night before, her arms reaching for the infant she had lost long ago. The best, the most, he could do for her would be to find the child, and bring them together.

Meanwhile Augusta paused on the gangplank to look back at the busy wharves. The sun shone on her hair: silver locks glistened in the red-gold waves. She wore a lavender hat, and a lavender gown with a wide purple sash. She was slim, and erect, and moved lightly as she turned back to climb up the gangplank with a swirl of skirts and lace petticoats.

The Callahan children trooped behind her. But they were grown now. Kevin was twenty-one. He wore the blue uniform of the Fall River Line, and already he had on his sleeves one gold strip. He was very tall, with his grandfather Marcus's height, but he had the thick chest and forearms of his father. Ray, twenty, was tall, too. They both had sandy red hair. Gussie was the dark one, and small, with an elfin look and laughing eyes. At eighteen she was very much her own person. Like Ray, she lived in Boston, where she attended nursing school, while he worked for a shipbuilding firm.

Augusta knew they had planned a surprise for her, thinking that she'd forgotten it was the sixtieth birthday of the line, and her sixtieth birthday too – May 19, 1907. She determined not to spoil it for them.

She kissed Diane and Caleb, wondering if all was well

between them. She hadn't expected the marriage. Ever since Rosalie went away with Peter, Caleb had seemed unable to love.

'It's such a nice idea,' Augusta told her daughter-in-law. 'Inviting us down to Newport for your party tomorrow.'

'I've been wanting to for a long time,' Diane answered. It was true, although the ruse had been Kevin's.

When Augusta went to get her key, the purser relayed the captain's compliments and said he wanted to know if Augusta would do him the favor of stepping up to the wheelhouse once the ship was under way.

She promised she would, remembering those long-ago days when her father had taken her to see Commander Comstock on the *Bay State*.

Later she and Kevin visited the captain, and he presented her with a bouquet of red roses. She laughed, and thanked him, and took them to her stateroom.

There, alone, she sat down to read the Fall River *Journal*. She scanned the concert program, then read the notes of Fall River history. She was taken aback to discover several incorrect items. It confirmed to her that memories were short. Only recently she had seen an advertisement for the Fall River Line that said not a single passenger life had been lost in all its years of service. But she recalled the *Empire State* explosion, and the men who had died then, and knew it wasn't so.

She rose, stretched. She ought to have brought reading matter with her. How handy it would be if there were a newsstand on the main deck: journals and papers, perhaps stationery, and, of course, pipe tobacco and cigarettes. She sank down on the bed, smiling. Luke would say she was meddling. Nevertheless, she resolved to mention the idea to Caleb.

'Grandma!' It was Gussie calling. 'What are you doing? We're going to arrive in Newport any minute!'

Augusta opened the door. 'I'll come up with you.'

They stood together at the rail. A breeze whipped across Long Wharf, sending paper flying and belling out the ladies' skirts. One man lost his hat and went chasing after it.

When Augusta saw Barbara and Luke coming aboard with their son Tom, she realized that the celebration was to be held on the ship, and not in New York as she had surmised.

Caleb confirmed the thought, suggesting that the party go in to dinner.

With Gussie on one side and Caleb on the other, Augusta entered the dining saloon.

A long table was set up. Two flower centerpieces laid brilliant color on the linen.

Caleb led her to the head of the table. The others, even restless young Tom, stood by their chairs. The stewards hurried to pour champagne.

Then Caleb lifted his glass. 'To Augusta Kincaid Wakefield, and the Fall River Line!'

Augusta waited until the others had drunk. Then she too raised her glass. 'To our future and fortune!' Smiling, she sank into her seat. 'What a wonderful surprise!'

'Did you think we'd forgotten, Grandma?' Gussie asked.

And Kin said, 'Oh, Mama, how could we?' He went on, intoning, '"It was the day of my birth, May 19, 1847. The *Bay State* made her first voyage..."'

'Kin,' Barbara said in a hot whisper, 'do shut up! Your mother won't realize you're teasing.'

'*She* will,' he retorted. 'Even if you don't.'

Over the years Kin had become tired of being maneuvered, disgusted with the offer of Barbara's body in exchange for his docility. He had taken a mistress who welcomed him because she wanted him. When Barbara realized he no longer desired her, she managed to get herself pregnant, thinking that way to keep him. The birth of small Tom four years earlier hadn't helped. Kin thought constantly about leaving her. She thought always about how to prevent it. So they quarreled incessantly over the trivial and avoided talk of the important.

Augusta had long suspected that there was trouble. Now, seeing the hostile looks they exchanged, she was certain. She was relieved that the dining stewards provided a distraction by serving the meal previously ordered by Caleb.

When they had finished eating, they visited the grand saloon. There, in groups of three, members of the crew came to pay their respects and wish Augusta well.

As soon as she could, she excused herself, telling Gussie that she wanted to walk on deck to savor the evening.

Outside, the salty breeze lifted her hat. She settled it more firmly as she went to the railing, and leaned there, listening to the shish-shish of the paddle wheels and the snap of the lines. Sweet and familiar sounds... the music of her life. It was good now to be here like this. Alone. All her own person. Much as she missed Luke, and being a wife. Much as she was sometimes aware of her body's yearning, it was good, too, at this time to be beholden to no one and independent.

She raised her face to the wind, smiling.

'Augusta,' the familiar voice said. 'It *is* you!'

She turned slowly. A tall form approached from the shadows. 'Jim! Where did you come from?'

He took her hands in his. 'I've been to Boston on Pinkerton business.'

'And we've met by chance?'

'Not exactly. I spoke to Ray. He told me about the surprise.'

'You ought to have joined us.'

'Oh, no. I'm not family.'

She ignored that to say, 'And how are you?'

He smiled at her. 'The same. I'm always the same.'

She understood his meaning, but ignored that too.

He went on, his voice deep, 'I'm here for a reason. Your grandchildren are grown now. There's nothing to keep you in Fall River. Come to Omaha with me.'

She waited through a long still moment. What was she to say to him? How could she make him see? He had been for too long accustomed to think of himself as a constant lover, with no obligations or responsibilities. He hardly knew by now what he really felt for her. At last she said softly, 'Oh, dear Jim, forgive me. I can't. I really can't. I've been alone for too long, and I'm set in my ways.' And suddenly, laughing, she seized his hands. 'You'll thank me for this one day, believe me. For it's the same with you. I know it's so. You've been a bachelor always. Can you imagine how it would be, you trying now to be my husband? To change everything, your style, your home, your hours of work and play, perhaps even your friends, to try to suit me?'

He looked stricken and bewildered at the same time. 'Augusta, I've loved you since I was a boy of twenty-five.'

'My dear, of course, and that's part of the trouble. It's habit. You've never allowed yourself to think of anyone else.'

'I didn't want to,' he said, but he was smiling. He knew that at least a part of what she had said was true. He was comfortable in his bachelorhood. It was like an old suit of clothes to him.

They spoke a little longer, and then she told him, 'Good night, Jim. And God bless you always.'

He wanted to walk her down to her stateroom, but she refused to allow it. 'I know the way,' she told him, 'and I can go alone as I always do and always have.'

'I'll see you in the morning when we dock,' he said.

She smiled, knowing he wouldn't, and walked quickly away. At the door, she turned back to wave once before she went inside.

The orchestra was still playing. She hummed along with it as she made her way to her stateroom.

It was filled with the scent of roses. That had been good of the captain. When she turned on the light and saw the Fall River *Journal*, she thought that yes, she must speak to Caleb about a newsstand and see what he said.

Later, lying in bed, listening to the ship's familiar sounds, she saw a beacon signal swing slowly past the porthole. It filled the room with momentary brightness. As it faded the *Priscilla* whistled three times, and lifted and swayed, and then sank down only to lift and sway again. Point Judith and the Atlantic Ocean, Augusta thought. Then there'll be Block Island and Montauk Point and the Long Island Sound. And after that Watch Hill, and rising into the moonlight dangerous and dark Latimer's Reef. It was there, at Latimer's Reef, that she drifted gently into contented sleep.

PART III
1907 to 1937

Chapter 33

On a misty evening in late September of the same year, 1907, Augusta and Marge Gowan, with four members of the study group, stood together on the deck of the *Priscilla* as she headed into Mount Hope Bay.

Augusta ignored the excited chatter of the others, enjoying the moment of departure as always.

The ship was crowded, and more passengers would board at Newport. A year earlier, 444,450 tickets had been collected on the *Priscilla*, a record for the line. This in spite of the competition to which she had just been witness... Porters from the Joy Line, shouting, 'This way to the *Tennessee!*' and from the Neptune Line, 'Here's the *Connecticut!*' The quarrels between agents on Baylies Street and Turner Street... Pedestrians carrying baggage besieged on Central Street. A relentless war was being fought for passengers, driving down rates, and freight costs too. Now a barrel of sugar sent to New York shipped for five cents and a barrel of oil for eight. Passage was three dollars, and included a free first-class berth. Staterooms went for an additional one or two dollars. There was, in Fall River, worried talk about the condition of all the different lines. But Augusta was sure the Fall River Line would best the others. Contracts had already been let for the ironwork of a new ship, now being built by William Cramp & Sons of Philadelphia. Ray had told her that each of the two sidewheels weighed a hundred tons. She would have 421 staterooms, 1,290 passenger berths, and carry 2,000 passengers. The crew would exceed in number that of the *Priscilla*, which was 196. By all accounts this new ship would be the finest to sail Long Island Sound, and Augusta hoped that she would have made her own contributions to it. She had spoken persuasively to Caleb about her idea for a newsstand; and struck by another thought at that moment, she had also suggested that the many businessmen and politicians traveling the line would be glad to have on board a stenographer to work for them as needed. Caleb had promised to speak to the designer, Mr. Gardner, at the Newport shops, and to the board. Augusta didn't mind that he was her surrogate. Who accomplished the task didn't matter. That it be accomplished was what mattered to her.

She smiled, thinking how much she was looking forward to stepping on board the new ship. But now there was a tug at her elbow.

Marge Gowan said, 'Oughtn't we to go in? It's very cold.'

Indeed, Marge did look chilled. Her face was pale and her lips pinched. She clutched her cloak tightly around her. But her eyes blazed with excitement. Several years before, when Marge was serving tea to the study group, going in and out with cups and cake plates, Augusta had noticed how she lingered at the threshold, lingered and listened. Augusta had insisted that she join in, and was delighted with her contributions. Marge knew the lot of the mill girls and understood the role of the unions. She was eager to learn what she did not know. From that time on, she had been a part of the group.

When they first spoke of the trip, Augusta had insisted she must go too, if she wanted. Marge had asked, 'But what of Kevin?' He was the only one left at home, aside from Augusta. 'Kevin's a grown man,' Augusta had told her. 'He can look after himself for those few days we're both away.'

'Then I'll go,' Marge said, and ran to see if she had anything respectable to wear.

Now Augusta walked slowly with the others toward the grand saloon. They had planned this excursion some seven months before, having read in the *Daily Herald* of a demonstration by English suffragettes who had stormed the Houses of Parliament to demand the right to vote. Sixty of them had been roughly handled by the police, some knocked to the ground, and all had been arrested and jailed.

'There's surely something wrong when women aren't even permitted to present their case,' Augusta had said. 'What do the men fear so, I wonder?'

'My husband says such actions damage the cause.' It was Bertie Branscombe speaking, the youngest member of the group at thirty-five. She always quoted her husband.

'Which actions?' Marge Gowan asked tartly. 'What the women did? Or what the police did?' She expected no answer and received none.

'That's typical of what men say,' Alice Peabody, older and more cynical than Bertie, remarked. She went on, 'At least that's what they say when they prefer to keep us in the kitchen and away from the polls.'

'But what does it accomplish?' another woman asked.

Augusta had smiled. In her mind she could hear Luke saying, 'You're meddling again, Gussie.' And smiling still, she said aloud, 'It's clear that such demonstrations are written about. Even our own paper reported this affair in London.'

There were murmurs of agreement. Before the meeting ended, the nine women had decided to go to Washington to demand the vote for American women and to show support for their English sisters.

But only four had embarked with Augusta. Bertie Branscombe had confessed with a blush that her husband had forbidden her to go. Alice Peabody's youngest son had the measles. Another admitted that her father had stopped speaking to her after she discussed the journey with him. One simply didn't appear at sailing time.

Augusta accepted these defections with equanimity. If all the others had withdrawn, she would have made the trip alone with Marge Gowan.

She had been amused by the reactions of the children. Kevin had bitten his mustache. Caleb had looked worried, saying, 'Listen, Grandma, are you sure you have to do this?' Ray had grinned, then caught her by both hands and swung her around, crying, 'Go get them, Grandma.' And young Gussie had said softly, 'Do you have to? Are you lonely? Are you sorry Jim went away again?'

Now, as she and her group approached the wide doorway of the grand saloon, she saw Caleb engaged in conversation with one of the ship's officers. How like her father Marcus he was these days. Not in his looks but in his movements. His whole body was expressive of what he was saying. Arms, shoulders, hands underscoring his words. Even his walk, which shook the deck beneath him. As she watched, he caught sight of her. A moment later he came to her.

He greeted the ladies, then drew her aside saying that he needed to talk to her.

She told Marge Gowan and the others that she would join them to hear Stannis Hoppe conduct the orchestra in a little while. Then she and Caleb sat in a quiet corner. But once they were settled, he seemed not to know how to begin. He started a sentence and stopped.

'What is it?' she asked.

'I know you'll be disappointed, and perhaps surprised. But I've considered it carefully and decided to give up my job with the line.'

She *was* disappointed, but not at all surprised. She had realized for some while that Caleb could not go on as he was. He had not enough time with Diane, for she remained at Cliff Mansion in Newport. It was not a good way to begin a marriage, Augusta considered. Yet she was troubled for Caleb himself. How would he fare without an occupation? Would he be happy?

He said, 'I'm needed, you see. Diane's father is no longer able to deal with his affairs. And Mrs. Gorgas has never concerned herself with them, nor has Diane. Someone must take over. There are twelve inns in the Gorgas chain. The managers and lawyers need supervision and prodding.'

'I see,' Augusta said. 'Then you *will* have a job.'

He nodded. There was more, but he felt no need to put it into words. Diane needed him, and he needed her. Not for a few stolen hours that made them seem like lovers instead of husband and wife, but for days and nights, for the small moments as well as the large. It seemed impossible now that when he had first seen Diane, he had thought of her only as a conquest to be made. His feelings had changed. Having fallen in love, and finally won her, he was a different man. He would miss the ship, his friends. But Diane – their life together – was more important.

'I'm sure it's for the best,' Augusta said.

He smiled at her, relieved. 'I am too.' He went on, 'And there's another thing. I spoke to young Luke when I was in New York the other day. He came down to the dock to see me. Kin and Barbara seem not to know it, but he's bitterly unhappy.'

'He didn't want to go back at the end of summer,' Augusta said.

'So he said. I don't understand the problem, but I'm worried about him.'

'I hoped he'd feel better once he was at home, and beginning college.'

'If you could talk to him, Mama...'

Augusta considered. Then: 'Tomorrow, when we arrive in New York, we'll have several hours before we take the train for Washington. I could stop at Barbara and Kin's to see Luke, and meet the ladies later at the station.'

Caleb asked softly, 'And what would you say?'

'I don't know,' she admitted, rising. 'I'll have to think on it.'

Caleb went with her as she hurried to rejoin her friends, but before they reached the grand saloon, there was a bustle in the corridor. Whispers and whistles and applause rang out.

Caleb said, 'I forgot to mention that the president is on board.'

'Mr. Roosevelt?' Augusta asked. Memory brought sudden pain. She saw small Amy rushing after Rutherford B. Hayes, and calling out to him.

Caleb was saying, 'He, and some of his family. They've been to see their son settled at Harvard.'

The president and his party soon came through the big doors. Theodore Roosevelt was a short, blocky man. He had a large head, and wore heavy spectacles. His smile was wide beneath a thick walrus mustache. His wife and two of their children were with him.

The captain of the ship was saying, 'If there's anything I can do, Mr. President...'

'Nothing just yet,' the president answered, as the captain bowed at Augusta, and then said, 'Here's a lady you'd enjoy meeting,' and drew her to his side to make the introductions.

The president smiled warmly. 'How nice to meet you, Mrs. Wakefield.'

'It's an honor, sir.'

The captain mentioned a bit about Augusta's father and her interest in the Fall River Line. 'Our Augusta would be captain of this ship, I think, had she been a man.'

Augusta was not content with such speculation. She said, dimpling, 'Mr. President, my friends and I are on the way to Washington.'

'Indeed? And what will you be doing there?'

She said gently, 'We'll be walking with banners in front of your house. I hope you don't mind.'

'Banners?' His laugh was a good-natured bellow. 'What sort of banners?'

'We'll be asking for the right to vote.'

'Ah,' the president said. 'I see.'

The captain coughed. 'My dear Augusta...'

'But I should like so much to hear the president's position.'

'Augusta.' The captain looked pained.

'And I don't mind telling you, my dear,' President Roosevelt spoke softly but firmly, 'I'm not opposed to women's suffrage. In fact, I favor it. However, important issues confront us. We can't waste time on so trivial a concern. Some time, perhaps in the future –'

'Trivial?' Augusta echoed. 'But, sir, surely the rights of women who are the mothers of your children and the keepers of your home...'

President Roosevelt, smiling still and looking about, said loudly, 'Where's Alice gotten to? Wasn't she with us? And what's happened to Nicholas? Have the two of them slipped away?' With these words and a nod at Augusta, he moved off, his party trailing after him.

'I didn't accomplish much with that encounter,' Augusta said ruefully. 'Perhaps we shall do better in Washington.'

'You're a stubborn woman, Mama,' Caleb said. 'Will you be as insistent on young Luke's behalf?'

'I'll try to be,' she answered.

Jeanette had met young Dottie Devanta on the main deck, and thinking that the girl would amuse Bennet, had brought her to meet him. But now, seeing how fondly Bennet looked at her, Jeanette was sorry. She passed a hand over her forehead, saying,

'I do have such a headache, Bennet. A migraine, I fear. I think I'd better go to bed.'

Bennet had never heard of a migraine headache. He suspected Jeanette had invented it because he'd taken such a fancy to Dottie, who was a deck passenger on her way to New York to work in a factory. It was Bennet's thought to provide the girl with a fine stateroom, so that once in her life she could sleep in the luxury she'd never before been able to imagine. He hoped she'd invite him to share it with her for a few hours, but if she didn't, that would be all right too.

'I'm sorry,' he told Jeanette.

When he didn't offer to go with her, she hesitated, looking first at Dottie, then at him.

'I hope the rest will help you,' he said politely, as she left him.

He spoke a few words more to Dottie, then excused himself to go to the purser's office. When he returned, she was waiting for him. She was thin, and very pale. She had large brown eyes and a mass of silky black curls. She accepted the key he put into her hand, saying, 'Mr. Graystone-Fields, are you sure you mean for me to have this?'

'Of course, my dear.' He smiled at her hopefully. 'And now perhaps we can have a glass of champagne together?'

'Champagne!' Her brown eyes glistened. 'I never had champagne before.'

'You'll enjoy it, I promise you.' He took her arm. 'We'll go to the grand saloon.' And, seeing the awe in her face, he went on, 'Have no fear.'

'But I was never there before.'

'You've never been to New York either, have you?'

She shook her head. 'But I know what I'm after there.'

'And you'll soon know what you're after, as you put it, here.'

It was what he most enjoyed. It rankled in him, however, that Jeanette refused, this time, to assist him in playing the fatherly teacher. 'Dear Miss Devanta,' he said, leading her to a deep chair, 'do you mind if I call you Dottie?'

'I don't mind.' But her brown eyes slipped nervously away from him to stare at the ladies sitting nearby. She was out of place in her simple gown, with the ribbon in her hair. Yet it didn't seem to matter. She was too fascinated to care. Where but on the *Priscilla*, whose comings and goings she had heard of for years, would she ever have had the chance to see what she now saw before her?

Bennet spoke to her, but she found it difficult to concentrate on him. There was so much to look at: the soft light of the chandeliers, the thickness of the red and gold carpet, the silks enwrapping the ladies, and their fur cloaks and scarves, the plumed hats, the narrow bejeweled slippers. All that, and yet she was expected to attend to the fat old man who sat beside her. In a little while, heady with champagne, she said, giggling, 'I want to explore.'

Bennet sighed, but acquiesced. He limped along after her while she cooed at the sight of the various dining saloons and danced along endless corridors, and stood gaping at the gallery where the musicians played. Finally, asserting the need for fresh air, she led him outside. There, in the dark, she said softly, 'My Ben'll never believe this.' She clutched Bennet's arm. 'You see, that's why I'm going to New York. To be with my boyfriend. He's a foreman at the Triangle Shirtwaist Factory, and he's going to get me a job there. As soon as we can, we're going to be married.'

'I see,' Bennet said sadly.

'My father and mother, they're mad at me. They didn't want me to go. But I have to be with my Ben.'

'I see,' Bennet repeated.

Then she went up on her toes and kissed his cheek, whispering, 'Thank you for everything.' Clutching the brass key to the stateroom he had gotten for her, she scurried off.

When Bennet joined Jeanette, she sighed from her stacked pillows, 'What time is it?'

He told her.

'Did you enjoy yourself?'

He said that he had, but he fumed inside. It was her fault that he was restless and unsatisfied. She was supposed to arrange these things. He didn't know how and didn't want to know how.

'Did you order champagne for us?' she asked.

'No.'

'Oh, Bennet,' she wailed. 'And I have such a bad headache.'

'Sorry,' he said, and settled himself to sleep.

*

Later, the concert over, the women of the study group had retired. Augusta sat alone in the grand saloon, thinking about young Luke and Kin and Barbara, and how to help the boy.

Nearby there was sporadic conversation. 'We'll soon have real competition from Japan,' a Fall River man was saying. 'The Kamgafuche Spinning Company at Kobe is a well-built mill, with machinery from England. Three quarters of its employees are women, working for ten to fifteen cents a day. How will we deal with that?'

'We needn't worry,' another man said. 'In spite of the panic earlier in the year, Massachusetts is the richest state in the union. Every wheel and spindle is turning. The mills and factories are running overtime. They employ thirty to forty thousand people, with room for more, and produce a billion yards of cotton yearly. The Pocasset Mills are going to double their capital and pay a one hundred percent dividend.'

'But the American Woolen Company has closed down for two weeks,' a third man put in sourly.

'Bad management,' the first man said.

Augusta was inclined to agree with him. Plainly there was vast opportunity in Fall River. She wondered if she could convince Kin and Barbara of that.

The next day, listening to the two of them bicker across the breakfast table, she decided not to try. It was the wrong time.

But there was still Luke to consider. He was abed now, Barbara said, although he ought to be at the university preparing for registration.

'He's become so irresponsible,' she went on to Augusta. 'I certainly didn't expect that when I agreed to allow him to spend the summer in Fall River with you.' As she named the town, her lips curled.

The accusation was plain, but Augusta didn't rise to the bait. It would accomplish nothing if she and Barbara were to quarrel.

Kin said nastily, 'If you weren't always at the boy, perhaps he'd be willing to stay at home where he belongs.'

'*At* him,' Barbara cried, her face reddening, 'and what do you mean by that, I'd like to know?' She turned to Augusta. 'You see? That's his attitude. He wants to blame me for his own neglect. If Luke had a proper father...'

Augusta thought it was no wonder the boy didn't want to be at home. Why should he, if this was the sort of argument to which he was constant witness. And she had no doubt it was.

Moments later young Luke came in.

At the sight of his dark tousled hair and his eyes, silver in his pale face, Augusta's heart shook within her. He was so like her own Luke as he had been at seventeen. Thin, serious of mien and bearing. This Luke had had everything her own Luke had not. Yet the boy winced when his mother said archly, 'Oh, there you are, my darling. You're just in time for a surprise visit with your grandmother.'

Augusta saw the look bestowed upon the boy. It was the same look that Barbara had once given Kin. Barbara accused Luke of irresponsibility, but she wooed him as she might woo a lover. It wasn't a nice thing to see or think upon.

She said, 'Luke, will you go with me to the station?'

Barbara began a protest, but was drowned out by Kin's hearty 'That's a fine idea, Mama. If you do insist on going. There could be trouble, couldn't there?'

'There could be.' Augusta was serene. 'If so, I'll call you.'

Barbara said nothing, but her face showed what she thought. Augusta and the study group were ridiculous. There was no need for women to have the vote. There were other ways in which they could express their will, and did, and always had, and always would.

Augusta rose as small Tom bounded into the room.

'Here's Grandma,' Barbara trilled.

The boy buried his face in Augusta's skirts. He was very blond, and unusually well spoken for a four-year-old. But now he said nothing.

Luke tousled the boy's hair. 'Cat got your tongue?'

'I want to go on the ship,' he said finally. 'Take me with you, Grandma?'

Augusta began to explain that she was going to Washington by train, but Barbara interrupted. The question had been too much for her unsteady temper.

'You see!' she exploded. 'It's an infection. An affliction. It's all I ever hear. The ships! The ships! The Fall River ships! And that – that stupid and provincial town. From Luke, from Tom.' She swung on her husband. 'And I suppose you'd say the same, too, if you dared. If you were to give even a little of that interest to Gavin and Gavin, my brother Tom wouldn't have to work nearly so hard.'

Kin's face tightened, but he didn't answer. He took out a cigar and lit it, retreating behind the thick pall of smoke.

Barbara flounced to her feet. 'I hope you have a good journey, Mother.'

Augusta thanked her, kissed Tom, and nodded at Kin.

When the two were settled in a hansom, Luke said miserably, 'You can see how it is.'

'You're not at fault. And what happens between your parents is no concern of yours.' But Augusta knew the words were useless. He was present. He heard and saw and felt.

'I don't know what they want of me,' he said. 'I don't know what to do.'

'I think you must go to school. Next summer you'll come to Fall River with me.'

'And then?'

'You'll be a year older. You'll know your own mind more surely.'

'I know it now.'

He was plainly not convinced that she was right, but he went on, 'I'll do what you say. For this year.'

She told him that she knew he'd never be sorry.

When he bade her goodbye at the train station, he said, 'Thank you, Grandma. Be careful in Washington.'

'I will be,' she said, kissing him on the cheek.

But there was no need for care in the capital.

The group checked in at Willard's Hotel on Pennsylvania Avenue. Within the hour they had unfurled their banners and walked the two blocks to the White House. There they spent the long afternoon and early evening promenading back and forth.

They were eyed with suspicion, amusement, and some disapproval. A few passers-by made disparaging remarks. One or two hooted, others sneered. Two ladies stopped to remonstrate with them. Three paused to express agreement.

At twilight, with aching feet and sagging spirits, they rolled up their banners and returned to the hotel. When they discussed the day, they agreed that they'd shown where they stood, but it

361

hadn't mattered. Marge Gowan put into words what they'd all been thinking.

Their long walk before the White House had been too peaceable. The few who noticed it would soon forget. No one beyond those few even knew about it. They'd learned a lesson for the future. A lesson the English ladies had already learned.

As they sat over coffee a young woman came to their table. She introduced herself as Betty Townsend, and asked if they were the suffragettes who had marched that day at the White House. When they admitted to it, she pulled up a chair and sat with them. She had, she told them, heard of their protest from a reporter for the Washington *Star*, who had seen them.

'He didn't talk to us,' Marge Gowan said.

He had told her that, Betty explained. She went on to say that their group was too small to attract attention. They must join with a larger one. She described the National American Woman Suffrage Association, which had met in Chicago the past February, and took their names and addresses for its mailing list.

When she had gone, Marge Gowan said, 'That's a sensible girl. And I think she's right.'

Augusta agreed thoughtfully.

The group boarded the *Priscilla* again for the return home.

It was the same day that the Cunard Line's *Lusitania*, the world's largest steamship, with a gross tonnage of almost 32,000, had docked in New York after her maiden voyage from Liverpool. Augusta had hoped to see her, but there'd been no time.

She was resting in her stateroom when Kevin knocked at the door, and asked how her journey had been.

'Uneventful,' she said.

'You sound disappointed. You wanted a brawl.' He grinned.

'It's what was needed. At least I, and Marge Gowan, and the other ladies, have come to that conclusion.'

'Will you become a troublemaker?'

'Perhaps,' she said.

Later, Kevin told Caleb, 'I didn't like the sound of it. I think Grandma's plotting something.'

Caleb chuckled. 'You can't stop her if she is.'

'No. But we can be on the alert, can't we?'

'I don't think my mother would be pleased to hear you say that. Although she'd surely be thankful you care what she does.'

'Care?' Kevin rubbed his sandy red beard. 'More than care. After all she did for me, and Ray and Gussie too.'

'She loves the three of you, Kevin.'

'I hope she'll love Ann as well.'

'It'll work for you,' Caleb told the younger man, and leaving him at the purser's office went on to make his rounds.

Settling at a desk, Kevin took up a ledger. But his thoughts were on Ann. Ann Whiting. She was the girl he was going to marry. He was waiting only because her father believed her too young, at sixteen, to know her mind, and Kevin too young at twenty-one to know his. Mr. Whiting was an unusual man, a bookish loom-fixer at the Pocasset Mills, with independent ideas. It was no use trying to persuade him that many girls marry at sixteen. All Kevin could do was patiently wait.

Kevin had met Ann, and the rest of her family, at Betty Gowan's funeral, which he attended with all the Wakefields. He had noticed Ann's small trim figure first in the chapel. Her pale blond hair under a black hat had seemed a beacon of light to him in the gloom. Watching her, he heard nothing of the service. Later, at the house on Highland Avenue, he had spoken to her while she was undertaking to entertain ten-year-old Rafe, Gowan Raleigh's son. The boy was active and bright and something of a brigand. Kevin's conversation with her had been brief and frequently interrupted. But he'd thought about her for weeks afterward, and finally he'd gone to call on her. That had been the beginning. She worked as a carder at the Atlantic Mill. Kevin wanted a home of his own, a family. He wanted Ann Whiting with all his heart and soul.

Now, though, the hoarse bellow of the ship's foghorn sounded. He raised his head, and nearly jumped.

Bennet Graystone-Fields was standing at the purser's window, smiling apologetically. 'Good evening. I'm sorry to trouble you. I wonder if there's a stateroom available for me?'

'A stateroom?' Kevin repeated, bewildered by the request, and by the knowledge that this was the second time he'd had it from Bennet. 'Mr. Graystone-Fields, you already have four.'

'Yes. And now I want another. If you don't mind.'

'The four are satisfactory, aren't they?' Kevin was certain he had used exactly the same words responding to the same request when the *Priscilla* had made her trip down to New York.

'Very satisfactory,' Bennet said, and waited.

Kevin's young face was too expressive. The 'why?' in his mind was clearly reflected there.

'I wish to be alone tonight,' Bennet murmured.

Last time, Kevin remembered, Bennet had said, 'It's a surprise for a young friend.'

Kevin told himself that the man was rich enough to do whatever he wanted. Aloud he said, 'Of course. As you wish,' and offered Bennet the big brass key.

The older man accepted it with a shy smile and a whispered, 'Thank you,' and walked slowly away, limping heavily.

It had been, for him, a difficult encounter, just as difficult as it had been when he was forced to it on the way to New York. It was Jeanette's fault, and he blamed her for it. This kind of thing was her responsibility. He didn't have the strength for running about the ship, attending to arrangements.

He sighed as he went into the stateroom Kevin had assigned to him.

By this time, in addition to the Duryea, he had a Pierce Arrow and a Welsh Tourer. In case he wanted to feel old-fashioned, he had a carriage and a surrey as well. He owned a house in Boston and a brownstone in New York. But he was full of sadness.

He brooded over his pain until there came a tap at the door. It was Jeanette. She said, standing over him, 'The purser told me you'd be here. I don't understand. What's wrong?' There was a shrillness in her voice.

He repressed a shudder. The sound was familiar.

'Tell me,' she said. And then more softly, 'Please, do tell me what's wrong. The girls are hurt. You've paid no attention to them. Not going to New York. And not now either.' And when he didn't answer, she said in a small, breathy voice, 'And I'm hurt, too.'

'It's nothing,' he said at last. He hadn't wanted the girls. He'd wanted Dottie Devanta, now lost to him forever. Jeanette should have arranged it.

'The girls...' she began.

'I'm bored with the girls,' he said softly.

364

'Bored?' The word was close to a scream.

It was clearly audible outside in the corridor. Caleb, passing by on his rounds, shook his head and grinned to himself. A late night quarrel between husband and wife . . . it was the very least that he'd heard during his years on the line.

And soon they would be over.

He continued on, passing a stateroom from which came the rumble of men's voices and the click of chips. A poker party in progress. There was always a lot of gambling on board. The porters in the glory hole throwing dice. Card games of every kind in the staterooms; one more diversion, along with drinking, and walking the decks, and listening to the bands' concerts.

He was thinking about Diane when he climbed up to the bridge. Soon now there would be no more separations. It was what she wanted, and what he wanted too. Yet he knew he would miss the ships.

It had been a few months after their marriage that he learned her sad secret. They were in their apartment at Cliff Mansion, a luxurious suite of several rooms decorated in white and gold. They'd just finished dining with her parents. William Gorgas had been as quiet as always, but his wife had been talkative enough for the two of them. She'd been reminiscing about Diane's childhood. They'd been treated to a discourse on all that Mary had done for, sacrificed for, her only daughter.

Listening, Diane had grown pale. At last she burst out, 'Oh, Mother, what does it matter? Caleb doesn't care about those days. Nor about Lillian Russell, nor Jim Brady. He knows them. He knows all your so-called friends.'

'It matters,' Mary Gorgas said grimly. 'Though of course it's obvious that what I did for you goes unremarked.'

Diane flung down her napkin, pushed back her chair, and leaped to her feet. '*You* know what I mean, Mother.'

Mary shrugged plump shoulders. 'Really I am glad that we don't have guests this evening. Your display of manners . . . I wonder at your breeding.'

'You can pretend it didn't happen,' Diane shouted. 'You can close your mind and heart, and shut out every memory, but I can't. I can't, I tell you.' With a wild glance at Caleb, she fled from the room.

He had made his excuses to her parents and gone after her.

She stood waiting for him, small hands clenched at her sides. Her face was wet with tears.

As he took her into his arms, he thought how often he had seen her crying, but never before when she was wakeful. Often in the nights that they were together, she would moan and thrash and when he held her, she would weep, speaking blurred and incomprehensible words to his whispered question.

This time, though, she had put her head against his shoulder and held tightly to him, saying, 'Don't judge me harshly for my disrespect for my mother. I have cause. You don't know.' And then, in a low, monotonous voice, she went on, 'I must tell you, Caleb. I can bear it alone no longer. What my mother did for me was for her own ambition.'

'Surely she meant the best for you,' he protested, thinking of Augusta and all that she had done for him.

Diane said, 'No, no, it was for herself.'

'Perhaps it was a combination of both. But what does it matter now? You have your own life. We'll be happy together.' It embarrassed him that he sounded like a father instructing his child. But he had to say what he believed. There must be honesty between them always.

'That was just what I thought. That we could be happy together.' She drew a deep, ragged breath. 'But we can't be, Caleb. Not with a lie between us...' She stopped, raised her head from his shoulder to look at him. 'I haven't told you all of it.'

'Whatever it is, I forgive you,' he said quickly. 'What counts is that we're together.'

'So you say.' He saw the quick beat of a pulse in her throat as she withdrew from the circle of his arms. 'Listen to me. And then tell me truly how you feel.'

Standing away, straight, tall, more beautiful than ever, she told him about Jesse Light, and the child that had been taken from her arms. 'I'm not whole, you see. I never shall be. Not until I have my daughter back again.'

He had vowed in that moment that he would find the girl, and return her to Diane. And for Diane's sake, and his own too, he would try to be in that child's life what Augusta had been in his.

Now, as a bell rang in the pilothouse and the ship's whistles signaled the Borden Flats light, he looked at the first glimmer of dawn streaking the horizon and silently repeated to himself the promise he had made then. He would find Diane's child and bring her home, and then Diane would be happy as she had never been before.

Chapter 34

It was more than a year later that Caleb found the twelve-year-old Fania Devanta.

By then his life had been unalterably changed, and he himself had changed as well, although it was some time before he realized it.

When he left his job with the line, he left a part of himself. Forever after he listened, when he was in Newport, for the three-whistle signal that meant one of the ships, of his ships, was approaching Long Wharf. Sometimes, although it was always late, he was at the docks to see the passengers boarding and the cargo loaded. Polo ponies, blindfolded and led up the gangplank. And very often, automobiles, first drained of their gasoline, and then, with a stevedore behind their steering wheels to guide them, pushed by muscular men into the hold. Often he went to the window of his bedroom, looked past Cliff Walk to the Atlantic, and imagined he saw the great *Priscilla* sailing there, or the *Puritan*. When he traveled to New York on Gorgas Inn business – and that was often – it was always on one of the ships where he had spent so much of his life before. Though he didn't regret what he had done, he learned that he was no longer the same, and accepted that too as part of his love for Diane.

In those first months as he began to organize his time, he discovered that she hadn't really supposed he'd want to deal with the hotel empire's affairs. When he questioned her, she said, 'The lawyers can handle it. Or ask my father, if you insist.'

It was of no use to question William Gorgas. He was only forty-nine years old, but seemed much older in mind and body. He was slouched, and thick in the middle. His face was seamed. His hair and beard were white-streaked, and his hands and head shook noticeably. He no longer knew, in any detail, what he owned, nor cared for it. He liked to speak of his childhood, and how his father had come home, one-armed from the war, and found him, and about the woman he called Ellie, who had helped raise him. He wouldn't discuss the Gorgas Inns. Mary made it plain that she had never had any interest in the hotel business, and refused any discussion of her husband's affairs.

Caleb spent several months familiarizing himself with the chain by visiting the inns, speaking to the managers, examining the account books, and then going over the whole organization's ledgers with the lawyers who oversaw them.

It was during that activity that, among other papers in the lawyers' office, he came upon an old and dusty notebook that listed a house run by Lottie Dimot, and of another two run by women with names he had never heard before. The pages were blurred, the handwriting scarcely legible, but after some puzzling, Caleb understood that these had been properties that had belonged to old Willie Gorgas. The entries seemed odd to Caleb. Curiosity led him to investigate. He soon realized the truth. But he spoke of it to no one. The knowledge amused him. Old Willie had come far from such improper beginnings. And a new light was cast on his in-laws and the pretensions of their lives in Cliff Mansion.

At the end of January 1908, he began in earnest the search for Diane's daughter. One morning, while Diane was still abed, he found Mary Gorgas in the breakfast room. She was dressed to go out, although at that season there was not much to do in Newport. She was years too old for the Gibson Girl outfit she wore. Charles Gibson had designed it for a slender girl, but Mary's waist, even in her Gavin corset, was too thick for the gown's wasp waist and her arms too thick for its sleeves. And her flat and beribboned hat didn't suit her jowly face. He said to her, 'We must talk, Mrs. Gorgas. If you'll give me a moment.'

She cast an impatient glance at the door. 'Ah, yes, but I have an appointment. What is it, Caleb?'

'It's about Diane.'

Mary Gorgas sighed. 'Yes?'

'She's told me about her marriage to Jesse Light, and the annulment you forced on her. And she told me what came after, too.'

'Indeed? And what came after?'

'The child, Mrs. Gorgas.'

Her eyes seemed to bulge. Color swept into her face, dyeing it a strange and terrible red, but at the same time her lips went white. After a moment she asked hoarsely, 'What child?'

'The one you took away.'

Mary didn't speak until she had drawn three long breaths. At last she sighed. 'I'm sorry you must know of it. I'd hoped it was over. But poor Diane – how she torments herself for nothing. For nothing, I tell you. Why does she do it? Why has this come upon her?'

'What do you mean?' he demanded.

'I'd hoped it would never be necessary to explain,' the older woman said. 'The poor girl . . . it was her mind. For months we had to restrain her. Ask William. Ask whomever you like. For you see, there was no child.'

'No child?' he repeated blankly. Stunned, he stared into his mother-in-law's bloodshot eyes.

'She imagined it.'

'How can you say that?'

'Because it's so, Caleb.'

Already his shock had faded. He asked himself if it was possible that Mary Gorgas was speaking the truth? Had there been no pregnancy, no daughter born to Diane? If so, wouldn't William have known? And the servants? How could Mary Gorgas expect to support such a lie?

'You say,' he said at last, 'that Diane was demented then, and still believes in a child that never existed?'

'Just so.'

But it wasn't just so to him. He was sure enough to tell her, 'Forgive me, but I don't believe you.'

'I can't help that.'

'I'll learn the truth,' he said quietly, and went on in words that surprised him, for he'd never known cruelty in himself before, 'There are so many things to discover. Families have extraordinary secrets. And yours seems to have more than most.'

'You're ridiculous,' Mary said.

'At least Willie Gorgas seems to have had such secrets.' Caleb knew at once that his words had struck home.

Her red face became empurpled. A sheen of sweat suddenly appeared on her brow. But, with stubborn dignity, she drew her fur cloak around her shoulders. 'I believe you must be demented, too. And now, if you'll excuse me...'

She went into the hallway, and stepped into the small birdcage elevator that had been installed when, because of William's failing health, they had decided to remain in Newport through the winter. The gilt door soundlessly slid shut. With a click the elevator moved downward. Caleb watched as she disappeared from view. Then he returned to his bedroom.

Even as the birdcage had begun its descent, Mary had clutched her head so that the big flat-brimmed hat fell to the floor. She leaned against the wall, her fur cloak dropping away from her shoulders. Her breath became a hard loud rasp.

When the cage reached the foyer level, it appeared to be empty. An hour afterward, the downstairs maid opened the gilt door, thinking to dust it. She saw the large, still body of Mary Gorgas and screamed loudly.

Three days later, Mary Gorgas was buried. Lillian Russell and Jim Brady came to Newport for the funeral. They consoled Diane and commiserated with William.

By then Caleb knew for certain that Mary had lied to him. He'd spoken to William. The man had sat nodding his head as he answered, 'I never saw the child. But I know there was one. It was born here in Cliff Mansion. Mary took it away almost immediately. She would never speak of it again.'

Caleb found it impossible to decide if Mary had deliberately lied or if she had convinced herself that Diane had never had an infant. He was more determined than ever to find the child, although William could help him in no way.

It was while he was going through some old household account books, preparing to destroy them, a chore Diane adamantly refused, that he came upon a list of names and addresses of the domestic staff employed at Cliff Mansion in 1896; he had overlooked, until then, the most likely of all possibilities. Were a woman to want to dispose of an infant child, how would she go about it? At the question his heart began to pound. Suppose his father hadn't been able to bring him home to Fall River, to Augusta? What would his mother have done? Dying, helpless, would she have allowed him to die with her? Or would she have given him away? Without money, friends, family to aid her, what *could* she have done? He had thought of it rarely in his adulthood, but now, briefly, he wondered how it had happened that his own father Luke, in the first year of his marriage to Augusta, had lain with her sister and with her conceived him. From that moment the child Diane had lost seemed to Caleb the child that he had been, or might have been. Their two fates were bound together forever.

He saw that his mother's situation had been different from Diane's. Her mother had money and connections. Mary Gorgas could easily have given the child to someone to care for. Who would be most willing to accept such a chore? A woman who needed money – perhaps an available servant.

He began, systematically, to attempt to trace the people who had worked for the Gorgas family at Cliff Mansion.

It took time and traveling to do it. He went to New Bedford and Tiverton and Providence; he went twice to New York. In mid-February, through information developed elsewhere, he went to a Newport neighborhood unfamiliar to him. He saw Mrs. Heck, a cook, who shook her head, denying knowledge of a child at Cliff Mansion. 'But oh how that woman tormented young Diane! Why, she kept her locked in her room for months. And for nothing, as I see it. The girl went on a short boat trip by herself. As if Mary Gorgas hadn't done the same.' Mrs. Heck waxed indignant. 'I remember it well. My sister was sick and I'd gone to see her. When I came back there was Diane, a prisoner in her own house. And Mr. William making a fuss about it, too. And how white and thin the child was when she was finally allowed out.' Mrs. Heck paused, frowning. 'But Susan Walker worked upstairs. She might know. Susan Walker. Yes.'

It was a month before he found Susan Walker. She had left Newport years before. Now she lived in Chelsea, Massachusetts. She was a stout woman in late middle age, but her face was small, vixenish, and surprisingly young looking.

She said, 'Don't ask me. I don't know anything. I hardly remember the Gorgas family. On Bellevue, you say? Cliff Mansion?' He knew it was pretense and mentioned that Mary

Gorgas had recently died. 'Oh, I see,' Susan Walker said. Now she was thoughtful. He saw avarice in her eyes, and told her about the reward he was offering. That helped joggle her memory. She suddenly recalled that Mary Gorgas had given her a thousand dollars to take an infant child away from Cliff Mansion. Where the baby girl had come from, whose it was, she had no idea. But she had found caring for an infant not to her liking. When a neighbor offered to have the child, she'd been happy to give it away. Seeing the look on his face, she'd added quickly, 'It was for the child's own good. They were a proper family, with children of their own.'

'I want their names, the address they had then.'

'Oh, in Newport somewhere. I don't recall the street.'

He reminded her of the reward.

'And how do I know I'll get it?' she asked.

'You can trust me.' He wondered as he said it. How could she believe that? A woman who'd proven herself to be unworthy of anyone's trust? Would she know honesty in another?

She cackled. 'I can trust you, can I? Then I shall. But I don't know where they are now, only where they lived then.'

'And where did they live then?'

She told him, adding, 'And they may not have the child any more. Mr. Devanta was angry about it. He already had two daughters. If the baby had been a boy, it would have been different. But as it was . . .'

'I must see them to find out.' Caleb started for the door, but turned back when she protested loudly that she deserved the reward. 'You'll get it,' he went. 'But only when I've located the Devanta family.'

In fact she never received the money he had promised her. When, late in April, he returned to Chelsea to deliver it, he found the city in a shambles. Virtually a third of it had been destroyed by fire. There were 10,000 homeless. Susan Walker was either dead or one of them. He never learned which.

Meanwhile, though, he had been to the Devantas' last address. The neighbors knew nothing of them. But at a nearby grocer he heard that they'd had a fisherman friend who often came to visit. After some time, he located him and learned that they had moved to Fall River. The father worked in a fish-packing plant. The fisherman had seen them a year ago. Two children were grown; the youngest, called Fania, was now twelve years old.

That same night Caleb took the *Providence* to Fall River. The men in the public rooms were talking about politics. Would the Republicans nominate William Howard Taft for the presidency? Would the Democrats put up William Jennings Bryan? Had everyone heard of Wilbur Wright's unbelievable feat of flying thirty miles in forty minutes?

Later, in the dining saloon, he saw a large party of Japanese seated at five long tables. He knew from the chief steward that they were bankers, merchants, and educators, on a 20,000-mile around the world voyage, finishing the United States part of it on the *Providence*. For their convenience, breakfast and dinner menus had been prepared in Japanese.

Wakeful in the black of night, Caleb heard the ship's whistle at the Borden Flats light. He was dressed and ready when she docked.

Though it was six-thirty when he left the *Providence*, he stopped at High Street. Augusta would probably be up. Yes, he thought, seeing the light at the windows, she doesn't change. He thought it again when she opened the door to him. It confounded him that she remained so much the same. She was sixty-one, but her smile was a young woman's. The two dimples near her mouth were as deep as ever.

She gave him coffee and johnny cakes, asking what brought him to Fall River, and how Diane was. He said Diane was fine, but was vague about his errand. There would be time, later, to explain.

After an hour he went down to the first of the two packing plants he knew of, and it was there that he learned Simeon Devanta's address, for the man was listed on the weekly payroll. He didn't try to speak to him, but hurried away to see what the place was like and who was about.

He lingered for three hours in the chill. There were few trees on the road, the aged house plantings had long since died. The house was a dingy three-story tenement. It was afternoon and nearly dark when he saw a young girl approach.

Fania Devanta gave him an inquisitive glance as she passed him by and climbed the steps and disappeared inside.

He was suddenly warm, heated with the pulse of inner

373

excitement. He had found her – he had found her for Diane! He stood looking after the girl, wanting to hold her, to tell her who he was and why he was there. But he must think first and plan. There was no doubt in his mind that he had found Diane's daughter. The girl was tall for her age, and very slender. Her body was already beginning to show signs of womanhood. Unlike Diane, whose hair was very smooth and blond, the child's was a mass of thick shining black curls that fell down her back. He'd had a single glimpse only of her eyes, but he knew they were dark. She had something about her of William Gorgas.

His heart thumping with triumph, he climbed the hill to High Street again. He asked himself what to do next. He didn't know. He had to consider. In his eagerness to conduct the search, he had made no decision about what he'd do, or how he would do it, once he was successful.

Augusta said, 'Oh, I'm glad you've come back,' and drew him inside. 'Kevin is here. And Gussie's down from Boston.'

Having greeted them, he asked, 'And what brings you to Fall River, Gussie?'

She glanced at Augusta, then announced, 'Nobody knows it yet, so it'll come as a surprise to Grandma and to Kevin, but I'm ... I'm coming home.' There was shame and defiance on her small pixie face.

Augusta glanced at her quickly, but said nothing.

Kevin scowled, 'Giving up on nursing! I had thought you were all afire for it.'

'I've changed my mind.' Gussie's throat worked. At Kevin's grin, she cried, 'And don't laugh at me! I don't want you to play big brother now. It's just what Ray said you'd do.'

'I'm not laughing, Gussie. I just don't understand it.'

'People change, don't they? Maybe I was ... was wrong.'

'And what do you intend to do here?' he enquired.

'Now, Kevin ...' Augusta began.

But Gussie cut in. 'I'll find work, of course. You needn't worry about me.' But her voice shook so that the words came out a trembling whisper. She wasn't going to explain. No, no, she couldn't. Not in front of Caleb and Kevin. When she and her grandma were alone, then perhaps she'd say it all. Grandma would understand.

Augusta said, 'I'm delighted with your news, Gussie.' And, deliberately changing the subject, 'How is William Gorgas managing without his wife, Caleb?'

'As well as can be expected.' Caleb's voice was cool. He'd felt no loss at Mary's death. He found it hard to think of her without anger. How cruel the woman had been to Diane! And the lie . . . the lie . . . He felt no guilt either.

'What news is there of the new ship?' Augusta asked Kevin. 'Has she been named?' She already knew that there would be a business office with someone to take stenography and to typewrite for those who needed such services. And, much to her delight, a newsstand was planned too. Caleb had brought her that information before he left his job.

Kevin said, 'The *Commonwealth.*'

'The *Commonwealth.*' Augusta repeated the name as if tasting it. 'Yes, I like it.'

Later, the two men embarked on the *Priscilla.* Kevin went to the purser's office, and settled himself behind the carved window capped by its elaborate fanlight.

Caleb spent most of the stormy trip to Newport in the pilothouse, reminiscing with crew members he had known for years.

When they were alone, Augusta and Gussie sat in the kitchen over tea.

Gussie asked softly, 'Are you sure it's all right for me to come home? Will it be too much for you?'

Augusta waved the questions aside. 'Are you sure you want to give up nursing? You *did* seem so certain.'

Gussie's face paled. Now was when she had to explain, to put it into words. Her throat grew tight and dry. Her breath failed her. She looked into Augusta's face, lips working and eyes brimming.

'Gussie! What is it?'

'I don't know how to say . . .'

'Just tell me what troubles you.'

'I don't want . . . I wish I could . . . If only there were some way.' Gussie put her hands over her face. 'Grandma, I just can't stand it. I want to. But I can't.'

'Nursing's a hard job, I imagine. On your feet hour after hour. Bedpans, trays, sheets – no, no, it can't be easy.'

'It isn't the work, grandma.' Gussie went on in a pained whisper. 'It's the... the death.' Her voice failed her. She sat staring at Augusta.

Poor child, the older woman thought. She remembers. And seeing Gussie's working lips and straining throat: No, it can't be. She rose, took the girl into her arms. 'Come home.'

'You're disappointed.'

'I'm glad you'll be with me.'

A fervent Gussie answered, 'And so am I.'

But as the days passed after her return and her relief grew, her enthusiasm faded. She was accustomed to hard work and long hours and being needed. Although she tried to make herself useful, there was little for her to do. Marge Gowan resented any incursion into the kitchen. Augusta looked after herself and had her own activities. Gussie spent some time with the study group, interestedly listening to its discussions. But the ladies were much older than she was. Very soon she gave that up.

She brooded. She had tried nursing and failed. Failed because of an old terror that had come back to haunt her. The chill of her mother's body soaking into her; the heart that had stopped as she lay curled to the soft flesh. At the hospital she had been assaulted hourly by the memory of it. When she had come upon a patient choking and sinking and reaching blindly toward the light, she had fled screaming into the corridor. Screaming for help, when she ought to have offered it. That was why she couldn't go back. And why she brooded, and why, when she was alone, she wept.

Then, one afternoon, she walked with Kevin to the docks. It struck her that everyone there had a purpose. There were women hurrying into the offices. The longshoremen were hauling cargo. White-gloved porters hurried about. The *Priscilla* was being polished by deckhands. In the distance tugs hooted, and bells rang.

Her shoulders sagged. A scowl darkened her face.

'What now?' Kevin asked.

'I don't like being useless. Nor being a burden on Grandma, either.'

'Then stop it.' He didn't smile to soften the words. 'I've been wondering just how long you intend to go on with this.'

'I don't know,' she said miserably.

'Then it's time you started finding out. You *are* a burden on Grandma. And just when she doesn't need it.'

'I know.'

'Then stop playing the baby.'

He was right, she knew. She couldn't argue with him. When he left her, she stood alone on the wharves. As the sky darkened, a wind came up. A newspaper blew around a corner and caught against her feet. She kicked it away, then saw a flash of words. 'Help Wanted.' She picked it up, and moved under a light, straining to read. Perhaps...

Woman, for counter work, rm brd 25 mo. Telegraph Boardwalk Inn New Bedford.

Ladies to learn to be typewriters. The new Remington will be the most desired. Apply to...

Now she laughed for the first time in months. 'That's what I'm going to do,' she cried aloud.

It was only as she hurried up the hill toward High Street that she realized the wind had brought with it spinning snowflakes as well as the newspaper that had shown her the way.

Caleb's inclination was to rush to Diane with the news that he had found her child. But he knew he couldn't. First he had to be absolutely certain that there was no mistake.

Two weeks later he stood before the dingy three-storey tenement again. He drew a deep breath as he knocked at the door. How happy Diane would be if he were right. If Fania Devanta was her daughter...

Simeon Devanta was a small man with a thin black mustache and the big scarred hands of a fisherman. He listened impassively while Caleb introduced himself, and explained why he had come. His wife was plump, her hair graying. Her brown eyes filled with tears as Caleb spoke.

'What do you want of us?' Simeon demanded.

'My wife would like to have her daughter back,' Caleb said gently. 'To know her, love her.'

Mrs. Devanta made a small sobbing sound, but her husband said, 'It's up to Fania. Let her hear what you say, and decide for herself.' He got up and went to the door, and shouted, 'Fania, come here!'

In moments the girl came into the room, trailed by her older sister Blanche.

Before Caleb could speak, Simeon Devanta said, 'This man is Caleb Wakefield. He's married to your real mother.'

Caleb broke in to say, 'Please, don't be frightened. I know this is a shock to you...'

She closed her mind to his persuasive voice. She didn't want to listen to him. She didn't want to hear any more.

She had known for a long time that she had been taken in by the Devantas as an infant. Her sister Blanche had burst out with that in a fit of anger years before. Fania had asked her mother, who said calmly that it was true but made no difference. Fania had been young enough then to accept the answer. Later her mother had told her that a neighbor had had her first and been unable to care for her, so the Devantas had taken her. They knew nothing of how the woman had come by her. Fania soon stopped wondering about it.

Now this man was here, in what had always been her home, talking of a woman named Diane, a place in Newport. Fania swallowed a lump in her throat. She was too frightened to speak.

He said, 'Your mother wants desperately to see you, to have you back...'

Fania trembled. The woman who claimed to be her mother was a stranger to her. A stranger, who wanted to change Fania's life forever.

Caleb said, 'If you came to Cliff Mansion for a few days, just to see her – to become acquainted...'

Her sister Blanche said tartly, 'Of course she'll go. Why not? It's her real mother after all.'

The Devantas said only that it was up to her to decide. Fania thought it would be different if her sister Dottie had been there. But she was in New York. Dottie'd have said, 'No, Fania, don't do it. We're your family.' Fania didn't know what to do. She looked at the Devantas, at Blanche. She looked into Caleb's gray eyes.

At last she said ungraciously, 'All right. I'll go. But only for a few days.' And in a shaking voice, 'It will only be for a few days, won't it? You won't make me stay there, will you?'

'I promise,' he told her.

Chapter 35

On July 1, 1907, the *Commonwealth*, then the world's largest sidewheeler, sailed from Fall River on her first scheduled trip. She had been designed for the New Haven Railroad to be used by the Fall River Line at the Newport repair shops by J. Howland Gardner, under a general contractor, Quintard Ironworks of New York. The hull was built in Philadelphia by William Cramp & Sons Ship and Engineering Company. The interior was done by Poitier & Stymus in New York, and contained seven distinct architectural styles in separate but interconnecting rooms.

On the upper deck, fifty feet above the water, there was the dining saloon and grill room. Dozens of windows made the outer walls appear to be of glass. The ceilings were formed by three domes, lit by hidden lamps. The papier-mâché finishing was in shades of gray. The draperies and fabrics were red, and the carpets a blend of mulberry and red. At the forward and aft ends of the room there were mirrored walls, which seemed to make it longer.

Off the dining saloon was a men's café finished in chestnut woods, with walls paneled in nail-studded leather, and English Renaissance furniture.

The grand saloon was two decks in height, with columns topped with carved corbels. The ceiling was of groined vaultings, each decorated with medallions depicting sea emblems. The gallery deck formed a balcony, and there was also a mezzanine musicians' gallery from which the orchestra played its concerts.

On the main deck there was a garden café. The forward gallery deck had a writing room, a library, and the newsstand. There was also the business office, with a large desk, a Remington typing machine, and a vase in which there stood a single red rose. Outside the door was a notice informing passengers that wireless telegrams could be sent from Stateroom 212.

When the *Commonwealth* arrived earlier in the day, the whole of Fall River had turned out to welcome her. Crowds gathered on the wharves and filled the waterfront, excitedly discussing her construction and decor. Her whistles shrilled and were answered by the wail of the mill whistles. From the cannon on the Stapes Coal Company Wharf a welcoming volley was fired. A great cheer went up as the *Commonwealth* was docked.

That evening at sailing the festive welcome was repeated in a joyful and noisy farewell.

Gussie Callahan sat nervously in the business office on the forward gallery deck. Some people had looked askance at the use of space for a typing machine and stenographer. She would feel reassured only if there was money in the desk drawer to prove the service desirable.

She had worked hard at mastering the Remington and learning the stenography. She was slow at the first and hesitant at the second. But she was accurate at both, so she ought to do. At least that's what Augusta said. Hoping for a dignified look, Gussie had turned her curls into smooth rolls that framed her face. Her skirt was black and straight, her shirtwaist white and severe.

When the door opened, she looked up with a quick smile.

Jeanette Graystone-Fields asked, 'Are you the typewriting lady?'

'I am,' Gussie said. 'And what can I do for you?'

'Not for me, for my husband,' Jeanette answered. She wore a brown traveling suit. The collar and cuffs were flounced, the skirt was drawn five inches above her ankles and pinned with a rosette, exposing a silk-clad calf. A choker of pearls completed the outfit.

Gussie waited, hoping.

Jeanette's eyes moved slowly around the office, then swung back to study the younger girl from head to toe. 'You take dictation?'

'I do.'

'You typewrite what you wrote down? On that thing?' She pointed to the Remington.

'Yes,' Gussie said, and wondered if the small, henna-haired woman was addled.

Jeanette smiled at her. 'Then I'll be back.'

Hurrying out, she congratulated herself. It had been pure chance that led her to investigate the notice she'd seen in the Fall River *Journal*, and chance again that the girl stenographer was young and pretty. Surely Bennet would be enchanted with her.

She found him sitting disconsolately in the garden café. He was alone, having disposed of the four girls he'd been enamored of only a year before. Through Jeanette, of course. She had returned one to school; another had become engaged. Two had been so openly mercenary that he'd paid them off and their aunt as well. But now he was lonely. He peered up at Jeanette, his gentle brown eyes dull in the plumpness of his face. 'Where have you been?'

'I have a surprise for you, Bennet,' she said in a lisping whisper. 'A beautiful surprise.'

His look brightened at once. 'You do?'

'You'll be delighted, I know. But you'll have to think of some work that needs doing.'

'Work?' He was alarmed. He didn't work. He paid his lawyers to do that. He paid his servants to do that. He didn't work. He didn't even like the sound of the word.

'You don't want to hear about it?' she asked.

'I do.'

'There's a girl,' Jeanette said lightly. 'Very pretty indeed. A stenographer. But not like your – oh, you know, not like those you called your typists. I mean, she has a Remington machine and knows how to use it.'

'You don't make sense,' he said sulkily.

'You must devise a letter you want written,' Jeanette said. 'That way you can spend a little time with Miss Gussie Callahan.'

'Ah,' he said. And then, 'But what letter?'

'To your lawyer maybe?'

'I've nothing to say to him at the moment.'

'Think, Bennet.' Her voice had risen slightly. She made an effort, and went on more softly, 'Surely there's some small thing.' She sat in silence, but only for a moment. Then, 'I could do one for you. Just a few words, say. And when you had the sense of it, you could go and seek her, and have her typewrite it as you want it.'

'Yes,' he agreed hastily. He called a steward to order champagne. When they had been served, he raised his glass to her. 'Thank you, Jeanette.'

'I only want you to be happy,' she told him, smiling.

A little later he went to the business office. It was as Jeanette had said it would be. He was so charmed by small, dark-haired, black-eyed Gussie that he nearly forgot the letter he wanted her to do for him. He hemmed and hawed and stared at her, and finally was able to tell her what to put down. It took only a few minutes. He spent a few minutes more reading it over three times, then thanked her, and paid her the fee she told him. Still, even though she turned back to her desk, he lingered, and looked at her ankles, and waited for her to make herself available to him. He lingered so long that she suddenly said, 'Mr. Graystone-Fields, is there anything more I can do for you in this office?'

He looked around. It was a pleasant enough room, but not that comfortable. There was not even a settle to lie down on. 'No, not here,' he said, wishing Jeanette had made matters simpler for him.

'In that case,' Gussie said, 'I do hope you'll forgive me. But I have work to do.'

'Oh, certainly. I understand.' Red of face, sweating, he pushed himself up from his chair and limped toward the door as fast as he could go. His embarrassment made him incautious. He tripped over nothing. His left leg gave way. He crashed to the floor with a terrible noise, and lay there with tears starting from his eyes.

Gussie cried out and ran to help him up. It was no use. He couldn't move himself, and though she tried, she couldn't move him. She raced to the newsstand for help. It took three men to raise Bennet to his feet. He thanked them, brushed himself off as well as he could, and went in search of Jeanette. Damn her! It was all her fault.

He found her in the garden café. She sat alone, an empty wineglass before her. When he flopped heavily into a chair, she asked brightly, 'And did you get your business done?'

'You know I didn't. Why didn't you arrange it properly?'

'I tried,' Jeanette said. 'Gussie Callahan was unwilling.' And smiling archly, 'I couldn't kidnap her for you, you know. But I did think that she'd change her mind when she saw you. Still, since she didn't, don't feel bad. It happens that way sometimes.'

Later, lying beside him, she pushed her head into his shoulder and said, 'You've got me, Bennet,' and repeated, 'So don't feel bad.'

On the dome deck, Caleb looked at Fania Devanta's pale face, and said gently, 'Don't be frightened. There's no need.'

'I wish I hadn't come,' she said. 'All I want to do is go home.'

'And you will. Unless you change your mind. Once you've met your mother . . .'

'I don't know her.' Fania's mouth felt dry. There was a churning in her stomach. She tried to think ahead, to imagine the woman she would meet. It was impossible. There was no way to picture her.

'You'll get to know her, Fania. She's a beautiful woman, and loves you dearly.'

'Loves me?' Fania cried. 'How can you say that? She doesn't know me, and never has. My mother is home in Fall River. The Devantas raised me. I want to be with them. We belong together because we're a family. Oh, why did you come?'

'Your mother wanted you. She looked for you for a long time but couldn't find you.'

'Did she really try?' the girl demanded.

'Yes. But there was no way. I discovered your whereabouts only by lucky accident.'

'And I wish you hadn't.'

Caleb leaned forward. 'Before you say that, learn more about your real family. And about me. You promised the Devantas that you would.'

'I'll try,' she said in a small voice.

He reminded himself that she was only twelve. And that, at whatever age, it was natural to be shaken by what had happened. He knew. He had himself been older, yet he'd thought the foundations of his world washed away. Only time, and love, would help her. That was why, since he had spoken to her for the first time in early May, he had only visited with her a few times, and suggested only gently that she come to see Diane, until now, finally, she had agreed.

'Tell me what she's like,' Fania said after a long moment.

'Soon you'll see for yourself.'

She picked at the lobster he had ordered for her, then pushed it away. 'And after a few days you'll take me home?'

'I've told you so,' he said quietly. 'I've promised.'

He was remembering that promise as he led her off the ship at Long Wharf. There, under the lights, Diane stood waiting near the Packard she had just learned to drive. Her face was pale. A large plumed hat dipped over her brow. Her gown was light blue, her cloak a darker blue.

Caleb led Fania forward, introduced her.

For a long moment, Diane stood immobile, and then, with a cry, she swept the girl into her arms and held her tightly, held her as if she were an infant and the twelve years past could be wiped away in a second.

Fania was rigid, resistant. She tried to free herself, sorry that she had come. The hugs, the kisses, the hot and demanding warmth repelled her. But Diane held her fast until Caleb interposed himself, saying lightly, 'Now, then, this is a happy reunion.'

Finally Diane brushed away her tears. 'Oh, my love, I'm so happy to see you.' At Fania's silence, Diane went on, 'We've so much catching up to do. And you must see how I've decorated your room, and what I've bought for you. You must learn your new home. Oh, we'll be so happy together.'

Fania said quickly, 'But didn't he tell you? I'm here just for two days.'

Diane didn't answer. With a veil thrown over her hat and a duster over her cloak, she settled behind the wheel of the Packard, saying, 'And you'll learn to drive. But of course you'll have your own carriage too. And we must think of a school.'

'I've only come for a visit, Mrs. Wakefield,' Fania said firmly, flashing a quick black glance at Caleb.

'Mrs. Wakefield!' Diane's voice was sharp. 'My dear child, I'm your *mother*!' and ignored Caleb's light warning touch on her hand.

As she spun the automobile around a cart, loudly blowing

the horn, he frowned. She was frightening Fania. The girl was shivering, although the air was warm.

Diane continued, 'Yes, I'm your mother. And you must call me that. Tell me that you feel for me what I feel for you. Call me Mother!'

Fania stared ahead, her lips pressed together, swearing to herself that after the two-day visit she would never never come back.

Later the same evening, after Fania had gone to bed and Diane and Caleb were alone in their apartment, she said softly, 'I didn't believe it would happen. And that you could do this for me, Caleb. I'm so grateful.'

'There was luck involved, you know.'

'But you did it.' She pressed close to him. 'We're a family at last. It's what I've always dreamed of.'

'You must go slowly with Fania. You don't realize what persuasion it took to bring her here this first time.'

'Go slowly? How can I? She's mine, and finally I have her.'

'I promised to take her home after a two-day visit. I shall keep that promise.'

'Oh yes, of course.' The words were quick, impatient. 'Certainly you'll take her home. This time. But she'll come back. And when she does, she'll want to stay. *Want* to. Of course she will.'

'We can't be sure.'

'She has to. She's my daughter, Caleb. Don't you understand that?'

'I know how you feel. But you must try to understand how Fania feels as well.'

'She's only a child. What does she know? How can she realize the life I can give her?'

'She doesn't care about that. Perhaps you can lead her gently, but you can't force her.' Although he didn't mention it, he was thinking now of Mary Gorgas.

Diane was saying, 'Force her? Why would I? And why would I need to? She'll see for herself, believe me. Tomorrow I'll take her shopping. We'll start a wardrobe for her. Did you see that shirtwaist she was wearing? And that skirt? How she can walk in those awful boots...'

385

'Her family has little.'

'Her family?' Diane dismissed the Devantas with a wave of her hand. '*I* am her family.'

It was the beginning of a fantasy that Diane quickly believed. She had always had Fania. She had raised the child from infancy and knew her baby smiles and laughter, and remembered her first step, and recalled the sound of her first word. She felt as if it were true and couldn't accept Fania's cool reticence.

When they shopped, Fania accepted what was bought for her with little interest. She said nothing, not even thank you, when they started back to Cliff Mansion, the Packard loaded with bags and boxes.

She hardly listened and didn't speak when Diane excitedly detailed for Caleb and William their purchases. 'Three gowns, each perfect for Fania, two shawls, and four pairs of slippers. And a silver brush and haircomb, just to start with,' she crowed.

'Good,' William said. 'You must show the loot to us, Fania.'

She gave her grandfather a dark sideways look, and shrugged.

He chuckled, his head nodding up and down. 'You see? I know that look. It's old Willie all over again.' He explained to Fania, 'That's your great grandfather, old Willie Gorgas.'

'Oh, never mind, Papa,' Diane said.

Fania turned to Caleb, 'What time will we leave?'

'The *Priscilla* will depart for Fall River at about four-thirty in the morning. I'll make sure you're awake in plenty of time.'

'You see?' Diane shuddered. 'That's a ghastly hour. Stay another day.'

'I can't,' Fania said.

'But I want to take you to a school I have in mind'

'I have my own school in Fall River.'

'When you live here, Fania...'

'Perhaps I won't,' Fania retorted.

'But of course you will.' Diane smiled. 'You'll decide that you want to. We mustn't be separated again. So do stay another day.'

Fania's mouth set in a way that Caleb was coming to recognize, and though Diane pleaded and persuaded, the girl refused to change her mind. She was going home that evening, as Caleb had promised her.

William Gorgas knew her expression too. 'You see?' he said. 'Just like old Willie.' He smiled at Fania. 'One day I'll show you where your great grandfather is buried in Fall River. And I'll tell you all about him.'

'Papa,' Diane said coldly. 'Fania's not interested in your father.'

'How do you know?' He leaned toward Fania. 'You'd like to know about your old great grandfather, wouldn't you?'

She looked straight at Diane and said, 'Yes, yes, I would, Mr. Gorgas.'

Fania had told herself that she'd never go back to Newport, but she changed her mind in the month that passed before Caleb, determined to give her time, returned for her.

It had begun with her sister Blanche, who tried on the four pairs of new slippers and winced, saying sulkily, 'But none of them fit me, Fania.' And who used Fania's silver brush and comb, saying, 'I wish I had a set for myself.'

Several times Fania's father, as she still thought of him, asked thoughtfully, 'You mean she really didn't give you any money?' and when she had answered, 'No, no. Why should she?' had grumbled under his breath.

Only her mother had hugged and kissed her and said she was glad Fania was home. And only her sister Dottie, writing from New York, bothered to say: *Tell that woman you belong to us, and forget her, Fania. It's too late for her to decide she wants you back.*

Fania cherished those words while Blanche kept at her, asking, 'Couldn't you get something out of her for me?' And Mr. Devanta wondered aloud, 'She's really rich, isn't she?'

So when Caleb came in the last week of September, she went with him. They sailed from Fall River in dense fog. All the way to Newport, where Diane joined them on the *Commonwealth*, the ship's horns bellowed raucous warnings into the white-shrouded night.

It had been Caleb's idea that they take Fania to New York. They would dine at Delmonico's, see a matinee, ride through Central Park in a carriage. Diane had agreed with enthusiasm to the idea.

But Fania seemed indifferent when he told her about it,

shrugging, 'Whatever you want,' and retreating into silence again.

She roused only when Caleb took her to the business office to meet Gussie, who smiled at her and formally shook her hand before asking, 'Would you like to try your fingers on the typewriting machine?'

For half an hour, until a man came in with documents to be typed for him, she investigated the Remington with glee, poking at its keys, moving its carriage, and saying happily to Gussie, 'I must learn to do this properly one day. It would be useful, wouldn't it?'

And later, when she and Caleb had gone to the grand saloon to listen to the orchestra conducted by E. L. Ney, she said, 'Tell me again. What is Gussie to you?'

'My niece. The daughter of my younger sister. Her name was Amy.' To forestall further questions, he added, 'She died a long time ago.'

She was roused to enthusiasm only once more during the trip. That was when Augusta and Marge Gowan came and sat with her and Caleb. The older women were going to New York to meet with Betty Townsend. They had had several letters from her since they had spoken with her in Washington, and now, at her invitation, they would attend a small conference of the National American Woman's Suffrage Association.

Augusta said, smiling, 'Fania, I'm happy to meet you at last. Caleb has told me about you. I hope you'll come to see me in Fall River often.'

Her warmth was disarming. Fania said, 'Oh, thank you.'

'Do you know that when I was young I knew your great grandfather?' Augusta's dimples deepened. 'It was a long time ago, and on another ship, but I remember him well.' She went on to speak of how Willie Gorgas had been involved in helping her escort two runaway slaves to freedom, and then again how he had saved her from falling during the explosion on the *Empire State.*

Fania listened, fascinated.

Observing her look, Augusta thought how different it was from the time she had tried to tell the same tale to Diane. Caleb's wife had stared at her. 'Willie Gorgas? My father's father? I never met him.' It had been odd, Augusta thought then. Now

Diane's daughter listened and asked questions, plainly wondering about the great grandfather she could never know.

When the *Commonwealth* finally docked at Newport, and Diane came aboard, Fania retreated into silence again.

They went to the dining saloon for their evening meal. She hardly ate. Diane attempted conversation to no avail. Very soon Fania asked to be excused. She was tired, she said. She would like to go to sleep.

When Caleb and Diane were alone, she said, 'It won't do, you know. We'll never get anywhere like this. She must come and live with us. That's the only way.'

'I'm afraid that if you force her to, she'll never forgive you,' Caleb said. 'Just wait a little.'

'I've waited a very long time already,' Diane retorted.

'Try to be patient. It'll be all right.'

After the meal, they had a short visit with Augusta and Marge Gowan, and walked for a little while on deck before retiring to their stateroom.

The ship moved slowly, her foghorns sounding continuously as she rounded Point Judith.

Down on the quarterdeck, a passenger was completing his business. 'Two shares,' he said. 'Very good. And you won't be sorry. One day soon these will double in value.'

'I'm certain of it,' the purser said, smiling.

'Your receipt.' The passenger wrote his name in a small neat hand – Alexander Graham Bell. 'And now I must go to bed.'

'Rest well,' the purser told him. 'And thank you.'

'Thank me when your investments pay off,' the passenger said.

Up on the bridge the captain peered through the big glass windows into a curtain of white. The ship was approaching the Race, having passed Watch Hill. He tilted his head, listening. There went the *Commonwealth*'s deep bellow sounding every thirty seconds. He tensed. In the echoing silence between his ship's blasts he thought he'd heard a whistle. There, now. This time he was certain. 'It's too close,' he cried to the pilot. Then, 'Sound the bell!' The engine-room gong rang full steam astern. But in that instant the *Commonwealth* shuddered with a terrific blow.

The pilot shouted into the tube, 'All hands on deck! All

hands on deck!' And then, 'Life-saving crew report to your stations! We've hit another ship.'

As the crewmen rushed to their positions, they saw that a big vessel hung on the *Commonwealth*'s bow. They watched the fog swirl around it, and then, with a grinding and rending crash, it rode down the *Commonwealth*'s side and slipped away from sight.

Within six minutes the Norwegian tramp steamer *Voland*, bound for Windsor, Nova Scotia, sank in Long Island Sound.

The life-saving boat, along with three others, was lowered. Rope ladders were thrown over the side of the *Commonwealth*. The fifteen-member crew of the *Voland* were all saved.

The *Commonwealth* had suffered a tremendous tear in her bow. There was a delay of two hours. Then, escorted by other ships of the Fall River Line, she slowly completed her journey and arrived in New York at eleven o'clock.

As they left the ship Diane slipped her hand under Caleb's arm, and smiled. She was pretending that nothing had happened, Caleb knew.

But something had. They were both jolted awake when the *Commonwealth* rammed the *Voland*. He had leaped up, immediately reaching for his clothes.

'What's the matter?' Diane cried, clinging to him, and weeping. 'Are we sinking?'

'No, no. But I must see if I can help. And then I must go to Fania.'

'Don't leave me,' Diane pleaded. 'I'm frightened. I don't want to be alone.'

But he dressed quickly, and as he went out, he heard her cry, 'Damn you, Caleb! You care more for the ship and Fania than you do for me.'

The words rang in his ears as he heard the excited talk of the other passengers, awake now and milling about. He remembered them as he spoke to the first mate, and saw that all was under control, and hurried to Fania's stateroom.

The girl had been thrown from her bed and sat, dazed and shaking, in the midst of shattered porcelain. He helped her up, relieved that she was unhurt, still remembering Diane's petulant cry.

But now Diane was smiling. 'We're going to have a lovely

time.' And to Fania, 'Tell me, my love, what would you like to do first?'

'I don't care,' Fania answered.

Diane's smile faded a little. It brightened again when a friend of her mother's came up, saying, 'Why, Diane, I thought I saw you on board, but when I went to talk to you, you were gone. How are you, my dear?'

The woman was elderly, stout, wrapped in a sable-trimmed coat. Diane introduced Caleb to her, and then turned to Fania, 'And this is my daughter.'

'And what's your name, dear?' the woman asked.

'Fania,' the girl answered. And with a baleful look at Diane, 'Fania Devanta.'

Red stained Diane's cheeks. Her eyes glinted.

'Devanta?' the woman asked. 'And what kind of name is that?'

Diane bade her goodbye and turned away. When they were in a hansom she said, 'Devanta is not your name.'

'I always thought it was,' Fania answered. 'And I still think so.'

The *Commonwealth* spent six weeks in dry dock undergoing repairs and then went into winter storage in Newport.

In November Republican William Howard Taft was elected to the presidency, defeating Democrat William Jennings Bryan.

By early January 1909 the *Plymouth*'s staterooms were all engaged by New Englanders planning to see the inauguration in Washington on March 4. Thus the *Commonwealth* was withdrawn from her winter berth, and on February 28 she made a special voyage to New York with every passage sold out. That same night the *Plymouth* also sailed from Fall River, transporting units of the Massachusetts Sixth Infantry Division and troops of cavalry on their way to join the inaugural parade.

Chapter 36

On March 25, 1911, the Triangle Shirtwaist Company in New York City burst into flame. Within the multistoried building, where the exit doors were locked to prevent stealing, smoke rose in thick choking curtains. Some 145 workers, most of them women, were trapped inside and died. Among them was a young girl named Dorothy Devanta.

Fania was on one of her visits to Cliff Mansion when she heard of her sister's death.

Pale, her eyes shining with tears, she told Diane, 'I have to go home right away.'

'I understand that you want to see the Devantas. You're kind to care for their loss. But *this* is your home.' Diane's voice was calm, although her hands trembled on her knees. 'All this time, since Caleb brought you to me, I've been patient, waiting.'

Caleb paused on the threshold. He'd heard these last words. It was wrong of Diane to choose this moment to speak what she was thinking. Fania had room now for only one idea – she must go home to her parents. He could understand that. He said quickly, 'I'll go with you, Fania. There'll be a train in two hours. Get ready.'

The girl gave him a grateful look. As she left the room, she said to Diane, 'It's my loss too. Dottie's my sister.'

Diane didn't answer, but when she and Caleb were alone, she said, 'I don't want her to go.'

'Be reasonable. You must know what she feels.'

Color burned on Diane's cheekbones. She said in a shaking voice, 'You're on her side. Always, always. No matter what I say or do, I know that you are on *her* side. If it weren't for you, she'd be happy to be living with us. But no, no, you kept saying don't press her. So she does me the favor of visiting once a month.'

'And would you rather you didn't see her at all?'

Diane didn't heed his quiet words. She cried, 'You're sorry you found her, aren't you?'

'No,' he said. But in a way, he was. Without wanting to, or even knowing it, Fania had come between Diane and himself. She had come between them by changing Diane. He saw her differently now. She was no longer the lost, vulnerable woman he had once known. Now she was petulant and demanding by turns, quick to take offense where none was intended, and caring only for her own feelings. He wanted back the woman with whom he had fallen in love, but didn't know how to find her. His thoughts frightened him.

She said, 'You're jealous of her, aren't you? That's why you don't persuade her to move here.'

'No,' he said quietly.

'Then I don't know why you oppose me. And have from the first moment you brought the girl to me.' With that, she left him.

He stood near the window, looking down at Cliff Walk, but thinking. The girl – too often Diane called Fania that. She had wanted to change Fania's name. Wanted the child to accede to being called Dolores, and use Gorgas for a last name. Fania had resolutely refused. She would be Fania Devanta as she had always been. Diane insisted that Fania move to Cliff Mansion; Fania said she would visit once a month and no more. Diane would have gone so far as to use legal means to enforce her desire, but Caleb had been able to discourage her from that. When Caleb went to Fania to escort her back to Newport, she always asked for his promise that he would return her after the two-day visit was over.

He had wanted to make Diane happy. He had hoped to give her what she most desired. But in doing so he had brought dissension into their lives. For these last three years Diane had lived for nothing but to convince Fania that she must live at Cliff Mansion, must change her name, must behave and speak and even think as if she had spent her life there.

Caleb found it impossible to explain to Diane that the more she pressed, the more the child would resist. He understood Fania's questions, the sense of pain and loss she suffered. He understood her refusal to give way. But he found it increasingly difficult to talk with Diane on the subject. And the subject appeared to be the only one in which Diane had an interest. She was obsessed by Fania. Even when the girl was not with them, Fania was all that Diane thought of, spoke of.

The woman on whom he had placed all his hopes and love seemed gone from him, and another had taken her place.

It was a bitter cold, windy afternoon. When they arrived at her Fall River home, Caleb said, 'I'll come in with you, Fania.'

'You don't need to.'

'There may be something I can do.'

She tapped lightly, then opened the door. The room was long and narrow. Its only light came from a high window at the far end. Mrs. Devanta half-lay, half-sat in a straight-backed chair. Mr. Devanta leaned on the table. Blanche crouched on the settle, her head in her hands.

'Mama,' Fania said, breaking into tears, 'Papa, I came as soon as I heard.'

This time Mr. Devanta didn't wonder aloud about Diane's money. This time Blanche didn't ask Fania to bring her back some pretties. This time Mrs. Devanta didn't look regretful.

There was an instant of silence. Within it Fania heard the blood drumming in her ears. She felt her heart beat in her chest. The people she had always called parents looked at her. Fania knew what they were thinking. Fleeting, flickering, words risen on some primitive tide... Why had it been Dottie? Why couldn't it have been Fania instead? Though it was for only an instant, Fania sensed what was there. She froze in mid-step.

Then Mrs. Devanta opened her arms. Fania went to her. She knelt at the older woman's feet, and put her head on her lap.

But the brief moment in which she had stood frozen was one from which she never recovered.

After an hour she rose to go, saying, 'I must go back to Cliff Mansion now.'

That evening Caleb and Fania boarded the *Plymouth*. They stood at the railing together. As the ship gave her departing signal and left the docks, Fania said, 'You know, don't you, that I'm not going back.'

He told her not to be hasty in her judgments.

She gave him a bitter smile. It reminded him that she was

now no longer a child. It was three years since he had first seen her. And those three years had changed her. She was fifteen, on the brink of young womanhood. There was, he saw pityingly, a new knowledge in her dark eyes.

'My great grandfather's buried here in Fall River,' she said, her voice soft. 'That's what Grandfather William said. I must go one day to see the grave.'

As they were going in to dinner, she said, 'I won't use the name Devanta any more. May I call myself Wakefield?'

He felt a quick rush of joy. 'Of course. If it's what you want.'

But even as he spoke, he wondered what Diane would say.

The purser knew the woman the instant he saw her. He was about to greet her by name when she said, 'I'm Caroline Nibbs. Do you have my stateroom key?'

He smiled, handed over the key. Yes, she was in the ledger as Caroline Nibbs. But there was no doubt that it was Carrie Nation. She was nearly six feet tall, with a high bulging forehead and gray hair pulled back in a knot. Her face was square, full at the jaws. She wore a black hat from which there dropped black veils, and a full black gown. Everybody knew about Carrie Nation. She had been advocating temperance, by which she meant prohibition, for the last ten years. He wondered if she were carrying the ax and Bible that had made her famous – the ax to chop open barrels of spirits; the Bible to convince the argumentative. The purser had no intention of arguing with her.

He wanted to say, 'Have a pleasant journey, Mrs. Nibbs.' It came out, 'Have a pleasant journey, Mrs. Nation.'

'I'm traveling incognito,' she hissed. 'Don't tell.'

'Of course not,' he agreed hastily.

But what she might do worried him. There were spirits aplenty on the *Plymouth*, and not many prohibitionists. As soon as she was gone, he sent word to the captain.

An hour later she appeared in the men's club room and said in a loud angry voice, 'You'll ruin your livers and your lives with what you drink. You'll call down the wrath of Almighty God!'

The college boys grouped at a table nearby began to laugh.

'Laugh now,' she said, 'for later you shall weep.'

'Go away,' one of the boys said. 'We don't need your advice.'

'Then whom will you listen to?' she demanded.

'Be still,' they yelled, and murmured to each other, 'What does she know?' and turned away from her to attend to the mugs before them.

The captain, watching from the threshold, asked himself what he should do. He was fearful of neither man nor beast nor sea. But he suspected he didn't know how to handle the redoubtable Carrie Nation. Then, with relief, he saw that she held nothing in her hands but her reticule. The most damage she could do would be with her tongue. He decided to leave her to it, and returned to the wheelhouse, while she continued her harangue of an audience that had stopped listening.

Jeanette Graystone-Fields was in her stateroom. She took off her hat, smoothing a long perfect curl over her right ear, and then her left. When she replaced the hat, she smiled at herself in the mirror. Not bad for a lady well past forty. Her face was still thin and small. Her eyes were big and bright, though not so bright as the jewels she wore on her wrists. She smoothed the silk ruffle at her throat, ignoring the lines she saw there.

It was a joy for her to travel alone for a change. She had left Bennet in Boston, entertaining a small young friend, as she had arranged it, and glad to see her go. He'd be glad to see her return, of course. For by then he'd want a new diversion. Which was all right with Jeanette. Except that she too needed a diversion.

She brightened her lips, powdered her face, and went to the grand saloon.

In a little while she had met a dark-haired young man named Derek Davids. They had a drink together, and walked on deck, and then they went to her stateroom. She ordered up a bottle of champagne – and still drunk in the early morning murmured a sleepy farewell to Derek when he left her.

When she awakened later, she found that her jewelry was gone. If she'd been completely sober she'd have written off the loss, knowing that she could cajole replacements from Bennet. But she was still befogged by champagne. She screamed into the corridor. A cabin attendant came running. Sobbing, she told him that she'd been robbed. She mentioned Derek by name. Before the *Plymouth* docked, she had her jewels again.

The following month she was once more on the *Plymouth*, but this time Bennet was with her.

The cabin attendant said to him, 'I'm glad your missus is all right, and that she got her jewelry back.'

Bennet asked what he was talking about.

The man realized he'd told Bennet what he hadn't known, and trying to recover, said he'd made a mistake. But Bennet kept up his questions and soon had the whole story as the man knew it. Bennet said nothing to Jeanette until they were on their return voyage to Boston, this time on the *Priscilla*.

But he had spent the past few days thinking. Thinking was an effort. What was effort did not suit him, and what did not suit him he dismissed quickly.

Thus he said to Jeanette, as they sat sipping champagne, 'I shall support you, of course, as I have for so long, but I believe it best that we parted.'

She stared at him, her hazel eyes blank. 'What are you talking about?'

'I enjoy you, I always have. From the beginning when my mother hired you. We've been a good twosome, I think.'

She winced at the mention of Mabel Graystone-Fields. Jeanette did not much bother with the past.

'I've never criticized you,' he went on. 'I shouldn't like to now.'

'What do you mean?' she demanded. By then she had forgotten Derek Davids and the incident on the *Plymouth*.

'I never thought you couldn't be trusted to travel alone,' he told her quietly.

Now she understood. She'd done it one time too many – and this time she'd been caught. By whom didn't matter. She was attached to her daily champagne, to her jewels, her furs, and her way of life. She didn't propose to forfeit all because she had lost her head over a few baubles.

She said bluntly, 'It won't happen again.'

He sighed, tented his pudgy hands. His soft brown eyes looked past her, as if planning an escape route. 'I know you believe it. But please, let's not argue.'

She shrieked, 'Damn you! I've always done what you wanted, haven't I? What if I did get drunk once and act foolish. I'm human too.'

He couldn't tolerate the shrill voice. He heaved himself to his feet. 'All right, all right. We won't talk of it.'

That same evening Jeanette found Carrie Hartwell for him. Carrie was seventeen, on the way to New York to try for a stage career. She had startling red hair and deep amber eyes. Her cheeks were round and dimpled, her mouth a natural cupid's bow. Jeanette introduced her to Bennet. Before the ship docked, he had convinced her to return with them to Boston and come to live with them. Bennet saw to it that Carrie had dancing and singing and elocution lessons, and sat through them, watching, cheeks pink, chins bobbing, breath wheezing in his throat. Soon she called him Uncle, and traveled with him and Jeanette wherever they went.

Six months later, sailing on the *Commonwealth*, Jeanette fell into conversation with a man named David Griffith. In a soft Kentucky accent he told her that he was a director for a company called American Biograph, which produced motion pictures. She thought of Carrie, and soon introduced Griffith to Bennet. Bennet was charmed by the man, more charmed when he saw talent in Carrie, and wanted to see what she could do before a camera. When the journey ended, Bennet was an investor in American Biograph. He and Jeanette inspected the company's brownstone at 11 East Fourteenth Street, settled Carrie in a good womens' hotel, and bade her goodbye.

They never saw her again, and Bennet soon forgot about his investment in the moving picture company. By then, he had also forgotten that he'd once wanted a separation from Jeanette. She, however, had not.

It didn't reassure her that she had stocks and bonds in safety deposit boxes in Boston and New York. She had savings accounts in both cities, too. There were four coats of fur in her closet, and dozens of gowns. Her jewelry was adequate to supply a small shop. She still wanted the security of Bennet's fortune. But there was the pre-nuptial agreement in which she had renounced any right she might have had to his estate, except for what he willed to her.

The will interested her, but she knew nothing about it and had never seen it, so she didn't know what it said about her or anyone else.

After long and careful consideration, she decided on a plan of action.

She waited until she and Bennet were on the *Commonwealth* again. It was in the spring of 1912. Bennet was in a good mood. The ship's surroundings always soothed him. He found the kitchen exceptionally fine and the service caring. He had eaten an enormous meal and finished almost a full bottle of wine himself. He sat silent but smiling as the moon rose beyond the great windows of the domed dining room.

Jeanette said, in a quiet little girl voice, 'I've been thinking lately that I ought to make a will.'

'You? A will? What for?'

'You know what for. To dispose of the property I own.'

Bennet shrugged. 'Why worry about that?'

'I want you to have it,' she said. 'That's why.'

'I believe I'll have another portion of the cream pie,' he told her.

'And I want you to help me write it out,' she went on.

'Me help you?'

'Who else?'

'I don't know how to do it. Go to a lawyer.'

She asked sweetly, 'The way you did?'

He paused, looked at her. Then, with a nod, he said, 'Yes. The way I did.' But he had made no will, nor did he intend to. He was unconcerned with what happened to the Graystone-Fields fortune after his death, though he understood her interest and what her words actually meant.

'So, if you've done it, then you know what I should say,' she finished triumphantly.

It was too much trouble to argue. He agreed he would help her.

As soon as he had finished his cream pie she led him, grumbling, to the writing room on the gallery deck. It was a comfortable place done in tones of French gray with ornately carved chairs and a polished writing table on which lay a neat stack of stationery embossed with an outline of the *Commonwealth* and the New England Steamship Company's seal.

She put paper before him. 'Tell me what to say.'

'Do it yourself. It must be in your own hand.'

'Oh no. I'll take it to the typewriting lady. You remember her, don't you? Gussie Callahan?'

'I remember her,' Bennet said. It was something Jeanette had not handled well. He had been embarrassed. Now Jeanette wanted him to face her again. He wouldn't and he told her so.

'Oh dear,' she laughed. 'You've misunderstood. You don't have to go; I will. I'll do it but you'll have to help me so I don't become confused.'

'I, the undersigned,' he dictated, thinking of his mother's will, 'being of sound mind, do hereby declare –' He looked at Jeanette, 'What do you want to declare?'

'I'll leave everything to you. I've told you that.'

Instead of thanking her, he asked, 'Don't you have relations?'

'No.'

'All right. Then put it down. You want to leave everything to Bennet Graystone-Fields.'

But her hand didn't move. Her eyes searched his face. Had he done the same for her or had he not? She still wasn't sure. In any case, she would go ahead. If she didn't need the document, she could destroy it.

She wrote quickly. But when she read back to him what she had written, he said, 'No, no. That's not the right wording. Do it again.'

She took fresh paper. It was nearly an hour before she had completed the brief statement to his liking. There were many scratchings out, corrections inserted. But when it was done, she was satisfied.

She walked Bennet to the grand saloon and saw him comfortably settled with a lit cigar in his mouth, a glass of champagne at his elbow. Then she hurried to the business office.

Gussie sat at the desk. Her back was straight. Her head was bent over a notebook and her hand seemed to glide across the page leaving a coded scrawl behind. Across from her, watching intently as he dictated, sat a young man.

Jeanette looked at him and then at Gussie and smiled to herself. She knew what was happening between them even if they didn't.

'Miss Callahan,' she asked, 'will you be busy long?'

Gussie frowned at the interruption, answered, 'Perhaps half an hour.'

Jeanette withdrew. When she returned, the young man was gone.

Gussie typed the document, and Jeanette returned to Bennet in the grand saloon. Soon after, they retired to their stateroom. They didn't speak of the will, now folded neatly into Jeanette's handbag. Jeanette thought that Bennet had forgotten about it, and pretended that she had too. Now that she had it, as she had altered just a few words, she felt safe. She could write Bennet's name as well as he could. If she had to, she would do it.

But Bennet was not Mabel Graystone-Fields's son for nothing. When Jeanette was asleep, he rose. He took out the will, and examined it. As it had occurred to him there might be, he found a change. The will purported now to be the last testament of one Bennet Graystone-Fields. It was, as yet, unsigned, but he supposed she had some plan to deal with that. He smiled faintly, and tore the paper to shreds which he burned in an ashtray. Then, still smiling, he lay down beside Jeanette and went to sleep.

The young people walked side by side, talking quietly. A spring moon laid a silver path on the quiet water. The stars seemed especially brilliant. A watchman's light glowed briefly, then disappeared.

Gussie said, 'Oh yes, I like my job.'

'I like working in the law, too. There's plenty of variety.'

'My cousin was studying law, but he gave it up.'

'Where was that?' John Carrier asked.

'Columbia.'

'I graduated from Columbia,' John said.

'I wish Luke had. Although he's doing well working in the Fall River Line office.'

'And are you content to spend all your time on the *Commonwealth*?' He laughed softly. 'I'll tell you quickly, I hope your answer is no.'

'I used to think I was. But now . . .' She didn't finish. She was twenty-three, still living at home with her grandmother when she wasn't aboard the ship. An emptiness was beginning to consume her. Time was passing too quickly.

'Now?' John was asking.

'I hope there'll be more to my life.'

He tipped her face up and looked down into her eyes. 'I'm glad you said that, Gussie.'

Later, after they had separated, she went over every moment of their time together and what he had told her of himself. He was twenty-seven. He worked for a big law firm. He had studied at Columbia, and had returned to Boston, where his parents had lived, when he graduated. They had since died, and now he lived alone. He had brown eyes and brown hair and wore neither beard nor mustache. He liked music, and walking, and cats. She was smiling when she fell asleep.

The next morning, at breakfast with Augusta, she said, 'I've met the most wonderful man.' She went on to speak of how tall and straight he stood, and how deep his voice was. Then she sighed. 'But he lives in Boston, and I'll probably never get to see him again.'

'Why don't you send him a note and ask him to come for dinner your next night at home?' Augusta replied.

Chapter 37

When, in May, Augusta's sixty-fifth birthday was celebrated on the *Priscilla*, John Carrier was among the party, and in mid-September Gussie and he were married by the minister of the Central Congregational Church in the wheelhouse of the *Commonwealth*, while the gulls swooped overhead and the setting sun faded through pink and mauve mists.

Afterward the whole of the wedding party sailed for New York. Kin and Barbara had come up with Tom, tall and blond, and very reserved for a twelve-year-old. Kevin and his Ann were there, too. Their son Taft, most often called Tafty, was three now, a stubborn handful.

At Gussie and John's wedding supper in the domed dining saloon, Augusta looked at Tafty, thinking what a miracle it was to see one's great grandchild. Yet even he didn't make her feel old. She knew that the red gold of her hair had faded somewhat. There was white in it now. Fine lines fanned from the corners of her eyes into her temples. Her smile had permanently marked her mouth. But nothing of herself was changed within. She felt the same as she had felt at sixteen. The thought made her smile. Young Luke caught her eye and laughed. 'You look like a bride yourself, Grandma.' Ray winked at her, his face flushed and merry.

After the wedding toasts, the group was served an elaborate meal. Soon Tafty became restless. Augusta took him by the hand and led him along the corridor. They passed several groups. At one the men spoke of the sinking of the *Titanic* four months before. At another there was a heated debate about the coming Democratic National Convention, and whether Woodrow Wilson, the governor of New Jersey, could win the nomination to run for the presidency against Republican William Howard Taft, the incumbent. Near the stairs two gentlemen spoke of the songs coming out of Tin Pan Alley, and whistled fragments at each other.

Small Taft paused near them. The men grinned down at him. He turned red, and with an awful yell, flung himself at the pin-striped thigh of the slighter of them.

'Tafty!' Augusta pulled him away. She smiled apologetically at the two men. 'Forgive the child.'

'I'm afraid he doesn't like our music,' one said as Augusta hurried away to return Taft to Kevin and Ann.

Soon Kin and Barbara excused themselves. Gussie and John went to walk on the deck. Augusta left the dining saloon with them, but at the grand saloon, she sent them on and paused to listen to the orchestra playing on the gallery. It was a song she recognized. She hummed along with the music.

A man paused beside her. 'Have you disposed of the little boy?'

'I must apologize to you,' she said. 'I don't know why he behaved so badly.'

'As I said, I think he didn't like my music.' He tipped his head, listening to the orchestra. 'That's mine, you know.'

'Yours?'

'May I introduce myself? I'm Harry Von Tilzer.'

'Ah yes, of course,' she said. 'I've seen your name on the concert program.'

'And what about you? Is this your first trip on the *Commonwealth*?'

She laughed softly. 'No. I've been traveling on the Fall River Line all my life.'

'How's that?' he asked, interested.

She told him about her father Marcus and the *Bay State*, and about her Luke, and when he asked about this particular trip, she told him about Gussie and John, and how they, like so many sweethearts before them, had first met on the ship.

Von Tilzer's eyes glowed. His smile broadened and his right foot tapped the floor. He was charmed by her, by what she told him about the ships and the men who had sailed them and the passengers they carried.

When Augusta and he parted, he walked the deck alone, seeing the ship through her eyes. He was humming when he went to bed. Months later, after long hours of work, those few gay bars would become a song called 'On the Old Fall River Line', and would be whistled and sung all over the world.

Meanwhile, as Augusta spoke to Harry Von Tilzer about the ships, Kevin was watching his younger brother Ray, whose face was redder than it ought to be. It was one thing to celebrate Gussie's marriage to John, Kevin thought. It was another to appear before Augusta and the family almost drunk. He wondered what was wrong.

When the moment arose, he drew Ray aside, saying, 'We haven't talked for a long while.'

Ray grinned. 'You're a busy man. A wife, a son, a job.'

'You could have the same,' Kevin told him. But there had been something in Ray's voice that led Kevin to ask, 'What about your job? Don't you like it any more?'

'What job?'

'You're not working?'

'Not at the moment.'

'But what happened? You've been with them for years.'

'They objected to having me punch my foreman in the nose.'

'For God's sake!'

'The man deserved it.' Ray's red face grew redder. 'I'd do it again, if I had the chance.'

'And what now?'

'I'll find other work. Maybe I'll go to sea.'

'How about the line? I could probably help you.'

Ray shook his head. 'No, thanks. There've been enough

Callahans and Wakefields on the line.'

'I think you're making a mistake,' Kevin said.

'It won't be the first.' Ray shrugged.

Gussie, clutching her bouquet of white roses and radiant of face, joined them. 'So serious. What is it?'

Kevin hugged her. Ray kissed her cheek. Then John came and swept her away.

Later, within the quiet walls of their honeymoon suite, she smiled at him. 'Now I have everything I want in life.'

'I hope so,' he said.

'Yes,' she whispered, leaning against him. 'Everything.'

And, for the next year, it seemed that way to her. They had a small flat in a not very fashionable part of Boston, but John's prospects with the firm were good. He bought a Model T Ford as soon as he could afford it, and both he and Gussie learned to drive. She went to Fall River often to see Augusta.

On one of those visits she told Augusta that she was expecting, and with her began to plan the layette the two of them would make together.

They spent many happy hours at their work. Augusta, although she didn't speak of it, was grateful for the company and the job to do.

It helped her over those first weeks of loneliness after Marge Gowan had gone away. In late February Betty Townsend had come to Fall River to visit Augusta and Marge. She told them about the suffragette march to be led by the National Women's Party to be held in Washington on March 3. She asked if they would come. Marge agreed, and Augusta too thought they should go, although when Kevin and Gussie heard of the plan, they protested vehemently.

Augusta ignored their comments. She and Marge sailed on March 1 on the *Priscilla* to New York, where, with Betty, they took the train for Washington.

The three women were in the front line of the parade as it set out along Pennsylvania Avenue for the White House. It was a cold and windy day, but the sun was bright. There was laughter and singing as the ranks marched, shouting: 'The vote for women! Women count too!' led by young Alice Paul of the National Women's Party.

Then, suddenly, at the edges of the parade disorders

developed. A man spat on a young girl who was passing by. Another thrust his lighted cigar into her veil. There were screams, scuffles. One man seized Marge by the arm and slapped her. Augusta saw it, and was immediately at Marge's side, shouting, 'Stop that, you fool!' He turned, his hand upraised, and met her angry look. 'You're old enough to know better,' he said, and skulked off.

Others remained. Men stood on the curb, shouting curses. Some snatched at the marchers' hats and shawls. There were even women who joined in with disapproving jeers. The police displayed as much animosity as many of the onlookers.

Augusta remembered briefly the day in 1907 when she and her study group had paraded with banners before the White House and no one had taken note of them. It was a big change, and meant something was happening. Here were five thousand women showing what they stood for and believed in.

Before it was over, forty women marchers had to be hospitalized, and it took the cavalry from Fort Myer to restore order to the street.

Afterward Marge Gowan had said to Augusta, 'We've been together so long, it's hard for me to imagine it any other way. But I'll return to Fall River with you for only a little while. When you have someone else to help you, I'm going to join Betty in her work. We've talked of it before, and she says I have a good deal to offer. I must try it and see.'

Within ten days Marge had found a woman named Nina Baras to come daily to help with the house and cooking, had packed her things, and with a promise to write often, had embarked on the *Plymouth* to meet Betty in New York.

So it was Nina Baras who served Augusta and Gussie tea as they sewed on the layette. She was a small woman in her mid-thirties, with black hair and snapping black eyes, and a faint accent to her speech, although her family had come to Newport from Portugal three generations before. She was artful at embroidery and lacemaking, and soon she too began to work on the layette for Gussie's expected child.

But it was never used. For early in 1914, when Gussie was delivered of her infant, it died almost immediately.

'I never held him in my arms,' she told Augusta bitterly. 'Never. Not even once.'

Augusta pitied her with all her heart. She smoothed back the younger woman's hair and wiped the tears from her cheeks, but didn't answer. There was nothing to say.

Within the same year Gussie was pregnant again. That time she miscarried at the fifth month.

Augusta was waiting when John brought her home from the hospital. In the twelve days since her pregnancy had ended, she had become very thin. The bones stood out in her face.

John helped her into a chair, worriedly asking what he could do, bringing her a blanket, a book. She was unresponsive, only greeted Augusta, then sank into dismal silence.

Augusta sat with her after John had gone to the office. Finally Gussie roused herself. 'I'll never have a baby, will I?'

'You will. A miscarriage is only a mistake. Next time it'll be all right.'

But Gussie shook her head. 'No.' Her voice dropped to a hoarse whisper. 'There's something wrong with me.' Tears spilled from her eyes. She sobbed, 'Don't you know? I thought you did.'

Augusta moved close to her, held her. 'No, no, what are you talking about?'

The words came in a breathless flood, anguished, choking words. 'It's the death in me, Grandma. How can I give birth to life? I remember it clearly. The night it happened, the night it touched me. I could feel her heart beating, and her warmth, as I felt the hearts of my two babies beating, and felt their warmth inside me. And then . . .' Gussie began to wail, beating her small fists on the arm of the chair, '. . . then it happened. Her heart stopped and her cold invaded me, and that's how it was with my babies. I felt their heart beats fade away, and now . . . now . . . there's only . . .'

'No,' Augusta said. 'No, stop it, Gussie,' and when the girl's screams grew louder, Augusta caught her one hand and clutched it tightly, and then, weeping herself, she slapped Gussie as hard as she could.

The girl fell back, panting, sobbing.

Augusta said, 'Now listen to me. There's no death in you. What a strange thing to say. Your mother died because she was sick with consumption. She was hurrying home with you and the boys because she knew she was ill. She loved you. So she was bringing you home.' Augusta's voice broke. 'She was making sure you had life.'

Soon the girl's sobs faded. She wiped the tears from her cheeks. 'I'm sorry, Grandma.'

'Yes,' Augusta said, and went to make tea.

When she returned with a tray, Gussie lay back in her chair with her eyes closed. 'But I'm afraid I'll always be empty.' She managed a smile. 'I'll just have to get used to it, won't I?'

It took her a long time to regain her strength. When she had, she visited John's office, but not to see him. She went to the chief partner to ask that he recommend her for a job to anyone he knew. Instead, he offered her a position as a receptionist. She accepted on the spot, and although John argued against it, from then on they went to the office every morning together, and every evening, when the day was done, they returned home together.

She thought then that that was how they would live the rest of their lives.

One evening in October of 1914 Bennet sat near the window of his apartment, watching the traffic pass by. Twilight was falling. The street lights gleamed, and in the wet pavement pale reflections shimmered. A carriage rattled to a stop before the building.

Bennet watched Jeanette alight.

She wore a thick fur stole draped around her shoulders, a wide-brimmed hat with three long tassels. From that distance, and in that light, she looked like the girl he had known years ago. He sighed. Time had changed her. She was round at belly and breast now. Her eyes were smaller in her chubby face.

Briefly he thought of how she had conspired to trick him with a will first written by herself, then altered to appear to be his own. She hadn't been very clever. And once it was burned to ash, it meant nothing. Which was why he had done nothing about it. It hadn't been worth the trouble.

She came in, smiling. 'At your window again, Bennet?'

'It's pleasant to see the world go by,' he told her.

'It's nice to be part of that world, too.'

But he wasn't, and never had been. He saw no reason, and no way either, to change that now.

Jeanette sank down in the opposite chair. She twitched her skirt aside so that he saw her ankles. They were still slender. He smiled at her.

'Everybody's talking about the war,' she said.

In late July of that year the Archduke Ferdinand, heir to the Austro-Hungarian throne, and his young wife Sophie, had been killed by an assassin in Sarajevo. Austria-Hungary, believing that the murders had been instigated by Serbia, immediately declared war on its small neighbor. Within days, Germany, for its own reasons, declared war on Russia and France, and invaded Belgium. At that point Great Britain declared war on Germany.

The American people were divided. Many believed the conflict did not concern them. Others felt that German aggression had to be stopped.

Bennet considered that the war would be good for business, and said so.

'Maybe,' Jeanette agreed. 'But how would you know? You never go out any more. It can't be good for you. You need to be with people.'

'No doubt.' He was amused to hear her. Of recent years her speech had changed. She spoke now like a grande dame, comfortable with herself and her position.

'You're getting to be a hermit. As I say, it can't be good for you.'

It had been weeks since he left the apartment. Yet he didn't mind. The less he went about the better. It required so much effort for him to move himself. He preferred to sit thus, to have his meal, his wine, and smoke his cigar in peace.

'We ought to go to New York,' she told him.

He had wondered what she had in mind. Now he knew. But that was all right. She had, lately, developed a circle of friends. Pleasant people, he thought, who expected little of him.

'And I've heard that Carrie Hartwell is in a moving picture. Wouldn't you like to see her?'

'Perhaps.'

'Bennet,' her voice was soft, 'it would do you good.'

'All right. Whenever you make the arrangements,' he said agreeably, since it was easier to give in than to argue.

The following month they sailed on the *Priscilla*.

They were no sooner on board than Bennet settled into his stateroom. He was tired. His leg ached. He arranged to have a barber come to shave him. He ordered dinner for that evening and breakfast for the following morning. He had champagne brought in.

Jeanette said, 'Won't you have a walk on deck with me? We could watch the departure.'

'I've seen it before,' he told her.

'We used to have fun,' she sighed.

'Hand me a cigar, would you please?'

She gave him one with a flourish he didn't acknowledge. Hands on her hips, she stood still, regarding him wistfully.

'A match, Jeanette?'

She supplied that too.

He thanked her from behind a cloud of blue smoke.

'Bennet?' she said softly.

'Hmm?'

'Then I shall take a walk alone.'

'Certainly.'

She drew a mink wrap around her shoulders, settling it with a small wriggle of pleasure. 'Back soon,' she told him. The door closed behind her with a sharp click.

Bennet smiled faintly. He wondered if her quick little mind was still working on the problem of his will. But decided it didn't matter. He thought suddenly how wise his mother had been. The pre-nuptial agreement was the greatest protection. Her purpose had been different from his. But it had served and would continue to serve. As long as Jeanette had her furs and jewels and time in New York, she would never leave him.

He let his head drop back to rest on the chair. He was too big to be quite comfortable, but he was too tired to rise and go to his bed. He watched the blue smoke drift slowly past his eyes.

He was forty-six years old but he felt as if he had lived much longer. The days of his childhood seemed bleaker than ever before. He remembered the shrill of his mother's voice, and his father's gentle touch. It had all been to no purpose. His birth, his life. He had expected nothing, given nothing, received nothing. He was certain it was his own fault. He ought to have done something. But what? Jeanette had tried. For whatever reason, she had provided him with the small life he had had. He ought to have gone walking with her.

He pushed himself to his feet and stood still, gasping. The stateroom seemed to swing slowly around him while pale mists gathered in the corners. Then, as he turned toward the bed, his bad leg collapsed under him. His heavy body toppled forward and he crashed to the floor. His cigar fell away. It burned a small hole in the carpet before the embers went cold.

Bennet's pudgy hands scratched for a little while and then were still.

'She's *my* daughter,' Diane said. 'I won't have you interfere, Caleb.'

He said very quietly, 'I don't intend that. I want only what's best for you.'

'Oh, do you?' she cried. 'How I wish I could believe that. But you always side with her. As if no matter what I do, I'm in the wrong. You don't understand. Fania's so wonderful. She could be perfect, but...'

'No one is or can be perfect. You ask too much.'

Diane rushed on, 'But she's been badly taught. If she listened to me, if you supported instead of opposed me...'

'I tell you, you're alienating her unnecessarily.'

'I ask only what's right.' Diane walked quickly to the door. Her cheeks were red, her eyes glinted. 'I'll talk to her. Alone.'

Caleb said nothing.

'You think I oughtn't to?'

'Yes,' he said. 'You so often embarrass her, though you don't mean to. "Fania, sit up. Elbows off the table." All that. She isn't a child any more.'

'But I'm ashamed when she sits like a shop girl or walks like a...'

Caleb shook his head.

'She must learn. When she has her debut –'

'Which she doesn't want.' Then, softly still, 'Don't you realize her happiness is most important?'

'She doesn't know where her happiness lies. One day she'll thank me.'

'She's eighteen now. Surely, at that age, you knew where your happiness lay.'

Diane thought fleetingly of Jesse Light, their short time

411

together, and how she had felt when her mother had taken her home, and how the marriage had been annulled. But that had been different. She told Caleb so. 'There was my mother...' Diane's voice faded.

He waited, but she didn't go on. She didn't realize how like her own mother she had become. She had Mary's single-minded determination to have her own way.

'I'll be back soon,' Diane said.

Caleb didn't reply. He lay down on the blue and white spread with the New England Steamship Company emblem and folded his arms behind his head, asking himself if he ought to have known what would happen when he brought Fania back to Diane.

A few doors away, in Fania's stateroom, Diane said, 'I hope you're ready to apologize.'

'What for?' Fania asked.

'You know what for. Your behavior is outrageous. It's hard to believe that you're really my daughter.'

Fania threw back her head. 'Perhaps I'm not.'

'You mean you wish you weren't,' Diane said accusingly.

'Maybe you're right,' Fania retorted.

'That's impertinent. And it's also not true. You came to me of your free choice. I could have done it differently. But I didn't. I waited, oh, how it broke my heart too, but for three years I waited patiently, certain you'd some time know your own mind.'

Remembering why she had left the Devantas hurt as much as it had at the beginning, Fania thought.

Diane said, 'Fania, please,' with her voice breaking, 'why do you hate me? I only want your happiness.'

'Hate you?' Fania echoed. 'I don't.' She drew a deep breath. 'It's myself! I can never be what you want me to be. I can never satisfy you.'

'You do, you can. These are small things only.'

'No, no. These small things are *me*,' Fania cried.

'Of course they are not!' Diane retorted, and then, softly, she said, 'Oh, if only you understood how I love you.'

Later, when Diane had left her, Fania threw herself on the bed. Why does she talk about love? she asked herself. How can she love me when she doesn't want me as I am but must try to remake me. What she wants to change is me. What I am, whether I want to be that or not. I was never the Devantas' child. Not in their hearts. Then why have they marked me so?

Since the day she had walked from that room of mourning for Dottie, she had seen none of them again. Neither seen nor heard from them. Even in her bitterness, though, there had been a small part of her that ached for them, and hoped they would write to her, or come, or at least send her word that they thought of her. But there had been nothing from them, only the long-lasting silence. She was given over to Diane to remold and re-form, as if there was no real Fania but only a lump of clay to shape until it suited Diane's purpose, whatever that was, or to fulfill a dream she had once had and remembered only faintly.

A week later, Diane and Caleb and Fania had returned from New York together. They didn't speak of the quarrel on the ship, Diane and Fania pretending it hadn't happened, while Caleb waited, knowing it wasn't over.

One afternoon, feeling restless, Fania took her hat, wrapped a heavy lace shawl around her shoulders, and went to walk in the grounds of Cliff Mansion.

Most of the gardeners were spreading mulch around the rich plantings near the tall iron front gates. But Jim Cruz was working closer to the house. He was a tall boy, sun-bronzed and muscular, with dark eyes and an unruly cap of blond hair. He had seen Fania come and go and had wished her 'good morning' and 'good evening' many times since he'd been hired to work on the estate a year before.

But now, when she paused beside him, he didn't know what to say. For this time, after her 'good afternoon,' she lingered beside him. He was twenty-two, and had a girlfriend in town, but that only made it worse. He bent to his work, too conscious of her nearness. He thought she must be the prettiest girl in the world.

'What do you call that – that stuff that you're spreading around?' she asked.

'It's just old pine needles from the trees, miss.'

'And why do you put it there?'

'It keeps the earth warmer.'

'I see,' she said thoughtfully. She went on then, feeling his glance follow her all the way to the edge of the property.

From there she could see Cliff Walk below, and the ocean, where the sun made a gleaming silhouette of a distant sail.

As it disappeared beyond the horizon, she turned away. Her grandfather was coming toward her. He was very stooped now, leaning on a thick black cane. His hair and beard were white and his face was grooved with deep wrinkles.

'Admiring the view?' he asked, when he stood beside her.

She nodded.

'And thinking about escape too, I'll warrant.'

She didn't answer.

'You won't, little Fania. People never do. You see your mother? She tried once. You're the result. She's her mother's daughter now though. And you'll be the same.'

'No,' Fania said. 'I couldn't be.'

'That's what you think now. I thought the same about my father, about old Willie. I went to school, and learned to speak as he never could. And I married above myself. I made my life as different from his as I could make it. But I'm old Willie. I am. Inside me.' After a pause William added, 'And so of course are you.'

'Perhaps,' she agreed.

'He was a man,' William went on. 'Big, rough. He scrubbed the decks of the *Bay State* when he was a boy. And made his first money in whorehouses.' William laughed. 'I remember how it got started. We were living in Ellie Franger's house then and a girl named Lottie was bringing in men. Papa didn't like it. He was worried for me. It oughtn't to happen where I could see. So he ran poor Lottie out. Later on, though, he set her up in a house. And then there were others.'

'Are you making that up?' Fania demanded. It was hard for her to be sure of her grandfather. There were days when he seemed scarcely to know who he was, days when he rambled almost senselessly about people she had never known or heard of before. But he had other days too.

'Oh yes,' he said. 'I'm making it up. How could it be true? After all, we Gorgases live in Cliff Mansion on Newport, don't we? We belong to the best of society. At least that's what Mary would have had you believe. But why do you think Diane was never allowed to know old Willie?'

'It *is* true then.'

William grinned at her. 'What do you think?'

She grinned back at him. 'I think it's very funny.'

He roared with laughter. 'So do I.'

That evening at dinner Diane told Fania, 'You're slumping again. A lady never allows herself to look as if she's going to fall into her soup.'

Fania reddened, then snapped, 'It must be the old Willie in me.'

'What?'

Caleb tried to distract her. He suggested that they take a ride the following afternoon.

But Diane ignored him. 'What about old Willie?' She knew the name of her father's father, but that was about all. She remembered how her mother froze on the few occasions it was mentioned. She thought she recalled seeing old Willie once, but only for a moment. She'd gone into the parlor, and a man was there, and her nanny had quickly pulled her away.

'Old Willie,' Fania said deliberately 'Your grandfather, who made his money in whorehouses.'

Diane sat very still, her slender hands clasped in her lap. The color rose in her cheeks and her eyes glittered with anger. At last, when she had caught her breath, she demanded, 'What is this nonsense?'

'No nonsense,' Fania said. 'You're very high and mighty with your manners and airs and speech and rules. That's the cream. But what's beneath is altogether different. Your grandfather was a deckhand you wouldn't have said "good morning" to, and when he was older he made his money from the whorehouses he started. And now you tell me that I laugh too loudly.'

White-lipped, Diane turned to her father. 'Have *you* told her these lies?'

'No, my poor deluded Diane.' He laughed. 'I've told her these truths.'

Diane flung down her napkin and rose, remembering the thousand and one slights Charles Farr had visited upon her, and how she had fled, determined never never to be shamed again. Now this . . . this . . .

Weeping, she ran from the room.

Caleb found her crumpled on a chaise in her bedroom. She clutched a small silk handkerchief in her shaking hands. Her face was wet with tears.

He sat beside her. 'What does it matter?'

'You're laughing at me. Everyone will laugh at me. Either to my face or behind my back.'

'No,' he said. 'No one will care.'

'But they will. You'll see it. As soon as they know. And of course Fania will tell.'

'But no one cares what your grandfather was,' he said reasonably.

'I care.'

'More fool you,' he said. 'You should be proud that he made his way, not ashamed of how he did it.'

'You wouldn't understand how I feel,' she told him.

'No, I suppose not. But I want to try.'

'You *don't* want to try,' she said shrilly. 'You're always against me. Always, always. I wonder now why I married you, Caleb.'

'I sometimes wonder too,' he answered.

Later, unable to sleep, he paced his room. Finally he walked into the quiet night and wandered along Bellevue Avenue. Hours passed. He found himself at Long Wharf. It was two-thirty in the morning. The eastbound *Commonwealth* was just being tied up.

Soon the debarking passengers came down, while others boarded. Cargo was unloaded and other cargo was carried on. Two automobiles were pushed from the hold. There were shouts and laughter, and somewhere close by a tired infant screamed.

Withdrawn in the shadows, Caleb watched, benumbed.

In a little while, the activity ended. The automobiles had been driven off. The wagons and surreys had rattled away into the night. The porters and passengers and stevedores had disappeared. Only the great lighted ship remained. From her bridge there came into the quiet the soft sound of a fiddle.

A faint smile touched Caleb's lips. All was well aboard the *Commonwealth*. Her captain was making his music.

Soon, though, the music faded away. The hawsers were freed from the bollards. The sidewheels began slowly to turn. Three times the ship's whistle blew and then she steamed into the night.

Caleb remained where he was. He followed the ship's course in his mind: now she was at Rose Island. She would pass Gull Rocks. Then there would be Gould Island. In her kitchens great vats of coffee would soon be set to boil. The stewards would be preparing grapefruit and prunes. Breads and rolls would be already baking. She would pass Conanicut Island; after would be Prudence. The Hog Island light would be next, and then Mussels Bed Shoals, Bristol Ferry and Borden Flats, and the wharves of Fall River.

The Borden Flats light. Fall River. He turned to make his way through the sleeping roads of Newport back to Cliff Mansion. But a part of him had gone with the *Commonwealth*, and he understood what was to come. But not yet. Not while there was still Fania to consider.

Chapter 38

Though the New Haven Railroad Company was based in New Haven, Connecticut, its affairs had been of great interest to the town of Fall River ever since 1893, when the New Haven absorbed the Old Colony Railroad and leased from it, for ninety-nine years, the Fall River Line, beginning a monopoly that would eventually affect all transportation in New England.

Thus anything that concerned the New Haven was well covered by the *Daily Herald*. In early June of 1907 it stated that the head of the New Haven, Charles S. Mellen, chosen for the job by J. Pierpont Morgan four years before, had been called to testify before the Massachusetts Committee on Railroads on an anti-merger bill proposed by Louis D. Brandeis.

This was the same Louis D. Brandeis who would one day become a Supreme Court justice, and Mellen's appearance would prove to be only the first of many before state and federal agencies, as the New Haven management and methods became a subject of public knowledge and dispute.

In April of 1910 the *Daily Herald* reported that Senator Robert M. LaFollette of Wisconsin had charged in the Senate that the New Haven deliberately engaged in legal delays until the president in office when suit was brought was no longer presiding by the time it should have been heard.

From June 1911 to November 1912 there were mentions of numerous accidents on the New Haven trains, in which twenty-eight were killed and several hundred injured.

In July of 1913 an Interstate Commerce Commissioner opened hearings into the New Haven's finances and service. At the end of the month it issued a report that condemned the company's operations and deceptive accounting practices. It was then that Charles S. Mellen resigned. By that time the value of New Haven stock had dropped sharply, and in December it passed dividend payments for the first time in forty years.

The *Daily Herald* wrote of these events, too, and when Augusta had read of them she frowned uneasily. She would manage, she thought, but it would be more difficult. Prices were rising. Coffee was now selling for twenty cents a pound, Porto Rico molasses for sixty cents a gallon.

She put aside the newspaper and went to the mantel. There beside the girandole stood the carved ivory dog with ruby eyes, the celadon lion, and the cloisonné vase. They had been there for as long as she could remember.

She would never sell them, she told herself. Without touching Marcus's follies, she turned to survey the room. It was much the same as when she had been growing up there, when Luke had been with her and the children were young. Caleb stamping about, and laughing as he no longer laughed; quiet Kin; and bright-faced, rebellious Amy.

Augusta and Luke had added a few pieces of furniture, and only shortly before he died nearly fifteen years ago, they had replaced the carpet with a new Axminster. The house needed painting inside and out. The garden was overgrown, although still beautiful in summer with roses and honeysuckle.

That evening when she heard the *Providence*'s signal at the Borden Flats light, she went up to the widow's walk. It was almost impossible now to see the wharves and the terminal building. The trees were grown tall and there had been much new construction. But she watched the lighted ship until she disappeared into the shadows of Mount Hope Bay.

Then, having gotten a lantern, she went into the attic. One of the old sea chests was already empty, but the second was still full, and the third nearly so.

She had taken out a piece here, a piece there, unwrapped each carefully. It was as if she could feel the presence of her mother and father.

Later Nina Baras called her, and she went down to dinner, telling herself that no matter what happened to the New Haven Railroad Company, the Fall River Line would survive. It was too firmly woven into the fabric of New England life to disappear. Like the human family, growing, changing, spawning new generations, it would live, accommodating to good times and bad, just as she would accommodate to changing circumstance. That night, with pen in hand, she sat down to plan those savings made necessary by the line's condition.

In April of 1914 the *Daily Herald* reported that the Interstate Commerce Commission, after a resolution by Congress that it investigate the New Haven's conduct, had opened new hearings.

In its July report, the Commission recommended that the New Haven give up its control of a number of New England railroad companies and steamship lines or face prosecution under the Sherman Anti-Trust Act. However, by agreement with the Justice Department, ownership of the steamship lines was to be dealt with in talks with the Interstate Commerce Commission. It would be years before that issue was resolved.

When Augusta read about the report, she thought of the New Haven's lease of the Fall River Line, and the competition for passengers and cargos which could only be worsened by the new canal being built across Cape Cod. Sitting still, with the paper clutched in her hand, she wondered, for the first time, how it would end.

Not long after that, Gussie and her husband John came down from Boston. They had a pleasant dinner together, then settled in the parlor. They talked of inconsequentials briefly, until John said, 'Grandma Wakefield, I know you've been reading about the New Haven's troubles, and wondering how it'll affect the line.' When she nodded, he went on slowly, choosing his words, 'It's a serious situation.'

'Yes,' she said.

'The stock's down to fifty-nine and a half, so you can do nothing at the moment. But it'll rise again, although probably for only a short time. When it does, you must salvage what you can.'

'Salvage?'

'Sell out for the most you can get.'

Gussie sat silent, biting her lip.

Augusta knew the child was torn. She worried for Augusta, but she realized the solution offered was painful. Gussie didn't know which way to go. John, untouched by the past, was unconfused by it. He spoke only out of concern.

At last Augusta said, 'I'll think about it,' and realized even as she spoke that she would do no such thing.

Chapter 39

May 7, 1915: A stir of excitement swept the Cunard Line's *Lusitania* as the light fog lifted and her passengers saw the beautiful Irish coast for the first time.

Even Ray, far below decks and with no view, felt it. He grinned. Almost to Liverpool. And then . . .

He remembered those years when he worked on the Fall River Line ships. It had been fun, with Kevin beside him, Gussie watching enviously when the two boys departed each evening, and being awaited by the tall slim silhouette of their grandmother, watching for them each morning from the widow's walk atop the house on High Street. But those years were long gone.

He wasn't sorry he'd gotten himself fired from the job in the shipyard. It was inevitable. He'd had too many bosses, too many orders. He needed to be his own man. But the other thing, and that business with the petty cash – he regretted all of it. For Grandma, especially her. But for the others, too. Somehow, some time, he'd have to make it up to them. And he would.

It was the same here, with too many bosses and too many orders, but at least he was out of Boston, where Callahan was still a name that brought sneers. But he was careful. He wasn't going to get in trouble again.

With a quick glance around to be sure he was alone, he took a bottle from his locker and gulped down a long fiery swallow. Then, putting his cap on his head and settling his uniform jacket, he went to the cabin deck that was his station.

Jeanette Graystone-Fields leaned at the rail, her eyes fixed on the rocky coast. She had treated herself to the trip, and brought along the handsome young man beside her, as a consolation prize. She'd felt she deserved something special. Bennet had made no will, his lawyers had told her. And when she remonstrated with them, they reminded her of the pre-nuptial agreement she had signed, read it to her word for word, and cited the $10,000 consideration she had been given. She'd cried, 'He said that didn't apply to what he left me in his will!' But there was none, they repeated. Bennet had left no will, no kindred, no issue, and no spouse eligible to receive his fortune. When she demanded to know who then would receive it, they looked so unhappy that she believed them. The state would receive it – the state.

That had hurt; but then she reminded herself that she had her stocks and bonds invested in Wall Street. Jewels, furs, a small circle of friends in New York, a few in Boston. She contented herself with what she had. But there had been that unpleasantness over another young man she had befriended whose mother had objected in an embarrassing public scene.

Jeanette decided a swift change of atmosphere would do nicely, and besides, she was due for a present after all she'd been through.

The *Lusitania* was the most talked of ship that season; she didn't care about the war. So she booked passage on her. They'd had a pleasant voyage. She looked forward to her stay in England.

Now, raising plump bejeweled hands, she straightened her

hat and turned to the young man beside her with a smile. 'Talk to me, Parker. I'm bored.'

'It's a beautiful sight, isn't it?'

'Yes,' she agreed. 'And . . . ?'

He looked at her blankly, not knowing what she expected.

She laughed. 'I mean "Yes, yes, but go on."' And thought how dumb he was.

'England will be exciting, won't it?'

'We'll see,' she answered, thinking of Bennet. Then, abruptly, 'Let's go get some wine.'

That same afternoon the *Lusitania* was hit by a German torpedo. She sank within twenty minutes. Nearly 1,200 lives were lost, more than a hundred American. Among them were Ray Callahan and Jeanette Graystone-Fields.

Augusta heard the shrill of the bicycle bell at the gate and went to look. The garden was still. A bluebird, frightened by the sound, had taken wing. The lilacs were in bloom, their thick blossoms lavender in the afternoon sunlight. The Western Union boy vaulted the closed gate and came up the path to the door.

By then, she was waiting, her hand outstretched.

'Morning, Mrs. Wakefield,' he said.

Her voice shook as she answered the greeting, taking the telegram from him at the same time.

She waited until the boy had backed off and vaulted the gate again to mount his bicycle. When he had disappeared down High Street, she tore the envelope open. The message was from Gussie. She had been notified by the Cunard Line that Ray was one of those lost on the *Lusitania*.

It was hard to take in, to believe. Augusta held tightly to the door frame. From far away she heard the hoot of a tug. A barge bell rang somewhere. A wasp buzzed at the step nearby.

She saw him as he had been the day Caleb led him into this house for the first time. Small, wide-eyed. She saw him pale of face, and breathless, when he came weeping to her, 'Kevin's lost at the quarry. And it's my fault.' She remembered how prideful he'd been when he offered to her the first pay he'd earned working in the baggage room of the *Bristol*.

Now, shaking, she withdrew into the house. With the door

422

shut, the small out-of-doors sounds were muted. She heard Nina at work in the kitchen.

Slowly Augusta looked around the room, smoothing the telegram between her fingers. Everything here reminded her of Ray. He had been enchanted by the celadon lion, and his dearest wish, when he was a child, was to be permitted to take it down and play with it. But she had never allowed that. How many hours he had spent, lying on the floor near the hearth, listening while she read to him with Kevin and Gussie close by. How many more hours had he and Kevin spent at chess, crouched over the table near the window.

As she sank into a chair, she remembered that last time she had seen him, only ten days before.

His eyes had been alight. He spun his derby on one finger, and grinned at her. 'Grandma! It worked just like you said it would. I talked to the man you sent me to on the New York pier, and I've got me a job. Everything's going to be all right.'

She'd been pleased, and told him so.

'The *Lusitania*, Grandma. Cunard's best. She sails on Saturday, the first of May. I'll be a cabin steward. I wasn't sure I'd get it, not having that experience. But they're short-handed. So many of their men have gone into the Royal Navy.'

She'd said, 'I'm glad. I hope things will work out for you.'

'Don't worry. I've learned my lesson. I've been lucky and I know it.'

Lucky, Augusta thought now, and buried her face in her hands as a thick current of anguish swept her.

The memorial service was short. The minister spoke of Ray's youth and accomplishments and how his family had loved him. Then, quietly, but with passion, the minister spoke of the distant war that had made Ray its victim, and of the brutality of the Germans who had sunk, without warning, an unarmed passenger ship carrying women and children.

In a little while the small group returned to the house on High Street. Nina had set out a cold lunch of ham and salad, and filled all the vases with flowers; now she hovered anxiously over Augusta, offering her food and drink.

Augusta waved her away as Kin came to sit near her. He had come alone. His hair was nearly white. There were deep blotches under his eyes. His hand trembled when he took hers.

He said, 'I didn't have the chance to say so before, but Barbara asks me to tell you she's sorry she couldn't come with me. Tom has a fever and is in bed.'

Augusta nodded. She rarely saw Barbara, or Tom either. Barbara blamed Augusta for young Luke's decision to come to Fall River to work for the line. But the boy was happy, and doing well, and that was all that mattered. 'I hope it's nothing serious with Tom.'

'A bad cold.' Kin sighed. 'I can't believe it's true. Ray. The first of that generation.'

Soon Gussie came to sit beside her, saying softly, 'Is it real? Is this how it ends?'

'Gussie . . .'

'We did all we could.' The younger girl's lips trembled. Her eyes filled with tears. 'And look how it turned out!'

'We couldn't have known,' Augusta answered. And then, 'Let Nina bring you a slice of ham and bread and butter.' The girl was so pale, Augusta thought. And thin too. Much too thin, even for her small frame.

'What does it matter?' Gussie said. 'I keep thinking of Ray.'

But it wasn't Ray that she thought of. It was her own barrenness, the hunger within that neither food nor sleep could quell. The ache was constant and deep, and she couldn't get away from it. She had pleaded with John to adopt a child, but he had refused. He wanted a son, but his, his blood. She knew what her grandmother would say: children come or they don't. She must make do with what life gave her, and be glad of it. But how be glad? And now Ray was dead.

Soon young Luke came up to make his farewells. His silver eyes were bloodshot. He hugged Augusta tightly, saying he'd be back later. He had, Augusta realized, hardly spoken to his father.

Kevin and Ann led five-year-old Tafty to be kissed. Augusta lifted him to her lap and hugged him. He squirmed restlessly, demanding, 'Why is everybody mad?'

'No one's mad. But everybody's sorry.'

'Why, Grandma?'

'Because your Uncle Ray has gone away,' Ann said quietly. She was a pretty girl, with a round face.

Gussie said she was stupid, but Augusta feared that Gussie didn't like any woman who had no trouble conceiving.

When she was finally alone, Augusta stood irresolute in the middle of the room. Her spirit was unquiet; sadness weighed her down. Ray. Ray. Amy's youngest. Though Nina was somewhere about, the house seemed empty, silent. The grandfather clock in the corner ticked time away, ticked life away. And in her mind there was the sound of her voice, telling Ray that he must leave Boston, that he must ask an acquaintance of hers on the New York pier to find him a job.

Augusta straightened her shoulders. She went up to the widow's walk that her father had built for her mother so she could see the *Bay State* depart and return. There, at the docks, though she could hardly see her, the *Commonwealth* lay moored, her lights agleam.

From below Nina called, urging Augusta to rest.

Downstairs, Augusta said, 'I can't rest.' While Nina protested, she wrote a short note to young Luke, telling him what she was going to do, and packed a small overnight bag. Then, taking her light coat from the halltree, she went quickly into the fading twilight. It was nearly time for the *Commonwealth* to leave.

When she reached the docks, the boat train's locomotive, *Plymouth Rock*, was getting up steam for its return trip to Boston.

She boarded the ship. Kevin greeted her at the purser's window. 'What are you doing here?'

'You know,' she said.

'Are you all right?' Without waiting for an answer, he went on, 'Kin's in the men's bar. I'll have someone run and tell him you're here.'

'No,' she said. 'I want to be by myself. Just give me a stateroom.'

He handed her the key, but asked again, 'Are you all right?'

'I will be,' she told him. 'This is better.'

And it was true.

With the deck under her feet, and the crowds moving around her, she was back in her own world.

She walked around the deck until the ship moved slowly into the channel. Then she went along the gray corridor to her stateroom. The orchestra was playing a familiar tune. As she heard it, she smiled. 'On the Old Fall River Line' – the song Harry Von Tilzer had written two years ago. She remembered the night of her sixty-fifth birthday, the line's birthday too. Tafty had been unpleasant to Mr. Von Tilzer, but the composer had been nice to her, and interested in stories about the ships.

Ray had been there that night, too. Sighing, she went to her stateroom. In a little while, she was in bed, silence and dark enfolding her. Ray, she thought. Ray, Ray. Again anguish overwhelmed her. She had sent him to the *Lusitania*.

Soon though there was the muted whisper of the paddle wheels. Soon though there came the occasional flash and fade of the light ships, and the low moan of the buoys.

By the time the ship reached Newport, she was asleep.

Chapter 40

In 1914, soon after the war in Europe began, President Woodrow Wilson had issued a proclamation of American neutrality. At the time, although there were some active pro-Allied groups, most Americans agreed with that position. Meanwhile the president attempted to persuade both the Germans and the British, as well as the French, to accept arbitration of the issues dividing them. He sent his aide Colonel Edward M. House, on several secret missions to Berlin, London, and Paris. These attempts failed.

In the three years that followed the sinking of the *Lusitania*, public opinion changed. Although William Jennings Bryan resigned from his position as Secretary of State, believing the president's protests over the incident had become too strong, most Americans supported the president, and the new Secretary, Robert Lansing. At that time, Germany apologized and offered reparations, but other sinkings of neutral merchant craft occurred, with more loss of American lives.

On April 16, 1916, the president issued an ultimatum to Germany: American relations would be broken off unless Germany ceased submarine attacks on merchant ships. The Germans accepted the ultimatum on May 4.

In November the president was reelected in a race with Chief Justice Charles Evans Hughes. The campaign emphasized the president's success at keeping America out of the European war.

However, at the end of January 1917, Germany announced that it was resuming unrestricted submarine warfare, and the president responded by arming merchant ships. As more ships and more American lives were lost, and acts of sabotage in the United States increased, preparedness efforts were stepped up. In March the *Laconia* was torpedoed; there were many American dead. Two days later the newly inaugurated president requested Congress to declare war against Germany. It did so in early April. The president signed the document on the 6th.

That same night, as the *Commonwealth* rounded Point Judith, the winds began to die. The clouds that had earlier obscured the full moon drifted slowly beyond the horizon.

In the shadow of the lifeboats on the starboard deck, Fania and Jim Cruz stood close together. Those casual 'good mornings' and 'good evenings' had developed into longer conversations, real ones. Jim stopped seeing the girl he had been walking out with. Fania spent more and more time wandering in the Cliff Mansion gardens. They had become more adept at arranging private meetings.

A day before, when she knew that she and her mother would be sailing on the *Commonwealth*, she had told Jim. He'd come too as a deck passenger. During the concert, Fania had yawned and told Diane that she was tired and going to bed.

To Jim, Fania was like an exotic goddess – her tall slender form, the deep-set burning black eyes, the heady scent of patchouli she wore... To Fania, Jim was solid, earthy – his work-calloused hands, the smell of sweat about him, the white flash of his smile in his sunburned face.

Now, voice breaking, she said intensely, 'What are we to do? They'll conscript you, Jim. You'll go away and I'll never see you again.'

It was likely, he knew. Nothing had happened yet, but soon a drafting law was sure to be passed. He didn't answer her. Instead, he took her into his arms and kissed her, and they stood in silence, holding onto each other as tightly as they could . . .

On a deck below, in her stateroom, Diane lit a cigarette, coughed, and put it out. She had only begun to smoke lately, and in private. She didn't enjoy it much. But within moments, she had lit another one.

What was she to do about Fania? The girl was impossible. She had refused a debut. She ignored the many young men who made overtures to her. And now this.

Savagely, Diane pressed her cigarette out in a white porcelain ashtray, not noticing the blue likeness of the *Commonwealth* on the bottom.

The girl would throw her life away on a gardener. Everything Diane had hoped for her, done for her, would come to nothing. She had no respect for herself, for Diane. For the past she had come from. Fiery heat flooded Diane's cheeks as she thought about that. How could Fania have respect?

Diane damned Willie Gorgas, the grandfather she had never known. Damned the whoremaster. It was all his fault.

And it was his fault, too, that Caleb had become a stranger to her. How long had it been since he held her in his arms? How long since he had said he loved her and been her strong shoulder to lean upon, to look to with hope?

She knew what contempt lurked behind his quiet courtesy. Once, when she had charged him with it, he had looked startled, and laughed. 'My dear Diane, every family has its skeletons.' But not of course the Wakefields and Kincaids. She was as certain of that as she was certain Caleb thought her not good enough for him.

Outside in the corridor there was a stir, the whisper of skirts, a breath of footsteps.

Diane raised her head, listening. Someone off to a clandestine meeting. She remembered when, long ago, she had gone just so to be with Jesse Light.

With the thought came a more recent memory; Fania leaving Stanis Hoppe's concert to go to bed early.

But Fania was not asleep in her room Diane was certain. Something was indeed brewing between Fania and that surly boy. Diane's fists clenched briefly. Then she threw a shawl

428

around her shoulders and hurried out.

She knew where to look. She had, after all, sought out such places herself. But the *Commonwealth* was large. Indoors there were many public rooms. She hurried through them quickly, ignoring those that were crowded. Fania and the gardener would want privacy, darkness.

On the portside deck she thought she had at last come upon them, but when she drew near, she saw that it was another couple, nestled together like two bananas on a stem. She cut through the ship, stepped out on the starboard deck, and walked quietly forward.

There, in the shadow near the lifeboats, she saw them. She watched from a distance. The gardener held Fania in his arms. They were silent, unmoving. The paddle wheels dipped and rose, murmuring faintly. Far away a bell rang. The light of the full moon slowly moved closer to them.

Moments passed while Diane watched the two. Finally she roused herself and went to them.

She settled one hand on Fania's shoulder, the other on Jim's. 'So this is how you sleep, Fania,' she said. And to Jim, 'How dare you touch her?' Her voice was harsh. The moonlight glittered in her blond hair.

'Mrs. Wakefield!' Jim said, despairing. 'Please.'

'Leave us alone,' Fania cried. 'There's so little time.'

'Be quiet the both of you.' Diane stared at Fania. 'And you, go down to your stateroom.'

'We'll be married,' Fania said. 'You can't stop us.'

'I can't? We'll see,' Diane answered.

'I won't let you ... ' Fania began, but Diane's gloved hand whipped across the girl's face. Fania staggered back, crying out.

'Go to your stateroom,' Diane told her. 'We'll speak later.'

'Fania, please ... ' Jim's words were a whisper.

'Don't let her spoil it,' Fania cried before she fled.

Jim started after her, but Diane stopped him. 'Wait. I have something to say to you.'

'I love her,' Jim said. 'I won't hurt her. Don't you know you've nothing to fear from me?'

'You love her!' Diane's laugh was cold, cutting. 'That's the most stupid thing I've ever heard. You won't hurt her, so you say. But you already have. Now listen to me. Fania's life can never be yours. Never, never. I made the same mistake she wants to make now and I've paid for it with bitter tears. I know what will happen. If you really love Fania, you'll go away and never come back. You'll free her to be the person she must be.'

'Go away?' he repeated.

'Return to Newport as quickly as you can. Leave Cliff Mansion. For Fania's sake, you can't see her again. If you do, I'll disinherit her. She'll have nothing from me. So if it's her fortune you have in mind, then forget her. You'll have no benefit of it. And think what you can do for her. For Fania Wakefield, of Cliff Mansion.'

With that she turned on her heel and left him.

Fania's stateroom door was locked. She didn't answer Diane's peremptory knock. She didn't pick up the telephone when Diane called her.

Jim remained on deck until dawn. When he finally went below, he knew what he must do.

They were on the way to the dining saloon, moving slowly through the crowds anticipating the arrival in New York. Fania searched every face, hoping for a glimpse of Jim.

'You needn't look for him,' Diane said. 'I'm sure I made myself as plain to him last night as I did to you.'

'I'm sure,' Fania agreed bitterly.

Diane's voice softened. ' Fania, please, it's for you. For your own sake. Forget him. We'll pretend it never happened.'

Fania didn't answer.

In the dining saloon, a steward soon seated them. He brought a silver pot of coffee, and toast with Florida orange marmalade and Maine raspberry jam. Neither of them touched the food.

'He only wanted your money. When I told him I would disinherit you, he changed his tune.'

'I don't believe you,' Fania said.

'You'll never see him again,' Diane retorted.

'I don't believe you,' Fania repeated, but once again her eyes made a swift circle around her. Where was he? Why didn't he come to her?

He wasn't on the various decks. He wasn't in any of the public rooms. And when the ship finally docked, Fania couldn't find him. At last she allowed herself to be persuaded to go with Diane.

The following day, when the two women returned to Newport, Jim was gone, with no word left behind.

Once Diane had walked in anguish in the gardens of Melford House at Long Melford. Now Fania, feeling the same anguish, walked in the gardens at Cliff Mansion.

Caleb reread the small notice in the faint light on the *Plymouth*'s main deck. He had been carrying it for a week. It was rumpled now, its print blurred, but he knew the words by heart: *Automobile mechanics and drivers for service in France. 37 to 50 years old. Ask General Secretary at Fall River YMCA or Overseas Motor Transport Service in Boston, Mass. 331 Little Building.* Caleb was too old by a year. But he was fit and strong and he knew automobiles and how to handle them. He *wanted* to go. Wanted to.

He and Diane lived like strangers. They *were* strangers. All vestiges of the woman he had loved and married were gone from her. She was as beautiful as ever, but her laugh was brittle, and a faint feverish blush always burned on her cheeks. She didn't need him, and made that plain. The lawyers handled the hotel chain as they always had before, so he wasn't needed there. As for Fania, he had found he could do nothing for her.

He waited at the gangplank. As soon as it went down, moments after the *Plymouth* was docked, he hurried off the ship.

It was a crisp October day. The sun hadn't risen fully, but the eastern sky was pink. The mist hanging over the river was pink too. Gulls swooped and screeched in the early morning stillness.

It was too early for his errand. He walked the streets. North Main into South Main. Past South Park and St. Anne's. Along Middle Street to Second, and then on Second, past the house in which the Bordens had died so long ago, to Central. The roads were astir now. Mill workers carrying their lunch pails. Carts loaded with lumber and coal, ice wagons drawn by work-worn horses.

Since April, when the United States had entered the war, the conscription law had been passed, requiring every man aged between twenty-one and thirty to register. The Liberty Loan drives, begun in June, were already proven successful. The Fall River Line cargo holds were full, bringing 44,638 bales of cotton in a two-month period to the town's mills. Even so they were operating at 75 percent capacity due to a shortage of skilled workers, many of whom had gone to munitions plants, where wages were higher, and others into the Army.

When the Town Hall clock struck nine, Caleb presented himself at the YMCA. The general secretary had known the Wakefields and Kincaids for years. His questions were brief. Caleb said his baptismal certificate had been lost in a fire. The general secretary shrugged that aside and asked after Augusta's health. He didn't return to proof of birth. Surely Caleb knew his own age, and his own mind. There were a few papers to fill out, and then it was done. Caleb was to report here, to join with his group, within seven days.

From there he went to the house on High Street.

Nina let him in, beaming. 'You'll have breakfast, won't you?'

Augusta threw her khaki-colored knitting aside to kiss him. Then, softly, she said, 'You've only just missed young Luke. I wish you hadn't.'

'What's happened?'

'He's been called up.' Augusta pressed her lips together. 'He seemed glad of it.' Her voice was doubtful. She didn't understand Luke's excitement nor approve or it, either. She had too many memories of war.

Caleb was saying, 'I'm sure he is glad of it, Mama. No one wants to be left out.'

'No one?' Augusta gave him a sharp probing look. 'What are you thinking about, Caleb?'

'It's done, Mama.'

'Yes?' she whispered dryly. 'You too? You've been conscripted?'

'I've volunteered for the ambulance corps.' He smiled at her. 'And lied about my age to do it.'

She closed her eyes briefly, remembering when she and Aria had bid Luke goodbye. Aria's dreadful weeping. Her own aching, silent tears. And Luke's return – his face scarred. The white streak in his dark hair that never faded.

'I had to,' Caleb said.

She said breathlessly, reaching for her knitting, 'I think you know how I feel.'

'Men are foolish,' he said lightly.

'Ah, yes,' she agreed, lightly too. But Caleb, whatever he was, was never foolish. There was something else. He wanted to be away. He never spoke of it, but she knew he was unhappy. His marriage to Diane hadn't proved what he had expected. He was moody, restless. The war would be his escape. But she said, 'I wonder about Kevin.'

'He's over age too, but in any event, I think they'll need men for the line's ships.'

The knitting needles clicked steadily for a little while. Finally she said, 'God be with you, Caleb. I'll pray for your safety.'

He was saved from having to answer, for Nina came in to say that a good breakfast was ready for him. He sat down, Augusta having coffee to keep him company, and with the best appetite he'd had in a long time fell upon the sausage and johnny cakes.

That same night, Caleb left the *Providence* after her docking, but lingered on Long Wharf. He was in no hurry. Everywhere he looked he saw signs of how Newport had been affected by the war. The Naval Station had been enlarged, and other naval facilities added. Giant searchlights moved constantly across the harbor, where an anti-submarine net was being installed. When it was finished, traffic wouldn't be allowed into the port after dark. Newport would then temporarily become the terminus of the Fall River Line once again.

He watched until the *Providence* departed, then went to Cliff Mansion. He found Diane alone in their apartment and told her what he had done.

She stared at him, silent with disbelief. Then she burst into tears. 'How could you do this to me?'

He said quietly, 'Let's be honest with each other this one time. You're hurt that I'm leaving. But you're relieved as well.'

It was true, and she knew it, but she cried, 'No, no, no,' and flung herself down weeping. It wasn't pretense. She wished it weren't the truth. But neither weeping, nor wishing, could change it.

She was composed, though, the day he left to join his group in Fall River. 'You'll take care of yourself, won't you?'

He touched his lips to her cheek. 'Don't worry about me.'

He didn't mention Fania, but he thought of her, and Diane knew that he did.

The girl had been distraught when she heard the news, crying, 'What will I do without you?'

He had hugged her. 'The same as when I've been here. I haven't done for you what I hoped.' He had drawn a deep breath. 'But if you should ever want for a home to go to, remember my mother in Fall River. She's fond of you.'

As he drove out of Cliff Mansion and into Bellevue Avenue, a weight seemed to slip from his shoulders. He found himself whistling. He didn't know what lay ahead of him, but in that moment, with a new sense of freedom enfolding him, he decided he would never come back.

Chapter 41

In the year and a half after the United States entered the European war, nearly three million men were conscripted for service with the armed forces.

The state of New York amended its constitution to allow women to vote, and it was announced there that a Wall Street broker named Bernard Baruch had been chosen by the president to head the War Industries Board and improve coordination for the war effort.

In Boston, the Navy had purchased a number of ships for various uses. Among these was the *Massachusetts*, a Fall River Line freighter that had been converted to carry passengers and then sold. The Navy recommissioned her as the U.S.S. *Shawmut*, and as such she served in North Sea mine lanes. Later, in 1928, she would be renamed the U.S.S. *Oglala*. As a minesweeper in the South Pacific, she would be sunk at Pearl Harbor by Japanese kamikaze pilots on December 7, 1941. Still later she would be raised, repaired and returned to the South Pacific as a service ship.

In Fall River the mill whistles had begun to blow earlier in the morning and later at night. Their smoke stacks belched black clouds for most of the twenty-four hours in each day. The waterfront area had become busier than it had ever been. One after another, freighters were loaded and moved out. Coal barges and oil tankers came and went.

The Fall River newspapers had begun to carry stories of sabotage in New Jersey and submarine sightings off Point Judith, and most issues had a letter written by a soldier in faraway France. By then there were 1.8 million Americans serving in Europe. The town's Liberty Loan quota had been reached, and bonds in the amount of $7,368,000 had been sold.

Augusta wrote to young Luke and Caleb often, and anxiously awaited their replies. She'd heard only twice from Luke, once from Caleb. She forced herself to keep busy. Always, when she sat, which was not as often as Nina would have liked, she worked on the khaki-colored yarn that she turned into sweaters for the Army. Three times a week she rolled bandages at the Red Cross. The study group, its number dwindled to four, met twice monthly, but now the talk was always of the war and how long it would go on. Still, for all her activities, time hung heavily on her until one hot July day.

She came in from shopping on South Main Street, and still wore her hat, though she had set aside her parasol. She heard a knock at the door and started for it, but Nina was there first, and when she opened the door, Fania said, 'May I come in?'

The light was behind her so that her face seemed no more than a dark shadow with glittering eyes, and her slender young body slumped with exhaustion.

Nina led her in, and Augusta hugged her, while she said in a ragged whisper, 'Caleb told me before he left that if I ever needed ... ever wanted ...' She faltered, then went on simply, 'Can you take me in for a little while?'

'Certainly,' Augusta said without hesitation. 'There's plenty of room.'

The house was big, almost empty now, and quiet. It seemed to be waiting. As Augusta herself was waiting these days.

Fania said, 'I can't stay with Diane Wakefield.'

Augusta thought it odd that she herself never thought of Caleb's wife as Diane Wakefield, but always as Diane Gorgas.

'I'll explain it one day. But just now I can't.'

'You needn't explain,' Augusta said, and went on matter of factly to suggest a room for the girl, and to begin to get her settled.

At the end of the week a trunk was delivered to the house. 'My clothes,' Fania said when she looked at it. 'I don't want them.' But Augusta said Fania needed them, and surely Diane wouldn't wear them, so the girl unpacked the skirts and chemises, and hung them in the wardrobe. No further word came from Newport.

Fania seemed content to stay close to home, doing the small chores Nina and Augusta asked her to, spending hours at reading or listening to records on the gramophone that Caleb had bought for Augusta at Steiger Cox Company not long before he left.

One day Augusta received a letter from Marge Gowan, and wrote back, saying she'd be coming to New York soon, and wanted to meet with Marge. She didn't mention that on reading Marge's words she'd had an overwhelming compulsion to see the younger woman. They arranged to meet, and with Betty Townsend too, on Friday of the last week of August.

Augusta invited Fania to join her, but Fania declined, so Augusta decided she would go alone.

When Gussie heard of the plans, she said, 'Why don't you take the train? It's a through trip, and quite pleasant.'

'The train?' Augusta repeated. 'Oh my dear, no. I couldn't do that.' And then, laughing, 'I'd never find my way around New York if I didn't start at the pier.'

But Gussie hadn't laughed with her. 'Grandma, I'm serious,' she said. 'It may be too much for you.'

Augusta folded her hands in her lap. 'I have my health, thank God. And my faculties. I believe I can manage.'

She said the same thing on the *Priscilla* when Kevin greeted her and then said, 'Will you be all right?' as he handed her her key.

'I believe I'll manage,' she said, and this time there was a tart edge in her voice.

It was nice that the children cared, but they needn't think she had to be treated like fine old china. She was as capable now as she ever had been.

In her stateroom, she took off her hat and stood before the

mirror smoothing her hair. It was pure white, combed back from her forehead in waves, and drawn into a high knot secured by tortoise-shell combs that had been her mother's, perhaps even her grandmother's. Around her neck she wore a black grosgrain ribbon with a cameo medallion Kevin, Gussie, and Ray had given her one Christmas many years before. She touched it now, remembering. Ray. Her face was momentarily bleak. She turned from the mirror, and with her shawl over her arm, left the stateroom.

The grand saloon wasn't crowded. Travel was light these days. There were a few groups of young soldiers. Two Army nurses sat together. A salesman tried to interest a resistant young couple in his jewelry cases.

The windows were heavily draped, the lights not nearly as bright as they used to be, because of wartime precautions. Every bar on the ship was closed, all liquor locked away as the ship neared Newport, which by government fiat had become a dry area for the duration. Past the five-mile limit, beyond the Beaver Tail light, the bars would open again.

After dining alone, Augusta went out on deck. It was a dark, moonless night. The air was moist and salty. The ship seemed to move within a black shroud, as the bow watchman stood at his post scanning the shadows, alert and ready to sound an alarm.

Then, from nowhere, it seemed, a patrol boat appeared. Lights swept the *Priscilla* from prow to stern. A voice called over the throb of motors, 'Give your password and destination!'

An answering voice called out the password and added, 'New York.'

The patrol boat's lights went out. The ship went on.

Those on deck whispered to each other, 'Did you see it? They're looking for subs.'

Augusta was having breakfast the next morning, and thinking how good it would be to see Marge again, when the steward said, as he brought her coffee, 'It's just about here that a submarine was sighted last week.'

The words were hardly out of his mouth when a rustle of alarm swept the dining saloon.

'I'm going to have a look,' the steward said, and rushed away.

Augusta took up her cup, held it for a moment. The faint

vibrations of the engines remained unchanged. There was no alarm bell. Smiling, she took a sip of coffee.

Around her, the tables emptied. There was a general rush to the door. Meanwhile she refilled her cup and buttered her toast.

Soon the others came trickling back, some grumbling, some laughing. In a little while the steward told Augusta that a passenger had seen something glinting in the dawn. It might have been a floating bottle or bit of debris. But the passenger had yelled, 'Sub! Hey, look!' and word had spread instantly throughout the ship.

'It's bound to happen,' he said ruefully. 'I'll be glad when it's over, won't you?'

She was thinking of that when the *Priscilla* docked. How glad she would be when the war was over. When Caleb and Luke were home again.

Marge Gowan, there to meet her alone, explained that Betty wasn't well and sent her apologies. Augusta thought that Marge herself seemed ill, although she didn't say so. Marge had a deep hacking cough, and her eyes glittered. She was scarcely forty, but looked older. When Augusta complimented her on her role in helping to get the New York State constitutional amendment concerning women's votes passed, Marge said hoarsely, 'It'll help. New York is important. But we must have a federal amendment. So far each time it's come up in the Senate, it falls on the two-thirds rule.'

They spent most of the day together, and more than ever Augusta was glad she had come. But she was concerned about Marge's health. The woman grew tireder by the moment, and more gray. When she accompanied Augusta back to the ship for the five o'clock sailing, Augusta urged her to go home and rest and take care of herself so that she could soon have a visit to Fall River. Marge promised to write.

In fact the next thing that Augusta heard was from Betty. She had recovered from the influenza, but Marge had succumbed to it several days earlier.

By then the disease had been reported all along the East Coast. Eventually it would spread to forty-six of the forty-eight states, and before the epidemic was over, some 500,000 people would be dead.

By October 2, there were 907 new cases in Fall River. The

Women's Union on Rock Street was distributing soups and custards for the ill.

Augusta and Fania, along with Nina, had worked all the day before in the kitchen. Now they left some large canisters there and went outside. It was a gray day. In the distance a trolley car clanged. Horses clip-clopped on the cobblestone road. An automobile backfired loudly at the corner.

Fania said that she'd like to do an errand if Augusta didn't mind, and Augusta agreed, pulling her coat collar tighter around her neck. There was a cold edge to the wind. She wondered if it might snow by dark.

'Then we'll stop at the Academy of Music. They've advertised for an elevator operator. I want to ask if I would do.'

Augusta allowed the girl to help her into the runabout. Its seat creaked under her. It was old, and would have to be replaced soon. The same was true of the horse. Augusta eyed the Model T that chugged by, and wondered if she could learn to deal with one. She saw no reason why not.

Fania was only a little while at the Academy of Music. The job had already been filled, she explained.

'There'll be something else,' Augusta said.

Within a few days Fania found a job in Porter's Stationery Store on North Main Street. The hours were long, the pay small; the work would last only until the clerk down with the flu was able to return. But Fania was content. She was *doing* something, and not sitting like a useless lump on a soft couch at Cliff Mansion. She lived with Augusta, helping in every way she was permitted to. She didn't allow herself to think of Jim Cruz except sometimes in the night.

Then she would remember that terrible afternoon in Cliff Mansion when the downstairs maid had said, 'This just came for you by post, Miss Fania.'

The reception hall was full of flowers, yellow roses and white ones. Their scent was strong in her nostrils. She opened the package and pulled out the Sam Browne belt, not knowing what it was at first. The medal fell to the rug. The maid picked it up and handed it to her.

Inside there was a note that said: *These belonged to Jim Cruz. He wanted you to have them. He asked me to make sure you did. He died yesterday. I'm sorry.* 'Yesterday' had been nearly six weeks before. Jim had been dead all that time and she hadn't known. She stood frozen, as if in a nightmare.

Diane came down the steps. She was wearing a riding habit. Her blond hair was pulled tightly back under a black derby. 'What do you have there?' she asked.

Fania held out the belt and the medal.

Diane took them, turned them in her hands. 'You've heard from the gardener then?'

In a hoarse whisper, Fania said, 'He's been killed.'

'I told you you'd never see him again.'

'It's *your* fault. *You* made him go!'

'I did you a favor,' Diane said coldly. And then: 'Well, I'm glad that's over. Now you can forget him.'

She tried. It was easier in Fall River. But sometimes when she was alone, she would take out the Sam Browne belt and the bronze medal, and read the note that had come with them. *These belonged to Jim Cruz... He died yesterday. I'm sorry.* It was signed *Rafe Raleigh.*

It was close to eleven o'clock. The ambulance moved slowly through the dark of the French countryside. The road was narrow and still wet, although the rain had stopped, leaving puddles through which the vehicles lurched uncertainly. Behind it, at the Meuse, there was a continual barrage from heavy artillery and the sky glowed with lavender fire. Ahead there loomed a nothingness as the ambulance rolled without lights through the shadowed trees.

Caleb wished he could drive faster. The men were badly wounded. He could hear the moans of one, the murmurings of the three others. He had some thirty kilometers to go before he reached the hospital. He wasn't sure of what waited along the way.

Borden Flats, he whispered in his mind, seeing the wind-stirred waters of Mount Hope Bay, Bristol Ferry, Mussels Bed Shoals, Hog Island ...

The ambulance bumped into a rut. The wheels slid. There was a questioning shout from the back. 'It's all right,' Caleb called. 'We'll make it.'

As he spoke a light winked in front of him, and a shrill whistle stabbed the dark. Directly ahead, the road exploded, spewing rock and dirt and fire..

On November 2, in New York, a Brooklyn Rapid Transit System train suffered the derailment of five cars. One hundred people died in the accident. One of them was fifty-two-year-old Kin Wakefield.

Hours later, Gussie received word in Boston. She and her husband John immediately went to Fall River. White-faced and trembling, wondering how she would say it, Gussie knocked at the door.

Augusta led her in, alarmed at her appearance. She gave John a questioning look, but he said nothing, while Gussie said, 'Sit down, Grandma. I have to talk to you.'

Augusta took a chair. Her hands had already begun to tremble. Caleb, Luke. They were so far away. Each day she read the casualty lists, fearful of what she might see.

Gussie said, 'I have bad news. It's Kin. He's dead.'

'Kin? Did you say Kin?' Augusta's voice was a whisper. 'But what's happened? He's not... he wasn't... In New York?' she ended.

Gussie wailed, 'I can't... I can't...' and put her hands over her streaming eyes.

'There was a train wreck,' John said. 'A hundred people died.'

'A train wreck,' Augusta said, her voice flat with disbelief. 'A wreck, you said?' His words, her words, made no sense to her. They were speaking of Kin. The disbelief faded under an onslaught of pain. Kin dead. Her first born. A part of herself gone. Gone along with Amy.

And Gussie wailed, 'Grandma, Grandma, please don't, don't!'

Augusta breathed slowly. She folded her hands tightly to still their trembling. Through tear-clouded eyes, she looked at the younger girl. 'We must go to Barbara and Tom. They'll need us,' she said hoarsely.

The three women, Gussie, Fania, and Augusta, were accompanied by John when they sailed from Fall River that evening.

When Kevin heard the news, he looked worriedly at Augusta. Later he told Gussie, 'You oughtn't to have taken her with you,' and Gussie answered, 'I couldn't have left her alone.'

It was a quiet and uneventful trip, although wherever the passengers gathered they talked of the war.

The first thing Barbara said when she saw them was, 'But why was he on the Brooklyn train?' She fixed her feverish eyes on Augusta's face. 'I don't understand it. Why was he on that train?'

Barbara received no reply, and expected none. She had asked the same question repeatedly ever since she first heard the news. It was her way of denying the reality, Augusta supposed.

Tom, now sixteen, and tall, with his mother's blond hair and blue eyes, sat rigidly in a chair near the window. His uncle Tom Gavin stood next to him.

'But why was he on the Brooklyn train?' Barbara said again, coughing. 'I had telephoned him at the office and told him I was ill. He said he'd come home. But if he was coming home, he wouldn't have been on that train. And if he hadn't been, then he'd be alive today.'

Her brother Tom could have told her that Kin had been going first to see his secretary, who had also been his mistress, ill with influenza in Brooklyn. At least that was Tom's guess. But he said nothing. What good would it do?

The next day Barbara collapsed at Kin's graveside.

She lingered for three days, coughing, choking, sometimes whispering Kin's name, and then she too died, another victim of influenza.

Shocked, but doing what had to be done, the family arranged for and attended her funeral. It was after that that Augusta drew the older Tom aside, and said to him, 'Now what of Tom? We must help him. I'd be glad if he came to Fall River and lived with me.'

Tom Gavin shook his head. 'No, no. That's not sensible. You're ... forgive me, Mrs. Wakefield, but you're too old.'

'I'm not young,' she agreed dryly. The two dimples near her mouth suddenly became deep. It was the first time she'd smiled since hearing of Kin's death. 'But Tom's my grandson. He should have his family about him now that both his parents are dead.'

'And I'm his uncle,' Tom Gavin answered. 'I know what Barbara would want.'

'We're not adversaries,' Augusta answered. 'We both want what's best for the boy.'

'Then we'll ask him,' Tom Gavin answered.

When it was put to Tom, he said, in what sounded like Barbara's voice and inflection, 'I don't want to go to Fall River. I'd rather stay with my uncle.' After a pause, he added, 'But thank you all the same, Grandma.'

John Carrier returned to Boston on the *Plymouth* that evening, but Augusta stayed on with Fania and Gussie. The three women packed Tom's belongings and had them moved to his uncle's house. They disposed of furniture and kitchenware and clothes once worn by Barbara and Kin. Without the help of the two younger women, Augusta couldn't have managed the sad disposal of two lives. But at last it was done.

On the evening of November 10, they left New York on the *Providence*. The ship was crowded. Every stateroom was taken, and all berths in the public rooms were filled. Among the passengers were many soldiers.

Fania looked at them and thought of Jim Cruz.

Augusta looked at them and thought of Caleb and young Luke, so far away. She had heard nothing from either of them for a long time.

The three women sat together in the grand saloon. Augusta took out her khaki knitting and bent over it.

Fania was aware of a soldier standing near a pillar. He was tall, with blond hair. His shoulders were wide, his legs long and slim in puttees. One of his arms was in a sling.

Deliberately she turned away and leaned toward Gussie to ask, 'Do you think it'll really be over soon?'

'It's hard to say. After the false reports of an armistice today, nobody knows what to think.'

From around them Fania heard snatches of conversation.

'It must end. The Germans can't go on much longer.'

'And what of Wilson, his Fourteen Points? Did Colonel House accomplish anything for him?'

She listened, but hardly understood. No one knew what was happening.

At close to midnight, Gussie yawned and said she was going to bed, and suggested that Augusta do the same.

Fania left the grand saloon with the others. Once again she

noticed the tall blond soldier. As she passed him, Gussie asked, 'Will you go to work tomorrow, Fania?' and Fania saw him start and stare at her, and take a step toward her. Wondering at that, she hurried on. She didn't know him, she was certain. She'd only looked at him because he made her think of Jim Cruz. Perhaps he'd been aware of her look and misunderstood.

Soon the three women were settled in for the night. But as they neared Newport, a sudden excitement swept through the sleeping ship. Bells began ringing. Whistles hooted. There were excited voices in the corridors. Fania opened the stateroom door. The steward grinned at her as he hurried by. 'It's over,' he shouted. 'The war's over. They've signed the Armistice.'

The women dressed quickly, and hurried out.

Shouts and prayers and joyous cries rang from every deck. The Armistice had been signed: wireless from New York had just brought the news to the *Providence*.

There was to be no more sleep on that journey.

The saloon chandeliers were lit once more. The orchestra regrouped and began to play. This time Fairman's musicians played 'The Star Spangled Banner', and 'America the Beautiful', and 'Over There!', followed by passenger requests.

Strangers kissed each other, and the saloons, which had never seen dancing before, were suddenly filled with cavorting people.

It was in the midst of this joyful confusion that Fania felt a light touch on her shoulder. She turned to find the tall blond soldier smiling at her.

'Happy Armistice!' he said.

'And to you, too,' she answered.

'Are you Fania?' he asked. 'I mean, are you Fania Wakefield?'

She stared at him, startled and uneasy. 'Yes, I am. But why do you ask? How did you know?'

'One of the ladies with you said your name before. I heard it.' His eyes were green, very bright, staring into hers. 'It's such a coincidence, you see. It took me aback, so I didn't say anything then. But I was ... I was coming to see you in Newport.'

'You were? To see me?'

'I'd better explain. I know I'm not making much sense. But my name's Rafe Raleigh ... and ...'

'Raleigh,' she said softly. Suddenly the floor seemed to tilt under her. She swayed.

444

He put a hand out to steady her.

'You sent me the belt,' she whispered. 'You knew Jim.'

Rafe's fingers tightened on her arm. 'Come outside. Please.'

It was a cold night, with an icy wind. There were no stars shining and no moon. He took off his blouse and put it around her shoulders. Only the faint lights of the ship touched them, and the bay's silence, while from inside there came occasional bursts of laughter and excited conversation and the sounds of music. Now they were playing Von Tilzer's 'On the Old Fall River Line.'

Rafe waited while a couple passed by, whispering, and a ship's watchman swung his lantern in a wide arc. Then he said, 'Yes, Fania, I did know Jim. I was with him when he . . . when he . . . got it. And I decided then, as soon as I got home, to see you. I live in Fall River . . .'

'So do I,' she said, 'now. If you'd gone to Newport, you wouldn't have found me.'

'Coincidence,' he told her.

'Yes,' she said. And, 'It's so long since I saw him. I don't remember what he looked like any more.'

Rafe put his arms around her and drew her to his chest. She crumpled against him while tears poured down her face.

The tinsel on the Christmas tree shone faintly in the dim light. The children were gone now. Augusta sat alone near the hearth, where the fire burned low.

There had been no word of young Luke, of Caleb.

She folded her hands tightly, and bent her head, and prayed for them, for their safety, as once, long ago, she had prayed for her own Luke, gone from home to another war.

Chapter 42

It was now some six weeks since the signing of the Armistice agreement that had ended the war. President Wilson had arrived in France to attend the peace conference. For the past month Fall River rumor had had it that the president and his aide Colonel House, or perhaps Colonel House alone, had held secret meetings with a number of Allied leaders on board the *Priscilla* to discuss the Fourteen Points of the president's peace program. It was also rumored that Senator Henry Cabot Lodge had been the host at a different secret meeting on the *Priscilla*, where he and a handful of other senators had discussed their disagreements with the president's proposal.

Now, in the late afternoon of the last day in December, it was snowing hard. The bare trees were white skeletons and the pines seemed swathed in ermine. From the harbor there came the sound of foghorns, and occasionally the muted boom that meant dynamite charges were being set off to free barges and ships frozen in place by surface ice.

On High Street more than a foot of snow had accumulated on the roadway and the sidewalks. In Augusta's front yard tiny footprints showed where hungry squirrels had been foraging.

A little while before, Rafe had come to pick up Fania. He was taking her to the New Year's Eve dinner at his parents' home on Highland Avenue. It was to be her first meeting with them, and for a good part of the day she had worried about what to wear and how she must look, and tried on one gown after another before she settled on a soft rose-colored velvet that set off her dark hair and eyes.

Augusta had been concerned about the weather, but Rafe had said his Packard could make it, and besides it wasn't far to go.

Augusta liked Rafe. She remembered him faintly as a small boy. She had known his great grandfather, George Raleigh, and Gowan Raleigh, his father. She was sure the boy's attentions to Fania were serious, and sure that Fania was falling in love with him. But there was something about him that made Augusta uncertain. She sensed a kind of wildness. More than anything Fania needed a man she could depend on, who would never surprise her. Was Rafe Raleigh that sort of man? Augusta wasn't sure.

It was nineteen years since Luke's death at the turn of the century. She still missed him. Sometimes she still felt his arms close around her. Sometimes she reached for him in the night...

Snow crunched on the path and then on the steps. The doorbell rang. She set aside the *Colliers* that had lain unread on her lap and went to see who it was.

The postman said, 'How do, Mrs. Wakefield. I wanted to wish you a happy New Year, and many many more.' There was snow in his hair and on his hat. He grinned as he put an envelope into her hand.

She wished the same to him, waited until he had gone, and then closed the door.

She shivered a little as she returned to the parlor. It was cold, and the fire that Rafe had stoked up before he and Fania had gone had already burned low.

She would put another log on, she told herself. But first – the return address was the Overseas Motor Transport Service, in Boston. She frowned. What was that? Why would they be writing to her?

She tore the envelope open, and as she read its message, she crumpled into a chair. *I regret to inform you that on or about November 1, 1918, near the Meuse River, France, your son Caleb Wakefield was injured while transporting wounded soldiers to a hospital. He died trying to help his fellow man.*

Each word stabbed through her, dagger sharp. Caleb was dead. Dead. She would never see him again. It was the worst that could happen to a human being. To be alive and know that her child was dead. All of them, all three of her babies, all three parts of herself, were gone. Kin, Caleb, Amy. It was impossible to bear, yet it must be. To keep from screaming, she put her hand in her mouth and bit down as hard as she could.

The next day, Fania sat weeping. 'I can't believe it,' she said. 'I can't believe it would happen to him.'

Augusta had been calm when she told the girl the news. Now, with new tears stinging her eyes, she said nothing.

'Jim,' Fania said. 'And now Caleb.'

Rafe, who had listened in silence for a long while, got to his feet and went to her. He drew her up and held her. 'I know it's terrible,' he said. 'But remember, you have me. You're not alone. You'll always have me.'

Two weeks later, Kevin told Augusta that young Luke would soon be coming home. She immediately began to make plans. He must have the big front upstairs room. She must go to meet him when his troopship landed in New York. She discussed schedules and shopping lists with Fania. Time seemed to drag. She telephoned Kevin often to know if he had yet had further word.

Finally, on a cold day in late February, Kevin came to the house to see her. After making some uncomfortable small talk, he said, sighing, 'It didn't work out as we thought it would. Luke's back. In fact, he's in Boston. But...'

'But what?' she demanded. 'Why wasn't I told he's already arrived?' Her voice was tart, yet fearful. Why was Kevin so uncomfortable? What was he hiding? What had happened to young Luke?

'It's complicated, Grandma.'

'But where is he? I want to see him. I want to have him home where he belongs.'

'He's not well, you see. He's in the hospital.'

Her heart began to beat quickly. 'He's badly wounded then? Is that what it is?'

'It's not physical.' Kevin rose and paced the floor, pausing to look at the ivory dog on the mantel.

'It's his mind? Is that what you're trying to tell me?'

'Yes,' Kevin said. 'They call it shell shock. It's partly exhaustion, I think. And partly, well... I don't know.'

'And where is he?' She had risen. Slender. Straight of back. And very determined.

'It would be better to wait a little while.'

She went to the door to call to Nina to get her coat, explaining that she was going to Boston right away.

Kevin protested, 'You can't do that. I don't even know if you'll be able to see him.'

'I'll see him,' Augusta said.

'Nor even if he'll know you.'

'He'll know me, Kevin.'

'Grandma, you can't wish this away, I'm afraid.'

She smiled faintly. 'Trust me,' she said.

In the end Rafe drove her to Boston, and Fania went with them. When they arrived at the hospital, both of them wanted to go in with her. But Augusta insisted on going in alone. She stepped from the Packard and presented herself at the locked iron gate.

A guard came out of the sentry box and spoke to her through the bars, bending his head to hear her soft query. He said he didn't know, but she could ask inside, and swung the gate back. When he'd locked it behind her, he gave her careful directions.

She went slowly up the long driveway, past snow-encrusted dead pyracantha bushes and beds once planted with lilies that were now raw brown mud.

Within the prison-like building she was stopped again. Once more she explained her errand. A slender Red Cross volunteer smiled at her. 'I know your grandson. I've read to him sometimes. Let me take you to him.'

On the way she said, 'My name is Norrie Williams. I'm originally from Fall River too,' and when Augusta said, 'Is that so?', the girl hurried on, 'We're moving back any day. My father's bringing his factory up from Pasaic. He has a mill a few blocks off Ferry Street.'

Augusta listened with only half attention. She was thinking ahead to the coming meeting. How would Luke be? What was shell shock? What was wrong with him that he was kept here behind locked doors and iron bars? How could she help him? When could she bring him home?

At the door at one end of a long gray corridor, where the windows were barred and the light bulbs shielded behind wire mesh, Norrie stopped. 'Mrs. Wakefield, don't expect too much. He may not know you. He's been through such a lot.'

'He'll know me,' Augusta said.

'He might, or might not. You see, sometimes he seems

perfectly all right. But then...' Norrie's voice shook. 'He's a lovely man, Mrs. Wakefield.'

Augusta smiled. 'I know.' But now, for the first time she noticed how pretty a girl Norrie Williams was. Her blond hair was long enough to wrap in a braid around her head. Her features were small and even. Her eyes were a dark blue.

'I just wish –' She stopped herself, sighed, and tapped with a small hand at the door. In a little while, it swung open. A nurse looked out. 'Luke Wakefield's grandmother,' Norrie said.

At the nurse's nod, Augusta went into the large ward. The door closed behind her. The sounds, the smells were overwhelming. She stopped as if she had walked into a stone wall. There were groans, and curses, and whispered prayers, all mingling. Thuds, and cracks, and claps, and stampings. Men lounged on their beds, or paced. Some crawled on their hands and knees.

At the far end of the place, a single soldier wearing dingy pajamas marched in proper posture and cadence from one corner to another. He carried a mop handle in place of a rifle, and wore no hat. But in all else he appeared to be on sentry duty. With a stamp and a present arms, he counted off his steps. Then, with a careful heel-to-toe turn, he swung about and started back again. A mock sentry, doing guard duty at some post, in a war now over.

The soldier was Luke.

Augusta went to him quickly, hands out, saying his name. He seemed not to hear her, seemed not to see her.

'Luke.' She said his name again. 'It's Grandma.'

He didn't respond, but continued his quick march. When the nurse approached, Augusta waved her away. For half an hour, Augusta stood watching in silence.

Then, suddenly, as if he had heard a signal, Luke presented arms, leaned the mop handle against the wall, and sank onto the edge of his bed. Sweat shone on his face. His hands trembled as he tried to wipe it away. 'How did it happen?' he asked in a hoarse whisper. 'Where did they come from? Was I sleeping? Is that why I didn't know?' And then, screaming, 'Oh, God, God, why didn't I know until they were there on top of me?'

Augusta took his thin shaking body into her arms and held him, and felt his tears scald her shoulder as they soaked into her gown. Though she gave no sign of it, she wept too. For him. For what he had been through.

There was a soft footstep. Norrie Williams came and stood close by.

'We don't know,' the doctor said. 'We've no real experience with it yet. It's still too soon.' He was plump and disheveled in an ill-fitting uniform.

'I shall take him home,' Augusta said firmly.

'It's a risk, Mrs. Wakefield.' The doctor's sad eyes swept her up and down. He was thinking of her age, Augusta knew. But she said nothing. He went on, 'I don't believe you realize or understand the problem.'

'I understand the boy,' she said. 'I shall take him home.'

Chapter 43

That spring Luke planted a garden in the backyard, following a design Augusta had laid out for him on a brown paper bag. Norrie came to help him with the seeding, and later with the weeding too. Slowly his pallor faded and he gained weight. The brightness returned to his silver eyes. He began to sleep through the nights, and only occasionally got up to march as though on guard duty. He pruned the lilacs in the front garden, and the roses along the fence.

Kevin and Ann often came to visit. Sometimes their son Tafty was with them; more often he wasn't. He was too active a boy, at ten, to sit for long with a houseful of adults, Ann said. Kevin spoke of the virtual closing down of the Newport Naval Training Station, and how, already, the Fall River Line had begun to feel the effects of it. And it wasn't just that. The fishing industry was turning more and more to trucking at the same time. Where once the ships were four hours at Long Wharf, and mainly to pick up cargo, now a half-hour stop sufficed.

Gussie and John drove down from Boston once a month.

There were faint lines of bitterness in Gussie's face now, and she rarely smiled. She spoke of her job sourly. She worked as hard and as well as the new young men recently hired, yet she was paid less and had no chance of a promotion. John talked politics to Luke, speculating about who would be nominated by the Republicans for the presidency at the convention next year. It would be, he thought, anyone that Senator Henry Cabot Lodge supported. Perhaps Senator Harding of Ohio.

When Fania and Rafe came by, Rafe was careful never to mention the war. He talked mainly about business, the new automobiles and trucks coming out of the factories, the new roads and bridges being built. He opened a bottle of whiskey he had brought with him, and served drinks, laughing about the 18th Amendment, which had gone into effect in January, and about the National Prohibition Act, soon to be discussed. Fania always made sure she sat close to him. She spoke little, but smiled often.

Luke was responsive to these conversations but seemed to have no ideas of his own and offered no opinions.

Norrie brought him new records for the gramophone. 'Smiles,' 'Waters of Venice,' 'The Blue Rose Waltz,' and 'The Yanks Are at it Again.' He played them repeatedly, except for the one about the war.

Then, one day when Augusta was on the widow's walk, looking down at the harbor, she heard the music suddenly lower in tone and slow until it was no more than a long ugly moan. She went down to the parlor. Luke stood at the gramophone, a hand on its crank, staring blankly at the wall.

'What is it?' she asked.

'I was thinking about Tom,' he said. 'He must feel very much alone, Grandma.'

When she had first told him that both his parents had died of the influenza, he had winced, and then been silent for a little while. Then he had asked, 'What about my brother Tom?' She explained, and Luke nodded. 'Yes, I see. Tom was always more Gavin than Wakefield, wasn't he?'

Now Augusta said, 'I'm sure he *is* lonely. I write to him and sometimes he answers. But he doesn't say very much. We'll go to see him, if you like, when you feel ready.'

'When I'm ready.' A flush rose in Luke's face. 'I'd want to be sure nothing happened.'

As she said, 'Nothing will happen,' he rewound the gramophone, and adjusted the needles, and soon 'Smiles' was playing. But later she heard the sudden drumbeat of his march . . .

He left the house rarely. One Saturday Nina suggested they go for a walk, and led them, smiling, into a small white and green ice-cream parlor. It was new, just opened by her nephew, Joey Baras. Her other nephew, Joey's older brother, Richard, was there too. He was a tall man, lean and saturnine, and looked amused while Joey welcomed them joyfully, eager to show them the marble soda fountain and its gleaming fixtures. Black eyes snapping, chubby face alight, he told how he had chosen the color scheme, in honor of spring, and done the painting himself. He had even laid the black and white floor covering. Nina listened, and didn't look at Richard as she said proudly to Augusta, 'He's a good boy, that Joey.' Finally he settled them at a round wrought-iron table and treated them to tulip-shaped glasses full of chocolate ice cream topped with hot fudge and thick whipped cream.

Luke enjoyed it, and thereafter, once weekly, he suggested that the three of them return.

Soon he and Norrie began to make short excursions. They walked down to the waterfront and wandered on the wharves, watching the freighters come in and load. They picnicked in North Park when it wasn't too hot. One day they took the trolley to Tiverton. As Norrie climbed on, clutching the small bouquet of roses Luke had bought her, her long hobble skirt split along its seam all the way to her waist. She sank into a seat, trying to hold it together, whispering, 'Oh, what'll I do? I'll not be able to get off.'

Luke laughed at her distress. He thought it was funny. He'd always said the hobble skirt was dangerous.

She sputtered furiously. 'But I can't stay on the trolley forever! And what a display I'll make when I have to get off.'

'It's nothing,' he told her, taking the rose bouquet. Slowly, carefully, he undid the wire that held it and broke it into pieces from which he fashioned neat homemade pins. While she made small sounds of protest, he pinned together the split in her skirt from waist to hem. Finally, he sat back, no longer smiling. 'It's not perfect. But it'll do.'

'Thank you,' she said softly. 'I ought to have known you'd

think of something.' Her voice shook a little. She could still feel his touch. How warm it had been even through the thickness of petticoats . . . how gentle his hands.

'Call on me any time,' he said lightly. But he wanted to sweep her into his arms. And he didn't dare. Not yet. He wasn't sure enough of himself. He didn't know what might happen.

At summer's end he told Augusta that he wanted to go to New York to see Tom. She wrote Tom to tell him, and at the beginning of the following week, she and Luke sailed on the *Priscilla*, now returned to her prewar schedule.

They spoke to Kevin when they boarded, and later he joined them for coffee in the dining saloon. He mentioned that the ship wasn't full that evening; passenger traffic was light; the holds were half-empty. Even so, when he left them, and Augusta and Luke went to the grand saloon, the place seemed pleasantly full. Fairman's orchestra was playing. Luke tapped his foot to a one-step, 'Hindoo Lady,' but when the song 'Romance' from *Maytime* began, he grew restless.

They went to walk on the deck. Luke carefully took Augusta's arm lest she stumble in the dark. The bow light winked ahead of them. The lifeboats creaked and swayed. After a long silence he said abruptly, 'I'm in love with Norrie. What should I do?'

'Tell her,' Augusta said, smiling. 'That's the first thing.'

'Do you think I'm all right now?'

'Very nearly so.'

'If I could only be sure. If there was only some way . . .' his voice trailed off. Soon though he said softly, 'There was a small farmhouse built of stone. It must have been very old. It was still smoking when we entered it. There were four dead Huns inside. And in the cold cellar, a family of five. Five, Grandma. A man, his wife, their three children. Their bodies made it easy to bury the men we'd killed.' His voice became no more than a whisper as he went on to describe that night and the next, and the one after that. In the distance they could hear sporadic shelling. They'd been ordered to hold on, no matter what.

The six of them took turns at keeping watch, two on while the others slept. They were all tired; it had been so long since they'd had real rest. They had to walk to stay awake. They couldn't whistle, nor smoke, nor even speak to each other, except in the softest of voices.

On the third night it stormed. The distant guns were still, but thunder rumbled beyond the nearby woods. Suddenly, through the hiss of rain, there came a rustle of unidentifiable sound. By the time Luke had cried an alarm, it was too late. Had he been sleeping on his feet? How had it happened? His buddies had died. He himself was left for dead beside the flaming farmhouse...

His voice faltered. 'Oh God, it's too terrible to remember!'

She waited a long time. She remembered how he had looked when she first saw him in the hospital ward. His thinness and pallor, the dull look of his eyes, his hands rigid around the broken mop handle. She thought of him rising from his bed to march and pause and march again. At last she said, 'You must tell Norrie how you feel.'

'Are you sure?' he asked. 'Will it be all right?'

'I know,' she told him. 'Tell her.'

The restaurant in which they met Tom was small and quiet. They had a table at the back with a good view of the other guests. Augusta was amused to see how differently the city women dressed. Their skirts were short enough to expose four inches of leg above the ankle. Their hats were small, many without veils. They wore long earrings and carried tiny beaded purses.

Conversation with Tom was difficult. He was rigid in his chair, giving Luke quick sideways glances, occasionally turning his blue eyes on Augusta. He had asked Luke about the war, where had he served and what had he done? Had it been scary or exciting? Luke went pale, shrugged the questions away. Tom sighed that he wished he hadn't missed it. Luke closed his eyes and didn't answer.

Now there was silence. To break it, Augusta mentioned the ladies' new fashions.

It surprised her to see Tom turn red and then white. 'Yes, and that's the trouble,' he burst out. 'I don't know what I'm going to do. Everything's changed.'

'What are you talking about?' Luke asked. 'What does that have to do with you?'

'Uncle Tom's business,' Tom answered. 'I was supposed to

go back to Bullis in Washington next month. But now he says I can't. I'll have to stay here in New York. There's not enough money left, he says. Because the women don't wear corsets any more. So there's hardly any money left. And my aunt says they have their sons to think of.'

'And is that so terrible?' Luke asked. 'You can finish high school here. And then, if you like...'

'But if I don't finish at a good prep school, how will I get into Harvard? That's what I was planning on. It's where Uncle Tom went, and where he always said I would go.'

'I'll speak to your uncle,' Augusta said.

And Luke leaned across the table. 'We'll figure something out for you. Don't worry, Tom. There's only you and me, and Grandma. We've got to stick together.'

Tom leaned back in his chair, suddenly relaxed. 'I'm glad you've come to see me.'

When the waiter brought his food, he ate it hungrily.

But Luke, Augusta saw, only drank his coffee, and hardly said a word until it was time to tell Tom goodbye. Then he repeated, 'Remember, don't worry. We'll figure out something.'

Later, when they had boarded the *Priscilla* for the return trip home, he said, 'I have to help him,' then sighed, 'and I don't know how.'

'We'll see him through school one way or another,' she told him. 'But I wish he was closer to us. I'd feel better about it.'

They sat to hear the evening concert. Hoppe's orchestra played a one-step called the 'Indian Blues.' A young couple spun out in a dance, immediately joined by two others. Within moments, stewards were there, speaking softly. The dancers retreated to their seats after some small conversation.

'It's no good,' Luke said. 'Dancing's in vogue now, Grandma. It's old-fashioned and impractical not to allow it. The line must keep up with the times.'

A month later he told Augusta the same thing. 'They're still doing business in the same old way. The ordering, the bookkeeping, the shipping manifests. Times are different now, and they're not looking ahead.'

He had, without saying anything to Augusta, gotten together with Kevin the night they returned from New York on the

Priscilla. He asked Kevin to put in a good word for him at the line's office. Kevin asked if he was sure he was ready to go back to work. 'I have to be,' Luke said, thinking first of Norrie, then of Tom.

Within the week he reported to the line's office at the terminus building. From where he sat at his desk, he could see the docks, the *Priscilla* moored there, or the *Providence* or *Plymouth*. He could watch the *Commonwealth* load. That was the only part of his work that he enjoyed. His salary was low. He saw no future.

Just before Thanksgiving he resigned and went to work for Norrie William's father at the American Yard Goods Company just off Ferry Street. From his window he could still see the Fall River Line terminus and hear the boat train's bell when it pulled in from Boston. But he hardly bothered to look out any more.

He arranged with Tom Gavin that his younger brother finish at Bullis, and he and Augusta managed to pay the bills.

At the end of the year Luke and Norrie were married. The wedding was held in Augusta's parlor. Nina cooked the food, and the drink was supplied by her nephew Joey. Joey had gotten it from his older brother Richard, who owned a saloon that would soon have to be closed. The whole family was there when Luke and Norrie exchanged their vows.

Ten months later, in November of 1920, their son Theo Wakefield was born.

By then the Senate had failed to muster the necessary two-thirds vote, so the Treaty of Versailles negotiated by Woodrow Wilson, and accepted by the Allies and the Central Powers, was rejected, and with it the president's dream of a covenant between nations.

Henry Cabot Lodge, the senator from Massachusetts, had led the opposition, maintaining that the president's treaty would entangle the United States in foreign alliances. The president toured the country, seeking support, but had fallen ill in Pueblo, Colorado, and returned to Washington, where he suffered a stroke soon after. Two months later William Gamaliel Harding defeated Woodrow Wilson for the presidency by a massive 60.3 percent of the vote.

The 19th Amendment to the Constitution had finally been

ratified, giving women the right to vote regardless of state laws. On November 2, 1920, Fania drove Augusta to the Quequechan engine house on Prospect Street near Highland Avenue.

Before entering it, Augusta paused. There was a faint blush of excitement on her cheeks. She imagined a fanfare of trumpets, thundering drums. Instead, the scene was commonplace, matter-of-fact, and orderly. The nation's flag snapped briskly above the wide-open doors of the firehouse. A long table and a desk replaced the wagons usually there. A few men spoke quietly near the potbelly stove. Yet this election day was different. For the first time, women too could vote for those who would govern them.

'Ready?' Fania asked.

'I've been ready for a long time,' Augusta answered, thinking of Marge Gowan, dead these two years, and Betty Townsend, still working for the cause, of the women force-fed in Washington's jail and manhandled on Boston's streets, who had, with so many others, made this moment possible. It was for all of them that she was here.

Smiling, she made her way inside and put her name in the registrar's book. Smiling, still, she accepted her ballot and went to the desk. She marked her choice firmly. Done. Done. Done. How sweet that moment! Exulting, she had turned away.

By then, too, prohibition had been in force nearly a year. Richard Baras had given up his saloon and moved his business to another location, where he sold drinks to patrons who knew the right word to whisper at the bolted door.

Little Theo had thick reddish-gold hair and deep blue eyes and a sturdy body with noticeably square shoulders. The first time he was brought to Augusta's house, Luke said, 'There's something you must do for me,' and led the way upstairs to the room where Augusta had been born, the room where Luke had spent so much time recovering after the war. 'Tell him, Grandma,' he said, putting the infant into her arms.

She held Theo, feeling his warmth against her breasts. For a long moment she couldn't speak. She looked down past the neatly pruned bushes in the front yard and the bare trees of the roadway to the harbor's steel gray shimmering, to the gulls that swooped over the tugs, to where the *Plymouth* lay moored.

'Look, my Theo,' she said softly, at last finding her voice.

'Can you see the stone arches and the big roof? That's the terminus of the Fall River Line. Long ago, my father, your great great grandfather, that is, helped to build the Fall River Line. It was in 1847 that it started. And he held me in his arms as I hold you now, and showed me its first ship, called the *Bay State*, and said to me, as I say to you, "She'll be the making of our future and fortune..."'

The same day, in Boston, Gussie pinned up her dark hair before the mirror in her bedroom. Avoiding her own eyes, she watched John's reflection as he buttoned his stiff collar.

She couldn't tell if he was angry. He was a quiet man; he kept his feelings to himself. Perhaps that was what was so wrong. If he faced her with it, accusing, complaining, then maybe she could explain it to him. How useless it seemed to her: to lie in bed, coupling, and for nothing. She was barren, dead inside. His ardor, which once had warmed her, now only made her cold. The silence between them made her cold too.

She gave her hair a final pat and turned to him. 'We must buy a nice present for the baby. And go to visit him soon.'

'Yes,' John agreed. 'After I come back from seeing the attorneys for Sacco and Vanzetti in Braintree.'

'I don't see why you're bothering,' she said. He'd been talking about it for days. Until now she had listened but never expressed an opinion. But what had happened during the night lay like a shadow in her mind. John had drawn her close, kissed her. She had turned her mouth from his, wriggled from his arms, saying in a strident whisper, 'No, John. Leave me alone.' He hadn't answered, only turned away. Now guilt made her perverse. She went on, 'In fact, I think it's downright silly. There's nothing you can do.'

'I feel I ought to try. At least find out.'

'It has nothing to do with you,' she said sharply, 'and I doubt that the partners will like it.' Whenever she said 'the partners,' there was dislike in her voice. At the beginning it had been different. She had admired them. But she'd given up hope of a promotion for herself, and John hadn't yet been taken into the firm as she thought he ought to have been.

John busied himself with his tie. He wished she would keep quiet. He knew she couldn't help being upset that Luke and

Norrie had had a son so soon after their marriage. But it was time she learned that the success of other women at childbearing was no reflection on her. In any event, he didn't want to talk about it now. Not when his temper was still uneven over her coldness the night before. Not when he had something he considered more important, for the moment, on his mind.

It had begun the previous May. They were on the *Commonwealth* together, returning from a business trip to New York. He had been reading the *New York Times* and only half-listening as she said, 'They ought to make you a partner soon. It's really wrong of them. You do all the work. We both know that.'

John had wished she took less interest in his career. He understood that she concerned herself with it because she had so little else to think of. If they'd had children, he supposed, it would have been different. But after her two miscarriages, nothing had happened. She rarely spoke of it now, and had stopped trying to persuade him to agree to adopting a child. Instead, she told him how to deal with his cases, and how to handle the partners. Since she still worked in the office, she knew what was going on. He guessed it could be worse, but he didn't like her interference. Particularly since she cared neither for logic nor law, but based her advice solely on her own intuitions.

As he grunted a response to her, he read on. Then he'd made a sudden exclamation.

'What's the matter?' she'd asked.

'The Braintree robbery and murder. You've heard about the case, haven't you? It says here they've arrested a couple of Italians, a fish peddler and a shoe-factory worker.'

'Have they?' she said, with not much interest.

'I wonder why they think they have the right people?'

'Why not?'

'They're both working men. They have jobs. Why would they do it?'

'A sixteen-thousand-dollar payroll is a lot of money.'

'Yes.' But there had still been doubt in his voice.

Later, when they were in the dining saloon, Gussie and John heard two men at a nearby table speaking about the case.

'Anarchists and murderers,' one said. 'They should be taken out and hanged.'

'Arrested with guns on their persons,' the second said. 'That's proof enough for me.'

'You see?' John said quietly. 'They haven't even been tried yet, and they've already been sentenced.'

'You're exaggerating,' she told him.

But over the months, he had followed the case carefully. He was less than convinced.

Now she reached for her hat, saying, 'I'm sure the partners won't like for you to involve yourself.'

'I have to,' he told her.

She saw the set of his mouth and gave up the argument.

The next day he went to South Braintree. He talked to the attorneys who were representing the plaintiffs and persuaded them to make it possible for him to meet with the two men. He saw Nicola Sacco first, then Bartolomeo Vanzetti, and listened to what both of them had to say. They had stolen no payroll, murdered no guard. They were, they both admitted, political radicals. They carried guns because they feared for their lives. The times were dangerous for men who had unorthodox beliefs. Didn't John know of the government raids and jailings and deportations? They both had heavy foreign accents. Neither was easy to understand. John left convinced of their innocence and determined to do whatever he could for them.

One afternoon while he was in South Braintree interviewing possible witnesses, one of the partners stopped at Gussie's desk. 'Mrs. Carrier,' he said. 'Do you know where your husband is?'

'He had a matter in Braintree?'

'And what was that?' the man demanded.

She didn't answer.

'When he returns, will you have him call me at once? At home, if need be. But at once, mind you.'

'I told you,' she said, when he came home that night. 'I knew it would happen.'

John didn't answer. He telephoned the partner and was told to come immediately to the man's home.

When he arrived, both partners were waiting for him.

There were no greetings, no pleasantries exchanged.

One said, 'You're not giving your full attention to your job with us.'

The other said, 'Have you lost your mind? Why are you involved with those anarchists and murderers?'

461

'I believe them not guilty,' John answered. 'But regardless, they're entitled to a fair trial.'

'Not on our time,' the one said.

'Nor on our reputations. You've no right to involve us,' the other threw in.

When the interview was over, John returned home. He told Gussie that he had been asked to resign and had done so.

'You're relieved, aren't you?'

'I think so. But I don't know what we'll do next.'

'Well, there's only the two of us to worry about,' she answered. 'We'll manage somehow.'

The next morning she went to the office as usual. She cleared her desk, and without a word to anyone, walked out for good.

John continued to work on a volunteer basis on behalf of the two imprisoned men. Meanwhile he sought a connection with another Boston law office. Word had gone out, however; he was marked as unreliable, a friend of anarchists. There were no jobs for him.

Within a month it was plain he'd never find work in Boston. They moved to Fall River and rented a house on French Street, a few blocks from Maplecroft where Lizzie Borden lived. With Kevin's help in providing instructions, John was able to get a place in the legal department of the New England Steamship Company's Fall River office. He liked the job, but remained obsessed with Sacco and Vanzetti. Even from that distance, he did what he could for them, and when their trial began at the end of May, he went to Dedham. He said little on his return, but it was plain that he wasn't hopeful. That night, wanting to comfort him, Gussie reached for him and held him and soon led him into making love.

By July of 1921, when Congress had at last ended the state of war between the United States and Germany and Austro-Hungary, and when Sacco and Vanzetti were found guilty after a six-week trial, Gussie suspected she was pregnant. In February of 1922 she was delivered of a healthy baby girl she and John named Tessa.

Though they were both ecstatic with delight and busy with the infant, John continued to help as much as he could on the appeals of Sacco and Vanzetti, as controversy grew around the conditions of their convictions.

*

That year in May, Augusta turned seventy-five years old. When she mentioned to Norrie that she planned a trip to New York, the younger girl looked pained. 'Do you really think you should?'

Augusta smiled at small Theo, who sat on her lap chewing the end of her jabot, and said to Norrie, 'Of course I should, and why not?'

'But, Grandma... well...' Norrie paused, trying to think how to say it.

'At my age, you mean,' Augusta said helpfully.

'You *do* have to be careful,' Norrie said, blushing.

'I don't see what of,' Augusta retorted. She was determined to do as she planned. She had an errand in New York that wouldn't wait too long. Besides, it was the line's birthday, as well as her own. How could she allow it to pass unremarked?

Norrie told Luke, who told Kevin, and Kevin came by for a cup of coffee and mentioned before he left that he thought it would be a good idea if Augusta were to stay at home that year. Then Gussie came with Tessa, who curled on Augusta's shoulder and stared at her admiringly with light brown eyes.

Fania said, 'Grandma, you take too many chances. At least take someone with you.'

Augusta finally agreed that Nina would accompany her, although what good Nina would do, she didn't quite know. When Augusta climbed to the attic now, on her way to the rooftop widow's walk, she moved more slowly than she used to. She was careful how she put her feet. But it was Nina who stood below, grunting and groaning with every step Augusta took, and calling out useless directions. It was Nina who panted, when Augusta came down, 'Those steps are too much for you,' while Augusta smiled and shrugged. They weren't too much for *her*.

She was still fortunate in her health, and with the children. They came often. She saw less of Tafty than she would have liked, but understood that at thirteen he was too active to sit with her. She saw more of the babies, and enjoyed them.

One day, a week before the sailing, when Gussie was visiting, Augusta heard Joey Baras's voice in the kitchen. He came rarely to the house. Usually she saw him when she and Nina went to the ice-cream parlor. She wondered what was wrong and went to see.

Joey sat at the kitchen table, his face disconsolate. He was losing the ice-cream parlor, he told Augusta. The building was being bought out from under him. He didn't have the money to start elsewhere. Augusta commiserated with him, and with Nina, who said, 'Can you imagine it? He was the first in the family to have his own business since my grandfather lost his fishing boat fifty years ago.' She didn't count her other nephew, Richard, who had a speakeasy, and was prospering with it.

Augusta had heard that there'd been trouble with the concession for the newsstand on the *Commonwealth*. She didn't speak of it to Joey.

But when she and Nina sailed on the *Priscilla* on May 19, she told Kevin about Joey, and asked who he ought to see about getting to run the newsstand.

Kevin supplied the information, and she and Nina went to their stateroom so Augusta could make certain that her luggage had been brought down. The bag was important. It held two small pieces from the trunk in the attic. She hoped she could get a good price for them. Luke was helping, but to send Tom through Harvard took no small sum. She saw him rarely, although she wrote often and had an occasional reply. He was, as Luke had once said, all Gavin. He was nineteen now, going into his junior year. She had written to ask him to spend the summer with her, and to work on the line while there. Many college boys were hired for the busiest months. She knew one, a young Negro, who was a dining steward, earning his way through medical school with his pay and tips. Tom still hadn't answered. She hoped she'd hear from him soon...

Below, in the purser's office, Kevin leafed through the passenger reservations. There was an Oelrich, due to board at Newport; also a Whitney; a Mrs. Diane Gorgas. Two judges had come on the boat train from Boston, along with lawyers, an editor of the *Atlantic Monthly*, some drummers, and any number of housewives bent on spring shopping in New York.

Still, boarding was almost completed, and there were many unoccupied staterooms. It bothered him that some trips were like that. He wondered what was going to happen. He couldn't imagine his life without the line. He was thirty-six years old, and he'd never known anything else.

He sighed and rubbed his mustache, wondering what was wrong with him. He seemed always, these days, to be filled with a faint queasiness. He wasn't exactly sick, but he wasn't right either. He worried about Tafty, who could never settle down to anything, or be interested in anything either. Kevin had tried to get him to know the ships, but Tafty had been so resistant that Ann said he'd better give it up. She fussed over the boy too much. What could you expect of a woman with only one chick?

A passenger stood before the window, gave his name.

Kevin checked, handed the man the brass key, and saw someone else approaching. He smiled, relieved to be busy at last.

Augusta sold the two small pieces for close to six thousand dollars, and then returned home. Several days later Nina heard from an excited Joey. He was to take over the newsstand on the *Commonwealth* when she began her summer season on June 1.

Soon after that Tom came to stay with Augusta, and John was able to place him on the *Providence* as a deckhand. He lasted only one round trip. On the way to New York, he developed blisters from handling the hawsers without gloves. On the return on a foggy June morning, the *Providence* went aground at the Dumplings near Newport and had to be towed off. Back at Fall River, Tom immediately telephoned a friend still at Cambridge to set up an excuse. The next evening he received a telegram asking him to meet his friend and family in New York, and to spend the summer traveling with them in the west. It was, Tom said, an opportunity that he mustn't miss, and apologizing while he packed, he quickly made his escape.

'Did you hear the news?' Norrie's father asked. 'President Harding has just died in San Francisco.'

'I knew he was sick,' Luke answered, 'but not that sick.'

The next day, August 3, 1923, Calvin Coolidge was sworn in as president.

That same day Luke was in his office reading about a bill then being discussed in Washington that would give veterans of the war a bonus. It was already known that Coolidge was opposed to it.

Luke set the paper aside and leaned his chin on his folded hands, his eyes fixed on the scene beyond the window; but he neither saw the busy yard where trucks rolled past nor heard the shouts of the drivers. He didn't notice the smoke from the mill stacks drifting by.

He was wondering if he would ever be truly well again. If he would sleep through a night without hearing gunfire in his ears. If he would have a day when he would be free of the sudden onset of shivering. He no longer rose up to do sentry duty. He no longer seized a broom or mop or whatever was at hand, and put it over his shoulder and strode, peering to left and right, from one corner of a room to the other. But the compulsion was there. He felt it, he recognized it. The feeling was there inside him. He controlled it, but it remained. He knew that Norrie watched him, hurried to protect him from distraction when the bad times were on him. He could tell that she sensed his uncertainty as if it were her own.

The doctor had said he was better than many, and that time would take care of his memories.

Luke sighed, wondering if the doctor was right.

He was glad that Rafe Raleigh was shown in at that moment. He didn't want to think about it any more. The two men shook hands. Luke asked how Rafe was.

'I'm always fine,' Rafe answered, with a wink of one green eye, and a grin. 'What about you?'

'Well, thank you. And Fania?'

'Pregnant. And happy for it.'

'So I hear from Grandma. I'm glad for you both.'

With the pleasantries out of the way, they settled down to business. Luke thought that there were better ways of transporting American Yard Goods products than by the Fall River Line ships, whether freighter or passenger type. He wanted facts and figures before he made a decision.

Rafe, having rented out trucks several times to Richard Baras, had concluded that he should, aside from leasing, establish his own trucking business. He had brought the information Luke needed. 'We can truck it cheaper,' he assured Luke, and proved it by the numbers. In a little while, they had agreed on price and schedule.

'It's good for us and good for them,' Rafe told Fania later.

'Poor Grandma,' she said. 'She'll feel that we, and Luke too, are betraying the line. And her, in a way.'

'Times change,' Rafe answered. 'We have to change too.'

She looked at him doubtfully. Augusta and her family were all the family that Fania had. The older woman had become her rock. Nothing must hurt her. Nothing – ever. She told Rafe that.

'Luke wouldn't do anything to hurt her, would he?'

'No,' she agreed.

'Well then.' He grinned. 'What are you worried about?'

When he left her after dinner that evening for a few more hours of business, Rafe thought of his words. He had made one kind of a deal with Luke that afternoon. Now he was about to make another.

Times change. Raleigh's had to change, too. In his great grandfather's time it had been George Raleigh. Hostlers. They'd dealt with carriages and carts and wagons. Next it was George Raleigh and Sons, Automobilists and Hirers. Now it was Raleigh's Automobiles and Trucks, and Shippers. The cars and trucks were for sale or for lease, and for neither did he ask why they were needed, or what would be transported in them. He received a good price and had, so far, lost none.

The bootlegger with whom he did most of his business was also his personal supplier. Rafe liked his whiskey and cared nothing for prohibition.

He met Richard Baras at a speakeasy. They had a drink together while they made the arrangements. Richard wanted four trucks for two nights. Later he would need them again. He had shipments coming in to be picked up at the Canadian border. But he would soon have more shipments arriving at various points along the Taunton River.

They settled on a price, and had another drink together. Richard sent his regards to Fania when Rafe left.

But Rafe didn't mention that to Fania, nor say who he had been with. He never discussed that part of his business with anyone. He said only, 'I'm going to need a few more trucks. We'll be expanding. Want to go to Boston with me tomorrow?'

It was a hot night in mid-September. A truck was flagged down by two men. When its driver leaned out to ask what was wrong, he was knocked unconscious. As he lay by the roadside, his crates were shifted to another rig. His truck was soon a mass of flames.

The ruin was traced to Raleigh's. In the early morning hours the police came to Rafe's house on Highland Avenue. He agreed that the truck was his, and shrugged. 'But what of it? I don't ask what my rentals are for.' He told them who had rented it from him, giving a name that he and Richard Baras had agreed on earlier.

When he returned to the bedroom, Fania was up and waiting. Her eyes blazed at him from her pale face. 'What have you been doing?'

'Nothing,' he said. 'They just had a couple of questions.'

'About what? I want to know. I have the right to know.'

He couldn't dissuade her, nor distract her. So finally he told her.

She said unbelievingly, 'You're involved with bootlegging?'

'Why not? It's a small thing. They make laws, they cancel them. It's dumb. They're not going to stop people from drinking.'

'I don't care about that,' she cried. 'It's you. You! Suppose something happens?'

'Nothing is going to happen.'

She screamed, 'You don't *know*! And I couldn't bear it! I won't let you – you're all I have. You're my mother and father and lover and husband all in one. There was Caleb and he was killed. And now it's only you.' Weeping, she collapsed on the bed. When he went to put his arms around her, she pulled away, sobbing. 'No, no, don't touch me! Suppose something happens . . . who will love me? Who will care?'

'All right,' he said softly. 'All right. I'll get myself out of it. Don't worry about it. Don't cry any more. I'll give it up, if that's how you feel.'

That time when he touched her, she fell into his arms and clung to him, still weeping.

He held her and rocked her until she fell asleep.

In the morning, he solemnly promised her he'd avoid any business with bootleggers. Later that week he arranged for the rental of two more trucks to Richard Baras.

Chapter 44

On the Wednesday afternoon before Thanksgiving in 1925, students from all of Boston's colleges and universities had converged on South Station. They sang, they yelled. One party of twelve organized an impromptu snake dance around the mounds of baggage with which the redcaps were struggling. Hawkers sold chrysanthemums and steaming water chestnuts. Here and there, furtively, bottles changed hands.

Tom Wakefield waited impatiently near the place where the *Pansy*, the New Haven's boat train for Fall River, would be loading. He had turned twenty-two that year, and was tall and slender and blond, with the understated good looks attractive to both men and women. He had arrived first as usual. He was always a little early for his appointments, eager to get started at whatever he was going to do. For the tenth time in ten minutes, he checked to be sure that he'd brought his flask. He looked at his ticket, and compared his watch with the big clock on the wall. It was five-thirty; the *Pansy* wouldn't leave until six. He had been looking forward to this weekend for weeks. November was the month in which both his parents had died, and his life had been changed forever. Now his Uncle Tom Gavin was bankrupt and working for somebody else. Tom jammed his hands into the pockets of his baggy pants, suddenly breathless. Had he lost his wallet? No. It was there. He sighed his relief. Money – God, how he wanted it! Lots of money, and he'd have it too! By the time he was thirty, he'd have a million dollars!

His thoughts were interrupted by the arrival of Carter Caynes, a friend from college. Both were seniors now.

Tom grinned. 'Finally! I've been waiting nearly an hour, you cake eater, you!'

Carter laughed at the compliment. Being called a ladies man was good; he was extremely shy, though attractive to girls. He wore a dark brown snap-brim fedora and a raccoon coat, and carried a banjo.

Mac Fielding and Peter Baker, the two men they expected to join them, were in the same class, and the same clubs. They made a good foursome. Except, Tom thought, that the other three had money, and he was always just a little short. If it hadn't been for what his brother Luke and Grandma Augusta gave him, he wouldn't be in school at all.

Now, once again, Tom looked at the wall clock.

Carter was singing 'Alexander's Ragtime Band.' It was his favorite song, although it was fourteen years old. He stopped to say, 'They're coming. Hang on to your horses.' And to Mac, and Peter, 'We almost gave up on you. Why're you late?'

'No taxis,' Peter said.

The boat train was opening for loading at that moment. The four pushed their way through, Tom ahead, and Carter last, having paused to grab a chrysanthemum from a hawker and to throw a dollar at him as he went on.

On the Pansy, out of breath, laughing, they took seats at the end of the car and sat facing each other, long legs angled to fit into the narrow space. The bells rang. The whistles blew. White steam billowed from the smoke stacks. The conductor stood on the platform swinging his lantern. 'All aboard!' and jumped on as the train began to move.

When it had cleared South Station, he came through to collect tickets. As soon as he had left the car, Tom asked softly, 'What about it! Are you ready for some giggle water?'

'I was hoping you'd ask,' Carter said. He took the flash Tom offered him. His eyes shone with tears as he swallowed. 'Tiger's piss! Where'd you get it?'

'The usual place.'

'Awful!' Peter licked his lips, then grinned. 'I'd better bring back some of my father's stock. It'll kill us if we keep up with this stuff.' Peter's father was a banker. He had the best brands bootlegged in from Canada. Peter gave the flask back to Tom. 'Boy, it feels good to get away from the books...' It was just talk. He was an English literature major, and he loved books. But mostly American ones. He had read F. Scott Fitzgerald's *This Side of Paradise* five times. The Fieldings' money came from bonds and stocks. They lived in New York. Mrs. Fielding was a prohibitionist. Mr. Fielding had promised Tom a job when he graduated.

Carter took the flask from Tom, but quickly held it under his seat. The conductor was coming down the aisle, offering stateroom keys. When he went on, Carter swigged the whiskey. They had a long way to go, the others protested. He was taking more than his share. Mac was the most vociferous one.

'When we kill this, we start on mine,' Carter said. 'I've come prepared, old pals.'

Peter looked at Tom. 'I hope you know what you're doing.' There was a question in his voice.

'Trust me,' Tom said. 'There are always plenty of girls on the *Commonwealth*.'

'Is it true about the necktie ladies?' Carter asked.

'Sure,' Tom answered. 'They each have a couple of ties. They go along the corridors, watching out for the crew, of course. And they tap at the stateroom doors. If a woman answers, they say they're just checking, and go on. If it's a man, they start selling him neckties.'

The boys guffawed.

'Would I like that to happen to me!' Peter said.

The boys considered Tom the expert on the Fall River Line ships although they'd sailed them themselves many times. Tom had told them about his grandmother Augusta, and her family, the Kincaids. He'd talked about his brother Luke and cousin Kevin. He'd even told them how he'd worked as a deckhand on one of the ships. He didn't say that it had been only for one trip. Even Carter, with whom he'd gone traveling in the west that summer, was foggy about that.

Carter took up his banjo and began to play. First *'Dinah,'* then *'Tea for Two.'*

The train chugged on, whistling at the crossings. The air turned blue with smoke. Finally, with its bell clanging, it slowed and rolled under the stone archways of the Fall River Line terminus.

The boys walked the few yards across the crowded ramps to the *Commonwealth*.

As always when he came to Fall River, Tom felt guilty. It had been a good while since he'd seen his grandmother; it was the same with his brother Luke. He knew he ought to see them more, but he didn't really want to. They had nothing in common. If he spent the day with them tomorrow, practically the whole family would be there, sharing Thanksgiving. But he'd have nothing to say to any of them. They were hicks; he was bigtown.

As he passed the purser's window, he flushed. Kevin gave him a big smile. He waved his key in response and hurried on.

Carter's avid gaze followed a girl down the deck. Her legs were long and slim, her skirt short, barely reaching her knees. 'That's for me,' Carter sighed.

'The cat's meow,' Tom agreed.

After the ship sailed, they toured the various public rooms. The mens' bar was closed. It would open as the *Commonwealth* rounded Point Judith. Once the ship was in Long Island Sound, it would close again.

But that was no problem for the passengers. The boys settled in Tom's stateroom for pre-dinner drinks. Others did the same. After steaks and potatoes in the dining saloon, Carter said, 'This is all very good, but...'

'Soon,' Tom said in a whisper, watching a group of girls nearby. They were young, pretty, with bobbed hair and heavy eye makeup.

They left before Tom could figure out how to approach them. The boys retreated to his stateroom. They drank more, listening hopefully for the knock of the necktie ladies, but heard nothing.

They talked about what they would do after June, when they'd be graduating. Peter planned to join his father's bank. Mac wanted to go to Paris for a year to write, but he wasn't sure his father would allow it. And Tom intended to take up Mr. Fielding's offer and start on making the million dollars he was counting on.

Mac suddenly got up and vomited in the sink. He was green and sweaty and shaking. The others worked him over with wet towels. Soon his color was back, and he was laughing and having another drink.

The conversation went back to girls. The group eyed Tom. He'd said it was going to be easy.

He was thinking that it was lucky that the *Commonwealth* had been taken out of storage for the holiday weekend. On any other ship, he'd not have known what to do. As it was he said, 'Let's go down to the newsstand, and see what's happening there.'

Joey Baras welcomed them with a grin. He sat on a high stool, watching the boys thumb through magazines, knowing that wasn't what they wanted. Finally he asked, 'Something I can do for you?'

Tom said, 'I've heard there's a way to make special arrangements.'

'You mean you've run out of joy juice?'

They hadn't but Tom didn't want to say so. Maybe buying a bottle was part of the deal. 'In a manner of speaking,' he said.

Joey rummaged in a nearby box. 'Just name your poison.'

Tom asked for whiskey.

Joey accepted the money, handed over two bottles. 'And what else? Some friends maybe?'

'Yes.' The chorus was quick and relieved.

'Sure,' Joey said. 'Give me your stateroom number. They'll be along pretty soon.'

Later he sat on the high stool and counted his cash – three hundred and forty-three dollars. He grinned to himself. Bless his Tia Nina. And bless Mrs. Wakefield. And his brother Richard, too.

Business was good. Joey sold newspapers, magazines, cigars, cigarettes, and souvenirs of the Fall River Line. But most of his earnings came from what was not listed on the inventory sheets.

The door opened. A pretty young woman came in. Her face was made up; her dress dipped low in front. She wore lacy stockings and very high heeled shoes. She said, 'Hi, Joey, I guess it's time to pay up. It was three, wasn't it?'

'Three, kiddo.' Joey smiled. 'Fifteen for me.'

She smiled back and gave him his cut.

Now he had three hundred and fifty-eight dollars. He put away the money and looked expectantly at the door. There ought to be more coming in soon.

'Did you see Tom?' Fania asked.

'I couldn't have missed him,' Rafe said.

'He was very drunk.'

Rafe grinned. 'Not very. Just some. Boys, at that age...'

'I know. But just the same . . .' Fania sighed. 'I wonder why he isn't at Grandma's.'

'For the same reason we're not, I guess. He had something he wanted to do more.'

'I don't feel comfortable about it.'

'But you agreed. I didn't force you into it. I just felt like getting away for a couple of days. And this was a good time.'

'I know. And it's all right.' She looked around the grand saloon, thinking about Caleb. He'd been dead eight years now, but still, sometimes, she had the feeling that he would appear from somewhere and she'd become the twelve-year-old girl he'd taken to Newport. When the early concert ended, Rafe suggested that they have dinner.

She said she wanted to have a look at the baby first.

'Why do I pay a nursemaid?' Rafe asked.

'Rafe! You worry about the baby as much as I do.'

'I'll go down with you,' he answered.

Diane Gorgas had a glimpse of them as they disappeared into the pale gray corridor. She had boarded the ship a little while before at Newport. Suddenly breathless, she went on to her stateroom where she took off her pink cloche and fluffed her hair. She powdered her face and reddened her lips. Bending close to the mirror, she examined her face. At forty-six, was she beginning to show her age? No, she didn't think so. She couldn't. Beside she had always looked young. She fluffed her hair again. It had been a pleasant trip to Newport, and it was always nice to visit friends, but she was glad to be going home to New York.

She had sold Cliff Mansion as soon as her father died. That was only months after she had learned that Caleb had been killed in France. She had also dropped the Wakefield from her name so that now, once again, she was called Diane Gorgas. She'd felt better as soon as she'd done it. It was easier to forget him, forget that he'd known about old Willie.

Her life was pleasant. By day she rested. She had a masseuse who kept her body smooth and trim; a hairdresser attended to her hair daily. She spent a lot of time on her clothes. Her nights were passed in various New York speakeasies with various escorts. She was serious about none of them, but always careful that they were men of quality reputations with wealth equal to her own. No fortune hunters for her, thank you.

When she thought of Caleb, which was rarely, she wondered why she had married him. Sometimes she wanted to weep, without knowing why. She never allowed herself that luxury. It would be bad for her looks.

Now, standing before the mirror, she saw her eyes brighten and blinked quickly. No, it wouldn't do. Besides, there was no reason to cry.

But still, in her mind's eye, she saw Fania. And the man with her. Who was he? Fania's sweetheart, her husband?

Diane considered how extraordinary it was that she didn't even know if her own daughter were married. What would happen if they were to meet face to face? Would Fania speak? What would she say? Would Diane herself answer? And what would *she* say?

It was very still in the stateroom. Diane took her beaded purse and went to sit on the bed. For a little while she smoothed the white coverlet, traced its blue stripes with her finger. Then she took a small packet from her purse. Carefully, she unwrapped the paper. It was filled with white powder. She held it to her nose and sniffed, breathing in deeply.

Later, bright-eyed, smiling, she went to the top deck. She was about to enter the dining saloon when Fania and Rafe came out.

Diane paused, held her breath, waiting.

So did Fania. Her mouth was dry. Her eyes burned. At last she said, 'How are you?' and turned to Rafe. 'This is my mother, Mrs. Wakefield. My husband, Rafe Raleigh.'

'Mrs. Gorgas,' Diane said crisply. And, 'How are you, Fania?'

'I'm well,' Fania answered, remembering an old anger, but feeling nothing of it now.

Diane said nothing more.

With a nod at her, and a tug at Rafe's arm, Fania went on, saddened but relieved. That part of her life once touched by Diane was over.

Now that the ship had left Newport, it was quiet at the purser's office. It would stay that way until an hour or two before the docking in New York at Pier 14.

Kevin was glad of the company of Ralph Beard, a Boston

475

stockbroker who spent a lot of time on Wall Street. He had read about the *Priscilla*'s rescue, a year and a half before, by an Eastern Steamship Lines ship, and asked if Kevin had been aboard the *Priscilla* then.

Kevin had been. He told Ralph Beard about it. The Eastern's *Boston* had been a new ship, only weeks in service. On a foggy night in July, she left India Wharf in Boston, steamed through the Cape Cod Canal, which made the all-water route possible, and ran into fog in Buzzards Bay. Whistles blaring, she proceeded toward Point Judith as the fog thickened. Somewhere close by a schooner was heard but not seen. The *Boston* stopped until there seemed no danger of a collision, then went on. Almost immediately there was a whistle at the port side. The *Boston* gave three warning blasts, but it was too late. The tanker *Swift Arrow* had cut through the *Boston*'s bow and into eight staterooms. An immediate SOS was broadcast.

It was heard on the *Priscilla* forty miles away in Long Island Sound. The captain ordered that the ship turn and steam at full speed back to Point Judith.

Kevin had felt the *Priscilla* respond and heard the constant blaring of her foghorn. The *Boston* was carrying 640 passengers – the SOS had said the ship was being abandoned. Kevin had helped swing lifeboats out so that when they arrived, they could pick up survivors as quickly as possible. It took one hour and fifty minutes for the *Priscilla* to reach the *Boston*, the first of a number of ships to arrive. Many passengers had been picked up by the *Swift Arrow*; others were taken aboard by the *Priscilla*. Afterward the *Commonwealth*'s captain had the *Boston* lashed to her side and towed the disabled ship to Newport.

'It must have been exciting,' Ralph Beard said, 'to see that. The *Commonwealth* is a more powerful ship than I'd thought.'

'She is,' Kevin agreed. 'She has ten boilers. It takes forty men in the engine room to keep her going, and she carries 200 tons in her coal bunkers. In a single hour she uses eight and a half tons.'

The stockbroker laughed. 'If you put that much interest into the market, you could be rich, purser.'

'Me?' Kevin shook his head. 'I'm a ship man, and that's all.'

'You could make a killing,' Ralph Beard said. 'Everybody's

investing. Why should you be left out?'

'It's tempting,' Kevin admitted, 'but I wouldn't know how to begin.'

'I can get you started. And I'd be glad to. It's my business, after all.' Ralph Beard laughed. The diamond ring on his hand sparkled as he raised his cigar to his lips. Around a puff of smoke, he said, 'You just think about it. When you decide, let me know.'

Kevin watched as the stockbroker walked away. He wore a fine suit; his shoes were of the best leather; his shirt was certainly silk. The market had treated him well, no doubt of that.

Kevin worked longer hours, was away from Ann and his boy Taft more than he was with them. He had some savings, and the house. All he had to show for the long years he had given to the line.

It seemed to him that everybody was more prosperous than he. And it was from the market. Night after night, as he listened to the passengers, he heard the same story. 'Made fifteen hundred on the market today. And seven hundred yesterday.'

No matter how many raises he got, and he didn't expect one soon, he could never earn anything near that.

And he couldn't predict the future. The Eastern Steamship Company's *Boston* and *New York* were stiff competition for the Fall River Line, so were its freighters. Gussie's husband John had told him that the government was probably going to buy the Cape Cod Canal, and eventually widen it. That would give the all-water route to New York an even greater boost. As much as Kevin liked his own ships, he had to admit that there was some convenience in boarding at Boston and getting off in New York, without having to take the boat train to Fall River. It was hard to figure out how things would go in the future.

People said that now Calvin Coolidge was elected, business would boom. But he didn't expect any of that to come his way. And he had to admit it would be good to go down street and buy an automobile. To tell Ann to outfit herself from head to toe. To send Taft to a good prep school. It was tempting to think about. The stock market . . . Still, something held him back. He wasn't sure. Suppose he lost all his earnings? Then where would he be? And Ann and Taft . . .

He said nothing to Ann about it when he arrived home. After he'd stamped the snow off his boots and washed, they had breakfast together. Taft was home that day, Ann told him. He had gone to bed with a cold, and Ann had decided, since the weather was so bad, that she would let him sleep it off.

Kevin read the newspaper for a while, then went to bed. He awakened to hear Ann say, 'Tafty! What do you think you're doing?'

'*Tafty!* Mama, I'm too old for that,' Taft said.

Kevin grinned into his pillow. The boy was sixteen now. Sometimes he acted it and sometimes he didn't; but he didn't want Ann to baby him.

Now he was saying, 'I'm a lot better.'

'But you certainly shouldn't go out. It's snowed again during the night and it's very cold. With you sneezing and coughing . . .'

'I'll wrap up good, Mama. I want to go down to High Street to see Grandma for a little while.'

It was the one reason that would convince her, Kevin knew. Taft didn't visit his great grandmother often enough. Kevin turned on his side and went back to sleep.

When later he came downstairs, Ann was on the telephone. 'I'm surprised he isn't there yet,' she was saying. 'He left two hours ago.' And then, 'No, no, I'm sure it's all right. But if you'd tell him to call me.' She hung up the receiver and turned to Kevin, frowning. 'I don't understand it.'

'I'll see if I can find him.' Kevin got his coat, pulled on his boots.

'He's probably stopped somewhere along the way,' Ann said uneasily.

'Probably,' Kevin agreed. 'Don't worry. I'll bring him home, and give him a piece of my mind on the way.'

It was a gray afternoon. The wind was cold. The snow was deep and hard-packed, covered with a thick layer of slick dirty ice.

Kevin hurried, taking the shortest route between his house and Augusta's, certain that Taft would have done the same. A coal-delivery wagon passed by, its horses straining against the load they pulled. A few automobiles steamed and backfired as they climbed the hill and disappeared. The wind, gritty with smoke from the mills' stacks, stung his cheeks.

He reached the hill crest and paused to catch his breath. Below him a long steep slope fell away. Not far from its bottom there was a crowd just beginning to gather. He could pick out the brown and red of knitted caps and dark coats and flying scarves. Distant shouts came to him. He realized that something had happened. Something was wrong.

Panic seized him. He broke into a run. The breath whined in his throat. 'No,' he cried. 'No, Taft. Please God, please, please...' The crowd was thick now. A woman was crying. A man cursed softly. Another said, 'He did it three times, maybe four. I saw him from my window. And then –'

Kevin pressed his way through, asking, 'What's the matter?'

'A boy on a sled. He came down the middle of the road and shot off into that tree.'

Even as Kevin forced his way past yielding bodies, trying to remember if he'd seen Taft's sled leaning against the front steps, he knew. Still, he was unprepared for the first sight of Taft's limp body, twisted legs awry.

'Taft!' Kevin whispered. He looked wildly around. 'It's my son!'

Union Hospital became home to them.

Augusta hurried there as soon as she learned of the accident. She sat close by Taft, saying his name softly, while Ann watched in frozen silence and Kevin leaned against the wall, his eyes averted, and the room echoed with unspoken accusations.

Still saying Taft's name aloud, Augusta thought of the two beside her, Ann, Kevin, each gripped in separate pain and fear. They must be together in this. Together, not apart. You're about to meddle, she told herself, and answered, So be it.

Later she held Ann, felt the girl tremble, and said gently, 'You mustn't blame yourself.'

'If only I hadn't let him go out! If only I'd stopped him!' Ann cried.

Augusta took Kevin's hand, drew him close. He looked beyond them to where Taft lay, asking himself, Why did she let him go?

Augusta's fingers tightened.

He looked at her, saw the question in her eyes, and knew she was asking him to consider himself. Why hadn't he gone down to tell Taft he couldn't go out? At last he said hoarsely, 'No, Ann. You're not to blame. I could have stopped him too, but I didn't.'

Then, somehow, she was in his arms, her head buried in his shoulder, weeping, and he wept with her.

By the end of the week they knew that the boy would live. But by the end of the month, it was plain that he would never walk again.

Kevin saw the bills mount, and looked into the future and became ever more frightened. In January he told Ralph Beard, 'I have five hundred dollars. Do you want to invest it for me?'

'I can do more with more,' Ralph told him.

'That's it for now,' Kevin said. He didn't dare use all his savings. He didn't know what would happen. John said that the planned installation of hot and cold water facilities in Fall River Line staterooms wouldn't help. It would be half a million dollars down the drain, he insisted. Competition from the Eastern Steamship Lines would cut into passenger and freight. To make matters worse, there'd been several mill closings, among them the Pocasset. Taft's condition and Kevin's own uncertainties encouraged him to invest, but with restraint.

Two months later, however, he gave Ralph Beard another five hundred dollars. He had seen a paper profit of fifteen hundred on the first outlay. He soon saw the same paper profit on the second.

'You've got to get out,' Kevin said. 'Come on the ship with me.'

'In this thing?' Taft patted the arms of his wheelchair. 'That'll be fun,. won't it?'

'Please,' Ann said. 'Just try it. Just this once.'

Taft looked from his mother to his father. They'd both said nearly the same thing a dozen times before. Slowly, he nodded. Anything to shut them up. It had been a year since he'd pulled the dumb trick that had made him a cripple. He couldn't stand how they worried over him. He was all right. At least he would be, if they'd just leave him alone.

The end of that week his father wheeled him onto the *Commonwealth*. Until then he'd never cared much about the ships. But suddenly he realized that they were great big floating worlds that he could explore. The idea excited him. And then his father took him down to the newsstand to meet Joey.

At Joey's suggestion, Kevin left Taft and went to the purser's office. When they were alone, Joey said, 'It must be close to hell for you. Being stuck in that thing.'

Joey was the only person, except Taft's grandmother Augusta maybe, who didn't pretend to be blind to the chair, to not realize he was a cripple. The first person willing to talk about it. Taft's parents tried to pretend nothing had happened, and at the same time, they babied him so much he couldn't stand it. All he wanted was to get on with his life, if only he could figure out how. Taft said aloud, 'It's close to hell all right.'

'What're you going to make of it?' Joey asked. 'You're sixteen years old. You've got a long way to go.'

'I'm working on it,' Taft answered. It felt good to be talking like that. It took some of the inside pressure out of him.

'One thing. You ought to thank God you've still got your head. Maybe you can't use your legs, at least not now, but you can sure use your head. So you've got to get your schooling.'

Taft nodded.

'And do everything that you can.'

'I'm willing to try. But you know, my folks – they worry.'

'I can maybe help you there,' Joey said.

He was as good as his word, too. He told Kevin that he could use somebody in the newsstand. Whenever Taft was out of school, he could work for Joey.

Soon Taft knew about the bootleg whiskey, and about the girls. He also learned from Joey how to make up accounts and pay bills. And meanwhile, he earned a wage for every trip, plus tips for his deliveries.

He was happy because he'd learned he could take care of himself.

One evening, Augusta came upon him laughing with Joey in the newsstand, and saw how changed he was. How strange life is, she thought. Joey told Nina about his trouble years ago, and I told Kevin. Now look what Joey's done for Kevin's son.

A year later, when Taft was eighteen, Kevin calculated that he was worth a hundred thousand dollars.

He talked about pulling out of the market with Ralph Beard, but didn't do anything about it.

In May of 1927 Charles A. Lindbergh flew a monoplane called the *Spirit of St. Louis* some 3,600 miles across the Atlantic Ocean and landed in Paris.

In August after a long series of appeals Nicola Sacco and Bartolomeo Vanzetti, still proclaiming their innocence, were executed in the electric chair at Charlestown State Prison in Massachusetts.

That evening John Carrier stood at the window and stared past the draperies into the silent street. Fireflies winked in the trees. There was a hazy red ring around the moon.

Gussie tucked five-year-old Tessa in, and kissed her, then came downstairs. For a little while she watched John from the doorway. Then she came and stood beside him, and leaned against him. 'I know,' she said softly.

'I believe them. I believe they were telling the truth,' he told her. 'We've done murder, Gussie.'

'It's over. You did all you could. There's nothing to do any more.'

'Except remember,' he said heavily. 'Remember. And wonder how it could have happened. And when it will happen again.'

Chapter 45

The *Commonwealth* left Pier 14 on a gray day of late October in 1929.

Ralph Beard, the Boston stockbroker, stood watching from the aft deck as the wharves receded. He was as well dressed as ever, his black fedora brushed, his shoes shined. As the ship went under the Brooklyn Bridge, he went down to the purser's office where a few passengers remained, some leaning against the corbel-topped oak columns and speaking in whispers.

Kevin saw Ralph Beard coming. His heart gave a single quick knock against his ribs. All week long he had believed what he heard on the ship: *The market will turn up. The banks will move in to save it. They wouldn't let it happen.* But it *had happened.* His hands began to tremble. He pressed them against the counter to steady them. When Ralph nodded to him, he said, 'I wondered if you'd be aboard today.'

'I'm going home,' Beard answered heavily.

'How was it? Judging by what I've been hearing –'

No one passing the purser's window had spoken of anything else. The stock exchange, knee-deep, thigh-deep in ticker-tape... the screams of anger, the confusion, pandemonium outside on Wall Street... Kevin had listened silently, telling himself, *Wait, wait. You don't know.*

Ralph Beard said. 'It wasn't good. But maybe it's not as bad as it sounds.'

Kevin's face tightened. He felt sweat gather at the back of his neck under his collar. 'Maybe not as bad...'

The stockbroker shrugged. 'It's too soon to tell.'

'When will you know what I have left?'

'Another few days, I suppose.'

From there Ralph went to his stateroom. He rested for several hours, and then went to the dining saloon. He ordered roast lamb with mint jelly and potatoes, and a fruit compote for dessert. He finished off the meal with a pot of black coffee and two double brandies. He paid his bill with the last of the cash in his pocket, and returned to his stateroom to stretch out on the bed, with his arms folded behind his head and his eyes fixed on the ceiling.

The past four days had been a nightmare – and today, the climax of it. He could still hear in his ears the roar that had risen over the clack of the ticker-tape machines and the ringing of bells in the stock exchange. By the time the market had been closed, he was ruined. Bank account, cars, and house were gone. It would be only a matter of days. Men like him, on the inside, knew. Those like Kevin, on the outside, didn't yet realize what had happened.

Much later, at about the time that the ship began to roll on the swell near Point Judith, he got up. Slowly, he went down the staircase and through the almost-empty grand saloon, and down again, until he had reached the main deck. It was dark and very cold. He leaned against the railing, his eyes fixed on the white foam churned up by the paddle wheels. Somewhere close by a buoy moaned . . .

In the newsstand on the forward gallery deck, Joey Baras was saying, 'You want to make a delivery, Taft?'

'Sure, where?'

'Outside the business office. He'll meet you there. You don't have to worry about the stairs this time.'

Taft grinned. 'I don't worry. Not here. There's always somebody around to give me a hand.'

When Joey gave him the package, he wheeled himself to the appointed place. A man was waiting for him. 'You from Joey?' Taft nodded. The man paid him, gave him a dollar tip, and disappeared down the corridor.

Taft started back to the newsstand. Somewhere outside a bell clanged. There were shouts. The ship's rhythm changed. He wondered what was happening.

On the main deck a lifeboat was swung out. Searchlights moved in long slow crescents over the dark sea. A watchman said shakily, 'I'm sure. It was a man all right. I saw him climb over the rail and hang there and then let go. He went overboard so fast there was nothing I could do from where I was. Nothing but yell, that is.'

The ship had stopped by then. The lifeboat was lowered. An hour's search proved fruitless.

The *Commonwealth* went on to Newport, and then to Fall River. At that time, when the ship was docking, a cabin steward told Kevin that Ralph Beard was not in his cabin and hadn't slept in his bed. Soon afterward it was confirmed that he wasn't on the ship. It was assumed that he was the man the watchman had seen go overboard.

Kevin knew then that he had lost everything he had put into the stock market. He could expect nothing back from his investment. Of the one hundred thousand dollars he had had on paper, there was nothing left. Gray-faced, he put Taft into a taxicab and climbed in beside him.

How had it happened? Why? He'd intended only to build up some capital. For Taft. Only for the boy – so he would have something. Why, Kevin asked himself, hadn't he gotten out?

He'd thought of it, and done nothing. And now there was nothing left. All these years, since he'd started on the ships handling baggage with Ray, he'd been content with what he had, and prudent. Suddenly he'd been seized by greed. He told himself it was for Taft, but now he wondered.

He looked out as they passed the blackened remains of the Granite Block, destroyed in a disastrous fire a year ago. The cleaning up had begun. One day new buildings would stand there. Fall River had rebuilt before. It would do so again.

Taft cleared his throat, asked, 'Did you know the man who... who died, Papa? Was he a friend of yours?'

'He was my stockbroker,' Kevin said.

'I see. Then you were in the market, too?'

Kevin nodded.

'And you've lost everything?'

Kevin shut his eyes. Nausea rose in his throat. He was hot and cold at the same time. It had all been for Taft, but the boy mustn't know. The poor crippled child must never realize.

Taft was saying, 'Maybe it's not as bad as you think.'

'I don't want to talk about it.'

Taft fell silent, gritting his teeth. That was the trouble. Neither his father nor mother would talk to him. They didn't seem to understand. He was twenty years old now and they still wanted to treat him as a child.

Kevin said finally, 'I'm sorry. I guess I'm just too tired to think.'

'One thing, Papa. You still have your job, and so do I. And there's the house. We've got a roof over our heads.'

'We'll make out,' Kevin said. 'Don't worry.'

'Listen. Don't you understand?' Taft answered. 'I want to worry. I have to. It's like Joey says. There's nothing wrong with my head, only with my legs. And I'll tell you what my head says. You earned some money on your investments. Then you lost it. Both the investments, and the money you earned. But, really, you only lost what you put in. You never had the rest, did you?'

Kevin stared at Taft for a minute. He'd never felt so close to the boy as he did then. It was a wonderful thing to have a son. A grown son. Kevin felt as if the weight of the world had slipped from his shoulders. He put his arm around Taft and hugged him, laughing. 'You're right. At least that's one way of looking at it. Yes, yes, I couldn't have lost money I never had, could I?'

Later, at home, the two had breakfast with Ann. She asked Taft how the trip had been. He told her it had been fine. Neither he nor Kevin mentioned Ralph Beard.

A week later Tom Wakefield stood in line before the ticket office on Pier 14. It was almost time for the *Priscilla* to leave. Ahead of him there was a short, stout woman wearing a hip-length mink jacket and a round, brimless hat with a nose veil. In her arms she carried a small dog whose collar and dangling leash sparkled with brilliant stones. The man with her was whistling as if he hadn't a care in the world.

Baggage carts rattled past, porters shouted at each other, and there was the constant clamor of taxi horns and brakes and slamming doors.

Tom watched the movement, heard the noise, but both seemed far away to him. He was numb, his senses blunted. Everything he'd worked for in the past three years was gone. He had enough in his pocket for a ticket to Fall River, and perhaps for a meal, and debts he couldn't calculate any more.

The last time he'd come here had been to meet his grandmother, Augusta. She had traveled down to spend the day with him. He'd taken off from Fielding's and they'd had lunch at the Palm Court at the Plaza. It had felt good to be with her. She was so – so serene.

The line moved. It was Tom's turn. The clerk stared at him. Tom hesitated, then said, 'No, thanks. I've changed my mind,' and walked away, trying to make sense of his feelings. He was a grown man of twenty-three. His grandmother, and brother, had already helped get him through school. He had to stand on his own. He couldn't ask them for more. And he was scared. Okay, so he was scared. So what? He jammed his hands in his pockets, and started walking.

The effects of the stock market crash of 1929, beyond those on the ones most immediately involved, spread slowly over the next three years. Many banks failed, businesses collapsed, farmers lost their lands to foreclosure, and factory workers lost their jobs. There were soon twelve million unemployed in the nation, and bread lines, soup kitchens, and beggars – some of them veterans – in the cities.

In Fall River, the mills began to close down. The textile workers lost their jobs and moved away. The population soon dropped to 115,000 and then even lower. Millions of square feet of factories were abandoned. In 1931 an emergency committee was formed to help victims of the depression for a period of twenty weeks; it raised $116,000 in contributions. Those who had work gave 1 percent of their salaries.

The revenues of the Fall River Line fell sharply. Freight income, which had been dropping for years, dwindled even more. Passengers seeking the cheapest means of transportation began to use inter-city buses. The New Haven ran one such line. Through bus fare from Boston to New York went as low as one dollar and fifty cents.

In that period the legal office in the line's Fall River office was closed, and John was let go. He had guessed it might be coming and told Gussie so, but she had brushed his fears aside. More and more in recent years John saw only the dark side. It had become a matter of contention between them.

He told Gussie, 'It's too late for your grandmother. Her shares will never be worth the paper they're written on. She ought to have listened to me.'

'But she couldn't,' Gussie said.

'It wasn't sensible.' John paused. Then, 'I wonder if . . . her age . . . perhaps her mind?'

'You make me sick,' Gussie flared. 'There's nothing wrong with her mind. The line means something to her you couldn't understand, a way of life, maybe, and her . . . her youth. She can't let them go. And why should she?'

Tessa was sitting on the floor, jacks between her knees, holding a small ball. She looked up, her light brown eyes serious. 'Magus knows what she's doing,' she said softly. Magus was her way of saying Grandma Augusta when she was first learning to talk. Now at ten she still used it.

'Of course she does,' Gussie said. 'Grandma's the same as she ever was.' And with a sharp look at John, 'At least *she* doesn't change.'

For the first few weeks when John was without work, he sat in a chair in the living room, staring into space. Gussie said little then. But finally she persuaded him that he must open his own office. She put a desk in the living room, and set a vase with a single rose in it on one corner. She found a file cabinet. She hung a sign on the front door. She wrote announcements and sent them to everyone she could think of.

Rafe Raleigh was John's first client. His trucking company was doing well, although the sales were down on his cars and the rentals had disappeared. Soon John had a few other people coming in. He didn't earn much but he was busy, and he knew the family would survive.

'That's the thing,' he said heavily, talking to Luke. 'To survive. This year, next year. To hang on. Because things aren't going to get better.'

Luke had brought his father-in-law's business to John. The American Yard Goods Company was running three days a week, but looking ahead. He told John so; John only shrugged.

Listening from her desk in the corner, Gussie sighed. He was different from the man she had married. Something had happened to him, gone out of him. Once he'd loved music, and walking. Once he had laughed. No longer. It had begun five years before, when Sacco and Vanzetti were executed. She remembered how he had stared out of the window as if into a nightmare. He'd lost faith, and it had aged him. His shoulders were slumped now and he moved slowly. He even spoke slowly.

Later, when Luke had gone, Gussie said gently, loving him, wanting to help. 'Why don't you forget it? Why don't you try?'

She didn't have to explain. John knew what she meant. He said simply, 'I can't, Gussie. And I can't even try.'

In midsummer of 1932, Luke and Norrie were returning from New York on the *Providence*. Luke had spent two days there on his father-in-law's business, while Norrie had been window-shopping. Now they sat in the grand saloon. Fairman's orchestra was playing a waltz. The lights of the chandeliers cast a soft glow. Couples walked about, the ladies in dresses that fell several inches below their knees, the men in dark loose-fitting suits. The conversation was of the depression, when it would end, and how.

Luke took a *New York Times* from a seat nearby, and opened it. After a few moments Norrie noticed that his expression had changed: his mouth tightened, his eyes narrowed, his shoulders hunched. She watched him, nervously wondering what he was reading. It was impossible to guess what would affect him. His moods were unpredictable. She'd learned that much in the thirteen years they'd been married. Another thing that she'd learned was that he hated being asked how he felt, or what was wrong, or what he was thinking. So she watched him instead. It was something she couldn't help. Because of the way he had been.

Suddenly he threw the paper aside. 'I should have been there,' he said.

'There? What're you talking about?' She ran her hands through her cropped hair, still missing the long braids she had worn around her head until recently.

'In Washington, with the veterans.' His voice was low. He didn't look at her.

'Oh,' she said worriedly. 'The bonus marchers, you mean.'

He had spoken of it before. How the House of Representatives had voted a cash payment to veterans of the war, and 17,000 of them had come from all over the country to Washington to persuade the Senate to do the same. The Senate had refused. Most of the veterans had dispersed, but two thousand of them had remained. When he first told her about it, she'd said, 'But Luke, you have a job. You needn't go.' She'd been frightened. Anything that reminded him of the war was bad for him. He'd answered then, 'I belong with them anyway.' But he hadn't gone after all.

Now he said, 'There's been trouble. Two veterans are dead — and two policemen. Hoover called out federal troops.'

She put her arm under Luke's and snuggled close. 'Never mind. When Roosevelt's elected in November everything's going to be different, you'll see.'

'But I should have been there,' Luke said.

That night he didn't sleep. He lay beside Norrie imagining what it had been like. The police and soldiers moving in. Cars and trucks and tanks and horses. The fire and smoke and screams as the shanties on the Anacostia Flats were pulled down . . .

In the morning, his silver eyes were dull. His face was haggard. He saw that Norrie looked at him nervously.

She had been upset — and concealing it — all during the trip. It had been hard to leave Theo for the two nights at Augusta's. In March, twenty-month-old Charles Lindbergh had been kidnapped from his home in Hopewell, New Jersey; in May, the infant's decomposing body had been found only six miles from home. Norrie hadn't spoken of it. She'd been unable to. But she'd felt as if her heart had withered within her. Suppose it had been her Theo? Suppose she would never see him again? And Luke was again dreaming his terrible dreams . . .

When the *Providence* docked, they went to get Theo.

He was twelve now, a tall slender boy with his father's light gray eyes and reddish-gold hair much like what Augusta's had once been. He greeted them happily, but soon grew quiet. He knew Luke's moods.

Nina served coffee and cake, and Augusta asked about New York. Norrie answered her questions, while Luke smoked one cigarette after another.

When the three of them returned home, Luke said he would go in to the office. He started down street, but never made it. He spent the day wandering along the waterfront, watching the gulls.

That night he dreamed of a small stone farmhouse and awakened covered with cold sweat, and fell asleep to dream again, and suddenly Norrie was pulling at him, and screaming: 'Stop it, Luke! Stop it! You haven't done that for years and years!' But he didn't know it was Norrie then. It was black, so he couldn't see. There were faint outlines, shadows in the trees. A sudden movement close by. Too close. *They were on him.* He threw his arms out. His hands clutched a throat . . .

And then Theo was pulling at him, crying, 'Papa, no, no!' and Norrie was weeping.

His hands dropped. He stared from one to the other. 'Sorry,' he said thickly. 'I was dreaming.'

'You were marching,' Norrie whispered, horror in her eyes. 'You haven't done it for years. But you were doing it again.'

He touched Theo's hand, then put his arms around Norrie. 'Dream's over,' he said. 'Let's go back to sleep.'

They never spoke of it again.

Chapter 46

On November 8, 1932, Franklin Delano Roosevelt was elected president by a margin of 7 million votes with a large Democratic Congress to support his programs. He was inaugurated on March 4 of 1933.

Augusta and Nina sat by the radio listening, as his deep resonant voice filled the room. 'Let me assert my firm belief that the only thing we have to fear is fear itself ... nameless, unreasoning, unjustified terror which paralyzes needed effort to convert retreat into advance.'

Tessa, facing Theo across the chessboard, raised her head. 'What does he mean?'

'We can accomplish what we want to, as long as we're not afraid.'

Three years later at the Durfee Theater on North Main Street the Pathe News showed scenes of wind-scoured farmlands in the midwest; Jim Braddock fighting Max Baer in New York; and goose-stepping soldiers shouting '*Sieg Heil!*' as they paraded before Adolf Hitler in Berlin.

And the parents of Fall River anxiously watched their children. For on July 15 a case of infantile paralysis was reported, and between then and late September there were 120 more. An untold number were left permanently paralyzed. Five died.

It was in that same year that the New Haven filed bankruptcy proceedings, and trustees were appointed to oversee its affairs. Permission was granted to discontinue the Providence and New Bedford lines. The Fall River Line became the last of the New Haven's shipping operations.

Tessa heard John and Gussie talking about it.

'I knew it would happen. I told you,' John said.

'You needn't sound so self-satisfied about your doom-saying,' Gussie retorted.

'What's your grandmother going to do?' John demanded.

Tessa retreated to her room. She didn't like it when her parents talked like that. She wasn't sure what bankruptcy was, but plainly, it was bad. And it had something to do with Magus.

Tessa straightened the wooden model of the *Commonwealth* that Taft had given her. She smoothed the *Priscilla* banner over her bed.

Later she discussed her uneasiness with Theo.

He said, 'They're going to go out of business pretty soon. That's what I think.'

'But why?'

'I guess they're not making enough money.'

Tessa thought that over. Then, 'What about Magus?'

Theo saw the fright in Tessa's eyes. 'Don't you remember the president's speech?' he asked. 'He said not to be afraid.'

'Magus isn't, is she?'

'No,' Theo answered. Of that he was completely certain, although there was much he did question. He wondered about his father's moods. Sometimes he was smiling, wanting to talk. Then there were other days. He was quiet, brooding. That was when Theo's mother was watchful – and Theo, too, never quite sure that what had happened once wouldn't happen again. The not knowing made Theo uncomfortable at home. He spent as much time as he could at his great grandmother's house, or at Rafe Raleigh's place, where he was learning the insides of motors and how to drive Rafe's cars. His parents didn't seem to notice.

He was correct in believing that Augusta was not afraid when she heard of the New Haven's bankruptcy proceedings. She was troubled, saddened, but not frightened. She was certain that something somehow would save the Fall River Line. It was old; it was needed. It would survive.

As for herself, she required little. She continued to live as she always had. Neither the Kincaids nor the Wakefields had ever been much for showy luxuries. Luke and Kevin kept the house and yard in good repair. There was enough to pay Nina, who kept the inside clean. Two of the old sea chests in the attic were now empty. But a few small pieces of chinoiserie remained at the bottom of the third. The ivory dog, the celadon lion, and the four-inch cloisonné vase stood on the mantel where Marcus had first put them.

Augusta still rose at dawn, as she had for so many years, and went up to the widow's walk to see the ships come in. There were fewer now, and not as many tugs and coal barges and freighters either. The same was true of the mills. In the 1920s there had been 123 in operation; now there were only fifteen left. So many smoke stacks rising against the sky, but black and cold . . .

In the evening she returned to the widow's walk to see the ships leave. She would hear the ship's whistled signal, and the sound of the trolley cars not far away.

She leaned a bit on the stout stick that Fania had brought her.

One bright afternoon in May she was returning from an around-the-block walk with Theo and Tessa.

The grocery delivery boy was at the gate. 'How do, Mrs. Wakefield,' he said. 'I'm glad I didn't miss you after all. I'll just carry the box in, if you like.'

She unlocked the door for him. When he had set the box on the kitchen table, he straightened up, grinning. 'I'll bet you didn't know, but I'm going to get married.'

'Billy,' she said. 'Why, that's wonderful.'

'I was wondering . . . I just happened to think . . . we've saved up ten dollars between us. For a honeymoon, you know. Only we're not sure – we've got two days. What can we do with ten dollars?'

'What can you do?' Augusta repeated. Her eyes sparkled, her dimples became deep. She knew what the young couple must do. But ten dollars! How to arrange it? She said, 'I'll be down street tomorrow. If I have an idea, I'll stop by and tell you.'

He thanked her and left.

Theo studied her face. 'You already have an idea, haven't you?'

She sat down at the table and rested her chin on her folded hands, humming a chorus from 'On the Old Fall River Line,' and thinking of Harry Von Tilzer, and Taft when he was a tiny boy. 'What about the *Commonwealth*?'

'The *Commonwealth*!' Tessa cried. 'Oh, Magus, that's a wonderful idea!' And she looked at Theo. 'Isn't it?'

He agreed that it was, and his face reddened, and he looked at Tessa.

Augusta's sharp green eyes caught the exchange of glances. Was it possible? she asked herself. It was, she decided. She knew. She had loved Luke when she was thirteen as Tessa was now, and loved him forever after too. And these two were always together. But they were second cousins. What would Gussie say? And young Luke? She could hear her own Luke saying, 'You're meddling again,' and put the thought from her mind. What would be would be. Meanwhile there was the grocery boy and his bride to consider.

She looked at her wristwatch. Fania and Rafe had given it to her for her coming birthday. It was a pretty gold case and bracelet, but the face was small. A bit hard to see these days. Her birthday! She would be eighty-eight years old. And she still didn't feel it. Oh, perhaps she moved a bit slowly and felt an occasional creak in her joints, but what of that?

It was interesting that Rafe and Fania continued so prosperous in a time when everyone else was feeling the pinch. Augusta had her own ideas about that, but would never mention them. After all, the 18th Amendment had been rescinded several years before. Rafe was a good husband and father, and Fania was happy. Reminding herself about the grocery boy, she looked at her watch again. Kevin ought to be home. When she called, he answered the telephone himself. He laughed at her question. 'Sure, Grandma, I can do it. Tell him to come to the purser's office and talk to me. I'll sell him a couple of passages on the ship and book them free into a honeymoon suite. There's sure to be one standing empty anyhow. And when they're ready, I'll have dinner for two laid on in the dining saloon, and maybe I can arrange a ride for them on Bellevue Avenue when they get to Newport.'

She was laughing when Nina brought the mail in.

There was a card from Tom.

Augusta read its few words, smiling, even as her eyes stung with tears: *Happy birthday, Grandma. All's well here. I've finally got a steady job. Love, Tom.* He'd remembered. After all this time, and all the miles he'd traveled. She hadn't seen him since the spring of 1929. She'd had a card from him, written in St. Louis, saying there was no work there, and he and Mac would go on to Kansas City. It was several years before she heard from him again. He was in San Antonio at that time.

She didn't know that he and Mac had gone across the country, working at odd jobs, dancing in marathons, riding in empty boxcars when they had to. Now Mac was running an elevator in Los Angeles and Tom was a handyman at M.G.M. in Hollywood.

That evening, after Tessa and Theo had gone, Taft and Joey Baras came by. Taft was full grown at twenty-six, his shoulders broad from rolling his wheelchair or dragging himself about on crutches. He was a happy man, always joking and smiling, and people liked him for it. He and Joey were partners now in the newsstand on the *Commonwealth*, and Taft ran that business while Joey had a small luncheonette, named after the ship, on North Main Street. Its walls were covered with pictures of the ship, and on the table next to the cash register there was a ship's ashtray. He spent most of his time there.

Now Taft was showing off a small kitten. She was black with white paws and a white throat. 'This is Minnie, Grandma. Minnie, say how do to my great grandmother.' The cat arched and meowed. Taft grinned. 'Sometimes, when it gets too quiet, I need a little company.'

'I've offered him better company than that,' Joey said, laughing.

Augusta supposed that he meant he'd offered to arrange a date for Taft. She hoped that he had. She would like to see Taft going out with girls, getting married, having a home. He was happy, busy with his life, for all that Kevin and Ann worried too much about him. But he *was* alone.

'One thing at a time,' Taft told Joey. 'For now my Minnie will do me.'

Two years later, Minnie was perched on the counter at the purser's office when Augusta came on board the *Commonwealth*.

It was May 19, 1937, Augusta's ninetieth birthday, and the ninetieth birthday of the Fall River Line.

The ship was glistening white, her brass gleaming in the sinking sun. Flags and pennants snapped on the wind-stirred halyards. The orchestra was playing. All about her Augusta saw the familiar excitement of departure.

The porters, catching up the baggage...

The cars and trucks rolling by...

The white steam floating over the boat train that had just arrived...

Augusta wore a silk dress of dark blue, a small blue hat, and at her throat the black grosgrain ribbon with the cameo. A light shawl lay around her shoulders, and under one arm she carried a copy of a new book called *Gone With the Wind* by a southern lady named Margaret Mitchell. Augusta was interested to know how it compared to *Uncle Tom's Cabin*, the book written by a northern lady so many years ago.

Now she paused on the gangplank, looking back at the wharves. She no longer wore the long sweeping gowns and petticoats she once had. It was the same here. The wharves no longer teemed with wagons and carts; but their spirit remained. Just as inside she was the same as she had always been.

As she went on board, Nina said anxiously, 'Be careful,' and stumbled herself. Augusta smiled, leaned on her stick.

They stopped at the purser's office. Kevin said. 'They're all aboard, and waiting for you. Even Theo and Tessa, out of school for the day.'

Augusta stroked Minnie's ears, then went to her stateroom. She passed several deckhands. Once she had known them all. Now she knew only a few. She remembered Willie Gorgas, and thought of how a bit of him remained with her in Fania, his great granddaughter.

The heady scent of roses hung in her stateroom. A large bouquet stood on the nightstand. The attached note said: *Happy Birthday from the captain and crew of the Commonwealth.*

'They remembered,' Augusta said softly. Among all the new faces, the so very young faces, there were some who knew her. It was a good feeling.

Others remembered the ninetieth anniversary of the Fall River Line. Crowds gathered on the waterfront, and cheers, shouts, and music blended when the *Commonwealth* pulled out.

Augusta stood at the railing, the family around her, until they passed the Borden Flats light. Then, on the way to an early dinner, they passed through the grand saloon. The orchestra was in the gallery mezzanine and playing. Augusta paused a moment, listening to the music, and then went on, humming the tune. 'It's "Harbor Lights",' Tessa told her softly.

'A nice song,' Augusta said, thinking of the dancing there would be later in the garden room, and below in the old main deck library, now converted into a Parisian sidewalk cafe.

The chandeliers sparkled under the three-domed ceiling of the dining saloon. Kevin had seen to it that a long table was prepared. He sat at one end of it, Augusta at the other. They were all there. Kevin and Ann, and Taft. John and Gussie, and Tessa. Rafe and Fania, and their two young ones. For they too were family now. It was what Caleb had intended when he sent Fania to Augusta, she knew. Luke and Norrie, with Theo, completed the party.

But as Augusta smiled at them, she saw the faces of those that were missing. Tom, so far away in California. Amy, Kin, and Barbara. Caleb. Ray. And her own Luke.

For a moment she was breathless. So many gone. So many parts of her.

Then Kevin rose, lifting his glass. 'First, I want to say I'm glad that prohibition's over. At least we don't have to wait for Point Judith and the three-mile limit so we can make the toast I want to propose.' He smiled at Augusta. 'To you, Augusta Kincaid Wakefield, grandmother to some of us, great grandmother to others, and dear to us all. Your future and fortune.'

'To our future and fortune,' she said softly. 'And to the Fall River Line.'

Nine weeks later, attorneys for the New Haven Railroad Company trustees appeared before a judge in the Federal Court at New Haven to petition for permission to abrogate the ninety-nine-year lease which gave them effective ownership of the Fall River Line, and to suspend services permanently.

Although in February the trustees had said they saw no reason for the discontinuance of the line, there had been constant warnings and rumors for some while.

It was said that the *Commonwealth* was to be sold for use as a girls' school, that the *Priscilla* and *Providence* would soon be turned into scrap, that the *Plymouth* was to end up as a daily excursion boat on Chesapeake Bay. While these stories were told in Fall River, a jurisdictional fight for control of the New York waterfront developed between the A.F. of L. and the C.I.O. Sitdown strikes were called against the Eastern Steamship Company, operating out of Boston. At one point the Eastern's passengers were transferred to the *Plymouth* of Fall River, so that schedules could be maintained. Then the crews of Fall River Line ships sat down in support.

That was when John said, 'Now it's going to happen. This is the excuse they've been waiting for.'

'You always look on the worst side of things,' Gussie told him.

'You don't realize that the New Haven has been itching for years to get rid of the line. They've always been railroad people, and that's what they remain. It goes back to when Mellen was president. The New Haven had something like 336 subsidiary corporations. And every one of them has been drained to support financial transactions having nothing to do with the companies themselves. Now that they can't get any more out of the line, they want to let it go.'

Within hours of that conversation Gussie heard that the agent for the Fall River Line in Fall River had stood on the dock near the *Commonwealth* surrounded by one hundred and twenty-five policemen and read the notice of suspension, while in New York, aboard the *Priscilla*, the same notice was read.

It was after that that the New Haven requested permission to suspend service permanently. A hearing was set for July 27.

Learning of it, Augusta was determined to go. But when she mentioned it to Luke, he said, 'What's the use? It's a hot four-hour drive to New Haven. And what can you do?' She spoke to Kevin, and he said, 'You don't want to be there any more than I do.'

Theo, seventeen by then, tall, with serious eyes and his grandfather Luke's faint smile, came to see Augusta one afternoon. 'You want to go down, don't you? You want to be at the hearing.'

'I do,' she said. She'd been there at the beginning. It seemed almost as if she remembered it. The bright sunlight . . . the *Bay State*, her flags snapping in the breeze . . . the steam swelling

498

like a white cloud over the boat train's locomotive . . .

'Grandma . . .' Theo leaned closer to her, and spoke in a near whisper, 'Grandma, is it – is it all right? For you, I mean.'

'Oh, yes! I must be there. I must be.'

'Then I'll take you. Tessa and I will. I've already arranged to get a car from Rafe. Tell me what time you can be ready.'

'Early,' she said, smiling. 'Yes, very early. We must be sure to be on time.'

It was hot that July day. The sun was scorching, the sky cloudless. The journey to New Haven was uneventful.

Augusta, her mind full of memories, spoke little. Theo concentrated on driving. In the back seat, Tessa prayed silently: *Please, God, don't let it happen.*

The courtroom was crowded. The mayors of New Bedford and of Fall River were there. People from Providence, and even Boston.

The trustees presented a single witness. He was a man Augusta had known for nearly forty years. He had started at the bottom of the line, become chief steward, then superintendent, and finally vice president in charge of traffic. He spoke softly of the depression, expenses, and losses.

Officials from Fall River testified to the public need for the line. Others from Newport and New Bedford said the same.

The hearing lasted one hour and forty minutes.

A hush fell as the judge prepared to render his decision.

Tessa clutched Theo's arm. Augusta sat quietly.

The judge said, 'The petition is granted forthwith.'

It was over.

'Grandma,' Theo whispered, 'I'm sorry I brought you for this.'

'I had to be here, Theo.' Augusta rose.

Tessa took her by the arm. The girl wouldn't allow herself to cry, but her eyes were wet and shining. Theo took Augusta's other arm, wondering if she had suddenly shrunk. She reached barely to his shoulder. He remembered her as being tall.

'And now we'll go home,' Augusta said, as they helped her into the car.

But when they reached Fall River, she said, 'Let's stop at the docks. I want to see the *Commonwealth* one more time.'

He drove her to the wharves and parked. The terminus building loomed large and quiet before them. Their footsteps echoed as they approached the ship. In response the gulls rose up in a white cloud and drifted overhead in eerie silence.

It was nearly twilight. There should have been white-gloved porters handling baggage, stevedores pushing automobiles, rolling barrels, and carrying crates. There should have been the boat train steaming in. And people. Everywhere there should have been people.

But no one was about until, when they had walked up the gangplank, a man appeared to ask, 'What do you want?' and then, with a closer look at Augusta leaning on her cane, to tip his hat and say, 'Oh, it's you, Mrs. Wakefield. How do.'

'How do,' she said. 'We've come for a last look. You don't mind?'

'Go right ahead,' he mumbled, turning away. 'I'm the only one left. I'll be down in the engine room, if you want me.'

They walked slowly through the entrance hall and then up the staircase to the grand saloon.

Augusta sighed, sank into a chair.

'Maybe we should go,' Theo said.

'Not yet.' She smiled. Then, 'It's so beautiful, you know.' Smiling still, she leaned back and closed her eyes.

Tessa and Theo exchanged looks and stood close beside her.

It was quiet. A hornet buzzed at one of the windows. The air was very warm.

Augusta pictured the children's faces. Tessa, Theo. How like her they were. How like her Luke, too.

Her Luke . . . running down the companionway of the stout *Bay State* . . . her father Marcus's booming laugh on the jinxed *Empire State* . . . the canaries singing on the *Providence* and the *Bristol*, where Jim Fisk strutted. The *Plymouth* . . . *the Puritan* – the princess, the *Priscilla* – the queen; the *Commonwealth* . . .

Then, from far away, she heard the ship's three-whistle signal. She was sailing now. She heard the muted thump thump of the paddle wheels. And suddenly there was gay music – music that sang of love – Harry Von Tilzer's song.

And there were strong arms around her. She heard a deep familiar voice saying, 'That ship, the one you call yours, is our future and fortune. And so is her line.'

The arms holding her tightened, and a young anguished voice cried: 'Grandma! Grandma! What's the matter? Are you all right?'

She forced her eyes open and looked into Theo's. 'I'm fine.' But the words were a whisper on fading breath.

'I'll get a doctor.' Theo pushed Tessa, and pointed to the door, silently mouthing, *Run for help!*

The girl raced away. Behind her, padding on silent feet, went the cat Minnie.

Augusta saw, smiled a little. Her slim hand brushed Theo's fingers. 'You stay, Theo. Be with me. But don't be sad.' She waited a long still moment. Then, 'It's the end of one dream, but the beginning of another.'

His young face was wet with tears. He choked, trying to answer.

Her eyes widened. Her smile was eager and welcoming. She heard the whistles blow, and felt the big ship throb as its engines heaved and the paddle wheels slowly turned. Soon they would be in Mount Hope Bay, and passing the Borden Flats light, then Bristol Ferry and Mussels Bed Shoals . . . And far far away there was the song: 'On the Old Fall River Line.'

The long-awaited sequel to the bestselling
APPLE TREE LEAN DOWN

MARY E. PEARCE
SEEDTIME AND HARVEST

_____90362-6 $3.95 U.S.

The triumphant conclusion to her powerful and moving saga of English farming life, set in the troubled years of World War II.

"Poignant and evocative" —James Herriot

"[Mary Pearce] writes with unfailing musicality."
—*The Washington Post*

NOW AVAILABLE AT YOUR BOOKSTORE!